Critical acclaim for T

'Nunn's talent for storytelling will have you chewing
up the 600-plus pages with compelling ease'
Sunday Times (Perth)

'*Territory* is a gem. With a fascinating riddle of plots and
subplots, it will have you glued till the last page'
That's Life

'Nunn skilfully blends threads of fact and fiction to
produce a story that is very real'
The Weekly Times

'A really good read. Nunn effortlessly weaves
diverse narratives into a seamless whole'
Australian Bookseller & Publisher

'A powerful family saga set against the battle for Darwin,
Cyclone Tracy and the building of a great cattle station'
Illawarra Mercury

'A passionate, tautly constructed yarn'
TV Week

'A great read'
Bendigo Advertiser

From stage actor and international television star to blockbuster best-selling author, Judy Nunn's career has been meteoric.

Her first forays into adult fiction resulted in what she describes as her 'entertainment set'. *The Glitter Game, Centre Stage* and *Araluen*, three novels set in the worlds of television, theatre and film respectively, each became instant bestsellers.

Next came her 'city set': *Kal*, a fiercely passionate novel about men and mining set in Kalgoorlie; *Beneath the Southern Cross*, a mammoth achievement chronicling the story of Sydney since first European settlement; and *Territory*, a tale of love, family and retribution set in Darwin.

Territory, together with Judy's next novel, *Pacific*, a dual story set principally in Vanuatu, placed her firmly in Australia's top-ten bestseller list. Her following works, *Heritage*, set in the Snowies during the 1950s, *Floodtide*, based in her home state of Western Australia, and *Maralinga*, have consolidated her position as one of the country's leading fiction writers. Her eagerly awaited new novel, *Tiger Men*, will publish in November 2011.

Judy Nunn's fame as a novelist is spreading rapidly. Her books are now published throughout Europe in English, German, French, Dutch and Czech.

Judy lives with her husband, actor-author Bruce Venables, on the Central Coast of New South Wales.

Territory

JUDY NUNN

An Arrow book
Published by Random House Australia Pty Ltd
Level 3, 100 Pacific Highway, North Sydney NSW 2060
www.randomhouse.com.au

First published by Random House Australia 2002
This Arrow edition published 2003, 2007, 2011

Addresses for companies within the Random House Group can be found at
www.randomhouse.com.au/offices

National Library of Australia
Cataloguing-in-Publication Entry

Nunn, Judy
Territory / Judy Nunn

ISBN 978 1 86471 246 9 (pbk).

A823.3

Typeset by Midland Typesetters, Australia
Printed in Australia by Griffin Press, an accredited ISO AS/NZS 14001:2004
Environmental Management System printer

To my brother Robert Marshall Nunn, with gratitude not only for his invaluable assistance, but for his encouragement and belief in this book. And to our mother Nancy, who inspired in us both a fascination for the history of the *Batavia*.

ACKNOWLEDGEMENTS

I would especially like to thank my husband, Bruce Venables, my agent, James Laurie, and my friends and work mates at Random House, Jane Palfreyman, Kim Swivel and Emma Rusher.

A special thanks also to Major Tony Young, Susan Mackie, Robyn Gurney, Dr Grahame Hookway, Ben Taylor and Maarten Smies.

For assistance in the research of Darwin and the Northern Territory my thanks to the following:
Phil Jackson and Anna Johnson of the *Northern Territory News*, George Manolis of Dymocks Books in Darwin, Dr Ella Stack, Carrie Elton, Katrina Foong Lim, Danny Thomas, Gerry Blitner, Eddie Quong, Brett Midena, Norman Fry, and members of Darwin's Chung Wah Society, Adam Lowe, Eric Lee and Albert Chan, who were most receptive to my visit and most helpful with my queries.

Amongst my many research sources, I would particularly like to recognise the following publications:
Amsterdam, Hans Koning, Time Life International, 1978.
Batavia, Philippe Godard, Abrolhos Publishing, 1993.
Islands of Angry Ghosts, Hugh Edwards, Hodder & Stoughton, 1966.
The Territory, Ernestine Hill, Angus & Robertson, 1955.
The Surveyors, Margaret Goyder Kerr, Rigby, 1971.
Hell West and Crooked, Tom Cole, Collins, 1988.
Sitdown Up North, Ted Egan, Kerr Publishing, 1997.
The articles of historian Peter Forrest, published in the *Northern Territory News*.

IN MEMORIAM

As a schoolchild I was taught of the many battles in which our brave troops fought and lost their lives. Of Gallipoli, the Somme, Tobruk, El Alamein, the list goes on.

Like most Australians, I was never told of the bombing of Darwin and the consequent battle which raged in the Top End.

Historians believe that the final figure of 243 dead in the bombing is not only conservative, but decidedly incorrect. The true casualty figure is estimated to be in excess of 500.

In memory of those who lost their lives on 19 February 1942, when Australia experienced warfare upon its own soil.

It had been Foong Lee's wisdom which had helped Paul
Trewinnard through what he called his 'dark years', the
years of despair when he'd first come to Darwin to escape
the horror of his life. And Darwin was a good part of the
world to escape to, a remote outpost where no questions
were asked and no judgements made.

These days, no longer in need of escape, Paul based
himself principally in Darwin simply because he loved
both the place and its people. For many years now the
Hotel Darwin had become intermittent home to Paul
Trewinnard, and Foong Lee had become his closest friend.

He raked his thick greying hair back from his brow, his
forehead already damp. Not that the heat particularly
bothered him. To Paul, the human body's perpetual state
of perspiration throughout the aptly named 'wet' season
was all part and parcel of Darwin's sensuality. He'd go
down to the dining room and have a light breakfast, he
decided, easing his gangly frame up out of the wicker chair.
That would at least get the day started.

In her small weatherboard house on the Esplanade, not
far from the Hotel Darwin, thirty-two-year-old Aggie
Marshall, school teacher, sat at her desk completing
her newsletter for the Country Women's Association. She
applied herself diligently to the task despite the fact that
there was no-one to send it to, all the members of the CWA
having evacuated Darwin, along with the majority of
women and children, and many of the men too, following
the fall of Hong Kong on Christmas Day. The fall of Singapore only four days ago had made those who'd stayed even
more aware of their precarious existence and the Government had evacuated the last boatload of people at noon
just the previous day. The Japs could attack at any
moment, many said.

Aggie had stayed in Darwin for the simple reason that
she had nowhere else to go. Which wasn't exactly true,

she could have returned to her elderly parents in Perth, they telephoned regularly begging her to do so, but the thought of being in the same city as her ex-husband made the prospect unbearable. And Perth was hardly a city in the true sense of the word, more like a large country town; it was not unrealistic to presume he would hear of her return and seek her out. For the first twelve months after she'd come to Darwin, Aggie had lived in fear that he might even have followed her north. Now, five years later, having reverted to her maiden name, her hideous marriage a thing of the past, Darwin had claimed Aggie. She'd discovered herself here, found a strength of her own she'd never known existed, and even the threat of a Japanese invasion could not drive her away. Darwin was where she belonged.

The school at which Aggie taught had been closed down so she'd set herself up as a one person secretarial office doing volunteer work for the war effort. She corresponded with various branches of the Red Cross, coordinating the parcels to be sent overseas, she typed endless circulars and lists of supplies and necessities, and she steadfastly continued to write her CWA newsletters. Mainly about courage in the face of adversity, now and then including a frivolous observation to boost morale, and she posted them up on noticeboards, in the post office and anywhere else she thought people might see them. It was something to do.

Aggie gathered together the pages of her newsletter. She was looking forward to a hearty chat with her friends at the post office. So few of her old acquaintances remained in Darwin, and the armed forces seemed to have completely taken over the town lately, but she enjoyed the company of the new friends she'd made at the post office. Many of them were recruits who had responded to the call for staff in this time of need, and they were young, vital and stimulating company.

She jammed on the brown felt hat that had seen better

days without bothering to check in the mirror—Aggie cared little about appearances. Her lack of vanity surprised some people because Aggie was a rather good-looking woman, tall and strong-boned. But she chose to wear her dark hair in an unfashionable bob (it was more practical that way), took little time with her dress (thank goodness trousers were acceptable, they were far more comfortable than skirts or frocks), and with the exception of a touch of lipstick (in the evenings, and when she remembered) she eschewed makeup.

As she opened the front door, Aggie noted that the wall clock said only nine-thirty. No, she decided, closing the door, she'd give it another fifteen or twenty minutes. Just until the post office had set up for the business of the day, then the staff would have time for a chat.

In Cavenagh Street, Foong Lee was carefully arranging his display of goods preparatory to opening his shop. Under normal circumstances he would have opened the shutters for business much earlier, or rather his eighteen-year-old son would have, Foong Lee himself having left before seven o'clock to visit the wharves or the market gardens or the number of subcontractors with whom he traded. But things had changed. Since the evacuation of Darwin business was poor, and his son Albert was in Adelaide looking after the rest of the family whom Foong Lee had sent south.

Most of the Chinese community had fled Darwin. As was to be expected, Foong Lee thought, the Chinese were not stupid, and he would most certainly have accompanied his family had it not been for the fragile condition of his father, who was unfit to travel. Foong Lee persuaded himself, with his characteristic commonsense, that it was just as well he had remained in Darwin, to protect not only his own interests but those of his friends.

Foong Lee was a highly successful businessman and leader of his community, not only loved and respected by the Chinese but recognised by the Europeans, which was unusual in Darwin where the two communities rarely intermingled.

Despite the fact that he was always well dressed (which was to be expected, since amongst his many interests he owned one of the major tailor's shops in Darwin) Foong Lee didn't look like an influential businessman. He looked and behaved more like 'one of the boys'. But a tai pan he was, nonetheless.

Born in Darwin on 22 January 1901, he had taken his first breath, he said, 'in the same hour that Queen Victoria took her last'. At times he spoke like a colonial English-man, and at others like an outback Aussie, depending upon the occasion and who he was talking to. As a result, in the eyes of the European community, Foong Lee so contradicted the image of the inscrutable Oriental that he qualified unreservedly, albeit a little patronisingly, as a good all-round chap by some, and a bonzer bloke by others. In actuality, Foong Lee was perceived by all exactly the way Foong Lee wished to be perceived.

Having prepared his shopfront display—an extra-ordinary selection of goods, both European and Chinese, from general groceries and photographic supplies to silks and lanterns and Eastern delicacies—Foong Lee walked through to the living quarters at the rear. Perhaps his father may want some breakfast, it might be one of the old man's good days. But it wasn't.

In the living area which looked out over the large back courtyard, Foong Shek Mei was a crumpled heap on the sofa. He'd slept there last night. Again. As he had for the past week or so. When the family had been present he had at least attempted to scrape himself up from the sofa and retire to his bed. It saddened Foong Lee beyond measure to see his father reduced to a skeleton, his eyes dim and befud-dled, his mind obscured by the phantoms which haunted it.

Foong Shek Mei's addiction was no secret amongst the

elders of the Chinese community. There were a number like him, remnants of the old days, habitues of the opium divans of Hong Kong and Singapore, who secretly fed their habits behind closed doors in little rooms at the rear of shops and shanty dwellings in Chinatown. Although the Darwin Chinese upheld the law and indeed did not approve of the opium trade, they sympathised with those few elders amongst them to whom, throughout their lives, the drug had been readily and legally available and whose inner peace could now only be attained by 'chasing the dragon'.

The once-strong body of Foong Shek Mei, the body which had served him so well when he'd arrived from Singapore in the nineties to work as a coolie on the goldfields, was now a wasted skeleton. A lifetime of opium abuse had taken its toll, and over the past decade his mind too had decayed to the point where he'd become childlike, dependent. Foong Lee now purchased the opium necessary to assuage the relentless demands of his father's addiction. He was reluctant to do so but aware that he had no option. Foong Shek Mei was too far gone, and the opium was now necessary to ease him into a painless death.

Foong Lee warmed some soup and sat beside the old man, cradling the emaciated body against his. Gently, he touched the bowl to the parched lips.

'*Lei yiu yam, Baba.*'

Foong Shek Mei's eyes slowly opened. But glazed, unfocussed, they saw nothing.

'*Lei yiu yam,*' Foong Lee repeated, imploring his father to drink.

The old man's head leaned forward slightly, the cracked lips parted and, like an obedient child, he sipped. Very gently. Twice. Then he rested his head back on his son's shoulder and his gaze focussed on the hand which held the bowl. His eyes slowly became alive and he turned to look at Foong Lee.

'*Lei hai ho jai, Foong Lee,*' he said. Both the voice and the smile were gentle. Faded and distant, as if they came from far away, but they were genuine nonetheless. Foong Lee was indeed a good son and Foong Shek Mei wished very much to tell him so.

Foong Lee smiled fondly back. '*Lei yiu yam, Baba. Ho gan yue.*'

But the old man's head lolled against his son's shoulder, he'd fallen asleep.

Foong Lee rose. He eased his father's head comfortably back upon the sofa, then he walked through the house to the shop to prepare for his morning stroll. It was his custom these days to walk the streets of Chinatown, to greet those few of his friends who remained in Darwin and to check on the properties of those who had left. The closed and shuttered shops were an advertisement to the lawless element who might wish to take advantage of the current situation. Foong Lee considered it his duty to keep his eye on things, to check the shopfronts for any sign of forced entry which may have taken place under the veil of night.

Before embarking on his walk, he checked the day's 'specials'. Despite the fact that business was poor, Foong Lee liked to vary the array and to have some tantalising offer displayed daily out front. Satisfied that all was in order, he stepped into the street. He would open the shutters for business upon his return.

Toshiro Kurasoto flinched. He couldn't help it. The voice that cracked like a whip through his headset momentarily startled him. It shouldn't have done so, he'd been expecting the break in radio silence from the moment their flight path had approached Bathurst Island. Fifty miles north-north-west of Darwin, Bathurst Island was the point at which the attack force was to receive its specific orders. After the continuous monotone of the engine, however, the sudden sharp noise caused Toshiro to flinch, involuntarily and barely perceptibly, but he cast a glance to his left nevertheless, hoping his commander had not observed his inappropriate reaction.

Lieutenant Akira Nakajima was far too intent upon the information and instruction he was receiving to take any notice whatsoever of his young copilot. The US destroyer *Peary* had returned to the port of Darwin for refuelling within the past hour. It was a stroke of luck. Her presence had not been anticipated when the attack plans had first been laid out. And she was to be Nakajima's prime target. After the initial high-level assault upon Darwin, the dive-bombers would take control of the attack. And Akira Nakajima determined that it would be he who would erad-icate the US destroyer. The whole of Darwin would be under attack and its installations annihilated, that was the plan, but the *Peary* would be the personal jewel in Akira's crown.

Having breakfasted, Paul Trewinnard lounged about in the luxury of the Hotel Darwin foyer observing, through the potted palms, the comings and goings of the few remaining guests and staff. It was one of his favourite pastimes, studying human behaviour. After ten minutes or so, he decided to wander down to the wharf to look at the warships. The US destroyer *Peary* had arrived this morn-ing, the desk clerk had told him.

'Huge thing,' the clerk had said, 'quite terrifying really.'

She'd be worth a look at, Paul thought, donning his Panama hat. He nodded to the uniformed doorman as he stepped out into the glare of the morning.

Aggie Marshall walked down the Esplanade on her way to the post office. The Esplanade formed the harbourside boundary of Darwin's township, sweeping down the coast-line and turning in an L-shape north-east at the wharves.

The streets of Darwin were busy, mainly with military personnel. Many of the older buildings along the

Esplanade had been commandeered by the military, and men went about their business. The streets leading off to the left from the Esplanade and into the town centre were busy too. The civilians who had remained in the town were also going about their business.

Foong Lee stepped out of his shop and started down the broad avenue of Cavenagh Street, walking beneath the welcome shade of the endless verandahed shops and crossing the small laneways which dissected the major streets of Chinatown. Just ahead, to his right, was Gordon's Don Hotel on the corner of Bennet Street and beyond that, to his left, was the *yung si*, the massive banyan tree which stood at the far end of Cavenagh Street only half a block from the wharf end of the Esplanade. The *yung si* was a dominant feature of Chinatown, particularly to the children who played amongst its branches. Foong Lee made a habit of turning into Bennet Street just before he got to the *yung si*, then he'd walk up Smith Street and back into Cavenagh to complete his around-the-block stroll. It was a pleasant twenty-minute walk in all, at a leisurely pace.

The attack force had crossed the coast of the mainland to the east of Darwin. Upon instruction, they swung round to approach the town from the south-east, with the sun behind them. Far in the distance, and from twenty thousand feet up in the sky, Darwin Harbour looked magnificent. And vulnerable. Ships of every description sat like tiny dots on the vast blue water. Forty-five in number. And tucked away, on its tiny peninsula within the massive harbour, was Darwin itself. Most vulnerable of all. Innocently waiting. Undefended. A lamb to the slaughter, Akira Nakajima thought.

'Tora!' The command barked through Nakajima's headset. 'Tora! Tora!'

Akira Nakajima commenced his dive.

Paul Trewinnard had strolled down Lover's Walk to the wharves and was studying the ships in the harbour when he heard the warning sirens. He thought it was a military exercise at first. Until he looked up.

Aggie Marshall was outside the Hotel Darwin and just about to cross Herbert Street when she heard the wail of the sirens. An awful sound, it always unnerved her, even when she knew it was only an exercise of some sort. Then she looked up.

Having turned the corner from Bennet into Smith Street, Foong Lee was outside the Bank of New South Wales when the sirens sounded. An air raid, he thought in the instant he heard them. He shaded his eyes and looked up.

The whole of Darwin looked up. It was two minutes before ten o'clock on a Thursday morning and people stood in the street staring up at the sky in disbelief, unable to comprehend what their eyes perceived.

Time stopped as the menacing horde swooped down from the sun. For the hundreds watching from the town, it seemed an eternity. Then, suddenly, the planes were overhead, so many they all but obliterated the sun. The light seemed to dim, the sky no longer seemed blue, and by ten o'clock, Darwin was under massive attack from the Japanese Imperial Air Force.

The *Peary* was hit aft by a dive-bomber. Her bridge ignited and the crew worked valiantly to extinguish the flames. Then again, another direct hit. But she fought on. Upon her captain's orders her guns still fired as she drifted ablaze on the harbour waters.

The *Neptuna*, berthed at Main Jetty, was hit amidships. She burned fiercely. A time bomb, the intense heat threatening at any moment to ignite the heavy ammunition and depth charges she carried.

The *Zealandia* and the *British Motorist*, both at anchor, were hit and sank at their moorings. The harbour was an inferno, erupting in pockets of flame and belching black smoke and, as shells screamed through the air and explosions showered the shoreline with debris, the township of Darwin too became a blaze of destruction.

Foong Lee ran up Smith Street. His one aim was to get back to his father whom he knew would be in a state of utter terror and confusion. People were screaming in the streets, panic-stricken. He passed C.J. Cashman's store and, halfway up the block, the force of an explosion caused him to stagger. He fell to his knees, hauled himself back up on his feet and looked over his shoulder. Cashman's had been hit. Sheets of galvanised iron had been hurled across the street and smoke billowed from the windows of the gutted building. Two bodies were sprawled on the pavement. Foong Lee ran on.

Paul Trewinnard made no attempt at all to run for cover. What was the point? In his opinion there seemed no specific place in Darwin any safer than another. There had been no preparation for an event such as this, although there damn well should have been, he thought. Where were the Government-built bunkers? Where was the massive defence force which should have been present to drive away the marauders? He was as fearful as the next man, he'd be the first to admit, as he sqatted, covering his head with his arms, water and debris showering about him, but he might as well stay where he was. If he was going to be killed then he'd watch the spectacle first.

And as he watched, Paul's fear was mingled with awe. Out on the harbour, the *Peary*, already twice hit and adrift, her guns still bravely blazing, suddenly destructed. The vessel's magazine exploded and, in the instant before she was engulfed in flames, Paul could swear he saw men flying through the air. Black oil flooded the harbour, black smoke billowed up into the morning air and the once-proud *Peary*, now a massive ball of fire, burned on the water. His own fear now forgotten, Paul thought of the men who, only seconds previously, had been firing those guns. This was Armageddon, he thought. The annihilation was total.

After the first hideous moments of shock, Aggie Marshall ran for cover. The post office was only a block away, on the bend of the Esplanade, so she headed there. If she was to die then at least she'd be with people she knew. She crossed Bennet Street, the post office was right ahead of her. Then she was thrown backwards by a force so strong it lifted her off her feet. The noise was deafening. Surely her eardrums must have burst, she thought briefly. Then she knew nothing as she hit the pavement and was showered with rubble.

Foong Lee ran down Knuckey Street to the corner of Cavenagh. All about him others were running, screaming, wailing, terrified, and the air was thick with smoke and the sickening smell of cordite. It seemed to him that the whole of Darwin was exploding. He looked up Cavenagh Street. His shop was a block away. He stepped from the kerb. But he had barely crossed Knuckey Street before the force of another explosion threw him to the ground.

When the smoke had cleared and he'd struggled to his feet, there was no shop a block away. There was no block at all. Just wasteland. Amidst the pall of smoke and dust, there was no delineation of streets and houses. There was nothing but rubble. Half of Chinatown had been obliterated.

Foong Lee walked towards where his shop and his home had been. As he walked, he ignored the mayhem which surrounded him. He ignored the fire which crackled about his feet, licking at the dried timbers which had once been verandah posts. He walked slowly, there was no point in running. He'd check the wreckage, he thought numbly, then he must help the others, those who lay maimed and bleeding amongst the ruins. He prayed that Foong Shek Mei had not awakened from his drug-induced state, he prayed that the gods had been kind and that his father had known no terror. As he stepped over the threshold into the smouldering remains of the small room which had once served as his office he saw the valuables safe. It sat upright, still locked and unscarred, apparently impervious to the Japanese bombs. With a numb sense of irony, Foong Lee walked past the safe and commenced the search for his father's remains amongst the destruction.

At 10.40 a.m. the all-clear sounded. The Japanese attack force had departed as quickly as it had appeared, and Darwin lay devastated in its wake.

Fire engines and ambulances screamed through the streets. Rescue work started immediately; there were those trapped beneath rubble, the wounded and the dying.

Foong Lee went to the aid of a child. A little boy. He was badly burned and, as Foong Lee gently lifted him, the child's skin came away in his hands. Mercifully, the boy was dead. Foong Lee was not a man given to the expression of emotion, but he fell to his knees and wept for the human race.

It was an army Landrover, serving as an ambulance, which transported Aggie Marshall to the hospital. She regained consciousness as they lifted her from where she lay in the street and, as she did, she realised that she was not in pain, but she couldn't seem to move. Her body was a dead weight and yet she felt extremely light-headed. A strange combination.

Good heavens, she thought when she saw the firemen fighting the flames which were devouring the post office. It's gone. The post office has gone. She wondered if all of her friends who worked there had gone too, surely nobody could have survived such destruction. She wanted to ask one of the two kind men who were so gently carrying her what had happened to her friends. She raised her head and opened her mouth to say something, but then she noticed the blood. All over the stretcher, all over her clothes. Such a lot of blood. Was it hers? And she seemed to have lost her left shoe, she noticed as they laid her gently in the back of the Landrover. But then she seemed to have lost most of her left foot as well. She couldn't really tell for the blood.

Whilst emergency rescue work and firefighting continued there was no time to ponder what had happened, or even to mourn the dead. There was so much to do that it seemed the battle was still being fought and, as if to emphasise the point, the time bomb berthed at Main Jetty suddenly exploded.

The *Neptuna* had been burning fiercely for close to an hour and, at 11.15, the heat aboard the 6,000-ton vessel reached such an intensity that the high explosives aboard finally ignited.

Giant jets of flame propelled wreckage high into the sky like an erupting volcano, showering the harbour with smouldering debris. In the town the force of the explosion shattered the windows of those buildings left standing as the whole of Darwin trembled from the impact of the shock waves.

The gigantic black cloud which followed the explosion billowed over the harbour and the township like a huge exclamation mark. Surely it indicated the end to the battle, to the unspeakable events of the morning. But it didn't. Barely thirty minutes later a fresh horror presented itself.

At 11.58, two hours after the initial assault on Darwin, fifty-four unescorted land-based bombers attacked the RAAF base four miles north-east of the town. The attack lasted twenty-five minutes and the base was virtually annihilated. The gateway to the north lay ruined. The Japanese had successfully destroyed all RAAF strength in the north-western area of Australia, known as the Top End. The vast land to the south was now more vulnerable than ever.

BOOK ONE

BOOK ONE

CHAPTER ONE

1628

*F*rom his little writing desk in the corner by the door, young Pieter Grij stole another furtive glance at the woman as he dipped his quilled pen in the inkwell. And, yet again, he quickly averted his gaze to concentrate upon the giant leather-bound ledger before him, lest his father should catch the naked admiration in his eyes. But old Gerrit Grij's attention was focussed upon the locket which he held in his hands. Seated at his showcase table, he lovingly buffed the silver with a fine silk cloth then delicately, reverently, and with a touch of regret as if loath to part with this newborn gem of his creation, he placed it in the black, velvet-lined presentation case.

Another glance from the youth to the woman. Once again his gaze quickly averted lest she herself should turn and perceive his unashamed adoration. Painstakingly, the tip of his tongue protruding from his lips, Pieter concentrated upon his task. 'Quantity—one—Silver pendant with diamonds inset . . .' he wrote, the nib of the pen scratching on the rough paper as he entered the description and the *payment into the ledger, all the while longing to look up and once more feast his eyes on her. For nineteen-year-old Pieter had never seen so beautiful a woman. A woman of breeding, it was obvious. Tall, slender, her face framed by a heart-shaped bonnet, her thick auburn hair captured by the bonnet's lace cowl. Even as Pieter entered the sum in the ledger, he could see, through the shadows of his sandy eyelashes, the aquiline profile, the proud tilt of her chin and the regal bearing of her shoulders as she gazed out of the window. Pieter daren't look up. Any moment she might turn, and those magnificent, ice-blue eyes might scorn him, that fine, arched brow might furrow with disapproval, for he was far beneath her. He, the lowly youngest son of a diamond merchant, albeit a master craftsman, and she a fine lady. Why, she might read something untoward in his admiration. Something sinful. And Pieter would feel shamed.*

But Lucretia van den Mylen did not turn from the window. She stood in the second-floor showroom of the merchant's house and continued to stare out over the Keizersgracht. What an elegant city Amsterdam was becoming, she thought. Even now, before the final stages of the Prinsengracht construction had been completed.

The three major canals, the Herengracht, the Keizersgracht and the Prinsengracht, were an engineering feat of which all Amsterdammers were justifiably proud. They started at the harbour, where the walled city of Amsterdam sat snuggled within the immense womb of the Zuider Zee, and they arced around the township to meet the Amstel River. Tall slender houses, like the diamond merchant's, had already sprung up beside the canals, wealthy merchants and traders willing to sacrifice breadth of frontage for fashionable canal views.

It was an afternoon in late September, and Lucretia watched a young couple, huddled together to ward off the autumn chill, as they walked along the cobbled street beside the canal. Now and then they disappeared amongst the row of elm and linden trees which lined the street, but still she watched until they were out of sight around the bend. They made her think of Boudewijn and how she missed him, and how she longed to feel his arms around her. In one month's time she would be on her way to him, she thought. Just one month. The voyage would take a whole further nine and God alone knew what perils lay ahead on the high seas, but each day would bring her closer to him, and to Lucretia that was all that mattered. Of course she would miss Amsterdam, she thought as she watched a small barge being punted along the canal, but . . .

'Here she is, Vrouwe van den Mylen.' The merchant's voice startled her, lost in reverie as she had been. 'A thing of great beauty.' Gerrit Grij checked himself. Although he always referred to his favourite pieces in the female gender, lavish comments upon his own work were uncharacteristic of him, he did not wish to sound proud. 'I hope she meets with your requirements,' he added.

He eased himself carefully from his chair, stifling a grimace at the pain of the arthritis in his hip, and held the open presentation case at arm's length. Ceremoniously he lowered it to the table in front of him. Lucretia crossed to the table and looked down at the locket.

A tiny but audible gasp of astonishment caught in her throat and her lips parted in a smile of sheer delight; the jeweller was right, the locket was a thing of great beauty. Circular, no more than an inch in diameter, it was made from solid silver, and engraved on its face was a rocky mountain. Not an etching, not an outline, but the very texture of the rock appeared to be carved into the heavy metal, as if it had been eroded by the elements themselves. And behind the mountain's peak rose a mighty sun, a cluster of diamonds, perfectly cut and set into the silver to reflect the maximum light from every direction. The two were entwined: the sun caressed the mountain, and the *mountain basked in the sun, its peak of a lighter hue than its base, as if it were reaching for the sun's embrace.*

'*It is glorious,*' *Lucretia breathed softly as she lifted the locket from the case, 'truly glorious.*'

She had spoken in depth with the jeweller about the design, and she had trusted in the quality of his work, for Gerrit Grij was far more than a merchant and a jeweller, he was a diamond cutter and an engraver whose crafts-manship was held in the highest esteem.

'*Boudewijn is the sun to me, as I am the earth to him,*' *she had said.*

Gerrit Grij had wondered briefly whether the request bore any astrological inference. As a devout Protestant he sincerely hoped not. But as an artisan the challenge excited him.

'*The sun and the earth,*' *he had mused. '*Yes, yes, the sun must be a cluster of diamonds. Perfect diamonds set to reflect its rays from all directions. And the earth—the earth must not be flat, not like Holland. There must be texture and depth. The earth must be a great mountain.*'

Lucretia had agreed. Now she marvelled at the result.

*Gerrit Grij was gratified by Lucretia van den Mylen's reaction, the locket had been a labour of love, it was his finest piece and he was inordinately proud of it. The joy in Vrouwe van den Mylen's magnificent eyes gave him far more pleasure than he would ever admit. '*The chain is strong,*' he said, '*each link is welded, you see?*' He reached out his hands and gave the chain a brisk tug.

'*Oh.*' *Lucretia was startled by the brutality of his gesture.*

'*You need have no fear of it breaking,*' *he added. '*Open it.*'

Gerrit's stern face, brow furrowed from forty years in his trade, softened as he watched the slender fingers turn the locket and press the catch on the side. A woman of such beauty deserved a thing of such beauty. He supposed that was why he had given the piece his greatest care and attention. And she had spoken of her husband with such love.

'I go to meet him in the East Indies,' she had said. 'And I wish for a memento of some sort to travel with me. As if we were together. As if, by the grace of God, Boudewijn were there to protect me.' The light of love was so strong in her eyes that Gerrit put aside his laughable notion of any connection with the occult art of astrology. The motif was born purely of devotion.

'The token must be in the form of a locket,' he had said, 'with the initials of you and your husband engraved on each side of the interior.' He hadn't added 'with a chain long enough that the pendant may rest against your heart', but he'd made the chain of such length anyway.

Lucretia opened the locket. 'L v.d. M' was engraved in perfect copperplate on the left, and on the right, 'B v.d. M'. 'It is perfect,' she said, and she pressed the open locket to her breast.

The gesture touched Gerrit Grij more than he could say. 'You are happy with the length of the chain?' he enquired as Lucretia closed the locket. 'Allow me.' He undid the clasp and Lucretia turned, lifting her hair in its lace cowl, allowing him to secure it about her neck.

Pieter was by now unashamedly staring. His father and the beautiful woman were both too intent upon the locket to notice him anyway. He could see the nape of her neck. White. Arched. Leaning forward as she was to assist his father. Arched, like a beautiful swan.

'Yes, I am very happy with the length of the chain,' Lucretia said. On her wide lace collar, the locket rested over her breastbone.

'With a chain of this length,' Gerrit explained, 'you can wear the locket at all times. As an adornment on the outside of your garment or, if you fear for its safety, it can remain hidden.'

'Extremely practical,' Lucretia agreed, although she had

a feeling the choice of the length of chain displayed the same understanding as did the design and craftsmanship of the locket itself. But she said nothing, once more bending her neck and lifting her hair as he unclasped the locket.

A swan, Pieter thought. A glorious white swan.

'And you will encounter times on your voyage when you will no doubt fear for its safety,' Gerrit continued, replacing the locket in its case. And for your own safety, he thought. He admired the woman for embarking upon such an arduous trip. Another measure of her love, he determined, and he prayed for her safety. Any number of disasters could befall her. Pirates, shipwreck, not to mention starvation, deprivation, and illness; ships were not known for their comfort and the voyage to the East Indies could take a year. Shipboard life was no life for a woman of breeding, as Gerrit knew well.

Lucretia read into the man's words what he was truly saying. 'I have little to fear,' she assured him. 'I shall be travelling aboard the finest ship ever to set sail from Amsterdam.'

'I am glad to hear of it,' Gerrit Grij said, handing her the case. 'I wish you well, Vrouwe van den Mylen. God speed you safely to your husband.' Then, to cover his display of sentiment, he barked at his young son, 'Pieter, see Vrouwe van den Mylen safely downstairs.' He gestured apologetically towards his walking stick.

Pieter opened the door and led the way down the narrow staircase.

'Pieter is it?' Lucretia said as they arrived at the little front shop which opened on to the cobbled street. She had been fully aware of the youth's surreptitious glances. She had not found them offensive, accustomed as she was to the admiration of men. Indeed, she had realised that the boy was painfully shy.

Pieter nodded. She had spoken to him! Directly to him!

'Perhaps one day if you work very hard you may

become a great craftsman like your father.' She smiled encouragingly.

She had smiled at him! He found his voice. 'I hope to,' he said. 'And I do work hard. Very hard.' He glanced nervously upstairs as if his father might hear him. 'Father is a stern taskmaster.'

'It is apparent in his work,' Lucretia said. 'He is a great artist. And great artists are meticulous. They must be. And you must be too, Pieter, if you wish to become a master craftsman like your father.'

'Yes,' Pieter said, 'I know, that is what he tells me.' She was talking to him! Actually talking to him! He wanted to keep her there in the shop, so that he could look at her and talk to her some more. But she had opened the front door. The shopbell tinkled. He must make conversation!

'What ship do you sail on?' he asked.

'The Batavia,' she said, and her smile was radiant. 'The Batavia. Her maiden voyage. Goodbye, Pieter.' The shopbell tinkled as the door closed behind her.

CHAPTER TWO

'They've bombed Darwin!' Flight Lieutenant Terence Galloway stared at the opened newspaper on the table before him. Page five. Only a small article, no picture. 'Japanese Attack Australia', it said, 'Air Raid on Darwin', and a short column followed. 'Just look at that!' He pushed the newspaper across the table to Robbie seated opposite. 'They've bloody bombed Darwin!'

It was Monday morning in the officers' mess at the RAF Fighter Command Base, Biggin Hill, Kent, approximately fifteen miles south-east of London.

Robbie Roper swallowed the last of his toast, shoved his cleanly mopped-up breakfast plate to one side and examined the article. 'Doesn't say much,' he commented, picking up his mug of tea and taking a swig. 'Last Thursday, that's four days ago, and just a mention like this.' He gave a laconic shrug. 'Probably means bugger all. A Jap reconnaissance flight, I reckon, and the locals have overreacted.'

'I don't think it's a recce at all,' Terence disagreed. 'The Japs have been flying recces over Darwin for months, Dad tells me.'

The homestead of Bullalalla cattle station, where Terence had been born and raised, was only sixty miles from Darwin, and his father, an ex-military man, kept Terence regularly posted with the news. Indeed Jock Galloway's recent predictions had been of an imminent attack.

'Better check it out with Harry then.' Robbie took another swig of his tea, slurping as he did, and annoying Terence further. A lot of things about Robbie annoyed Terence, most of all his indifference. Some saw his lackadaisical attitude as a sign of strength, and Terence reluctantly agreed that to newly trained pilots about to face combat Robbie's nonchalance was probably a comfort. But to Terence, the man's lack of passion was both uncaring and soulless, and his reaction to the newspaper article typified his apathy. He was an Australian for God's sake, didn't he care that his country might be under attack?

'Yes, I'll do that,' Terence replied and he all but snatched the paper from Robbie's hand as he rose abruptly to his feet. 'I'll get Harry to check it out right now.'

Robbie watched as Terence crossed to the far end of the mess where Harold Crighton-Smith was sitting with his cronies. It was quite obvious that he'd somehow annoyed Terence, but Robbie couldn't for the life of him think what he'd done wrong. It was often like that. As the only remaining Aussie pilots on the base one would suppose they'd have more in common, particularly having been through so much together, but they were chalk and cheese, all right.

Terence and Robbie, like many Australian airmen, had been seconded to London during the Battle of Britain. They had been amongst the lucky survivors, seeing many about them die, and when the battle was finally over they'd been offered positions as Spitfire pilot instructors at the Royal Flying College in Cranwell not far from Biggin Hill. Robbie had jumped at the opportunity; he would willingly live out the war as an instructor, at thirty he was getting too old for battle. It surprised him, however, when Terence accepted the offer. He'd have expected Terence to insist upon a posting to the Middle East. In his mid-twenties, intrepid and reckless to the point of foolishness at times—in Robbie's opinion, anyway—Terence Galloway had a lust for battle.

It was ego which had dictated the decision, Robbie had decided. Terence's ego would have demanded he accept the position of chief flying instructor at an establishment like the Royal Flying College, it was the consummate endorsement of his skill. A skill which Robbie would be the first to acknowledge. Terence Galloway was the finest pilot he'd known, and Robbie himself was no slouch. Now, however, well over a year after the Battle of Britain, Robbie could sense the frustration in his countryman. Terence had flown on a number of operations but it wasn't enough, Robbie could tell that he longed to be back in the thick of it.

Robbie couldn't understand why. Bloody awful business, war, he'd decided, and he couldn't fathom Terence's desire to do battle. But then there was a lot he couldn't fathom about Terence. In Robbie Roper's opinion, Terence Galloway was a strange bastard.

Harold Crighton-Smith was the base's intelligence officer and an obliging chap, particularly when it came to Terence Galloway whom he very much admired. Terence possessed all the criteria necessary for hero status. Tall, handsome, dashing, daring, he was everything Harold had always longed to be.

Terence knew full well that Harold had a 'crush' on him. There was no evidence of homosexuality in the man's behaviour, but Terence was scathing of him nevertheless, considering him soft and weak, despite the fact that Harold was extremely efficient and very good at his job. 'Typical Pommie public school boy,' he'd said to Robbie on numerous occasions. Terence did not suffer what he considered to be any form of weakness kindly. But he was not averse to using Harold when he felt it was necessary.

Harold knew nothing of the attack upon Darwin, he said, but he would get on to the War Office and have information for them by lunchtime.

As always, Harold was true to his word. He met Terence and Robbie in the mess shortly before one o'clock.

'The Japs made two raids,' he said in his precise, clipped tones. 'Twenty-three aircraft were destroyed and the RAAF base virtually demolished.' Terence and Robbie exchanged a look of incredulity. 'Five merchant ships and three warships were sunk,' Harold continued, 'and thirteen other vessels damaged or beached.' He reeled the list off without referring to any notes; he rarely made notes. 'It was a massive raid evidently. Reports, as yet unsubstantiated but rumoured to be true, are saying that the Japs dropped more bombs on Darwin last Thursday than they did on Pearl Harbor.'

Shocked from his normal complacency, Robbie looked at Terence aghast, but Terence continued to stare at Harold who, in turn, continued to reel off the inconceivable facts.

'They're not releasing the death toll as yet.' Harold spoke dispassionately as he always did when dealing in statistics, particularly the horrifying ones. 'But casualties are likely to be considerable, a lot of the town was destroyed.'

It was only then that Terence looked at Robbie and, when he did, each read the fear in the other's eyes. For the first time in its history their country was experiencing warfare upon its own soil. Both men were deeply shocked.

But several days later Harold's contact at the War Office divulged the most horrifying news of all.

'Been looking for you everywhere, old man, thought you'd want to know as soon as possible.' Harold caught up with Terence in the carpark, Terence having just returned from a trip into nearby Bromley.

'They're not publishing the facts in Australia,' Harold told him, 'not to the general populace anyway. The Government's decided to keep the public in ignorance. For fear of panic or whatever.' There was a flicker of criticism in Harold's normally bland eyes. 'Heaven only knows why, surely the Australians have a right to the truth, the people are strengthened when they can share their losses. I tell you, the English wouldn't stand for it, being kept in the dark.' Then, quickly back to business. 'The official toll at this stage is at least 238 dead, including women and children, and between 300 and 400 wounded. But that's a conservative estimate,' he added, 'the numbers are probably far greater.'

My God, Terence thought as he stared at Harold in horror. *Oh my God. The war has landed in Australia.*

'Five pounds!'

There was a moment's silence. Most present were thinking 'that's a week's wages', while they peered behind them to see whose voice it was that had shouted from the back of the crowded Masonic hall.

Henrietta peered, along with the others. In her Red Cross volunteer's uniform, lined up with WRENS and WAAFS and ATS, there were fifteen of them in all, she stood on the stage and searched the servicemen's faces as they jostled each other and waved and laughed. Who amongst the sea of men in army, air force and navy uniforms had bid a whole week's wages just for a dance? And with her!

One by one, the girls had been called to the stage and introduced, each receiving a generous round of applause. Then they'd lined up in front of the dance band, beneath the huge portrait of King George which hung from the proscenium arch, and the bidding had begun for each girl.

One by one, numbering from the left and starting at five shillings a pop. Girl number five, a pretty blonde WREN, was so popular that her final bid had come in at two pounds five shillings.

Fourteenth in line, Henrietta had waited, cursing her stupidity in volunteering. 'Go on, Henrietta,' her workmates had urged, 'it's all in good fun and it's for a good cause.' It had seemed harmless enough at the time. Until the volunteers had been called up on stage. To Henrietta's horror every one of the servicewomen looked as though she'd stepped out of a beauty pageant, or off the pages of *Vogue*. Willowy and elegant, or petite and pretty, their hair perfectly coiffured, their makeup immaculate, Henrietta felt large and clumsy and untidy in their company. She'd dreaded the arrival of her turn. What if nobody bid? Well, some poor sod would probably feel sorry for her and offer five bob, but how humiliating!

'I bid five pounds for Miss Henrietta Southern!' The voice with the lazy drawl repeated itself strongly from amongst the balloons and streamers which festooned the walls at the back of the hall. There was a huge round of applause.

'Thank you, sir, most generous,' Alfie, the cockney MC announced through his microphone. 'If you'd just make yourself known to one of our two stewards, we'll move right along.' No point in trying to push up the price, nobody was going to go higher than that. Funny choice though, Alfie thought, the big girl with the unruly copper-coloured hair. Good looking enough, he supposed, but he would have gone for the little blonde WREN himself. And the bidding moved onto the next and final girl.

This was the highlight of the NAAFI Ball, the moment everyone had been waiting for, the buy-a-belle dance to raise contributions for the Orphans Welfare Scheme.

As the girls stepped from the stage, the dance band struck up a rendition of 'Amapola'.

'Flight Lieutenant Terence Galloway,' he stepped out of the crowd and introduced himself.

'Henrietta Southern, how do you do,' she said and they shook hands. She was taken aback. He was tall and well built, sun-tanned and sandy-haired, with arresting hazel-green eyes. In fact he was so handsome that Henrietta was shocked. She'd expected her benefactor to be a middle-aged philanthropist—who else would have five quid to spend on a dance?

'You're Australian,' she said, noting the RAAF uniform. She'd thought he was a Yank from the twang of his accent.

'Yes,' he replied. 'Shall we?'

He offered his arm, she took it, and he led her through the jostling throng and onto the dance floor.

From the moment he'd seen her up on the stage, Terence had known he must meet her. Her chestnut curls bouncing disobediently whenever she moved, her skin, free of makeup save for a touch of lipstick, glowing with vitality, she had put the other women to shame, he thought. Their prettiness was manufactured, synthetic beside the natural beauty of Henrietta Southern. Just in case other potential bidders had been thinking the same thing, Terence had cut to the chase and bid five pounds. He'd recently received a money order from his father so he could afford it.

She wasn't a nurse, hers was the uniform of a volunteer worker. 'What do you do?' he asked. 'For the Red Cross, I mean.'

'I drive,' she replied. 'Courier cars, supply trucks, you name it.'

He smiled as he nodded. She looked like she could handle a truck. Practical. Capable.

There was a wry twist to his eyebrows, she noted, and his mouth was a little lopsided when he smiled, none of which detracted from his looks, if anything they made him even more attractive.

'Where are you based?' she asked by way of conversation. He was a good dancer too.

'At the moment, Biggin Hill,' he said a touch evasively. 'Where do you live?'

'Chelsea. With my grandmother,' she added, although she didn't know why. Perhaps it was because he was so direct. She wanted him to know that she wasn't one of 'those' girls, just in case he was wondering.

It charmed him even more. She could dance too. 'Chelsea, that's not far from here, is it,' he said.

'About a half a mile.'

'Perhaps I could walk you home after the ball,' he said, and then quickly added, 'Taxis'll be hard to come by with this crowd.'

'Perhaps.'

'Amapola' had finished and the band now began to play the introduction to 'The White Cliffs of Dover' as the MC stepped onto the stage and took the microphone from its stand.

'Would you like a glass of punch?' Terence asked. He wanted to get her away from the dance floor before another prospective admirer cut in. 'Or a cup of tea?' he suggested at her slight hesitation. Lined along one wall of the hall was a row of trestle tables with tea urns and huge bowls of punch. The table at the end, with crates of beer, was surrounded by men; he'd steer clear of that one.

'Yes. Punch. Thank you.' It was a warm June night and the air in the crowded hall was close. Too hot to drink tea.

'Our special guest for tonight,' the MC was announcing. 'A young lady who has sung her way into all our hearts. Take the arm of the girl of your dreams, gentlemen,' Alfie was milking it for all he was worth, 'and dance the night away with our most loved songstress! Our mistress of melody! Our very own . . . Miss Vera Lynn!'

The music swelled and there was a huge ovation as the singer appeared. The band repeated its introduction to

'The White Cliffs of Dover', Vera Lynn took the microphone from Alfie and, to hushed silence, she started to
sing.

   '*There'll be blue birds over . . .*'

   'She's wonderful, isn't she,' Henrietta remarked, accepting the glass of punch Terence handed her. But she blinked
rapidly, feeling the hot familiar sting in her eyes. She
wanted to get away from 'The White Cliffs of Dover', it
had been one of their favourites and even now, nearly
two years later, such reminders could reduce her to tears.
A fact which Henrietta found embarrassing in public.

   People were drifting back to the dance floor. Keeping
a sharp lookout, Terence had noted two men making a
beeline for Henrietta. 'Would you like to duck outside for
a bit of fresh air?' he said. 'I could do with a smoke and
it's stuffy in here.'

   She smiled gratefully. How tactful of him, she thought,
how sympathetic. And, just as the men arrived, one on
either side of Henrietta, Terence took her hand and
elbowed his way towards the main doors.

   Once outside, he led the way down the several steps to
sit on the low stone wall out the front of the hall.

   'Thank you,' she said, fumbling for the handkerchief in
the pocket of her uniform.

   'What for?' He proffered his packet of Craven A but she
shook her head.

   'I was a bit upset,' she said, briskly blowing her nose.
'Terribly embarrassing, I'm sorry. Thanks for getting me
out of there.'

   'I was getting you away from two blokes who were
going to ask you to dance.'

   Henrietta burst out laughing, it was the best remedy he
could have offered to break through her brief maudlin
bout.

   He liked her laugh. It was open and honest, and he
liked the genuine humour which shone from her clear

blue eyes. 'Why were you upset?'

'Oh,' she shrugged, tucking her hankie back in her pocket, 'just the song. Reminding me of things. You know how it is.' It was time to change the subject.

'What things? A boyfriend, I suppose.' He struck a match. 'A great love?' he asked as he lit his cigarette. If there was any cynicism intended she couldn't read it from his tone, but the question was impertinent, she thought.

'No,' she said, just a trifle brusquely.

But he didn't get the message. 'What then? What did the song remind you of?'

The intensity of his interest unnerved her a little. 'You're very persistent,' she said.

'I'm a fighter pilot, I have to be.' His non sequitur puzzled her. 'Our life-expectancy isn't rated very high,' he explained, 'and I've learned to get to the point. I can't afford the luxury of taking months to get to know you, Henrietta—you don't mind if I call you Henrietta?' He didn't wait for a reply. 'I want to get to know you now. I want to know everything about you.'

Henrietta had been sexually propositioned along similar lines on a number of occasions. 'I'm going into battle, I may never come back . . .' But even as she'd felt for the young men, she'd never once been tempted to succumb. This was different, she thought. 'Why?' she asked. 'Why do you want to know everything about me?'

'I'm not sure,' he said honestly enough, but even as he said it he had a feeling he did know why. He had a feeling that this was the woman he wanted to marry. He couldn't tell her that. It was madness. 'But please let me know you, Henrietta.'

She looked away for a moment at the several other couples who had escaped the hall and were whispering quietly or embracing, heedless of those about them. 'The song reminded me of my parents,' she said, 'they were killed in the first heavy bombing.' September 10, 1940, she could have said but she didn't. 'Nearly two years ago now.'

She was glad of his reaction. He didn't say he was sorry he'd asked, he silently accepted the information and waited for her either to call a halt to the conversation or to continue. For some strange reason she continued.

'We lived in Battersea,' she said. 'The whole block was destroyed, razed to the ground. It was around midnight, and I would have been killed along with them if I hadn't been safely out of London for the night.'

Henrietta was surprised to hear herself say it without bitterness. There would have been a sarcastic edge to such a comment once. For a full twelve months she had felt shockingly guilty that she hadn't died with her parents. As if, by escaping their fate, she had deserted them. In fact, talking now to Terence Galloway, Henrietta was pleasantly surprised that she didn't feel at all emotional. It was quite liberating to simply state the facts to a person who was neither embarrassed nor dripping with concern for the tragedy of her life.

'I wasn't driving trucks then,' she said. 'I only did the occasional job for the war effort so that I wouldn't feel guilty about not helping. When the raid happened I was in Amersham with twenty children who'd just been evacuated. I was supposed to come back the same day but I missed the afternoon train to London and had to stay the night.'

'That was lucky.'

'Yes,' she said. He was right of course. For a long time she'd blamed herself for missing that train. 'Yes, it was very lucky.'

He stubbed out his cigarette and rose. 'Do you want to go back inside?'

Vera Lynn was singing 'A Nightingale Sang in Berkeley Square' when they returned. Then the band played a bracket of upbeat American swing numbers, and Henrietta was whisked off her feet by a succession of enthusiastic Yanks. But Terence was waiting when, giddy with exhaustion, she finally refused all offers. 'I'm sorry,' she panted to a disappointed GI, 'I need to get my breath back, I really do.'

'Punch?' Terence was holding a glass out to her.

'Thank you.'

The last dance she reserved for him. At least he made sure that she did. He was by her side in an instant.

Vera Lynn was back on the stage.

'*Goodnight sweetheart, 'til we meet tomorrow, goodnight sweetheart, tears will banish sorrow . . .*'

They swayed to the music, to the melody and the woman's glorious voice. There was no need to talk any more.

He'd told her about his father's cattle station as they'd sat drinking punch.

'I thought they were called ranches,' she'd said.

'That's in America.'

And when she'd asked if all Australians were such good dancers he'd said 'No, probably not, but my sister Charlotte is and she taught me. She doesn't dance any more, though; they call her Charlie now and she musters cattle.' She hadn't really understood the comment but he'd grinned as he'd added 'and she's bloody good with a rifle', and she'd thought how fascinating his family must be.

He'd asked her about her family too; she didn't sound as though she came from Battersea. Her mother was Irish, she'd said. She'd lived quite a lot of her early life in Ireland.

'Ah, that explains it,' he'd said. He loved the slight lilt to her voice.

'*Dreams enfold you, in my arms I'll hold you . . .*'

There was nothing more to say as they swayed to the music. There was no need for words.

'*Goodnight sweetheart, goodnight.*'

Terence Galloway and Henrietta Southern were in love.

He walked her home to her grandmother's flat in nearby Chelsea and shook her hand as he said goodnight, although she wouldn't have minded at all if he'd kissed her. He was going away for a while, he told her, but when he returned may he call on her? Of course she said yes.

She thought, regretfully, that she'd never see him again. But two weeks later he was back. He took her out to lunch on the Saturday. To a little café in Soho an RAF mate had told him about that sold good food, and they talked. Or rather he did while she listened. He didn't talk of the war or the missions he'd flown, but of his home in Australia. The Northern Territory, he called it. She'd never heard of the Northern Territory. And the cattle station. 'Bullalalla'. She thought it was a beautiful name.

'You can travel a dozen countries at Bullalalla,' he told her. 'You can gallop your horse across the the Pindan country where, at dusk, the spinifex glows red like fire. And you can look down into gorges hundreds of feet deep, and you can climb rocks the size of castles.' Her rapt attention drove Terence on. 'In the wet season, when the rivers flood, all you can see for miles is green, and then the dry comes and whole riverbeds and lakes disappear.'

She looked as if she didn't believe him. 'They do,' he insisted. 'They just dry up. They burn to a crust, and you can drive a thousand head of cattle across something that was once an inland sea or a raging torrent of water.'

Never in his life had Terence waxed so poetic. But then never in his life had he needed to. Where had such passion come from? He really didn't know. But one thing he was sure of, he wanted this woman for his wife, and he needed to paint a picture she would wish to see.

On the Sunday afternoon they walked along the Chelsea Embankment. Holding hands. As if they'd known each other for a very long time. She looked at other couples holding hands. A soldier and a girl were embracing, clinging tightly to each other.

'I'd like to meet your grandmother,' he said, surprising her.

'Flight Lieutenant Terence Galloway,' he said. 'How do you do, Mrs Southern.'

A very formal introduction, the old lady thought. There'd be a reason for that. Currying favour of course, but to what end? Any young Lothario out to bed the girl didn't need to seek the approval of an old woman. Henrietta was twenty-two years old, she'd make up her own mind.

'How do you do,' she said, shaking his hand. She was in her favourite armchair by the window, overlooking the small park, her crocheted rug tucked about her knees. It was where she spent most of her time.

Henrietta had led Terence through the front door and up the stairs. 'Grandma doesn't get around much these days,' she'd explained.

He was a handsome devil all right, Winifred Southern thought, Henrietta had said that he was. 'Will you get the tea, Henrietta?'

'Of course.'

As her grand daughter left the room, the old lady said, 'I'm sorry we have nothing stronger, Lieutenant, I wasn't expecting you.'

'Tea's fine, thanks.' She was tough, he thought, but he respected her for it. She didn't look at all like Henrietta. Small, and frail in body—well, she must be about eighty— she had white hair which would once have been black judging from the beady brown eyes which were studying him intently. Henrietta must have got her looks from her Irish mother.

'How long are you stationed here?'

'Not for much longer,' he said. 'I've applied for a transfer to Darwin. The Yanks have set up bases there and the Dutch are sending forces from Batavia.'

'Darwin?' she queried politely. 'Where's that?'

'The Northern Territory.' She looked a little blank. 'The north of Australia,' he said, 'we call it the Top End.'

'Ah.'

'Darwin was heavily bombed six months or so ago. In February.'

'Who by?'

'I beg your pardon?' He was confused by her question.

'Who bombed Darwin?' Winifred Southern asked. Why in God's name would the Germans want to bomb northern Australia, she was wondering. What on earth could they gain by it?

For a brief moment he wondered at the stupidity of her question. Then he realised that civilians experiencing the horrors of the European war probably wouldn't even know that the battle had spread to the Pacific. And they probably wouldn't care if they did. Why should they? Their lives were being torn apart right here at home.

'The Japanese,' he said, and added, not impertinently but with the vestige of a smile. 'The Japs are in the war too, you know.'

'Ah yes, of course.' She made no apology. 'Here's the tea. Do sit down, Lieutenant.'

She was calling him Terence, by his request, when he left nearly two hours later, but for all the charm he'd laid on he wasn't sure if she liked him. She was certainly adding him up, trying to read his intent, which was what he'd expected. After all, Henrietta was the only family the old woman had.

'When my son and his wife were killed,' she'd said in her brittle matter-of-fact way, 'Henrietta was immensely strong. I was not well myself, I believe it was grief which brought about my physical decline.' She spoke of grief as if it was the croup, and Terence could imagine little affecting the old lady emotionally. 'She came to live with me in order to look after me, and she devoted herself to her Red

Cross work. She was always a good driver. She drives trucks, you know.'

'I know.'

'Yes,' the old woman nodded proudly. 'She does the work of a man. Devoted to it too, quite devoted.'

'Well I wasn't any good at knitting socks and vests, Grandma,' Henrietta said lightly, wishing her grandmother would stop speaking about her as if she wasn't there.

'A very strong girl, my Henrietta. Very strong. Very capable.'

Terence wondered exactly what sort of message the old woman was sending him. He was trying to read her, just as she was trying to read him. On the one hand she seemed to be telling him that she needed Henrietta to look after her, and on the other she was extolling Henrietta's virtues as one did a brood mare.

'I shall be leaving for Australia within the month, Mrs Southern,' he said as he bade his farewell.

'Shall you be paying a visit before your departure?' she asked. The beady brown eyes were asking 'a visit not only to Henrietta, but to me'. The old woman knew that he wanted to marry her grand daughter, Terence could tell. Was she for him or against him? She was giving away nothing.

'I most certainly shall.'

'I look forward to that, Terence. Goodbye.' She shook his hand.

Henrietta took him downstairs and saw him to the front door.

Winifred returned her attention to the little park out the window. Well, his intentions were honourable, that was obvious, he wanted to marry the girl and take her to Australia. Young people moved so quickly these days, but then there was a war on, they had to.

There was a little girl in the park, playing with a dog.

A puppy really, half grown. Both young and exuberant. Winifred remembered the puppy she'd had as a small girl, so boisterous it would bowl her over. Life went on, didn't it. God, but she was old. So very, very old. She snapped her mind back to the present.

The lieutenant came from a wealthy family it appeared. Cattle people, a property with the rather ridiculous name of 'Bullalalla'. Four thousand square miles no less. She'd found it impossible to believe at first.

'Don't you mean acres?' she'd asked.

'Nope, square miles, that's the way we measure it where I come from.'

'But that's half the size of Wales.'

'Is it?' He hadn't appeared particularly interested in British comparisons. 'In the more arid areas there are stations ten, twelve thousand square miles and more,' he'd said, 'but Bullalalla's good country, the homestead's only sixty miles from Darwin, along the Finniss River, you can double your stock on land like ours.'

Winifred had been aware of the sales pitch, but he hadn't been lying, she was sure of that. Yes, she thought as she looked out the window, Henrietta would be well looked after. And she'd be in Australia. A foreign country, so very far away. But Australia was safe, the Lieutenant had assured her. The cattle station was isolated. Far from the bombs. And that was what Winifred wanted more than anything, the safety of her grand daughter. The death of her only son had devastated her, she must protect his daughter at all costs. When Terence proposed marriage, as it was obvious he was going to, Henrietta would agonise over leaving her grandmother. Well, Winifred would convince her that she must. The next-door neighbour would do her shopping, she would say, and if necesssary she could employ a helper. That's what old people with means did, she would say, and she was not without means. She would make it easy for the girl, who was so clearly in love.

Winifred would miss Henrietta sorely, she knew it. But perhaps the absence of her grand daughter would help her to die. Since the death of her son she had longed to die, Henrietta had been the only thing keeping her going. Perhaps the loneliness would help.

She only hoped the lieutenant would be kind to Henrietta. There was a hardness behind his eyes. Perhaps it was because he was an Australian, from 'the outback' no less. She couldn't really picture 'the outback', but he'd spoken of it with such pride and passion. And he was a fighter pilot, they certainly needed to be hard, perhaps that was it. Winifred fought back any misgivings she might have had. Terence Galloway was the best thing that could have happened to Henrietta, she told herself. Her grand daughter would go to a safe life in a safe haven with a man who loved her.

'Did you like him, Grandma?' Henrietta was back. 'Did you really like him?'

He obviously hadn't proposed, Winifred thought, or Henrietta would have burst through the door announcing it. But her grand daughter's cheeks were glowing and her eyes were shining, and any tiny doubt Winifred might have had disappeared in an instant.

'Very much,' she said. 'And you're right, he's very handsome.'

Henrietta was the only one of the three of them, Winifred thought, who had no idea of what had gone on that afternoon.

CHAPTER THREE

*I*f it were not for the company of Commandeur
Pelsaert, life aboard the Batavia would be intolerable,
Lucretia often thought.

No, not intolerable, she now decided, as she stood upon
the deck looking out over the sullen ocean, the huge sails
flapping idly overhead, the ship rocking gently, silent,
becalmed on this strange, still sea. No, she would tolerate
any hardship life could deliver so long as each day brought
her closer to her beloved Boudewijn. But, amongst the
deprivation and rigours of shipboard life, and the close
proximity of rough and vulgar men, Lucretia blessed the
companionship of Commandeur Francisco Pelsaert, a man
of breeding and sensitivity.

The convoy had set sail with all the pomp and ceremony
Amsterdam had to offer and, as they'd swept through the
Marsdiep, the principal channel connecting the Zuider Zee
to the North Sea, they had indeed presented an awesome
sight. The Batavia, the flagship leading the convoy of
eight, the grandest of them all. The most magnificent
vessel ever to set sail for the East Indies. Built of seasoned
oak, she was 140 feet in length, forty feet in the beam and
forty feet from deck to keel. She carried 600 tons of cargo

and, within the cramped space below decks, she housed no less than 300 soldiers, passengers and crew.

But it was her decoration which made her unique. Her hull was painted bright green and gold, and around her massive stern were carved figures to ward off the evil spirits which might cause her harm. Likewise, all about the vessel were ornately carved heads and life-sized figures, watching over the ship from every vantage point, guarding her safety, and proclaiming the superstitions of the Dutch seamen. But most impressive of the carved symbols was the figurehead. Rearing from the prow of the ship, below the massive bowsprit was the Lion-of-Holland. Three times the size of a man, bright red with a golden mane, the Lion-of-Holland snarled its rage, defying the domination of the elements.

And above the Batavia's gaudy magnificence there towered the three masts whose virgin white sails, as yet unblemished by the salt of the sea, embraced the wind, forever speeding them on towards the East Indies.

For all of her splendour, however, and despite the fact that she was by comparison to others a luxurious ship, any sense of comfort aboard the Batavia was short lived.

The convoy had barely entered the North Sea when they were beset by a violent storm, most of the ships losing sight of each other. As the Batavia pitched and rolled and reared and dived, the many inexperienced travellers aboard her were convinced they must drown. When the Lion-of-Holland disappeared into the waves and the bowsprit itself speared the sea, they felt the vessel must surely plunge to the bottom of the ocean never to return. But she reared back up again, like a wild horse refusing to be broken.

Like the others, Lucretia had thought she might die from the sea sickness, but she had recovered and found her sea legs far better than most. Now she weathered the storms like a seasoned sailor. She was better housed than most too, and she knew it. The sailors slept and ate huddled amongst the twenty-eight cannons. The soldiers, some seasoned regulars, some military cadets, others conscriptees bound for national service in the colonies, were restricted to the closely confined quarters above, where there was not space enough for a man to stand upright. There they crouched for eleven hours at a stretch before being allowed their brief respite on deck. And the working-class passengers found space where they could. Only the commanding officers had cabins of their own.

In consideration of her social standing, Lucretia had been allocated an alcove which she shared with her maid, Zwaantie, and she ate with the officers in the dining room at the stern of the ship. The one grand room aboard the Batavia, the dining room converted to sleeping quarters at night, but during the early evening, at mealtime, the select dozen or so were seated in a civilised fashion around the large oak table.

Not that the company was civilised, Lucretia thought. With the exception of Francisco Pelsaert, she loathed the men with whom she was forced to socialise. Particularly the ship's captain, Adriaen Jacobsz. For all of his renown as an excellent sailor, and for all of his personal pretensions to intellectual superiority, Lucretia had decided upon their first meeting that the man was a pig.

Jacobsz, although a handsome man with an imposing figure, was an unashamed hedonist who ate and drank with gusto and boasted openly of his sexual exploits. Convinced of his own fatal charm, he had very early on set about to impress the aristocratic and beautiful young woman. But the harder he tried, the more Lucretia retreated behind her haughty façade, openly displaying her preference for Pelsaert's company, which further annoyed Jacobsz. As Commandeur of the fleet, Pelsaert was his superior in rank, Jacobsz accepted that, but it was quite evident both Lucretia and Pelsaert also considered him of *inferior social standing, which was an insult. He was after all the captain of the vessel. Jacobsz turned his attentions instead to Lucretia's maid, Zwaantie Hendrix, and there found instant gratification.*

It irked Lucretia that her maid was conducting an affair with the detestable Jacobsz, and she grew to despise Zwaantie. She knew too that the loathsome pair were whispering obscenities about her and Pelsaert. Nothing was secret aboard the Batavia. *The Commandeur had recently taken ill and Lucretia regularly visited him in his cabin, to take him a bowl of soup which the cook had brewed or to bathe his fevered brow. Some troublemakers amongst the men considered the Commandeur a malingerer. 'Lying back in his cabin enjoying the trip, who does he think he is,' they said. And the lascivious rumours spread by Jacobsz and Zwaantie Hendrix did not help matters. Lucretia van den Mylen was Pelsaert's whore, they whispered, and others listened.*

Well, let them talk, Lucretia thought now as she gazed up at the luffing sails, savouring the moment of calm. And let them listen. She would rise above them all, she did not need them. She had the locket to keep her company, to guard her against all evil. The symbol of Boudewijn and the love they shared nestled against her breast.

At night, Lucretia would take the locket from its concealment beneath her clothing and she would caress its face. She could not see it in the darkness, but she could feel the ridges of the mountain, and the thrust of the rays from the diamond sun. Even as she cursed Adriaen Jacobsz and his like—and there were others on board, she knew it, who lusted for her, who considered her vain and arrogant, and who would wish to degrade her—even as she cursed them all, she clung to the knowledge that each day brought her closer to Boudewijn.

CHAPTER FOUR

The bombers were clearly visible in the early dawn light. Twenty-four of them in all, and twenty-five fighters.

But there could have been hundreds, Bernie thought, you could never tell from down here, the sky seemed full of them. Enemy planes wherever you looked, relentless and menacing. They'd been bombing the Top End military and air force installations for a whole bloody year now.

'Fuse 2-0!' The order rang out from the command post.

'Fuse 2-0 set!' Young Bernie Spencer, gunner with the 31st Heavy Ack-Ack, yelled in response.

'Fire!'

Crouched beside his 3.7 heavy mobile ack-ack, dug into the ground and wedged with sandbags, Bernie and the other three gunners in the battery fired at the bombers overhead.

'Enemy bombers three o'clock high.' The Wing Commander's voice sounded composed, almost detached, as he ordered his squadron to climb, preparatory to attack. But Terence Galloway, Spitfire pilot of No. 1 Fighter Wing, felt anything other than composed and detached. Adrenalin was pumping through his body, he could see the flak of their own anti-aircraft guns, already the sky was becoming a furnace, and the dogfights hadn't even started!

Twenty thousand feet. Now! The order sounded and Terence wheeled his aircraft to dive on the bombers below.

The Jap aircraft seemed to come from nowhere. Four Zeros. They must have been taking cover in the bank of cumulus cloud to the east, Terence thought. Clever bastards.

The enemy fighters dropped their belly tanks and dived. Terence banked sharply, turned and, as two of the Zeros crossed the nose of his aircraft, fired a long burst through each. One kept diving, an angry streak of orange flame streaming from its fuselage. It was out of commission and heading for home, Terence doubted it would make it. The other Zero turned, banked, and the dogfight was on.

Terence was aware that all about him the air was an inferno of machine-gun and cannon fire and, amongst the haze of smoke, he kept a lookout peripherally for any other enemy fighter attack, but his main focus was concentrated on the Zero he'd chosen. Or the Zero who had chosen him, he thought as they both wheeled and climbed and turned and fired, then dived and rose again to resume the deadly fight. Once, they were so close he could see the Jap's face. A good pilot, Terence thought. But not good enough. One of us will die, my friend, and it won't be me!

Terence was revelling in the thrill of the chase. This was what he'd been missing, he thought. This was what he lived for, what he was prepared to die for. But not today. Oh no, not today!

The Jap had missed his opportunity. For an instant Terence had thought it was he himself who had lost. He heard a series of thuds and felt his plane jump. He'd been hit. But not badly. And the Jap had lost concentration. Perhaps thinking he'd won, he'd been slow on his turn. There he was! In Terence's sights long enough for him to rake the whole fuselage from tail to nose. He watched as the orange flame streaked from the tail of the Zero. Then he watched as the aircraft plunged to the ground.

'Cease fire!'

Young Bernie Spencer flopped back against the sandbags, sweat pouring from his brow. The sun was barely up in the sky and yet it was stinking hot. But then he wasn't in Adelaide now, this was the Northern Territory and it was early March, what did he expect? His rotting shirt clung wet to his back and his Bombay bloomer shorts were grimy with the red outback soil.

After four months at the Bullalalla station gunsite, Bernie was accustomed to the discomfort, but it was the boredom which grated with him and the other blokes. Not this morning, though. This morning had been a beauty. This morning they hadn't sat around taking potshots at a Jap reconnaissance plane travelling too high to be bothered by the ack-ack. They'd had a say in things this morning.

One of the lads, another gunner, stood up and cheered, waving a fist to the sky and the retreating aircraft. Then the whole of the battery stood and applauded, over twenty in all, and nineteen-year-old Bernie Spencer joined in. Well, they wouldn't be whingeing about the Top End being the arsehole of the world today, he thought. No bellyaching today about the mossies and the ants and the heat and the flies, and why they hadn't been sent overseas to fight the war. Today they'd served a purpose. Two bombers, on fire, had headed out to sea, the rest had turned tail and fled. The Jap raid had been a dismal failure. Between the Spits above and the ack-ack below they'd sent the yellow peril home with their tails between their legs. 'Go home, you bastards!' Bernie yelled along with the others.

Terence wanted more. But the fight was over. The bombers had departed. He followed them long enough to see one still burning in the sea just outside the port of Darwin, along with six enemy fighter aircraft. Then he set his sights for home.

Bernie shielded his eyes. 'Here he comes!' he shouted to his mates as he watched the Spit emerge from the haze of battle and fly towards the homestead over the ridge ten miles south of the gunsite. All the men stood and cheered, waving their hats. They'd seen the pilot do it before. Often. For no apparent reason he'd buzz the homestead. They didn't know why he did it, what his connection with Bullalalla cattle station was, but they admired his antics, he'd helped fill in the tedium of many a long day.

'Here he comes!' Unwittingly echoing young Bernie Spencer, Jock Galloway's voice boomed through the homestead as he opened the front door from the verandah and yelled with all the force his lungs could muster. 'Everybody outside! At the double! He's coming!'

This was the moment old Jock had been waiting for. He'd stood on the verandah for the past hour, mesmerised by the smouldering sky and the cacophony of artillery fire. He knew that, inside the house, Margaret, Henrietta and Charlotte would be glancing nervously from the windows wishing it were over, and Nellie and Pearl would be whimpering with terror, as Aborigines always did at the sound of machine gunfire. But they should have been standing here with him, outside on the verandah, glorying in the spectacle of it all.

Every military fibre in Jock's body responded to the sight and the sound and the smell of warfare. But he was no mere spectator, he was a contributor to the entire exercise, the armed forces were on his property. A battery to the north, and to the south an airstrip and RAAF base. Following the bombing of Darwin in February the previous year, and the consequent destruction of any

RAAF strength in the north-western area, the air force had built their Top End airfields with one simple strategy in mind—dispersal. And Jock Galloway had been only too eager to offer to the military and the RAAF any area they chose of the four thousand square miles of Bullalalla cattle station. As a veteran of the Great War, he was proud to be of assistance; he'd declared, it was his bounden duty to King and Country.

But his proudest moment was to hand right now. The moment when Terry would salute him. Fresh from battle, his son would circle the homestead. It was a triumphant tribute shared between father and son and, each time, Jock felt his chest would burst with pride. The boy was a chip off the old block, all right.

'At the double!' he bellowed again. 'Outside! He's here!' And, belying his sixty-one years, he bounded down the several steps from the verandah with the agility of a man half his age.

His wife Margaret, and Charlotte his daughter, quickly joined him. But Terence's young English wife reluctantly followed in their wake.

It wasn't that Terence's antics particularly worried Henrietta, but she failed to see why Nellie and Pearl must be forced to endure something which so obviously terrified them.

'It's all right,' she assured them as she always did. And Nellie gave her customary tight smile and nod, grateful for the assurance, but the whites of her eyes shone nervously in her normally placid, brown face and she kept a tight hold on her twelve-year-old daughter's hand.

'Could you not tell your father to let them stay inside?' Henrietta had asked Terence in the early days of his aerobatics when his father had taken to demanding that the entire household stand in the baking heat to applaud his son. 'Nellie and Pearl are absolutely terrified, every single time.'

But Terence hadn't appeared particularly concerned. 'It'll do them good,' he'd shrugged. Then by way of explanation, 'Teach them they can't run away every time they're frightened. Besides,' he'd added, realising his answer had not satisfied her, 'you try telling Dad to do anything.'

She'd had to accept that. It was true, nobody told Jock Galloway to do anything. But she'd found it unsettling to later discover that, after buzzing the homestead, Terence took delight in dive-bombing the native camp several miles away. It was the start of the dry season and the Aboriginal stockmen and their families had moved into the tin huts and humpies there preparatory to the annual muster. 'They ran like scared rabbits,' she'd overheard Terence boast to his father one day, and it had chilled her to hear him say it. Had he changed, she was beginning to wonder, or had there always been a cruel streak in him which she had failed to recognise in London?

Three months in the Northern Territory had opened Henrietta's eyes to many things, not least of all the gradual metamorphosis in the man she had married.

Now she stood with the others, fifty yards from the house as Jock always instructed, and, hand shielding her eyes from the blinding sun, she gazed up at the approaching aircraft.

The Spitfire circled the homestead three times, as it always did, lower and lower each time. Then it ascended, turned and dive-bombed. Involuntarily, Henrietta wanted to duck, or to turn away, even to run, but she had learned to stand her ground and watch, just as Margaret and Charlotte did.

Margaret Galloway, although subservient to her husband, was as strong as old Jock in her own way, her back as ramrod straight as his, her thin, weathered visage as stern. Charlotte too, Terence's older sister, once handsome, was hardened by the living conditions and the harsh northern sun. Not yet thirty-one years of age, her thick hair, always pulled back in a practical ponytail, was iron grey, and her face was as rugged as a man's. Both were outback women, tough and resilient like the landscape itself. They had adapted to the adversities of life in the Territory, and Henrietta supposed that it was her duty to mould herself the same way, although she couldn't imagine how she was to go about it.

The Spitfire dropped like lead from the sky and was coming straight for them. Was it her imagination, Henrietta thought for an instant, or was it flying lower than usual? She glanced briefly to her side. Old Jock's arm was raised in salute and Margaret and Charlotte continued to gaze ahead without even shielding the sun from their eyes. The roar of the engine was horrendous. Behind them, the windows of the homestead rattled, and the branches of the impressive lemon-scented gums which Jock's father had planted as saplings and which lined the drive to the house, swayed and swirled as they did in a gale.

The aircraft seemed all but upon them when young Pearl broke away from her mother and ran shrieking towards the verandah. Nellie stared down at the ground, longing to put her hands over her ears, visibly trembling, tormented by the scream of the engine.

Then, as quickly as an eagle having swooped successfully upon its prey, the Spitfire was back up in the air and Henrietta could have sworn she'd heard Terence laughing. Or was it Jock? Jock was certainly laughing now. Laughing and waving proudly to his son. Henrietta put a reassuring arm around Nellie, and Nellie shamefacedly beckoned Pearl back to her side.

Terence was pleased with himself. It had been a particularly good dive, he thought, barely fifty feet from the ground, he could swear. He decided against a further show of aerobatics, the aircraft was displaying a distinct and repetitive shudder, he'd better get back to base and have them check the damage he'd copped from the Zero. He briefly contemplated dive-bombing the native camp, but decided against that too. The muster was well under way now, only women and children would be there. The stockmen would be out bush, rounding up the cattle on the plains, penning them in the bush stockyards, sorting the steers from the breeding stock and the new season's calves from their mothers.

The first time Terence had buzzed the homestead and the camp he'd been showing off. It put the fear of God into the native stockmen, he knew it, but he was just playing a game, a boyish prank, that was all. But when his father had called his performance 'a salute of triumph', he'd quickly changed his views. The old man was right of course, it was a victory celebration. Hell, if anyone knew about the triumphs of battle, it was Jock Galloway.

He descended and circled the homestead one more time, smiling proudly at the sight of his father once again standing stiffly to attention. He noted with irritation that Henrietta was comforting the two blacks. He'd told her not to in the past and she was disregarding his orders, as she did on occasions when she disagreed with his views. It annoyed him. Not that he wished to break Henrietta's spirit. It was her spirit which had first attracted him. She was such an interesting contradiction, such a mixture of strength and naivety. Like a healthy young mare, Terence often thought, not a racehorse, she was not elegant enough for a racehorse. High-spirited as she was, she lacked the neuroses that accompanied a racehorse's inbreeding, and that was fortunate. But she possessed all the natural beauty, all the strength and enthusiasm of a healthy young mare. And she was a chestnut, what's more. Terence had always been fond of chestnuts.

His annoyance faded and he felt a wave of affection for his young wife. He would admonish her for fussing over Nellie and Pearl when he got home, certainly, but he would not round on her. In time he would teach her and she would become accustomed to the ways of the outback, he had no wish to change the essential Henrietta. God forbid that his wife should grow bitter like his sister Charlotte, or worse still, humourless like his mother. Much as Terence respected his mother, he was the first to admit that Margaret Galloway singularly lacked a sense of humour. He turned his aircraft and headed south towards the base. A beer with Hans and the boys and an exchange of exploits and tactics was the next pleasurable item on the agenda.

Jock gave a final salute to the receding Spitfire. 'He's fearless, that boy,' he announced to the sky, 'utterly fearless.' A chip off the old block, he was thinking. A son any man would be proud to call his own. And the boy worshipped him. Always had.

Jock recalled the barbecue at a neighbouring homestead when Terry had been barely ten years old. Asked how he wanted his steak cooked, the boy had loudly stated, 'Same as the old man, rare and bloody, it's the *only* way.' Then, encouraged by his father's delighted guffaw, he'd added, 'Just cut its horns off and wipe its arse.' He'd heard his father say it in male company on a number of occasions.

The women had been disapproving, and Terence's two younger brothers had ducked for cover, fearing their father's wrath. But, far from angry, Jock had laughed fit to burst. 'A chip off the old block,' he'd proudly said to his mates when he'd regained his composure. 'That boy's a chip off the old block.' He'd been saying it ever since.

And now his son was a hero. Defending his country just like his father had. And, just like his father, he was fearless in the face of battle.

Over the years, Jock had conveniently forgotten that he had never fired a shot in combat. He was a Gallipoli veteran and you didn't get a more honourable war record than that. The truth was that Jock could remember, in the dead of night, climbing down the rope netting, full tackle on his back, and into the boats. And he could remember the boats being towed by the pinnaces away from the ships and then released near the shore. He could remember rowing with all his might. They'd chanted as they'd rowed and he'd concentrated on the heaving back of the man in front of him, just as he knew the man seated behind him was concentrating on his back. 'Heave! two, three, four . . .' They were a team, 'two three four . . .' Then all hell had broken loose. That was the last thing Jock remembered. The noise! The unspeakable noise!

Then nothing but silence. He barely remembered the hospital ship. A month or so later, he recalled the English nurses and the crisp cotton sheets of the sanatorium, but all remained silence. Six months later, back in Australia, honourably discharged from the army on medical grounds, his was still a world without sound. It was nine months before his hearing started to return, and then only slowly.

Jock had been sorely cheated. Like so many, keen for adventure, eager to fight a war, he'd been quick to volunteer, even at the age of thirty-three. He'd lied about his age and, as he'd looked every bit as fit and strong as the men ten years his junior who were enlisting beside him, no-one had raised an eyebrow. He'd suffered no guilt at leaving behind a wife with a three-year-old daughter and a new baby son; King and Country called, he said. And he'd revelled in training camp. He loved army life and the rigours it entailed, he was a natural soldier who ached for battle. And he'd never got to fire one bloody shot! He'd been cheated, all right.

It didn't help, after the war at Anzac Day reunions, when old army buddies said, 'Jesus, Jock, you were well out of it, count your lucky stars, mate.' At first he'd thought they were mocking him. But he soon realised they weren't. 'Bloody hideous war,' they said. 'Nothing noble about it, I can tell you.' 'You can stick the army right up your arse, mate.' They all seemed to be in agreement, but Jock did not concur one bit. A military life was a noble life and if a war was thrown in then all the better.

He stopped going to reunions where he might meet disenchanted fellow veterans and, from the stories of others, he created his own history. But his was a noble history and his battles were glorious. Over the years, nobody, his wife, his four children, even his domineering father, ever doubted the veracity of Jock's stories. Jock Galloway was a Gallipoli veteran, with his medal and discharge papers to prove it.

The Spitfire was a speck in the distance. Soon it would disappear over the far-off hill to land at the RAAF base beyond. Jock turned to discover Henrietta standing barely ten yards away, she too apparently lost in thought. Margaret had hustled the Aborigines back to their chores, Nellie and Pearl only too happy to obey, and Charlotte had left her father to his reverie as she always did, Jock invariably watching until the aircraft had disappeared from sight. But this time Henrietta had remained. Just as she should, Jock thought. Paying tribute to her husband, it was only right.

'He's a fine man, the man you married,' he said.

'Yes.' It wasn't what Henrietta had been thinking.

'Put on a hat if you're going to stand around in the sun.' Jock's voice was as gruff as always but his intention was kindly enough. Although Margaret would have preferred an Australian daughter-in-law, Jock approved of his son's choice. A good strong body, shapely, but not plump. A healthy bosom, good child-bearing hips, a sound young filly when all was said and done. Jock had always likened women to horses. No insult was intended, indeed more often than not he considered his comparisons a compliment to the woman to whom they were directed. They certainly were in this case. Henrietta was a filly with excellent breeding prospects. A chestnut into the bargain.

Chestnuts had always been Jock's preference. 'Or else come into the house,' he said, 'the sun's not kind to complexions like yours.'

'I'll come in when I've fed the chickens,' Henrietta replied. She wanted to be on her own for a while.

'Chooks, girl! When will you learn? Chooks!' But he smiled his leathery smile as he said it.

'Chooks.' She smiled back. 'Chooks. Yes.'

Henrietta watched him mount the steps to the verandah. She watched the flywire door slap shut behind him. The heavy wooden front door remained open, as all the doors in the homestead did on still days like this, to channel through the house any available vestige of breeze.

The flywire door had amused her at first, it was at odds with such an imposing house. 'Designed by my grand-father,' Terence had proudly informed her three months previously, as he'd pulled the Landrover up in front of Bullalalla homestead. 'Built entirely from imported Tasmanian oak.'

Two storeys high, the house was surrounded by verandahs on all four sides, and large front balconies opened out from the upstairs bedrooms. A succession of elegant lemon-scented gums lined the last fifty yards of the driveway. They were around thirty feet tall with graceful white trunks and silver-green leaves and, just beyond the gums, where the drive dipped down to the homestead gates and the private road beyond, was the grove of mango trees, glossy green in foliage, rich and luscious. The mixture of sub-tropical and Australian-outback flora was striking, and typical of the area Henrietta was to discover.

'Two storeys is a bit of a luxury,' Terence boasted. 'Grandpa Lionel owned a stud in South Australia. Race-horses. He was very successful. Very wealthy. He only bought the Bullalalla property as an investment, running buffalo for pet meat, it was big business back then. He hadn't planned on falling in love with the place, but he did,

so he built the sort of house he wanted to live in. Personally,' Terence added with a grin, 'I think the old bloke
wanted to show off a bit of southern style to the locals.'

Terence could barely remember his grandfather, Lionel
Galloway, but the stories he'd heard from Jock were
romantic and intriguing.

'Grandpa left the place solely to Dad in his will,' he continued. 'Dad was always his favourite, because of his war
record and all that. When Grandpa built this homestead,
Dad says it caused a lot of comment in Darwin, people
thought that Lionel Galloway had tickets on himself.
But so what? Good on him! That's what Dad reckons.'

Henrietta nodded happily. The house was beautiful, she
agreed, but it was Terence's boyish enthusiasm which
she found most engaging. She loved him, and she was
going to love this house, and Terence's family, and this
strange new country. Henrietta intended to embrace it all.

'Grandpa Lionel even built a full-scale racecourse, I'll
take you to see it tomorrow. We have an annual race
meeting on the station, people come from all over, jockeys
and bookies, the lot. Of course it's all been put on hold for
the duration of the war, but you just wait, Henrietta.'
And she laughed as he swept her off her feet and carried
her up the porch steps. 'One day you'll be the belle of the
Bullalalla Races!'

He was about to carry her over the threshold and that's
when she'd commented on the flywire screen door. It was
incongruous, the ugly mesh screen masking the magnificence of the hand-carved oak door with its huge horse's
head door-knocker in gleaming brass.

On the other side of the doorway, Margaret Galloway
had gathered the family, including Nellie and Pearl, in the
hall beside the grand staircase. Even Jackie, Nellie's
husband and head stockman, had been called from his
duties. Jackie, Nellie and their daughter did not live in
humpies like the other natives but in a small cottage a half

a mile from the homestead, and Margaret had insisted that all concerned with homestead life must be present to greet the new wife of her eldest son. Jock had wanted to stand on the verandah and wave and yell at the Landrover as it pulled up, but his wife had maintained that, as an Englishwoman, Henrietta should be greeted with a touch of formality, along the lines to which she was no doubt accustomed. Jock had agreed readily enough, it was acknowledged that Margaret had full reign in the running of the house; it was a woman's job, after all, and no doubt his wife knew best in such matters of protocol.

Now, Margaret's lips pursed into a hard, thin line as she heard her daughter-in-law's disparaging comments about the flywire screen door. Already the girl was being critical. Well, we won't have any hoity-toity behaviour here young miss, she thought.

Terence laughed. 'Every door and every window in the place has a screen,' he said. 'You'll find out why soon enough.'

And she had. The flies and mosquitoes had driven her mad for the first few weeks. But she'd quickly taught herself to become accustomed to them. Just as she'd taught herself to become accustomed to the erratic weather.

'It comes with the territory,' Terence had laughed, but Henrietta had been suffocated by the humidity on her arrival. They'd been married in London and Terence had flown home shortly after the ceremony for briefing and training with the defence unit. He'd been there to meet her ship and, from the moment she'd stepped ashore and he'd walked her through the streets of Darwin, or what was left of Darwin since the bombing, she'd felt as if she was walking under water. Wading through a wet haze, her legs heavy, her head engulfed in the clammy, moisture-laden air.

'That's where the post office used to be,' he'd said, pointing out a pile of rubble with tufts of grass growing through it and chickens running about amongst the ruins. 'Ten postal workers killed, mostly young too.'

'How terrible,' she'd said, and she'd meant it, but, as pockets of damp seemed to hit her in waves, all she could think of was the fact that, at any minute, she might faint.

Then, two weeks later, an almighty thunderstorm had broken out. It had raged through the night and Henrietta had been fearful, sure that at any moment one of the great jagged bolts of lightning must strike the homestead. But Terence and the other members of the household had taken it all in their stride, unbothered by the show of nature's force. The storm had been followed by torrential rain which had lasted a fortnight, turning the red earth into mud. Where was the pattern to such weather, Henrietta had wondered. It was the monsoon, Terence told her, the 'wet' season, the weather was always erratic during the wet season, she'd find the 'dry' more comfortable.

Henrietta soon realised that extremes were a daily occurrence in the Northern Territory and, as a result, the Territorians' reaction to drama was, on the whole, rather placid. To Henrietta everything around her seemed dramatic. The size of the landscape, the ferocity of the storms, the intensity of the heat. She must learn to adjust, she'd told herself.

She was aware, however, that there was one adjustment which she would find very difficult to make, and that was the change in moral outlook. In particular, Terence's explanation of European and Aboriginal relations which had shocked Henrietta immeasurably.

'It's not talked about, although it's common knowledge,' Terence had said, shortly after she'd met the Aboriginal family whom she'd presumed to be house servants, 'but Nellie is Dad's half sister.'

Henrietta had been more mystified than shocked at first. The fact was very difficult to assimilate, Nellie being so distinctly Aboriginal in appearance, and a good twenty-five years younger than Jock. But Henrietta had tried to cover her nonplussed reaction as she waited for Terence to explain.

'There are hundreds of half-caste blacks wandering about the place,' he'd said, 'the offspring of white station owners and the wives of black stockmen. They take the boss's Christian name as their surname—Nellie was Nellie Lionel before she married.' He grinned. 'The whole thing's a bit of a joke, really. In pubs all over the Territory there are white blokes skiting about the number of black kids running around with their Christian name—kids they've fathered by stockmen's wives.'

'Don't the stockmen mind?' She wondered how she could sound so calm as she voiced the question.

'Good God no,' Terence scoffed at the suggestion, 'on the contrary, they're proud if the white boss takes a fancy to one of their wives—they usually have two or three, sometimes more. Quite often they'll offer the services of whichever lubra the boss has an eye for, and the boss'll give them a present in return. Tobacco's the most popular.'

'Oh, I see.' Henrietta's reply had been followed by a breathless gulp, and that's when Terence had suddenly realised that she was shocked.

He'd cursed himself. Of course she'd be shocked, it would all be so foreign to her. She needed to be broken in to their ways gently, he should have been more careful.

'Well, that was a while back now,' he assured her, 'times have changed.'

They hadn't really. Terence knew full well that his own father had had his fair share of dalliances with Aboriginal women in the past. Discreetly of course, for fear of incurring the wrath of his wife. And Terence himself, encouraged by his father, had lost his virginity at the age of fifteen to the eighteen-year-old daughter of a black drover. Jock had boasted of the fact to his mates. 'The boy's developed an early taste for black velvet,' he'd said, and Terence had felt like a man.

Henrietta still looked rather shaken and Terence realised she needed further reassurance.

'My grandfather was a good man, Henrietta,' he said, 'he did the right thing by Nellie. He gave her a decent education at Port Keats Mission, and he found her a husband, and I'll tell you something else,' he added with pride, 'you won't find another black family around here who can boast their own cottage a half a mile from the homestead! Built on the boss's orders, I might add.'

It was true, Lionel Galloway had been a good enough man, and he'd been fond of Nellie in his own way. Her arrival shortly before his fifty-second birthday had imbued him with fresh blood, made him feel young again. And she'd proved an asset furthermore.

His wife's intense annoyance had been appeased when, at the age of fifteen, the girl had returned from the mission to take up her role as a hard-working domestic, costing the household no more than her keep. And when Nellie had caught the eye of young Jackie Yoorunga, the horsebreaker from Queensland and the best at his trade, she'd been worth her weight in gold. The quickest way to keep Jackie on the property had been to offer him the boss's daughter and a cottage to boot. Lionel Galloway had been a good man, but also a practical one, exceptionally astute when it came to business.

'Now don't look so shocked as if we're all monsters,' Terence said teasingly. 'Remember, the sins of the grandfather should not be visited upon the grandson.'

Terence was right, Henrietta thought, this was a different world she now lived in. She must learn not to be so easily shocked.

'I need to be tougher,' she said in all seriousness the following day, having thought long and hard on the matter. 'More like Charlotte and your mother.'

'Oh no,' he insisted, 'don't you dare.' He kissed her fiercely and affectionately. 'Don't you dare become like

Mother and Charlotte, you stay exactly the way you are.'

During the several days' leave he'd had after her arrival in Darwin, he'd taken her for a drive and shown her the countryside. As much of it as he could, he said, in a Landrover.

'The only way to really see it is on horseback,' he'd told her. 'When Charlotte's taught you to ride, I'll show you the gorges and the waterfalls. And rock formations that look like cities. And at the end of the wet season I'll show you the rivers and the plains.'

But she'd seen enough to impress her. From the rough bush track in the high country she'd looked down over the wetlands and marvelled at the lush vegetation and the wildlife. She'd thrilled to the sinister shapes of the salt-water crocodiles which Terence had pointed out to her, basking amongst the pandanus trees on the banks of the swollen creeks. And the birdlife fascinated her, the flocks of honking magpie geese and the noisy blue-winged kook-aburras. The sulphur-crested cockatoos, the corellas, the Major Mitchell galahs and the lorikeets, she'd never seen birds of such colour. She had thrilled to it all and Terence had delighted in her excitement.

Yes, she thought, she had delighted him then. So what had happened?

Henrietta had finished feeding the chickens in the coop at the rear of the house—'chooks' she reminded herself, 'chooks'—but she didn't want to go inside, despite the intense heat and the clamminess of her white cotton blouse and the fact that, without a hat, the sun was indeed making her feel light-headed. She wasn't in the mood for Margaret, she decided, as she stood in the shade of the huge water tank, high on its stilted wooden platform beside the chicken coop. She wouldn't mind having a quiet cup of tea with Charlotte, she'd come to like Charlotte strangely enough, but it would be lunchtime soon, little chance of that.

The back flywire door swung open and Pearl appeared with a basket of laundry. She crossed to the clothes lines which stretched between the chicken coop and the hessian-covered vegetable garden (Margaret's pride and joy) and set the basket down on the old wooden table.

'I'll do that, Pearl.'

The Aboriginal girl was startled, she hadn't noticed the young missus standing silently in the shade of the water tank. She hesitated.

'You go inside and help Nellie with the lunch.'

'Yeh, Miss Henrietta,' Pearl said with reluctance. She hoped she wouldn't cop it from the old missus, she'd copped it once already this morning, for running away from the aeroplane.

Henrietta understood the girl's hesitation—Margaret Galloway ran the household with a rod of iron. 'You tell the missus,' she said very firmly, 'that I told you I wish to hang out the clothes.'

'Yeh, Miss Henrietta.' Pearl smiled, that would get her off the hook. She liked the young missus.

Henrietta watched her go inside. She liked Pearl too. She wasn't sure whether the girl was lazy or shy, probably a mixture of both, but she was devastatingly pretty when she smiled.

Henrietta hung out the clothes in a desultory fashion, buying time, waiting to be called in to lunch, wondering why she felt depressed. Terence buzzing the homestead in his Spitfire, she supposed; she'd grown to hate it. And he'd be home in a couple of hours, fired with adrenalin and excitement, and she knew what would happen then.

It wasn't the lovelessness of Henrietta's sex life which was making her unhappy. A virgin at twenty-two, she had realised, on her wedding night, that sex was a woman's duty and that, despite romantic novels and girlish gossip, it did not involve affection on the part of the male. Ensuing sexual relations with her husband had led her to accept this as her lot in life, but what had become of the affection which Terence had displayed when she'd first come to the Territory? And in London? He'd been a different man when he was courting. She'd naively said as much to Charlotte.

'Well of course all men are different when they're courting,' Charlotte had replied. She'd offered her friendship to Henrietta from the day the girl had arrived. Someone should, she'd thought, feeling sorry for her brother's young wife.

'But he was romantic in London.' Henrietta knew she sounded like a deluded schoolgirl, but she was grateful for Charlotte's support, and was determined to speak her mind no matter how foolish she sounded.

'He wanted to win you.' Charlotte too was prepared to speak her mind. She always did. And she could see no change in her brother. Terence had always insisted upon control, and that's what he was doing with his pretty young wife, taking control, Charlotte had no doubt of it. Perhaps, in his own way, her brother loved Henrietta. But in what way was that? The same way he loved a horse he'd broken in? 'He does love you, Henrietta,' she'd said, hoping to be of some comfort, 'in his own way.' And she'd left it at that. She refused to lie.

But Henrietta had brought the subject up again and again; Charlotte was her only ally. Exasperated, Charlotte had finally spoken her true mind. 'Have you ever thought you might be a breeding mare, Henrietta?' She was gratified by the shock she saw in the girl's face; she'd intended to shock. But she'd shocked herself also in the saying of it.

In the silence which followed she added, 'We all are, you know. All we Galloway women. It's why my husband deserted me when he found I was barren.'

They were seated in the big open kitchen, by the windows, and Charlotte's expression was bitter, her eyes hard, as she stared unseeingly out at the water tank. 'It's why

Terence treats me with such disdain. Well, he doesn't so much now,' she corrected herself. 'He respects me now that I do the work of a man.' It was true, Charlotte could handle a rifle, ride a horse and round up cattle along with the best of them. The men called her Charlie and accepted her as a fellow drover on many a muster. 'But he didn't always respect me,' she concluded, turning to Henrietta. 'Not when I was supposed to be a breeding mare.'

Charlotte's comments indeed shocked Henrietta. But self-preservation persuaded the young Englishwoman that her sister-in-law's views were the result of a deep and understandable cynicism. Charlotte was barren, her husband had deserted her, of course she would feel cynical where men were concerned.

Charlotte realised she had gone too far. 'You've come to know our father,' she said as reasonably as she could. 'Terence has spent his whole life training to become the man his father is. He's intent on building a dynasty, just like the old man, he's the next Galloway in line, the next leader.' Charlotte shrugged, in her opinion it was the truth, so why not tell it. 'Even my brothers recognise it, you wait 'til you meet them, you'll see what I mean. They jump to his command just as if he was Dad.' Her smile was scathing. 'That's why they both married young, I swear it—to get out of home before Terence took over.'

'You're very observant, Charlotte.' Henrietta was saddened by the loss of her only ally. She would not speak again of her husband, she did not believe Charlotte. She could not afford to.

'Observation is my hobby.' Charlotte knew that Henrietta would no longer confide in her, and perhaps that was just as well, for Charlotte refused to play girlish games. Not that that was what Henrietta was seeking, the girl merely wanted assurances. But Charlotte refused to offer false encouragement, Henrietta would find out in time. Every Galloway woman did.

Their relationship had changed since that day. They were still friends, Charlotte patiently teaching Henrietta the ways of station life, but Henrietta no longer invited intimate conversation and Charlotte was grateful for it.

At times, in the deepest recesses of Henrietta's being she wondered whether Charlotte could possibly be right. I must conceive, she told herself. It was her duty, after all, to have a child. Perhaps when she'd had a child, Terence would revert to the man he'd been in London. The man with whom she'd fallen in love.

CHAPTER FIVE

In the distance, young Bernie Spencer watched the Spitfire complete its final circle in the sky before turning south and heading for the RAAF base. He continued to watch until it disappeared from sight.

To Bernie, the aircraft signified their utter isolation. It was a link between everything he couldn't see. He couldn't see the homestead beyond the ridge and he couldn't see the RAAF base far to the south.

Bernie looked around at the gunnery campsite. The cookhouse made of bark with dirt floors, the fires where the men did their own cooking, the lean-to shelters with the beds that they'd made themselves from tree forks shoved in the ground and corn sacks. Christ, it was the back of beyond.

He wondered about the bloke in the Spitfire. Why did he buzz the homestead? Jeez, I'd love to find out, Bernie thought. Then he had an idea. That's what he'd do with the two days' monthly leave he had coming up, he'd pay a visit to the homestead and find out. Hell, it'd have to be better than Darwin.

Bernie had wasted his last month's leave hitching a ride into Darwin with some Yanks on their way through from the US base near Katherine. Darwin was a desolate place. Sad, Bernie thought. No shops to speak of. Not that he had any money to spend, his payroll went home and his two bob a day allowance didn't buy much. But it was sad to see a town with no shops. 'Course there wasn't much need for shops as such, most of the civilians had fled or been evacuated. Jeez, why would you want to stay if you didn't have to, Bernie thought, the place was a mess, ships sunk in the harbour, even Chinatown a thing of the past.

Bernie had heard wonderful tales of Darwin's China-town. Of the smell of incense and cooking spices wafting through back alleyways, and of open-fronted stores selling strange and wondrous things, and he'd longed to eat exotic foods and explore bustling markets. But what little was left of Chinatown was in ruins and the place deserted. Well, the Chinese were no fools, were they? They'd fled Darwin along with the others.

Yeah, that's what he'd do with his next leave, he decided. He'd hike over to the homestead and meet the people who lived there. He'd find out about the bloke in the Spitfire too. Reg might want to come with him. The people at the homestead might even give them a feed, might let them camp the night in one of their sheds. You never knew your luck, Bernie thought. Hell, it'd be some-thing different.

Terence was preparing to land, but something was wrong. As he turned into his landing circuit, the rudder jammed. But how could that be? He'd been circling the homestead only a short while ago. Something was jamming the control cables. His aerobatics had cost him dearly, the hit from the Zero was making itself known. Damn it, he should have come straight back to the base.

With the rudder jammed he wouldn't be able to control the aircraft on landing. A Spitfire needed full left rudder to land, otherwise it would swing hard to the right. Terence knew well what to expect.

Gently, very gently, he brought her in. He was doing less than ninety miles an hour. And he touched down in the very centre of the dirt airstrip with such delicacy, the aircraft obeying him as she should. Responding to his command. Like a good horse, heeding his every wish. The landing was perfect. But that was all he was able to do, the rest was beyond his control. He turned off the ignition and the petrol, and braced himself.

Hans van der Baan, bomber pilot, had left the mess hut to stand by the airstrip and wait for his friend. The other Spits had come in, but Terence hadn't been amongst them. Stupid bastard, Hans had thought, he was buzzing his father's house again. When would he learn?

Now, watching the Spitfire's approach, Hans sensed that something was wrong, Terence was bringing her in so very carefully. He watched the aircraft gently touch down, he could see the damage to its side, then he watched as it turned hard to the right. The rudder was jammed, he thought. Even with the brakes Terence wouldn't be able to control her. Nothing could. The Spitfire circled in a cloud of dust. Round and round, chasing its tail.

Harnessed safely to his seat, Terence watched the world spin by through the cockpit window, waiting for the moment when the aircraft would come to a halt and go up on its nose. That was the moment when the Spit could catch fire, Spits had a nasty habit of catching fire in such situations. He'd have to get out quick.

Finally the aircraft came to a halt and, as it went up on its nose, Terence unharnessed himself, opened the cockpit window, and scrambled out onto the wing.

Men had gathered to watch amongst the trees and the scrub which lined the bush airstrip. Terence could see Hans waving him to get clear, but he didn't need any encouragement. He leapt onto the ground and sprinted as hard as he could.

When he'd put enough safe distance between himself and the Spitfire, Terence turned back and breathed a sigh of relief. She wasn't going to burn. Thank Christ, he thought. If she'd gone up in flames, his late return might have been commented upon and some bothersome questions asked. As it was, he'd probably be congratulated on bringing a damaged aircraft safely home.

He pulled off his goggles and leather helmet and swaggered up to Hans. 'Rudder jammed,' he said.

'I could see that.'

'Pretty good landing, though,' Terence grinned. 'Neat and tidy, don't you reckon?'

'You stupid bastard,' the Dutchman growled in his thick guttural accent. 'You'll kill yourself one day.'

'What do you mean?' Terence asked innocently.

'She's damaged, man,' Hans waved an expressive hand at the Spitfire. 'Just look at her. You go showing off in a damaged aircraft, you're just asking for it, I tell you.'

But even the dour Dutchman couldn't dampen Terence's spirits. He felt elated. And alive. So very alive. 'Come on,' he said, clapping his hand around the beefy shoulder of Hans van der Baan as they walked towards the mess hut. The men were very good friends and admired each other's skill, sharing endless discussions on tactics. 'We'll get a mug of tea while I tell you what went on up there.'

Henrietta heard the Landrover pull up. So did Margaret. They were seated beside each other at the huge, paper-strewn desk in the office downstairs. The office had been a sitting room in the old days, big and grand, with huge bay windows where people lounged in armchairs and looked out across the verandah to the tree-lined drive and the mango tree grove beyond. The view through the bay windows was the same but people no longer lounged, for this was now the hub of the station. Here was where

Margaret kept her books. Her ledgers and log books and accounts, her records of stock, and of stores and supplies for the native workers. It was from here she supervised, day to day, month to month, year to year, the running of Bullalalla cattle station.

'Some stations employ a full-time bookkeeper,' she'd told Henrietta, 'but I believe it is a wife's duty to take on such responsibilities.' And Henrietta must learn to do the same, she was instructed. In time she was to take over the role. Margaret and Jock would retire when the war was over, they'd go south to enjoy the autumn years of their lives and Terence would inherit Bullalalla. Henrietta would need to know her job.

Margaret put aside her accounts books and her ledgers when she heard the Landrover pull up. 'He's home,' she said. Unnecessarily, Henrietta thought as she heard her husband yell, 'I'm home!' But she rose dutifully from her chair and followed her mother-in-law into the hall.

Jock was already there. 'Terry!' he bellowed, as his son burst through the door. 'Terry, my boy!' And he pumped his son's hand, they never embraced. 'What a triumph!' Pump, pump. 'What a salute!' Pump, pump. 'I'm proud of you, son!'

Terence returned his father's handshake with equal fervour. But where was Henrietta? He was on fire. He looked about, and there she was, to his left, standing behind his mother at the office door. And she looked so desirable.

'There she is, my gorgeous wife!' He picked her up, whirling her about while he continued to talk excitedly to his father. 'What about that dive, Dad! A beauty wasn't it? And with a damaged rudder as it turned out. I had some trouble landing her, I can tell you.'

Jock would love to have sat and talked with his son, to thrill to the camaraderie which only men of action could share. But Terence was already starting up the stairs, his arm around his wife's waist, half dragging her, half carrying her, Henrietta laughing self-consciously.

Ah well, Jock thought, he'd hear it all later, over the dinner table, he always did. Besides, when a man had faced death, it was only right he should seek the pleasures of his wife, any red-blooded male would do the same.

'Can we eat early tonight?' Terence called before he disappeared upstairs. 'I skipped tucker at the base and I'm starving!' A final hushed whisper from Henrietta and they were out of sight.

Jock exchanged a glance with his wife. Margaret did not return her husband's grin, which frankly she found a touch lascivious, but she too approved of Terence's healthy libido. The sooner that girl conceived the better, she thought, not only for the provision of an heir, but because Margaret sensed a quiet rebellion in Henrietta. The girl needed to be taught her place.

Upstairs, in the bedroom, Terence ripped at Henrietta's clothes, his mouth engulfing hers as he thrust his groin roughly against her. Henrietta returned his kiss, opening her mouth to him, desperately willing herself to respond, wishing that she could find a passion which could meet his. But it was always the same.

Each time on his return home, despite her self-consciousness at his overt behaviour in the presence of his parents, Henrietta loved being the object of Terence's desire. She loved the thought that she could give him pleasure. But once alone, it was not pleasure he sought, it was brute satisfaction.

A first she had tried to dampen his ardour, just a little, enough to give her time to undress. 'Gently, gently,' she'd whisper, 'you'll tear it,' and she'd try to ease off her blouse.

But he'd tear it anyway. 'I'll buy you five more,' he'd say. Sometimes he'd curse her for wearing trousers. Sometimes he'd just hoist her skirt up and rip off her panties before thrusting himself into her. Henrietta had learned to simply succumb to his wishes.

Today, however, she had decided upon a different tack. She had planned for his return. After lunch she had removed her brassiere, hoping nobody would notice the fullness of her breasts beneath the white cotton shirt, and she had changed into a very light skirt, easily removable, just a button at the waist. She didn't know why. Perhaps her actions were inspired by her reminiscences this morning as she'd stood in the shade of the water tank. She'd thought for a long time of their days in London, and she so wanted to be a good wife.

Although she'd anticipated his return with her customary resignation, Henrietta had determined to try harder. Perhaps the fault really did lie with her, perhaps if she could teach herself to respond to his passion . . .

'Yes, yes,' she now breathed as she undid the button and let the skirt drop to the floor. He barely noticed, one hand behind her neck pulling her to him, the other fumbling with his belt buckle.

Fervently she returned his kiss although she could feel the stubble of his chin rasping her skin as he ground his mouth against hers. She slid her panties over her hips and they slithered down her legs to the floor.

Terence released her long enough to pull off his trousers, noticing as he did so that she stood before him virtually naked, clothed in nothing but the sleeveless cotton shirt. It was open and her breasts were displayed, full and milky-white against the tan of her arms, her belly rounding perfectly to the mound of ginger-gold hair between her thighs. The sight of her raised the fire in him to fever pitch.

He forced her back onto the bed, his hands ripping her legs apart.

'My darling,' Henrietta breathed, 'my darling.' She stroked his face with her hand as she said it, willing him to look into her eyes. But he didn't. As always, he neither looked into her eyes nor said her name as he buried himself deep inside her.

Although it was painful to start with, she tried to meet his thrusts, to let him know that she wished to give him pleasure. But by the time the pain had disappeared and she could concentrate upon the desperate rhythm of his body it was too late. Raised on his arms above her, his eyes rolled back in their sockets, he was unaware of any movement in her body as he ground himself mindlessly into her. Two more thrusts, then a guttural cry, and Terence was spent.

He flopped down beside her, gasping for air. Once again she caressed his face, still seeking a moment she might share. And finally he did turn to her. He laughed, a triumphant laugh as if he'd proved something, then gave her a brief resounding kiss and rolled on his side, his back to her. It was what he always did. He would sleep now, for exactly half an hour, and when he woke there would be no display of tenderness, no affectionate embrace in recognition of their intimacy. He would awake full of energy, revitalised, and spring from the bed ready to get on with the rest of the day.

Her attempts to share his passion had failed dismally, Henrietta thought. She was disappointed but not surprised as she lay quietly beside him. She never rose from the bed until he awakened, never washed herself after their coupling. She lay there, not daring to move, her vaginal muscles firmly clenched, holding his seed inside her, praying that this time she might have conceived.

CHAPTER SIX

'It's a boomerang.'
'Yes.' She stroked the wooden crescent with her
fingertips. Flat and smooth, delicate to the touch,
it was a beautiful thing. 'Yes, I can see that.'

Bernie was surprised. He hadn't expected the young
Englishwoman to know what a boomerang was. 'Do you
know what it does?' he asked.

'You throw it and it comes back to you,' Henrietta said
simply. Jackie Yoorunga, the head stockman, had shown
her; Jackie was a master of the boomerang.

Bernie laughed. 'Well, it comes back to them,' he corrected her, 'the Abos. That is if it hasn't killed or stunned
something they've chucked it at first. That's what it's for,
you know, it's a weapon, but I've never seen a white bloke
who could make the things work. Come on, let's give it a
burl.' He jumped up from his seat on the front verandah
and offered her his hand as they walked down the front
steps. He didn't know why, offering his hand by way of
assistance to young women wasn't the sort of thing Bernie
did. But then he often behaved in a peculiar fashion when
he was with Henrietta Galloway. Perhaps it was because
she seemed such a lady, with her creamy skin and her

lilting voice which sounded almost Irish. 'Better get away from the house in case we bust a few windows,' he said, self-consciously releasing her hand at the bottom step. She laughed her agreement and they walked down the slope towards the stables and the barn.

It was Bernie's third visit to the homestead, and the second time he'd gone AWOL. He hoped they wouldn't miss him. 'Just going for a walk,' he'd said, aware of the strange looks from the others at the campsite. Where the hell was there to walk to, they were thinking. All except Reg, that was. Reg knew where he was going.

Bernie hoped he wouldn't cop it when he got back. They hadn't missed him the last time but hell he was pushing his luck—two times in a row. What the heck, it was worth it.

Reg had been with him on the first visit he'd paid to Bullalalla station, and Bernie hadn't been AWOL then. He and Reg had both had two days' leave, and Reg had agreed to join him on his hike to the homestead. Old man Galloway had given them a right royal welcome. They'd arrived at the gates, about a half a mile from the cluster of buildings which formed Bullalalla station, and were admiring the fine homestead set amongst its trees when Jock had cantered up to them on his whopping great chestnut.

'What are you boys doing so far from home?' the old man had bellowed, then without waiting for an answer, 'Come on up the house and have a beer.'

Bernie had grinned, about to say 'Good on ya mate', but Reg had quickly replied 'Love to, sir, thank you very much.' The two young soldiers were the best of friends but twenty-three-year-old Reg found Bernie very young and very gauche at times.

'Make yourself known to the missus. Just on my way home myself, be with you when I've watered down The Baron here.' Jock touched his heels to the horse by way of introduction and the stallion wheeled on the spot in response to his master's command. Jock knew they looked impressive. The Red Baron stood nearly seventeen hands and, as Jock constantly boasted to his mates, looked a dead ringer for Phar Lap. 'Tell her the boss said to break open the icebox,' he called before he took off in a cloud of dust. Jeez, for an old bloke he couldn't half ride, Bernie thought.

It was a good thirty minutes later when Jock burst through the back door and into the kitchen where Bernie and Reg were starting on the ice-cold beers Margaret had placed before them. Both had been a little uncertain as to their reception from the dour mistress of the house, but Jock quickly dispelled their misgivings.

'Jock Galloway's the name, lads,' he said. 'Good to see you. One for me too, love.'

Margaret fetched him a beer, although she didn't approve of him drinking during the day; he never did normally. But then normally they didn't have visits from soldiers. When the lads had arrived and Bernie had said, 'G'day missus, we met the boss and he said to break open the icebox,' she knew it wasn't just cheek on the young man's part, the words were pure Jock Galloway. Her husband was keen for the company of military men so that he could boast of his own exploits, she'd seen it all before.

They'd been chatting for a good half hour, Margaret opening a further two bottles of beer, before Henrietta arrived. Reg and Bernie had introduced themselves and Bernie had asked about the bloke who buzzed the station and Jock had proudly announced that it was none other than his son, whereupon he'd launched into a boastful account of Terence's exploits.

'Learned to fly at the Royal Aero Club of South Australia no less, made me send him down there when he was just a boy, not much older than you, Bernie.' Bernie bristled just a little. He'd be twenty next month, but everyone took him for seventeen or eighteen, and it annoyed him.

'Mind you, he wasn't aiming on being a fighter pilot

then,' Jock continued. ' "Light aircraft's the way of the future, Dad," that's what he told me, he was no more than eighteen at the time. "We'll be one of the first stations to have our own airstrip".' The old man swigged from his glass, wiped the foam from the stubble of his upper lip and laughed with pride. 'Well, we haven't quite got around to that yet, but he always was a forward thinker, my Terry. Just like me. A chip off the old block. Ah Henrietta, come in and meet the lads.'

Reg jumped to his feet as Henrietta entered and Bernie followed suit, gathering it was the right thing to do.

'This is Reg from Sydney and Bernie from Wagga Wagga. My daughter-in-law Henrietta.'

'How do you do, Mrs Galloway,' Reg said.

'G'day,' Bernie nodded, 'Mrs Galloway,' he added.

'A beer, my dear?' Jock asked expansively, and before Henrietta could say she'd get herself a cup of tea, Margaret interrupted.

'I'm sure Henrietta would prefer a cup of tea.'

'No, a beer would be lovely, thank you.' Damn it, Henrietta thought, why had she done that? She didn't set out daily to annoy Margaret, it was just that, on occasions, she couldn't help herself. Oh well, too late now. 'It's rather stifling, isn't it?' She smiled at the older woman with a touch of apology.

It wasn't, Margaret Galloway thought. It was a mild day by normal standards. And who ever said 'rather stifling' anyway? The girl was mocking her.

'Let me,' Henrietta said as Margaret went to the icebox to fetch more beer.

'No, no,' Jock insisted. 'Sit down, sit down and entertain the lads. Look at them, they're so polite they won't sit until you do. Come on, come on, sit, girl, sit.' Henrietta did as she was told, no-one disobeyed Jock.

'Charlie'd be here to entertain you too,' Jock said to the boys, 'but she's out mustering.'

Reg and Bernie exchanged a bewildered glance as they sat.

'She's been out bush for three days now,' Jock added, 'she's a damn fine stockman, but if she was here she'd be proud to entertain two fine members of the Australian armed forces.' Jock hadn't eaten since breakfast and the beers were going to his head.

Margaret plonked Henrietta's beer down in front of her. She was far more annoyed with her husband than her daughter-in-law now. Entertain the armed forces indeed! She was the one doing the entertaining and yet he didn't cast a look in her direction, just roared for more beer. She contemplated calling Pearl in from the laundry tub to dance attendance upon the men, but decided that it wasn't worth it. The aftermath would be unbearable. 'These are the men defending our country!' he would roar at her later, in private, 'They deserve to be entertained by the woman of the house!'

'Thank you.' Henrietta said in acknowledgement of the beer, and she smiled encouragingly at her mother-in-law, but Margaret merely turned away. The woman was offended, and Henrietta understood why. It was justifiable too, she thought, Jock was often very hurtful to his wife.

As it turned out, it was Jock who provided the entertainment. Talk quickly turned to The Great War, he made sure of that, and the nobility of battle for one's King and Country.

Reg listened avidly. His father had died at the battle of the Somme, a hero, the reports said. Reg believed in his father's noble death and it upset him when some of his dad's returned servicemen mates talked about the bloody waste of war. 'Cannon fodder, we were,' that's what some of them said. Reg hated it. Jock's stories were far closer to the truth, and he leant on the old man's every word.

Bernie, however, was barely aware of Jock's rantings, he couldn't take his eyes off Henrietta. Perhaps it was because it had been a long time since he'd been in female company, or perhaps it was because she was the most sensual and attractive woman he'd ever seen, he didn't bother to analyse which.

Margaret, having heard all of Jock's stories a hundred times, observed every facet of the proceedings and it annoyed her that Henrietta appeared totally oblivious to the boy's fascination. She called Pearl in to prepare food for the men, they were not going to get drunk in her kitchen.

After they'd eaten, Jock took Reg and Bernie on a guided tour of the homestead and its immediate surrounds. The large outhouse to the rear of the station was the store-room, he explained, from where they doled out the clothing, rations and provisions for the stockmen and their families. The flywire-encased shack beyond that was the meatroom where they hung the bullock carcasses before butchering, and beyond that, in the distance, was the slaughter yard, where, fortnightly, they killed two steers to supply the homestead and native families with meat.

They'd walked around to the front of the homestead, Jock enjoying playing lord of the manor, and he pointed out the stables, which was a tack room really he explained, and the barn, both about a hundred yards or so to the left of the house.

'Take your pick, boys,' he said, it had been agreed they would stay the night. 'In the stables you'll get horse shit—normally the horses are out in the paddock, but Molly's about to give foal—and in the barn you'll get mice, maybe rats. Take your pick.' Reg and Bernie opted for the stables.

'You'll sleep well tonight,' Jock assured them, 'with one of Nellie's stews inside you, you'll sleep like babies.'

He'd been right. The stew was the best meal they'd had since they'd left home. And Pearl delivered ample bedding supplies to the stables. With real pillows! Christ, Bernie said, a bloody sight better than camp!

The breakfast the following morning had been even more unbelievable. Steak and eggs! Reg and Bernie looked at each other across the table. Beef that wasn't tinned? Eggs that were fresh? Bernie tried not to eat like a pig.

Margaret thought Jock had gone too far in his offer of hospitality. There was room enough at the kitchen table, certainly, with Charlotte out on the muster and Terence staying at the base as he often did, but surely Pearl could have delivered the men something to eat at the stables. She said nothing of such thoughts to her husband but as Reg and Bernie took their leave and Jock said heartily, 'Any time lads, any time, pay us a visit,' she thought, over my dead body.

Two days later, on his return from the base, Terence's thoughts had been much the same. 'They stayed the night, Dad?'

'Yes, in the barn.'

'And had breakfast in the kitchen!'

'They're soldiers, Terry!' The old man couldn't comprehend his son's lack of understanding.

'They're bludgers, that's what they are.'

Terence had heard the whole story from his mother. 'They drank beer for hours,' Margaret had told him, 'then they had lunch, then dinner, then stayed in the barn, then they had breakfast, right here in the kitchen, before they left.'

Terence didn't like the sound of it at all. They were privates too, his mother had said, no rank, just two young soldiers out for a free ride.

'Bludgers,' he repeated, 'bloody young bludgers.'

'Listen boy,' Jock said, and the baleful glare which Terence remembered well from his childhood days, was as grim and malevolent as ever, 'these are soldiers! These are men fighting for their country! Just like I did! Don't you ever forget that! If I meet a man who's fighting for his country, then he's a mate of mine, don't you ever forget it!'

Jock had made his point, he knew it from the look on his son's face. He smiled. 'Just like you're fighting for your country, Terry, and I'm proud of you. Hey, they're gunners, son!' He clamped his hand around Terence's shoulder. 'These are the men who protect you up there. You owe them, boy. You hear me?' He gave Terence's shoulder a hearty thump. 'You owe them!'

Terence left it at that. His father was still boss, for the time being anyway. But Terence wasn't at all happy when he'd heard that young Bernie Spencer had paid another visit.

The boy had been on his own this time, and he hadn't stayed the night. Of course he wouldn't have dared, Terence thought, he'd have gone AWOL, he wouldn't have had another day's leave so soon. But why the hell was he bothering to hike ten miles to the homestead, spend a few hours and then hike the ten miles back to camp?

'What did he do?' Terence asked his mother.

'Had a cup of tea, your father wasn't here so I didn't offer him a beer, and talked to Henrietta.' The look on her face spoke multitudes.

Terence had later queried Henrietta, but she made light of the episode. 'He's just a boy,' she shrugged, 'he's lonely.' And Terence said no more on the subject, but he seethed. Just one more time, mate, he thought. You try it just one more time!

And now Bernie was back. Barely a fortnight later. He had a present for Henrietta, he said to Margaret, knocking back the reluctantly offered cup of tea—Margaret knowing full well that if Jock were there he would expect her to offer tea at the very least—and she watched disapprovingly through her office windows as the two sat on the front verandah and examined the boomerang.

When Bernie took Henrietta's hand to assist her down the steps and they walked together towards the stables,

Margaret continued to watch for a moment or so, then rose and walked purposefully into the kitchen where Charlotte was making herself a cup of tea.

'That cheeky young devil's on the make,' she said, 'he just took her hand.'

'Oh Mum, give it a rest.' The muster was over and Charlotte was assisting Jackie in the roundup of pack horses from the home paddock in preparation for the annual drive when 1,000 head of beef would be herded 600 miles to the meatworks at Wyndham. Charlotte had no interest in her mother's fanciful gossip. 'He's a boy and he's lonely,' she said, repeating Henrietta's words to her. 'There's nothing more to it than that.'

But Margaret appeared not to hear. 'Terence is coming home this afternoon, he has three days' leave. He told me so.' She poured herself a cup of tea as she added, with some relish, 'He could arrive at any minute and I wouldn't like to be in that boy's shoes when he gets here.'

Charlotte wondered briefly whether she should warn young Bernie. What the hell, she thought, and she sipped her tea.

Bernie Spencer had racked his brains trying to think of a present he could give to Henrietta. Something that would impress her. Then it had hit him. Of course. The boomerang. It was his most prized possession, but that didn't matter, he didn't mind parting with it one bit if it would impress her.

He was a bit disappointed to discover that she knew what a boomerang was, but her laughter as he chased after the thing, retrieving it and returning to her like a faithful puppy, was reward enough.

Finally, exhausted, he draped himself over the fence poles of the yard. His antics with the boomerang had taken them around the back of the barn to the horse-breaking yard at the rear of the stables. 'I reckon you better keep it just as an ornament,' he panted, 'it doesn't work too good, does it?'

'You really mean to give it to me?' she asked. 'It's such a lovely thing. Surely . . .'

'Yep, it's yours,' he interrupted, and he scuffled his feet in the sand, not looking at her. It was the possession that he valued above all else and he dearly hoped that she would accept it. 'I'd like you to have it.'

'Thank you, Bernie.' Henrietta was in a dilemma. She'd been a fool, she suddenly realised. Naive, stupid. The boy was infatuated with her. She had ignored Margaret's disapproval and Terence's possessiveness, they were both overreacting, she'd thought, to a lonely young man starved of female company. If her Terence were marooned somewhere in the outback and enjoying the company of a woman she would feel no jealousy. But now, as she realised the importance of the boomerang, the value of the gift she was being offered, she knew she'd been wrong. She would have to tell Bernie not to visit the homestead again.

She turned the beautifully carved piece of wood over and over in her hands, caressing the smoothness of its surface, buying time, wondering how to say the words without being too hurtful.

'It's made out of ironwood,' Bernie said, proud that she was so taken with his gift. 'They make a lot of their spears and woomeras and boomerangs and things out of ironwood.'

'Where did you get it?' she asked.

'From Talc Bay, it was where we were sent first when we came up here. It's the south side of the harbour, pretty remote, and there's lots of Abos there who don't speak English. Not even a word of Pidgin, they just live in the wild the way they have for thousands of years. It's something to see, I can tell you.'

Bernie's young face was flushed with excitement in the telling of his story. 'Really friendly they are too. At least they were to us. We used to give them the leftover catch from the net and they'd carry on like kids being given a present, jabbering away and dancing about.'

Henrietta looked bewildered, and Bernie made himself slow down as he explained to her how the men in his unit would set up a complex fishing trap to augment their supply of fresh food. 'With thirty-foot tides, you've got to go out a long way,' he said. 'We'd lay a couple of wings of wire netting out into the sea. Twelve-foot wide and 100 yards long, with a big mesh trap at the shore end. The fish sweep around a bay at high tide,' he explained, 'and if they bump into something they follow it.'

He told her how he and the others would service the net at low tide. 'There'd be hundreds of fish all flapping about,' he said, 'trevally and bream and baby shark, good eating. We used to deliver fresh fish by barge across the bay to the other units posted around the place.'

From where they were, behind the stables, well away from the house, neither Bernie nor Henrietta heard the Landrover pull up in front of the homestead.

'You had to be careful when you were sorting out the catch, though,' Bernie said, 'baby crocs'd get in the trap, and stingrays. Dozens of stingrays, and they were the worst, they hurt like a bastard! I beg your pardon,' he hastily added, then aware that he hadn't offended, he continued, 'They've got a barb under their tail, you see, and the sting's really poisonous. One of our blokes, Goliath, giant of a fella just like his name, got stung by a whopper, right in the joint of his ankle, and three seconds later he's yelling in agony. That was nearly a year ago and Goliath still gets pain, and his anklebone sticks out all crooked like he's got arthritis, it'll never be the same again he reckons. I tell you I'd rather cop a bite from a baby croc than a stingray.'

Bernie realised that he was babbling again. 'Anyway,' he said, 'when we were sorting out the catch and chucking the stingrays away, the Abos kicked up a fuss—there was always a few Abos gathered around to watch us—they thought we were mad not keeping the things. So we chucked the rays to them, and that was the start of it. We got to be mates and they gave me that boomerang. Good people, they were. And they can do things like you've never seen . . .'

Henrietta was enthralled. So much so that she had momentarily forgotten her decision to tell Bernie he mustn't visit again, and was listening and watching in rapt attention. And Bernie, aware that he had a captive audience, was spurred on to even greater heights.

'Like the way they spear fish! I've seen a black bloke stand still for an hour amongst the mangroves. Like a statue. Spear raised above his head like this,' Bernie struck a pose, 'not moving a muscle, just staring into the water. You can't see a thing yourself, the water just looks green. Deep green, like jade. Then suddenly *thwack*!' Bernie hurled the imaginary spear with such force that Henrietta jumped, startled, 'And there's this bloody great fish on the end of his spear! Honest, it's amazing!'

'They've got the quickest reflexes you could possibly imagine,' he continued. 'You can be standing next to a bloke—just passing the time of day—and suddenly his hand's moved faster than you can see and he's plucked a march fly out of the air. He gives it a squidge between his fingers, chucks it away, and doesn't even know he's done it. Like magicians, they are.'

Henrietta knew what Bernie meant, she'd seen Jackie Yoorunga do exactly the same thing, but she didn't want to interrupt so she nodded for him to go on.

Neither of them heard Terence's customary call from the front verandah, 'I'm home.'

'One time, me and Reg and Goliath made a canoe out of a log of wood,' Bernie enthused. 'The way the Abos do. They showed us how, and it took us over a month, but we didn't mind. We had nothing else to keep us busy, there was no action, the odd Jap recce that was all, and we were bored. Well, when the canoe was finished it looked pretty good, I can tell you. Over fifteen feet of hollowed-out log, a work of art Reg said, and the Abos seemed to reckon it was all right too. They inspected the thing and jabbered away and patted us on the back and grinned a lot. They were always grinning. And the day we launched it they were all there, along with the rest of the unit, must have been close to forty people watching. Reg had worked out how we were going to do it, he used to be a surf life-saver at Bondi, you see.'

Henrietta obviously didn't see, but she wanted to know, Bernie could tell. 'Bondi's a beach near Sydney,' he explained, 'it's pretty popular and lots of people go swimming there, and when they get into trouble the local lifesaving blokes launch a wooden boat into the surf, and jump into it and belt out and rescue them, it's dramatic stuff.'

'Ah,' Henrietta nodded helpfully. Whether or not the picture in her brain was the correct one was immaterial, it was certainly colourful.

'They're famous the Bondi lifesavers,' Bernie continued, 'and Reg used to be one of them so we left it to him. He said that Goliath'd have to sit in the stern to keep the nose up which made sense, but we had a bit of a disagreement about how we got the thing into the water. Reg told us that him and me had to carry the bow between us, one either side, and Goliath had to carry the stern and we had to belt along the beach and into the surf and then throw ourselves into the canoe and paddle like hell as if we were on a rescue mission. Well Goliath doesn't like a lot of fuss, and he pointed out that there was no surf—which is true, the water there's like a millpond—and that nobody was drowning, so why didn't we just drag the boat along the sand and plonk her in, and Reg said "where's your pride mate!" and I have to say I agreed with him.'

Terence tapped on the open door to the office. 'Where's Henrietta?' he asked. Then he saw by his mother's expression that something was not right.

'So there we were,' Bernie continued, 'me and Reg up front, Goliath at the rear, somebody yelled "go" and we belted for the water. We were up to our knees and everyone was cheering and we were looking pretty good, and then we dropped the canoe in the water, pushed her out and jumped aboard. Well, we didn't last one second. She rolled in an instant and we were all dumped in the harbour. Everyone laughed of course, particularly the Abos, but we didn't care, we were going to show them! We just didn't have the balance right, that was all. At least, that's what we reckoned. So we did it again, a bit slower. Same thing happened. Then we did it again. And again. We tried every which way to control the thing, but no matter how carefully we got in she just rolled on us. It was like trying to ride a greased pig.'

Bernie's laughter at the recollection was infectious and Henrietta's returning grin encouraged him all the more.

'By now, everyone in the unit wanted to have a go,' he continued, 'and blokes were laying bets they could last a minute, but no-one could, and the Abos were laughing fit to burst, they couldn't control themselves . . .'

Henrietta herself laughed out loud, not only at the imagery of the men and the canoe, but at Bernie's enthusiasm in the telling.

Neither was aware of Terence's approach as he rounded the side of the stables and walked slowly towards them. He came to a halt barely twenty yards away and stood watching.

'. . . and crikey those Abos could laugh!' Bernie swore, thoroughly enjoying himself. 'The blokes were squatting on the sand holding their ribs, the women were covering their mouths and pointing and squealing and the kids were rolling on the beach like hysterical puppies.'

Terence studied Bernie and Henrietta. The intimacy of their shared mirth angered him beyond measure. To Terence, the peal of Henrietta's laughter had the unforgivable ring of betrayal. Never had she laughed like that with him. He studied the soldier, no more than a boy. Terence wanted to kill him.

'Go back to the house, Henrietta!'

The steely edge of his voice cut through their laughter, which died in an instant. They turned to see him. He was so close by, how could they not have noticed him, Henrietta thought briefly, at the same time wondering what it was she had done so very wrong. Terence's face was flushed with rage and his eyes glittered with an icy anger she'd never seen before.

'I don't think you've met Bernie,' Henrietta said in an attempt to cover the awkward pause. 'This is . . .'

'I said go back to the house!'

Bernie himself had automatically jumped to attention, he was in the presence of a senior officer. 'I was just telling Henrietta where I got the boomerang, sir,' he said. 'It's a gift.'

Henrietta! He'd called her Henrietta! And he'd had the effrontery to bring her a gift! If Terence had had a gun he might have shot Bernie there and then. But he wisely decided on a different tack.

'Stand to attention, private,' he commanded.

Bernie, who was already standing to attention, visibly stiffened.

'You're AWOL, aren't you?' Terence demanded.

'Um, well, sir,' Bernie stammered, 'just for a few hours. I um . . .'

'And it's not the first time you've gone AWOL to come here, is it?'

Bernie hesitated for a second, then shook his head.

'If I see you anywhere near here again I'll have you court martialled, is that clear, boy?' Bernie nodded. Terence turned to discover Henrietta still standing there, frozen, the boomerang in her hand. 'Give it back,' he said.

Without a word, Henrietta handed the boomerang to Bernie and, without a word, he accepted it.

'Now get off this property!'

Bernie saluted. 'Yes, sir,' he said. Then he dropped the boomerang, picked it up, saluted again, and fled.

Henrietta was about to say something, but as Terence turned and marched back towards the house she knew it was her duty to simply follow.

He said nothing as he strode on ahead, and she had to jog to keep up with him. He said nothing as he crossed the verandah and entered the front door, and he was still silent as she followed him through the house and into the kitchen.

The female clan was present. Charlotte seated at the table, Nellie preparing the evening meal, and Margaret loitering. Charlotte was invariably to be found in the kitchen at this time of day, it was her favourite place. When she was not out working the property, she enjoyed sitting and chatting to Nellie as she cooked. It was unusual for Margaret to be present, however; as a rule she would still be ensconced in her office in the late afternoon. But today, recognising the storm about to ensue, Margaret had determined not to miss the action.

She gave Nellie a meaningful nod. Nellie took one look at Terence's face, stopped chopping her vegetables and left. She didn't glance at Henrietta as she went, although she wanted to. The young missus was in trouble, she knew it. Nellie liked the young missus and she wished she could have helped, but there was nothing she could do.

'Terence . . .' Why was he behaving like this, Henrietta thought, it was silly.

But he ignored her. 'Henrietta has decided to join you and Jackie tomorrow when you ride out for the kill,' he said to Charlotte. Henrietta said nothing, but the surprise in her eyes was evident.

Charlotte held her brother's gaze, she knew he was lying. Why would Henrietta want to ride out for the kill? But, after a moment or so, she shrugged her agreement, it was time Henrietta's horsemanship was put to the test. And the fortnightly ride out to the home paddock to bring in the two steers for homestead consumption was an easy one.

'She's ready enough,' Charlotte smiled encouragingly at Henrietta, 'she's had a good teacher.'

Henrietta returned her sister-in-law's smile. Charlotte had indeed been a good teacher. No natural horsewoman, it had taken Henrietta a whole two months and all of Charlotte's considerable skill to help her overcome her innate fear. For the past few weeks, however, she'd felt comfortable riding both of the two placid house ponies.

'They don't frighten me anymore, Charlotte,' she'd proudly announced.

'They're not meant to,' Charlotte had laughed, 'why do you think they're called Fast Asleep and Seldom Awake?' Fast and Seldom were not actually as lazy as their names suggested, it was rather that they were good-natured horses, docile and tolerant of beginners.

'I'll look forward to going with you tomorrow, Charlotte,' Henrietta now said, determined to show courage in the face of Terence's rather daunting announcement. 'I'll ride Seldom.'

'No you won't,' Terence corrected her, 'you'll ride Florian.'

Margaret had taken over the vegetables upon Nellie's departure and had been feigning indifference at the proceedings. Now she stopped attacking the carrots and looked sharply at her son.

'Don't be ridiculous,' Charlotte said dismissively, 'she can't ride Florian.'

Henrietta looked from one to the other, a little confused.

She knew Florian by sight, a big bay which Terence often rode, a much bigger horse than she was accustomed to riding.

'Why do you want me to ride Florian?' she asked.

'It's time you moved on from the house ponies,' Terence said. Charlotte was about to interrupt, but he cut her short. 'She has to learn some time, Charlotte.' Then he turned back to Henrietta. 'It's sometimes better to learn the hard way. Don't you agree, Henrietta?'

His eyes drilled into hers but she didn't glance away. She'd seen that look before, just as she'd heard those words before, and they'd shocked her at the time. She held his gaze and, as she did, the images flashed through her mind. The day he'd insisted she watch the slaughter of the steers.

'It's humane,' he'd promised her, 'and you need to learn, my darling, we need to toughen you up.'

It had made sense, she'd supposed. But as she'd stood by the slaughter yard and watched the stockman standing beside the pulley system, chains at the ready, and the other stockman's hands firm upon the rope about the beast's neck, and as she'd seen the rolling white eyeballs of the terrified steer, she'd wanted desperately to look away.

'Watch,' Terence had quietly ordered as he stood beside her, 'watch and learn.'

So she'd dutifully watched as the Aboriginal stockmen, a team of three, went about their work. The man with the rope looped it around a fence post and held the beast's head firmly in position whilst Jackie straddled the poles of the yard and, from above, pressed the muzzle of his .303 against the steer's skull. An explosion followed, then everything happened in a matter of seconds.

In the instant following the shot, the ropes about the steer's neck had been released allowing it to fall, and the moment it did, the man beside the pulley system was

shackling the chains to the animal's hind legs. Simultaneously, the rifle had vanished from Jackie's hands and a
butcher's knife had appeared in its place. As he'd jumped
from the railings, he'd moved so fast that Henrietta hadn't
even seen him take the knife from its sheath attached to his
belt. Before the beast's head had touched the dust of the
slaughter yard, its throat had been cut. That much Henrietta had seen only too clearly. With one swift, backhand
motion Jackie had sliced through the animal's jugular as if
it was butter and, as the carcass was hoisted into the air,
blood had gushed like water from a broken downpipe.
Never before had Henrietta seen so much blood. And the
eye of the dead steer seemed to gaze directly at her through
the thick, red stream which had once been its life's force.
She'd felt sickened by the sight, dismayed by the efficiency
which had so swiftly deprived such a strong and magnificent animal of its existence.

Somewhere, behind her shock, commonsense told her
that this apparently barbarous act was a necessary part of
survival here in the outback, and she'd turned to Terence,
expecting him to tell her so by way of support. That's
when she'd seen the look in his eyes. He had known she
would be sickened, she suddenly realised, and he had
relished her horror and revulsion. He didn't even try to
hide the fact.

'It's sometimes better to learn the hard way, Henrietta,'
he'd said. And when she hadn't answered, he'd raised his
voice so that the others could hear. 'It could be worse, you
know. When they make a kill in the bush, they shoot the
steer through the lungs so it can still walk. They're clever
like that, the blacks. Then they herd it towards the nearest
trees—could be a mile away—so that they can butcher it
in the shade. The skill is in the timing of course. You have
to keep the animal mobile while its lungs fill with blood,
you can't allow it to lie down and die until you're ready.'

She hadn't looked at him after that, but stood resolutely

through the slaughter of the second steer, aware this time of what to expect, disguising her revulsion, refusing to allow him the satisfaction of seeing her flinch.

'Well done, Henrietta.' He'd congratulated her as though she'd passed some form of test, the tone of his voice quite warm and friendly, the look which had so chilled her no longer in his eyes. 'It comes with the territory, my dear,' he'd smiled. Then he'd walked off towards the house and Henrietta had remained, still stunned and bewildered, watching Jackie's two helpers skin and gut the carcasses which were to be hung in the meatroom for butchering the following day.

'Jackie don' kill no animal like that, missus.' The voice had been right beside her and Henrietta had turned, startled, to see the coal-black face of Jackie Yoorunga. Never before in her life had Henrietta met a person as black as Jackie, and she was still a little fearful in his presence.

'Like what, Jackie?' she'd asked.

'That bush way the boss say. Shoot 'im in chest, make 'im walk. Some black fella kill that way. Not Jackie. Jackie give 'im animal no pain. Not 'im, not 'im.' He'd pointed to the carcasses of the two steers. 'No pain 'im there.'

Henrietta had never seen Jackie so animated and the realisation struck her that the man was aware of the distress she had felt in witnessing the killing. This coal-black man, so foreign to her, so efficient in the dispatching of large animals, was more sympathetic to her feelings than her own husband.

'Jackie take 'im breath away,' the Aborigine insisted. He gestured once again towards the carcasses, ''im big, strong fella. Live fella.' He held out his hand. 'Then Jackie take 'im breath away.' He snatched at the air and it was the act of a magician, one second his hand had been there, in front of her eyes, and then it had gone. 'No more breath,' he said, ''im dead fella. But 'im feel no pain. No pain, missus.'

'I know, Jackie,' she'd said. 'Thank you.'

It had been that day which had initiated the friendship between Henrietta and Jackie Yoorunga. But it had also been that day which had sown the first seeds of doubt in young Henrietta Galloway's mind. She would never forget the look in her husband's eyes, the sadistic pleasure he'd derived from his power to shock her. And yet he'd been proud of her when she'd passed the test. Had he expected her to burst into tears, she'd wondered.

And now she saw the same look, there was no mistaking it. Only this time she sensed there was a punishment intended. Because of Bernie. Well if Terence was searching for her weakness, he would not find it today, Henrietta thought. Nor tomorrow.

'I'll ride Florian,' she said.

Florian was not a mean-spirited horse, Jackie Yoorunga would have no mean-spirited horses at Bullalalla station, and he trotted along beside the other three obediently enough. But Henrietta recalled Charlotte's advice. 'When he takes off, hold onto his mane and sit tight,' she'd said. 'He doesn't like to be left behind and you'll never be able to hold him.'

Jackie had been surprised to see Henrietta on Florian. The missus would never control that horse, Jackie thought. That was a good horse but that was a stubborn horse. Took the bit between his teeth, needed a bloody good rider to control him. Jackie would have said something but he was further surprised to see Terence on The Baron. What was the young boss doing here? The young boss never rode out on the kill. So Jackie held his tongue, it was not his place to tell the young boss Galloway which horse his wife should ride.

It was seven in the morning and a pleasant day, the sun yet minus its sting. All four of them wore hats, however; it would not be long before the heat would make itself felt.

Henrietta wore khaki trousers and a sleeveless cotton top, but she carried a full-sleeved shirt for protection later.

They travelled at a leisurely pace, Jackie and Charlotte taking their horses slowly, allowing them time to warm up.

Riding close beside Henrietta, Terence seemed in excellent humour.

'I'll take you up there, my darling,' he said pointing to the far-off escarpment, 'just like I promised I would. And I'll show you waterfalls like you've never seen.'

She gazed at the distant rocky ridges which looked for all the world like the walls of an ancient city. 'That won't be very difficult, Terence,' she replied, 'I've never seen a waterfall in the whole of my life.'

'You want to though, don't you?'

'Of course.'

'Then all the more reason for today's ride.' He leaned forward and patted Florian's neck. 'Once you've mastered a strong horse and when you can take a hard day's riding, I'll show you a whole new world.' His smile was so affectionate that Henrietta wondered whether perhaps she'd been wrong. Perhaps today wasn't intended as some sort of punishment. She started to relax, just a little, and enjoy her surroundings.

They rode through the open forests and woodlands, the air thick with the smell of cypress pine, and they crossed the low-lying swamp ground, not long since flooded during the wet, where termite mounds towered like giant tombstones. Riding with Charlotte, Henrietta had seen the magnetic termite mounds on numerous occasions, but she never ceased to marvel at them. Aligned, as their name suggested, on a north-south axis, they towered ten feet and higher, and were so prolific that in parts the landscape looked like one massive burial ground.

After an hour's easy ride, they came to the home paddock, several square miles of fenced off woodlands and grassy plain where cattle grazed, unperturbed, and

Henrietta realised that this would be where the test began.

Jackie and Charlotte conferred and, the selection of the steers having been made, it was time to cut them from the rest of the herd. Charlotte gave Henrietta a warning glance, and the race was on.

As Charlotte and Jackie took off, there was no stopping Florian, he was after them like a bullet. Just as Charlotte had predicted, Henrietta found it impossible to hold him back and within seconds she gave up trying. She leaned over the horse's neck, grabbed clumps of his mane in her fists and clung on as best she could. But for a relatively big animal, Florian was extremely agile. He ducked and weaved like a stock pony and within seconds Henrietta had lost her stirrups. Another sharp turn and she was gone.

The ground came up and hit her so quickly that she barely knew what had happened. But somehow, instinctively, she'd clutched the end of the reins as she fell, perhaps recalling Jackie's advice in her early riding lessons. 'Never lose 'im,' he'd said as he'd helped her mount Seldom Awake. 'Long walk home, missus.'

Henrietta struggled to her knees, a little shaken and winded, but pleasantly surprised to find that nothing was broken or sprained. She was even more surprised, however, to find Florian quivering beside her, apparently more unnerved by the incident than she was. She felt sorry for the animal. He hadn't intended to throw her.

'Sorry, Florian,' she said and she patted his neck.

Several hundred yards away, across the grassy plain, Charlotte and Jackie had cut the two steers from the herd and were turning them towards the track which led through the woodlands.

As The Baron trotted up to stand beside Florian, Terence's expression was one of approval.

'Well done,' he said, and he meant it. She had control of the situation and she was comforting the horse, it was an excellent sign.

Henrietta's own reaction was a mixture of annoyance at her husband's apparent lack of concern and pride in her own lack of fear. But to her astonishment, and before she had time to question her actions, she found herself once more mounting Florian.

If she'd expected Terence to stop her she was destined for disappointment. He simply watched as Florian, having seen the other horses at work, wheeled on the spot and took off again, Henrietta once more leaning forward, clutching his mane, clinging on for dear life, and cursing her foolhardy bravado.

Florian galloped as if it was a race he must win, his tail streaming behind him, his mane flicking her cruelly in the eyes as he strove to overtake the others. He crossed the plain in minutes and suddenly they were in the woodlands. Charlotte's and Jackie's horses were only a hundred yards ahead, moving at a leisurely pace, droving the two steers along the bush track, but Florian decided on the short cut. He seemed to be revelling in it. He dodged and weaved between the trees—they might have been flags in a gymkhana event—and he faltered for only one second at a log which lay in his path. But in that second Henrietta was lost. She lurched forward and, as Florian jumped, she saw the log beneath her. She started to fall, reaching her hand out along the horse's neck, the ground spinning dizzyingly towards her and, as if in slow motion, she felt the bridle between her fingers, then the reins. She clutched at them and held on with all her strength to lessen the impact of the fall, but as she did she checked the animal's stride. In the instant she hit the ground Florian stumbled and she felt his hoof catch her in the leg. He staggered, recovered his balance and the reins were ripped from her hand.

Hearing the commotion, Charlotte and Jackie had turned and seen Henrietta fall. Jackie rounded up Florian, the horse was prancing about, nervous and badly shaken.

Charlotte cantered up to Henrietta who was sitting on the ground rubbing her shoulder.

'Are you all right?' she asked as she dismounted.

Henrietta's shoulder was hurting like hell. 'I think so.'

'That doesn't look too good.' Charlotte pointed at the lower right leg of Henrietta's khaki trousers where the material appeared to be tucked inside the fleshy part of her calf. A red stain was seeping through. Charlotte gently rolled up the trouser leg and eased the material out of the deep crescent-shaped gash into which it had been wedged.

'You held him on too short a rein,' she said. 'He was trying to get clear of you and you checked his stride.'

'Yes, I know.' Henrietta was grateful for Charlotte's business-like manner. She was in a slight state of shock, she realised, any sympathy and she might start crying.

'It'll need a bit of stitching.' Charlotte respected Henrietta. For a beginner, and an English one at that, the girl had a lot of guts. 'I'll give you a ride back to the house,' she said, gently helping Henrietta to her feet, 'Jackie can look after Florian.'

'What's happened?' Terence said as he rode up to them. 'Another fall?'

'Quite a nasty one,' Charlotte nodded, 'she's going to need stitches.'

'It's my fault,' Henrietta hastily added, parroting Charlotte's words, 'I held him too short and checked his stride.'

'That won't do,' Terence said. 'He could have fallen and broken his knees, quickest way to ruin a horse.' He didn't say it in anger, just mild criticism, but Charlotte flashed him a reproving glance and even Jackie looked surprised. 'It's a valuable lesson learned, Henrietta,' Terence continued affably enough, ignoring his sister's disapproval. 'It's why we ride with a long rein, after all.' He looked at Charlotte and the edge of criticism was back in his voice. 'I'd have thought Charlotte would've taught you that.'

Charlotte ignored the comment. 'I'm taking her back to the house,' she said. Smug bastard, she thought.

'No, I'm fine, thank you, Charlotte,' Henrietta heard herself say. 'I'll ride Florian back.'

Charlotte opened her mouth to say something, then decided against it. But it wasn't the sharp look from her brother warning her not to interfere which gave her second thoughts, it was Henrietta's resolution. What was going on between these two, she wondered. Whatever it was she would keep well out of it, but she admired Henrietta's guts all the more.

Jackie dismounted and held Florian's bridle, whispering gently and stroking the horse's neck as Henrietta prepared to mount. 'Talk to him, missus,' he muttered.

'I'm sorry, Florian,' she said gently. 'It was my fault, I'm sorry.'

As she put her foot in the stirrup, Florian's eyes rolled white and he gave a nervous snort, but Jackie whispered soothing words in a language Henrietta didn't understand and the horse stood still and allowed her to mount.

Jackie mounted his own horse, very slowly, talking all the while to Florian, then he gave a clicking sound with his tongue and, as they set off, Florian walked alongside Jackie's horse, the flanks of the two animals almost touching.

'You stay close, missus,' Jackie murmured, 'him fine now.' Then for Terence's benefit, he added more loudly, 'We take it easy, eh boss? Don't want 'im break 'is knees.'

Terence looked sharply at the Aborigine, but there appeared no insolence intended. Jackie simply walked his horse at a slow, steady pace, talking all the while in his strange foreign tongue to Florian who walked peacefully beside him.

During the ride home, her leg throbbing with pain,

Henrietta did not once cast a glance in Terence's direction. She resolved not to. Just as she resolved that he would never break her. If that was his intention, then let him try. But she would never give in. Never.

CHAPTER SEVEN

*I*t was a dark night, the occasional glimmer of moonlight filtering through the cloud cover and reflecting
silver on the blackness of the ocean. But the dark held
no fear for Lucretia as she stood on the deck enjoying the
slight chill of the evening. She was relishing her solitude.
It was May now, a full seven months since they had set
sail from Amsterdam, and she found the claustrophobia
aboard the Batavia at times unbearable. Particularly since
they had become separated from the rest of the convoy.
Lucretia had found the sight of the other vessels comforting, even when, for the most part, they were mere masts on
the horizon. These days there was nothing as far as the eye
could see but the vastness of the Indian Ocean.

When the Batavia had been separated from the convoy
in storms south of the Cape of Good Hope, Commandeur
Pelsaert had been quick to quell the fears of his passengers.
Such an occurrence was not unusual, he had stated.

'No matter,' he had announced, 'it is as God wills. We
may come up with them again in higher latitudes.'

In private, however, he had admitted to Lucretia that
the loss of the convoy worried him somewhat. It had been
of great comfort to have the man-o'-war Buren constantly

in sight. The Buren, *with her three decks of guns, was the perfect deterrent to the many pirates who roamed the high seas. The* Batavia *was well armed, it was true, she carried twenty-eight cannons, a company of soldiers and an arsenal capable of equipping every able-bodied man on board. But, amongst her cargo of wines and cheeses, cloths and trade goods, she also carried twelve bound chests of heavy silver coin worth 250,000 guilders and a casket of jewels worth a king's ransom. If the knowledge of this cargo had reached the ears of those bent on piracy, then she would most certainly present an irresistible temptation.*

'*We are quite safe of course,*' *he'd assured Lucretia, not wishing to worry her unduly.* '*We shall keep a sharp watch, and the* Batavia *can outspeed any vessel upon the seas, but I shall miss the* Buren.' *Pelsaert found it a comfort to converse with one of his own kind, they were of similar social standing, he and Lucretia.*

Lucretia hugged her arms about her chest as the wind whipped through her bodice. After the heat of the day, the evening seemed suddenly chilly. But she delayed her return to the stifling atmosphere below decks and the unpleasant company which she might encounter and which she went to great pains to avoid. Since Commandeur Pelsaert had once again been struck ill, she missed his companionship more than ever, although she continued to nurse him as his health waxed and waned. At times he was feverish and seemed near death, then he would make an apparent recovery only to be once more struck down.

During the periods of his illness, it was plainly obvious that Pelsaert found great solace in the presence of Lucretia van den Mylen, but the knowledge that certain elements aboard slandered their relationship angered him. And the degree to which the odious rumours abounded was unsettling. The Batavia's *skipper Adriaen Jacobsz was a loathsome creature, to be sure, and the crew rough,*

ill-bred men, but the venom of their attack upon the character of both himself and Lucretia was so personal and
vicious that it threatened to damage the general goodwill
aboard ship, something an experienced sailor like Captain
Jacobsz would normally avoid. Pelsaert was mystified
as to why the man should encourage such behaviour,
and as Commandeur he meted out punishments to instill
discipline in the men, but the disquiet continued.

Lucretia too was aware of the extent of the slander.
No longer was it mere innuendo spread by Adriaen
Jacobsz whom she had spurned as an admirer. Jacobsz
had been joined in his attacks upon her character by
the powerful undermerchant Jeronimus Cornelisz, and
together the two of them incited a hatred towards her
which was palpable. As she passed by members of the crew
they would hiss at her, make lewd gestures and mutter
obscenities which were not the comments of mere lustful
ruffians. Lucretia was accustomed to men's lust and even
that of base men instilled in her no fear, but she sensed
hatred in these men, and hatred was foreign to her.

It was Jeronimus Cornelisz whom she most feared,
however. He was the antithesis of the foul-mouthed,
heavy-drinking Jacobsz, and it was initially puzzling as to
how, and why, the two had become such close acquaintances. In appearance Cornelisz was a cultivated, attractive man. Thirty years of age, a former apothecary from
Haarlem, he spoke French and Latin and, with an evident
love of fine clothes, was impeccable in his attire. Fasti-
dious too, his long, brown hair always brushed and
gleaming, his moustache always neatly trimmed. As representative of the Vereenigde Oost-Indische Compagnie, the
United East India Company, Cornelisz was the third
highest ranking official aboard the Batavia, second only to
the Commandeur and the Captain, and so successfully had
he ingratiated himself with the Commandeur that Pelsaert
considered him a man of breeding. But due to either

feminine instinct or the fact that Cornelisz did little to disguise his lascivious feelings towards her, Lucretia had been quick to recognise the man's dual personality. His obsequious behaviour in Pelsaert's presence was in direct contrast to the cruelty he displayed to the underdogs aboard and the obvious pleasure he experienced in witnessing the regular physical punishments meted out for insubordination. As the lash of the whip ripped a man's back to shreds Cornelisz's eyes gleamed with exhilaration and the cruel curve of his lip revealed to Lucretia the man's true sadistic nature. In his company, she felt she was in the presence of the Devil himself, and all the more so because, as the weeks had become months, Cornelisz had taken a delight in displaying his evil for her and her alone. Whilst engaging others, particularly Pelsaert, with his wit and charm, he would whisper in Lucretia's ear quotes from Torrentius, the painter and philosopher whose beliefs were blasphemous to the extreme.

'All religions restrict pleasure,' he would murmur as she sat captive beside him at the dining table. 'Torrentius maintains that God put us on earth in order that we might, during our brief existence, enjoy without hindrance everything that might give us pleasure. It is an interesting theory, is it not?'

Lucretia would recoil at such blasphemy, and at the hideous intimacy of his tone as if he felt she might agree with his heinous beliefs. Then Cornelisz would give a merry laugh, intimating they had shared a witty story, and he would turn his considerable social skills to entertaining the table.

Lucretia avoided his company whenever she could, but privacy aboard the Batavia *was a luxury afforded to no-one.*

'Good evening, Vrouwe van den Mylen.'

Standing on the deck, lost in her thoughts, Lucretia was startled by the voice, but she knew immediately whose it was. There was no mistaking the silken mockery of his tone. She turned in the darkness to face him.

'Good evening,' she said as pleasantly as she could, she never addressed him by name these days, she could not bring herself to do so.

'It is late for you to be out on deck, is it not?'

Lucretia cursed herself. When the weather permitted, she took her customary walk upon the deck at dusk. Tonight, the seas being so calm, she had left the dining table whilst the men were still drinking, and she had anticipated a quiet ten minutes or so alone.

'Yes it is, and the air grows chill; I shall bid you good-night.' She half expected his hand upon her arm, his lips close to her ear to whisper more filth, but mercifully he did nothing.

'Sleep well, Vrouwe van den Mylen,' he called after her, 'may your dreams live up to your expectations.' And there was something in his tone that willed her to dream of ghosts and demons. Lucretia put her hand to her breast and felt the comfort of the locket beneath her bodice. The man wished to instill fear in her, but she would never allow him to know that he succeeded.

Cornelisz watched her go. The haughty bitch thought she was too good for him. Well it would not be long before she would be begging for mercy, it would not be long before she would be more than willing to share her favours. How he relished the prospect. Cornelisz made his way to the small aft cabin where the meeting was already under way.

He whispered the password to the man who stood close watch at the door, and was admitted entry. Gathered around the table, in the flickering light of a single tallow candle, sat the mutineers; now they awaited only one of their members, none other than the skipper himself, Adriaen Jacobsz.

'Where's the Captain?' muttered the High Boatswain, Jan Evertsz.

Cornelisz knew full well that the Captain was at the dining table still swilling back the raw genever gin he so favoured. 'He'll be present shortly,' he replied. 'In the meantime, Jan, I have a plan to further undermine our Commandeur. The skipper is in agreement, so listen . . .'

Cornelisz and Jacobsz had planned the mutiny from the outset of the voyage. They would pirate their own ship, they had decided. And they, together with all those who joined forces with them, would live like kings for the rest of their lives on the wealth of the Batavia's cargo. Systematically, they had set about stirring unrest amongst the men. During the heavy weather encountered around the Cape of Good Hope, Captain Jacobsz had altered his course, successfully losing sight of the rest of the convoy. Both men had prayed for the death of Pelsaert whose illness they took to be an excellent omen, but when their Commandeur had rallied, nursed back to health by Lucretia van den Mylen, they had recognised further fertile ground in which to plant their seeds of disquiet. Their plan had proved successful. Not only had the slander of Pelsaert and his 'whore' unsettled the men, all of whom had lustful feelings towards the aristocratic Lucretia van den Mylen, but the disciplines which Pelsaert had set in place to check this slander had been deeply resented. And furthermore, the men, who were denied the pleasures of the flesh during the long voyage, seethed at the thought that their Commandeur was experiencing such pleasure nightly. Feelings were rife, a highly successful breeding ground for inciting mutiny, Cornelisz and Jacobsz had found.

Pelsaert's fear of piracy was warranted, but the threat did not issue from foreign ships; it was gathering, like rancid pus, within the very bowels of the Batavia.

By the time Adriaen Jacobsz arrived at the meeting, drunk, his beard and moustache still wet with gin, plans for the final act of degradation had been made. An act

intended to so anger Pelsaert that he would mete out
punishments which would incite a riot.

It was dusk, the hour when others would be gathering to
dine. For the past two evenings, since her encounter with
Cornelisz, Lucretia had delayed her arrival at the dining
table. She had no cause to regret the fact that her lateness
might seem rude in the eyes of Commandeur Pelsaert, for
his illness continued to confine him to his cabin. Cornelisz
appeared to strictly adhere to the routine of his day, and
dusk was the one time when Lucretia felt safe to walk on
the deck without the risk of bumping into him. She
intended never again to find herself alone in the man's
company.

The breeze was quite strong and Lucretia had secured
her hair at the nape of her neck with a ribbon. She
breathed in the salt air deeply as she gazed out at the vast
expanse of the Indian Ocean, enjoying her solitude. The
sails billowed above and the masts' stays creaked as the
Batavia *cut through the white-flecked sea. They were*
making good speed, she thought, and she wondered, as
she did several times each day, how long it would be before
she saw her beloved Boudewijn. In the pale light of the
crescent moon, the silhouetted shapes of the carved
wooden figures, the Batavia's *guardians, were strangely*
comforting.

There was a noise behind her. A scuffling sound. She
turned. To her horror she was confronted by a man
wearing a mask. Then another. And another. Each
masked. In an instant she was surrounded. Lucretia
opened her mouth to scream, but rough hands threw her
to the deck. The ribbon was yanked from her hair, a rag
shoved in her mouth and the ribbon tied tightly to wedge
it in place. She writhed, gagging, as her skirts and petti-
coats were dragged up over her head. The men ripped at
her undergarments, tearing them to shreds, exposing her

naked from the waist. Then she felt the same callused hands wiping themselves over her buttocks and her thighs and her legs. They were covering her in something. What was it? Tar, she could smell tar. And something else. Oh dear God, the stench! The bile rose in her throat. She was sickened. The vileness! She started to choke. They were covering her in excrement.

They pulled her skirts back down from her face and slapped the filth on her cheeks and her throat and her bare arms. She was choking on her own vomit now.

'Do you like that, bitch?' she heard one man say amongst the panting and slobbering and grunting of the others. 'Put her over the side,' he said, and they dragged her to her feet.

She was gibbering, she could hear herself. The horror of it all. The stench was suffocating her, she could taste the filth. Strange animal sounds were coming from her throat along with vomit and saliva as she felt them lift her over the side of the ship. Let me drown, she prayed, let them throw me into the sea and let me drown.

But they didn't throw her into the sea. They held her by her ankles, her skirts billowing over her head, her hands catching the waves' spray each time the ship rolled to starboard, her legs and her private parts, covered with tar and faeces, fully exposed to the men above.

She didn't know how long they held her dangling there as she prayed for them to release her, to let her sink to the bottom of the ocean and find oblivion in a watery grave. Perhaps she lost consciousness for a moment, but she didn't feel them haul her back on board, she didn't hear them scuttle away into the darkness. She suddenly found herself curled up in a dark corner of the deck, still gibbering, still gagging. She pulled the ribbon and the rag away from her mouth and tried to breathe normally. She couldn't. She was shivering and her breath came in sharp gasps. She was alive, wasn't she? She should be grateful for that. But she couldn't think reasonably, the smell and the taste of her degradation were too vile. Then she thought of the locket. Had she lost the locket as they held her over the side? Feverishly she fumbled beneath her bodice. Something told her if she had lost the locket then she had lost her life. But it was there.

Between her fingers, Lucretia felt the carved shape of the mountain and the diamonds of the sun, and she clasped the locket to her breast as she sat rocking back and forth, whimpering in the darkness.

BOOK TWO

Book Two

CHAPTER EIGHT

Victory in Europe. On 7 May 1945, Germany surrendered. The Allies had won. But as Europe celebrated, the war in the Pacific raged on. Some said it was merely a matter of time, but men were still dying, Australia was still a country very much at war, and Darwin, broken and wounded as she was, remained of central military importance.

At Bullalalla cattle station news of the victory in Europe was greeted with jubilation, but Henrietta Galloway had double cause for celebration. She was eight months pregnant, a fact which had altered the course of her life.

A year previously she had visited a doctor in Darwin in an attempt to discover the reason for her inability to conceive.

'There's no reason at all as far as I can determine,' the doctor had said following his examination. 'It's quite possible your husband has a low sperm count, perhaps he should come and visit me.'

It was impossible, she replied, her husband was a fighter pilot. He stayed mainly at the RAAF base and was constantly on call.

'Ah yes, well there is a war on isn't there.' The doctor

didn't intend to sound sardonic, but there was something in his tone which intimated he had more important things to worry about than a young woman's fertility. 'Perhaps he could come and see me when the war's over, it can't go on forever. In the meantime, keep trying. These things sometimes take time.'

'What did the doctor say?' Terence asked.

'He said to keep trying,' Henrietta replied. 'These things take time, he said.' Low sperm count? No, she could never tell Terence Galloway that.

Now, as her healthy body bloomed with impending motherhood, it seemed all was forgiven. Her husband was loving, ever solicitous of her well-being, and in the eyes of her father-in-law she could do no wrong. She had become old Jock Galloway's favourite, the mother of his son's child.

Much as Henrietta was aware that, to them at least, she had finally fulfilled her duty, she couldn't help but respond to their kindness and she had never been happier. Even the reaction of her sister-in-law Charlotte, who might have been forgiven a touch of jealousy, was generous to the extreme.

'Well, you took your time, Henrietta,' she said in her usual blunt manner when she first heard the news, 'but good for you.' Then her weathered face broke into a grin, 'I was worried you were going to end up like me.' Henrietta had been very touched at the time and, as her pregnancy progressed, Charlotte continued to be responsive and caring. So much so that Henrietta had to insist she was perfectly capable of continuing with her chores about the house.

'All right, all right,' Charlotte agreed. But she insisted upon no more horseriding. 'Florian can live without you for a while,' she said.

It was sensible advice and Henrietta complied, although she missed Florian. She and the animal had become good friends. She still couldn't control him if another horse took off in his presence, but he no longer frightened her, and he behaved impeccably during her riding lessons with Charlotte. Henrietta had even insisted on riding Florian when Terence had taken her up to the escarpment to show her his long-promised view of the waterfall.

Henrietta was convinced that it had been that day—that glorious day which would live in her memory forever—that had been the turning point in her life.

The day had augured well from the very outset. Terence had been in one of his good moods, and when they'd completed their painstaking climb to the top of the escarpment the landscape had been as enthralling as he'd promised it would be. The rock formations, intricately carved by the forces of nature, were as ornate as the pillars and domes of ancient temples, and the gorges and the waterfalls were breathtakingly dramatic.

'The Northern Territory in all her glory,' Terence had boasted as they stood on the peak of a ridge and gazed across the gorge at the waterfall, cascading sixty feet to the blue-green pool below.

Henrietta had been overwhelmed. The waterfall symbolised something powerful, she realised as she looked down into the huge crater, surrounded by its towers of rock, to where the growth was lush and verdant and the animal and birdlife thrived. In all its majesty, the waterfall symbolised the very force of life itself. She'd stood in awe, and Terence remained silent beside her, gratified by her response.

They'd sat on a flat rock at the top of the gorge, sipping from the waterbag, watching the waterfall whilst the horses grazed quietly nearby, and he'd kissed her. So gently. Then a little more fervently as his passion grew. When she'd looked self-consciously about, realising that he wanted to make love, he'd laughed out loud.

'For God's sake, Henrietta,' he'd said with genuine humour, none of the customary sarcasm in his tone, 'who's going to see us? A few blacks maybe, and they wouldn't mind, they'd probably applaud.' At which she'd looked about again, nervously this time.

'No, my darling,' he'd assured her, 'no blacks, I promise, I was only teasing.' And they'd made love, high up there on the ridge.

Henrietta had experienced no fresh awakening. She was only slightly aroused by the time he climaxed, but she had long ceased to expect anything different, blaming herself for being unable to keep pace with his sexuality. But something else had happened, something far more important to Henrietta than her own satisfaction.

'I love you,' he'd said as he lay on his back looking up at the sky. Then he'd propped himself up on his elbow and looked deeply into her eyes. 'I love you more than you could possibly know, Henrietta, don't ever forget that.' There had been such passion in his gaze and in his voice that Henrietta, moved, had been at a loss for words. Then, only seconds later, he'd stood and helped her to her feet. 'Let's go,' he'd said as if nothing had happened. But it had. To Henrietta something vast had happened. For the first time since she'd come to this strange outback land she felt assured of her husband's love. And the assurance had been wrought by the very land itself, she was sure. High up here where the force of nature demanded truth, Terence had been moved to declare his love. In that moment, Henrietta felt at one, not only with her husband but with the land itself, and she was glad she had come to the Territory.

Terence teased her during the ride back down the escarpment. 'What would you have done if we'd been surrounded by blacks whilst we were doing it?'

'You said there weren't any around here.'

'Oh yes there are,' he replied in all seriousness. 'This is Warai land. We were damned lucky we weren't clubbed to death, they can be a pretty wild bunch.'

'Terence!' She was aghast, until he let out a burst of laughter and she realised he was joking.

'No, they're not dangerous,' he assured her, 'but Warai do live around the escarpment. They camp up here, and we have an agreement. Have had since my grandfather's time. If the odd dumb steer wanders up to the ridges then they're welcome to it, so long as they leave the rest of the herd alone. It works well for both sides.'

'Do you think they saw us?' Henrietta felt stupidly girlish, but she couldn't help blushing at the thought.

'No. But like I said, they'd probably have applauded if they had, they're a highly sexed bunch, they approve of that sort of thing.' He laughed as her blush deepened.

Two months later, when Henrietta discovered she was pregnant, she knew she had conceived that day up on the ridge. Just as she knew, in the very depth of her being, that the force of the outback had willed it.

There was only one person at Bullalalla who didn't appear particularly happy about the impending birth of Henrietta's child. Margaret was constantly disgruntled these days, which surprised Henrietta. Given the number of jibes she'd received from her mother-in-law about her barren state over the past three years, Henrietta would have expected Margaret to be the happiest of them all. Then she realised why she was not. It was old Jock Galloway. More than ever, he ignored his wife, lavishing attention on Henrietta every minute of the day. It was a simple case of jealousy, Henrietta realised, and she tried as hard as she could to redirect Jock's interest towards his wife, but with little success.

'Let me feel that grandson of mine,' he'd insist and she'd reluctantly stand by his chair as put his hand and his ear to her distended belly. 'Kick, boy, kick!' he'd demand, and the baby always seemed to obey. Then Jock would roar with delight. 'That's a Galloway in there! The next generation!' And Henrietta would look apologetically at

Margaret nearby, ignored and forgotten, and she'd wonder what on earth Jock would do if the baby was a girl.

The birth was two weeks premature, completely unexpected and very quick. It was mid-afternoon, Terence was at the RAAF base, Jock, Charlotte and Jackie were out fencing and it was young Pearl who discovered Henrietta. She was crumpled up outside the door of the chook-house, the feed bowl dropped at her feet, birdseed scattered in all directions and angry fowl squawking on the other side of the door, demanding to be fed.

Fifteen-year-old Pearl took one look, dumped her basket of washing on the old wooden table by the clothes line and yelled, 'Hang on, missus!' Then she belted through the back door to the kitchen screaming, 'Mum!'

But Nellie wasn't in the kitchen. Alerted by young Pearl's screams, it was Margaret who was the first to reach Henrietta's side.

'Can you walk?' she asked briskly, tucking one of her hands under Henrietta's armpit and circling her wrist in an iron-like grip with the other. Henrietta nodded.

'I can't find Mum,' Pearl arrived panting beside them.

'Take the other arm,' Margaret said, and between them they helped Henrietta inside.

They got her upstairs and Margaret started undressing her. 'Put some water on to boil,' she ordered Pearl, 'the big stew pot, then go and find your mother. And bring up some towels.'

'Breathe deeply,' she told Henrietta as Pearl scuttled out the door. Then, in one swift movement, she ripped the coverlet off the bed and laid Henrietta down. 'They're coming quite fast aren't they?' Henrietta nodded, trying to concentrate on her breathing. 'How long have you been having them?' she asked bluntly, in the same matter-of-fact manner with which she discussed the distribution of rations.

'A couple of hours.' Henrietta had felt the first pains at

the lunch table but she hadn't said anything. They couldn't be contractions, she'd thought, she wasn't due for another two weeks. 'I thought it was a false alarm.'

'No point in being heroic, girl,' Margaret said as she pulled the coverlet over her.

Nellie was at the top of a ladder picking mangoes, it took Pearl fifteen minutes to find her, by which time the labour was well in progress.

Margaret and Nellie were both efficient midwives, and when Jock, Charlotte and Jackie returned just before dusk, the baby was nestled comfortably against Henrietta's breast.

An hour later, when Terence arrived home, he was informed that he had a son.

Henrietta tried, in every way she could, to show her gratitude to Margaret. Her mother-in-law had been a tower of strength throughout the birth, stroking her hand and her brow, telling her when to push, when to rest. 'It's an easy birth,' she'd said, 'you're strong and you're healthy and it's going to be quick, there's no need to be frightened.'

Had Margaret forgotten how kind she'd been to a young woman fearful in the throes of labour? Surely not. But it would appear so. The more intimate the contact Henrietta attempted, the more withdrawn Margaret became. And again Henrietta knew why.

Jock Galloway was a tyrant, she realised it now more than ever. Just as she now realised that she had been scarcely more than an incubator during her pregnancy, as far as Jock was concerned anyway. She'd been an incubator for his precious grandchild. Nothing existed for Jock but his son and his grandson. Least of all his wife. His wife knew it, and she seemed to blame Henrietta. But didn't Margaret realise, Henrietta wondered, that she too was now redundant?

Henrietta could make no inroads with her mother-in-law so she tentatively approached Charlotte on the subject. 'Jock has other grandchildren,' she said. 'Your brothers have given him four grandchildren between them.' Henrietta had met neither the brothers nor their families, but she knew of them through conversation—with Charlotte more than Terence.

'They weren't Terence's children,' Charlotte replied simply. 'This was bound to happen.' Charlotte Galloway was fully aware of the problem. 'Poor mother,' she said, more to herself than to Henrietta, 'it was bound to happen.'

Henrietta found herself praying that Terence would not desert her now that she had produced a son. Surely she was not a mere incubator to him. But Terence was so like old Jock in so many ways, as Charlotte was always ready to point out. 'A breeding mare', that's what Charlotte had told her in the early days. Was it true? Was that all she was to the men of this family?

But Terence appeared as proud of his wife as he was of his son, and, even as he encouraged Jock's indulgence with the baby, hurtfully ignoring his mother, he displayed more affection towards Henrietta now than he had throughout their marriage. And grateful, Henrietta determined she would do everything she could to maintain his affection.

Little Malcolm Galloway was two months old. It was a pleasant afternoon in late July and Henrietta was sitting in the rocking chair on the front verandah, the baby asleep in her lap, when the flywire door slapped open and Jock appeared, a glass of beer in his hand. He pulled up a chair beside her, plonked his glass on the small coffee table between them, and held out his arms.

'Bring him here,' he said with an affable grin, but it was an order nonetheless, 'bring him to Grandad.'

'He's asleep, Jock.'

'Not when he's with Grandad, he always wants to give Grandad a smile, bring him here.'

Henrietta rose reluctantly, there was no point in

arguing, and, aware of Margaret watching through the bay windows of her office, she placed the baby in Jock's arms.

Jock jiggled the child on his knees. 'Wakey, wakey, Malcolm, give Grandad a smile,' and the baby dutifully woke, gurgled and grinned back at the old man pulling funny faces. Henrietta had to admit that Jock had a way with Malcolm.

'See, what did I tell you?' Jock said proudly. 'He loves his old Grandad, don't you, Malcolm?'

Tickling the baby's tummy with his left hand, Jock reached out with his right, grabbed his beer and took a swig. Then he saluted Malcolm with his glass. 'Not long before you'll be joining your Grandad in a beer, eh?'

He took another swig, put the glass back on the table and took the baby's tiny hands in his leathery fists, dandling the child like a puppet in his lap. Henrietta wondered whether the old man might be a little drunk. Not that he was as a rule, it was rare to see Jock drunk, and never during the day, but he seemed to be particularly jovial this afternoon.

The truth was that Jock was feeling strange, a bit out of sorts, weary and a little light-headed. It had come on him quite suddenly and he'd popped out to play with the baby by way of distraction.

He made a fool of himself, as he always did, pulling ugly faces for the baby's amusement, and he felt proud when the child smiled back at him. He seemed able to make special contact with Malcolm and he'd convinced himself that they had a particular bond. That, even at this tender age, Malcolm somehow sensed he was the favourite. Jock had been favourite of Lionel, Terence was favourite of Jock, and now here was little Malcolm ready to carry on the line as the favoured one. The chosen of the dynasty, the vital link.

Jock laughed with delight as the baby wriggled in his lap

and gurgled its laughter along with his. He was feeling
better by the minute. He reached once more for his beer
but, as he did so, he felt suddenly faint. Breathless. And his
heart was beating more quickly, irregularly it seemed.

'Take the baby,' he said suddenly to Henrietta.

'Are you all right, Jock?' Henrietta was on her feet in an
instant, the baby in her arms. Jock looked pale, he held his
hand to his chest. Was he having a heart attack? Should
she call Margaret?

'I'm not feeling very well,' he admitted. Was he having a
heart attack? Should he call Margaret, he wondered.
Margaret would take control of the situation, he could rely
on Margaret. But he was loath to call her. To do so would
be to admit his dependence. In his own way, Jock had
always known he was reliant upon Margaret.

'Don't worry, Henrietta. Don't worry, it'll pass,' he
waved a hand dismissively, commanding her to sit down
and stop fussing.

Henrietta returned to the rocking chair, and cuddled
the baby, watching Jock closely. He was insistent and she
wasn't sure what she should do; Jock's word was the one
that carried in this house.

'You see?' he said with a bravado he didn't feel, 'I'm
fine,' and he reached out for his beer. But his right arm
wasn't working properly. He tried to reach further, but his
arm wouldn't obey him. He shifted his weight in the chair
in an attempt to get his hand, which suddenly seemed
crippled, nearer the glass, but the whole right side of his
body wouldn't obey him.

Henrietta watched, horrified, as Jock's chair toppled
over, taking the coffee table and the beer glass with it.
She jumped up, clutching the baby to her, and looked
down at Jock sprawled on the verandah. He was in a state
of stupefaction, staring up at her, his hand clutched to his
chest.

'Margaret!' she screamed.

On 14 August 1945, the Japanese surrendered. Finally, the war was over. Australia revelled in a frenzy of celebration. But nowhere in the country was victory in the Pacific felt as intensely as it was in the Top End's gateway to the north. The people of Darwin, predominantly in the services, and those few civilians who had remained, had cause to celebrate beyond that of the rest of the country. They had defeated invading forces, they had fought and won a war which had threatened them on their very own soil.

As a married man with a young baby, Terence was amongst the first to be demobbed, but his welcome home was not that of the conquering hero as he would have anticipated it might be a month previously. His father was not waiting on the front verandah to embrace him and bellow, 'I'm proud of you, son.' In fact the whole household seemed to be in mourning.

It was little more than a fortnight since Jock's stroke and, at Margaret's insistence, the homestead had become a virtual hospital to cater for her husband, his needs and his hopeful recovery.

They had been advised by telephone that it would be unwise for the patient to travel and Margaret had carried out all instructions, arranging immediately for a specialist to be flown up from Adelaide. The prognosis had not been good. 'It's impossible to predict at this early stage,' the specialist had said, 'as to the degree of Mr Galloway's eventual recovery. We won't know for the next several weeks. Certainly, for the next fortnight he will have apparent remissions and relapses, after which, when he stabilises, he will need physiotherapy. Only time will tell.' But by the tone of the specialist's voice he didn't hold out much hope.

By the time Terence came home to stay, a nurse and a physiotherapist were living at the house, both flown up from the Stroke Unit at Royal Adelaide Hospital, and the homestead's large office, Margaret's pride and joy, had been converted to Jock's bedroom and care facility. No expense was to be spared, she had instructed the specialist, and he had taken her at her word. Jock's recovery was costing a fortune.

'What's the point?' Terence said to Henrietta as they sat in the front room, the old man curled over in his wheelchair staring at the floor, 'he's never going to recover.' Jock was indeed totally incapacitated, his right side immobile, his face contorted, and the sounds he made unintelligible as any form of speech. It was shocking to see.

Although, inwardly, Henrietta agreed, she was taken aback by Terence's callousness. This was his father. His hero. Wasn't he upset? More importantly, what if Jock could hear?

'The specialist said there's every possibility . . .' she started to say, but Terence interrupted.

'Rubbish,' he said harshly. 'The old man's had it, he should have died.' And he walked out of the room, just as Margaret arrived with the physiotherapist. Terence ignored his mother, and Margaret ignored Henrietta.

'Good morning,' the physiotherapist said.

'Good morning.' Henrietta nodded politely to the young man, then left the room. She didn't like to watch the physiotherapy sessions. Every movement the young man forced Jock to make looked painful. He would stretch out the old man's arm and pull at his hand and fingers, talking boisterously all the while. 'Come on Mr Galloway, you can do it!' And Margaret would join in. 'Try, Jock, try!' she would insist, 'it's for your own good,' and Jock would protest in his garbled jumble of noises. It was distressing to witness.

Henrietta felt deeply sorry for the old man. He may have been a tyrant, but no-one deserved to live in this state. No-one.

One afternoon, during Jock's sleeping hours, she slipped into the front room to see him. She had no particular intention, perhaps just to sit with him for a while.

He wasn't asleep, he was lying propped up in his bed, his body listing to the right as it invariably did. The bed faced the bay windows, and he could have looked out at the view if he'd chosen to do so, but he was staring vacantly down at the floor. Henrietta stood there, undecided. Why had she come, she wondered, she could do no good.

'Hello, Jock,' she whispered. There was no response, and she sat in the bedside chair and took his left hand in her own, stroking the work-worn skin. He'd always been a lean man, but he seemed to have withered, she thought, as she felt the bones of his fingers. 'I just thought I'd come and say hello.'

She looked at him, seeking a reaction as she stroked his hand. 'They don't mean to hurt you,' she said. 'Everyone wants you to get well, Jock.' Then, realising how inane she sounded, she started to talk about Malcolm. How big he'd grown, how strong he was. 'He misses you, Jock,' she said. 'You could always make him smile.'

When she felt the claws of his fingers curl gently around hers, her heart started to beat faster. He could hear, she was sure of it. She looked at him. He continued to stare unseeingly at the floor, but he was listening, she knew it, the insistent caress of his fingers urged her to keep talking.

The door opened and Margaret swooped into the room. 'He's supposed to be sleeping,' she said with a disapproving scowl.

'He can hear me, Margaret,' Henrietta said excitedly, 'I know he can. I was talking about Malcolm and he moved his fingers. Look.' But the old man's hand now lay still in hers.

'He often does that. I sit with him for hours at night.' Her tone was a mixture of hurt and accusation; *you didn't know that, did you*, she was saying. 'And I talk to him. I talk to him endlessly.' *You didn't know that either, did you?* 'And he often holds my hand, sometimes quite strongly.'

Henrietta refused to be daunted. 'Then you must believe he can hear you.'

'Of course I believe he can hear me,' Margaret said harshly, 'and he understands every word. So I'll thank you to tell Terence to stop speaking disparagingly in his father's presence, he takes no notice when I tell him.' She didn't allow Henrietta to reply but continued to issue orders as she walked briskly around to the other side of Jock's bed and started hauling him upright, propping his bad arm on a pillow. 'And if you must disturb his sleeping hours then I'd be grateful if you'd straighten him up. You know he's not supposed to lie crooked.'

'Yes, of course I will,' Henrietta said. 'I'm sorry, Margaret.' She wanted to say she was sorry for everything, for all the hurts and the blows Margaret had suffered, but she quietly left the room.

Barely three weeks later, Margaret made her announcement. 'I'm taking Jock to Adelaide,' she said to the family over dinner, 'In two weeks. Nigel and Sarah are accompanying me.' Nigel and Sarah were the physiotherapist and the nurse. 'I have booked us into an excellent nursing home where there are family quarters and I can stay there with him.' Margaret had arranged it all without saying a word to the others.

Henrietta and Charlotte exchanged amazed glances and Nellie stopped clearing the plates to stare in surprise at the missus. Only Terence appeared unmoved.

'That's probably a good idea,' he said.

'Yes, I thought you'd approve, Terence.'

Terence ignored the sarcasm in his mother's voice. 'He needs full-time care,' he said.

'But he gets it here.' Henrietta, in turn, ignored her husband's sharp glance which warned her not to interfere. 'And he's made such improvement.' She addressed herself to Margaret.

It was true, Jock was communicating these days. Not

with words, but he would look others directly in the eyes, and he would make signals with his left hand. There had even been the vestige of a smile on his lips the other day when Henrietta had held Malcolm in his lap, and he'd stroked the boy's little fat legs with his fingers.

'I cannot give him my sole attention when I have station business to attend to.' It was as if Margaret hadn't heard. 'You are skilled enough to take over the books, Henrietta, and Terence, you shall take over Bullalalla as it was always intended.' There was an unpleasant twist to her mouth as she smiled. 'You will receive your inheritance a little earlier than you'd expected, I don't suppose you'll complain about that.' Then she turned to Charlotte. 'And Charlotte, you will come with me and live at the nursing home, I shall need your help.'

Whilst Charlotte stared back uncomprehendingly, Terence finally reacted. 'Don't be ridiculous,' he said, 'I need Charlotte here.'

'You do not, Terence. Charlotte has never been needed here, she's simply been free labour. You can employ another drover, it's no job for a woman.'

'It's a job I like,' Charlotte said. But she said it quietly, as if she was already conceding defeat.

'You'll like living in Adelaide better when you get used to it,' Margaret said, not unkindly, 'you can go to the theatre, and meet people.'

Henrietta looked at Terence, expecting some argument, but he offered none. 'It's probably a good idea,' he said again, then he added, 'for all concerned.' But he didn't look at Charlotte as he said it, he nodded to Nellie instead, signalling that she bring in the dessert.

It was a sad day when they left. To Henrietta anyway. She had only been a part of it for a short while, but it seemed to her that an era was ending. Nellie, Jackie and Pearl obviously felt the same way. Pearl was crying, and Nellie seemed not far from tears.

As they all gathered on the verandah, Jackie knelt and shook Jock's left hand. 'Bye, boss,' he said, and Jock clasped the Aborigine's hand in return and nodded, obviously moved.

Charlotte refused to give in to any overt display of emotion but it was quite obvious she too was moved. She clung to Nellie for a little longer than necessary when they embraced. And when she shook hands, man to man, with Jackie and he said 'Bye, missus, you take care down there in the big smoke,' she gave in and embraced him instead. But she refused to give way to tears. She seemed philosophical about the turn of events her life had taken.

'Who knows what I'll do?' she had shrugged earlier in answer to Henrietta's query. She didn't share with her sister-in-law the fact that she no longer wished to remain at Bullalalla under Terence's regime. To Charlotte an era had most certainly ended and, without knowing exactly why, she no longer wished to be a part of the next one. She would remain with her mother for as long as it proved necessary and, if life in Adelaide did not agree with her, as she predicted it wouldn't, then she would return to the outback. But not to Bullalalla.

'Mother needs me at the moment,' she'd said to Henrietta, 'I can tell.'

Henrietta wasn't so sure; Margaret appeared to need no-one. She wouldn't even let Terence drive them to the airport. 'Nigel will drive us,' she'd said, 'it's all arranged. He needs to return the car he borrowed to the garage anyway, it's more convenient this way.'

Terence hadn't insisted. 'Dad would probably rather say goodbye here,' he'd agreed, obviously thankful to be relieved of the duty.

As Malcolm wrapped his tiny hand around the old man's thumb, Jock seemed close to tears. It was apparent that he didn't want to go. Just as it was apparent that his wife couldn't wait to leave.

Margaret Galloway relished the prospect of having Jock to herself. For years she'd watched from upstairs as he'd walked down to the Aborigines' camp, knowing he was going to assuage his sexual appetite with a young black girl. For years she'd been ignored as he'd focussed his attention solely on his eldest son. And, until the stroke, it had appeared that for the rest of her life she was to be destined to the sidelines as his world revolved around his grandson. At last he was hers, totally dependent upon her, and there was no competition.

She made no attempt to return her daughter-in-law's awkward embrace; Margaret was not physically demonstrative at the best of times, but her words were kind.

'Bullalalla is in your hands now, Henrietta, and you'll do a fine job, you're a good wife.' Perhaps because Henrietta no longer presented a threat, or perhaps because, after all, she genuinely felt an affection for the girl, she said, with the utmost sincerity, 'It's your turn now, my dear. Good luck.'

She was not as receptive with her son, but stood rigid as he kissed her dutifully on the cheek. Terence's farewell to his father was equally remote.

'Bye, Dad,' he said. 'I'll be in touch regularly.' But it was obvious from his tone that he wouldn't.

The car wasn't even out of sight when Terence turned to Henrietta. 'We need to buy you a new dress, my darling.' He was in extremely high spirits. 'There's a garden party at Government House next week.'

CHAPTER NINE

Aggie Marshall clumped into the foyer of the Hotel Darwin, her wooden foot thumping heavily on the highly polished floors. Wood to wood, it was always the same. Most of the houses in Darwin also had wooden floors so it seemed she was always being noisy, always calling attention to her foot, or rather the lack of it. Not that she cared particularly. Friends told her that, now the war was over, there would be a huge call for prosthetic limbs, she should get herself a nice new foot and wear nice shoes for a change. As it was, Aggie always bought cheap shoes, it was a waste of money to spend any more when she only threw the left one away. She'd donated her dresses and skirts to charity and always wore trousers these days, which didn't bother her at all as she'd always preferred trousers, and she wore a carpet slipper on her wooden foot. It did little to muffle the thumping, though, because she tended to stomp—it was like having a pegleg, she said, she felt like Long John Silver. Her friends said she wouldn't walk so heavily if she had a proper prosthetic foot, but she didn't listen, she had better things to do with her time and money.

'Paul.' She saw a head of greying hair buried in a news-

paper across the other side of the foyer and recognised
Paul Trewinnard's lanky frame, the only person present,
apart from Aggie herself, who was not in uniform. Following the bombing, Darwin had been placed under
military administration and the Hotel Darwin taken over
as a mess and intelligence headquarters. Paul had
promptly disappeared, no-one knew exactly where, and
had only recently returned. Now, lazing about in a wicker
chair, his beige linen suit slightly crumpled, he presented
an image from the hotel's grand old days. But then, to
Aggie, Paul Trewinnard had always seemed a little like a
relic of a bygone era.

Paul rose as Aggie thumped her way over, the thumping
stopping for a moment or so when she hit the Persian
carpet in the centre of the foyer.

'Aggie.' He embraced her. They were good friends. Paul
liked Aggie Marshall immensely, even though she disapproved of the way he wasted his life, and lost no time in
telling him so.

'Do something useful,' she'd say. 'Get involved. If you
can't be bothered with yourself, then be bothered with the
community. Darwin needs its locals, particularly now.'
So he'd allowed her to inveigle him into joining the Garden
Party Committee.

He took the armload of papers she was carrying from
her and together they went into the Green Room, once the
hotel's central drinking hall, in more recent times a
military strategy room, and now a strangely deserted mess
of tables and chairs. There, they set up for the committee's
final meeting; the garden party was only a week away.

The Darwinese were limping home. That was Aggie's
phrase for it, and from Aggie it seemed rather apt. Not
many as yet, but in dribs and drabs they were finding their
way back, some with official permission, some without, to
start rebuilding their town. It would be no mean feat as
Darwin had been virtually destroyed; only 171 habitable

homes remained and these in various states of disrepair. The horrifying fact to those who had lost everything was the knowledge—quickly gained from those who had remained—that their loss had been incurred not only through enemy action but through the acts of Australian soldiers. And not only through random looting which abounded, and continued to do so despite the fact that troops were being withdrawn, but through the Department of the Army itself. Buildings had been gutted, including hotels and the public library, and a large number of premises had been demolished altogether. Either for 'strategic reasons', or in order to obtain supplies of material for 'essential defence works', it was reported.

The returning residents were forced to camp in abandoned army buildings or other vacated, half-ruined premises, and already rows of galvanised iron sheds were appearing in the commercial streets of Chinatown which had been totally destroyed.

Many basic services no longer existed, including the collection of night soil, so the newly returned Darwinese built 'flaming furies', as they called them, in their backyards, army style. A 44 gallon drum was placed over a pit, a hole cut in its top, sheets of galvanised iron placed around it for privacy, and once a week the pits were burned off. Newcomers were quickly taught how. 'Chuck in a bit of diesel, follow it up with a lighted match and then stand well back,' they were instructed. The pits would smoke for hours and the stench of burning sewage was ever constant in the town.

The rebuilding of Darwin would be a long, slow and painful process, and Aggie Marshall was convinced that 'morale boosters' were essential and that the first of these must be a Victory Garden Party at Government House. She'd shamed the local authorities by having the idea first. However, it had been 'very high on their agenda' evidently.

'But as you can imagine,' she'd been told, 'the Government has so many priorities to address that . . .'

She'd immediately been given full support from all quarters, to such an extent that everyone now thought the idea had emanated from the public service, a fact which Aggie didn't mind at all, just so long as everything went according to plan.

She and Paul prepared the table in the Green Room, setting out Aggie's minutes at each of the eight places, and the blank paper and the pencils she always brought for those too lazy or forgetful to provide their own. Aggie was very thorough, and meticulous in her insistence that everyone make notes of the duties they'd been allotted. 'If you've written it down you can't blame me if you forget it,' she'd say jovially.

Along with the Government and military officials, several prominent businessmen were on the Garden Party Committee, and the first to arrive was, as usual, Foong Lee.

The three greeted each other warmly. Foong Lee had been most surprised to discover that Aggie had managed to acquire the services of his old friend Paul Trewinnard.

'How did you do it, Aggie?' he'd enquired. 'And more precisely, what on earth does Paul have to offer?' But his pouched eyes had gleamed mischievously and he'd given Paul a hooded wink, he was only too delighted to see Paul Trewinnard about to do something productive with the time which he normally idled away.

Aggie had been quite defensive. 'He is going to write all of our literature,' she'd said. 'Our leaflets, our pleas to various departments, and he's going to publicise our events in his articles for the *Northern Standard*, now that it's started up again.' The *Northern Standard* had ceased publishing immediately after the bombing of Darwin and had only recently reopened for business. 'Paul is going to be extremely useful,' Aggie had said adamantly.

'Of course, of course, I have no doubt.' He didn't tell her he'd been joking. When Aggie was fervent about something there was little point.

Foong Lee had been delighted when Aggie had asked him to join the committee, and he was generously donating countless supplies for the event. By mutual choice, the Chinese and Europeans had always lived in separate communities and Foong Lee was of the firm opinion that segregation should play no part in such a celebration. Both parties must participate.

'It is a common victory we celebrate, Aggie,' he had said, 'your garden party must be for the whole of Darwin.'

'Well, for those of us who are still here,' she'd corrected him, even as she'd nodded in vociferous agreement.

It was the weather which was her main worry. 'Early October,' she'd said, 'the start of the wet, it's a tricky time to plan a garden party.'

'I wouldn't worry,' Foong Lee assured her, 'they say it's going to be a long dry season.' She looked at him sceptically. 'It's true,' he swore, 'I heard a long-term weather forecast yesterday on the wireless,' and it was impossible to tell whether or not he was lying. 'Besides, we shall plan for indoors as well,' he announced, 'Government House is very large.'

Foong Lee was well acquainted with Government House, from as far back as 1930 when he'd been one of the representatives to present the aviatrix Amy Johnson with gifts from the Chinese community at a welcoming ceremony in her honour. He'd been just twenty-nine at the time, already a successful businessman, and since those days he had been a guest at many a Government House function.

'It's simply a matter of gaining permission,' Foong Lee advised. 'I'm sure Government House will "come to the party" . . .' His eyes disappeared into slits as he smiled at his pun.

Aggie was grateful for Foong Lee's support, he was a very calming influence, she decided.

Now, as the Garden Party Committee gathered in the Green Room of the Hotel Darwin, Aggie was pleased to announce that Government House had been most supportive and that the ballroom would be at their disposal should the weather prove inclement.

Everyone clapped, and the Government House representative, a grey birdlike woman who was somebody's secretary, graciously accepted the applause, but Paul and Foong Lee knew where the true credit lay.

'We shall demand the ballroom,' Aggie had said to them in private, refusing to accept the suggestion that the verandahs would surely supply adequate shelter in the event of rain.

The two men now exchanged a smile. As usual Aggie had won.

As it turned out Aggie's fears about the weather proved groundless. The day of the garden party was clear, sweltering and sticky as was to be expected but, come late afternoon, when guests started arriving a shadow of a breeze promised a cool evening.

Government House stood grandly on its promontory overlooking the harbour, surrounded by its beautifully landscaped lawns and gardens. Miniature rainforests, tropical groves with exotic plant species and arbours of native trees were linked by terraced walks. The grounds on the western side, near Lover's Walk, had received a direct bomb hit during the first Japanese raid of February '42 and remained partially destroyed, but the rest of the gardens and the spacious house with its louvred verandahs had survived unscathed throughout the attacks.

The House of Seven Gables, as it was known, presented an oasis in the war-torn town as guests arrived at the carriage-loop and started to mingle.

Terence was proud of Henrietta, she looked magnific-
icent, her chestnut curls piled on top of her head, her
yellow sleeveless cotton dress with the little mauve flowers
accentuating the curves of her body. She hadn't allowed
him to buy a new dress, it was far too much trouble,
she'd said. And she had dresses in her wardrobe which
he'd bought on her arrival that she'd never even worn. But
she'd taken a lot of trouble with her hair. She wanted to
wear it 'up' for a more 'formal look', she'd said. It really
didn't want to stay there, however, and Terence thought
the threat of its falling made her doubly attractive.

His pride was mingled with a touch of wary aggression
as they sauntered through the milling crowd and he sensed
men's admiring glances. He was proud to have a creature
like Henrietta on his arm, but let one man overstep the
mark! Henrietta was his, and Terence was at the ready.

'Terry!' It was Hans van der Baan. Henrietta was
momentarily surprised, she'd heard no-one but Jock call
Terence 'Terry'. But as the big Dutchman swooped upon
them, with several of his friends in tow, it appeared that
Terence was 'Terry' to all of his air force mates. They
slapped each other on the back and raised glasses of beer,
and, one arm around Terence's shoulder, Hans grabbed a
glass from the tray of a passing waiter and thrust it into
his friend's hand.

'A toast!' he exclaimed. They all raised their beer glasses
and drank to the 457 Spitfire Squadron, then to the 319
Bomb Group's Squadron, then to Victory, and it was only
after that Terence thought to introduce his wife.

In the grip of camaraderie, Terence's feelings of possessiveness disappeared and Henrietta was quickly ignored as
the men reminisced. Not that she minded. She accepted
a glass of wine from a waiter and wandered down the
terrace to admire the giant banyan tree which stood in
the south-eastern corner.

'You're Mrs Galloway aren't you? From Bullalalla?'

Henrietta turned to confront a tall, handsome woman with short dark hair and apparently little sense of occasion—she was wearing trousers.

'Aggie Marshall,' Aggie said, and she held out her hand.

'Henrietta Galloway,' Henrietta returned the handshake which was as firm as that of a man's; it rather reminded her of Charlotte.

'You've been here for years and yet I've never seen you in Darwin,' Aggie said. 'Bullalalla's only two hours' drive, you must come in and join us from time to time.' Whilst Henrietta wondered how Aggie knew so much about her, and whilst she pondered about who the 'us' might be, Aggie didn't draw breath.

'I do a bit of work for the Country Women's Association,' she said, which was putting it mildly. Aggie devoted her every waking hour to fundraising events which she herself orchestrated under the banner of the CWA. 'And we need all the members we can get. Or rather all the "helpers" we can get, should I say. There's so much to be done, isn't there?' She was about to continue but a voice broke in.

'She's lining you up to do something, I can tell. She's incorrigible, don't listen to her.' It was Paul Trewinnard. 'You're Mrs Galloway from Bullalalla station, aren't you? Paul Trewinnard, how do you do.' And he offered his hand.

How did everyone know about her, Henrietta wondered as she returned his handshake.

'This is Darwin,' his grey eyes gleamed a warning, he was aware of her bemusement. 'Everyone knows everyone in Darwin, and they know *of* everyone within a hundred mile radius. The grapevine is alive and well, despite the war, and nothing is sacred.'

'How is your baby?' Aggie interrupted, ignoring Paul and compounding his theory, 'he must be three months old now.'

Henrietta was nonplussed, but charmed nonetheless, she couldn't help but be. Despite the surprising discovery that she'd apparently become hot gossip, the enthusiasm Aggie Marshall displayed was genuine and very engaging. 'Malcolm,' she smiled, 'he's just over four months actually.'

As the women engaged briefly in baby discussion, Paul Trewinnard started to drift away in search of a waiter, his wine glass was empty. But Aggie wasn't about to let him off the hook.

'Paul has agreed to play chauffeur when I go out to the boat which arrives the day after tomorrow, haven't you Paul?' She stopped him in his tracks.

'Glad to help,' he replied, as he tried unsuccessfully to catch the attention of a waiter who was too far away to notice them.

'I have trouble getting down to the wharf,' Aggie explained, 'so Paul always drives me when a boat comes in.' Henrietta hadn't noticed that Aggie was lame, but she nodded politely wondering where the conversation was leading. 'If you could make yourself available, Henrietta— you don't mind if I call you Henrietta do you?' Before Henrietta had time to nod, Aggie continued, 'I think it would be an excellent idea for you to accompany us. The boys love to see women on their return, and one as pretty as you would be a special treat.'

'What boys?'

'She means the POWs,' Paul explained, waving frantically at the waiter. 'Aggie goes out to the boats and planes to meet the returned prisoners, they've been coming back in droves for several weeks now.'

Aggie Marshall had been working closely with the Australian Women's Army Service and had made it her job not only to greet the returning men, but to search for news of husbands, fiancees and relatives who had been enquired after through the AWAS.

Henrietta hesitated.

'I told you she'd try to bulldoze you into something,' Paul said. 'Leave Mrs Galloway alone, Aggie, she has a young baby for goodness' sake.'

'Henrietta please,' Henrietta corrected him.

'Bring Malcolm along, he'd be more than welcome.' Aggie wasn't about to give up.

'Dear God, woman, you're a bully.' Paul's frantic waves had finally caught the waiter's attention.

'No, really, I'd love to help,' Henrietta said, pleased to have been asked. 'But I'll have to check with my husband.'

'Excellent,' Aggie grinned enthusiastically. 'Let's say the foyer of the Hotel Darwin, shall we? Two o'clock, Tuesday afternoon.'

The waiter had arrived. Paul insisted they all top up their glasses, and he proposed a toast. 'To new acquaintances,' he said.

The crowd was then called to attention by a spokesman of the official party who had now gathered on the verandah. The Government Administrator, Charles Lydiard Aubrey Abbott, was about to give his address. Paul and the two women wandered back up the terrace to join the throng and it was only then that Henrietta noticed Aggie's severe limp. She saw the carpet slipper protruding from the grey slacks and noted the heaviness of Aggie's gait. Did the woman have a false leg, she wondered.

Following the administrator's address, there was a brief but boring speech from an army general about 'the fine job our servicemen have done in the defence of Darwin'.

'They've done a fine job looting the place too,' Paul muttered to Henrietta. He'd been disgusted at the damage his beloved Hotel Darwin had suffered. The jewel of the southern hemisphere, as she was so often referred to, had survived the carnage inflicted by the Japanese, but she hadn't escaped the violation of her own protectors. 'It's a downright disgrace,' he added, this time just a little more loudly. The military were not popular amongst the locals.

Foong Lee was then called upon to speak on behalf of the Chinese community. He stood on the verandah, a penguin-like figure, dwarfed by the general and the administrator, and spoke his King's English with an Aussie twang, and yet his were the words which carried the most dignity and meaning.

He said that although he'd been asked to speak on behalf of the Chinese, he preferred to speak on behalf of all those present who had a love of Darwin. 'The rest of Australia doesn't know what we've been through,' he said, 'and we've acquitted ourselves well in a war which nearly destroyed us. We must now acquit ourselves well in peacetime.' He glanced at the general.

Paul gave a 'bravo' under his breath, Foong Lee's words were a direct dig at the military. Charles Abbott nodded his agreement, he too had no doubt as to where the blame lay for much of Darwin's destruction.

'We must rebuild our fine city, and we must do it together,' Foong Lee said. 'Our strength lies in our unity. On behalf of my own community and all those who love Darwin, let us work together in raising her from the ashes.'

There was a warm round of applause as he finished speaking and, after a series of photographs taken by the *Northern Standard* photographer for inclusion in Paul's forthcoming article, the official business of the afternoon was over and done.

Paul sought out Foong Lee and his family and brought them over to meet Henrietta.

'How do you do, Mrs Galloway,' Foong Lee said. 'My wife, Lin Mei, and my son, Albert.' He introduced the young man at his side with great pride. Albert Foong was very good looking and towered a full five inches over his father.

'Good heavens above, Albert,' Aggie said, 'I'd barely have recognised you.' Foong Lee's family had returned to

Darwin only the preceding week, and Aggie hadn't seen Albert for four years. 'How old are you now?'

'Twenty-one,' Albert replied, with an accent as Australian as his appearance was Chinese. 'Had my twenty-first in Adelaide last month.' He grinned at his father. 'I told Dad he missed out on a beaut party, it went on all night.'

The group of them posed for the *Northern Standard* photographer who was taking shots for the society page. From time to time Henrietta looked about for Terence to make sure he wasn't annoyed by the fact that she was mingling. But he was getting so happily drunk with his air force mates gathered around the beer table, that she'd probably be in the way if she joined him, she decided, so she relaxed and enjoyed the company of her new-found friends instead.

She'd forgotten how pleasant it was to socialise, and she suddenly realised how isolated her life had been over the past three years. Aggie was talking about her plans for socials and fundraising events, and saying how much she'd love to include Henrietta on her planning committee and, as she chatted on, Henrietta would dearly have loved to have accepted every offer there and then. She wanted to do something useful and productive, certainly, but most important of all, she wanted to have a friend. A friend like Aggie Marshall. She decided, however, to take it in easy stages. One never knew what Terence's reaction might be, he was so unpredictable.

'I shall be at the Hotel Darwin next Tuesday at two, Aggie,' she said, feeling that was bold enough to start with.

Paul Trewinnard, whose main pleasure in life was the study of human behaviour, had been watching Henrietta closely. He observed the anxious looks in her husband's direction, and he observed her relax and enjoy the company of others as she realised she was not under threat. Was her husband violent towards her, he wondered. There was something at odds in Henrietta Galloway. A woman as generous in body and features as she was should be vivacious, confident of her femininity, but he sensed she was not. Whatever the situation, Galloway had certainly kept his wife out of circulation. Paul hoped Henrietta would join forces with Aggie Marshall. Aggie would work her mercilessly, but it would do the young woman good.

The rain had obligingly held off for the afternoon, despite the gathering clouds, but at seven o'clock, as the proceedings were winding down, the deluge started and people fled for the verandahs. Aggie gave Foong Lee a look which said 'so much for your wireless and the long-term weather forecast', and Henrietta sought out Terence to suggest they go home.

At first he was loath to leave, he was having too good a time and there was plenty of beer left, he said. But when Hans and two more of his mates accepted the offer to come home to Bullalalla, Terence couldn't wait to go. The men unashamedly grabbed armloads of beer from the ice crates by the serving table, and Terence happily allowed Henrietta to drive whilst the others followed in Hans' Landrover. The boys were going to make a night of it.

Henrietta drove slowly through the pouring rain, glancing from time to time in the rear-vision mirror to make sure Hans hadn't driven off the road, the man really was far too drunk to be behind a wheel.

Well, she thought, now was as good a time as any. 'You know Aggie Marshall?' she said, broaching the subject with care.

'The school teacher? Yeah.' Terence took a swig from the beer bottle he'd just opened. 'Met her when she first came to Darwin. She had her foot blown off by a bomb, I heard.'

So that's how it had happened, Henrietta thought. 'Yes, she was there today.'

'Oh?' He didn't appear particularly interested. 'I didn't see her.'

Henrietta smiled, he hadn't seen anyone except his mates. 'She seems very nice.'

'Yeah, she's all right, bit of a busybody.'

'She does a lot of good work. Community stuff. Fundraising and things.'

'Oh yeah?' Another swig.

Henrietta took a deep breath, she hoped her timing was right. 'She wants me to go with her to welcome home the prisoners of war, there's a boat coming in on Tuesday.'

'Oh that's nice.'

She looked sideways at him. Was he drunk enough that he might not remember in the morning, she wondered? But he wasn't falling about or slurring his words. She went one step further. 'I enjoyed her company, I'd like us to be friends.'

'Good idea,' he said affably. 'You could do with some friends, you should go into Darwin more often if it makes you happy.'

It had been that easy.

Henrietta was shocked. Aggie had warned her, but she was still shocked. The returned prisoners of war were in a dreadful state. Emaciated, skin hanging from bones, eyes huge in the sunken sockets of gaunt faces. She was glad she'd left Malcolm at home in Nellie's care instead of bringing him with her as Aggie had originally suggested.

She found the experience harrowing, but also very uplifting. One thing every man had in common, whatever his physical state, was his happiness to be home. Each and every one of them was ecstatic.

'Jeez, will you look at that,' a voice would croak, 'a real Aussie sheila,' and men would laugh, wheezy laughs that turned into coughs, and they'd feel the cloth of her dress in pleasure, as if paying homage.

Henrietta wanted to cry, but she flirted instead. 'We have to be careful, I wouldn't want my husband to find out about us,' she warned with a twinkle in her eye as she held a man's hand or lit his cigarette.

Aggie was thrilled with the success of her enterprise as she and several members of the AWAS went about the boat conducting their enquiries, seeking out the missing. Henrietta was a Godsend, she thought. And Paul Trewinnard, who had come out with them on the pilot launch, stood to one side watching, enthralled. Was this the real Henrietta Galloway emerging, he wondered? She was glorious.

There was a dance on that night as there always was, courtesy of Aggie and her organising committee, for those POWs fit enough to attend, and the men were disappointed when Henrietta said she couldn't be there. 'You'll be the belle of the ball,' they said, which had a familiar ring somehow. She declined but, even as she did, she wondered whether, next time, she might not arrange to stay the night in town.

Henrietta had found a purpose in life and she blessed her new friend Aggie Marshall.

CHAPTER TEN

When Lucretia van den Mylen had been discovered by the night watchman in a dark corner of the deck, defiled and whimpering with terror, Commandeur Francisco Pelsaert had been beside himself with rage. The whole ship must suffer, he decided, every blackguard aboard must be flogged.

It was his interview with Lucretia herself the following day which would alter the direction of his thinking. Amazingly enough, Lucretia was lucid—the event should surely have been enough to drive any woman insane, Pelsaert thought—and she even named the one person whose voice she had recognised. That of Jan Evertsz, the High Boatswain. It was his words she'd heard amongst the general mutterings of the others.

As Lucretia had scrubbed her body throughout the night, with sea water and rags so harsh that they abraded her skin, refusing all help apart from the delivery of more water, she had pondered the facts. The relentless cleansing of her body had helped keep her mind clear, and some instinct told her that Evertsz had been acting under orders. If he and the rest of the rabble had wished to have their way with her, then they would most surely have done so.

The object of the exercise had been her humiliation,
Lucretia thought as she scoured the filth from her flesh.
But why?

Commandeur Pelsaert now assured her that strong
disciplinary measures would be taken, that men would be
flogged and Jan Evertsz slapped in irons to await trial.
Lucretia found herself interrupting.

'No, Francisco, that is not the way.' He stopped mid-
sentence. Surely the woman wished to seek vengeance.
'It is what they want, I am sure of it. Cause to rise against
you. It might well be why certain rumours were set in
place from the outset.'

He knew of a sudden that she was right. The two of
them had never spoken of the slander which abounded
with regard to their relationship, but each had known
that the other was aware of its existence. Who was setting
about to cause such dangerous mischief, Pelsaert
wondered, and to what purpose? But Lucretia was right.
In the light of his illness and his estrangement from the
crew, Pelsaert knew that if he brought further and heavier
punishment down upon the men he would risk a revolt.

'We will avenge these terrible acts upon your person,' he
assured her, 'when we are safely in port.' He was lost in
admiration for the woman's dignity as she took her leave
and departed his cabin.

Lucretia credited the preservation of her sanity to one
thing and one thing only. The locket. If it had not been
for the locket, during those hours between the attack and
her discovery, she was convinced she would either have
thrown herself into the sea or gone stark raving mad. The
locket was her saviour. If she could withstand the abomi-
nation of the preceding night then she could withstand
anything; the locket had decreed it so.

She kept well away from the men, fetching her meals
directly from the galley and eating them alone in the small
alcove allotted her; Zwaantie, her maid, had long since

deserted her for the company of Adriaen Jacobsz. The only person with whom Lucretia communicated was Pelsaert, and the only time she ventured on deck was when she was in his company.

The mutineers were momentarily thwarted, their plan had gone awry. What had happened to the heavy punishments Pelsaert was expected to have meted out, the prospect of which Cornelisz had particularly relished. They had been on the threshold of taking over the ship, Pelsaert's fury had been all they needed.

But it was a force above that of their Commandeur, and above that of their own mutinous actions, which would decide the destiny of the Batavia. The force of the elements themselves.

It was two hours before dawn and, under full sail with the southerlies behind her, the Batavia cut smoothly through the slight swell, her decks deserted but for the steersman and night watch, the Commandeur and his passengers sleeping soundly below.

Two other figures leaned on the lee rail also keeping watch: the captain, Adriaen Jacobsz and Hans Bosschieter, the gunner. On the open seas, with a mild swell, the watch was relaxed, no masthead lookouts had been ordered to their posts, and the two men were chatting, enjoying the balminess of the night air.

'Jesu!' Jacobsz suddenly exclaimed as he thought he saw white water ahead. 'Breakers!'

Hans Bosschieter peered into the distance. The moon was fickle, appearing and disappearing amongst the clouds overhead. 'No, skipper,' he said reassuringly, 'it's only the moonshine on the water.'

Jacobsz relaxed. Of course, what else could it be? The dreaded Houtman Abrolhos, the reefy islands which had seen the destruction of many a vessel, lay far to the east. They were still a good 600 miles from the Great South Land, the way ahead was perfectly clear. He thought of

Zwaantie lying in his bunk, warm and inviting, he would join her at dawn.

Zwaantie was a very obliging mistress, only too willing to indulge him in any way he pleased. No longer in the service of the haughty whore van den Mylen, she had been won by his promises that he would make her a fine lady. An impossibility, Jacobsz grinned to himself, but he would keep the girl for as long as she satisfied him, and the thought of Zwaantie's huge breasts brought a stirring to his loins.

Jacobsz's lecherous musings were interrupted as he was thrown violently against the lee rail; Hans Bosschieter too was caught off balance and clutched at a mast stay to keep from falling.

With the horrifying sound of rending timbers and rudder bolts being torn apart, the Batavia *met the reef. She staggered drunkenly forwards, crashing and lurching. Relentlessly, she struggled on, as if with all her great might she could plough her way through the object set in her path. But she couldn't. And finally, trembling with the shock of her own destruction, she heeled to starboard and settled in a mist of spray, the white water churning angrily about her hull.*

Even in the instant of disaster, Jacobsz recognised his mistake. In losing the convoy he had become complacent, he had failed to keep accurate track of his ship's latitude. They were several degrees off course, too far to the south, and these were the treacherous reefs of the Abrolhos.

He cursed himself as he rounded on Bosschieter. 'That was surf not moonlight, you fool! God's death!'

Pelsaert appeared on deck. He'd been thrown from his bunk in the collision and presented a rather ludicrous figure in his nightgown as he now hurled abuse at Jacobsz.

Jacobsz, in turn, hurled accusations at Bosschieter, as passengers, soldiers and sailors poured out onto the deck, Lucretia amongst them, terrified at the sight of their ship in her death throes and the booming surf which surrounded them.

On 4 June 1629, little more than seven months after leaving the port of Amsterdam, the proud Batavia had foundered on the infamous islands of the Houtman Abrolhos.

CHAPTER ELEVEN

Since meeting Aggie Marshall, Henrietta's life had changed irrevocably. She hadn't realised until now how lonely she'd been, and she blossomed. Her visits to Darwin increased until she was making the trip once a week. She even stayed overnight occasionally, at Marrinah House, a tasteful hostel for women located on the Esplanade not far from Aggie's house. She'd declined Aggie's offer to stay with her.

'Good heavens, Henrietta,' Aggie said time and again, 'it's such a waste of money. And I have one of the few remaining houses in the whole of Darwin (a slight exaggeration, Henrietta thought), so why not let me put it at your disposal.' No, she didn't wish to impose, Henrietta insisted. Secretly, she was very much enjoying her independence.

For the first month or so she had kept waiting for Terence to call a halt to her new life of freedom, but strangely enough he hadn't. He seemed genuinely happy for her. She'd invited him to come with her to the first dance she'd attended for the returning POWs, aware that he would not have allowed her to go on her own, and he'd satisfied himself that there was no cause for alarm.

Between Aggie and that strange Paul Trewinnard she was quite adequately chaperoned, Terence decided, and besides, he'd been bored witless watching his wife shuffle around the dance floor with emaciated soldiers.

'It's a very nice thing for you to do, my darling, I'm quite happy for you to go on your own in future,' he'd generously agreed. So Henrietta kept up her weekly visits to Darwin and happily devoted the rest of her time to her son and to keeping the books in order at Bullalalla, a task which she undertook with all seriousness, determined to 'run a smooth ship' as Margaret used to say.

Terence had little reason for complaint, the change in Henrietta delighted him. She was once more full of the spirit and enthusiasm which had first attracted him. Totally unaware of the influence his unpredictable moods had had upon his young wife, Terence decided that she'd become withdrawn over the past few years because of her isolation and the depressive presence of his mother.

Terence didn't miss his parents for one minute. He thought of his father as dead, it was easier that way. More pleasant to remember Jock Galloway as the hero he'd been. Terence was thoroughly enjoying being the boss of Bullalalla. He'd employed a full-time overseer and intended to return Bullalalla station to its pre-war grandeur.

His first mission in doing so had been to rid his land of the eyesores which remained as reminders of army occupation. The roads built by the military had been left littered with remnants of their camps, from abandoned huts and equipment to old jeeps and staff cars. Terence took what he could use and disposed of the rest. He was free to do so, the Government having set in motion a strategy called the Marshall Plan as a preventative to profiteering. The plan dictated that, in the interests of the country's economy, there was to be no selling off of army or air force equipment, and that all military property was to be left in the scrub to rot. The plan even went so far as to allow planes to be shoved overboard from ships and buried at the bottom of Darwin Harbour. Nobody was to profit from the sale of parts.

Following the cleaning up of his property, the next priority on Terence's agenda was the Bullalalla Races. Their re-introduction, he decided, would prove to everyone just who was the king in these parts. The June 1946 'Victory' Bullalalla Races would go down in local history.

'The Bullalalla Races, good heavens. So there's to be a return to normalcy so soon after the war, I'm most impressed.'

Henrietta was never quite sure how to take Paul Trewinnard. She sometimes wondered whether his air of cynicism was just an act or whether he really was as world-weary as he appeared. And she wondered now whether his comment was indeed cynical or whether he actually was impressed. He was a confusing man.

'Terence is very excited about it,' she said a little defensively, 'and he said I'm to ask my new friends as official family guests. And that means you two.' She directed her words to Paul, despite the fact that Aggie was sitting beside her.

'Me too?' Paul deliberately misunderstood.

'You *two*!' Henrietta emphasised with frustration, including Aggie.

'Oh, you mean me and Aggie.' Lightening dawned.

'Don't listen to him, Henrietta,' Aggie said dismissively. 'I'll be there of course, wouldn't miss it for the world, you'll drive me, won't you, Paul?'

'Delighted of course. How exciting.' Paul had been to the Bullalalla Races before the war, in Jock's time, and had enjoyed himself very much. He'd simply turned up, however, along with the hundreds of others who'd done so, he hadn't been formally invited. 'An official family guest, thank you,' he said, 'what an honour.' He meant it sincerely, he couldn't help it if others misread him.

'You must bring Foong Lee too,' Henrietta said. She'd met Foong Lee on a number of occasions and, although she didn't know him particularly well, she was aware that he was a very close friend of Paul's.

The three of them were lolling around in Aggie's untidy study, a preliminary meeting of the 'rebuilding of Darwin' subcommittee in progress. Except that they hadn't progressed, Henrietta having been so excited about delivering her invitation that she'd jumped the proceedings.

Aggie was seated in her comfortable armchair, her carpet-slippered foot supported by the old leather pouffe she always favoured when her leg was tired. Henrietta was seated beside her and Paul was leaning against the window frame, the open windows which looked over the Esplanade affording the only air available, it seemed, in this stiflingly close space. It was the end of the wet season, but the weather remained uncomfortably humid, he thought. But then perhaps it was just Aggie's place. She didn't even have a ceiling fan, just a small, useless contraption which sat on the corner of her desk whirring noisily and doing little but blow her papers in all directions. She was forever plonking paperweights and bowls and ashtrays about the place.

'The Races will be held in two months' time,' Henrietta continued, 'and family and guests are to join us in the grandstand. Well, Terence calls it a grandstand, but if that's what it really is then it's a very miniature version.' She laughed.

Henrietta had certainly changed since their first meeting, Paul thought. He approved of her exuberance, in his opinion she'd never looked lovelier.

Paul Trewinnard would have quite willingly admitted, had anyone bothered to ask, that he had a bit of a crush on Henrietta Galloway. 'Good heavens, what man wouldn't,' would have been his reply.

'It's to be a two-day affair, people are invited to camp the night,' Henrietta chattered on, 'and Terence is going to set up huge spits to roast sides of beef in the evenings. There'll be the family gymkhana events on the first day and the big races on the second, and he's planning it all for the second weekend in June.'

'Thank God for that.' Paul fanned himself with the papers he held in his hand.

'Stop complaining,' Aggie barked, 'it's a beautiful day.' The heat never seemed to affect Aggie the way it did others. 'It all sounds wonderful, Henrietta, and we shall most certainly be there, now let's get on with some work, there's so much to be done.'

The Bullalalla Races was a more spectacular event than Henrietta could possibly have imagined, even though Terence had promised that it would be.

'Up to a thousand people used to come,' he'd told her, 'bookies and jockeys and spectators would pour in from miles around. Of course that was before the war,' he'd corrected himself, 'with so many evacuated from the area we probably won't get half that number, but it'll be something to see, I promise you.'

Henrietta had prayed that it would be a success, for Terence's sake, he'd worked so hard and it was so important to him, she couldn't bear the prospect of his disappointment.

Now, as she stood in the grandstand, little Malcolm in the perambulator at her side, preparing for the arrival of friends and family, she looked out at the crowd and was overwhelmed. Men were mingling around the perimeters of the track socialising, parents were watching the scores of their children taking stocky little ponies through their paces in preparation for the morning's gymkhana events and, beyond the track, yet more families were busily setting up camp amongst the trees by the creek.

'There must be hundreds,' she murmured to Terence who was beside her, shaking hands, slapping people on the back, mostly fellow station owners and managers, proudly introducing them to his beautiful young wife in her pretty floral dress and his year-old son gurgling happily in his pram.

'And this is only the first day,' he laughed in reply. 'Just you wait 'til tomorrow when the big boys turn up to put the money on.'

Terence was in his element. Even he had not expected such numbers. Where had they come from? It was as if the war had never been. Perhaps that was it. People wanted to forget. Those from Darwin were only too happy to leave their troubled lives behind for two magic days, to forget that they were living in hovels trying to piece together a new existence, whilst others were willing to travel from far and wide for a taste of pre-war style cele-bration. Whatever it was that had brought them, they were there in numbers, and the atmosphere throughout was one of festivity.

The dusty oval racecourse was carved out of the scrub, the gymkhana courses set up in the centre. The track railings had been painted bright green, as had the several open shelters around the perimeter, which Terence had had built to provide shade for the elderly and women with babies. He'd gone one step further with the grandstand enclosure. The grandstand was bright yellow with green trim—'the same as the Sydney Cricket Ground,' he'd boasted, 'makes it look official.' Amidst the vast Territory scrubland, the overall effect of the Bullalalla racetrack was bizarre but attractive.

Hans van der Baan, who had married an Australian girl, a nurse he'd met during the war, and was now living in Perth, had flown up for the occasion and Terence was overjoyed. The two men opened a bottle of beer from one of the several iceboxes and were soon lost in conversation, leaving Henrietta to converse with the station managers and their wives.

An hour or so later, the children's gymkhana events under way and the crowd roaring enthusiastically, Henrietta excused herself to feed and change the baby in the family tent, a comparatively luxurious affair in the shade by the creek. It was close to noon now and he needed to be out of the heat, she said. Nellie was waiting for her and the two women chatted, Henrietta thankful for the break. She hoped that Paul and Aggie wouldn't be too much longer, she could do with some allies, and she would need them more than ever when the family arrived. Terence's two younger brothers, whom she'd never met, were flying up from Adelaide with their wives and were expected to arrive in the early afternoon.

She left the baby with Nellie and, upon returning to the grandstand, was thankful to find that Paul and Aggie had arrived. They had driven out in Paul's newly acquired Austin and were standing to one side waiting for her, Foong Lee and his son Albert with them. She greeted them warmly, ushering them to seats in the front row alongside her.

She sensed a slight change in Terence as she sat next to him and hoped he wasn't about to have one of his unpredictable mood swings. He'd been in such good humour of late.

'Is something the matter?' she whispered.

'I told you to invite your *friends*,' he muttered.

'I did.'

'Since when have you been friends with the Chink?' He said it a little louder, obviously for Hans van der Baan's benefit, she noted, as the big Dutchman nudged him and nodded vigorously in agreement.

Henrietta was shocked and felt herself flush. She looked quickly sideways at the others, but Aggie, seated beside her, was in deep conversation with Paul, and Foong Lee three seats further to the right could surely not have heard, he certainly showed no signs of having done so.

'He *is* my friend,' she whispered fiercely, turning back to Terence, humiliation lending anger to her voice, her eyes flashing a warning, 'and I'll thank you to remember that.' She was as confused as she was angry. Terence had never displayed any malignantly racist tendencies, and amongst the crowd there were many Chinese and Aborigines. It was Hans van der Baan's influence, she realised with an instant surge of dislike, and she gave the Dutchman a withering glance.

For once, Terence backed down. 'All right,' he said, placating her, 'all right, fair enough.' But he scowled as he took a swig of his beer, looking neither at her nor at Hans.

When the Dutchman had said, 'What are you doing inviting a Chink to the grandstand,' Terence had replied, 'I didn't', and he'd felt annoyed with Henrietta for having taken it upon herself to do so.

Given the potpourri of Darwin society and the Territorians' general acceptance of racial differences, Terence had always kept his disdain for Asians and Aborigines in check, but secretly he was of the opinion that Hans van der Baan and his ilk had the right attitude and he rather wished the Australian authorities had followed the line of the Dutch colonial administration of Indonesia.

'They're not called the Dutch East Indies for nothing my friend,' Hans had boasted to him on more than one drunken occasion. 'We kept the Malays and the Indonesians in their place right from the start. And even when the Jews of Asia came in for a slice of the action (Hans always referred to the Southern Chinese as 'the Jews of Asia') they were soon taught their place. They can run their laundries and shops, they're good at that, but they've got to learn they're second-class citizens. I tell you, man, we'd never have allowed them the business foothold they've got in Darwin, this is a white man's country.'

The Dutchman had fired Terence up on a number of occasions and, although Terence had been guarded against voicing his agreement when they were in the company of others, Hans van der Baan had successfully fed his contempt, particularly for the Chinese. Now, because the 'Chink' in question was none other than Darwin's tai pan Foong Lee, and because if others had heard his comment he might be howled down, Terence had been forced to accede to his wife which he knew didn't look good in his friend's eyes. Bugger them all, he thought. Bugger the Chink for coming, bugger Henrietta for inviting him, and bugger Hans for having brought up the issue. Terence tried to shake off his annoyance as he downed his beer, none of them was going to spoil his day.

They picnicked in the grandstand and cheered the little girl with freckles and plaits who won the under-twelve mixed jump event and everyone was in excellent spirits. Henrietta announced that she was entered in one of the adult gymkhana events during the afternoon and Aggie and Paul were most impressed. Foong Lee, always a keen punter, asked if there was a book being run on it so that he could bet on her, and when he was informed that, although the official bookies weren't coming until tomorrow, there was always a book being run somewhere, he and Albert went in search of it.

Around the entire racetrack was a feeling of carnival as an official lunchbreak was called and people ate and drank whilst prizes were awarded to the children. Announcements were made through a loudhailer by Terence's overseer, Frank 'Buff' Nelson. Buff was a tough, likeable man in his mid-forties. An ex-buffalo hunter, he'd been a top drover, then station manager in his time, and Terence paid well for his services. As Bullalalla's representative, Buff announced the winners from a rostrum at one end of the oval, then called the excited children up and presented them with their ribbons and prizes. Terence himself would present the awards during the following day's race meeting but, in the meantime, Buff Nelson was having a high old time, enjoying the kids' enthusiasm.

Shortly after lunch, the other Galloways arrived. Michael and James, with their wives Helen and Miriam were introduced to Henrietta, and Nellie brought Malcolm up from the tent in his pram. The wives clucked over him appreciatively and Henrietta enquired after Helen and Miriam's children, two apiece, each of whose names she had committed to memory. The family seemed pleasant enough, albeit a little withdrawn. They hadn't seen each other for so long, and Henrietta had expected a little more of a reunion, but the brothers and their wives were quite deferential in Terence's company.

She noted too the change in Terence's manner, and Charlotte's words, from so long ago, came back to her. 'They jump to his command just as if he was Dad,' Charlotte had said. And what else? 'They couldn't wait to get out of home before Terence took over,' something like that. Then why had they come today, Henrietta wondered. It didn't take her long to find out.

'Dad's talking now,' she heard Michael say to Terence as the three brothers stood together at the grandstand railings. Michael and James visited their father intermittently at the Adelaide nursing home.

'Oh?' The response was lacklustre.

Henrietta hated the fact that Terence didn't even bother to disguise his indifference. Chatting with her sisters-in-law, she gave only perfunctory replies to their polite conversation, as she busily eavesdropped on the men.

'Not much, mind you,' Michael said. 'But he's communicating, it's certainly all up here,' and he tapped his head.

'He's physically very frail, though,' James added, 'we don't know how long he's going to last.'

As Terence gave a disinterested nod without even bothering to answer, Henrietta fought the urge to interrupt.

'This is your father they're talking about!' she wanted to yell at him.

James, the younger and bolder of the two, decided to get straight to the point. 'We need to talk about Grandad's stud, Terry.'

It was then Terence realised why his brothers had come to the races; like Henrietta, he too had wondered at the reason. 'I see,' he finally responded.

Henrietta was aware that she hadn't been the only one eavesdropping. Both Helen and Miriam gave up all pretence of conversation and openly observed the men.

Lionel Galloway's original horse stud had been in the hands of a highly competent manager for years. It ran smoothly and turned over an excellent profit, there was certainly no cause to alter the arrangement. Terence knew that, in the event of Jock's death, the Galloway stud would be left to the three of them, Jock had told him often enough.

'You'll get the pick of the lot when I die, Terry,' the old man had said on a number of occasions. 'Bullalalla will be yours. So it's only fair the stud goes to the three of you. But I'd strongly advise you leave it in Gordon's hands, he knows horseflesh better than any bloke in the country.'

Did his brothers worry that Jock might have left the property to him alone, Terence wondered; they hadn't seen the old man for several years prior to his stroke. Surely Margaret would have told them the facts. But then perhaps not, his mother was perverse at the best of times, perhaps she was enjoying watching them squirm.

'Yes, I've been wondering about the stud myself,' he said. He hadn't, but if Michael and James were thinking of taking over the property they'd better think again. 'With the army gone the bottom's dropped out of the local beef market and I've been seriously contemplating a move south.' A brief glance in Henrietta's direction, as she stared at him wide-eyed, warned her not to say a word. 'The

Galloway stud would be the perfect solution, how long do you reckon Dad's got?'

There was a stunned silence. The feeling of shock was palpable. Hans van der Baan stopped swilling his beer and wondered what was going on. Even Paul, Aggie and Foong Lee, standing nearby, surreptitiously turned an eye to the proceedings.

'How ridiculous, we're not thinking of moving south at all.' Henrietta couldn't help herself, the sight of the brothers' faces, and those of their wives, all four white with dismay, and Terence's obvious enjoyment of their discomfort was more than she could bear. 'He's joking, aren't you Terence,' she said with the brightest of smiles. 'He couldn't bear to leave Bullalalla.'

Terence looked at her, his face expressionless, but Henrietta refused to be daunted. 'It's very naughty of you, darling,' she said cheerfully, then to Miriam she added, 'He's a terrible tease.'

Miriam and Helen exchanged a hopeful glance. A 'tease' was the last term they would have applied to Terence Galloway, but perhaps their brother-in-law had changed since his marriage.

Terence turned to his brothers and smiled. 'Of course I was joking,' he said, 'it'd be a stupid proposition for any of us to interfere with the Galloway stud, don't you agree?'

Michael and James relaxed and grinned back, but before they could answer, Terence said to Henrietta, 'It's time for you to change for your event, my darling; I'll have Jackie saddle up Seldom Awake.'

He was angry, she could tell. Very angry. His eyes were always dead like this when he was angered.

'But I'm riding Florian,' she said, a little confused. It had been agreed she would ride Florian. The two house ponies, Fast Asleep and Seldom Awake, had only been brought to the races for the enjoyment of any children who might wish to ride them.

'No, I don't think so . . .'

'But, Terence . . .'

'You could hurt yourself,' he said. Then he loudly announced to the assembled company, all of whom were now openly watching, 'Florian's very difficult to hold, she's come off him twice before.'

'That was two years ago!'

'Please, darling,' he kissed her lightly and there was a world of concern in his voice, 'for my sake and for Malcolm's, don't ride him.'

But his eyes were still dead. He was playing a game with her. She was to be publicly humiliated. Put in her place.

'All right, Seldom Awake it is.' She laughed as she turned to the others. 'I'm terribly sorry about your bet, Foong Lee.'

Buff Nelson announced the event through his loudhailer. It was a ladies' race and the rules were simple. When he blew the whistle, the twelve competitors were to gallop to the far end of the oval, dismount and pick up, in their teeth, the stick which rested on their individual 44 gallon drum. They would then remount and return. After crossing the finish line, the first to gallop to the rostrum and personally present him with her stick would win the race. Everyone applauded, these events were the fun part of the day.

Henrietta lined up with the others, hardened outback women wearing battered men's hats, sitting easily on feisty horses, all prancing and raring to go. Seldom Awake's hooves were planted firmly in the dust, and Henrietta sat perched on his broad back, feeling silly in her jodhpurs and smart riding helmet. She and Seldom heaved a joint sigh of resignation, it seemed they both knew what they were in for.

Buff blew the whistle and they all took off, including Seldom, he was an obedient animal and he knew the rules. But he took off at a snail's pace and, as the stock horses burst into a gallop, he continued to plod, Henrietta's frantic heels in his well-padded sides raising him finally to a trot and that was as fast as he'd go.

Jackie appeared from out of the crowd and ran alongside them. He urged the horse on in his foreign tongue and amazingly Seldom broke into a canter. A lazy, sloppy gait. He was not used to cantering, but for Jackie's sake he was trying.

Even Jackie's incantations could not work miracles and, in the distance, through the swirling dust of the others, Henrietta saw the women dismount and pick the sticks up in their teeth whilst their horses snorted and danced, impatient to get back in the race. One rider dropped the reins and her mount left her behind to take off after the others. Henrietta was only halfway to the 44 gallon drums when she met them on their way back. Sticks in their mouths, they waved to her and she waved in return as Seldom lumbered on.

The crowd was laughing and cheering with delight. This must be the comic turn. The stockmen were laughing at Jackie Yoorunga, speaking in the tongues of horses to a fat, lazy animal who wasn't listening, and everyone else was laughing at the station owner's wife, in her jodhpurs and smart riding helmet, making a fool of herself. They'd never seen anything like it.

Henrietta dismounted by her 44 gallon drum. Beside her, Seldom waited patiently not moving a muscle. 'Good boy,' she muttered, but Seldom was only too grateful for the brief respite. Henrietta picked the stick up between her teeth, her mouth dry and tasting of red dust, and remounted.

'Don't drop him, missus,' Jackie said, and he pointed to the stick. Then he sprinted off, reaching the finish line before Seldom was halfway there.

Seldom plodded his weary way back, the crowd roaring its approval. Without Jackie's influence, he refused to canter and even slowed from a trot to a walk. Henrietta gave up and simply sat on his back, waving to her right and left and grinning inanely with the stick in her mouth. She felt like a retriever dog, but if they all wanted a laugh, then fine, she would join in the joke.

As she reached the finish line, the outback women who had long completed their race, were waving their sticks in the air and cheering. Henrietta felt the whole world was laughing at her. But, strangely enough, she didn't care. If this was what Terence wanted, so be it. If she did not show her humiliation, then he would have no victory.

'Good boy, Seldom,' she muttered through her teeth which were clenched firmly around the stick, and she patted the horse's neck as he obediently plodded up to Buff Nelson who was standing on the rostrum.

'The winner!' Buff yelled through his loudhailer and, whilst Henrietta presumed this was all part of the joke at her expense, he explained to the crowd.

'The rules were clear,' he yelled, 'each rider must report to me with her stick in her mouth. The other contestants took their sticks from their mouths before reporting to the judge, they are therefore disqualified.'

The rules hadn't been at all clear, Henrietta thought. She'd been so self-conscious she'd simply forgotten about the wretched stick. She looked at Jackie who stood by the rostrum, smiling his gappy-toothed grin. Was this Jackie's doing? Or was it Buff's? The smile on Buff's leathery face was just as broad. The female riders were waving their sticks and grinning too. And the crowd was applauding generously. Everyone was delighted that Henrietta had won. What a good sport the boss's wife was, they all thought.

The joke was on Terence, Henrietta decided as she dismounted and walked up the steps to the rostrum.

'The winner!' Buff roared again as she took the stick from her mouth and presented him with it. 'Mrs Terence

Galloway!' And he held the stick aloft as evidence of her triumph.

Henrietta pulled off her riding helmet and curtsied as men whistled and women cheered. She played up to the crowd, bowing and blowing kisses in every direction, particularly towards the grandstand.

'Well done, my darling.' Terence embraced her when she returned to the grandstand surrounded by her friends. Paul and Aggie, Foong Lee and his son Albert had all run to the track to meet her as she left the rostrum. On their way back, she'd stopped to shake hands with drovers and their wives and people from town, she'd been the most popular person present, she realised with a sense of surprise and delight.

Now, as Terence embraced her and the family cheered, she looked for the sign of his disapproval. His eyes should be dead, but they weren't. There was even a touch of admiration in them as he said, 'You did very well. Didn't she, Hans?' he added, glancing at the Dutchman. Henrietta sensed it was a test she had passed. He admired her for it, certainly, but the rules remained his.

'It was fun,' she smiled as she returned his embrace.

Paul Trewinnard had witnessed the exchanges between man and wife from the very beginning. At first he'd thought Terence wished to humiliate Henrietta, and he'd felt annoyed and protective. But when Henrietta had taken the riding helmet off and shaken those glorious chestnut curls free and curtsied and blown kisses to the crowd, he'd decided that it must be some sort of game they played. A game of one-upmanship. And now, watching Terence toast his wife and embrace her as he clinked glasses with the Dutchman, Paul felt strangely disillusioned, he had not thought of Henrietta as a person who played games. How naive of him, but then he was not experienced at marital game-playing, his own marriage hadn't had time to get that far. He joined in the toast to

Henrietta's success. It was their marriage after all, what
business was it of his, he told himself as he fought off his
vague sense of disappointment.

Following the gymkhana events, the Aboriginal stockmen gave an exhibition of horsemanship, Jackie Yoorunga
leading the troops. At a flat gallop, he swung down from
the saddle, took two steps beside the horse, leapt back
in the saddle, then swung off again to the other side,
repeating the exercise a number of times. Then he swung
under the horse's belly where he clung to the girth strap,
and was suddenly once more back in the saddle. Even by
stockmen's standards, Jackie was the most remarkable of
horsemen.

As dusk gathered, those who were not camping out for
the night took their leave, most of them returning to
Darwin with the promise that they'd be back the next day,
but the crowd numbers did not decrease. If anything they
swelled with the arrival of the serious racing fraternity.
Those owners and riders with the earnest intent of winning
settled their horses down for the night at Bullalalla so they
wouldn't have to travel the animals on the day of the races,
then they themselves prepared for a party. It appeared a
tired racehorse was a crime, but a tired jockey was perfectly acceptable.

Tarpaulins were spread on the ground as families laid
out the provisions they'd brought, many pooling their
resources. Women buttered bread and shovelled potatoes
into the coals of the two large cooking fires, whilst on
smaller fires billies were boiled to brew tea. Men handed
around bottles of beer, or tots of rum, and all the while the
smell of roasting beef wafted tantalisingly over the entire
racecourse.

Two large pits had been dug, and the fires erected in
them had been lit at dawn. By mid-morning they had been
reduced to hot coals, and the two carcasses of beef
donated by Bullalalla station had been steadily turning on

their spits for the past eight hours. Now, people were encouraged to simply hack off what they wanted.

'You'll stay and eat, surely,' Terence said to Henrietta's friends as they took their departure.

'It smells wonderful, but no thank you,' Paul spoke for the others, he was driving them back to Darwin and they'd agreed it was time to leave, 'It's been an extraordinary day.' He shook Terence's hand.

'Most extraordinary, I agree,' Foong Lee also shook Terence's hand, as did his son Albert.

Henrietta, watching closely, was relieved to see Terence return their handshakes. 'You must come back tomorrow,' he insisted.

'I would be delighted,' Foong Lee replied. He had heard Terence's comment upon their arrival and he had appreciated Henrietta's defence, but Foong Lee always put racial discrimination down to ignorance and, as he secretly felt superior to ignorant people, he wasn't in the least bothered. Besides, it was to his advantage to return the following day, he was very much looking forward to the races, and the big betting opportunities they promised.

The feast continued well into the night. People gorged themselves on the beef, children held chunks of bread under the dripping carcasses to catch the fat, ignoring the fruits and salads their mothers had prepared. Finally, everyone having sated themselves, youngsters were put to bed and adults gravitated to each other. Someone in one bunch had a banjo, someone in another a mouth organ and they joined forces, others gathering to sing along or clap in time to the music. The man on the mouth organ struck up a polka and a circle was formed, spontaneously creating a dusty dance floor in the dying light of the fires and the many kerosene lamps which hung from nearby trees and tents. Men boisterously grabbed women and whirled them about as the crowd clapped along to the rhythm.

Henrietta had been disappointed when Paul and Aggie had left. She hadn't realised how much she'd come to depend on their company, they really were her only friends, she thought. She'd visited the tent to check on Malcolm, wondering whether she might use the baby as an excuse to bow out of the evening altogether but, upon Terence's instruction, Nellie and Pearl were taking turns to look after him so it was hardly a valid excuse, and she knew he wanted her to mingle.

Now, as she was whirled off her feet, she didn't have time to miss Paul and Aggie. She was the queen of the bush polka, the men all eager to dance with the boss's wife who was such a good sport.

'I told you you'd be the belle of the ball,' Terence said, joining her by the track railings. She'd begged off the next polka and had left the crowd in order to catch her breath.

'You don't mind, do you?' she asked. He'd seemed so involved with the bunch of men gathered around the fire, drinking and regaling each other with stories, that she hadn't been aware of him watching her. Henrietta sensed a strangeness in his mood and, following the afternoon's episode, she felt she was walking on eggshells, unsure what he expected of her.

'Of course I don't mind,' he replied just a little too brusquely.

'I won't dance with them if you don't want me to.'

'Oh for God's sake, Henrietta,' he snapped, 'don't be servile, it doesn't suit you.' Terence was also confused. He wasn't sure what it was that he wanted. He had been proud of her this afternoon, certainly, what man wouldn't be proud of a wife like Henrietta? When she'd won her race and the crowd had bellowed its approval, he had derived great pleasure from the knowledge that she was his. And tonight, although he hadn't enjoyed watching her in the arms of other men, he'd been proud to see them all queuing up for a dance. Under normal circumstances they wouldn't dance with the boss's wife, no matter how good looking she was, they'd be too inhibited. They were relaxed in her company because she'd shown herself to be a 'good sport', several of the men had said as much to his face. Terence was in a quandary. He didn't wish to break her spirit, but she trod a fine line. How much leeway should he give her?

Henrietta herself was in a state of utter bewilderment. Earlier in the day she'd been too outspoken, now she was too servile. What did he want? He was a mercurial man and she had learned to accept his mood swings but if only, just now and then, he could talk to her, offer some reason. It was as if he was toying with her, playing a game. If they could only talk openly, she thought, and for once she decided to confront him.

'Terence . . .' She hesitated momentarily as she looked at him in the dim glow from the nearby lamp which hung on the railing. Then, what the hell, she thought and she blurted it out. 'I wish you wouldn't play games.' She tried desperately to read the reaction in his eyes as she said it.

'What games?' There seemed to be no reaction whatsoever.

'The gymkhana event this afternoon,' she said, 'why did you . . .' But he didn't give her a chance.

'I don't play games, Henrietta, you should know that by now.' Still no reaction, and he was not angry, his eyes were not dead. But they were very serious. 'I never play games,' he said, and perhaps there was just the touch of a warning in his voice.

'Then if you're displeased about something, why can't we *talk* about it,' she continued desperately, 'why can't we *talk* instead of . . .'

'But we *do* talk, my darling!' He smiled as he imitated her emphasis, 'we *are* talking! And as I said before, and I'll say again now, *I was very proud of you this afternoon!*' He kissed her lightly on the lips, still smiling. 'And I'm very proud of you tonight. Now,' he continued, changing the subject completely, 'have another dance if you like, but I want you to go to the tent in the next half hour or so, the men have a lot of grog in them and things can get a bit rough.' He took her by the arm and started walking slowly back towards the crowd. 'I'll get my kit from the tent now so I don't disturb you, I'll be sleeping under the stars tonight.'

She looked at him uncertainly. Another game? Some sort of lesson? Was she to sleep alone as a form of punishment? But there was humour in his smile as he added, 'I'm expected to get a bit drunk with the boys, the boss can't be seen to sleep in a tent.'

'Of course.' There was to be no talk, she realised. 'I'll go to bed now, I'm tired,' she said, 'I don't want to dance anymore.' Henrietta knew that no further mention would ever be made of today's gymkhana event.

The Bullalalla Races were in full swing and Terence was in his element. It was a rough, tough day, a men's day, as horses thundered down the track, big money changed hands and the odd fight ensued over placings. Buff Nelson had to break up one heavy dispute and, as the boss of Bullalalla, Terence was called upon to be judge, referee and linesman all in one. He called the race a draw and the matter was settled, but not before the protagonists had laid into each other and scored a couple of heavy punches apiece, much to the crowd's enjoyment.

Foong Lee and Albert were cleaning up in the betting stakes. Foong Lee had a good eye for horseflesh and was down at the track, keenly inspecting both horse and rider before each race, and placing his bet at the very last minute.

Paul Trewinnard was betting very little. He enjoyed a gamble as much as the next man, but he enjoyed Henrietta's company more, so he remained seated beside her in the grandstand. He noted that, although her husband was revelling in the day, the gaiety seemed to have gone from Henrietta.

'It's a tiring business, the Bullalalla Races,' she smiled by way of explanation.

Henrietta was annoyed and frustrated. She'd thought long and hard as she'd tossed and turned in the tent last night, comfortably enough bedded but unable to sleep as she'd listened to the men's drunken guffaws grow louder. She was annoyed with herself for not having forced her confrontation further, and frustrated because she knew, if she had, it would have led nowhere. Terence would always close her out, a fact which she found depressing.

Now, for Paul's sake, she tried to shake herself out of her mood, not wishing to be poor company.

'Will you place a bet for me, Paul?'

'Of course.'

'The race after this. Jackie's riding Florian.' She gave him a grin. 'I suggest you put money on it too, it's a sure-fire combination.'

As Paul went down to the track to place the bets, he recalled Aggie's words. She had not accompanied them today, but when he'd dropped her at her house the previous night, he'd mentioned Henrietta and the gymkhana episode, not by way of gossip, he'd wanted a female point of view. Aggie had been very positive in her opinion.

'They weren't playing a game,' she'd said. 'Terence is a tyrant, and he'll wear Henrietta down if he can.' It was the voice of experience, Aggie knew only too well what it was like to live with a tyrant. 'She needs us, Paul. She needs her friends.'

'Come on Florian! Come on Jackie!' Henrietta and Paul waved their hats in the air and screamed at the tops of their lungs. It wasn't necessary, Florian led from the moment the field took off, and he crossed the finish line a full body length ahead of his nearest contender. Henrietta and Paul collapsed in each other's embrace as happy and excited as school children.

Jackie cantered by the grandstand. Standing in the stirrups, he saluted Henrietta who jumped up and down as she waved back. Paul poured two cold beers and they toasted their win, he once more delighting in her exuberance. A woman like Henrietta should never be unhappy, he thought.

Aware that this evening promised to be a far more raucous affair than the previous night, Henrietta was grateful when Terence suggested she take Malcolm home.

'It's just like the old days,' he said happily. 'They're drunk already, and there'll be fights before long, it's no place for you and the baby.' Terence was delighted, the races had been a phenomenal success.

Henrietta readily agreed. Most of the families with young children were packing to go home, to leave the final evening to the men and those bent on a night of rowdy dissipation.

Nellie helped her settle Malcolm into the Landrover. She and Pearl were camping out for the night, and Terence was already drinking with the men around the spit.

'You want me to come with you, missus?' Nellie asked.

'No, of course not, Nellie,' she said, 'you stay and have a good time, you've earned it.'

Then she said goodbye to Paul. He was about to head back to town and she wondered whether she should ask him to the homestead for a drink, she would have liked to talk to him. She wasn't sure why, perhaps just to wind down, it had been a hectic two days. But it would be a good hour and a half out of his way and it was already dark.

'Goodnight, Paul,' she said, 'thank you for coming.' She kissed his cheek warmly, wishing she could tell him how grateful she was for his company, the day would have been miserable without him.

'Thank you for asking me,' he said. 'Are you all right to get back to the homestead? It's over an hour's drive and it's getting dark.'

'I think so,' she laughed. 'I drove trucks in the war, you know.'

'Of course,' he said, 'I knew that.' She didn't need him at all, but he wished she would ask him home for a drink. Just a drink and a bit of a talk. He so wanted to be in her company.

'Thanks, Paul,' she said, 'for everything.' And she climbed into the driver's seat, wishing he was coming with her.

'Henrietta . . .' he said through the open window.

'Yes?' She'd already started the car.

Paul wondered whether he was feeling the effects of the beers he'd been drinking throughout the day. He was a heavy drinker, Scotch mainly, and he rarely felt the effects of alcohol. Beer to him was a soft drink, 'mother's milk' he'd say, but today, for some reason, he felt light-headed. He decided to speak his mind.

'You know I'm your friend, don't you?'

'Of course.'

He was leaning down, his elbow resting in the open window, his face quite close to hers, grey hair flopping over his brow, and he seemed concerned. Gone was the cynical twist to his mouth and the sardonic twinkle in his eyes. Why is he so serious, she wondered.

'If you're ever in need, I'm here, you know.'

'Thank you, Paul.' It occurred to her suddenly that he might be drunk. She'd never seen Paul drunk before, although he invariably had a glass in his hand.

'If you're ever in need,' he repeated, 'I hope you'll call on me for help.'

How very formal he sounded. 'Yes, of course I will.' She patted his elbow.

'You must never be unhappy, Henrietta.' He took her hand in his.

She smiled. 'I'll try not to be.' He was most certainly drunk. Who would have thought it? Sentimentality from the hardened, cynical, heavy-drinking Paul Trewinnard. She squeezed his hand. 'Drive carefully.' And he stood back as she put the car into gear. 'Bye,' she called.

'Bye.' She thought he was drunk, he realised as he waved at the car and she waved back through the window. Perhaps it was just as well. And perhaps he was drunk, why otherwise would he have made his little speech? But he knew full well why he had.

At some point during the afternoon, Paul had realised that he was hopelessly in love with Henrietta. Not that he intended to do anything about it, any attempt would be futile. But then his entire life had been futile, hadn't it. He would simply be her friend, it was all he had to offer. And as Aggie said, Henrietta needed friends.

CHAPTER TWELVE

'*Happy birthday, dear Malcolm, happy birthday to you.*' The four adults sang in unison and the little boy delightedly clapped his hands. It was Malcolm's second birthday and Nellie had baked him a special cake, she and Pearl presenting it to him while Henrietta and Terence applauded loudly.

They all sat around the kitchen table, Malcolm in his highchair, and as Henrietta cut up the cake she wondered how she would broach the subject of the children's party in Darwin next week. Terence had been very moody of late. She understood why, he was under a good deal of pressure. His comment to his brothers at the races last year had been prophetic, the departure of the army had strongly affected the beef market and business was not good. Henrietta had curtailed her trips into town, he seemed to find them irritating now.

'You could be a little more supportive, Henrietta,' he'd say, although she couldn't think how. He was gone most of the day, the station's books were in order, stocks and supplies were up to date, and each Friday she personally distributed the rations from the store shed to the native stockmen's families who'd recently arrived for the forthcoming muster. The homestead was running smoothly. If simply being by his side would help, then she was only too happy to oblige, but once again Henrietta felt she was walking on eggshells. When he came home of an evening, sullen and irritable, she did her best to cajole him, and when it appeared she was an annoyance she would leave him alone, but then that would annoy him further and he'd demand her presence again. It seemed she could do nothing right. Nellie and seventeen-year-old Pearl kept well out of the boss's way and Henrietta only wished she could do the same.

She longed to accept Aggie's invitation to the children's party in Darwin. She needed to be free of the claustrophobia of Bullalalla, she told herself, if only for a day. She didn't wish to admit, even to herself, that it wasn't Bullalalla she wished to escape from at all, it was the oppressive company of her husband.

'We haven't seen you for nearly a month,' Aggie had said the last time they'd met, and that was a whole two months ago now.

'Business is not good, Terence needs my support.' Henrietta had decided to be honest.

Aggie wanted to say 'you need some support too', but she didn't. The man was wearing Henrietta down, she could tell. There was the same anxiousness, the same wariness in Henrietta as there had been when Aggie had first met her, and Aggie knew all the signs. She wanted to say 'leave him, get away', but of course she couldn't. The woman didn't recognise the depth of her problem and, besides, she had a young child. Aggie briefly considered telling Henrietta her own story, but she knew it would do no good.

'There's to be a party for the children at the end of May,' she'd said instead. 'It's really a part of my consolidation campaign but we're calling it a children's party.'

When the school had reopened, Aggie had once again taken up her teaching post but, far more, she had taken up her 'consolidation campaign'. It entailed regular meetings between families, both parents and children. 'We must keep establishing our bonds,' she insisted. 'Government assistance and labour are not enough, bricks and mortar might rebuild the town, but it is the people who will rebuild the spirit of Darwin.' And true to form Aggie had taken on the rebuilding of Darwin as her personal crusade.

She had then plonked another ashtray on the papers which threatened to be blown away by the silly little fan on the corner of her desk and said, 'I think you should bring Malcolm in to town to meet the other children.'

Henrietta laughed, Aggie was a breath of fresh air. 'He's hardly old enough for school,' she'd said.

'He's never too young to meet other children,' Aggie responded, austere and insistent.

'He's barely two years old, he's a baby.'

'What better time to meet others?' Aggie knew she was being bossy, but she hoped Henrietta would accept the invitation, for her own sake far more than her son's. 'It's a very isolated life for a child, even of that age. He should be given the opportunity to meet other children, you owe it to him, Henrietta. And you must stay the night here,' she'd said emphatically, 'with me.'

It was an attractive offer and Henrietta had been thinking about it for the past two months. She decided that this afternoon's birthday party was the ideal time to broach the subject; Terence seemed in an approachable mood.

'Of course you must go,' he replied, when she came downstairs having put Malcolm in his cot; the excitement had exhausted the child.

Henrietta wondered whether he'd heard her, he seemed distracted. 'Aggie wants me to stay the night.'

'Why not?' he said with a complete lack of interest. He'd poured himself a whisky, she noticed, and it was barely five o'clock. Terence seemed to be drinking more than usual lately.

'Are you sure you don't mind me going?'

'Of course I'm sure,' he snapped, and she decided to leave it at that. But, several minutes later, it was Terence who pursued the subject, obviously having given it some thought. 'It's probably a good idea for you to go into Darwin,' he said, 'you could do with the break, why don't you stay a couple of nights?' He sounded amicable enough and Henrietta couldn't believe her luck. But she hoped he wouldn't change his mind at the last minute, it was quite possible he would.

A week later, the day before her trip to Darwin, he told her he was going bush for a few days to meet up with Buff Nelson and check on the muster. It was a month into the dry season and Jackie and his team were out mustering the herds. Henrietta immediately assumed he was about to renege on their arrangement, but he wasn't. 'Leave instructions for Nellie to hand out the rations on Friday,' he said, 'I'll be gone first thing in the morning.'

He made love to her that night in his customary brutal fashion, and although, as always, there was no pleasure for Henrietta in the act, she was gladdened by the knowledge that he still desired her. He'd made no sexual advances for the past month, a fact which, coupled with his irritability, made her feel very insecure about his affections.

She was still drowsy with sleep when he left at dawn and, when she awoke an hour or so later, Henrietta felt excited, like a small child about to go on a holiday. She was to meet Aggie at the Hotel Darwin, Paul was taking them all to lunch.

'But I'll have Malcolm with me,' she'd said when Paul had telephoned, delighted to hear that she was coming to town.

'He doesn't eat much, does he?' Paul had replied. He had insisted they all dine at his beloved Hotel Darwin in order to celebrate its recent reopening. Michael and

Chrissie Paspalis, who had won their bid to lease the hotel from the Government, were just the people needed to return the 'Grand Old Dame' to her pre-war grandeur, Paul maintained, and they'd certainly started out the right way. The Hotel Darwin had reopened with a gala ball, and Paul had moved back in with alacrity, grateful to be out of his poky little room at the Victoria Hotel.

Paul was full of plans for Henrietta. After lunch he would take them for a drive, Aggie always enjoyed being taken for a drive, he said. And, on the Friday evening, following the kiddies' party in the afternoon—'or rather should I say "Aggie's consolidation campaign",' he added, his tone heavy with irony—perhaps she'd agree to have dinner with him. Her trip to town was perfectly timed, he told her, he was due to leave for London on the Monday. 'It's a six-month assignment,' he explained, 'a series of articles for *National Geographic* on post-war Europe. A farewell dinner would be perfect.'

'Thank you Paul, but no,' she'd laughed, 'I'll have the baby with me.'

'Aggie said she'd love to babysit Malcolm.' He hardly drew breath. 'And she also said, as you're not leaving until Saturday, perhaps we could have a picnic lunch at Mindil Beach before you go.'

Henrietta sensed the collusion. Between the two of them Aggie and Paul had it all worked out. 'We'll see,' she smiled, feeling a little swept off her feet.

Shortly before midday, she left explicit instructions and lists with Nellie, packed Malcolm and the suitcase into the Landrover and waved goodbye to Pearl who stood on the front verandah waving back.

Lunch in the vast and splendid dining room of the Hotel Darwin proved to be a far more relaxed affair than Henrietta had anticipated. She'd worried a little about Malcolm, it was hardly the place to take a two-year-old child. But the waiters were very accommodating. A highchair was instantly fetched and, as Henrietta fed him, she made sure the bowl was well out of his reach so that he couldn't throw food about, which was his favourite trick. Several times he got a little demanding, letting out a squeal as he smashed his fist on his tray-table, but no-one seemed to mind, least of all Aggie and Paul. It was so good to see them.

'What a change from beef,' she said as she tucked into her grilled barramundi.

They chatted about Aggie's new foot. When they'd met in the foyer Henrietta had been surprised by the absence of the carpet slipper. Aggie still wore trousers but protruding from the cuff of the left leg was a smart walking brogue and, as the three of them had proceeded through to the dining room, she no longer clumped. Even her limp was minimal.

'I'm very impressed,' Henrietta remarked over lunch.

'You sound like Paul, that's exactly what he said.'

Paul nodded, his mouth full of eye fillet.

'It's a proper prosthetic foot, the latest thing,' Aggie proudly boasted. 'I should have had one fitted years ago, it's far more comfortable, but I'd probably never have got around to it at all if it hadn't been for the school.' Henrietta looked mystified. 'The carpet slipper was too distracting,' Aggie explained, 'so was the way I clumped about, the children paid far more attention to my pegleg than they did to their lessons.'

After lunch they called in briefly at Aggie's house to drop off Henrietta's suitcase and leave the Landrover behind. Then they all piled into Paul's Austin and he drove them to Nightcliff where they walked along the clifftops, Malcolm perched on Paul's shoulders.

It was an impressive vista. The ragged splendour of the sandstone cliff face stretched for miles and the water was at low tide, exposing the vast shelves of rock which extended out to the sea.

Aggie sat on a bench with Malcolm whilst Paul and Henrietta walked down a track to the beach. When they returned half an hour later, Paul's pockets were bulging with the pebbles and stones Henrietta had insisted upon collecting.

'Next time we'll take a bag,' he complained good naturedly as he emptied them out onto the grass, 'or you can wear trousers for a change.' Henrietta's skirt and blouse were pocketless.

Malcolm had a splendid time arranging and rearranging the different shaped stones which were velvety to the touch, worn smooth and perfect by the sea. There were little round pebbles like marbles, and there were wafer-thin elliptical dishes, and triangles and oblongs, and flat-based domes like miniature Ayers Rocks, and all in every colour imaginable, from the deepest of oranges and burgundies, to the lightest of pinks and lavenders.

'We'll put them in a very special bowl when we get home, darling,' Henrietta promised the child when he protested strongly as she started packing the stones away in her carry bag. 'And you can play with them whenever you like. Come on now, we have to go.' She hoped Malcolm wasn't about to throw one of his tantrums. 'He's tired, he's getting a bit crotchety,' she apologised to the others. Mercifully he fell asleep on the drive back to Aggie's house.

'You're going to come in for a drink, Paul?' Aggie asked.

'Of course.' Paul pocketed the flask of whisky he always kept in the glovebox of his car. Aggie was the only person he knew whose invitation to 'come in for a drink' meant a tea or coffee. To anyone else in Darwin 'a drink' meant a gin or a whisky, or at least a cold beer. Paul always travelled prepared.

He carried the sleeping child inside but the moment he deposited him in the spare room Malcolm woke up, thoroughly energised and ready for mischief. Henrietta emptied the stones out onto the scatter rug by the lounge room windows and, instantly, the child once again became engrossed in his arrangements.

'I shall forgive you the sand in my pockets,' Paul said approvingly, 'that's the perfect distraction.'

'Yes, isn't it,' she agreed, 'I've just become a devoted rock collector.'

'Would you care for something a little stronger than Aggie's tea?' He took the flask from his pocket. 'Miss Marshall runs an alcohol-free house.'

'Not today,' Aggie said as she disappeared into the kitchen and returned with an icy bottle of champagne and three glasses. 'Today she's laid on supplies. There's another bottle in the fridge.'

'Good heavens above,' Paul exclaimed as he took the bottle from her and started to open it. He looked at the glasses. 'And I didn't even know you possessed champagne flutes.'

'I didn't until yesterday.'

'You should be flattered, Henrietta.' Paul eased out the cork and poured the champagne.

'I am.' She was more than flattered, she was very touched.

'Here's to your return to town,' Aggie said and she raised her glass. 'You mustn't leave it so long between visits, we've missed you, haven't we, Paul?'

'We most certainly have,' Paul agreed, and he meant it far more than Henrietta could possibly realise. But after one glass of champagne he left the women to talk. He and Aggie had agreed they were worried about Henrietta, and he hoped that Aggie might be able to help in some way.

Aggie had every intention of trying to draw Henrietta out with regard to her problem, the young woman needed someone to talk to, she was convinced of it. But Henrietta was evasive. Yes, she was quite happy, she replied, perhaps a little tired, Malcolm was a handful, and the beef business wasn't doing well so Terence was a bit tense lately. She wouldn't go any further than that, but turned the conversation back to Aggie. Was she enjoying teaching again, Henrietta asked. But they'd talked about the school over lunch. Drastic measures were required, Aggie decided.

She opened the second bottle of champagne. Aggie normally drank very little and the alcohol had gone straight to her head. Emboldened by its effects, she decided to tell Henrietta her own story, to use herself as an example in order to help the young woman.

'Did I ever tell you about my marriage, Henrietta?' she asked filling her own glass. She went to fill Henrietta's but it was untouched. 'You're not drinking,' she remarked.

'I've already had three glasses,' Henrietta smiled, 'another one and I'll be on my ear. I didn't even know you'd been married.'

'For five years, I was very young at the time, just twenty-two.'

'The same age as me,' Henrietta remarked, 'I was twenty-two when I married Terence.'

'Yes.' Aggie had known that, just as she also knew that Henrietta had been married for five years. 'It wasn't a happy marriage from the outset,' she continued, 'but I wouldn't admit that, least of all to myself. It took five years for me to realise that things would never change and that he was destroying my life.'

Why was Aggie telling her this, Henrietta wondered. Why did she feel the need to talk about her marriage, it had been years ago? It was probably the effects of the alcohol; Aggie certainly wasn't accustomed to the amount of champagne she'd drunk, and now she was draining the glass.

'I blamed myself,' Aggie barged right on as she reached for the bottle. 'For years I thought I was responsible in some way for his moods and irrational behaviour.' She poured herself another glass, the taste already souring in her mouth, but the alcohol was certainly giving her Dutch courage. 'Even when he hit me I blamed myself.'

'He hit you?' Henrietta was shocked.

'Oh yes, quite often, when he was drunk. Of course he'd be full of remorse the following morning.' Aggie realised that Henrietta's shock was genuine. Well that's something, she thought, at least Terence doesn't hit her; she and Paul had wondered if he did. 'Strangely enough, though, the physical violence wasn't the worse part. I'm actually grateful for it now.'

Aggie suddenly realised that she was rather enjoying her one-sided conversation. She had never spoken this way to anyone and, after ten years, it was interesting to analyse her past. 'I left him because of the violence. Perhaps if he hadn't hit me I'd still be with him,' she took another swig from her glass. 'I'd still be thinking it was my fault, still being manipulated, forced to play his games. The games are the worst part, Henrietta. The mental games, when a man plays with your mind and makes you feel insecure and uncertain of yourself.'

Henrietta felt distinctly uneasy. This was sounding too familiar, was Aggie trying, in a clumsy way, to compare their respective marriages?

'I'm sure women can do the same thing to men,' Aggie rambled on, 'but I'm not talking about other women, I'm talking about us.' She threw caution to the wind as she drained another glass, convinced that Henrietta's attentiveness was a sign of her recognition and agreement.

Anger surged through Henrietta. 'We're not talking about us at all,' she said coldly, 'we're talking about you, Aggie. At least *you're* talking about you. How dare you make such a presumption.'

At the sound of his mother's voice, raised in anger, Malcolm looked up from his arrangement of stones.

'My husband doesn't beat me,' Henrietta said a little more quietly, her eye to the child, 'I have a happy marriage and I'll thank you to keep your opinions to yourself.'

It was Aggie's turn to be shocked. She'd assumed that Henrietta had been following her train of thought, identifying with her, even agreeing. 'I'm sorry, Henrietta,' she said, 'I only wanted to . . .'

Malcolm started to cry. 'He's tired.' Henrietta rose from her chair, end of conversation, her tone said.

'I'm sorry,' Aggie repeated, cursing herself for her stupidity.

'I'll give him his feed, he'll soon be ready for bed.'

When the child was asleep in the spare bedroom, the two women shared an uncomfortable meal, eating little, awkward in each other's company, and then they too retired.

Both had a sleepless night. Aggie, aware that she'd gone too far, felt wretched. And Henrietta, recalling Aggie's words, was filled with doubt. Did she indeed have an unhappy life? She hadn't wished to see it that way, but Terence did play mental games, and she often felt insecure and unsure of herself. But he loved her, she told herself. And he'd certainly never hit her, surely that meant her marriage was not on a parallel with Aggie's. She couldn't afford to listen to such innuendo.

Beside her in the bed, Malcolm woke several times throughout the night, and she comforted him and waited for him to go back to sleep. In the morning she awoke, exhausted and strangely depressed. She wished she was back at Bullalalla, on her own; what value were her friends if they made her feel like this? It was a conspiracy, she realised, and Paul had been part of it. He and Aggie were convinced that she needed rescuing, well damn the both of them.

When she emerged in the morning, she discovered that Aggie had been up for a good hour or so. Aggie was always an early riser, and the house was filled with the aroma of freshly baked bread.

'I popped out to Eddie Quong's.' Aggie sliced through the hot crusty loaf. Eddie Quong's bakery in Smith Street was famous, she said. 'I bet you've never tasted bread like this.' She chatted all the while as she cut up a mango and set out the jam and marmalade beside the sliced bread, and she carefully avoided any mention of the previous night, which she deeply regretted. And Henrietta made pleasant conversation back, wishing that she could put aside the doubts that Aggie had raised and shake off her depression. It had been the champagne, she told herself, Aggie hadn't meant any harm. But the harm had been done nonetheless.

Immediately after breakfast, Aggie left to set up the decorations and the presents for the children's party. She declined Henrietta's offer of help.

'No, no,' she insisted, 'I have a half a dozen volunteers who'll be there already. The party is supposed to be as much for the parents as it is for the children, so you stay here with Malcolm. Paul's picking you up at eleven.'

Mid-morning they gathered in droves outside the old Town Hall. A handsome stone building of intricate design, the old Town Hall faced Smith Street but was set well back from the road, shaded by trees and surrounded by a white picket fence. In bygone days it had been a picturesque and popular venue for many a function and historical event but, during the war, it had served as a drill hall and training centre for the navy. Although it was currently being converted into a museum and art gallery, Aggie had fought tooth and nail for permission to use the old Town Hall as the venue for her children's party. In keeping with her 'consolidation campaign' it was the perfect choice, she'd maintained. 'The old Town Hall is the spirit of Darwin,' she'd loudly declared. And as usual she'd won.

Parents and children, teachers and friends now flooded through the main doors. Upwards of a hundred people gathered in the welcome cool of the hall with its high ceilings and cypress pine floors. Aggie's team of helpers had done a fine job, streamers and balloons festooned the walls, small wooden tables were laid out with kiddies' treats, jugs of cordial and party pies, buttered bread colourfully sprinkled with 'hundreds and thousands', and in the corner of the hall, piled high on a white-clothed trestle table were gifts wrapped in glossy paper.

Standing by the table, doling out the presents, stood Foong Lee and his son Albert. Foong Lee had donated the trinkets from his new store, charm bracelets and hair ribbons and tiny dolls for the girls, miniature cars and aeroplanes and toy soldiers for the boys, and little mesh bags of sugared almonds for everyone. Albert had sat up half the night individually wrapping each and every one.

The day was an unmitigated success. The children wore party hats and played games and the adults mingled, catching up on the gossip and comparing notes. Henrietta spent most of her time with Paul, who left her side only when Aggie, who was tirelessly working, called for his help.

'Are you all right?' he asked when he returned from rigging up the pin-the-tail-on-the-donkey board. 'You seem very quiet.'

'Of course,' she replied, trying to dredge up a vitality she didn't feel, 'just a bit tired, Malcolm kept me up half the night.'

When the presents had been given out, Foong Lee and Albert joined them. Foong Lee was a very busy man of late. One of the founders of the Chung Wah Society, established to unite the Chinese community upon their return to Darwin, he had nonetheless found time to build a fine new house in Mitchell Street. And his new store and his tailor's shop were doing very well, Paul told Henrietta.

'And Albert has had the excellent idea of our opening a restaurant,' Foong Lee added, while young Albert, towering handsomely beside his squat little father, beamed with pride. 'It's been a slow process,' Foong Lee said, 'but things are coming along nicely.'

'A slow process?' Henrietta shared a smile with Paul. Foong Lee had obviously moved faster than anyone in Darwin to re-establish his businesses, whilst most others were still struggling.

As the party was winding down, Foong Lee asked Henrietta and Paul if they'd like to come to his house. 'I like showing off my new house,' he said, his eyes disappearing into slits as he smiled happily, 'and Lin Mei will make us some tea.'

'That's very kind of you, Foong Lee,' Henrietta replied, 'but I think I'll take Malcolm home to Bullalalla.' Beside her, she was aware of Paul's surprised reaction. 'It's been a long day and he's tired.'

'Of course,' Foong Lee agreed, 'another time.'

'I thought you were staying tonight at Aggie's,' Paul said, quietly easing her aside.

'I was, but I . . .'

'And I thought we were having dinner together.'

'I didn't say I would, if you remember.' She realised that she sounded brusque. She didn't mean to, she wasn't angry with Paul for his complicity, she wasn't even angry with Aggie anymore, they both meant well. But she needed to be on her own. 'I'm sorry if it's a disappointment,' she said, 'but . . .'

'It is.'

'. . . but I'd prefer to take Malcolm home, we're both tired.'

'Are we all going back to my place?' They were interrupted by Aggie, dishevelled, her hair a mess from being tugged at by tiny children, her clothes in disarray from playing hide and seek with the older ones, and her eyes sparkling with the success of her party.

'Henrietta says she's going back to Bullalalla,' Paul said. 'She won't listen to me, it's up to you to convince her otherwise, Aggie.'

Aggie was instantly deflated. A look of concern replaced

the sparkle in her eyes. 'Oh Henrietta . . .'

'Forgive me, Aggie, I really must,' Henrietta immediately interrupted, she couldn't bear to hear another apology. She hated seeing the regret in Aggie's eyes and she hated the knowledge that she was ruining the woman's moment of triumph. 'Malcolm didn't sleep well last night, he'll be much more comfortable in his cot at home.' She tried to make her excuses sound as reasonable and sincere as she could. 'And quite frankly, so will I,' she smiled. 'I was saying to Paul earlier, Malcolm kept me awake half the night, I really am exhausted.'

Aggie nodded guiltily and she looked so unhappy that Henrietta hugged her. 'I'm sorry, Aggie, really I am.'

'So am I,' Aggie said quietly.

'Don't be,' Henrietta whispered in her ear. 'I'm not angry anymore, thank you for caring.'

Paul looked at the women, bemused. What the hell was going on? But as Henrietta went off to collect Malcolm, Aggie refused to acknowledge the query in Paul's eyes; she wasn't ready to share confidences yet.

'I'll be here for hours cleaning up, Paul, you drive Henrietta back to the house, I'll get you the key.' She fetched her front door key from her handbag. 'Just tell her to leave it under the doormat,' and she disappeared.

They talked about the party on the drive back to Aggie's, Paul aware that Henrietta didn't want to discuss what had happened and Henrietta grateful for his sensitivity in not asking.

He packed her suitcase into the Landrover, strapped Malcolm into his seat and embraced her as he said goodbye.

'Don't forget, Henrietta,' he said, 'if ever you need me . . .'

'Yes I know, Paul. Thanks.' She kissed his cheek and got into the car.

Malcolm slept during the two-hour drive home to Bullalalla and he was still sleeping when she pulled up in front of the house, it was four o'clock in the afternoon. Gently she lifted the child from the car and carried him inside, she'd get him settled and come back for the suitcase later.

The house was deserted. Of course, Henrietta realised, Nellie would be at the storeroom near the slaughter yards handing out the rations, Pearl was no doubt helping her.

Henrietta carried the little boy upstairs and into the nursery, and he half woke as she undressed him and put him in his cot, but he was fast asleep again as she tip-toed to the door. Perhaps it was just as well she'd come home, she thought, the child was utterly exhausted.

As she quietly closed the door behind her, she heard muffled noises coming from the room next door. The master bedroom where she and Terence slept. Had he come home from the muster? She turned the knob and pushed open the door.

The black and white of their skin was shocking, it was the first thing that struck Henrietta. They were standing by the bed, both naked from the waist up, and Terence's sleek, tanned body looked strangely white against Pearl's blackness as he grasped her to him. In their struggle, neither saw Henrietta. Terence's back was towards her and he was ripping at Pearl's skirt. It came away and he threw it to the floor. Pearl's eyes were tightly shut and she was gasping as he pushed her towards the bed, tearing at her panties, his mouth at her throat as if he wanted to devour her.

She was shaking her head from side to side and trying, ineffectively, to push him away. He tore her panties from her and she opened her mouth as if to scream her protest, but she didn't. Her eyes opened wide instead and Henrietta saw in them not only revulsion but resignation. Horror-struck, she realised that the girl was prepared to accept her rape. And in that same instant Pearl's eyes met hers.

Terence unbuckled his belt, he didn't know why the girl had stopped fighting, he'd liked it better when she struggled, but obviously she knew her place and she'd given in. Then he saw the look in the girl's eyes and he turned.

Henrietta stood frozen at the door. There was a moment's silence. Then she said, 'Let her go.' Terence had already released his grip on the girl, but Pearl remained motionless, afraid to move.

'Go on,' Terence said, 'get out,' and Pearl ducked for the door.

'Collect your clothes, Pearl,' Henrietta said, 'get dressed and wait for me in the hall, I'll take you to your mother.'

Henrietta wondered at the calmness of her voice. The first jarring sight of them had sickened her, then seconds later, the recognition of Terence's intent to rape had repulsed her. Now she felt nothing. She was numb.

Pearl submissively gathered up her clothes and dived out the door, her eyes averted, terrified.

'What do you mean, you'll take her to her mother?' Terence, having recovered from his own shock of discovery, was derisive. 'The girl's a slut.'

'You were going to rape her.'

'She asked for it.'

Henrietta remained staring at him. Standing, still numb, by the door, wondering why she couldn't leave.

'For God's sake, Henrietta, do you think she's a virgin?' Terence buckled up his belt. 'She's been sleeping with one of the drovers for months, she's a slut, she's anybody's.' It had been driving Terence mad watching Pearl go down to the native camp the nights when the drovers came home. He'd lusted after her for years, but he'd always done the right thing. Pearl was, after all, 'family', in a bizarre way, and he'd sated his appetite for black velvet elsewhere. But now the girl was of age, and she was sleeping around, and Jesus all of his mates did it with the blacks, it was common knowledge. Just as it was common knowledge that the wives turned a blind eye. Terence knew he'd overstepped the mark by taking the girl into the bedroom, he was willing to concede that, and he cursed the fact that Henrietta had come home unexpectedly, but he really didn't understand that he'd done anything so terribly wrong. Henrietta's silence and her look of revulsion annoyed him.

'Christ, Henrietta,' he said, picking his shirt up from the floor, 'when will you realise you're not in the old country, things are different here. It's just a bit of fun, she's a black and she was panting for it.'

'No she wasn't.' Henrietta needed to get away, the numbness was wearing off and she couldn't bear to be in his company. 'I'm leaving,' she said, 'and I'm taking Malcolm with me.'

She turned to go, but in two quick strides Terence was upon her, whirling her about, his annoyance now blind anger. He struck her so forcefully across the face that she was knocked sideways and fell sprawling to the floor. She sat up groggily, her cheek aching, a ringing noise in her ear.

He stood towering over her. 'You'll never take my son. And if you ever try to leave me I'll find you, Henrietta.' He pulled her to her feet and she stood, still a little dizzy, as he supported her. 'I'll find you and I'll kill you.'

For the first time in the five years of their marriage, Henrietta recognised the madness in her husband. She'd seen flashes of it before, she realised as she stared back at him. Images spun through her mind. The day when he'd made her ride Florian. The day when he'd taunted her with the slaughter of the steers. But she'd not seen his behaviour as that of a madman, and she'd never feared him as she did now.

Terence was pleased with her submissiveness. He led her to the bed and sat her down. 'I'm sorry,' he said gently, 'I shouldn't have brought the girl into our bedroom, I'll never do it again.' As she looked up at him, something in her eyes, frightened as they were, must have prompted him to add, 'I'll never go near her again, I promise.' He reached out his hand and softly stroked her hair. 'And I'm sorry I hit you, I'll never do that again either, I give you my word. But you must never threaten me, Henrietta, you must never leave me. Besides,' he said, still stroking her hair, 'where would you go? How would you live?'

She seemed to have calmed down, so Terence crossed to the shirt which lay on the floor where he'd dropped it. He stooped and picked it up. 'And surely you wouldn't wish to cheat your son of his inheritance,' he said, slipping it over his shoulders. 'Not that you'd be able to take Malcolm with you in any event. If you walked out on our marriage, any court of law would grant me custody of the boy.' He sat beside her on the bed, buttoning up the shirt. 'It's silly to make threats, Henrietta. I love you, you know that.' He kissed her gently. 'I love you and you're mine. Never forget that you're mine, Henrietta, never ever forget that.' He kissed her more deeply and Henrietta, too fearful to resist, submitted to the kiss.

'There you see? It's all over.' He held her to him, caressing her tenderly. 'We'll forget that it ever happened.'

'Yes,' she whispered. She had to get out, she had to get away from him.

He took her face between his hands and looked at her. 'You do believe that I love you, don't you, Henrietta?'

'Yes,' she said, 'I do.' Despite his madness, she knew that he loved her, she could see it in his eyes, in the anxiousness with which he awaited her reply. It was his love that she most feared, she realised.

'Good.' He relaxed, rising from the bed to tuck his shirt into his trousers; it was evident that the episode was over.

Henrietta somehow found the strength to say, 'I'd like to

go back to Aggie's tonight, as I'd planned, if that's all right.'

'Why?' His eyes clouded once more as he turned to her.

'I promised I'd meet with the others this evening and help clean up the hall after the party.' Desperation lent her strength, it was as if her life depended on the credibility of her lie. 'I only brought Malcolm home because he didn't sleep well last night and he was terribly tired. I was going to leave him with Nellie and go back to Aggie's.'

'I see.' There was an ominous pause. 'And what will you tell your friend, Aggie?'

'Nothing.' Her response was not prompted by the inherent threat in his tone. Never would she tell anyone what had happened this afternoon. 'I'll tell Aggie nothing,' she said.

'Good.' Chameleon-like, he relaxed once more. 'It's all forgotten then?'

'Yes it's all forgotten.'

'I'll take your things to the car.'

'My suitcase is still in the Landrover,' she said, thankfully remembering she'd left it there. It added to the credibility of her story. 'I'll just check on Malcolm.'

Moments later, as she closed the nursery door behind her, Terence met her on the landing and they walked downstairs together.

Pearl was not waiting in the hall as Henrietta had instructed her, the girl was nowhere to be seen. It was hardly surprising, Henrietta thought, she'd probably heard the violence of Terence's reaction and run for her life.

Pearl had indeed heard the boss strike the missus, and she'd heard the missus fall to the floor. As she'd scrambled into her clothes on the landing, she'd heard everything. She'd scampered, terrified, downstairs to the back door. But she hadn't run away. She'd left the back door open to afford a quick getaway and she'd crept back through the kitchen. If the boss was killing the missus then she must run for help. But as she'd peered through the door to the main hall, all had been silent from above, and she didn't dare go back up to look.

Now, as the two of them came downstairs, she was surprised to see they were behaving as if nothing had happened.

'Malcolm will need to be fed in about half an hour,' the missus was saying.

'I'll do it myself,' she heard the the boss answer, 'and I'll get my own dinner, I'll give Nellie the night off.'

Pearl watched them walk out the front door together. Thank goodness the boss hadn't killed the missus. She ducked through the kitchen, she'd keep well out of the boss's way tonight. Thank goodness the missus had saved her from having to sleep with him, she'd hated him touching her. She wished he hadn't told the missus she was a slut, because she wasn't. She'd slept with no-one but her fella, they'd been together six months now, and they were going to get married next season. Pearl closed the back door quietly behind her, she hoped the boss wouldn't come at her again.

Terence opened the car door for Henrietta. 'What time will you be back?' he asked.

'About lunchtime, I suppose,' she answered automatically. She didn't know what to say, she didn't know if she'd ever be back, she needed to think, there were decisions to be made.

But during the drive into town Henrietta couldn't think. Not logically anyway. She could make no decisions, her mind was in turmoil. Images kept whirling about in her brain. The two of them, black and white, locked together. The look in Pearl's eyes as they'd met hers. The madness in Terence as he'd struck her. She tried to rid herself of the images and concentrate on his words instead, but they too whirled dizzyingly through her brain. *If you leave me I'll find you, Henrietta, I'll find you and I'll kill you . . . surely you wouldn't want to cheat your son of his inheritance . . . if you walked out on our marriage, any court of law would grant me custody of the boy.*

She must force herself to think constructively. A plan, she must make a plan. But Terence was right. Where would she go? How would she live? She could return to England, her grandmother had money. For the past five years Henrietta had corresponded regularly with her grandmother, but the thought of Winifred Southern brought no comfort to her now, for the old lady was dying. 'It's taking such a long time Henrietta, and I so want to go,' Winifred had written in the spidery hand which had once been so bold. 'But oh my dear I am so happy for the richness of your life. Of course I would love to see my great-grandson as you suggest, but under no circumstance do I wish you to return. I am well looked after, and the knowledge that you are happy gives me untold pleasure.'

Was she to deprive the old woman of her peaceful delusion, Henrietta wondered. And if she were to return to England it would be without her son, Terence would make sure of that. Unthinkable. Could she do as Terence had suggested? Could she forget that today had ever happened? Impossible.

As she drove into Darwin, Henrietta's brain felt on fire and she suddenly knew that she couldn't go to Aggie's. She couldn't bear to face Aggie's questions and she couldn't bear to face Aggie's answer. 'Leave him,' Aggie would say, Henrietta could hear her saying it. But it wasn't that simple.

She drove to the Hotel Darwin instead. 'Mr Paul Trewinnard,' she said to the desk clerk. 'Would you tell him Mrs Galloway is in the foyer.'

Paul appeared only minutes later. 'Henrietta, you're back,' he said, delighted. Then he saw her face. It was ashen, and there was an angry welt on her left cheek. 'Good God what's happened?' He led her to his favourite nook amongst the potted palms and held her hand as they sat together.

Henrietta couldn't help it. Not once had she felt the desire to cry, and now she couldn't stop. She didn't even try. She sat, head bowed, studying her hand in his, and she clutched it tightly as the tears poured down her cheeks.

Her body was shuddering and her breath was coming in tiny gasps, she was in a state of shock, Paul realised. He took her other hand in his and she clutched that too, staring down at the tightness of her knuckles as, over and over, she squeezed his fingers, it was as if his hands were her lifeline.

Paul said nothing, and they sat, linked together, for minutes which could have been hours. Finally she stopped shuddering and took several deep breaths. She released her grip on his hands as she looked up.

'I'm sorry,' she said.

He took his handkerchief from his breast pocket and offered it to her. 'I'll organise a room here for you at the hotel, is your suitcase in the car?'

'Yes,' she said, taking the handkerchief from him. 'Thank you, I'm all right now.' She dabbed at her eyes, trying desperately to stem another onslaught of tears.

'Of course you are. Are you parked out the front?' She nodded. 'Give me the keys.' She handed him her car keys and he rose from the chair. 'Only be a minute.'

Henrietta watched him walk over to the reception desk. She was drained and exhausted, but strangely relaxed. What a blessing, not to think.

'I'd like to book a room for Mrs Galloway, thanks Jimmy,' Paul said to the desk clerk, 'and could you have someone collect her suitcase from the Landrover out the front.'

'Of course, Mr Trewinnard.' Jimmy took the keys and Paul signed the registration form.

'On my account,' he said. 'We'll be in the bar, let us

know when Mrs Galloway's luggage has been delivered to
her room.'

'Certainly, sir.'

He was back at Henrietta's side within minutes. 'You
need a drink,' he said.

'I don't,' she answered with a wan smile, feeling embarrassed. 'Really.'

'I do,' he said. 'Really. Come on.'

They went into the bar and he ordered two Scotches.
'If you don't want yours I'll have it,' he said and she
actually heard herself laugh. 'But drink it if you can,' he
added, 'it'll do you good.' She took several sips of the
Scotch and to her surprise rather enjoyed it, or rather
the sense of relaxation it afforded her.

Paul had downed his drink quickly and ordered another
when the desk clerk arrived with the key. 'Thanks, Jimmy,'
he said, 'I'll see Mrs Galloway to her room.' Then he
turned to Henrietta, 'Do you want anything to eat?
Jimmy'll have something sent up.'

'No thanks, I'm a bit tired, I think I'll just go to bed.'

'But it's only seven o'clock and I'm starving. Send up
some sandwiches will you, Jimmy, a bit of a mixture,
anything'll do, and a couple of Scotches.'

'Of course, Sir.'

In her room, they stood by the open shuttered windows
looking out over the sports oval and the harbour beyond.
It was a beautiful evening. The heat had waned and the
dusk air was mild, the light over the water grey and
peaceful.

'I'll go if you want me to,' Paul said.

'What about the sandwiches?'

'I'm not really hungry, but I thought you should eat
something.'

'What about the Scotches?'

'I'll take them with me.'

She smiled. 'I don't want you to go.'

'Good, I don't want to.'

They sat by the windows. 'Thank you, Paul,' she said.

'My pleasure.'

'I can't tell you what happened.' She felt she owed him an explanation.

'I don't expect you to.' He could have said 'you don't need to', but he didn't. Aggie had been right, the husband was a bastard, he'd obviously hit her, there was no doubt about that. Paul wondered what she would do. Would she leave him? Probably not, she had a small son to think of. He longed to hold her. She looked so vulnerable.

The sandwiches and Scotches arrived. Henrietta found herself ravenously hungry. Paul sat and drank as he watched her eat.

'Are you sure you don't want some?' she asked.

'Quite sure.' She didn't realise that he simply wanted to watch her.

Henrietta couldn't believe that she was scoffing back sandwiches and enjoying herself. Some switch had mercifully clicked off in her brain. In this room, beneath this ceiling fan, Darwin Harbour gleaming through the open windows, in the company of this man who demanded no explanation, the agony had disappeared. It would be back, she knew, but for this moment, she didn't need to seek answers.

She finished the sandwiches and they sat chatting comfortably about Paul's forthcoming assignment for *National Geographic*, or rather he did. Then he finished his final Scotch and rose from his chair.

'Goodnight, Henrietta,' he said.

'Oh,' she didn't want him to go. If he went, she would start thinking again and the demons of indecision would come back. 'Don't you want to order up a couple more Scotches?' she asked hopefully.

'It's nine o'clock,' he laughed, 'if I do that the rumours'll be rife. We'll have settled in for the night.'

'Oh yes, of course, what a pity.'

'I could pop back to my room and grab a bottle.'

'Go on,' she urged. 'I'll have one with you.'

He was back only minutes later. 'I made sure I was seen going into my room,' he announced, 'but no-one saw me duck back here. Your reputation is intact, Mrs Galloway.'

'Thank goodness for that.'

Surprisingly enough, they didn't drink much, but they talked. Or rather Paul did, at Henrietta's instigation. She knew so very little about him, she said.

It occurred to Henrietta that nobody knew much about Paul Trewinnard. Even Aggie, who was a fund of information about everyone in Darwin, knew only that he'd been married at one time. 'I think the wife died,' she'd told Henrietta, 'ages ago.'

'You're a man of mystery, Paul,' Henrietta remarked.

'Not really,' he replied, 'just "a bit of a bad egg", that's what my father used to say.' Paul was prepared to talk about himself, not only to distract and comfort her, but in order to stay in her company.

'I can't believe that.'

'Oh yes. I was a lawyer with the family practice. Very old firm established by my grandfather. Frightfully respectable, don't you know,' he said with a toffy accent. 'Frightfully wealthy too, I might add. But I took a wrong turn and they threw me out.'

'What on earth for?'

Out of habit, Paul hesitated for a moment. Foong Lee was the only person in Darwin who knew his past but if, in telling Henrietta his story, he could momentarily deflect her pain then he was quite happy to talk.

'My wife and child died in an accident,' he said, 'a very long time ago.'

'Oh,' she hoped he didn't think she'd been prying. 'I'm sorry.'

'So was I,' he said. 'But the real problem was that I

killed them.' He was surprised at the ease with which he said it. 'A drunken car accident,' he continued, 'senseless deaths, an ignominious end to two wonderful lives. A good woman and a beautiful little girl, she was just two years old. And I was responsible.'

'Oh Paul . . .'

He didn't want her sympathy, it wasn't why he'd told her, he simply wanted to distract her, and he'd obviously succeeded. 'So, you see, I became a bit of a lost soul.' His tone was very matter-of-fact, 'no use to the family, no use to the firm, I just drank and wallowed in self-pity. They sent me to Singapore, ostensibly to manage their agency there, Trewinnard and Sons had a lot of wealthy clients in Singapore. They still have, despite the war. But I couldn't manage a thing, least of all myself, and I wasn't needed in Singapore, a cousin looked after the agency quite adequately.' He gave a wry laugh. 'Simon and I couldn't stand each other, he's a typical Trewinnard. Every male member of the family went into the firm, you see, I'm sure they still do, I've rather lost touch. They all studied law whether they liked it or not. And I didn't like it at all, so even before the accident I was the "bad egg" as father was wont to say. They just paid me a director's fee to keep me out of the way. They still do.' He smiled to lighten the mood. 'Australians have a perfect term for my sort of chap, "a useless bludger", it's very apt.'

Henrietta smiled in return and waited for him to continue, obviously intrigued, so he did.

'I came to Darwin in the thirties and met Foong Lee,' he said, 'and that's probably what saved me. Somehow he straightened me out. God alone knows how,' he gave a humorous shrug, 'he's such a funny little man, but he's damned effective when he sets out to do something.'

Paul knew exactly how Foong Lee had helped him, but there were some things he was not prepared to tell Henrietta. He realised, however, that he may have sounded

too flippant and he didn't wish to trivialise his friendship
with the Chinese, so he added more seriously, 'Foong Lee
is a priceless friend to me.' Then he laughed and the banter
was back in his tone. 'Of course even Foong Lee can't
accomplish the impossible, and I'm still a bludger, I serve
little purpose.'

This time Henrietta didn't laugh in return. She leaned
forwards in her chair, her face very close to his. 'You serve
a great purpose to me,' she said. 'To me you are a priceless
friend.'

He kissed her. He wasn't sure if she wanted him to, but
he couldn't help himself. It was a gentle kiss, and she
gently responded. But when she didn't break away, he
wasn't sure what to do. He desperately desired her,
he would have given anything to make love to Henrietta
Galloway, but how could he take advantage of her under
such circumstances. For one brief moment, as he broke
free of their kiss, her eyes remained closed, her lips parted,
and it took Paul every shred of willpower he could muster
to rise and say, as casually as he could, 'It's time you went
to sleep, Henrietta.'

She also rose. 'I won't be able to sleep,' she said. 'Please
stay with me.'

'Are you sure?' Did she know what she was asking? Did
she know how he felt, or did she merely need his
company?

Henrietta knew exactly what she was asking. In the
moment of their kiss she had recognised both his desire
and his love. She didn't question whether she loved him in
return. She so ached to be loved that she didn't think
beyond the fact that she wanted Paul to stay and she
wanted him to make love to her.

'I'm sure,' she said. 'Please. Stay the night with me,
Paul.'

They kissed again, more deeply this time, and as they
held each other close Henrietta felt that she had never

before experienced such tenderness, nor had she felt herself more deeply aroused.

They undressed each other slowly, their lips barely parting, their hands caressing each other all the while, and Henrietta's mind could encompass nothing but his touch. Her whole body was a receptor, it seemed. His fingers in her hair, upon her face, tracing a line down her naked back, and when he gently cupped her breast in his hand and bowed his head to her nipple, she shuddered with ecstasy. Never had she felt such pleasure.

He entered her slowly, and they made love as gently as they had caressed, tantalising each other until both were at the peak of their desire.

Paul fought to control himself for as long as possible, to give her as much pleasure as he could, but when he could last no longer, in his final moment, he looked into her eyes. Henrietta could not return his gaze, she was transported. Her eyelids were fluttering, her neck and her back arched as she offered herself to him, and sounds that she'd never known she could utter were emanating from deep in her throat.

'Henrietta,' Paul said her name as he gave in to his release, and she clung to him, her body frozen with his as if they were one. They quivered together in mutual ecstasy and Paul remained inside her until her body stopped shuddering and her eyes finally opened. Then, spent and exhausted, he withdrew to lie on his back and hold her to him.

Henrietta was dazed, astounded by her body's response. So that was what it was like, for years now she'd stopped wondering.

'I love you, Henrietta,' he whispered as she snuggled into the crook of his arm.

'I love you too,' she said. She didn't analyse whether it was truly love that she felt, she didn't know and she didn't care. She was simply aware of an overwhelming gratitude and affection as she drifted into a blissful sleep.

In the morning she awoke before he did and, in her moment of waking, she looked at the strange room and wondered if it had all been a dream. But his arm was draped across her and she could feel his breath against the back of her neck. Gently, so as not to disturb him, she rolled over and looked at him as he lay sleeping. He was snoring quietly and he looked quite beautiful in sleep, she thought, peaceful and tender. She should feel riddled with guilt, but she didn't, and she wondered at the fact. Did it mean that she loved him?

He gave a sharp snort, startling himself as he did so, and the snoring stopped. She thought he was about to awaken, but he didn't, he heaved a sigh and continued gently snoring again. She smiled. Yes, she loved him, she'd wake him up shortly and tell him so and they'd make love again.

Henrietta's smile faded. After they'd made love they would need to talk, and she knew what she must tell him. She loved him, yes, but not enough to desert her son. She knew what she must do, and she knew now that she had the strength to do it. She couldn't conduct a clandestine affair with Paul, she couldn't live such a lie. And, even if she could, Darwin was a small town, a hotbed of gossip, the truth would become known and Terence, she was certain, would not only kill her, he would kill Paul too. If she must live a lie, then for the sake of her son she must persuade herself that Terence was right, that there were outback ways to which she must adjust. And she must live the lie of sharing her life with a man she detested.

He gave another snort, louder this time, it was obviously his preamble to awakening. Then he sighed once more and made as if to roll over but he stopped, and his hand, now resting on her hip, caressed her as if in sleep he was wondering who was lying beside him. His eyes opened in an instant.

'Good morning.' He smiled, 'I thought I might have dreamed it.'

'So did I.' She grinned back at him. 'I didn't know you snored.'

'Well you wouldn't, would you? How unattractive of me.'

'Not really.' She wriggled closer to him and he could feel the fullness of her breasts against his chest. 'You weren't very loud, I found it quite disarming,' she said and she wriggled again, wantonly.

They made love, laughing this time, teasing each other's desire, and this time, in her final moment, she looked into his eyes.

'I love you, Paul,' she said when they were spent and lay on their backs holding hands and looking at the ceiling.

'Do you really?' he turned his head towards her and there was a joyful incredulity in his eyes. 'How wonderful.'

She wondered if now was the time to have their conversation, but before she could say anything further he'd jumped out of bed and was pulling on his clothes. 'It's seven o'clock,' he said, 'we have to cover our tracks. You order breakfast. Just for one of course, and I'll go and mess up my bed so the maids don't talk. I won't be long.' And he was gone.

She had a shower and waited, but it was a good half hour before he returned. Her bowl of fruit and toast and pot of tea arrived, and she was wondering what had happened to him when there was a light tap on her door and she opened it to discover Paul standing there, a pot of coffee in one hand and a plate of toast in the other.

He ducked inside and she closed the door. 'Coffee and toast,' he said, 'my daily start to the day, I thought it wise not to break the habit. And I waited until I saw the maid deliver your breakfast.'

They sat on the bed and ate together, like two naughty children sharing an illicit picnic. And when they'd finished eating, she kissed him, it was quite evident she wanted to make love again.

'Good God, girl,' Paul said, 'I'm not a young stud anymore, I'm forty-seven years old.' But it appeared, with Henrietta, anything was possible. He certainly felt like a young stud again.

As they lay, once more exhausted, in each other's arms, there was a knock on the door.

'The maid,' Paul mouthed the words, and Henrietta dressed quickly, calling out, 'Just a minute please.'

She opened the door several inches.

'Do you want your room made up, madam?'

'Not right now, thank you, I'll be booking out in the next half hour or so.'

'Very good, madam.'

She closed the door and turned to face him. The incident had had an instantly sobering effect on them both. 'It's time I left,' she said.

'Yes, I know.'

And it was time for the conversation, Henrietta thought, dreading the prospect. 'We can't ever do this again,' she said bluntly, she didn't know how else to put it.

'I know that too,' he said as he rose and started dressing. 'It's why I've been covering our tracks.'

She sat silently on the bed and watched him. She didn't know what she'd expected, perhaps that he might beg her to come away with him. But he wasn't looking at her as he efficiently tied up his shoelaces.

'It's just as well I'm going on Monday,' he said, 'I may stay away for quite a while longer, I think perhaps it's for the better.' The efficiency of his tone belied his feelings. He wanted to hold her and tell her he would love her for the rest of his life, but he had known she would go back to her husband and son, what was the point in prolonging it?

'Yes,' she said quietly. What more was there to say?

'Will you be safe, Henrietta?' He was worried for her.

'Yes,' she said, 'I'll be quite safe.'

He looked at her intently, 'Are you sure?'

She nodded. 'It's the first time he's hit me.' They hadn't discussed Terence once, but Henrietta knew Paul had guessed that he'd struck her. 'And there were circumstances,' she said awkwardly, her voice trailing off. 'It won't happen again, he's promised me.'

He took her in his arms. 'If you ever need me . . .'

'Yes, I know,' she said as they held each other. But she would never need him. Or if she ever felt she did, she would never call upon him, she daren't.

Paul knew exactly what she was thinking. 'I won't keep in touch,' he said, and she was grateful. 'But Aggie will always know where I am.' He eased her away from him and his eyes were deadly serious. 'Promise me, Henrietta. Promise me that if you're ever in danger you'll contact me.'

'I promise.'

They kissed gently, then he said, 'You get your things together and call the porter. I'll go downstairs and bump into you in the foyer.' He smiled. 'It'll put the finishing touch to the charade.' He stroked her cheek. 'My darling girl,' he said.

She brushed her lips against his. 'My dearest love,' she whispered. And, as she did so, she knew that it was true, that she would love Paul Trewinnard for as long as she lived.

He left quietly closing the door behind him, and fifteen minutes later they bumped into each other in the foyer.

'You're leaving, Henrietta,' he said brightly.

'Yes, it was just an overnight stay,' she answered.

'It's all right, Bob,' he said to the porter, 'I'll see Mrs Galloway to her car. You must come into town more often,' he said, picking up her suitcase, 'it's been lovely to see you.'

'Yes, I must,' she agreed as they walked out through the main doors.

They shook hands just before she got into the car.

'Goodbye, Henrietta,' he said.

'Goodbye, Paul.'

CHAPTER THIRTEEN

*I*n one of the many makeshift tents on the island, Lucretia van den Mylen knelt with the predikant, his wife Maria and their six children. It would soon be night, the night of the fourth day since the wreck of the Batavia, and Gijsbert Bastiaensz was leading his family in prayer.

Her head bowed, Lucretia held the hand of Judick, the eldest daughter, who had sought out her friendship, but Lucretia was not listening to the predikant whose pontificating sounded meaningless, she was praying in her own way. Simply and fervently. 'Dear God, if we are about to die, please let it be quick and merciful.' She tried to swallow but she couldn't, her mouth was so parched, her throat so dry. The scant supply of drinking water had run out and this, the fourth day, had been the harshest yet in their fight for survival. A miracle was needed. Another day like this and they would all be dead. Lucretia had seen people drinking their own urine. Others had drunk sea water and she'd watched them go mad. A number had died. With a hand to her heart, Lucretia felt beneath her bodice, the outline of the locket as she prayed. 'And please, dear God, should I die, look after my Boudewijn.'

*On the morning of the wreck, Lucretia had been amongst
the first forty passengers brought ashore in the longboat,
along with other women and the children. The island to
which they'd been transported was little more than a mile
from where the* Batavia *remained foundering on the rocks,
and the longboat had made three successive trips, bringing
the sick and the weaker of the men also, until soon 180
people were crowded onto the barren triangular-shaped
platform of coral. The island measured less than 340 yards
in length and on average 70 yards in width, and with the
meagre supplies allotted them, the hapless survivors were
forced to set up camp amongst the spindly bushes between
the two small coral beaches. The luckier ones acquired the
strips of canvas which had once been sails and made rudi-
mentary tents. It had been a relief, nonetheless, to be away
from the ship. The hours following the wreck, those two
hours of dark before dawn, had been a nightmare. Convinced they were destined to be plunged into the churning
black sea, panic-stricken passengers had screamed in
terror, soldiers had jostled the crew, demanding to know
what was going to happen, and sailors had been hindered
by the hysteria as they'd tried to go about their duties,
Captain Jacobsz screaming all the while above the melee.*

*'Let my sailors do their work! Quiet, you cattle!' But
no-one heeded him.*

*The morning light had brought little relief. The hysteri-
cal passengers still believed they were destined to drown.
And when Adriaen Jacobsz returned from his exploration
in the longboat to report to Commandeur Pelsaert that the
nearest island would not flood at high tide and could
accommodate survivors, hysteria reached its peak as
people fought to get into the longboat. The smaller yawl,
a dinghy which could take only ten passengers, threatened
to capsize as they clambered aboard. Weak, frightened
men trampled over women; women, parted from their
children, wailed; sailors tried desperately to fend the frail*

craft from the ship's side as they loaded barrels of bread and water.

Eventually, however, all those who wished to go ashore had been transported, and those left on the Batavia could then assess the damage and possibility of repair. There was none. The Batavia was crippled and dying. Jacobsz had known it. Cornelisz, the undermerchant, with his lack of seamen's knowledge, had hoped that somehow they might salvage her, float her and her precious cargo off the reef, leave the others behind and reap the riches. Jacobsz scorned such naivety.

'Her back's broken, you fool, she'll sink to the bottom like a stone,' he scathingly replied.

Jeronimus Cornelisz was displeased by Jacobsz's disdainful reaction, and later that day he watched from the bulkhead as Jacobsz took the Commandeur ashore; Pelsaert was needed to restore order and leadership to those marooned on the island, the skipper said. Did this mean that the skipper was no longer allied to him now that their mutinous plans had miscarried? Such a notion was dangerous. Was Jacobsz considering an alliance with the Commandeur whom he detested in order to save his own skin? Was he about to desert his colleagues in crime? Cornelisz surveyed the treasure chests and the wealth of cargo which had been hauled out onto the deck. No, he satisfied himself, Adriaen Jacobsz would never desert such riches, he would be back. In the meantime, with the Commandeur safely out of the way, they'd have fun tonight. The ruffians amongst the soldiers, those with no loyalty to the United East India Company, were already plundering the vessel and their drunken roars could clearly be heard from the hold where they'd broken open casks of gin and bottles of Spanish wine from the stores.

Not to be outdone, the sailors joined in the destruction, breaking into Pelsaert's cabin and making a mockery of his personal possessions, and Cornelisz himself took great delight in reading aloud from the Commandeur's journal. He was rewarded for his trouble by guffaws of laughter and ribald remarks when he parroted, in an imitation of Pelsaert's voice, the passage relating to the outrage perpetrated upon the person of Lucretia van den Mylen. When they had tired of this sport, they fouled the journal. 'Give it the same treatment afforded the van den Mylen slut,' Cornelisz suggested, and the men obeyed with alacrity. Then they tossed the journal into the sea.

A soldier attacked one of the money chests with an adze. Grasping the wooden handle of the adze, which was at right angles to the heavy chisel-like tool, he raised it above his head and, in a drunken frenzy, swung again and again at the chest until finally it burst open. Greedy hands grabbed coins and the men, staggering in their drunkenness and bellowing with laughter, threw the money in each other's faces.

That night Cornelisz gathered his fellow conspirators about him, at least those who were still conscious, and in the great cabin, the ship's main dining room, they gorged themselves on food from Pelsaert's larder and drank yet more wine from his fine personal collection. It was just a taste of things to come, Cornelisz assured them, he had plans and there were still riches to be had. He wasn't sure what his plans were, like the others he was too drunk to think or to care, but he had no intention of giving up his treasure.

Pelsaert and Jacobsz did not set up their encampment on the island with the marooned passengers, but rather on a small, rocky cay halfway between the wreck and the island itself. There, with their crew of seamen, having commandeered not only the longboat and the dinghy, but provisions and barrels of water containing some twenty gallons, they made their plans.

The following day, watching the Commandeur and the Captain from the larger island, the survivors named

*the cay Verraders' Eylandt, 'Traitor's Island', convinced
that those who were to have led them had deserted them.*

*Perhaps they were right, for forty-eight hours after the
wreck of the* Batavia, *before dawn on 6 June, the longboat
slipped away. Pelsaert had ordered Adriaen Jacobsz to set
sail, convinced there was only one possible chance of
survival for those remaining on the island. He must reach
Java and the city of Batavia, after which his ship had been
named, and he must return with a rescue vessel. Although
he trusted in Adriaen Jacobsz's ability to skipper the
longboat to safety, he did not trust in the man's integrity.
He doubted Jacobsz would return for the others, and so,
heavy-hearted with the enormity of his undertaking and
the fact that some would see it as desertion, Pelsaert took
command and set sail. Jacobsz himself had no such misgivings. The survivors were doomed and he was only too
eager to rescue himself.*

*The last instructions Pelsaert relayed to the seventy men
still aboard the* Batavia's *wreck were, 'Make some rafts
and leave the ship as quickly as you can, and God help
you.' Then, with his crew, which included his skipper,
Adriaen Jacobsz, the High Boatswain, Jan Evertsz and the
buxom Zwaantie Hendrix, Pelsaert left the survivors to
fend for themselves.*

*Barely twenty-four hours later, the smaller dinghy also
departed with a crew of ten; a speedier lighter vessel, she
sought to catch up with the longboat and sail in unison.
Small wonder that the 250 men, women and children who
remained on the island and aboard the rapidly disintegrat-
ing wreck felt abandoned.*

*At first Lucretia tried to defend the Commandeur.
'Perhaps he has gone in search of water,' she suggested,
and most certainly Pelsaert had made several explorative
searches for nearby water supplies, with little success.
Even on the fourth day, when people were dying of thirst,
Lucretia weakly maintained his innocence. 'He will return*

with a rescue ship,' she said, and although she believed this to be Pelsaert's intention, she did not think it possible. If he ever did return it would be to find them all dead.

On the fifth day the miracle happened. It rained. The skies opened and a life-saving deluge poured down upon the survivors, who held their faces to the heavens and wept with relief. When they had sated their thirst, they rigged their canvas tents to catch the rain and funnel it into barrels.

'God is merciful, he has not forgotten us,' the predikant cried.

The numbers on the island swelled as men risked the perilous swim from the ship which was fast breaking up, forty of them drowning in the process.

Jeronimus Cornelisz was the last man to leave the Batavia. His purpose in staying aboard was not a grand gesture, nor did he remain in order to guard his treasure; unable to swim, and having witnessed the deaths of others who'd made the attempt, he was simply terrified of drowning.

For eight days he stayed on board as heavy seas pounded the vessel and she splintered and broke apart beneath him. Then, finally, he had no choice. Sitting astride a section of the bowsprit, he braved the waves, leaving the hulk of the Batavia behind him as he made his way towards the island, a small plank serving as a paddle.

It took him two days and, when he was finally washed up on the island's shore, he was exhausted, floundering in the shallows, neither able to speak nor to walk.

He was granted a hero's welcome. People cried out with joy at the sight of him. The undermerchant lived, they had thought he'd drowned, and they carried him ashore and clothed him in warm garments and fed him water and then food when he had recovered enough to eat. At last they had a leader. With the departure of their Commandeur and their Captain, the undermerchant was the most senior member of the Vereenigde Oost-Indische Compagnie, and as the official representative of the VOC, he was afforded every entitlement his rank demanded.

When he had regained his strength, Cornelisz quickly realised that the situation was nowhere near as drastic as he had presumed it to be. There were barrels of rain water, and other barrels had been washed up on the shores from the wreck. And not only barrels of water, but of gin and wine, of food and cargo. A regular watch was kept to rescue any valuable debris which drifted past in the current. The mainmast had been rescued, supplying enough canvas in its sails to provide tents for everyone. Carpenters, of which there were a number amongst the survivors, were already constructing flat-bottomed boats from the wreckage timber. He would be able to salvage some of the wealth from the *Batavia's* hulk.

Given the leadership they had granted him, Cornelisz made his plans. A council had been set up amongst the survivors to protect their community and to mete out punishments for misdeeds, but Cornelisz displayed no interest in becoming a member. He had his own hierarchy, consisting of those loyal followers who had been part of the intended mutiny, and he was disturbed to hear from his men that word of the mutiny had spread in various quarters.

'It was the day the skipper left,' Coenraat informed him. Coenraat van Huyssen, a handsome young military cadet whose aristocratic exterior belied the true evil of his nature, was one of Cornelisz's most loyal supporters. 'Ryckert broke open a barrel of gin,' Coenraat said. 'He was staggering in the drink and he told anyone who would listen that Jacobsz had deserted him, said that he'd been prepared to risk the gallows for the skipper and this was his reward.'

Cornelisz glared angrily. Ryckert Woutersz, a gunner, was a weak milksop of a man, Cornelisz had known him

to be so from the outset, a man fond of talking and frightened of action. 'Kill him,' he said.

'We did,' Coenraat replied, 'that very night, a dagger
between the ribs. But his disappearance was remarked on
the following morning and the rumour persists, I don't
know how many believe it.' In his handsome eyes was the
gleam of a fanatic. 'We need to kill more, Jeronimus. We
need to kill them all. The food and water can't last forever,
what is the point in feeding so many useless mouths.'

'Calm yourself, Coenraat,' Cornelisz said smoothly. The
young man was impetuous but he was an invaluable
supporter. 'All in good time, we must tread softly, nothing
will be gained by frightening the people, there are too
many soldiers to protect them. We must gain their confidence and somehow rid ourselves of the military who are
loyal to the VOC. Keep your peace, you and the others,
laugh off the rumours as drunken foolishness and do
nothing to arouse suspicion.'

Over the days which ensued, Cornelisz not only ingratiated himself with the people, both he and his followers
imbued them with confidence. His hierarchy consisted of
the most senior and educated men amongst them, clerks
of the Company and officer cadets who came from aristocratic families. The common people were accustomed to
accepting the authority of such men.

It was these same men who had conspired to mutiny and
yet, if any person or persons now attempted to disobey
them, then they themselves would be accused of mutiny.
For, as Cornelisz dictated, he and his followers acted in the
name of the Company and, as the senior VOC representative, who could contest him? The irony of the situation
delighted Cornelisz.

Lucretia observed, with dire misgivings, the burgeoning
power of Jeronimus Cornelisz. Did the people not recognise his depravity? And she trusted none of those with
whom he surrounded himself. But Cornelisz manipulated

everyone with consummate ease, and even Lucretia had to admit that so far his plans had made sense.

The most urgent and basic requirement was a source of fresh water, the barrels would not last forever, they could not rely on the rain, and so Cornelisz had sent out boats on exploratory expeditions. One such expedition to the nearest island, a thin strip of land with visible clumps of vegetation, had revealed a colony of seals, and the two carcasses the men had brought back had provided a feast for all.

'Many more there for the taking,' they assured the others, 'and they're easy to catch, they just bask in the sun.'

'God is kind,' the predikant had proclaimed, 'we will not starve.'

During calm weather, Cornelisz had also sent boats to the hulk of the wreck, and they had returned with riches. A casket of jewels fit for a king and a chest of heavy silver coin. Brocades and gold braids, fine apparel and boots of best leather, and even a trunk containing the clothes and uniforms of Commandeur Francisco Pelsaert. The people were imbued with fresh hope, their situation had improved tenfold since the arrival of the undermerchant, they declared.

What good were caskets of jewels and silver coin, Lucretia thought. Furthermore, she'd seen the greedy gleam in Cornelisz's eyes, the man looked upon the treasure as his own. But she said nothing. To speak ill of the undermerchant would be regarded as traitorous by many. But when Cornelisz turned his charm upon her, as he so often did, she felt the bile rise in her throat. She could still hear his blasphemous whispers and the repugnant intimacy of his tone, 'Do you believe in the teachings of Torrentius, my dear?' She detested the man and she knew him to be evil. She tried, whenever she could, to avoid him.

Cornelisz was pleased overall, so far he had suffered just

one major disappointment. Of the twelve bound chests filled with heavy silver coin, eleven had sunk to the depths of the ocean, the only one retrieved being that which the soldier had broken open with his adze, and half the coin had gone, thrown about as it had been in the men's drunken frenzy. But the chest of jewels was worth a king's ransom, more than enough to set him up for life.

Cornelisz's plan was simple. He and his cohorts would seize the rescue ship when it arrived. He strongly believed in Adriaen Jacobsz's skills. If anyone could navigate the longboat to Batavia it was Jacobsz, and Pelsaert would return for the survivors, Pelsaert was an honourable man. There would be no survivors, however, except for Cornelisz and his followers. All others would have perished. At this point the plan became a little more complicated, for Cornelisz and his men were severely outnumbered, the soldiers loyal to the Company being of particular concern.

Cornelisz had won a number of soldiers to his cause, but there remained a hardcore group of older men, seasoned regulars, who were known to be incorruptible. He had not dared to approach them. It was a pity, Cornelisz thought, he could have made use of their abilities with a blade in ridding himself of the others. The soldiers' undisputed leader was Weibbe Hayes. The epitome of his kind, Hayes was tough and strong, a man of great courage and unswerving loyalty to the VOC. Cornelisz would turn the man's qualities to his own advantage by exploiting Hayes' commitment to duty.

Weibbe Hayes and his twenty or so men were to be sent on a life-saving mission, Cornelisz announced. 'The discovery of a fresh water source is imperative,' he instructed them. They were to be taken to the High Islands which could be seen on the horizon to the north. There they would be left to continue their expedition for as far and as long as necessary in order to discover drinking water. 'Our lives may well depend upon your discovery,' Cornelisz *emphasised. He then confiscated their arms just prior to their departure, weapons being a hindrance, he maintained. 'You will need all your strength to carry the water barrels,' he said. The soldiers were ordered to light a fire as a signal when they had discovered water, at which time, Cornelisz promised, the boats would come to collect them and their valuable cargo.*

'We shall never collect them and we shall never see such a signal,' he said to Coenraat van Huyssen as they watched the boats depart, 'there is no water up there.' One of his boats had returned from an expedition only a few days previously to report that the High Islands were a wasteland of rocks and sand and mudflats. He'd told his men to keep such knowledge to themselves. 'Weibbe Hayes can walk his feet off searching,' he said to Coenraat, 'I have no doubt he will, and then he'll die of thirst.'

Cornelisz's next problem was how to split up the survivors. There were simply too many to kill en masse. But it proved very simple.

'We are overcrowded,' he said to the assembled community, 'we must disperse our company. If only for the sake of hygiene and the gathering of firewood, it will be to all of our advantage.' None could disagree, the living conditions had become intolerable. Seals' Island was the perfect answer, Cornelisz said. It had an adequate water supply, he lied, and regular supplies and provisions would be delivered for all those who wished to escape the overcrowded confines of their present environment.

Forty-five men, women and children gathered on the small coral beach and were transported to Seals' Island where they were left to fend for themselves as best they could. There would be no provisions delivered and, if they didn't die, then in time Cornelisz would redress the situation. In the meantime he assessed the remaining numbers. Quite manageable, he thought. He dissolved the community's council and set up his own elected members

to govern the island. The island which was to become
known as Batavia's Graveyard.

'Now, Coenraat,' he said, 'now you can start killing.'
Coenraat van Huyssen and the other young noblemen
cadets had been secretly practising their swordcraft for
beheadings and disembowellings; their bloodlust was up
and they were craving to kill. 'The strong ones first,'
Cornelisz ordered. 'At night. And dispose of the bodies,
we'll tell the others they've gone to the High Islands.'

'But we'll keep some of the women,' Coenraat said, for
some time now he'd had his eye firmly fixed on young
Judick Bastiaensz, the predikant's daughter.

'Of course,' Cornelisz agreed, 'we'll keep the good-
looking women.' Now, at long last, Lucretia van den
Mylen would be his.

CHAPTER FOURTEEN

Henrietta was pregnant and Terence was delighted. Henrietta was delighted too, despite her certainty that the child she was carrying was Paul's. She did not doubt the fact for one instant. Just as she had known that her first child had been conceived that day on the ridge overlooking the waterfall, so she knew that this child had been conceived during her night of lovemaking with Paul Trewinnard at the Hotel Darwin.

Paul had not returned to Darwin. True to his promise he had kept well out of her life and, although she thought of him daily, Henrietta was grateful for his absence. To act out the charade of a casual friendship would have been unbearable for them both. She regularly received messages via Aggie, however, and recognising a code, she replied in kind.

'Paul's going to settle in London,' Aggie had said several months after he'd gone, 'I don't know why, he hates the place. He says it's because most of his work is based in Europe these days, but why doesn't he live in Paris? He speaks passable French.'

'He told me once that he loves Paris but he can't stand the Parisians,' Henrietta replied.

Aggie conceded the fact. 'Anyway, he sends his best and says he hopes you're well and happy.'

'Very well and very happy,' Henrietta said, knowing her message would be relayed.

Several times Aggie chastised her. 'Why don't you write to him as I do?' she said. 'We're his friends and he misses us.'

'I'm a terrible letter writer, Paul knows that.'

'Yes, he said that's why he doesn't bother writing to you himself, he knows he'll never get a reply.'

After a while Aggie gave up nagging and simply relayed the innocently solicitous messages back and forth. She was the reliable conduit through which Paul could keep a check on Henrietta and Henrietta could assure him of her safety.

Henrietta's visits to Darwin dwindled and she said nothing of her pregnancy to Aggie until several months down the track when, during a rare trip to town, her condition was only too evident.

'Good heavens, Henrietta,' Aggie exclaimed, 'so that's the surprise you mentioned, why on earth didn't you tell me?'

Henrietta laughed. 'I didn't bother over the telephone, I thought I'd come into town and show off instead. Six months now.' She lied, she was seven months pregnant. 'And Terence is ecstatic.'

The lie was necessary. If Paul was to hear the news of her pregnancy via Aggie, and he was bound to do so, he must not suspect the child was his. 'Terence is hoping it'll be a brother for Malcolm,' she chatted on, 'but I'm rather hoping for a girl myself.' It was easy to play the garrulous, excited mother-to-be, it was exactly the way Henrietta felt. Initially she'd agonised over the fact that her child's life was to be based on a lie, and she still had misgivings, but what other option was there? None. Perhaps, one day when the child was grown, she would admit to the truth. Perhaps not. Only time could tell as to the wisdom of such a revelation. In the meantime, she must ensure that her baby had a happy and healthy childhood. Having accepted such a priority, Henrietta once again glowed with the joy of impending motherhood; pregnancy suited her.

'Of course it doesn't matter at all whether it's a boy or a girl,' she continued, 'just so long as it's healthy. Oh Aggie, I'm so happy.'

After she'd said goodbye to Paul that morning outside the Hotel Darwin, Henrietta had wondered whether she would ever be happy again. For her son's sake, she knew she must live the appearance of happiness but, as she'd driven back to Bullalalla, she'd wondered how she would be able to face Terence. What would she say to him? She'd wondered whether she'd even be able to look at him. She had found the answers in Nellie.

Nellie had been waiting near the mango grove not far from the main gates. She'd been waiting and watching for the car all day and, when she'd seen the trail of dust in the distance, she'd gone to the grove.

Henrietta pulled up and got out of the car. The woman was agitated, obviously Pearl had told her mother what had happened.

'I knew you'd come back by and by, missus,' Nellie said, 'and I been waiting to say thank you.' She took one of Henrietta's hands in both of hers and held it to her chest as if she was praying. 'Thank you for saving my Pearl.'

Henrietta could feel Nellie's hands shaking and it was quite obvious the woman had been crying. 'It's all right, Nellie,' she said. 'Everything's going to be all right.'

Nellie pulled herself together. She wanted to make sense to the missus, it would not serve her cause to start blubbering. 'I know what goes on, missus . . . down the camp . . .' She was trying to be discreet, she didn't want to say 'I know the boss sleeps with the girls in the camp', not to the missus. '. . . but Pearl,' she continued, then she paused. It was very difficult to be discreet about the next part. 'Pearl is . . . family.'

Nellie had been shocked to the very core of her being that the boss had tried to have his way with Pearl. Nellie herself had been treated not only with respect but even a certain degree of affection by the old boss, Lionel, her father. He had built a house for her and Jackie. And Jock Galloway, tyrant as he was, had regarded both her and Pearl as valuable members of the household. He had even put Nellie on a modest weekly wage. That the young boss should force himself upon Pearl showed such a lack of respect that Nellie's world had been turned upside down and she didn't know what to do. When Jackie came home from the muster she would have to tell him, she and Jackie shared everything, and Jackie would ask her what they should do. Jackie always asked her advice, 'you bin school, Nellie', he'd tell her with one of his cheeky grins. That meant she was smarter than he was. And she would tell him they'd have to leave. But this was a top job Jackie had, and what other boss would build them a house? And she didn't want to leave the missus. The missus needed them, she shouldn't be left alone with the boss.

Nellie looked at the bruise on Henrietta's cheek, Pearl had told her the boss had hit the missus. Nellie was in a terrible quandary, she didn't want to leave but she couldn't risk the boss having another go at Pearl. Her daughter was not one to be had whenever the white boss felt like a black woman.

Mission-school educated, Nellie had been brought up in a white man's world. She could even read and write, the basics anyway. Jackie refused to let her teach him, in the early days he'd teased her about being a white lubra. The white man was there to be used, he'd tell her, they paid you and fed you and you could learn things from them, sure, but you didn't want to turn into one. Beneath his teasing, he was serious. 'You Warai, Nellie,' he'd tell her, 'you don' never forget that.' Jackie even went walkabout for a month during the wet when the work was slow and he was allowed time off. He would visit a clan of the Warai whose territory was the high rocky escarpments above the plains. He missed his own people in far-off Queensland and, through marriage, the Warai had become his family. Nellie never went with him, her place was in the home caring for the Galloways, but she liked Jackie's contact with her clansmen. He had taught her to be proud of her Aboriginality.

But Nellie could not relinquish her white upbringing. And with it came her own very strict set of rules, which included a strong disapproval of sexual promiscuity. She did not approve of polygamy, a man married one woman, just like her and Jackie. Jackie had no other wives, although Aboriginal law allowed him several. And she did not approve of sex outside marriage. She disapproved of Pearl's affair with the young stockman but at least they were to marry. She didn't know how to say any of this to Henrietta, she didn't have the words, and she didn't even know where to start.

'My Pearl's a good girl, missus,' she said, 'she going to marry her fella by and by, next season maybe. She been saving up the money I give her each week. She gonna have a proper dowry.' Nellie said it with pride, but she was becoming agitated again as she squeezed Henrietta's hand. 'I don't want us to leave, but we gonna have to. I can't take the risk, missus.'

'You don't have to leave, Nellie.' Recognising the unfortunate woman's turmoil, Henrietta clasped Nellie's hands in her own. 'It will never happen again, I promise you. He will never go near Pearl again, you have my word.' Henrietta felt very strong as she looked into Nellie's eyes. 'Do you trust me?'

Nellie nodded. She wondered how the missus could make such a promise, the boss was strong and he had a bad temper on him, but yes, she trusted the missus.

'Furthermore,' Henrietta continued, 'Pearl will be paid a wage for her work, just as you are, you don't need to give her money anymore, she shall have her own.' She released Nellie's hands and hugged her close. 'Will you stay?' she asked. 'Please.' Nellie nodded again, not trusting herself to speak. 'Good,' Henrietta broke from the embrace.

As she did so, Nellie put a hand gently to Henrietta's cheek, her fingers very softly touching the bruise. 'It was a brave thing you done, missus.'

'We'll never talk of it again, Nellie,' Henrietta said. 'Never.'

She got back into the Landrover and drove up towards the house.

'How was Aggie?' Terence asked as he came out to meet the car.

'I don't know, I stayed the night at the Hotel Darwin.' She got out of the car and suffered his embrace and the kiss on the cheek. 'I didn't feel like chatting to Aggie.' She'd briefly considered lying, then realised that she didn't care enough to bother. What would he do, hit her again? She didn't even feel frightened of him.

'Ah.' She seemed very calm, he thought, and a little remote, which was hardly surprising, he supposed. But he was so relieved she was back, he'd been secretly afraid that she might leave him and he hadn't known what he'd do if she did. Of course he wouldn't kill her, what had made him say something so stupid? He'd acted like a madman in the shock of discovery, it was all just bluster because he'd been caught out. And how could he have hit her, what on earth had come over him? He loved her, and if she ever left him . . . It didn't bear contemplation.

'I've been thinking, Terence,' she said as he took her suitcase from the car, 'about Pearl.'

'Oh yes?' Christ, here come the conditions, he thought. Well to hell with it, he'd get rid of Pearl, he'd get rid of the whole bloody family. It'd be a bastard, he'd never find a head stockman as good as Jackie, but he'd do anything to keep Henrietta happy.

'Yes,' she said briskly as they walked up the steps to the porch, 'she should be properly employed, just as Nellie is, it's disgraceful that she's treated as an unpaid servant.'

'Sure. We'll pay her a wage if you like.'

'What a good idea.' She smiled at him as if it had been his suggestion. 'She's been saving the money Nellie gives her, you know, she's going to marry her young man next season.'

Terence followed with the suitcase as Henrietta threw open the front door. 'Malcolm,' she called, 'where are you, darling?'

'Mummy!' The shrill cry of excitement came from the kitchen where Malcolm had been playing with Pearl, and mother and son charged towards each other, meeting in the doorway from the hall. She picked him up and whirled him about, the child laughing and squealing with pleasure.

Henrietta had never felt so strong. They all needed her. Nellie and Pearl and Jackie, and most of all her son. She could live the lie, she knew it.

'Has he been a good boy?' she asked Terence, so pleasantly, as if nothing had happened.

'Yes,' Terence answered. Thank Christ, he thought with relief, she was back and the episode was forgotten. 'He's been the best boy.'

'Look what I have for you, darling.' Henrietta took the suitcase from Terence and squatted on the floor as she opened it. She took out the bag and emptied the stones onto the floorboards. The little boy knelt beside her, immediately engrossed in the shapes and colours and the designs he could make with them.

With astonishing ease, Henrietta glanced up and

exchanged a smile with Terence before returning her attention to her son. Yes, of course she could live the lie, she thought. She looked at the stones, they would always remind her of Paul.

Three weeks later Jackie returned. He sought out Henrietta, she was feeding the hens in the chook yard.

He closed the wire gate behind him and stood gazing at her, his black eyes so intense that Henrietta was momentarily mesmerised. She would normally have given a bright 'hello Jackie', but she didn't, she just stared back at him. He was wearing an old khaki shirt, the sleeves cut out, his shoulders and arms glistening with sweat from the heat of the day. He crossed his arms, put his hands beneath his armpits, then wiped them down the wetness of his biceps. He said something in his strange language, took the several paces towards her, and put his hands to her face and her throat and her own bare arms. She could feel the dampness and she could smell his sweat as he patted it onto her skin, but she didn't feel afraid. And she didn't feel repulsed. His eyes signalled his actions as a ritual of friendship and gratitude. Several seconds later, the intensity in his black face vanished as he grinned his gappy grin. Jackie had a very infectious smile. She smiled back and offered her hand.

'Thank you, Jackie,' she said as they shook hands, and he left without uttering a word.

As the months passed, Henrietta knew that Terence still occasionally visited the Aboriginal camp to satisfy his lust. She didn't mind, in fact she was grateful, it meant his advances towards her were less frequent. She could no longer stand the touch of his fingers on her flesh or the taste of his mouth when he kissed her. And when they did have sex, which was thankfully not often, she gritted her teeth, blanked out her mind, and counted the minutes until it was over. Henrietta no longer thought of sexual intercourse as 'making love'. She knew what 'making love' meant now, and she realised that, in the five years of her marriage, never once had she and Terence 'made love'.

When she became pregnant, she used the baby as an excuse to plead off sexual intercourse as often as she could, pretending a morning sickness which she didn't experience. So long as she could avoid a physical relationship, life with Terence took on the semblance of happiness. She was constantly wary, always on the lookout for any signs of his madness, but there were none, Terence remained kind and considerate. In the meantime, Henrietta lived for her son and for the child she carried in her womb.

'I'd like to have the baby at home,' she said to him as her time grew near.

'Why?' Terence had presumed she would go into Darwin Hospital.

'Why not?' she answered simply, 'it worked last time, Nellie's an expert midwife. Besides,' she added, 'I'd like the baby to be born at Bullalalla.' The lie she lived never extended to the mention of 'our' baby, somehow she couldn't bring herself to say it.

Terence smiled. 'You've become a real outback wife, Henrietta,' he said as he kissed her, 'I'm proud of you.'

Henrietta intended to have her baby quietly and privately. When the child was two months old she would take it in to Darwin to show Aggie and no-one would know the exact date of its birth.

The child was born on 7 March 1948. A boy, and they called him Christopher. Terence was beside himself, two sons, the dynasty was assured. And Henrietta, as she studied the curve of her baby's lip and the shape of his brow, was glad that she'd had a boy. She was quite sure that she could see Paul in his face.

Two months later, Henrietta took her children in to Darwin to meet Aggie. Malcolm, who was nearly three years old, had trouble with his little brother's name. He called the baby 'Kitsopher', so they shortened it to 'Kit'.

'Here he is, Aggie,' Henrietta tucked back the blanket from the face of the infant she cuddled to her breast. 'Meet Kit Galloway.'

BOOK THREE

CHAPTER FIFTEEN

'Dig your heels in, Kit, you've got to make him know who's boss.' Ten-year-old Malcolm sounded exactly like his father.

Kit dug his heels in as far as he could but Seldom Awake didn't move. The horse wasn't being disobedient. Through the fleshy surrounds of his upper ribs he couldn't feel the seven-year-old's urgent kicks.

'Come on, boy,' Kit urged. 'Come on, get going.'

Seldom understood the vocal command and he quite willingly started to plod.

'That's it,' Malcolm yelled; he was riding Fast Asleep. Both horses, fat and thirty years old, remained good natured and reliable. But Malcolm was a more experienced, and far more aggressive rider than Kit, so Fast had been raised to a sluggish trot.

'That's it! Kick him!' Malcolm yelled.

Kit kicked for all he was worth. 'Come on, Seldom,' he cried, 'Come on, boy.'

Seldom realised that he was expected to keep pace with Fast so he obliged, and both animals trotted lazily out of the yard by the stables and set off for the home paddock.

Henrietta and Terence watched from the front

verandah. It was a Sunday, and the first time the boys had
been out riding for any considerable distance on their own.
They'd been told they could go as far as the home horse
paddock, then they must turn around and come straight
back. It was a test.

'Shouldn't we be with them,' Henrietta had asked, 'what
if one of them has a fall?'

'Then they'll get back up again,' Terence replied.
'Besides, Malcolm won't come off, he's a good rider, that
boy. And if Kit takes a fall and can't get back up then
Malcolm'll come home and tell us.' Henrietta looked
aghast. 'It's only a few miles,' he assured her, 'and they
have to learn to look after each other.'

It was another outback lesson, she realised. He'd
already made a habit of setting tests for the boys. Malcolm
met every one of the tests head on, but Kit didn't. And it
wasn't just the age difference, Henrietta was sure. The
boys were chalk and cheese. Malcolm was Terence and Kit
was Paul, even in appearance. Malcolm had his father's
strong body. Kit, although quite tall for his age, was slight
in frame. Malcolm had his father's sandy hair and hazel-
green eyes, Kit's eyes were grey.

'He has your eyes,' several women had commented to
Henrietta. But they were wrong. Kit's eyes were Paul's. He
did indeed appear to have inherited her hair, a little darker
in colour, almost auburn with deep reddish tinges. But
then, Henrietta wondered, had Paul, before he'd turned
grey, possibly been auburn-haired?

The differences between the two boys were so obvious
to Henrietta that she had worried others might notice, particularly Aggie. But paradoxically it had been Aggie who
had put her mind at rest.

'Look at them,' she'd said one day when Henrietta had
made a visit to town and they sat by the oval watching the
boys kick a football around, 'Australia versus England.'

'What do you mean?' Henrietta had been a little bewildered.

'They're so different, the boys.' In her guilt, Henrietta froze. 'Malcolm is Terence and Kit is you,' Aggie continued, 'it's quite amazing, isn't it?'

'Yes, I suppose it is.' Henrietta had relaxed after that.

The boys were the best of friends. Malcolm was protective of Kit, and Kit idolised his big brother. Strangely enough, it was Malcolm Henrietta most worried about. He so wanted to emulate his father, and she knew that the boy, despite his bravado, was often fearful of the tests Terence set for him.

Some of them were easy. 'How do you like your steak, son?' Terence would ask.

'Rare and bloody, it's the only way,' the boy would proudly reply.

'Cut its horns off and wipe its arse, eh?' Terence would whisper, it was a joke they shared. 'But we never say that in polite company,' Terence always added for Henrietta's benefit.

Kit refused to eat meat which was bleeding. 'I don't like it,' he stated, and no insistence from his father could force him to eat it.

When the lessons were a little harsher it was worse. Malcolm, at six years of age, had been forced to watch the slaughter of the steers. Henrietta knew the child had been terrified, but in order to earn his father's approval he'd stood through the ordeal. Kit hadn't. Several years later, when he was six and it was his turn, he'd run away before the shot had been fired.

'The boy's a coward,' Terence had complained to Henrietta.

'He's too young,' she'd said, 'give him time.'

'You're never too young to learn,' Terence had insisted. It was a quote of Jock's he'd heard many a time as a child. 'My father did it to me and I did it to Malcolm, and Malcolm handled it just as I did. Kit has to learn.' And then he'd accused her of mollycoddling the child.

Terence interpreted Kit's refusals to obey him as not only disobedience, but a sign of weakness. Henrietta considered it a show of strength and, although she worried about the friction which occasionally resulted between the two of them, her elder son Malcolm remained her most worrying concern. At the moment, his father was his hero, but if Terence kept pushing the boy too far Malcolm could well become a frightened person. She often saw fear in his eyes. Not only fear of the tests which Terence set him, but fear that he could not live up to his father's expectations. She prayed that Terence would not break the boy's spirit.

'They're home,' she called. She'd been watching anxiously and was relieved to see Fast Asleep and Seldom Awake plodding through the main gates towards the stables. She and Terence went down to the yards to help the boys unsaddle the horses. The children's ride to the home paddock and back had been a success.

'Kit came off,' Malcolm announced as the two boys slithered down from the horses' backs. Kit darted an anxious glance at his brother, he hadn't intended telling his dad that he'd fallen. 'And he got straight back up,' Malcolm boasted. He knew full well there was no crime in coming off a horse, in fact it was good, Dad said, it taught you a lesson, just so long as you got straight back up.

'Good boy,' Terence said, and Kit smiled gratefully at his brother. 'Did you hang on to the reins?' Terence asked.

Kit missed Malcolm's signal to lie. 'No,' he said without thinking.

'How many times have I told you,' Terence said sternly. 'You could be stranded a hundred miles from home if your horse bolts on you.'

'But Seldom doesn't bolt,' the boy replied. 'He just stands there.'

'That's not the point . . .'

'Did you hurt yourself?' Henrietta interrupted. The right

sleeve of Kit's checked shirt was torn.

'Yep,' he said with a touch of pride and he pulled his shirt up for her to inspect the graze on his elbow.

'How did you fall?' Terence asked. Henrietta wished he'd stop grilling the children, she wanted to take Kit to the house and dress the graze, it wasn't deep but there was grit in it, the wound needed disinfecting.

It was Kit's turn now to return the favour and boast on behalf of his brother. 'Malcolm got Fast to take a jump,' he said.

'Is that true?' Terence asked the older boy.

'Yeah,' Malcolm nodded with camaraderie to Kit. It had only been a little log, barely eighteen inches in height, but after much belting with a stick on Fast's healthy rump, the animal had clumsily lurched over it.

'That horse has never jumped in its life, well done, boy,' Terence gave a guffaw of delight, 'well done.'

'I tried to get Seldom to take the jump but he wouldn't,' Kit continued with his explanation. Seldom had followed Fast as he usually did but when he'd come to the log, he'd stopped dead in his tracks. 'And I came off.' But his father, still chortling with pride at his elder son's feat, wasn't listening.

'Come on,' Henrietta took Kit by the hand, 'we're going to clean up that elbow.'

'We're going to water the horses and brush them down first,' Terence said.

'You two can do that,' Henrietta firmly replied as she set off for the house, the seven-year-old in tow. 'We two are going to disinfect this arm.'

The following day was school for Malcolm. Henrietta drove him in to Darwin each morning in the Holden utility and collected him in the afternoon, occasionally taking Kit with her for the ride. Accustomed as she was to outback distances, four hours' daily driving meant little to her. Next year, when he would turn eight, Kit too would attend the school, but in the meantime Henrietta tutored him at home.

Aggie reported favourably to Henrietta on Malcolm's progress, but true to form she was brutally honest.

'He's a bright boy, and he enjoys learning,' she said, 'but he's very opinionated for a kiddie his age. According to Malcolm there's only one way of doing things, and that's his way. He becomes quite aggressive when the others don't agree.'

'It's his father's influence,' Henrietta admitted, with a freedom which rather surprised Aggie. Since their altercation years ago, Aggie had taken care to avoid any discussion of her friend's husband or marriage. Henrietta appeared, however, to feel no disloyalty at all in mentioning Terence, it was obvious that Malcolm was her main concern. 'I'm sure high school will change his attitude,' she added, trying to sound confident. She certainly hoped that it would.

In his thirteenth year, Malcolm would be sent off to boarding school in Adelaide. Henrietta would miss him, she knew it, and she'd worry about him desperately, but loath as she was at the thought of his leaving home, she was hoping that the absence of his father and the constant companionship of other children his own age would do him good. No longer would he be the oldest, and the first one to face each test as it came along. And no longer would he have to accept his father's entrenched opinions, he would be presented with options. Henrietta only prayed that it would not be too late.

Her favourite day of the week was Saturday. Saturday was a work day for Terence and, free of his criticism, she'd play games with her children. It started first thing in the morning; Terence always left at dawn to meet up with Buff Nelson at the overseer's cottage five miles from the homestead, and Henrietta and the boys had the house to themselves. She had made it Nellie's regular day off, and Pearl had long since married her young man and moved out, although she visited from time to time.

Henrietta always cooked boiled eggs for breakfast on Saturdays and she and the boys drew faces on the eggs before they ate them. It was a never-ending source of amusement.

From the outset, Kit had drawn an animal's face on his egg. 'That's a pig's egg,' he'd said the first time.

'Pigs don't lay eggs,' Malcolm had corrected him.

'My pigs do.'

After that it had become a running gag. 'That's a cat's egg,' or 'that's a horse's egg,' Kit would say. Malcolm would correct him, 'They don't lay eggs,' and Kit would reply in all seriousness, 'Mine do.' Then both boys would shriek with laughter. Henrietta found it very healthy, although she knew Terence wouldn't approve of their frivolity.

On Saturdays they played hide and seek or I-spy. When it was I-spy Kit would always pick things that Malcolm insisted didn't count. Like the air, or a breeze, or a smell. 'But you can't see them,' Malcolm would say.

'That doesn't matter, they're there, you can feel them.' In his own way Kit could be as pedantic as Malcolm. 'And that's what spies do, they feel things.' Kit was convinced that a game called I-spy must be about spies.

Sometimes Malcolm would become exasperated, and sometimes he'd find it funny, but Henrietta noticed that he was never aggressive towards his little brother. She'd been worried by Aggie's talk of his aggression at school and watched closely for signs of it at home.

Saturday was also the day they went hunting for stones. Henrietta knew she was flirting with danger. Terence didn't like Malcolm's preoccupation with his collection.

'He's obsessed with the things, it's not natural,' he said.

'He's a child, Terence,' she patiently replied, 'they're his toys, and children get obsessions about toys.'

But toys were of little interest to Terence unless the children could learn from them. Even Malcolm's toy gun had become obsolete now that he was being taught to shoot. In Terence's family a boy's tenth birthday meant an introduction to the use of firearms, and after several months Malcolm could already hit tin cans from thirty paces with a .22 rifle. 'There's nothing to be learned from playing with a pile of rocks,' Terence maintained.

So Saturday stone hunting was their secret, and the children seemed to understand that. They would sift through their collection when they got home, and play games with them, and then the best of the stones would go into boxes to be brought out the following Saturday.

The Darwin collection, Malcolm's pride and joy, was kept in a separate box. No stones on the property compared with his Darwin collection. The rocks of Bullalalla were harsh. Some were flat, some spiky, and they ranged in colour from light grey to black, and orange to red. They were dramatic, certainly, you could build a castle out of them, but there was no silky smoothness to the Bullalalla stones. Nor were there lavenders and pinks and apricots to be found, all the variables of colour which existed in the sun-parched, sea-worn stones from the beaches of Darwin.

His Darwin collection was very precious to Malcolm, but he shared it with Kit. On the kitchen floor, they would build a fortress from the Bullalalla stones, and in the centre they would make a mound out of the Darwin collection. These were the jewels, and they had to be protected from the marauders. The boys would attack the fortress with their tin soldiers.

Terence had approved of tin soldiers when Malcolm was little. Just as he'd approved of miniature fighter planes and warships. He'd considered them educational toys at the time and, when Malcolm had been five or six, he'd taught the boy battle manoeuvres. But he no longer played games with his firstborn son, Malcolm was too old for such nonsense, and Kit somehow didn't enter the equation.

Unbeknownst to their father, however, protecting the rock fortress and guarding the treasure was a favourite Saturday pastime for both boys.

One Saturday, only a fortnight or so after the boys' expedition to the home paddock, Terence arrived home in the early afternoon. He and Buff Nelson had been out surveying the fencing—the maintenance of fences on the vast property was a never-ending affair—when a dust storm had come up. Normally the men would have stuck it out. Huddled under their ground cloths or their oilskin jackets, they would have weathered the storm. But this was a bad one, there was no point in staying on, so they'd come back, Buff to his cottage and Terence to the homestead.

Caked in grit, his eyes, his ears, his nose full of the fine red dust, uncomfortable and irritable, Terence walked into the kitchen to see his wife and two sons sprawled belly down on the wooden floor studying a pile of rocks. And for the first time in years, the madness came upon him.

They were so engrossed that none of them had heard him. Terence, plodding wearily, had made little noise.

Suddenly, a large boot flashed before them, and the stones were viciously scattered, the fortress and its treasure strewn in every direction.

Henrietta grabbed the boys and pulled them to their feet. They could have lost an eye from the force with which Terence had sent the stones flying.

She saw the madness instantly.

'What have I told you about these bloody rocks!' he yelled at her. 'Get them out of here, do you hear me!' And he kicked at the stones once again sending them whistling through the air like missiles. 'Get them out of here!'

She didn't waste time collecting them, it was more important to get the boys out of the kitchen and away from their father. She hustled them into the hall.

'Go upstairs to your rooms,' she instructed, 'and don't come down until I tell you.'

'Will you save my Darwin collection, Mum?' Malcolm pleaded. 'Just the Darwin ones, please?'

'Yes,' she said, 'I promise. Now go upstairs.' The boys obeyed and she went back to face Terence and clear away the offending stones.

He was standing in the centre of the kitchen staring down at the tin soldiers, and he seemed perfectly calm. Had the madness left him so quickly, she wondered. She said nothing, but knelt and started sweeping up the stones with a dustpan and brush, careful to put the Darwin ones in their special box.

Terence stooped and picked up several of the toy soldiers, placing them on the kitchen table.

'They were playing military manoeuvres,' she said, hoping to mollify him.

'Yes, I can see that.' A number of the toy soldiers were time-worn and battered, they'd been Terence's when he was a child. He hadn't noticed them when the rage at the sight of the forbidden rocks had overtaken him.

'The soldiers were attacking the fortress,' she explained.

'It's a childish game, Malcolm's too old for toy soldiers. Tell the boys to come in here, I want to talk to them.'

He seemed rational, and Henrietta decided it would court far more danger if she were to question his orders. She finished clearing up the mess, threw the stones in the bin, and placed the box with the Darwin collection on the table.

'Malcolm! Kit!' she called up the stairs from the hall. 'Your father wants to talk to you.'

The boys tentatively entered the kitchen where Terence was seated at the table.

'Sit down,' he instructed, and they did. 'Malcolm,' he said, 'what would you do if your mates at school called you a sissy?'

Malcolm stared back. It was a test, but he wasn't sure of the right answer. Was he supposed to say that he'd fight them?

'You wouldn't like it if they called you a sissy, would you?' his father asked.

Malcolm shook his head vigorously, 'a sissy' was the worst possible thing a kid could be called.

'Good.' Terence continued to address his elder son quietly and authoritatively, but as an adult, 'You are ten years old, you can ride a horse and you can shoot a rifle, don't you think playing with toy soldiers and rocks is a little bit childish?'

'Yes,' the boy agreed.

'Good.' Terence said again, pleased with the response. 'I'll let you keep the toy soldiers as a memento of your childhood,' he continued magnanimously, 'but you'll throw out the rocks. Right now.'

Kit looked anxiously at his brother, not the Darwin collection surely, they were the jewels and Malcolm treasured them. But Malcolm didn't flinch, he nodded obediently.

'Can I keep them?' Kit asked, 'Just the Darwin ones?'

Henrietta jumped in quickly, aware that Terence was annoyed at Kit's interruption. 'He's only seven,' she said, it was a gentle reminder that the boy didn't have to become an adult for another three years.

Terence shrugged, he felt an intense irritation towards his younger son. He often did. There were moments when Terence disliked Kit. The boy showed no respect for his authority. 'He can do what he likes,' he said dismissively to Henrietta. 'Malcolm,' he rose from the table, 'there's still time for some rifle practice. I'll see you down by the tack room.' He left abruptly, Malcolm jumping to his feet to follow.

'I'll look after them for you, Malcolm,' Kit promised.

'What?'

'The Darwin collection. They'll still be yours, I'll look after them.'

'You can have them, I don't want them, they're for sissies.' Malcolm ran off to join his father.

'That was nice of you, Kit.' The little boy looked so hurt, Henrietta wanted to cuddle him, but she didn't. She knew he was trying very hard to be grown up. 'We'll look after them together.'

'Okay,' he agreed, and they took the box upstairs where Kit hid it under his bed.

Henrietta thought of Paul that night. She often thought of Paul, Kit was such a reminder. Just like his father, the boy was gentle, but strong.

Paul Trewinnard had disappeared from her life. Aggie thought that perhaps he was dead. 'Why else would he stop writing?' she had asked when Henrietta expressed shock at such a brutal assumption.

'Perhaps he's met someone,' Henrietta had replied, 'perhaps he's married now, perhaps he has a child and a whole new life.' She hoped that he had.

'That wouldn't stop him writing to us,' Aggie had scoffed, 'we're his best friends.' For years Paul had dropped the pretence of polite enquiries after Henrietta, his letters were always addressed to the two of them. 'Dearest Aggie and Henrietta,' he would write and then he would chat on about his assignments and travels. Paul's letters had been witty, amusing and often outrageous, and the women had taken great pleasure in reading them aloud to each other and chuckling at the latest irreverence.

The letters had always been posted to Aggie. Aggie had assumed Paul was avoiding direct contact with Henrietta in order to spare the woman any unpleasant reaction from her over-possessive husband, and she approved of the decision. God only knew what Terence's response would be to his wife's receiving regular correspondence from another man. In Aggie's opinion Terence Galloway was a megalomaniac who would brook no outside influence upon any member of his family. She was appalled with the way in which he was turning his elder son into a carbon copy of himself. She never commented on the fact to

Henrietta, however, as usual avoiding any discussion of Terence.

Then, abruptly, Paul's letters stopped arriving, and Aggie's own letters to Paul were returned 'address unknown'. When she'd tried to reach him through the family firm, she'd discovered they had no home address for him whatsoever. They never had. Just a post box number at St Martin's in the Fields GPO in Trafalgar Square. She'd received no response from there either, and for the past two years Aggie had given up trying to trace Paul Trewinnard, convinced that he was dead.

On Kit's first day at school, Aggie had been there to welcome him. She discovered very quickly, and to her relief, that the boy was not yet brainwashed by his father the way his brother had been. He was a friendly child and got on well with the others, displaying none of his brother's aggression, and yet Aggie sensed a quiet strength beneath the surface. He would need it, she thought, to survive a father like Terence Galloway. Thank goodness the boy had Henrietta's spirit.

Kit loved school. He enjoyed the company of other children and made friends quickly. When Henrietta picked the boys up each afternoon Kit would chatter on endlessly about his mates whilst Malcolm would look away through the open window of the ute and pretend disinterest.

'I don't know why you hang around with that mob,' he occasionally sneered, 'they're a bunch of sissies.'

'No they're not,' Kit hotly denied. 'What about the day Pete Mowbray fell out of the tree and busted his elbow.' Kit had boasted about the incident often, it had deeply impressed him. 'He didn't cry or anything, he just said "I think it's busted", Pete's really brave.'

'He's not brave,' Malcolm scoffed, 'he's dumb, they all are, that mob.'

When the conversation took such a turn, Henrietta

would change the subject, encouraging Malcolm to talk
about his own day at school, but by then the damage had
been done and he'd shrug sulkily and continue to stare out
the window. She realised that, deep down, he resented the
ease with which Kit made friends. It worried her to see
the boys argue, they had never argued in the past. But
when they got home to Bullalalla the tension disappeared
and the brothers remained the true friends they'd always
been.

Malcolm would offer to help Kit with his homework,
it was his way of apologising for having scorned Kit's
mates. He didn't know why he always made fun of
Kit's mates. Hell, he thought they were only little kids.
He just wished that Kit wouldn't gab on about them all
the time.

When Malcolm had something of his own to boast, he
always waited until he could announce it in the presence
of his father.

'I kicked the football further than Dennis Portman at
goal practice this arvo,' he announced at the dinner table.

'Oh?' Terence looked up from his roast beef.

'Dennis Portman's the longest kick in the team.' He had
his father's full attention now. 'And he's a year older than
me.'

'Good on you,' Terence congratulated him. 'Well done,
son.' And he returned to his roast beef.

Malcolm glowed with pride, but he knew better than to
chatter on any further about the episode, if he did he'd be
accused of boasting.

Henrietta never asked Malcolm why he hadn't told her
about his exploits in the car on the drive home. She knew
it was important to the boy that his achievements be kept
expressly for his father. But the only stories Malcolm
brought home from school were those involving competition in which he'd performed favourably. There were no
simple tales of comradeship. And if he'd experienced

defeat, no-one would ever know. Kit was exactly the opposite.

'I came last in the three-legged race,' he said the night after Aggie's fundraising fete at the school. 'Pete Mowbray was mad at me 'cos I kept falling over, he hates to lose.'

Malcolm looked at his brother in amazement, wondering how he could admit to defeat in the presence of their father. Terence didn't deign to comment.

It was a stifling November afternoon and Henrietta had just pulled up in the ute to wait for the boys outside school. She was early, as she usually was, it would be ten or fifteen minutes before Kit charged through the gates of the small wooden fence, Malcolm sauntering out a good five minutes later, wishing the others couldn't see his mother waiting for him.

Malcolm desperately wanted to ride his horse to school. Some of the kids who lived on the outskirts of town did, he'd said to his father, and there were stables nearby. But Terence had instantly dismissed the idea.

'Don't be ridiculous, boy, it'd take you hours,' he'd said, so twelve-year-old Malcolm had to suffer being collected by his mother as if he were one of the little kids.

Henrietta climbed out of the car. The plastic-covered seats of the Holden had been hot and uncomfortable and she could feel the dampness of her cotton dress clinging to her back and the trickle of sweat between her breasts. She felt claustrophobic when the air was thick and sticky like this, as if the elements were trying to stifle her. It was always the same in the wet, she'd never really adjusted to it. She wished the storm would break soon to relieve the oppressive humidity.

As she stood in the shade of the stringybark tree, fanning herself with the brim of her straw hat, she noticed a nearby car with its driver-side door open, someone else was waiting to collect a child. She wondered if it was one of the parents she knew, but she didn't recognise the car, a two-tone blue Holden sedan.

Then the man in the driver's seat got out, and Henrietta froze at the sight of the familiar figure. Tall, lanky, a Panama hat, and a beige linen sports jacket. No matter how hot, when others were in shirtsleeves, Paul had always worn a jacket.

'Hello, Henrietta,' he said as he started towards her.

'Paul.'

Two other cars were pulling up outside the school, Henrietta recognised the vehicles and the mothers driving them, but she didn't hesitate. Her hat fell from her hand and dropped to the ground as she walked into his arms.

'Paul, thank God.'

It was Paul who first freed himself from their embrace, not wishing to compromise her reputation.

'Aggie thought you were dead.' Henrietta held on to his hands, she didn't want to relinquish the physical contact.

'I know, she told me when I phoned her. "Welcome back from the grave", were her exact words. Rather apt under the circumstances.'

Henrietta suddenly noticed how tired and worn he looked. There were dark shadows under his eyes and, always a lean man, he was thinner than ever.

'You've been ill,' she said.

'Yes.' He gently extricated his hands from hers. 'I think you're expected to say hello,' he murmured. The two women had climbed out of their cars and were standing by the acacia trees near the gates; both were looking in their direction.

'Hello,' Henrietta called with a friendly wave, and the women waved back. Then once more she grasped his hands.

'Is this wise?' he smiled.

'What's wrong in holding hands with your very best friend?' she asked. 'Besides, it'll stop them coming over, let them talk if they want to.' She looked into the familiar grey eyes she'd so often seen in her sleeping and waking moments over the past decade. 'Tell me what happened.'

'In a little while,' he said. 'Perhaps, when you've collected the boys we could go for a drive to Mindil Beach?' he asked hopefully. 'While the boys are playing we could talk.'

'Of course.' She wondered briefly how he'd known she would be here collecting the boys, then she realised. Aggie, naturally.

'Do you think you should pick up the hat?' he suggested. The two women were still watching, and another car was pulling up. Henrietta swiftly scooped her hat up from the ground.

'Mum!' It was Kit, belting towards them. 'I won!' The Christmas essay competition results had been announced in class today, he explained, breathless with excitement, ignoring the man standing beside his mother.

Paul stared at the boy. He was seeing himself as a child.

'And I won!' Kit exclaimed.

'I'm so proud of you, darling.' Henrietta knelt and hugged her son. 'I'd like you to meet a very dear friend of mine,' she said as she stood. 'His name is Paul Trewinnard. Paul, this is my son Kit.'

'How do you do, Kit,' Paul offered his hand, not daring to look at Henrietta. Why hadn't she told him?

'Hello,' Kit shook the man's hand. 'I got a prize,' he said to his mother, 'look.' He took a bookmark from the pocket of his shorts. 'Read what it says.'

' "Christopher Galloway," ' she quoted. The bookmark was gilt-edged with gold stars on it and she recognised Aggie's handiwork. ' "Winner of the Christmas Essay Competition." That's wonderful, Kit, I'm proud of you.'

'It got a bit crumpled,' he said.

'We can iron it. And then we might frame it, what do you think?'

'Okay.' He grinned happily.

Malcolm was walking through the school gates in the company of several other boys, but Henrietta knew better than to call out to him. 'I wish you wouldn't do that, Mum, it's embarrassing,' he'd told her. He said goodbye to his mates and sauntered over to meet his mother and brother.

'Malcolm, this is my friend Paul Trewinnard,' Henrietta said.

'We've met before, Malcolm,' Paul shook the boy's hand. 'But you'd have been too young to remember.'

'We thought we'd go to Mindil Beach before we drive home,' Henrietta told the boys, 'would you like that?'

'Yeah!' Kit punched the air in his enthusiasm.

'All right,' Malcolm nodded, careful not to show too much enthusiasm, but Henrietta could tell he was keen on the idea.

As they drove to the beach, Paul following in his car, Kit chattered on about the essay prize and, for once, Malcolm didn't stare out the window pretending disinterest, he was nice to his little brother.

'Good on you, Kit,' he said, imitating his father. 'Well done.' Malcolm actually felt a bit sorry for Kit. Winning an essay prize wouldn't impress Dad much, he thought.

As the boys talked, Henrietta's mind was elsewhere. She'd been overwhelmed at the sight of Paul. And when he'd shaken his son's hand and she'd looked at the two of them, she'd wondered if he'd guessed at the truth. If he had, then he'd given nothing away. And if he hadn't, she would never tell him.

All four of them took off their shoes and sandals and walked along the beach by the water's edge where the sand was cooler.

'You might find some good stones up there, Malcolm,' Paul pointed towards the headland. Malcolm looked at him distrustfully. 'You used to like collecting stones when you were a little boy.'

'I don't anymore,' Malcolm replied.

'I do,' Kit jumped in quickly. Mr Trewinnard seemed like a nice bloke, he'd asked them to call him Paul, and Malcolm had sounded rude. 'I like collecting stones.'

'Off you go then,' Henrietta said with a look of rebuke at her elder son.

'I'll help you find some,' Malcolm said by way of apology; he hadn't meant to be rude.

'Don't go too far,' Henrietta called after them as they ran off up the beach, 'the storm's going to break any moment.' But the boys weren't listening as they quickened their pace, it had turned into a race to the headland.

'They're nice boys,' Paul said. 'They seem like good friends.'

'They are,' she smiled.

The two of them sat on the sand and watched the boys galloping up the beach like healthy young colts. 'Why didn't you tell me, Henrietta?' he asked.

So he'd guessed, she supposed it was inevitable. 'It would have made life too difficult,' she said after a moment or so, 'for all of us. But I'm glad you know now.'

'So am I.' She couldn't possibly know how glad, he thought. Of course he understood why she hadn't told him at the time, her life would have been intolerable. But the knowledge that he and Henrietta had a son, albeit a son he could not claim as his own, filled Paul with indescribable happiness.

They held hands like young lovers, and looked out at the black clouds gathering over the sea. The light was sombre, more like dusk than day and, despite the impending storm, Henrietta thought that she had never before felt such a sense of peace.

'I'd like to get to know him if I may,' Paul said, 'just as a friend of course.'

'So you're staying in Darwin?' Her response was so joyful that Paul looked away. He was careful in his reply, he must not encourage any hope, she must not become dependent upon his friendship.

'For a while at least.'

He seemed wary, she thought, circumspect, even afraid. Why? Did he think she wanted to resume a torrid affair? 'Don't worry, my love,' she kept her tone light and humorous, 'I'm not going to ravish you, I promise.'

'Just as well,' he said with a touch of irony, 'that part of me doesn't really work anymore, in fact not much of me does.'

Henrietta's smile faded. Suddenly she noticed how old he looked. He was fifty-seven years of age but he could have been a man in his late sixties.

'Tell me about it,' she said.

'Not much to tell, really, they did what they could.' He didn't want to talk about the cancer, the endless operations and treatments. 'And now they don't think there's any point in going further. For which I'm extremely grateful,' he added with one of his wry grins, 'I'm lucky to be here, and seeing you makes it all worthwhile.'

Henrietta looked down at his hand, their fingers entwined, remembering how, all those years ago, that hand had been her lifeline. And now he was dying.

'How long do they say?' she whispered.

'Oh Henrietta, my darling girl.' She looked so sick with concern, he hadn't wanted it to be that way. He took her face in his hands and kissed her. 'It could be a year, it could be two,' he said as their lips parted and he stroked her hair, 'I didn't want to make you unhappy, I just wanted to see you.'

He grinned to lighten the moment, and the boyishness of his smile lit up his haggard face. 'And now there's Kit as well. If I can see you both, just now and then, between the two of you, who knows, you might keep me hanging around for years.'

Henrietta returned his smile, forcing back the tears

which threatened, knowing it was not what he wanted. 'Between the two of us we'll try,' she said.

A bolt of lightning streaked across the horizon illuminating the world in the split second of its brilliance. They jumped to their feet.

'Malcolm! Kit!' she called. And in the distance the boys started running towards them.

The thunder roared, more lightning cracked, and then the rain started, a torrential downpour. The tropical storm had hit in seconds, as it always did in the Territory, and by the time the boys had joined them, all four were drenched.

'Let's get wet!' Henrietta yelled above the thunder, although it was impossible for them to get any wetter. And she stood with her arms outstretched, her eyes closed, and her face upturned to the deluge. The boys imitated her, they weren't normally encouraged to stand out in the rain and it was a good game as far as they were concerned.

Paul looked at the three of them. Oh God he was glad he'd come home. For this was his home, he realised. Darwin and the drama of her seasons, how he'd missed it, Europe had nothing to compare. He took off his Panama hat, closed his eyes and bent his head back to the sky. The four of them stood like that for a full minute or so, unafraid of nature's wrath which roared about them, their faces turned to the rain.

'Malcolm, Kit, time to go home.' Henrietta yelled. Suddenly aware of her motherly duties, she thought it was time to call a halt to the fun.

'Oh Mum . . .' they both whinged, they could have stood there forever.

'Time to go home,' she repeated. She looked at Paul, the two of them could have stood there forever too. 'You're at the Hotel Darwin.' It wasn't a question.

'Of course,' he shouted back.

'I'll ring you! Come on boys!' And they belted for the car.

Paul watched them go. He stood there in the storm, drenched and bedraggled, for a good five minutes or so before he walked up the rise and back to his car. He hadn't felt this happy in a very long time.

CHAPTER SIXTEEN

*L*ucretia watched, hollow-eyed, from the far end of
the table as he strutted about in his scarlet tunic, his
silk stockings and garters of lace. She recognised,
vaguely, that the tunic was Pelsaert's.

In his grand tent, Jeronimus Cornelisz was holding
court. A number of his men were present, including the
handsome young cadet, Coenraat van Huyssen.

Cornelisz unlocked the heavy wooden casket which sat
in the middle of the table, threw back the lid with a grand
flourish and stood aside in order that the riches within
might be admired. He himself never tired of caressing the
treasures, buffing the jewels with a fine silk cloth, holding
them up to the light. His favourite was the great cameo of
onyx, one of the largest in the world, Pelsaert had once
told him. Carved for the Roman Emperor Constantine in
the fourth century AD, and intended for the Indian
Emperor Jahangir.

'Now it is ours!' Cornelisz would proclaim to his
friends, but he really meant 'it is mine'.

Lucretia continued to watch dully from the sidelines.
The jewels were of no interest to her, nothing was of any
interest to her, except the mere matter of survival. These

were times when the only task at hand was how to exist
from one day to the next.

She had momentarily wondered at the presence of the
predikant. Gijsbert Bastiaensz was a weak man who could
serve no purpose to Cornelisz, and yet the predikant
appeared to be the guest of honour. Then she realised of
course that it was all part of the game. The predikant had
been invited along with his eldest daughter, not his wife,
nor his other five children, just pretty young Judick. And
Judick had recently become 'betrothed' to van Huyssen.
Was poor old Gijsbert being feted as the father of the
'bride', Lucretia wondered. It was a mockery in the eyes of
God, but it was a mockery which God Himself would
surely forgive, for the playing of such a blasphemous game
would no doubt save Judick's life.

The murders were becoming more blatant now. At first
people had simply disappeared. They'd gone to the High
Islands, the community had been told, in search of water,
or to Seals' Island to join the settlement there. And they'd
chosen to believe Cornelisz and his men; after all, it meant
more space and more provisions for those who remained.
But they could no longer close their eyes to the truth.
Remains of bodies fed to the sharks had been washed up
on the shore. The more handsome of the women, several
married, whose husbands had disappeared, were servicing
Cornelisz's men in order to stay alive.

The mock betrothal of Judick to the vile van Huyssen
mirrored Lucretia's own predicament. Jeronimus Cornelisz was wooing her. Like a suitor paying court, he called
upon her daily, and several times he had invited her to his
tent. Fearful for her life, she had attended and sat silently
witnessing such scenes as this. And after the jewels had
been admired, and they'd all eaten and drunk and the
others had departed, he would read poetry to her in Latin
and French and ply her with fine Spanish wine. He would
even offer her a jewel from the Company casket in his

efforts to seduce her. But, silent, repulsed, Lucretia had withstood his advances. Perhaps if he had held a knife to her throat she might have succumbed, she did not wish to die. But he didn't threaten her. He behaved like a frustrated admirer and allowed her to return to her tent unscathed. Lucretia wondered how much longer it would be before he tired of the game.

A man appeared at the tent opening, Cornelisz gave him a brief nod, and he disappeared. Lucretia observed the interchange, in her detached state little escaped her notice. The man was Davdt Zeevanck, Cornelisz's closest confidant and a ruthless killer. She wondered who it was they were going to murder tonight.

'Predikant Bastiaensz,' Cornelisz said with gusto, raising his glass, 'I drink a toast to your beautiful daughter and my young friend Coenraat.'

The assembled company followed suit, Gijsbert Bastiaensz accepting the toast as if it were a personal salutation and reciprocating with a vote of thanks to Cornelisz. How flattering to be so feted, he thought with an eye to the food which lay in wait, they didn't eat like this in his tent. The fear having momentarily left him, the predikant was pompous, jovial, and pathetic in his vanity.

Cornelisz gestured to his lackeys for the feast to be brought to the table.

Wybrecht Claes, young serving maid to the predikant and his family, answered the soft call from outside the tent. Her throat was slit in an instant and the five men stood and watched silently as she lay twitching on the ground. When death had clouded the terror in her eyes, they raised their adzes above their heads and stormed into the tent.

Cornelisz, in ordering the dispatch of the predikant's family, had himself suggested that adzes would be the most effective weapons in close and crowded quarters. 'Several

*can be felled with one blow,' he'd said, wishing he could
be present to witness the slaughter.*

Maria Bastiaensz, her three sons and two daughters, sat
eating their meagre meal in the light of a single lamp. A
man swung his adze, the lamp shattered and, in the near
darkness, the men set about their grisly task. The eldest
son, eighteen years of age, was the first to die, his skull
smashed in one blow. Then the men went into a frenzy,
swinging their deadly adzes in every direction.

The infant, Roelant, nearly made good his bid to escape.
Running between the knees of the murderers, he was at the
door of the tent when his silhouette was spied in the dim
light of the moon which issued from outside, and he was
felled by one of the men with a back-handed blow. The
child's skull shattered like a young melon, and all was
silent.

The bodies were dragged from the tent to a shallow
grave which had been dug in preparation, and there they
were unceremoniously dumped and covered in a thin layer
of dirt. The disposal of bodies was becoming more and
more slovenly, the murderers by now fearing no reprisals.

In Cornelisz's tent, the party continued. The men, having
gorged themselves, continued to guzzle from their
tumblers, wine running down sodden beards and dripping
to the ground. Led by Cornelisz, they were now singing.
The predikant was drunk, and his daughter Judick was
sitting in a corner with her young cadet, smiling as van
Huyssen whispered in her ear.

Lucretia watched them. They looked for all the world
like a young couple in love, she thought, sickened. Was the
girl deliberately blinding herself to the fact that her
handsome young man was the most bestial of murderers,
guilty of the foulest deeds beyond all imagining?

Cornelisz, who was in turn watching Lucretia, stopped
singing. The others continuing without him, he sidled up

to her unnoticed, bent and whispered in her ear. 'Young love is a beautiful thing, is it not?'

She jumped, startled, then quickly regained her composure. She made no reply, nor did she look at him.

'You haven't touched your wine, is it not to your palate?' Still she made no reply. 'Look at me, Lucretia,' he commanded, and she knew that she must.

He smiled as her eyes met his. 'I said, do you not like the wine?' he repeated gently.

She picked up the glass and took a sip. 'The wine is excellent,' she said obediently. Did he think he could beguile her with the smile of Satan? She did not flinch, sitting proudly at the table, her back ramrod straight, but inwardly she recoiled at the evil before her.

'You must stay and have a drink with me after they've gone,' he whispered.

'As you wish.' Yet again he would press his suit, she knew it, and yet again she would refuse him, wondering if this would be the night he would force her to his bed at knifepoint.

Cornelisz soon tired of the revelry, he wanted Lucretia to himself. Perhaps tonight would be the night he would win her. Abruptly, he ordered everyone to leave.

'My dear,' he said when they'd departed, 'have more wine.' He sat beside her and filled her empty glass, she had surreptitiously tipped its contents onto the ground as she always did. Then he sang to her softly, one of his favourite French ballads set to music, she had heard it a number of times before. 'Did you like that?' he whispered, his mouth so close to her ear she could feel his breath.

'It is a beautiful verse,' she replied. How dare a voice so vile profane words of such beauty.

'Lucretia,' he murmured. Her loveliness, the very sound of her voice, filled him with desire. 'Lucretia, my dear,' he raised her hand to his lips and kissed it. She suffered the caress in silence. Emboldened, Cornelisz leaned towards her, his breath *fanning her face, his mouth bent upon seeking hers.*

Lucretia rose from the table. 'I have told you before, I am married.' She could never bring herself to call him by name, much as he insisted she do so. 'I cannot commit adultery.'

Thwarted once again, frustrated beyond endurance, Cornelisz leaped to his feet. 'A kiss, woman!' he snarled. 'Jesu, just a kiss!'

She stood her ground. Was tonight the night he would kill her, or at least threaten to do so? And if he did, would she have the strength to die? 'A kiss is an act of adultery,' she said, and she added, 'I beseech you to accept my refusal.' No, she did not want to die.

A harrowing cry rang out through the night. 'Oh horror of horrors!' It was the predikant's voice. 'What cruelty!' he wailed. 'Oh horror of horrors!' And he fell into a fit of sobbing which echoed about the island.

Lucretia felt the blood drain from her face. So that was why the predikant and his daughter had been invited to the grand tent. She stared dumbly at Cornelisz who smiled as he stared back at her. Perhaps now, he thought, the knowledge of his power might force her to succumb.

Lucretia turned and stumbled from the tent.

Early the following evening, she received a visit from Davdt Zeevanck, the man with whom Cornelisz shared his innermost confidences.

'I hear complaints about you, Vrouwe van den Mylen,' Zeevanck said with a voice like ice. 'You do not comply with our Captain's wishes.' Cornelisz had long assumed the rank of captain with his men, and of late the entire community had considered it safer to address him as such. 'In his generosity,' Zeevanck continued, 'the Captain begs for your kindness, and yet you disobey him.'

Zeevanck himself was bewildered as to why Cornelisz had not taken the haughty bitch by force. 'Stick a dagger at her throat and she's yours, Jeronimus,' he'd said. But for twelve *days Cornelisz had wooed the woman like a lovesick school-boy. For twelve whole days she'd withstood his advances. Why, yet again, just this morning, he had said, most unhappily, 'Still she resists me, Davdt, what am I to do?'*

Zeevanck refused to allow such behaviour to continue, it undermined his Captain's authority. 'Leave it to me, Jeronimus,' he'd said. 'Tonight you shall have her.'

'You must make up your mind, Vrouwe van den Mylen,' he said, 'either you must do that for which we have kept the women, or you will go the way of the others.'

Lucretia had seen the shallow grave of the Bastiaensz family, the bloodied remnants visible beneath the scattering of earth. And she had seen the blood-drenched tent where the slaughter had taken place, the horror of it all was etched in her brain.

'The decision is yours,' Zeevanck said. The woman did not reply and he took her silence as acquiescence. He walked to the door of the tent and turned. 'I shall be back in one hour to escort you to your Captain.'

When he'd gone, Lucretia knelt and prayed. She did not question her strength to resist, she knew she had none. She prayed that God might take her quietly during the night, that when she had been defiled by the Devil, she might die. But she did not have the strength to offer herself up for a bloody death at the hands of the murderers, may God forgive her. She would do what she must to avoid becoming one of the corpses of Batavia's Graveyard.

She unfastened the locket from around her neck. When Cornelisz saw her in her nakedness he would surely take it from her. She made a pocket amongst the lining of her skirts and, as she kissed the symbol of her love, the mountain peak and the diamond sun, she wondered, if she were ever to survive, how she could allow her husband to touch her body which had been so defiled. Carefully she concealed the locket amongst her skirts, and awaited the return of Zeevanck.

CHAPTER SEVENTEEN

Henrietta saw Paul several times a week. After she'd dropped the boys at school, she'd spend the day with him and they'd walk along the clifftops, or take a picnic lunch to Mindil Beach. Sometimes they talked avidly, Paul regaling her with wicked and colourful stories of his past until Henrietta was hysterical with laughter. Or she would recount to him the latest mischief the boys had got up to. Paul took a keen interest in both children. He was always eager for news not only of his son Kit, which was to be expected, but also of Malcolm, about whom he appeared equally concerned.

Sometimes they felt no need to talk at all, and they would hold hands and look out at the sea, both overwhelmed with a sense of peace and contentment, and they would whisper their love for each other before they parted and she collected the boys from school.

From the outset she'd told Terence as much as she felt he needed to know. 'Paul Trewinnard is back in Darwin,' she'd announced. 'I'm going to spend the day in town with him every now and then.'

Terence's eyes narrowed. She was not asking his permission, she was telling him. 'Why in God's name?'

'Because he's my friend and he's dying.'

There wasn't much Terence could say to that. But when the visits became too regular for his liking, he decided it was time to check out his wife's story.

'I might come into town with you this morning,' he said casually one day, studying her reaction. 'Perhaps I could have lunch with you and your friend Paul?'

She ignored the sarcasm in his tone. 'Of course,' she said, 'I'm sure he'd be delighted to see you.'

Paul was indeed very interested in seeing Terence, and he insisted upon taking them to lunch at the Hotel Darwin. 'You're on my home turf,' he said with a smile, and throughout the meal he asked Terence questions about the homestead and the boys, encouraging the man to talk, and apparently enjoying the conversation.

Terence was relaxed and expansive over lunch, any misgivings he'd had having dissipated the moment he'd laid eyes on Paul Trewinnard. The man was a skeleton with one foot in the grave, he looked about seventy.

Paul could clearly see the bully beneath Terence's charm. And the man was as arrogant and self-opinionated as he'd always been, it was evident in his every gesture, even in the way he ordered a beer. Normally scathing of such men, Paul took great care to disguise his dislike; Terence Galloway was a violent and unpredictable man who could make Henrietta's life hell if he chose. He already had. Once anyway.

Paul would never forget Henrietta's distress all those years ago when she'd come to the hotel to seek his help. They often talked of their night together, the wonderful night when they'd discovered each other, but she had never told him what had happened that afternoon. It was the one thing she never spoke of and, until she felt the desire to do so, he had resolved never to ask her.

Now, as Paul looked at Terence, all he could see was the bruise upon Henrietta's cheek and her hands shaking uncontrollably as they clutched his own. He despised Terence Galloway.

'Really?' He laughed dutifully at the anecdote about Malcolm demanding his meat rare. 'Just cut off its horns and wipe its arse,' the boy had apparently said.

'Yes, he's a chip off the old block, that boy. It's become a bit of a family joke, you see, father to son,' Terence said with happy pride. 'For generations now. Can't wait to hear Malcolm's boy follow suit.'

Poor Malcolm, Paul thought, and poor Malcolm's boy. He didn't dare look at Henrietta for fear his smile might be readably intimate. He'd heard the joke before, she'd actually told it in defence of Terence. 'He's been indoctrinated,' she'd said. 'Old Jock did it to him, now he's doing it to his sons, what hope does any poor Galloway kid have?' and she'd said it with such ironic humour that he'd laughed out loud.

Lunch was a great success. 'We must do it again, Paul,' Terence said as the two of them shook hands. 'You must come out to Bullalalla.' If you live long enough, you poor bastard, he thought.

'Thank you, I'd love to.'

'Christ, he looks as if he's going to drop dead any minute,' Terence said as they drove to the school to pick up Malcolm and Kit.

'Please don't say that in front of the boys.'

'Why the hell not?'

'Because they like Paul, and they don't know he's dying.' God he could be so insensitive. 'And they don't need to know either.'

'All right, all right.'

Sometimes Henrietta and Paul would take Aggie for a drive during her lunchbreak. But, much as they both loved Aggie, it was out of a sense of duty, loath as they were to relinquish one moment of their time together.

Sometimes Aggie would hiss to Henrietta when Paul

was out of earshot, 'He looks terrible, what can we do?'

'Nothing,' Henrietta would reply. 'Let him handle things his way, that's what he wants.' She hated being reminded that Paul's days were numbered. She thought he was looking much better herself, he was rallying, she was sure.

Paul agreed. He hadn't felt this alive in years, she was the best medicine in the world, he told her. And perhaps he was right. A full year had passed with little apparent deterioration in his condition. He certainly looked the same, no better, no worse, and if the daily task of living was becoming just that little bit harder, then no-one but Paul knew. Well, no-one but Paul and his old friend, Foong Lee.

On the times when his medication did little to control the pain, Paul visited Foong Lee who, finally, approved of the opium pipe.

'On very rare occasions it can serve its purpose, I agree,' he said to Paul and, through one of his many contacts, he arranged a moderate but regular supply. 'No more than is necessary,' he insisted. He even set aside the small downstairs den as Paul's special room.

'My home is yours, Paul,' he said. The fact was, Foong Lee wanted to oversee Paul's use of the drug. He did not wish his dear friend to spend the last precious months of his life in an addled state, not when he was as happy as he was. For, despite the pain, Foong Lee had never seen Paul Trewinnard so happy. Gone were the cynicism and discontent, to be replaced by an inner peace, and it was all because of Henrietta Galloway.

Paul had told Foong Lee everything, relying upon the man's innate discretion, and Foong Lee was glad for his friend. The time would come when Paul would need to give in to his pain, and Foong Lee would be there to help him. In the meantime, every minute which belonged to Paul and Henrietta must be preserved. So Foong Lee monitored Paul's use of opium.

On Kit's tenth birthday Terence fetched the Browning semi-automatic .22 rifle, lessons were to begin in earnest. The boy had already been taught to handle an unloaded rifle, how to hold it and sight his target, now it was time for shooting practice.

Henrietta was exasperated. Surely it could wait until tomorrow, she thought. Surely the boy should be allowed to celebrate his birthday without having lessons forced upon him. Besides, it was a long weekend and Malcolm had come home from boarding school; he'd been in Adelaide for the past three months. Nellie had baked a cake and they were to have a special dinner. Jackie had even come home from the muster that morning to give the boy a present he'd made—he and Kit were firm friends.

Jackie's gift was a woomera which he'd carved from rainbow tree wood and he gave it to Kit on the front verandah, with the family gathered around.

Kit was deeply impressed. 'Hey, look Malcolm,' he said, examining the design which was ornately carved into the heavy reddish wood. It was the work of a craftsman. 'Gee,' he said in breathless admiration.

'I teach 'im throw spear good,' Jackie said to Henrietta, proud of the reception his gift had received.

'Not until he's proficient with a rifle,' Terence replied rather tightly, and that's when he'd fetched the .22. 'Just an hour's practice, that's all,' he said in answer to Henrietta's remonstrations. 'There'll be plenty of time to have a party and eat cake. Put the woomera down, son.'

Kit reluctantly left the woomera on the verandah and went with his father and brother to the horse yard by the stables where Terence lined the tin cans up on the far railing.

He hadn't expected his youngest son to show much proficiency, Kit seemed inferior to Malcolm in every way, but as the barrel of the gun flailed about in the air, Terence couldn't help feeling an intense irritation. The boy was useless.

'Keep it steady, boy, keep it steady,' he snapped.

Malcolm watched warily from the sidelines. He was nervous for his brother, if Kit made Dad angry he'd cop it for sure. He kept his fingers crossed, hoping Kit would get his eye in.

But the rifle was too cumbersome for Kit, it seemed a dead weight in his hands and, as he tried to concentrate on the sights, the barrel swayed about all over the place.

'Can I try it on the railing, Dad?' he asked. And Terence gave a taciturn nod.

Kit rested the barrel on the pole and focussed on the tins sitting atop the railings on the other side. The first tin was lined up in the rifle's sights, he fired. It flew up into the air. He set his sights on the next one, steady as a rock. The rifle shot cracked and the second tin spun into the air. And the next. And the next. He took his time.

Terence watched in astonishment. The boy had an amazing eye, he was a natural, who would have thought it?

Malcolm watched, equally astonished, his nervousness having turned to envy. He couldn't shoot like that when he'd started. Hell, he couldn't shoot like that now and he'd been practising for nearly three years.

'Good on you, son, well done,' Terence said.

They were the words Malcolm always longed to hear, he had devoted his entire young life to earning those words from his father, and he couldn't help feeling a stab of jealousy.

Kit too was surprised. Not only at the unaccustomed praise from his father, but at his own ability. He was going to enjoy target practice.

'You'll have to learn how to shoot without using the railings, though,' Terence said.

'Okay, Dad.' Kit was only too willing to try. 'What a beaut birthday, eh?' he said to Malcolm as they started walking back to the house.

'Yeah.' Malcolm tried to return Kit's grin, he didn't want to spoil his brother's day, but he could feel one of his moods coming on. He'd be back at boarding school next week. Not that he minded boarding school, he was one of the top footy players in his year and it made him a bit of a hero. But he hoped Kit's marksmanship wouldn't mean that, in his absence, his younger brother would become Dad's favourite.

A month after Malcolm had returned to Adelaide, Kit had his first 'live practice'.

'One of those galahs,' Terence said, pointing to the two pink-breasted Major Mitchells which sat close together on the branch of a lemon-scented gum.

They'd ridden several miles from the house and were in bushland. 'Live practice,' his father had announced when they'd tethered their horses, and Kit hadn't been quite sure what that meant. Shooting targets out in the bush, he'd presumed, and no railing for a support. That was okay, he'd mastered the rifle now, practising for hours with the unloaded .22, placing his weight, positioning himself, it was all a matter of balance, he'd discovered.

Now, having loaded the rifle and handed it to him, his father was pointing at the birds and Kit realised he was supposed to shoot one of them. Like Malcolm used to do before he'd gone off to boarding school. Malcolm had often come home boasting about the number of birds he'd shot, and Kit had never understood why. He didn't want to shoot birds, he liked birds. Besides, the Major Mitchells were a pair, what would the other one do without its mate?

'Can't we go back to the tin cans, Dad?' he asked hopefully.

But Terence wasn't listening. 'Come on, line them up, you might even get both of them if you're quick.'

Kit raised the rifle to his shoulder and sighted on the galah to the left. The stock felt perfectly balanced against his shoulder, his feet were firmly positioned, his torso balanced, it was an easy shot. But the birds were happily nuzzling each other and he didn't want to kill them. He waved the barrel a little, as if he'd lost the centre of his balance, and pressed the trigger. The shot rang out and, with an indignant screech, the galahs took off.

'Not to worry,' Terence was prepared to be patient, it was the boy's first time, 'you'll get the hang of it.'

They walked a little further into the bush and Terence told him to aim at a large black crow which sat patiently in a tree, a perfect target as it signalled to its mate with its plaintive cry. The same thing happened, the rifle barrel wavered, the bullet widely missed its mark and the crow flew off.

They tried several more times and Terence was becoming impatient. He took the rifle from his son and aimed it at a flock of large white birds which were roosting in a cedar. They were hanging upside down from its branches and screeching and playing the fool, the way only cockatoos could; the cedar looked like a Christmas tree decorated with fake snow. 'Now watch,' he said. He chose his target amongst the flock, 'Take your time, you see, easy does it,' then he fired.

The cockatoo dropped to the ground like a stone. Kit walked over to where it lay. He loved the sulphur-crested cockatoos, they were the larrikins of the bush, they made him laugh. He looked down at the carcass of the bird, dead but still quivering. What a waste, he thought, you couldn't eat it.

His father joined him. 'Right, now you try,' he said handing the rifle to Kit. 'We'll set up a railing for you, if you like.' That'll give the boy confidence he thought as he looked around for suitable logs and branches, he just needs to get his first shot in, that's all.

But Kit remained looking down at the bird. Terence noticed his distraction. Christ alive, he thought, surely the boy wasn't upset because a bird had been shot. He tried to curb his impatience.

'They're as bad as vermin in some parts,' he said. 'They have to be destroyed, they can put whole orchards out of business.'

'We don't have orchards.'

Terence looked sharply at his son, was the boy answering him back? He'd take no cheek, he'd belt the kid.

But the boy's clear grey eyes held no hint of mischief, he was genuinely puzzled as to why they should kill birds which were harmless. 'I'd shoot a dingo,' he said, trying his hardest to be helpful. Dingoes killed the chooks, Kit knew that, and they could even cause trouble in the calving season if a calf was stranded and sickly.

'You'll shoot whatever I tell you to shoot, boy.'

Kit looked down at the bird, then back at his father. He was too frightened to say the words out loud, but he couldn't kill unless it was necessary, something told him that he wouldn't be able to do it.

The words were not required, his eyes said it all, and anger surged through Terence. How dare the boy defy him. With the back of his hand he struck his son across the face with all the force he could muster.

Kit fell sprawling on his back. For a moment he lay still and Terence was shocked to his senses. Jesus, had he killed the boy?

Then, groggily, Kit raised his head. The world was spinning and there were dots in front of his eyes.

'Can you stand?' his father asked.

He nodded and slowly hauled himself to his feet, staggering a little as he did so.

Terence was relieved, but he offered no help. The boy was all right and it was a lesson learned. 'Get your horse,' he said, 'we're going home.'

When they got back to Bullalalla, Henrietta was concerned to see a cut on Kit's arm and there appeared to be a graze on the right side of his face.

'What on earth happened?' she asked as she inspected the arm.

'I came off,' he said, noticing the cut for the first time, he must have hit a rock when he fell.

Kit's answer came automatically, it was simpler to say he'd fallen from his horse. Besides, if he told his mother the truth, he might cop it from Dad again.

Terence heard the lie and was thankful. He would defend to the death his right to strike his son, the boy was wilful and disobedient. But if Henrietta were to disagree with his form of discipline, he knew it would bring on a fit of rage and he tried to avoid that whenever possible. He knew that, if he were ever to hit Henrietta again, she would leave him.

'Are you all right now?'

It was night. Kit was in bed, reading. Terence had been momentarily irritated, the boy always seemed to have his head in a book. And Kit, in turn, had frozen at the sight of his father silhouetted in the open door. The boy nodded.

Terence sat on the bed, he could see the fear on his son's face. Perhaps it was a good thing that he'd instilled fear in the boy, but he hadn't meant to hit him quite so hard.

'That need not happen again, Kit,' he said, 'if you do as you're told.' Why did those unwavering grey eyes so unnerve him, Terence thought. The boy was frightened and yet he met his gaze, was it defiance? 'We won't shoot birds anymore,' he said, not knowing quite why he said it.

'Thanks, Dad.' Kit replied gratefully. He had a feeling that in a strange way his father was saying he was sorry.

Damn his hide, Terence thought, the boy sounded as if he was accepting an apology. 'But we'll find a live target that you approve of,' he said with a touch of sarcasm as he rose. 'It's time you learned how to kill.'

Terence had to rethink his assessment of his younger

son. Kit was not a coward as he'd originally suspected, but he was wilful. Terence was grateful for the difference. Bravery could not be instilled in a coward, but discipline could be instilled in a wilful child. The boy would learn obedience.

The following weekend was the killing of the steers. Kit no longer found the process repugnant as he had at the age of six when he'd first been called upon to witness the slaughter. To the contrary, he appeared to find the efficiency of the exercise rather interesting and he would watch admiringly as the stockmen butchered the carcasses. But Terence decided that it was the killing of the steers which would present the ultimate test. One the boy would fail, and it would teach him a lesson.

The morning of the slaughter, he made the announcement. 'You'll kill one of the steers today.'

They were alone on the verandah, Terence had made sure of it, he would brook no argument from Henrietta.

Kit looked bewildered. Malcolm had never killed a steer. But then Malcolm had killed birds. He suddenly realised that this was his punishment. He thought about it for a second. The steer had to be shot anyway, it was food. And if he killed the steer it'd make Dad happy, and then maybe he could go back to taking shots at tin cans, he liked that.

'Okay Dad,' he said, aiming for a touch of bravado, trying to sound like Malcolm. I bet Malcolm'd love to shoot a steer, he thought.

'Slaughter yards in an hour,' his father said, 'Jackie and the boys should be back by then.'

And Kit was left on his own, suddenly fearful at the prospect. What if he missed the vital spot? What if the steer died in agony? He was thankful that Jackie was home this weekend. Jackie'd help him, he'd tell him what to do.

An hour later, he reported to the slaughter yards with his .22. His father was nowhere in sight, and Kit waited there patiently until, a half an hour later, Jackie and the boys arrived, herding the steers. It was only then Terence appeared. He gave Jackie a nod, said nothing to Kit, and stood at the far end of the yard silently watching.

'G'day, Kit,' Jackie called, and Kit waved back. His heart was thumping wildly and he hoped no-one could tell how scared he was.

The first steer was positioned for the kill, its neck rope looped around the pole, its head held firmly in position. The man on the pulley was standing by, and Jackie mounted the railings with his .303.

'Give the gun to Kit, Jackie,' Terence called.

'Sorry, boss?' Jackie yelled back across the yard above the bellow of the terrified steer. He must have heard wrong.

'I said give your rifle to Kit,' Terence shouted, 'Kit's going to kill the first steer today.'

Jackie stared at the boss, was he joking? But the boss didn't make jokes. The other two Aboriginal stockmen exchanged glances. Jackie looked at Kit, who was walking towards him, clutching his .22, ashen-faced with fear. The boss wasn't joking.

'I've never shot a .303,' Kit said quietly to Jackie, trying to keep his voice steady.

'.22 okay.' Jackie leaned his .303 up against the railing and gave Kit a confident grin. 'You be okay, Kit, you shoot real good.' The boy did too, Jackie had seen him shooting tin cans. And a bullet through a steer's skull was a lot easier than shooting tin cans at thirty paces. But the boy was frightened. It didn't seem fair to Jackie that the boy should have to do something which made him frightened. Leaning over the railings, Jackie pressed his gnarled black thumb against the animal's skull. 'You get 'im here,' he said. 'You get 'im here, 'im feel no pain.'

Kit nodded, swallowing nervously, and Jackie held the .22 as he climbed the railings to sit on top, the steer's head directly below him. When the boy was in position, Jackie handed him the rifle.

'I told you to give him the .303!' From the far end of the yard Terence's command was loud and clear.

'.22 okay boss,' Jackie called back. Was the boss crazy? Kit had never shot a .303, and he was little. A .303 kicked like a mule, it could break the boy's shoulder. '.22 just as good,' he called.

'I said give him the .303.'

The boss sounded angry, Jackie knew he had no option. He cocked the .303 and exchanged rifles with Kit, but he held on to the .22. If the boy made a mess of things, and he probably would, then Jackie would finish the beast off quickly.

'You hold 'im hard,' he said to Kit, patting the stock of the rifle, 'you hold 'im *real* hard, .303 'im can hurt.'

Kit dug the stock into his shoulder as hard as he could, feeling Jackie's hand firm against his back, bracing him. The gun was a dead weight in his hands, but he steadied himself, his stomach muscles tightening as he took aim at the steer's head, the muzzle only inches away from the creature's skull. He didn't feel frightened anymore as he concentrated on the spot where Jackie had rested his thumb. Very gently, he curled his finger around the trigger.

Terence knew what would happen. The rifle was too heavy for the boy, the barrel would waver and he'd miss. He'd shoot the animal through its eye or its ear and he'd cop a sore shoulder in the process. It'd teach the boy a lesson. After today Kit'd be begging to shoot birds with his .22.

Through his sights, Kit could see the imprint of Jackie's thumb, or at least he told himself he could. But the barrel was starting to sway, only slightly but enough, he couldn't seem to hold the weight of the rifle steady. He leaned forwards and placed the muzzle directly against the animal's skull, knowing as he did so that the stock was not firmly positioned into the crook of his arm. Too bad, he thought, and he pulled the trigger.

The gun roared, the steer dropped to the ground, and Kit was thrown backwards, a searing pain in his shoulder.

Jackie held on to him, breaking his fall, and the next thing Kit knew he was sitting on the ground, his shoulder aching like hell. In a matter of seconds, Jackie had leapt over the railings and slit the steer's throat and, by the time Kit looked up, a little dizzily, the animal was hanging in the air by its hind legs, well and truly dead.

'You okay Kit?' Jackie climbed back through the railings and squatted beside the boy, pulling aside his shirt and inspecting his shoulder. It appeared nothing was broken.

'Yep,' Kit said and he struggled to his feet. Jeez it hurt.

Jackie gave the broadest of grins. 'You kill 'im good, eh?' Then he yelled to Terence. 'He kill 'im good, eh boss?'

'Yes,' Terence called back, although he didn't appear too happy about it. 'Well done.' And he walked away. He didn't bother examining his son's shoulder, if there was any real damage Jackie would have reported it.

Kit watched his father walk off, he'd expected a 'good on you, son', maybe even a handshake, like his Dad did to Malcolm when he'd passed a test. But Jackie and his two mates gave him a round of applause and slapped him on the back which, although not helping the shoulder, did wonders for Kit's morale. He was a hero to them at least.

That night, at the dinner table, Kit couldn't raise his right arm. It hurt too much to try, so he left it dangling by his side and speared his food with his fork, left-handed.

'What's the matter with your arm?' Henrietta asked and, without waiting for an answer, she was by his side opening his shirt. 'My God, look at your shoulder! How did it happen?'

'Kit shot the steer,' Nellie said, delivering a fresh jug of gravy. 'Jackie said he done real good.'

'Kit did what?' Henrietta directed the question at her

husband, but it was Nellie who once again answered.

'He shot the steer,' she said proudly. 'With a .303, what's more. Big gun for a little boy, Jackie said. You done real good, Kit.'

Kit smiled at Nellie, enjoying the praise, but a bit worried that his mum looked cranky. He hoped there wasn't going to be a blue. Although his parents argued rarely, when there *was* any form of disagreement, Kit could sense a tension between them which unnerved him.

Henrietta insisted on examining the shoulder there and then. It was already swollen and discoloured. 'You're lucky it wasn't dislocated, or even broken,' she said. She didn't dare look at Terence, who continued to eat his meal, refusing to be unsettled by what he saw as Henrietta's overreaction.

'We'll put some liniment on it after dinner,' she said, determined not to cause a scene in front of either Nellie or Kit. 'You're going to have one hell of a sore shoulder for a while.'

'Yep,' Kit said happily. That's good, he thought, there wasn't going to be a blue after all.

When she'd dressed the shoulder she sent Kit to bed, although he didn't want to go. 'If you're not tired you can read a book,' she said, 'now do as you're told, Kit.'

'Okay.' she was a bit crabby tonight, he thought.

Whilst Nellie did the washing up, Henrietta fronted Terence in his study. 'This will stop as of today,' she said, the anger she'd kept under control throughout dinner threatening to break out at any minute.

'What?'

'These ridiculous tests you keep setting for Kit. He doesn't like them and they're not healthy.'

'What do you mean? The boy has to grow up, it comes with the territory.' Terence gave a derisive snort. 'Jesus Christ, he shot the steer today without a qualm, and he can't bring himself to shoot a bird, I don't know what's the matter with the kid.'

'He's not a chip off the old block, that's what's the matter with the kid!' She spat the words at him, Henrietta was as angry as she had ever been in her life.

Her anger so took him by surprise that Terence stared at her in bewilderment. What the hell was she talking about?

Henrietta fought to control her rage. She must try to make him see sense, angering him would serve no purpose. 'Terence,' she said, keeping her voice as even as possible, 'Malcolm has spent his whole life trying to emulate you.'

'So? I tried to emulate my father . . .'

Exactly! she wanted to scream. *And look at you!*

'. . . what's wrong with that?'

Everything! 'Nothing, I suppose.' Dear God what was the point, she thought. 'But Kit is not Malcolm, he's different. He doesn't want to do the things Malcolm does.' She wanted to say 'half the time Malcolm doesn't want to do them either', but this was Kit's battle she was fighting now. 'You can't treat both boys the same.'

'Why not? They're my sons.'

'And they're *different*!' Henrietta felt frustrated beyond belief. 'Can't you see that, Terence? They're individuals. They're as different from each other as they could possibly be . . .'

'And do you know why they're different, Henrietta?' Terence rose from his desk, irritated. Her overreaction to the shooting of the steer, which he'd taken as a typically female response, was really annoying him now. 'They're different because Kit is your favourite.'

Henrietta stopped in her tracks. Shocked. That wasn't true. Was it?

'You mollycoddle that boy,' Terence said, gratified that his comment had obviously received the reaction he'd desired. 'He's not a Galloway, you've turned him into something else. Some Pommie hybrid who plays with stones and reads books and doesn't want to shoot birds.'

Terence was surprised at the impact of his accusation.

She appeared to actually believe him, he could see it in her face. Henrietta was a fine mother to both boys and yet he'd struck a chord. Good, he thought, it was easier to blame her for the fact that he didn't particularly like Kit. 'You want to watch it, Henrietta, you'll ruin that boy, he won't fit in. I'm going to get a drink.'

Terence left the room, pleased that he'd turned the conversation to his own advantage and proud of himself for not having lost his temper.

Henrietta stood for a moment, still shocked, trying to come to grips with his accusation. Was he right? Did she favour Kit? It had never once crossed her mind. Surely it wasn't true. She'd agonised over Malcolm and the pain the boy went through to earn his father's approval. In fact she'd worried far more about Malcolm than Kit, who seemed to have an inner strength which Malcolm lacked. But then she remembered those lonely years when Kit was a constant reminder of Paul. When she'd dreamed of Paul at night and woken to see him there in the face of his son. Had she unwittingly favoured Kit all this time? Henrietta was riddled with guilt.

CHAPTER EIGHTEEN

Jeronimus Cornelisz had now embarked upon an orgy of torture. There was no longer any reason to his killing. It was mid-July and he had culled the numbers on Batavia's Graveyard to such a degree that provisions were ample and none of the remaining men posed a threat to his reign. Several younger males had been spared and recruited, under pain of death, to join his band of cut-throats. Many of them VOC clerks unaccustomed to any form of violence, the young men were forced to perform murders themselves to prove their loyalty.

No threat was anticipated from any other quarter, Weibbe Hayes and his men were presumably dead as planned, no smoke signal having been sighted from the High Islands, and Cornelisz had sent a party to Seals' Island to dispatch the survivors there, most of whom had been already near death. He'd sent a further party to Traitor's Island to execute those who had attempted to escape the carnage, and now there was no-one left to kill. No-one whose death was necessary.

But the killing continued, and more important to Cornelisz than the killing itself was the torture which preceded the death of his victims. Jeronimus Cornelisz had decided that, if he was to languish in this desolate place until his own bones were bleached white by the merciless sun, then he would practise the teachings of Torrentius. This, his last period on earth, would be one of unprecedented sensual pleasure. During the daylight hours he would indulge his bloodlust in a way no normal society would permit, witnessing with profound interest the ultimate in human suffering. And at night he would relive these experiences whilst sating his sexual lust with his personal concubine.

As he caressed the silken skin of Lucretia van den Mylen, Cornelisz savoured the images of his men at play that same afternoon. How they'd blindfolded a boy, convincing the lad it was a game, then decapitated him and kicked his head about like a toy. The memory afforded Cornelisz an exquisite pleasure as he felt the womanliness of Lucretia's body beneath him.

Lucretia now lived with Cornelisz in his grand tent, and was required to service him whenever he wished. She was his personal property and no man was to communicate with her. Should any man attempt to do so, he would be signing his own death warrant, and ever since the savage murder of young Andries de Vries, who had been seen in conversation with Lucretia, most men averted their eyes in her presence.

Lucretia had given up praying for death. Perhaps God intended her to live for some purpose, but she no longer cared why. For weeks after the brutal killing of Andries de Vries, she had felt guilt over his death, adding further pain to her nightly defilement. She could not have prevented the boy's murder, just a boy he'd been, barely nineteen years old, but she could have shown some compassion. She could have helped relieve him a little in his torment. Instead she had been repulsed.

'They made me kill, Vrouwe van den Mylen,' he'd sobbed. 'Eleven sick people in the infirmary tent, they made me slit their throats with a knife.'

She and Andries had been friends in the early days aboard the Batavia *and, risking the wrath of Cornelisz, the youth had from time to time visited her in secret. Despite the fact that Lucretia was his elder by only nine years, he seemed to regard her as a mother figure and sought the comfort of her company. But that last day perhaps he sought her as a kind of confessor to absolve him of his sins.*

'And last night they made me go back,' he sobbed, 'to finish off the remaining sick.' The boy could not rid himself of the dreadful eyes staring at him, reproachful in death, women and children and men weak from their illness. 'They said they would kill me if I did not do their bidding.'

But Lucretia had been unable to absolve him, just as she'd been unable to disguise her revulsion. 'Andries,' she'd said, 'I cannot believe it of you.' And when Andries had left, doubly tormented, a spy had reported his visit to Cornelisz and the boy was then set upon by three men with swords and hacked to death.

Lucretia now knew that far more vile acts were being perpetrated. Perhaps Andries' speedy execution of those ill people, no doubt destined for a lingering death, had been merciful. Perhaps he had been doing God's will somehow, albeit upon the instructions of Cornelisz. She wished she could have told him so.

These days Lucretia no longer tortured herself with guilt, what was the purpose, there was nothing she could do. She led a solitary existence, passing gaunt-faced and sunken-eyed amongst the others, speaking to no-one. Each afternoon, by way of exercise, she would wander through the tents to the far end of the island and there she would pace along the shore looking out to sea, ignoring the misery behind her, seeing nothing but the vastness of the ocean, her mind a blank; she'd trained herself to keep it that way. She no longer thought of Boudewijn, and she no longer caressed the locket hidden in the lining of her skirts. She often felt for its outline to make sure it was safe, but she no longer gazed upon it, nor did she trace with her fingers the contours of its engraving. There was nothing to be gained by dwelling on the past, and there was no point in contemplating the future.

Finally, she would return to the tent and prepare herself for Cornelisz's demands, closing her ears to the stories of horror she occasionally overheard along the way. She could not afford to know what was being relived in Cornelisz's mind, for she knew that he revelled in his atrocities as he drove himself into her body. She could tell by the brutality of their intercourse, and by the madness of his ecstasy. She avoided looking at the demon's eyes, tightly closing her own to keep out the sight of his face. It was the one merciful aspect to their coupling. Now that he had ceased to 'court' her, and since embarking upon his orgy of torture, Cornelisz no longer required her to look at him, he was lost in a world of depravity which was all his own.

One afternoon, as she passed amongst the tents, her eyes downcast as they always were, she was aware that someone had fallen into step beside her. A young man, judging by the firm young calves beneath his leggings. She glanced up briefly, recognising him. Dirck Liebensz, a clerk twenty years of age, he'd been a friend to Andries de Vries. He signalled her with his eyes. Was he about to speak to her? She looked away and moved on, increasing her pace. He walked with her. Was the young man mad?

She reached the far end of the island and he stood several paces behind her. 'I wish to speak to you, Vrouwe van den Mylen,' he said softly.

She stared out at the expanse of coral reef and the ocean beyond. 'You're insane, boy, they will kill you.'

'That would be preferable to what they ask of me. Please Vrouwe van den Mylen, I need to talk, there is no-one else.'

She recognised the agony in his tone. Dear God, was this to be another Andries, what did he want of her? 'Do not look at me as you speak,' she said.

He walked to the edge of the small coral beach, to where she could see him if she wished, but she did not turn to look. From the corner of her eye she could distinguish his form. Stocky, well built, a strong young man. She turned away and looked towards the settlement, no-one appeared to be taking particular note of them, and ten feet apart, their backs to each other, she listened to him as he spoke.

'Cornelisz killed a child today,' Dirck said, his voice a monotone as he forced himself to speak calmly of the horror. 'He made us watch, Salomon Deschamps and me.'

Lucretia knew young Deschamps. She'd met him often with the Commandeur, he had been Pelsaert's favourite clerk. He too had been a friend of Andries de Vries. She wished Dirck would be silent, she did not wish to hear of the atrocity, but she said nothing.

'He gouged out the infant's eyes,' Dirck paused, swallowing hard as he fought for control, 'and then, whilst the child still lived, he cut off its head.'

He inhaled deeply, then exhaled, a long slow sigh, and as he did, he felt the tightness in his chest relax just a little. He had said it. He had spoken out loud of the vile act. He didn't know why, but somehow it had helped.

Lucretia felt sickened. She swayed slightly and her fingers curled into fists. Why had he told her this? She of all people did not need to know. She must not know. For it would be these images which Cornelisz would bring to their bed tonight. As he sought pleasure in her body, she would know what was in the mind of the Devil himself and she would see those same images, she would be at one with Satan.

'Why do you tell me this?' she cried out in anger.

'Andries said that he often spoke to you in secret, he said that you were a comfort to him.' Dirck had not

wished to cause the woman fresh anguish. He had thought that as Cornelisz's mistress she would know directly from the fiend himself of such atrocities.

Lucretia started to weep softly. The young man had broken through her defence which she had thought impregnable. The image of the mutilated child would haunt her forever, just as the reminder that she had been of no comfort to Andries in his hour of need would haunt her.

'Forgive me,' Dirck whispered at the sound of her weeping and he turned to her.

'Do not look upon me,' she hissed. 'Turn away. Turn away.' He did as she bade him, and Lucretia stopped weeping. Her display of weakness was no help to the boy. 'What do you wish of me, Dirck?' she asked when she had regained her composure.

'I do not know, Vrouwe van den Mylen,' the young man said. 'Your blessing perhaps, there is no-one else to whom I can divulge my plans.' His voice was strong now, calm, it was good to talk freely, albeit from a distance. He sensed Vrouwe van den Mylen wished him well. 'I intend to escape from this island before I am put to the test.'

'What test is that?' she asked, shuddering at the prospect of whatever new horror Cornelisz had in mind.

'Tomorrow Salomon and I are to strangle a child for the sport of the men. We will be killed if we refuse. Salomon has told me he will do it in order to survive, I have pretended to agree.'

'How do you propose to escape? Others have tried.' Lucretia focussed upon the distant tents, people gathering whatever sparse kindling they could find for tonight's fires, women washing clothes and tending children. Was there a spy amongst them?

'Whilst the men are drinking tonight I will steal one of the smaller rafts.'

Satisfied that no-one was paying them any heed,

Lucretia said, 'Go to the far end of the beach, sit amongst the bushes there where you cannot be seen. I will join you shortly.'

After five minutes or so, Lucretia walked to the far end of the cove. She did not hide with him amongst the bushes, her daily constitutionals had been too regularly observed, but she strolled about beside the sparse clumps of vegetation as she so often did. If she were seen, it would be presumed she was alone. And they talked.

'A guard stands watch over the rafts,' she said. She felt strong now, she had a purpose. Perhaps even the purpose for which God had intended her. She would do whatever she could to aid Dirck Liebensz in his escape.

'I have a knife,' he replied, 'which can serve a better purpose than that of slitting the throats of women and children.'

'They will find you and kill you. They have killed all those who have escaped to Traitor's Island and Seals' Island.'

'They'll not find me there.' He looked up at her from amongst the bushes as she stood gazing at the horizon. She was magnificent. And a woman wise in the ways of the world. Andries had said that she was. Dirck was glad that he had shared his confidences with Vrouwe van den Mylen. The sight of her and the knowledge of her support were giving him strength. 'I will try for the mainland.'

She was startled. No attempt had been made to reach the mainland, which was no more than a vast shadow in the distance. Through rough, shark-infested seas, the journey was considered too hazardous. And should such a feat be accomplished, who knew what savages roamed the shores of the Great South Land.

'You will die in the attempt,' she said.

'It will be a better death than I will find here.'

There was such resolve in the young man's voice that Lucretia felt the faintest glimmer of hope. Not only for

Dirck Liebensz but for herself. This was surely why God had kept her alive. She fumbled amongst the linings of her skirt and withdrew the locket.

'I have something for you,' she said and she gazed for the last time upon the symbol of her love. Gently, she kissed the diamond sun, 'Farewell, Boudewijn,' she whispered.

Lucretia knew in her heart that she would never see her husband again, and she had no misgivings in parting with the locket if it would save the young man's life. There was no God on this island but perhaps a symbol of His mercy remained in the locket, which she was convinced had preserved her up until now. She prayed that its power would preserve the boy.

'Give me your hand, Dirck,' she said and, for the first time she looked at him. The young man held out his hand and she pressed the locket into his palm. 'If you survive, you will need to buy your way back to Holland. This may be of assistance.'

Dirck stared at the locket, the diamonds glinting brightly in the sun, never had he seen a thing of such beauty. 'Vrouwe van den Mylen . . .' he said, overwhelmed and he lifted his head to gaze up at her.

Lucretia smiled. She had thought she would never smile again. 'The locket will see you safe, Dirck,' she said, 'I know that it will. Take care and Godspeed.' She pressed his hand once more. 'Wait here for ten minutes after I am gone.'

Lucretia was animated tonight, Cornelisz thought. He'd become accustomed to her silence and he was pleased and flattered by the change in his mistress. And she looked more glorious than ever.

Lucretia had brushed her hair vigorously, and it hung, free of its snood, like a magnificent mane across her shoulders. She had pinched her cheeks until they flushed a comely pink and she had rubbed oil on her lips. She wished to look distracting tonight.

'*I am in the mood for company,*' *she'd said,* '*could we not invite Judick to dine?*' *If Judick were there, Coenraat van Huyssen would be present, and if van Huyssen came, then many others of Cornelisz's closest company would too. It would become a party, and the fewer of the mutineers wandering around the camp tonight the better.*

Cornelisz was only too delighted. '*We'll have a banquet,*' *he announced and he ordered his lackeys to break open the wine and prepare a feast for his company of friends.*

Lucretia pretended to drink the wine and she talked to Cornelisz's vile companions, all the while observing the actions of those in command. When the feast was being brought to the table, she saw Zeevanck issue orders to one of the men, and she knew it was around the time when they changed the guard.

'*Will you not favour us with one of your verses . . .?*' *she said to Cornelisz who sat beside her. She tried to say his name in order to charm him.* '*Please, Jeronimus,*' *she meant to say, but she could not bring herself to do so. Not because it would arouse suspicion; the man's ego was such that he was delighting in the amiability of his mistress, not questioning her change of heart, convinced that she found him attractive, as well she should. But even now, when Lucretia would do anything to aid the escape of Dirck Liebensz, she could not bring herself to utter the name of the Devil.*

Only too happy to oblige his mistress's request, Cornelisz sprang to his feet calling for silence, and launched into one of his favourite French odes. Everyone paid rapt attention. As Lucretia well knew, no man would dare leave the tent when their master was reciting.

'*Bravo,*' *she said when he had finished, and she swigged at her wine, pretending she was affected by the alcohol.* '*Another.*'

The assembled company followed suit. 'Another,' they cried. Anything to keep the Captain in good humour.

The following morning, one of the smaller rafts was discovered missing, and a guard was found with his throat slit. A head count revealed that the perpetrator of the crime was the young clerk Dirck Liebensz. Cornelisz gave orders for parties to be sent to the nearby islands, the boy would pay dearly for his crime. His would be a slow death.

But as the makeshift boats prepared to depart a cry went up.

'Captain!' One of the men was pointing to the far-off High Islands where a smoke signal clearly wound its way up into the sky. Weibbe Hayes and his men had found water.

Lucretia prayed. She gave thanks to God, convinced that this timely distraction was His doing, and, for the first time in months, she prayed for something other than her own death. She prayed fervently for the safety of Dirck Liebensz.

The young clerk was forgotten in an instant. Weibbe Hayes and his men lived! Cornelisz immediately set about making his plans.

An emissary would be sent to the High Islands to negotiate with the soldiers. Being seasoned soldiers loyal to the VOC, Cornelisz was aware that, under normal conditions, they would have little interest in accepting his terms. But these were hardly normal conditions. After all, he held all the weapons, did he not? His proposal was simple. Weibbe Hayes and his men were to enter into a pact with him, in return for which they would be granted special treatment. If they refused, they would be destroyed.

Lucretia listened throughout the night as Cornelisz composed his letter of negotiation and, the following day, she watched as the emissary set off for the High Islands, but she was not thinking of Weibbe Hayes and his brave *soldiers, although she prayed that they might somehow be spared. All of her thoughts were focussed on young Dirck Liebensz. May the power of the locket keep him safe, she thought, as she gazed at the mystical shadow on the horizon. The shadow of the Great South Land.*

CHAPTER NINETEEN

Paul was near the end, his body finally succumbing to the illness which ravaged it, and he could no longer deny the fact. For three years he'd deluded himself that his love for Henrietta could keep him alive forever and, in a way, it had. The past precious three years had been worth more to Paul Trewinnard than the rest of his existence. But he didn't want her to be with him at the end. He wanted to make his farewell in a lucid state.

'Will you spend Friday evening with me?' he asked.

'Yes,' she said. She knew it was time, he had been very open with her.

'I shall stay the weekend with Foong Lee,' he'd said, 'and on Monday he will take me to the hospital. I don't want visitors.'

She'd stared out of the car window at the raging storm and said nothing, determined not to cry, it was not what he wanted.

'And I rely upon you, my darling, to keep Aggie well away.'

She'd turned back to him and forced a smile in reply to his. 'I promise.' Then he'd asked her to spend Friday evening with him.

'Yes.'

They were sitting in Henrietta's car parked down by the docks, Paul no longer drove, not trusting himself at the wheel, and they were enjoying the ferocity of the storm over the harbour. It reminded them both of the storm they'd watched together on the day of his return. It had been November then too, Henrietta thought, nearly three years to the day. The most wonderful three years of her life.

'I'll spend every night with you, if you wish,' she added.

'No, that might be gilding the lily,' he laughed gently, 'just Friday evening will do. I'll book a room for you at the hotel.'

They drove to the school to collect Kit, who ran through the deluge to meet them.

'Can we go to Mindil Beach and watch the storm?' he asked as he scrambled into the Holden.

Henrietta looked at Paul, she knew he was in pain, he should go back to the hotel and rest.

'Of course,' he said.

Kit idolised Paul. The boy's imagination was fired with stories of far-off places, and he devoured the books Paul gave him, Rider Haggard and Buchan and Somerset Maugham. Kit would be thirteen in four months' time but his reading was far in advance of his years. One day he would travel to those places, he told himself, and one day, like Paul, he too would write. He'd already written several short stories, much to his father's irritation, and Paul had treated them very seriously, teaching him about structure and narrative and dialogue. But even while pointing out his errors Paul had told him he had a talent. Kit was inspired.

Kit had known for a long time that Paul was not well but, until recently, he had not realised the gravity of his illness.

'I'm going to boarding school next year, Paul,' he'd said,

'but I'll keep writing, and when I come home for the holidays you can read my stories and tell me where I've gone wrong.'

'I may not be here when you get back, Kit.' The boy was so eager that it broke Paul's heart, but he was deeply thankful. He'd been granted a lifetime's gift in the knowledge of his son, he must ask for no more than that.

Kit noted the expression on his mother's face as she and Paul exchanged a glance.

'In fact,' Paul added, 'I shall be saying goodbye shortly. It's probable that we shan't see each other again, and I shall miss you. But that's the way things are.' His smile was caring but his tone invited no discussion.

'Paul's dying, isn't he?' Kit had asked his mother that night.

'Yes,' she'd admitted. And when the boy cried, she comforted him, saying, 'He doesn't want you to be sad, Kit. You've made him very happy.'

'Where will you stay?' Terence asked. She'd told him, quite bluntly, that Paul was going into hospital on the Monday and that he wouldn't come out, and that she intended to spend Friday evening in town.

'Perhaps I'll stay at Aggie's,' she replied, knowing that was what he would prefer to hear. 'But then perhaps not,' she added, she couldn't be bothered lying. 'I'll probably stay at the Hotel Darwin.'

'He should have been hospitalised months ago,' Terence said. He'd seen Paul Trewinnard recently. In town buying supplies, he'd bumped into the man. Literally. Nearly bowled him over, he'd had to hold Trewinnard up as he'd staggered. Terence had barely recognised him, he was a walking cadaver, you could see the skull through the skin of his face. Well, what the hell, if she wanted to spend the evening with a skeleton, then let her.

Terence was glad that Paul Trewinnard would soon be

dead, he had become jealous of the time Henrietta spent with the man. And he knew that the books his younger son devoured came from the Englishman. Trewinnard was a meddlesome nuisance in Terence's opinion and he couldn't wait to be rid of him.

On the Friday afternoon, when Henrietta collected Kit from school, Paul said his final goodbye to his son.

'I'm going away, Kit.'

Kit looked at his mother. They had driven to Mindil Beach, their favourite place, and they were sitting on the sand. It was a hot, sweaty afternoon.

'Where are you going?'

Paul looked into eyes which could have been his own so many years ago. How he would love to acknowledge Kit as his son. 'I'm not sure,' he said, 'a long way away, we won't be able to keep in touch.'

'Mum told me . . .' Kit couldn't bring himself to say 'that you're dying', but his eyes held Paul's, steady and unwavering, and Paul longed to embrace the child.

'Yes,' he admitted, 'I won't see you again.' He fumbled in the pocket of his jacket and withdrew a book. 'I have a small gift for you.' He gave it to Kit. A slim volume, no more than a short story, really, but with a hard linen cover, prettily bound. 'It's a very simple narrative,' he said. 'A story of love, and of a good man who found a purpose to his life.'

Kit opened the volume and read on the first page, '*The Snow Goose*, by Paul Gallico'. Beneath the title, in Paul's neat handwriting, was an inscription, 'To Kit Galloway, from his friend Paul Trewinnard'.

'It has a purity of style which I think you'll enjoy,' Paul said, rather formally.

Kit knelt and flung his arms around the fragile body of his father, Paul mustering the last reserves of his strength to prevent himself from falling back on the sand.

Henrietta was concerned, Kit was being far too boisterous. But, as Paul maintained his balance and cradled his son's head to his shoulder, she realised it was the moment he had longed for.

Kit was crying, but trying very hard not to, he knew that Paul didn't like emotional scenes. 'Thanks for the book,' he said, his voice muffled.

'My pleasure.' Paul stroked his son's hair. Over the boy's head, his eyes met Henrietta's and he smiled his gratitude. 'It's time we were going, I think.'

Kit read the *The Snow Goose* during the drive back to Bullalalla. Henrietta said nothing but she was aware of the boy's rapt attention beside her.

'Did you like it?' she asked. They were nearly home when he closed the book and looked out the window.

'Yes.' He turned to her. 'Have you read it?' he asked.

'Many times,' she said, 'it's one of my favourites.'

'Why does Paul have to die?'

'It's his time, Kit. Just like it was Philip Rhayader's time in *The Snow Goose*.'

Kit nodded, but he returned his attention to the window and the passing bushland, it didn't seem fair somehow.

Less than an hour after their return to Bullalalla, Henrietta was once again setting off for Darwin. During the morning, Terence had offered to collect Kit from school, but she had declined.

'Into town and back twice in one day?' he'd queried, 'that's stupid.'

'I enjoy it,' she'd said, determined that Paul should not be deprived of his final moment with his son. 'I find the drive relaxing. Besides, I won't be coming back the second trip, I'm staying overnight, remember?'

'Ah yes, of course,' Terence had growled.

'So what time will you be home?' he now asked, as he put her bag into the back of the Holden.

'I don't know.' He'd have to be satisfied with that, she thought. 'Some time mid-morning, I suppose,' she called back through the open window as she drove off.

Terence stood in the early evening light watching the dusty trail of the car for quite some time. Thank Christ this would be the last of Paul bloody Trewinnard, he thought.

Paul had booked a room for her.

'I'd far rather spend the night with you,' she said.

'And compromise your reputation?' he queried, the customary twinkle in his sunken eyes.

'Bugger my reputation,' she replied, and they laughed.

'It might not be wise, my darling girl,' he added, 'the nights can be restless.'

'We'll see.'

They didn't eat in the dining room. Paul ordered a light meal in his room and they sat by the open shuttered windows, the evening breeze and the ceiling fan clearing the humidity of the sweltering afternoon. He'd ordered a bottle of champagne too for their final evening, but he was sipping a glass of water. Alcohol no longer agreed with him. 'It's one way to give up drinking,' he'd said on a number of occasions, with the old sardonic curve to his lip.

'Kit loved *The Snow Goose*.' Henrietta sipped at her champagne. She didn't feel like alcohol, but he obviously wanted to make their last night festive so she obliged.

'I hoped he would. The simplest pieces are so often the best, I think he already has the eye to recognise that.'

'One day I'll tell him who his father is, Paul.'

The glass of water remained poised at his lips for a second. Then he put it down on the table. 'Be careful, Henrietta.'

But she'd not said it in an idle moment. Henrietta had often deliberated over whether she would ever tell Kit the truth, and this afternoon, as she'd watched her son with his natural father, she had made her decision.

'Kit is your son,' she said. 'He doesn't know the man he presumes is his father. He's confused, he doesn't know why he doesn't fit in. And Terence keeps telling him that he doesn't. "You're not a Galloway," he says. He actually *says* that!'

Paul was looking rather sombre so Henrietta broke into one of her performances, as she often did in order to amuse him. She jumped to her feet and roared an imitation of Terence at his military best. 'You'll never fit in, boy, you're not a bloody Galloway!' Then she gave a hoot of laughter. 'My God, imagine the look on his face when he finds out he's right.'

Despite himself, Paul couldn't help but smile. Henrietta's performances were always so boisterous.

'The boy needs to know why he's different, Paul.' She knelt beside him, her hand resting on his knee. 'I won't tell him until he comes of age, I promise. But when he's twenty-one he'll learn the truth. And he'll be so proud to know that he's your son.'

Paul breathed a sigh of relief, there would be no danger if the boy was an adult and could look after himself. And the fact that Kit would one day acknowledge him as his father was the greatest gift Henrietta could have given him. 'I love you,' he said.

'And so you should. Can I get up off my knees?'

'I demand it,' he said as he rose, 'I have a gift for you, and you must sit here where the light is right.'

He seated her at the desk and turned on the lamp. Then he fetched something from his suitcase in the wardrobe. It was an object wrapped in beige kid cloth and he placed it before her.

She lifted apart the soft leather to expose a piece of jewellery. The lamplight illuminated the diamonds in all their brilliance. The diamonds were a sun which shone radiantly over a mountain peak, engraved deeply into silver.

Henrietta picked up the locket. It was heavy in her hand for something so small, no more than an inch in diameter.

She traced the engraving, thick and bold. She could feel the texture of the mountain, and the warmth of the diamond sun reflected perfectly upon its peak.

'It's beautiful,' she said in awe. 'Where did you get it?'

'From Foong Lee. He believes it to be a symbol of love. He offered it to me many years ago in return for a favour I did him, but I refused to accept it at the time. What was the point? I had no-one to share it with. He said he's been keeping it in trust for me ever since.' Paul grinned. 'The wily old fox, his timing is perfect, isn't it? Look inside.'

Henrietta opened the locket. Two faces looked at her from the interior. On the left hand side was a picture of herself, and there was one of Paul on the right. She remembered the photograph, the one and only time they'd been pictured together and it had been the day they'd first met.

'The garden party at Government House,' she smiled. The photograph had appeared alongside Paul's newspaper article the following day, Aggie had saved her a copy. Henrietta recalled there had been at least another dozen people in the shot. Paul had carefully cut their own faces out from the crowd.

'Yes,' he said, 'courtesy of the *Northern Standard*. I kept the photograph all these years, it was the only reminder I had of you.' He grinned self-deprecatingly. 'It's a bit soppy of me, isn't it? You can remove the pictures quite easily. Look,' he took the locket from her and, with the penknife on the desk, he carefully prised out the photographs, 'there're some beautifully engraved initials underneath.'

Henrietta examined the initials. 'L v.d. M' and 'B v.d. M'. She wondered who they were. When had they lived? What had become of them? Had their love continued to blossom into the autumn of their lives as hers and Paul's could not? She hoped so.

'It's the most beautiful thing I've ever seen.' She picked

up the photographs and painstakingly re-inserted them beneath the lips of the curved interior. 'And the pictures aren't soppy at all,' she said, 'they're perfect.' It was indeed the perfect token of his love, and she would treasure it always. She closed the locket and held the chain around her neck. 'Will you do it up for me, please?'

Paul was as happy as a schoolboy at Henrietta's obvious delight in his gift, but he was doing his best not to show it. 'We don't know the locket's history,' he said as he did up the clasp. 'It's antique of course, seventeenth-century Foong Lee thinks . . .'

She rose, took off her blouse and stood in front of the full-length mirror to admire the locket as it rested on her skin. It sat exactly where it should, she thought, upon her breastbone, close to her heart.

'. . . and possibly Dutch judging by its craftsmanship and the initials,' Paul rambled on. He gazed at her breasts, the glorious fullness of them couched in the lace of her white brassiere. How he wished he could make love to her. 'It's certainly valuable, you should probably have it valued and insured.'

She looked at him in the mirror and he hastily averted his eyes.

Henrietta undid her brassiere. 'Get undressed,' she said.

He sat on the bed, defeated and forlorn. 'Henrietta,' he said, 'you know that I can't.'

'Can't what? Get undressed? Oh for goodness' sake, Paul, then I'll do it for you.' She dropped the brassiere, knelt half naked at his feet and took off his shoes. He allowed her to do so and then she made him stand up, but when she started unbuttoning his shirt, he once again demurred.

'Henrietta, please . . .'

'Oh my dearest love,' she smiled as she kissed him with the utmost tenderness. 'I just want us to lie together naked, to hold each other whilst we sleep. I don't mean to be provocative.'

Paul looked at the sight of them in the mirror, a wizened old man and a voluptuous half-naked woman, and he burst out laughing. The laughter then turned into a cough, and when he finally recovered, he wiped the tears from his eyes and turned her to the mirror. 'Look at yourself, Henrietta, just look at yourself. You could be nothing other than provocative, you are a totally sexual creature.'

Henrietta looked in the mirror simply seeing herself half naked; she had never considered herself a 'sexual creature', but she was delighted that she'd made him laugh so wholeheartedly.

'So get your clothes off and give me a cuddle,' she said, 'I promise I won't do anything threatening.'

The laughter having relaxed him, Paul started undressing. 'It's a pretty tired old body, I must warn you,' he said.

'Well I can't have everything, can I? It's the body of the man I love,' she dropped her skirt to the floor, 'so it'll just have to do.'

'Can we at least turn out the lights?' He switched off the desk lamp, draped his shirt over the chair and started unbuttoning his trousers.

'Oh dear, the blushing bride.' Henrietta had stripped off her panties and stood naked before him, wearing nothing but the locket. 'If we must, I suppose.'

'On second thoughts no,' he said as she crossed to the light switch. 'I'd be a fool to deprive myself of such a vision.'

'Just the bed lamp? Then we won't have to get up.' Henrietta turned on the bedside lamp and pulled back the coverlets. After she'd switched off the overhead light she lay on the bed and waited for him, the locket gleaming between her breasts.

Paul finished undressing a little self-consciously and lay beside her. She cuddled herself up to him and the feel of her skin against his was exquisite. As they lay in each other's arms, he felt the tension float out of him like a rising mist. Even the pain, which was ever constant these days, seemed to lessen. It was a miracle.

'I'm sorry about the bag of bones,' he said.

'Well they're my bag of bones, aren't they?' she whispered. He was so frail and emaciated she was frightened to hold him too tightly for fear he might break, but she was overcome with a love so tender, like that of a mother with a newborn child.

Half an hour later Paul was sound asleep, and Henrietta lay for a long while cradling him with his head to her breast, before she too dozed off.

In the morning, he asked her to go to the room that he'd booked for her. She was to pull back the bedcovers and order breakfast for one.

'Really, Paul,' she smiled, 'I don't think that's necessary . . .'

'Please, my darling,' he insisted, 'it's the way I want it, please play my game. I'll be with you shortly.'

She humoured him, although she thought it was childish, but Paul wasn't really playing a game at all. The hotel was a hotbed of gossip, it simply was not worth the risk to Henrietta.

Forty minutes later, when she'd showered and changed and her breakfast had been delivered, there was a gentle tap at her door.

Paul stood there with his coffee and toast. 'I waited until the maid had gone,' he said. 'There's a certain sense of déjà vu about this, isn't there,' he added as he ducked into the room and she closed the door behind him.

But as they sat in silence sipping their tea and coffee, Henrietta experienced no sense of déjà vu. There was no element of illicit liaison in their companionship this time. Rather they were like a happily married couple, each warm and comfortable in the other's presence. They might have been together for twenty years, they so complemented each other.

'Foong Lee's picking me up in half an hour,' Paul said

when they'd finished their breakfast. 'Shall we meet accidentally in the foyer?' he looked at his watch, 'Say, in about ten minutes?'

Henrietta was shocked back to reality. So soon? Surely not. She had expected to spend the whole morning with him. She felt a sense of panic, the immediacy of their parting frightened her.

Paul knew that he'd shocked her. It had been deliberate. He'd promised himself there would be no lingering farewells. 'It's the way I want it, my darling girl,' he said, rising and holding out his hands to her, 'and it's easier this way. Besides,' he tried for a touch of his old flippancy, 'it rounds things off nicely, don't you think?'

As she stood, taking his hands in hers, he could still see the shock in her eyes. He kissed her. 'My love,' he said, tracing the outline of her face with his fingers, 'my Henrietta. You have made me happier than I have ever been in my life.'

'I love you, Paul,' she whispered.

'I know you do,' he smiled, 'that's what's so wonderful.'

They held each other close, and Henrietta did not weep. She could do that in the car, now was not the time.

'I'll see you downstairs,' Paul said. He didn't look back at her as he left.

'Henrietta,' he called out in the foyer ten minutes later, 'you're leaving?'

'Yes.' She remembered the words. 'It was just an overnight stay.'

He smiled gratefully. How brave and wonderful of her to play the game. But then that was his Henrietta. 'It was lovely to see you.'

'You too, Paul.'

He walked to the main doors with her as the porter carried her overnight bag.

'Goodbye, Henrietta.' They shook hands.

'Goodbye, Paul.'

CHAPTER TWENTY

Jeronimus Cornelisz hung from the gibbet. Mutilated, blood dripping from the stumps of his wrists, he twitched and shuddered in his death throes. 'Revenge!' he'd cried as the rope had tightened about his neck. 'Revenge!'

Lucretia had watched as his arms had been placed on the chopping block, and she'd watched the fall of the axe as it had severed both his hands. She'd felt nothing. And as he'd been hauled into the air, screaming his outrage, still she'd felt nothing.

Now, in the last seconds of his death, his eyes met hers. Had he sought her out? They were the eyes of the Devil himself, and she could see no remorse in them. But she did not turn her head. She remained staring at the monster until she knew that there was no life left in him. Then she walked away, down to the shore to stare across the brief expanse of sea to Batavia's Graveyard.

The executions were taking place on Seals' Island, and Cornelisz had been the first to swing. Seven other mutineers were to meet a similar fate, although prior to their hanging they would have only their right hand severed. Lucretia had no need to watch further.

Behind her, she heard the axe on the block, and a scream of agony, followed by cheers from several of the onlookers. She was not the only civilian who had chosen to see justice done that day.

Commandeur Pelsaert had been surprised when she'd accepted his offer to attend, but he'd said nothing. Perhaps it was right that she should observe the death of her tormentor, perhaps it would help release some of the demons which must plague her.

The unbelievable had happened. On 17 September, little more than three months after the wreck of the Batavia, Commandeur Francisco Pelsaert had returned aboard his rescue vessel the Zaandam. And the timing of his return was nothing less than miraculous.

Upon that same day, and at that same hour, the mutineers had launched their final assault on Weibbe Hayes and his men. Hayes had refused to join forces with Cornelisz, and he and his soldiers had withstood the mutineers' attacks on their position in the High Islands. After several weeks, however, their defence finally weakening, they would most surely have met their deaths had the Zaandam not been sighted, for upon the sighting the mutineers called an immediate halt to their advance.

Now, as Cornelisz swung lifeless from the gibbet, Pelsaert noted that Lucretia van den Mylen simply walked away, her bearing as regal as it had ever been. He wondered what was going through her mind. A woman like that, forced to suffer such horrors.

But Lucretia was not dwelling upon her horrors. Nor was she relishing the death of Cornelisz. He would haunt both her waking and sleeping hours for the rest of her life, she knew it, but for this brief moment she was free of him, she had seen him dead, and her thoughts once more turned to the boy.

In the weeks following his departure, Lucretia had clung to her thoughts of Dirck Liebensz. Without the locket she

*had felt lost and alone, and the hope for Dirck's survival
was her only comfort.*

*She did not regret giving the boy the locket, telling
herself that if she and Boudewijn had ever had a son,
perhaps he would one day have grown to become a fine
young man like Dirck. She had survived on such thoughts.*

*Since the arrival of Pelsaert and the fortnight of trials
and formal proceedings which had ensued, other things
had occupied Lucretia's mind, but now she was flooded
with thoughts of the boy. She gazed out across the barren
islands of the Houtman Abrolhos and wondered. Had
Dirck Liebensz lived? Had the locket guarded him as it
had guarded her?*

The locket gleamed brightly about the black neck of Gitjil
Djandamurra as he squatted and rubbed the firesticks
together. Women nearby were preparing fresh-water
mussels and gutting wallabies and goannas in readiness
for the cooking fire. Others were collecting wood. There
would be a feast after the men's corroboree tonight.

A little further along the valley, by the river, a group of
men painted each other's bodies with intricate designs. The
white of the burnt sea-shell lime and the kaolin clay was
stark against their black skin. Silent, concentrating on the
task at hand, they were mindless of the children at play in
the water. The youngsters splashed each other, and swung
from tree branches into the river, and squealed and giggled
with a boisterous and boundless energy.

Including women and children, this clan of the Yamatji
people numbered fifty in all, and Gitjil Djandamurra was
the chief of their elders.

A spark was ignited by the friction of the firesticks.
Then another and another, Gitjil patiently teasing the
sparks with a dry leaf until a small fire was ignited. He
rose, leaving the fire to be tended by the women and,
muttering several words in his harsh tongue, he gestured

for the young man standing beside him to follow.

Dirck did so, and they joined the other men, Gitjil instructing his own son, Yundjerra, to prepare Dirck for his first corroboree.

It had been a long trek from their previous campsite and Dirck was tired, unaccustomed to walking the distances the Aborigines quite happily travelled in a day. To them the fifteen mile hike from the mouth of the Hutt River across the Murchison Plateau to the valley had simply been a day's walk. But, already, Dirck's calf muscles were seizing up and his back was aching.

He forgot his fatigue, however, as Yundjerra decorated his body; he was excited at the prospect of this first step on the road to his initiation. Previously, when the men had held a corroboree, he had been instructed to stay with the women. Tonight was proof of his gradual acceptance into the clan.

Yundjerra, a strong young man around the same age as Dirck, daubed him with white lime and clay, and he and the others laughed amongst themselves at the paleness of Dirck's skin. The paint hardly showed up, they were saying to one another. Dirck grinned back at them, understanding the reason for their mirth. And, as he did, he recalled the terror he'd felt upon his first sighting of the black men. Was it only a month ago? It seemed a lifetime.

It had taken Dirck less than two days to travel the forty miles to the Great South Land. His small supply of bread and the fresh water in his flask had proved ample provisions and, with the aid of the south-westerly drift and the winds, he had travelled north to the mouth of the Hutt River.

But that was when his troubles had started, for the breakers picked up his small raft like a plaything. It was overturned in an instant and then he too became a toy at the ocean's mercy. He fought with all his might against the breakers and the rip, one minute being smashed towards *the shore, the next dragged back out to sea. He must have made some headway, however, for the sea, as though finally recognising his efforts, mercifully washed him up on the shore, half drowned, more dead than alive.*

His lungs heaving, he coughed and vomited sea water into the sand, which he couldn't fail to notice seemed strangely pink. When he'd recovered himself a little he raised his head and looked about. The shore and the coastal sandhills were indeed pink and quite beautiful, a result of the garnet in the rocks of the area. But Dirck was quickly distracted from the beauty of his surrounds, for the black men suddenly appeared out of nowhere. They circled him as he lay on the beach. There must have been at least a dozen of them, naked and as black as night, their spears raised. It was a fearful sight and Dirck relinquished all hope. So this was to be his fate. Exhausted, he sank his head into the sand and awaited his death, praying that their spears would be merciful and find their mark.

But Gitjil and his clansmen were intrigued. They had never seen a white man before. They rolled him over on his back and started stripping his clothes from him.

Dirck could hear them jabbering all the while. He watched as they lay their spears down on the sand, they seemed intent on having fun. Dear God, were they going to torture him?

They pulled down his breeches, pointing at his genitals, laughing and nodding approvingly, it appeared the white man was the same as them. It was a source of fascination.

Then one of them, a big man with a head of silver-grey hair and a white beard, startling against the blackness of his face, saw the locket. He gave it a gentle tug but the chain would not break, so he grasped it in his fist and fiercely wrenched it from around Dirck's neck.

Gitjil held the locket up to the sun. It was a thing of great power. The sun's rays darted off this thing he held in his hands, as if it were a tiny sun all its own. He knelt on the sand beside the white man, and he asked the white man what it was.

Dirck listened to the strange staccato tongue of the native. He was asking questions about the locket, and the others were standing around waiting for answers. Dirck realised that this man was the leader, or at least one who commanded the respect of the group. He was older than the others too, probably in his fifties, it was difficult to tell. One thing was quite obvious, however, he was fascinated by the locket.

Dirck heaved himself up onto one elbow and, in a rasping voice which sounded unlike his own, he said, 'It is yours,' and he waved his hand in a gesture of good will. 'A gift. You take it, it is yours.' He remembered no more than that. The small exertion of his energy made the world spin and he lost consciousness.

When he'd regained his senses he found himself in a cool, shaded grove beside the river. It was dusk and women were pressing moist leaves upon his face. They fed him a strange mixture from a sea-shell cup and all the time they jabbered and laughed and made obviously ribald comments. He was still naked and they were fascinated by his private parts. But it was good natured, he realised, they were not going to kill him. He did a lot of nodding and smiling back and they liked that, nodding and smiling in return. Dirck gave thanks to God for his deliverance.

That was barely a month ago, and sometimes he wondered whether the black men might have killed him had it not been for the locket. Possibly not, they seemed a peaceable people, but the locket had most certainly made him favoured amongst their leaders. The elders of the tribe sometimes passed it around amongst themselves as they sat together of an evening, treating it with great reverence. And at all other times Gitjil Djandamurra wore it on a length of twine about his neck, the broken chain dangling against his naked chest. It was because of the locket, Dirck was sure, that Gitjil had more or less adopted him, teaching him the ways of his people and the words of their language. He had even named Dirck Koo-ee-lung, which meant porpoise, because he had come to them from out of the sea. And now Dirck was on his way to becoming an accepted member of their society.

The corroboree started at dusk and, as he listened to the haunting sound of the didgeridoo and the clacking of the Aborigines' sticks mingling with the screeches of the birds winging their way home to roost, Dirck once again gave thanks to God. He didn't know what was to become of him. He had no plans. The civilised world seemed so far away from this untamed land. How was he ever to return to Holland? But he was grateful to be alive. And he owed his life to Lucretia van den Mylen and her locket, and to these strange black people who had befriended him.

CHAPTER TWENTY-ONE

Jock Galloway died in his sleep on Christmas Eve, 1960. Terence's brother Michael telephoned with the news.

'Your grandfather died an hour ago,' Terence bluntly announced to the boys as he returned to the lounge room where Henrietta was reading a book and his sons were sprawled out on the floor playing monopoly.

Neither Malcolm nor Kit was surprised. They'd visited Grandpa Jock once four years previously on a trip to Adelaide. He'd had pneumonia at the time and their mother had insisted they see the old man before his expected demise. To the boys he'd seemed older than Methuselah, and they'd hated the hospital, they couldn't wait to get out. Then Grandpa Jock had rallied and soldiered on for another four years.

'So much death lately,' Henrietta commented more to herself than anyone else.

Terence realised that she was referring to Paul Trewinnard, it was barely a month since the man's funeral. He felt intensely irritated by her comment.

'Jesus, Henrietta, stop sounding so tragic. Dad had a good innings, it's nothing short of a miracle he lasted this long, and Trewinnard should have died years ago, he was a living corpse.'

Henrietta was hardly aware that she'd spoken out loud, she wished she hadn't. 'Yes of course, you're right,' she said.

Paul had died barely a week after his hospitalisation. He'd willed himself to die, Henrietta was convinced of it, the time had been right and he'd held on for as long as he could. She'd taken Kit out of school for the afternoon to attend the funeral, much to Terence's annoyance.

'Why don't you come too?' she'd asked, knowing that he wouldn't and duly thankful when he refused.

Henrietta wore the locket to the funeral. The cherished locket which was the symbol of their love rested out of sight beneath her blouse, but she could feel it as it lay against her skin.

After the funeral, she returned the locket to its hiding place. She kept it under lock and key in a small silver jewellery case hidden amongst her underwear. And she resolved never to look at it again until she was free.

Henrietta had made plans. Her declaration to Paul that she would tell Kit the truth when he came of age had raised the question of her own future. Quite obviously she would no longer be able to remain with Terence after she told him the truth. But by then both her sons would be adults, there would no longer be any reason for her to stay. And she would have the means to support herself with the inheritance left her by her grandmother, who had died many years ago.

Henrietta was glad now that Terence had been too proud to accept her offer of financial assistance when, the beef market having hit an all-time low, she'd tried to persuade him to use her inheritance. 'I do not need money from my wife, Henrietta,' he'd said scathingly. She'd admired him at the time, she remembered, although she'd thought he was being pig-headed. Now she was thankful.

Having planned her future, Henrietta felt a great relief. Knowing that there would one day be an end to the fiasco of her marriage helped ease the ache left by Paul's death. She'd even gone so far as to transfer funds to an account in another name should Terence try to deprive her of her means of support. It was a positive action which emboldened her. She felt excited at the prospect that one day she would have a life of her own. In the meantime, she lived for her sons, although she dreaded the fact that in barely six weeks Kit and Malcolm would both be leaving for boarding school in Adelaide and she would be left on her own with Terence.

'Pall Mall, I've got you! That's mine!' Malcolm yelled triumphantly, Grandpa Jock's death forgotten in an instant.

'We must go to the funeral, when is it?' Henrietta asked.

'The day after Boxing Day. Why, for God's sake?' Terence genuinely couldn't see the point. 'Michael and James have everything in hand.'

'I'm sure your mother would appreciate us being there.' Henrietta tried not to sound arch. 'And Charlotte too.'

'All right, we'll go.'

Henrietta was surprised by his immediate acquiescence, she had been sure he was going to argue.

Terence had most certainly been prepared for argument. In fact he would have ended up telling her to go to the funeral if she wanted, and to take the boys for all he cared, but come hell or high water he wouldn't go with them. Then all of a sudden it occurred to him that a trip south would be very much to his advantage, he'd have a good look over the Galloway stud whilst he was down there. Jock's death may have been most timely. One third of the value of the Galloway stud might prove immensely useful over the next year or so.

Terence had said nothing to Henrietta of the approach by Vesteys to buy Bullalalla cattle station. At first there had been no point, he'd summarily knocked them back, having no interest in their offer. But the beef industry was tough for sole-property owners these days, and many were selling out to the big multi-national companies. And you didn't get any bigger than Vesteys.

Headed by Lord Vestey, the vast empire had strings of properties and meatworks not only in Australia but in Africa and Latin America; and the Blue Star Line, one of the world's largest shipping companies, flew the Vestey house flag. Lately Terence had found himself pondering upon their offer, which was certainly generous.

Perhaps now, he thought, with his share of the Galloway stud, it might be to his advantage to sell. With the finances from both properties he would certainly have impressive capital for investment and Darwin businesses were thriving. Rental properties were lucrative, new hotels were planned, there was a boom in the retail business, it was certainly worth consideration.

Terence, surprisingly, had no compunction about leaving the land and his childhood home, the prospect of becoming a powerful businessman was far too attractive. Furthermore, he had no qualms about the fact that the demand for his share of the Galloway stud in cash would probably force his brothers to sell the property. And the ultimate fact that the sale of both Bullalalla cattle station and the Galloway stud would wipe out the dynastic legacy of both his father and his grandfather was a thought which simply didn't cross his mind. They were his properties and his to do with as he wished.

Kit was excited about the trip to Adelaide, he'd flown in an aeroplane only once before and it was a huge adventure. Malcolm was far more blasé. He'd flown heaps of times, and when he went to military school in two years' time, he'd be parachuting from aeroplanes and jumping out of helicopters, just like they did in the pictures. Malcolm would soon be sixteen and he was blasé about a lot of things.

The adventure quickly soured when they reached Adelaide, however, even for Kit.

The boys sat uncomfortably on the hard wooden pews as the priest droned on, both of them wishing they were back home riding their horses.

Henrietta gave a little frown at Kit who was fidgeting, but she felt sorry for them, and she rather wished she hadn't insisted on their coming. She'd only done so in order to please Margaret, thinking it might comfort the woman to have her grandsons present. But Margaret had barely acknowledged them when they'd arrived at the church.

'Malcolm, Kit,' she'd said, giving them a brusque nod, then she'd offered her cheek for Henrietta to kiss. 'Thank you for coming, Henrietta,' she'd said, and she'd turned to Charlotte. 'Let's go in.' She'd paid no further attention to them after that, nor to the rest of her family. Michael and James with their wives and children were equally ignored as Margaret sat, steely-eyed, staring straight ahead throughout the service.

It was Charlotte who most worried Henrietta. It had been only four years since she'd sat companionably with her sister-in-law at Jock's bedside, but in those four years Charlotte seemed to have aged immeasurably. For a brief moment, when they'd first arrived at the church, Henrietta had thought that Charlotte was Margaret, and during the service as she'd surreptitiously glanced at them seated together, she'd been shocked at their likeness. Margaret looked the same as she always had, a little more weathered perhaps, but the same. Charlotte had lost any vestige of her youth. She had become her mother.

Henrietta sat in the backseat of the car with Charlotte as the cortege left the church for the cemetery.

'Are you all right, Charlotte?' she queried gently.

'Of course.' Charlotte was annoyed by Henrietta's solicitude. 'Why shouldn't I be?'

'What will you do now that Jock's gone?'

'Stay with mother of course. What else is there to do?'

'You could always come back to Bullalalla. Margaret too.'

'My mother will never go back to Bullalalla. She told me. She said "without Jock there is no Bullalalla".' Charlotte's tone was antagonistic. 'Those were her exact words.'

Henrietta knew that the antagonism was not directed at her, but at Terence. 'Oh Charlotte,' she urged, 'that doesn't mean that you . . .'

But Charlotte interrupted. 'Leave it, Henrietta,' she snapped. After a moment's pause, she added a little more gently, 'I'm sorry, I didn't mean to be rude.' She hadn't either, Henrietta's intentions were well-meaning enough, but Charlotte wished no interference in her life. 'I'll stay with mother. We'll get a place near the nursing home so that when the time comes . . .' She shrugged and looked out the window and there was nothing more to be said.

Henrietta felt very saddened. She had always admired Charlotte. Had Margaret broken her daughter's spirit, she wondered, or had it been life in the city which had destroyed her? Charlotte most certainly belonged in the outback. It was probably a mixture of both, Henrietta decided, but the fight had gone from Charlotte. The woman had given up.

Terence refused his brothers' offers to stay with them. Their properties were too far out of town, he maintained, it would be easier to get to the airport the following day if he and Henrietta and the boys stayed the night in an inner-city hotel. He'd booked in advance, it was all arranged. Michael urged him to cancel the reservation and come to the farm for several days so that their respective children could get to know each other.

'They're cousins, after all,' he said.

Henrietta thought it was an excellent idea, but Terence insisted he must get back to Bullalalla, she didn't for the life of her know why.

She was even more mystified when, the morning after the funeral, he got up at the crack of dawn and announced he wouldn't be back until mid-afternoon, just before they were due to leave for the airport.

'I'm going out to the stud to have a look around,' he said when she insisted upon an answer. 'And Michael and James don't need to know.'

Henrietta understood that it was an order for her to keep her mouth shut. Well at least it explained why he'd insisted upon hiring a car. She wondered what he was up to, but she didn't ponder the matter too long, she and the boys would have a wonderful time on their own in Adelaide.

And they did, Malcolm proudly showing off his knowledge of the city and Kit overawed, he'd never been in a place with so many people. They explored the shops and then they wandered down to the river, where they sat on the grassy banks eating meat pies.

They hired a rowboat, Henrietta watching from the sidelines as Malcolm taught Kit how to row, and laughing as they went around in circles. Once Kit had sufficiently mastered the art, the boys rowed ashore and insisted she get in. So Henrietta sat in the stern of the dinghy whilst her sons rowed her up and down the Torrens River. It was a beautiful day.

Terence was in a very good mood when he returned to collect them from the hotel. Kit was eager to tell his father that he'd learned how to row.

'Malcolm taught me,' he said.

'Good on you, boys, well done.'

'But he can't feather the oars yet, like they teach us at school,' Malcolm added.

'Oh well, when he comes to school next year they'll teach him, won't they.' Terence gave Henrietta a kiss. 'I'm glad you had a good day.'

Terence had had a good day too. The Galloway stud

would fetch an excellent price. Old Jock had been right. 'Leave it in Gordon's hands,' he'd said, 'he knows horse-flesh better than any bloke in the country.' Well Gordon certainly had, the property was a gold mine. A proper check would need to be done of course, a survey of the property, an accounting of the stock and of the books. In the meantime there was no need to bring up the subject with his brothers, it could all be done on the quiet, Terence's lawyers would inform Michael and James of his intentions. All in good time.

Henrietta found herself desperately lonely when the boys left for boarding school. She'd anticipated that she would, but the degree of her loneliness was beyond all expect-ations. She was busy enough, certainly. She was still the bookkeeper for Bullalalla station which involved endless paperwork and meetings with Buff Nelson, Terence being away more than usual on mysterious trips to Adelaide. But she'd been managing the books for so many years that they were hardly a distraction.

Occasionally she went for a ride with Jackie and the other stockmen when they rounded up the steers for the kill. Henrietta enjoyed Jackie's company, he seemed to have eyes everywhere, and was always eager to share with her his latest observation. They'd be riding side by side in silence and Jackie would suddenly say, 'Look, missus.' And soaring majestically far above there would be a wedgetail eagle, wheeling in never-ending circles, its curved wings motionless as it caught the thermal draft. Or he'd pull his horse up to point out a frill-necked lizard which, chameleon-like, was the colour of the parched rock upon which it sat as it basked in the sun. Henrietta found Jackie's love for life contagious.

Sometimes Henrietta would chat to Nellie in the kitchen, usually about Pearl and her two children—Nellie was a very proud grandmother. Sometimes she'd make the trip into town to see Aggie, but much as Henrietta enjoyed Aggie's company, she no longer enjoyed Darwin. Darwin reminded her too much of Paul.

For the most part, Henrietta was bored and disinterested, simply marking time until the school holidays.

Terence was aware of her listlessness. She missed the boys, it was obvious. Well, the boys wouldn't be with them forever. Malcolm would be going to military school in a couple of years, a fine career for a young man, and Kit would follow suit when his turn came. Henrietta would need to prepare herself for a life without her sons. She was not yet forty, still a comparatively young woman, surely she would welcome a change from her isolated existence at Bullalalla. One evening he tested her out.

'I had an offer from Vesteys a while back,' he said, sipping at his Scotch as they sat in the lounge room, Henrietta with her head in a book as usual.

'Oh yes?' Henrietta didn't take much notice. Vesteys were buying up every property they could lay their hands on, it was hardly surprising.

'What would you say to selling?'

'Selling what? Bullalalla?' She sounded incredulous, but at least he'd gained her attention, she'd put down the book. 'Yes.'

'Don't be ridiculous, Terence.' He was simply trying to get her attention, she knew her reading annoyed him, but then what was she supposed to do of an evening? Sit silently in his company? They had very little to talk about these days.

'I'm not being ridiculous,' the dismissal in her tone annoyed him. 'The offer's a good one, why shouldn't I sell?' he said belligerently.

He was being purposefully argumentative in order to engage her in a fruitless conversation, she thought. Bullalalla was in his blood, he would never sell. Henrietta refused to play his game.

'Because Bullalalla is your father's lifetime work and your sons' inheritance, that's why,' she said, and she returned to her book.

'My sons' inheritance?' Terence scoffed, 'Malcolm and Kit are going to have military careers, what will they want with a cattle station?'

But Henrietta concentrated on the book, turning a page to signal her indifference, although she wasn't reading a word. Kit didn't want to go to military school, he'd told her so. She'd said he wouldn't have to, that they'd face that bridge when they came to it.

Terence rose to refill his glass, quelling his anger. He'd say no more to her about the sale of Bullalalla, but he'd go ahead with his plans. By the end of the year they'd be moving to Darwin. Perhaps then, when she discovered she was married to one of the most successful businessmen in town, she might finally be impressed.

It was the end of first term. At long last. School holidays and the boys were home. And how had they managed to grow so much in only a few months! Malcolm was sixteen soon and he'd filled out, he'd have the body of his father soon, deep-chested and broad-shouldered. And Kit, at the gangly age of thirteen, had grown at least an inch taller. Henrietta blossomed in the company of her children.

The fact that she did so irked Terence. Her listlessness and indifference had annoyed him, and now that she'd returned to her old vibrant self, he was doubly annoyed. Why couldn't she be animated and engaging with him? Terence would never admit it, but he was jealous of his sons.

Malcolm did his best to appease his father's ill humour. He was the star goal kicker for the A-grade school football team and he eagerly demonstrated his skills to Terence, setting up goal sticks down by the stable yards and belting about with seemingly inexhaustible energy throughout the heat of the afternoons.

It helped. Terence was mollified by the fact that his elder son sought his approbation. If only his wife would do the same, he thought.

Kit loved boarding school. Henrietta was delighted. She had worried a little about how he'd fit in. For several years Malcolm's stories of camaraderie had all related to football, which she knew held little interest for Kit. Would he find friends to relate to, she'd wondered. But it was the study which Kit loved, particularly English literature, and he'd brought home some of his essays.

'I got the top mark in my class for this one,' he said proudly. 'It's about the bushfire we had two seasons ago, remember?'

She did. The fire had sprung up in the late afternoon, no-one knew how, but it had been kept well under control and had done no damage, burning off several square miles of bushland which would quickly regenerate. The boys had watched from the sidelines, well into the night, as the men contained the blaze. It had been an impressive spectacle, flames licking at silhouetted trees, sparks jumping like fireworks up into the blackness.

The following morning when they'd surveyed the bushland, blackened and still smouldering, Kit had been fascinated. 'It looked like a fairyland last night,' he'd said.

The bushfire and its aftermath had made a great impression on the eleven-year-old. Now, two years later, he'd written about it.

'You see this part here, Mum,' he said excitedly when she'd finished reading the essay, it was remarkably good, 'this part where she corrected me,' he was talking about his teacher, 'well, I don't agree with that.'

' "*The hypocrite, night, had cloaked the devastation . . .*",' she read. The teacher had crossed out 'hypocrite' and neatly printed 'hypocritical', her handwritten correction in the margin read 'adjective, not noun', and she'd given him nineteen out of twenty.

'Would you have got twenty out of twenty if it hadn't been for that?' Henrietta asked in all innocence.

'It's not the mark, Mum!' he said, impatient in his excitement. 'I knew that I was putting two nouns together, and that you're not supposed to do that, but it was the effect I wanted. And she turned it into an adjective, "hypocritical", you see?' He stabbed his finger at the word. 'But that's not what I wanted, and I think she's wrong.'

Henrietta wanted to laugh and cry at the same time. It could have been Paul Trewinnard speaking. Paul had always been impatient and pedantic in his love of the English language and its usage.

'I didn't tell her I thought she was wrong,' Kit continued, 'I just copped it, and it didn't matter about the mark. But if you're going to develop a personal style then you have to be allowed to take liberties. "Poetic licence", that's what Paul called it. "English is a living language, and the rules are there to be broken, so long as you make it work", that's what he said.'

She resisted the urge to hug him. 'I agree with you, Kit,' she said instead. And she did. 'I prefer it your way, it's more dramatic.'

'Yep.' He grinned, happy that she'd grasped his point. 'That's exactly what I thought.'

Terence was impatient when she and Kit huddled together with their books, reading their favourite passages out loud to each other. *The Snow Goose* featured quite often. He once again accused her of favouritism.

It was late afternoon on a Sunday. He and Malcolm had been kicking the football around and, when Terence walked in the front door, hot and sweaty, he was intensely irritated to see them poring over their books together just where he'd left them an hour and a half previously.

He said nothing, but went upstairs to shower and change for the evening. When he came back down the boys had gone out riding together, as they often did around dusk.

'Jesus, Henrietta, you're ruining that kid,' he growled as he poured himself a Scotch.

'How? He'd read with or without me, you know that, he's passionate about books.'

Aware she was right, Terence changed tactics.

'It's not that at all,' he said, although it had been. 'You're making it quite obvious he's your favourite and it's not fair on Malcolm.'

But this time Henrietta was not prepared to accept his argument and to allow herself to be riddled with doubt. This time she knew she was in the right.

'I can't talk to Malcolm about football,' she said, 'and Malcolm understands that. So if you can't talk to Kit about literature, then surely it's permissible for me to do so. Malcolm certainly doesn't mind.'

Her argument was irrefutable and Terence felt his anger grow. He put down his Scotch and walked over to the coffee table by the sofa where she sat. He picked up the book which rested on top of the pile and opened it. *The Snow Goose,* he read and, beneath the title the inscription, 'To Kit Galloway, from his friend Paul Trewinnard'.

Henrietta watched as his eyes deadened. It was always the first sign of his madness, and she prepared herself for the fit of rage which she knew he'd been resisting for so long.

But Terence didn't explode. He opened the book at its centre and methodically tore it in two through its binding. Then he dropped the pieces to the floor and picked up the next book. He opened it to the title page. *The Coral Island*, by R.M. Ballantyne, but there was no personal inscription. He tossed it back on the coffee table and picked up the next. *Dombey and Son*, by Charles Dickens. No personal inscription.

'Are there any others from Paul bloody Trewinnard?' he asked as he dumped it on the table and picked up the next. How dare that scrawny dead bloody Englishman have such an influence upon his son!

She shook her head, not daring to speak. But he systematically inspected the title page of each book, and there must have been a dozen, before he silently gathered his Scotch and left the room.

Henrietta got down on her knees and picked up the two halves of *The Snow Goose*. She could mend the binding with sticky tape, but the book must now be kept hidden from Terence at all times, she must tell Kit that.

It was the final straw for Henrietta. Less than eight years to go, she thought. She would start counting now.

CHAPTER TWENTY-TWO

1660

As the son of Gitjil, Yundjerra Djandamurra had inherited the locket. His father had died and Yundjerra had long since split from the clan, as many men did with their wives and grown children, to travel in his own family group. Yundjerra's family included not only his wife, his two sons and their children, but his sister and brother-in-law, their children and grandchildren. The group numbered twenty in all.

Koo-ee-lung and Yundjerra, now in their fifties, were as close as if they had been true brothers. And indeed they were, for not only had Koo-ee-lung married Yundjerra's sister, but Gitjil himself had adopted Koo-ee-lung.

Dirck no longer thought of his previous life. And on the past occasions when he had, it had not been with longing. In fact, if he were ever to lay eyes on a white man again, he doubted he would be able to communicate, either socially or even in a common language. It had been thirty years since he'd spoken his mother tongue, having quickly given up his arrogant attempt to teach the Aborigines

Dutch; they'd simply laughed at him.

Stocky and thickset, with his vivid green eyes and wild reddish beard, Dirck looked completely at odds with the group, even with his own pale-skinned children, each having deep brown eyes, and the blackest of hair. But the latest grandchild had surprised them all. A boy, with ginger hair, green eyes and the whitest of skin. Yundjerra had found the child a source of great amusement.

The locket continued to hold a place of importance amongst the group. Like his father and the elders of the clan, Yundjerra treated it with great reverence and, like his father, he called it minya yindi, *which meant 'small sun', and he painted pictures of it in caves they inhabited, just as his father had done before him. In the wealth of their combined travels, they had recorded drawings of the locket as far inland as the Great Sandy Desert.*

At no time did minya yindi *leave its place, resting against Yundjerra's naked chest, unless his brother wished to hold it, then Yundjerra would untie the twine from about his neck and pass* minya yindi *to Koo-ee-lung. But it had been many years since Koo-ee-lung had expressed a desire to hold* minya yindi.

When Dirck had occasionally thought of the old days, he had requested the locket from Yundjerra as they sat by the fire of an evening. And he had opened it and looked at the initials within. He had thought of Lucretia van den Mylen and wondered if she had lived. But the old days were gone now and the memories too. He no longer thought and he no longer wondered. He no longer even remembered.

As his grandchildren played in the river, and his strong young sons returned with their catch of turtle and black bream; as his sons' wives prepared the cooking fire and his wife cuddled his latest grandchild to her breast, there was nothing to remember. The man who had once been Dirck Liebensz no longer existed.

CHAPTER TWENTY-THREE

The situation between Terence and Henrietta had gone from bad to worse. The moment the boys returned to boarding school she was once again disinterested and he was once again annoyed by her lack of vitality. Where was the ready smile and the vivacity she displayed with her sons? Terence felt excluded, frustrated and powerless.

A week or so after the boys had left, he decided to woo her.

Henrietta had taken to sleeping in one of the guest rooms most nights, to escape his snoring, she said. She hadn't dared suggest that they have separate bedrooms, and he'd accepted the situation. In truth, Terence snored very little, but he wasn't to know that and it was the perfect excuse.

'Stay here tonight, Henrietta,' he said, as she sat in front of the dressing table brushing her hair. She looked very beautiful in her beige silk chemise.

She agreed, knowing that he wanted to have sex, she never denied him his conjugal rights. She'd stay, it would be over quickly, he'd soon be asleep and she'd retire to the other room. In the morning she'd tell him, quite amiably, that his snoring had kept her awake, and he wouldn't question her.

She slipped between the sheets. It was a pleasant night, warm but not too humid, and the ceiling fan wafted an agreeable breeze against her face as she lay waiting for him.

He pulled the sheet back and looked at her. He wanted to rip the flimsy chemise from her body, he enjoyed rough sex, but he resisted the urge, lying beside her instead, kissing her gently and caressing her breast.

She accepted the kiss. It was unlike him, Terence rarely kissed, and when he did it was brutal. He'd grind his mouth against hers, and bite at her lips, and her skin would be abraded from the stubble of his chin. This kiss was different. She felt his lips gently force hers apart, his tongue entering her mouth, exploring it tenderly, tracing the line of her teeth, flickering against her palate, as his fingers found her nipple and teased it erect.

Henrietta was powerless against her body's response. She was unable to stop her nipple from hardening, which she knew was exciting him as his mouth left hers to wander down her neck towards her breast. But emotionally she was unable to respond to his lovemaking. It sickened her. As she felt his mouth engulf her nipple, and his hand ease her thighs apart with all the tenderness of a true lover, she wanted to push him away. But she didn't. She lay there accepting his caresses, not daring to move as his fingers found their mark.

By now it was costing Terence every shred of willpower he possessed not to force himself into her. He could feel her juices, she wanted him he knew it. He wished she would caress him in turn. He wished she would make animal noises and moan her desire. But then Henrietta never behaved that way. It was her middle-class British upbringing, he'd always supposed, and he'd come to accept the fact that she didn't display her sexual craving. But as she lay there, acquiescent, her body responding to his stimulation, he knew that she wanted him as desperately as he wanted her.

He could stand it no longer. Ripping her legs apart, he forced his entry.

Henrietta was thankful. She preferred it this way, accustomed as she was to his brutality. Nothing was required of her, she was simply a vessel.

Soon it was over and, when he'd grunted his satisfaction and rolled on his side, he said, 'I do love you, Henrietta, you know that don't you?'

'Yes,' she said. She had known for many years that he loved her, in his own strange way, but the fact that he did was no comfort to her. The possessiveness of his love was rather something to fear.

As Terence drifted off to sleep, he thought of Bella. Bella was far more exciting than Henrietta in bed.

Since the men had left for the muster Terence had been regularly visiting Bella at the camp. Bella wasn't her real name. Her real name was unpronounceable so Terence had christened her Bella, telling her it meant 'beautiful', she'd liked that. And Bella *was* beautiful. The way only an eighteen-year-old black could be, he thought, with pert breasts and a firm round bottom and a slit between her legs of the brightest pink, like a wound in the centre of her blackness. She wouldn't age well, it was true, but in the meantime Terence couldn't get enough of Bella. And she loved being taken, she was like a tigress. Terence dreamed of Bella as he slept.

Henrietta rose quietly and left the room. It had been several months since he'd made any demands on her. She knew that he sated his sexual appetite down at the camp and she wished he would confine his activity to whichever woman there had won his favour. Perhaps his attempt at lovemaking had been a bid to gain her attention, she had certainly been remote since the boys had left. She couldn't help it, her life seemed so empty without them.

The following morning, Terence was affectionate. He apologised for the fact that he'd snored and she'd been forced to go to the guest room. 'But it was fun wasn't it?' he said as he kissed her. She smiled and kissed him back. She'd play the game, she decided, anything that curbed his irritability was to her advantage.

A week later Michael rang. Terence had gone into Darwin for several days, Henrietta told him, and she chatted on for a while before sending her best to the family and asking if Michael would like Terence to ring him back.

'You mean you don't know?' Michael asked, having listened, amazed, to Henrietta's innocent conversation. The solicitors had informed him of Terence's demands and he had presumed she was party to her husband's plans.

Henrietta was initially shocked when Michael told her, although everything now fell into place. Terence's visit to the Galloway stud after Jock's funeral, his ensuing trips to Adelaide.

'We'll have to sell,' Michael sounded sick with worry, 'James and I can't afford to buy him out.'

She confronted Terence when he returned three days later, but he obviously felt no guilt at forcing the sale.

'We can do with the money,' he said. 'And it's ours, after all.' He refused to be drawn into any further conversation.

Terence had said nothing to Henrietta about the impending sale of Bullalalla, which would be finalised at the end of the muster when a full account had been taken of the livestock. He had told Buff Nelson, swearing him to secrecy, and Vesteys would no doubt keep Buff on as manager, but he had seen no purpose in informing anyone else.

In the meantime, he was investigating some exciting property purchases, principally two large blocks on either side of Mitchell Street, cornering onto Knuckey, in the centre of town.

Now that the sale was definite and his plans were set in motion, Terence couldn't wait to move on. He'd been struggling long enough on the land, for little remuneration and even less recognition. He wanted to be rich and he wanted to be powerful, but above all else, he wanted to be admired. He would forge a dynasty, he'd decided. *Galloway and Sons*. He could just see it. Galloway and Sons would become the very hub of Darwin. One day when his boys left the army they would inherit a family empire which would be handed down to their sons, and to the sons of their sons, Terence had it all planned. And the new family home, the designs of which were currently being drawn up by a prominent architect, would be on the point at Larrakeyah. A grand house overlooking the water, it would be the envy of all.

Terence had decided he would make his announcement to the family in September, when the muster was over and the boys had returned for the holidays.

As the weeks progressed, Henrietta had no idea why Terence was spending so much time in Darwin. He seemed to take little interest in Bullalalla these days, leaving the station business to her and Buff Nelson. She didn't mind, she preferred it that way, and as he had made no further calls upon her sexually, she presumed he had a mistress in town. She was thankful and made an effort to be pleasant in his company, but she was once again marking time until the boys came home.

They all stared at him in dumb amazement. Terence had dropped his bombshell. He'd called a household meeting, Henrietta and the boys, Jackie and Nellie, and they'd gathered around the kitchen table. He'd considerately chosen the kitchen in deference to Jackie, who would not have been comfortable in the lounge room.

He'd methodically told them of his plans, brooking no interruption, then announced, 'We'll be moving at Christmas.'

Henrietta, who had tried to interrupt a number of times,

was now rendered speechless. So was everyone else, it seemed. He had confounded them all with the detail and finality of his arrangements.

Jackie and Nellie exchanged a look which Terence noted.

'I have no doubt that Vesteys will continue to employ you both,' he said, 'I shall certainly suggest that they do.' Then he rose from the table and peremptorily dismissed them. 'You can go now, I'll talk to you later, Jackie.'

When Jackie and Nellie had left silently through the back door, Henrietta finally found her voice.

'Do we have any say at all in this?' she asked coldly.

'No.'

Her shock was slowly turning to anger. 'You turn our lives upside down, you deprive your sons of their birthright, and we're to quietly accept it without saying a word?'

'You can say what you like, Henrietta,' he snapped, 'but it won't alter a thing. And I am not "depriving my sons of their birthright", as you put it, I am creating an empire which they will inherit.'

'And what if they don't want to inherit a business? They were brought up on the land.'

'Shut up, Henrietta!'

She wasn't about to, but when he added, 'They're old enough to speak for themselves,' Henrietta fell silent. He was right, and she hoped the boys would have the courage to speak their own minds.

Terence turned to Malcolm first. He tried to keep calm, Henrietta's reaction had infuriated him. 'You'll be off to Duntroon in a year or so, Malcolm, and from there God knows where the army will send you. I'm sure, after a fine military career, the last thing you will wish to inherit will be a struggling cattle station.' The sneer in his voice was intended for Henrietta, but when Malcolm remained silent, Terence demanded a reply. 'You do get my point, don't you, boy?'

Malcolm nodded obediently, although it was difficult to encompass his whole life so neatly mapped out before him. 'Will we be able to keep horses?' he asked.

Terence grinned, his fury instantly evaporating, he'd known that he could rely on Malcolm. 'Of course we can, we can keep a whole stable full.'

Malcolm grinned back, pleased that he'd come up with the right answer.

'And you, Kit,' Terence turned to his younger son. 'After you leave the army how would you feel about inheriting an empire? "Galloway and Sons".' He painted the sign proudly in the air with his outstretched hand. 'We'll own half of Darwin.'

'I don't want to go into the army.'

There was a moment's silence. Henrietta held her breath. She had known the day of confrontation would come, but not quite so soon, the boy was not yet fourteen.

Terence refused to take the declaration seriously. 'You'll feel different after you've been to Duntroon,' he said.

'I don't want to go to Duntroon.'

There was that look in the boy's eyes again. That unwavering grey stare. Terence once more felt his anger mount. 'What exactly would you prefer to do with your life?' he asked. His voice was ominously calm and Henrietta recognised the danger signs.

Kit apparently didn't. 'I want to go to university,' he said with ingenuous enthusiasm. 'I want to study English literature and be a writer.'

'I see. And how do you propose to go about that?' Terence's tone was blandly innocent, as if expressing a sincere interest.

Kit looked a little bewildered, 'University,' he said, 'an arts course . . .' He thought he'd answered that question.

'Ah yes,' Terence said, 'university, of course, but *after* university . . . how do you propose to become "a writer"?'

He was playing a cat and mouse game, Henrietta

realised, letting Kit feel he was free to express himself when, any minute, he'd pounce and tear the boy to shreds.

Relieved that his dad didn't seem mad about his not wanting a military career, Kit missed his mother's warning glances altogether and rattled on eagerly, presuming his father's enquiry to be genuine.

'Oh, I know I can't become a writer just like that,' he said. 'Crikey, maybe I'll never become a *proper* writer, you know like writing a book and getting it published and everything, that takes years. And besides, there's no point in writing until you've got something to write about, that's what Paul always said. "You've got to do a bit of living first," he told me.'

Fury burned white hot in Terence. That bloody Englishman again, he's influencing my son even from beyond the grave, he thought. Inwardly he cursed Paul Trewinnard. If the bastard was still alive I'd kill him, cancer or no bloody cancer, he thought.

Henrietta watched as Terence's eyes grew dead, and wondered if he was about to throw one of his fits of rage.

'But with an arts degree I'd be able to get a job in a newspaper,' Kit continued, 'I checked with my English teacher and she thought it was a good idea.'

By now Malcolm too could sense that his father's silence was not healthy, but Kit, excited and garrulous, still failed to recognise the fact.

'I don't care if I start at the bottom,' he said, 'just getting people cups of tea and stuff, but I'd work hard to be a journalist. I want to be a travel writer like Paul,' he eagerly added, 'and then you get to see all those places that you can write about later . . .'

'That's enough!' Like steel, Terence's voice knifed through the boy's chatter. The fingers of his right hand clenched into a fist which he longed to drive into his son's face, but he resisted the urge and wheeled on Henrietta instead.

Henrietta instinctively cringed in her chair.

'This is your doing,' he snarled. 'You and that English string of misery have done your best to ruin my son. Well, I'll have no more of this rubbish, do you hear?' He smashed his fist down on the table. 'Not one more word!' Then he turned again to his younger son, who was staring open-mouthed in bewilderment at his father's sudden rage.

'And you, boy,' Terence growled with utter contempt, 'you will go to military college when the time is right and you'll make a man of yourself. You're a Galloway and it's high time you started behaving like one.'

Terence strode from the room before his temper got the better of him and he started throwing punches.

The following weeks of the boys' vacation were not the joyous school holidays which Henrietta normally awaited with eager enthusiasm. Terence was in a constant ill humour and they all trod warily, fearful that the slightest thing might give offence and bring down the force of his wrath. Even the weather seemed to match the mood of the household. The wet season hit early and the days were either clammy and oppressive or beset with violent storms.

For the first time in years Henrietta was thankful when the boys returned to school. She didn't know which had been worse, the threat of Kit's rebellion, or Malcolm's desperate attempts to mollify his father.

Henrietta had promised Kit, privately, the very night after the confrontation, that he would go to university. She had funds of her own, she'd said, but he must be patient and wait. In silence. So Kit had wandered around, sullen, resentful, wanting to speak his mind but obeying his mother's wishes.

Malcolm, on the other hand, had been overanxious and determined to please his father.

'I've set the goal posts up, Dad, do you want to kick the ball around?'

'In this weather? Don't be bloody stupid.'

Time and again Malcolm had been left feeling humiliated and wretched, and each time he'd been spurned,
Henrietta's heart had gone out to him.

She did not attempt to confront Terence herself, she
dared not for fear he would take his black rage out upon
his sons. She pretended instead that nothing untoward had
happened. She was bright and breezy with the boys and
pleasant with Terence, and careful every minute of the day
that he should find no chink in their armour. No books
appeared during the holidays, there were no discussions
about literature, and she breathed a sigh of relief when Kit
and Malcolm returned to school.

'The house won't be finished until the middle of next year,'
Terence said pleasantly as he sipped at his Scotch in the
quiet evening of the lounge room.

He'd been going out of his way to be pleasant since the
boys had left, and in ratio to the re-emergence of his good
humour, Henrietta had reverted to silence and her books.
She had decided there was no point in trying to communicate with him, what was the use, but she was infuriated.
He'd made the boys' holiday hell and now he expected
everything to be back on an even keel. Well, bugger him,
she thought, as she buried her head in her book.

'So when we move to Darwin at Christmas we'll have to
stay somewhere else.' He ignored the fact that she was
paying him no attention. She was probably punishing him
for his behaviour when the boys were here, he thought. He
knew he'd been surly, but what did she expect? He'd
worked his guts out organising things to the best possible
advantage, ensuring Henrietta's middle years would be
comfortable and his sons would inherit an empire, and
what thanks did he get? Terence had been unable to shake
off his reaction to such ingratitude for weeks, but now that
the boys had gone, particularly Kit, whose presence had
been a constant annoyance, he was prepared to let bygones

be bygones. The fact that Henrietta was sulking and disappearing once again into her books irked him but he was determined to do his best to pacify her.

'I thought perhaps the Hotel Darwin,' he said.

At the mention of the Hotel Darwin, Henrietta looked up.

Good, he had her attention. He'd known that the Hotel Darwin would please her.

'What?' she said.

'The Hotel Darwin, that's where we'll stay whilst the house is being finished. I thought you'd be pleased,' he said, 'you've always liked the Hotel Darwin.'

'Yes,' she said. Dear God, no, she thought. 'But surely when the boys come home for the holidays we'll need to rent a house for the space.'

'They might rather like the novelty of the hotel,' Terence replied, 'and it would save you a lot of work.' He was doing his best to be agreeable.

'Perhaps. But then there are newer places than the Hotel Darwin, maybe we should try somewhere different.'

Why, he wondered? Because she associated the Hotel Darwin with fond memories of her precious friend Trewinnard? Terence pushed for an answer. 'Why?' he demanded belligerently.

Henrietta retreated. 'Oh for heaven's sake, Terence, no reason whatsoever, we'll stay wherever you like, let's discuss it closer to the time, shall we?' And she returned to her book.

'I'm going into town tomorrow to see Aggie,' Henrietta announced the following week, 'she's taking her class to a special art exhibition at the old Town Hall and I said I'd join them.'

'Fine.'

'I'll probably stay a few days, I haven't seen her in months.'

'Of course,' he replied pleasantly enough, although he

found her peremptory tone irritating. 'Tomorrow's Wednesday, I'll give Nellie the night off, she and Jackie might like to go to the pictures.'

Wednesday was the only night Aborigines were permitted to attend the picture theatre in Darwin, where they sat in the cheap seats up the back. In fact Wednesday was the only night Aborigines were allowed into town at all, 'between sunset and sunrise', and even then they needed to queue up for permits.

'That'd be nice,' Henrietta said, 'I'm sure they'd like that.'

Again the coldness of her tone irritated him, but then Terence had been in a constant state of annoyance for the past week. Despite all of his efforts, Henrietta remained remote. It infuriated him.

Nellie and Jackie were indeed delighted at the prospect of an outing to the Star Picture Theatre, and Wednesday night found Terence alone in the house. It also found him brooding and angry. Henrietta had turned her cheek to him when he'd kissed her goodbye that morning. She'd actually avoided his lips and proffered her cheek like a maiden aunt. Her action symbolised the coldness she'd displayed to him over the past fortnight since the boys' departure, and the more Terence brooded upon it the angrier he became.

The emptiness of the house aggravated his burgeoning ill-temper. The lack of Henrietta's presence seemed to taunt him, as if it was another gesture of hers intended to humiliate him, and he stalked about the place, Scotch in hand, wishing that she was with him. If she was here now, he thought as he poured himself another drink, he'd put her in her true place. And her true place was upstairs, naked, with her legs spread. He'd rip her clothes off her and he'd drive himself into her with all the force he could muster, and he'd bite her lips and her breasts until he drew blood. If she was here now he'd demand she serve him as a true wife should. Terence was frustrated beyond endurance.

Bella, he thought, he needed Bella. He slammed down his Scotch and left for the Aboriginal camp. But on the way there, he had a better idea.

Half an hour later, Terence returned to the homestead, and he brought Bella with him. The girl was nervous, she didn't want to come into the big house, and he had to literally drag her through the back door.

'There's no-one here, see?' He dragged her through the kitchen and into the hall. 'Big house empty. People gone.'

Bella stopped struggling and looked about, her mouth open, her eyes wide in wonderment. She had never seen such grandeur. She gazed up at the high ceilings of the hall, at the wide ornate wooden staircase, she peeked through the open door of the lounge room where the light from the wall brackets illuminated furnishings that she had never known existed. This was a magic place. A palace. She looked at Terence and smiled with childish delight.

The excitement in her eyes, the fullness of her lips and the whiteness of her teeth gleaming in the dim light of the hall intensified Terence's desire. He grabbed her hand and pulled her towards the stairs. Her nervousness returning, she baulked a little, but once he got her up to the landing, pushed the door of the main bedroom open and turned on the lights, she was once again like a child in fairyland.

Bella had never imagined a bed could be so big. She'd never actually seen a bed before, only an occasional discarded mattress at the camp, put to use during the muster and dumped as the families moved on. And the dressing table! With its huge gilt-edged mirror and silver-topped jars and brushes and combs . . .

She crossed to it and looked at herself in the mirror. She discovered that, if she stood back from the dressing table a little, she could see her whole body, from the top of her head to her knees. She'd never seen her whole reflection before. She didn't have long to wonder at the fact, however, Terence was beside her, ordering her to take her clothes off.

There wasn't much to take off, she wore no underwear beneath her light smock and, as Terence rummaged in the top drawer of the dressing table Bella slipped the smock over her head and admired her nakedness in the mirror.

'Put these on,' he told her, and he handed her a pair of white panties and a lacy white brassiere.

Bella giggled as she stepped into the panties, and he had to help her with the brassiere, she had no idea how to fasten it. Then she stood before the mirror admiring herself in the fancy underwear of the white missus. It would be uncomfortable to wear all the time, but it looked very sexy. She cupped her breasts and pulled them up higher into the brassiere; it was too big for her, but its lace looked lovely against her skin. She turned and looked over her shoulder, admiring her bottom in the panties. She liked what she saw.

So did Terence. As he sat on the bed watching Bella admire herself, the sight of his wife's stark white underwear against the girl's black skin excited him. He undressed, not taking his eyes from the girl for one instant, and when he was naked he stepped behind her and gazed at their reflections.

'Bend over,' he said. Bella knew what was expected of her, and she started to take off the panties. 'Leave them on,' he ordered.

Bella leaned her elbows on the dressing table, parted her legs, and arched her back, her rump pointing up invitingly at him.

Terence pulled aside the panties and entered her from behind. He tried to move slowly, to savour the image as he looked down at his groin and thrust himself through his wife's underwear into Bella's velvet interior. He looked at their reflections in the mirror. Bella was enjoying herself now. Her head lolled back, her eyes half open, her lips parted, she was making guttural sounds as she met his every thrust.

The sight of the girl's blackness and her wantonness in Henrietta's pristine underwear was both erotic and rebellious and Terence was losing control. He tried to slow down but it was impossible. The thought of Henrietta's debasement was giving him untold pleasure, and the harder and stronger he pumped himself into the girl's body, the more he was making Henrietta pay for her coldness.

Frigid bitch, he thought as he thrust more and more brutally and, as he reached his climax, the knowledge that he had defiled Henrietta in her absence, in her own bedroom, with her own underwear, afforded him the most exquisite pleasure.

As soon as he was spent, he dismissed the girl. 'Go home, Bella,' he said.

Bella was a little disappointed. She'd wanted to explore the grand house, but the boss was in one of his bad moods. He was funny like that. Sometimes after they'd done it he'd laugh and play with her, and sometimes he'd just walk off. Bella slipped her smock back on and disappeared.

The panties were damp and they smelled of his semen. Terence decided to destroy them. It was one thing to humiliate Henrietta in her absence, another entirely to be found out. Faced with the knowledge of his indiscretion she might well leave him, and that was a prospect which, deep down, terrified Terence. But he wondered, as he folded the brassiere and returned it to the drawer, whether she might smell the black woman next time she dressed. A musky smell which she would put down to damp, but the thought pleased Terence.

About to close the drawer, he noticed what looked like a jewellery case. Henrietta wore little jewellery. He'd been unaware that she had recently acquired this small silver box. And without informing him too. Terence was intrigued.

The case was locked. Even more intriguing. He searched briefly for a key without success. No matter. He'd break the lock easily enough, husbands and wives should have no secrets, after all. And he took the jewellery case downstairs to his study to attack it with his penknife.

CHAPTER TWENTY-FOUR

1878

B enjamin Sullivan liked to show off the locket. In Barclay's Room, a converted old store of the famous surveyor Goyder, where the elite of Port Darwin attended concerts or played dominoes and charades, Benjamin would sit in a corner chatting to the latest newcomer, and it would be only a matter of minutes before he produced the locket. It was always an excellent conversation opener.

'Where did you get it?' the newcomer would ask, suitably impressed.

'Exchanged it with a black,' Benjamin would lie, 'for a tomahawk, the blacks like tomahawks.'

Monsieur Durand, the dandified mining magnate complete with tamarind-blossom buttonhole and waxed moustache, who acted as master of ceremonies at Barclay's Room, would inevitably be holding court or introducing the latest performer, but Benjamin always preferred a quiet chat in the corner.

'I was a surveyor with Goyder's expedition in '69,' he'd

continue which, if not exactly a lie, was certainly an exaggeration. He'd been a cadet surveyor doubling as an axeman when the need demanded. Again the newcomer would be impressed, the year-long expedition of Goyder and his team was the stuff of legends.

In 1869 the South Australian Government had decided that the mysteries of the far-distant Northern Territory must be revealed. Who knew what pastoral lands might lie hidden amongst the vast tracts of unexplored country, or what wealth of minerals might lie undiscovered beneath its surface. George Woodroffe Goyder, Surveyor-General of South Australia, was the man chosen to lead the expedition, the purpose of which was the survey of a half a million acres of tropical territory in less than a year.

Not only did Goyder carry out his mammoth task but, two years later, the success of the 'Singing String' was considered largely due to George Woodroffe Goyder's Northern Territory Survey Expedition. The 'Singing String' was two thousand miles of overland telegraph line stretching from Port Darwin to Adelaide. Linked by submarine cable to Java, the line had thence linked Australia to the rest of the world.

A bit of the hero was bound to rub off on anyone connected with the Goyder expedition, and Benjamin Sullivan liked to be considered a hero. He always started off his tales with the locket, though, such a visual way to impress, before branching off into his adventures and the men with whom he'd shared intimate acquaintance.

'Goyder, yes, knew him well, a fine man.' He hadn't known Goyder well at all, taking most of his orders from one of the junior surveyors. 'And Bennett, tragic story Bennett, we were close friends.'

Benjamin and J.W.O. Bennett hadn't been 'close friends', but Benjamin had indeed known the young draftsman. They'd been the same age, just twenty-three, when Bennett had been stabbed in the back by natives.

There'd been a recent tribute to him in the Northern Territory Times. A retrospective article indeed, but an indication that Bennett's death remained a newsworthy item.

'Took him four days to die, poor fellow.' And Benjamin would shake his head, as if reliving the loss of his dearest companion.

Benjamin Sullivan was a striking looking man. Above average height, thirty-two years of age, he was strong and fit in the body. With thick, wavy hair which grew to his shoulders and an impressive beard and moustache, he looked for all the world like the rugged frontier man he wished to be. But for all the strength of his appearance, he was a weak man at heart. Perhaps he knew it. Perhaps it was why he needed his stories.

He was just as comfortable telling his stories in any one of Darwin's three hotels, each consisting of a bar and three rooms. There was the Pickford's Family Hotel, the Palmerston Club and the North Australian. But not being a drinking man himself, Benjamin preferred Barclay's Room. Gold miners, when they returned to their shanties near town and sought out the bars, were more intent on getting the grog into them than they were in conversation.

It was the pioneer families in their shack homes dotted about the scrub whose company Benjamin most enjoyed, the wives being particularly fascinated by the locket, and the varying stories he told of its acquisition—he always varied his stories about the locket according to the audience he was entertaining. These brave young wives had joined their husbands, many of whom had been members of surveying teams, and settled in Port Darwin, bringing with them a cultural and social change to the town. Benjamin wanted nothing more than to be one of those pioneer families. He had built his own modest home and intended a trip to Adelaide soon to find himself a wife, one who would bear him strong children.

Benjamin was in his customary corner at Barclay's

Room and this time he was out to impress the wife of James Masterson, a successful gold miner who had recently joined forces with Monsieur Durand. No shanties for those two, both men lived in fine houses, and no prospector's pan for them either; they employed whole teams of pig-tailed, palm-leaf-hatted Chinese coolies—and two whites with rifles to keep them in order—and at no initial cost. The South Australian Government had given free passage to thousands of Chinese in order to provide cheap labour for its northern province. With thirty Chinese to a team, each paid a shilling a day, tons of supplies and equipment could be carried in the baskets of their shoulder poles across the 120 miles to Pine Creek and the mines. And even if it took the teams three weeks, there was little cost to the mining magnates, the coolies lived on a bag of rice, and then they trekked back, their baskets laden with cakes of smelted gold. It was necessary to keep replacing the coolies, however; more often than not when the Chinese had received their first week's pay they purchased a pannikin, a shovel and dish and set off to fossick on their own. There were hundreds of them out there, it was told.

'It is certainly a most lovely thing,' Mrs Masterson said, holding the locket up to the light, 'how did you come by it?'

'Yes it is lovely, isn't it?' Benjamin agreed, admiring the line of Mrs Masterson's neck as she held the locket up to the light. She was a handsome woman, he'd like his wife to resemble Mrs Masterson. 'It was given to me by a black woman. Of the Larrakia tribe. A great beauty.'

Mrs Masterson handed the locket back to him and directed her attention to Monsieur Durand, who was introducing a soprano to the minuscule stage.

Benjamin realised she had taken offence. He'd meant no harm by his remark, he'd simply wished to gain her attention. But then Mrs Masterson was an Englishwoman newly arrived in Port Darwin and possibly fearful of the blacks. It was certainly obvious from the set of her pursed lips that she didn't approve of them. Personally, Benjamin didn't find the blacks at all offensive, he had come to know them during the expedition. Come to admire them in fact. Therein lay the huge weight of his guilt, but no, he mustn't think about that.

'I was a surveyor on the Goyder expedition at the time.' He hastily dropped his story of the Larrakia beauty and was about to launch into his adventures on the trail, but she cut him off dead in his tracks.

'Really,' she said without interest, her tone glacial and dismissive.

Annabelle Masterson had assumed Sullivan was offering the locket for sale and she'd been about to enquire as to its purchase price. Now she wiped her soiled fingers daintily on the lace handkerchief which she kept secreted in the sleeve of her gown. How dare the wretched fellow proffer her a tainted piece of merchandise. And his mention of the black woman's 'beauty', did that mean he'd had intimate relations with a native? Was she supposed to be impressed? Was he deliberately insulting her? It was indescribably sordid, and she signalled Monsieur Durand with a subtle lift of her eyebrows.

'Mrs Masterson,' Durand was at her side in a matter of seconds. He'd been keeping his eye on Sullivan, it had always irritated him the way the man paid no attention to the evening festivities. In fact Durand often wondered why Sullivan bothered coming to Barclay's Room at all. If he simply wanted to sit and talk then why didn't he frequent one of the hotels? He certainly looked as if he belonged in a bar, with his long hair and his untrimmed beard. It was appallingly obvious that he didn't even clip his moustache. And now it appeared he was annoying Masterson's wife.

Durand raised Annabelle Masterson's hand to his lips in the flamboyant gesture he extended to all the ladies; they loved it. 'Perhaps you would care to sit a little closer to the front,' he said, 'your view is somewhat obscured here in the corner.' Although bent upon rescuing his new business partner's wife, and although he neither liked nor approved of Benjamin Sullivan, Durand knew better than to directly offend the man who was, after all, a renowned surveyor.

'Thank you, that is most kind. Good evening, Mr Sullivan.' And Annabelle Masterson sailed away without so much as a glance at Benjamin, who sat, with the locket still in his hands, wondering exactly what he'd done wrong.

Benjamin had never received such a reaction before. Many of the pioneer wives had been titillated by his story of the Larrakia 'princess' whom he had befriended. The daughter of a native 'king', she had been a great beauty and he had saved her life, in return for which she had given him the precious locket. He always kept the story innocent and heroic. Unless there was a suggestive twinkle in the eyes of his listener, in which case he would look away and say modestly, 'she remains my friend to this very day', and allow them to read into his remark whatever they wished.

But it hadn't been like that at all. The locket had not been gained by heroic deeds, nor indeed by simple barter. No matter how many stories Benjamin invented, no matter how hard he tried to forget, every now and then something would jog his memory, as strangely enough Mrs Masterson's snub had just done, and the hideousness of that morning would return as vivid as ever.

It had been during the long sea voyage aboard the Moonta when they'd rounded the southern coast of Western Australia and headed northwards, bound for Darwin Harbour from where the Northern Territory Expedition would set out. They'd stopped at several ports en route to replenish supplies, and they'd set up camp in several protected bays during the voyage. They were well north of the Gascoyne River, bound for Port Hedland, when the orders came that they were to hove to, disembark, and set up their tents.

The following morning he and Harry Stafford had gone on a hunting expedition. So had a number of the others, whatever fresh meat or fish supply they could find was a welcome relief from the endless corned beef rations on board.

Harry Stafford and Benjamin had become good friends. Harry was a survey hand and, although lower in the ranks than Benjamin, far more of a leader. In fact Harry was trouble. A tough, wiry young man who enjoyed a fight and took on any dare offered him. Benjamin, six years younger, rather envied Harry and tried, when he could, to emulate him.

They were well into the bush, three or four miles from the camp, in a clearing beside a creek which augured well for their hunting prospects, when they heard a noise, something big in the scrub behind them, perhaps a kangaroo. Harry turned, revolver raised at the ready.

Yatamudtji was travelling alone with his wife Toolainah. She was carrying a baby in her belly and wished to give birth to her firstborn in the company of the women of her own people, the Kullari, far to the north. Yatamudtji had travelled across many tribal lands, he was now in the territory of the Ngarli and he wanted no trouble. At first, when he'd heard the tread of human feet through the bush he had thought it was people of the Ngarli, but the steps were too heavy, he'd realised. Then he'd seen the white men.

Yatamudtji had seen white men on two occasions before, from a distance, and although at the time they had done no harm to his people, he was very wary of them. They carried fire weapons which could kill in the blink of an eyelid. If he'd been alone he would have crept stealthily away, but they were nearing the place where his wife was resting, in the bark lean-to amongst the bushes by the creek. Any minute Toolainah might rise and startle them, and they might think she was some beast of prey and point their fire weapons at her.

Yatamudtji put down his spear, he must give them no cause to find him threatening. He would offer them the two goannas he held, strung together with twine. Then he had an even better idea, he would show them minya yindi, the symbol of peace. Yatamudtji wore minya yindi around his neck, his father had entrusted it to him as an omen of good luck, that his firstborn might be a son.

'Waminda,' Yatamudtji said, which meant 'friend', as he stepped from the bushes, and in his right hand he held up the locket.

Harry fired in the instant that he saw the black. Even as he pulled the trigger he was aware that the man carried no spear, but what the hell, he was a big healthy young buck, not one to tangle with, and God knew how many more of the bastards might be hiding in the bushes.

Yatamudtji was thrown backwards by the impact, his chest shattering as the bullet entered his heart.

'Take cover, Ben!' Harry yelled, 'they might have us surrounded.' He felt the thrill of battle as he circled the clearing, aiming his revolver at the bushes, prepared for attack from any quarter. Come on you black bastards, he thought, just try to take me. Just try, I dare you.

Benjamin was terrified. But, even in his terror, he'd registered that the native had been weaponless, and that he'd been holding up his hand. Surely it meant he was approaching them as a friend. But what if Harry was right? What if they were surrounded? Any minute hordes of black savages might come at them from out of the scrub. Benjamin spun about fearfully, searching in every direction, his revolver raised at the ready.

Toolainah had been shocked awake by a loud explosion. What could it be? She hauled herself to her feet and saw her husband on the other side of the clearing. He was sprawled dead on the ground and blood was seeping from the wound in his chest.

Her eyes wide with shock, her hand to her mouth,

Toolainah started to wail. She was not aware of the white men who whirled to face her, all she could see was Yata-mudtji.

'Shoot for God's sake!' Harry yelled, turning his revolver sights once more on the bushes, leaving the woman for Benjamin to dispatch, there was far more danger in the bushes. Any minute now they might charge.

'It's a woman,' Benjamin said rather stupidly, staring dazed, at Toolainah. Her wails had now reached the point of hysteria. How could he shoot a woman?

'So?' Harry snarled. 'Shoot the bitch.' Her screaming was getting on his nerves. But Benjamin remained frozen to the spot. 'Jesus Christ, Ben!' Harry turned, took aim, and fired.

Toolainah's screams were silenced as part of her skull blew away and her body fell backwards into the shallows of the creek.

Harry circled the clearing like a dervish. 'Any more of you out there?' His bloodlust was up. 'Come on you black heathens!'

Benjamin stood stunned, staring from the body of the man to the body of the woman. As her blood wound its way through the rocks to trickle downstream, he saw her protruding belly and realised, with a sickening sense of shock, that the woman was with child.

Satisfied, finally, that they were safe, that the savages had been travelling alone, Harry came to his senses. 'We'll have to cover the bodies,' he said, gathering foliage and dead branches and dragging them towards the stream. They would be in deep trouble, he knew it, if the slaughter of the blacks was discovered. Orders from the South Australian Government were that peace must be maintained with the natives at all cost. He threw the branches and foliage over the woman's body.

'God in heaven, man, lend a hand,' he growled at Benjamin.

'She was with child.' Benjamin still couldn't move.

'Good riddance, one less black bastard.' Harry was getting angry now, perhaps with his own hot-headedness, but he felt like strangling Benjamin; useless bastard, he thought. 'Drag him over here,' he ordered, jerking his head in the direction of the black man's body as he gathered together more foliage. 'Come on, man, move! Do you want to go to gaol for murder?'

Jolted from his state of numbness, Benjamin did as he was told. Harry was right, they would have to cover the bodies. As he grasped the black man beneath the armpits, he noticed the locket. Hanging by twine around the man's neck. This was what he had been holding up to them as he'd stepped from the bushes.

Benjamin glanced back at Harry who was paying him no attention. He slid the locket over the black man's head and slipped it into his pocket. He would look at it later. Then he dragged the body to the shallows of the creek where he helped Harry cover it from view.

They left the scene of the crime as quickly as they could, and approached the camp from a different direction. They travelled silently, Benjamin still horrified at what had taken place, and Harry cursing the fact that he'd been in the company of spineless young Benjamin Sullivan. Who would have thought such a fine looking specimen of manhood would prove to be such a coward.

When they came in sight of the cove where the ship was at anchor, and they could see the tents set up along the shoreline, Harry grasped Benjamin's arm and pulled him to a halt.

'What's wrong?' Startled, Benjamin looked about nervously. Was there something unseen in the bushes?

'Nothing. Yet.' The threat in Harry's voice and in the steely glint of his eyes was ominous. 'But there will be, I swear, if you don't play the game.'

'What do you mean?' Benjamin felt distinctly uneasy.

'If those bodies are discovered and questions are asked, you know nothing. We never saw any blacks, right?'

'Right, Harry.'

'Because if you say anything . . . anything to anyone at any time, I'll get you, Ben.'

There was murder in Harry's eyes and Benjamin was genuinely fearful of the man. Harry, recognising his fear, relaxed.

'Besides,' he said, releasing Benjamin's arm, 'there's only the two of us and if it ever came to light it'd be my word against yours. I'd tell them you did it because you were pissing yourself with terror at the sight of a couple of blacks, which of course they'd believe,' he sneered, 'and I'd say that I covered for you because you're so young and helpless.' He grinned contemptuously. 'And I'm a much better liar than you, Ben.'

'I won't say anything, Harry, I promise.'

Two days later, when the Moonta upped anchor and they departed the cove, Harry breathed a sigh of relief. The bodies had not been discovered.

It was presumed by some aboard that Harry Stafford and Benjamin Sullivan must have had a falling out. Not that there was any friction between them or that they ever spoke ill of one another, but they'd been such good friends and nowadays they were rarely seen in each other's company.

Now that their secret was safe, Harry had no time for Benjamin, whom he considered a coward, and Benjamin was relieved to be free of Harry's company. Harry's violence not only frightened him, but the mere sight of Harry Stafford was a reminder of that hideous morning.

Six months later, when they were working side by side on the survey team and news reached them that the young draftsman, Bennett, had been speared to death by natives, Harry felt thoroughly vindicated.

'See,' he hissed to Benjamin, 'I should have killed more of the murderous bastards.'

But Benjamin didn't feel that way at all. By then he had had many happy communications with the black people, there had been many employed along the way to work with their teams. And the more he came to know them, the more the image of the pregnant black woman lying dead in the rocky creek came to haunt him. As did the image of the black man, stepping out from the bushes, unarmed, the locket held up innocently in his hand as a peace offering.

Benjamin often looked at the locket. He knew it was wrong that he should own it, a thing of such beauty acquired the way it had been, but then what was his alternative? He could not return it to its rightful owners, and he could tell no-one his story.

So, when he returned to Port Darwin several years after the survey and started planning his life, building his modest home and investing the healthy sum of money which he had saved from the expedition, he invented stories about the locket. It was a good way to make friends, he found, an impressive introduction. And, as the years passed, the stories became quite real to Benjamin, until, every now and then, something brought back the memory.

He needed to find a wife, Benjamin thought as he watched Annabelle Masterson lightly tap her fingers together in applause for the soprano. He needed a woman who believed in him, a companion, he was lonely, and above all he wanted children. He'd hoped to find a woman locally, but single women were in short supply in Port Darwin. He must stop merely thinking about it, he must go to Adelaide, and soon.

Perhaps the locket would aid him in finding a wife, he thought as he slipped it back into the pocket of his vest. Women were always very impressed with the locket—well, with the exception of Mrs Masterson—perhaps he'd better invent a story other than the Larrakia 'princess' though. Certainly if he wished to attract the right sort of woman.

CHAPTER TWENTY-FIVE

If Henrietta had expected sympathy from Aggie regarding the sale of Bullalalla then she was destined for disappointment.

'I think it's wonderful news,' Aggie said as they sat in her lounge room drinking tea, 'for once I'm in agreement with Terence. And it is, after all, his prerogative to sell the property.'

Disliking Terence as she did, Aggie could nevertheless see his point of view. It was quite possibly a shocking thing he was doing, selling off the life's work of his father and grandfather, denying his own sons their heritage. But then if the station was struggling, and if he could get a good price and open a thriving business, then surely it was the practical thing to do. Aggie was not a sentimentalist, nor was she a hypocrite, and she did little to conceal her delight.

'It'll be a whole new life for you, Henrietta,' she said enthusiastically, 'you can become *involved* in things.' 'Involved' was one of Aggie's favourite words, and she waved a hand about airily, signifying the hundreds of things worthy of involvement, and the lack of necessity for her to be specific. 'And with the boys away you *need* to become involved.' With the boys away Henrietta needed something other than the sole company of her tyrant of a husband, Aggie thought, but forthright though she was, she knew better than to make any comment on Henrietta's matrimonial affairs.

Henrietta was annoyed by Aggie's over-simplification of the whole predicament, and her apparent empathy with Terence. 'It's not quite that simple,' she said a little archly.

'Oh but it is,' Aggie insisted, fully aware of Henrietta's irritation. 'You said the sale has gone through and Terence is locked into his plans, isn't that right?'

'Yes, but . . .'

'Then make the most of it, use the opportunity, move with the times. There's no point in sulking about it, just look at you.' Aggie scowled, mocking Henrietta's sullen expression, and Henrietta couldn't help but laugh. Aggie looked for all the world like a ferocious old lion with her mane of grey hair and her bushy greying eyebrows.

Now in her early fifties, Aggie had resisted her hairdresser's suggestion that she enhance her hair colour with a 'gentle blue tint' as many middle-class Darwin matrons did ('no dear, they look like hydrangeas,' she'd said), and she steadfastly refused to pluck and shape her eyebrows in the fashion of the day. Aggie remained a non-conformist.

The ferocity dropped away now as she smiled, and the twinkle in her eyes was that of a mischievous child. 'Oh Henrietta, we'll have such fun, you and I,' she said.

By the following morning Henrietta was feeling very positive and she left in high spirits. The two women embraced at the front door.

'You're a tonic as always, Aggie.'

'Oh my dear, I can't wait for you to come into town.'

Terence was waiting for Henrietta upon her return. She was a little surprised, she'd presumed he'd be out working on the property.

'I thought we might spend the day together,' he said pleasantly as they walked up the front steps, 'go for a ride, maybe take a picnic lunch up to the waterfall.'

It was an odd suggestion. In all these years they'd never once been back to the waterfall. No-one went there, he'd said, it had been a special treat. And certainly no-one went for long rides and picnics in November.

'Bit of a risk,' Henrietta remarked as she stood on the verandah and looked up at the clouds gathering overhead.

'No, it's going to blow over,' he said with confidence, 'I heard the early forecast on the radio.' He smiled encouragingly. 'I thought you'd like the idea of a picnic.'

'I do,' she replied. She couldn't help but feel suspicious. What was his motive, she wondered. But it was wise to agree if it kept him in such an affable mood, and besides, she'd enjoy the ride. 'I think it's a lovely idea.'

He opened the flywire door for her and they went inside.

Half an hour later when she'd changed into her riding gear she found him in the kitchen with Nellie, who was quite happy to pack them a picnic lunch but a little wary of their plans.

'Going to be a storm by and by, boss,' Nellie was saying.

'No, it'll blow over, I heard it on the radio.'

But Nellie still had misgivings. 'I dunno,' she said with a shake of her head, 'not good to go too far.'

'We're not going far, just to the home paddock.' Terence turned as Henrietta entered the kitchen. He joined her at the door. 'No point in worrying her,' he muttered, indicating Nellie, who was still shaking her head as she ferreted about in the refrigerator.

Henrietta rode Florian and Terence was on Blocker, the big bay stallion which was his current favourite. Florian was twenty-one now and somewhat calmer than in his youth, although still spirited enough to take on a dare.

Past the home paddock and out on the flats, Terence urged Blocker on and Florian gave chase. For a short while they were neck and neck but the older horse quickly ran out of wind and had to concede defeat. Reluctantly, he allowed Henrietta to rein him in, panting and puffing, and she laughed and patted his neck.

'Good boy, Florian,' she said. 'Good boy.' She loved the animal. He'd been so much a part of her introduction to this wild country, it was as if they had grown up together.

Way ahead, Terence wheeled Blocker about and cantered back to join them.

'He's still got some spirit in him,' she said proudly, keeping Florian to a walk although, panting as he was, the arrival of Blocker brought a skip to his gait as if he wanted another race.

'So have you, Henrietta,' he said, a little strangely she thought. Then he smiled. 'You're a very good rider now, you handle a horse excellently.'

She laughed. 'Only Florian,' she said, 'he knows me so well.'

'Yes, he does, doesn't he.'

Terence was quiet as they rode together, and she presumed he was enjoying the peace as she was.

'It looks as if your weather forecast was right,' she said, looking up at the clouds which seemed to have moved on, revealing patches of blue high above.

'Yes,' he said. And they rode in silence until Henrietta felt the need to say something. Aggie's words had remained with her.

'I'm sorry if I've been selfish, Terence.'

'In what way?'

'About the sale of Bullalalla. It's your property, after all,' she said parroting Aggie's words, 'it's your prerogative to sell if you think it's the wisest move, which it obviously is.'

'And what's brought about this change of heart?'

'Aggie. She told me you were doing the practical thing and that I should stop sulking and move with the times.'

'What a wise woman.'

There was mockery in his tone. What had happened to his affable let's-have-a-picnic disposition, Henrietta wondered, but she no longer tried to fathom the reasons for Terence's mood swings. She hoped he wasn't about to spoil the day.

'She's a very good friend isn't she, your Aggie?'

The mockery again, the sarcasm. 'Yes, she is,' she said shortly, and she ignored him, looking about at the countryside, wishing now that they were not going on a picnic.

Terence was wondering if Aggie knew about the locket. About Trewinnard, and about Kit.

The moment he had opened the cherished locket which his wife had kept locked and hidden away, Terence had recognised the face of his son in the image of the Englishman. It had explained everything. How could he have been so blinded to the truth? The boy who had always seemed such a stranger to him was not his son. Hatred had consumed Terence. And fear too. The fear of discovery. Did Aggie Marshall know that he had raised another man's bastard? And if Aggie knew, who else might she have told? He glanced at Henrietta. He would find out soon enough. But Henrietta was ignoring him, she had closed off, he could see it. Oh no, he wouldn't have that.

'You're lucky, Henrietta,' he said with a sincerity which surprised even himself, 'very lucky to have a friend like Aggie.' He actually meant it, he realised.

She looked at him with suspicion. Another game?

'I mean it. Friends are hard to come by. I don't think I have any. Hans perhaps, but then I see him so rarely.' He gave her his most winning smile. 'I'm glad that you have a friend like Aggie. I really am.'

She would never understand him, and she no longer loved him, that much she knew. But there were times when she realised why she'd married him. He looked so warm and so loving, and so handsome; the realisation came as a bit of a shock.

'I'm glad too,' she said simply and she smiled back at him; for the moment his mood was forgotten.

They rode warily as they travelled up the escarpment, occasionally dismounting and leading their horses, it was dangerous territory, particularly in the wet. The recent downpours had rendered the terrain slippery and difficult for the horses to negotiate.

After a long and arduous trek, they reached the top. Henrietta was panting when they got there, they'd had to walk a lot more of the way than the last time they'd visited the waterfall. But it was worth it, she thought as she looked out over the panorama which surrounded her. And the waterfall itself, swollen from the rains, thundered magnificently to the rocks sixty feet below. She walked to the edge and looked down. The pool was obscured by spray and mist. As far as the eye could see, heavy pockets of mist clouded the valleys and the gorges. It was a different view entirely, she realised, than the one she had seen all those years ago. Strange and mysterious, but just as impressive, mirroring the changing image of the Territory's seasons.

Terence had tethered the horses while she'd been admiring the view, and now he crossed to stand beside her at the edge of the precipice.

'It's superb, isn't it,' she whispered, still a little out of breath.

'Yes,' he said, but his eyes didn't leave her, he had no interest in the view. She was superb too, he thought. As beautiful as the day he'd met her, perhaps even more so, the fine lines around her eyes and her mouth giving an added strength to her face. And her chestnut hair, with its barely discernible flecks of grey, tumbled as magnificently as ever to her shoulders. Her arms, bare in her sleeveless shirt, gleamed with the sweat of her exertion and her breasts still heaved a little as she panted. *What a pity she's a whore*, he thought.

Henrietta turned to him, aware that he was studying her and not the view. How strange. 'Shall we set up the picnic?' she suggested.

'No.' His reply was brusque. 'We won't have time for a picnic.'

She looked up at the angry clouds. He was right, the storm would break soon, they'd have to start heading for home.

She was glad they'd revisited the waterfall though. Her first son had been conceived up here. She remembered that magic day so vividly, she'd like to have stayed a little longer.

'What a pity,' she said.

'Yes it is, isn't it.' *A very, very great pity*.

That tone again, his foul mood was back. The moment was broken for Henrietta and she started towards Florian. But he stopped her.

'I have something to show you,' he said, reaching into the top pocket of his shirt. And she watched as he produced the locket.

He reached out his arm and dangled it before her eyes, and Henrietta stood mesmerised, speechless.

'It's very pretty,' he said, as he swung it teasingly in front of her face, 'valuable too by the looks of it. I wondered where it had come from when I first discovered it. Then I found out.' He opened the locket and thrust it into her face, involuntarily she flinched. 'It came from your scrawny English lover didn't it?' His voice was no longer teasing. He was keeping his anger in check, but it was a challenge, defying her to deny the truth. 'From the father of your bastard child no less. Am I right?' *Whore! Whore!*

'Yes,' she whispered. What else could she say? She stared at the pictures in the open locket. They told it all, how could she lie?

He snapped the locket shut and closed his fist around it

as if to crush the images inside and Henrietta was forced to meet his eyes. They were dead, she realised.

'What will you do, Terence?' She spoke as calmly as she could whilst she measured the distance between herself and Florian. Impossible to get away, she realised. The horse was tethered, and even if he hadn't been, Florian was no match for Blocker, Terence would run her down in no time.

'Kit is recognised as my son.' Terence's voice was as dead as his eyes. 'He will remain my son. No-one will know that you were unfaithful to me, Henrietta. I won't have that, do you understand?'

She understood fully. It would be more than Terence's pride could possibly withstand. What did he want of her? Was she to go away? To simply disappear? She would. She would promise him anything. Her mind was racing as she looked at the madness in his eyes.

'Do you want me to go away?' she asked, trying to keep calm. Don't panic, she told herself, don't panic. 'I will, I promise.' She could come back for her children, she thought, if only he would let her get away now. 'I'll leave, and I'll never tell anyone the truth.'

'Oh yes, I want you to go away,' he said. *I want you to go very, very far away*. 'But there are a few questions first. Does Aggie Marshall know?'

She shook her head.

'Does anyone know?'

Again she shook her head.

'Good.' It was the answer Terence needed, and he believed her. Despite her brave front, he could see that she was too terrified to lie.

'Because if anyone *did* know, I would not only kill you, Henrietta, I would kill your bastard child. You believe me, don't you?'

She nodded, she believed him implicitly.

'No-one is ever to know that Kit is not my son.' He took

her right hand and held it out, placing the locket in her open palm. 'No-one is ever to know that my wife was a whore,' he said as he closed her fingers around the locket. 'You keep this, Henrietta, I'm sure that you earned it.'

Henrietta stared down as he made a fist of her hand and held it in both of his, the grip slowly tightening.

'What was he like in bed, your scrawny Englishman?' The images had plagued Terence throughout the night. Henrietta in the throes of ecstasy beneath the skeletal body of Paul Trewinnard, it disgusted him. *Did you moan and writhe for him in a way you never do for me?* his mind screamed. How could she have chosen Trewinnard over him! Trewinnard of all men! *Did he give you orgasms?* he wanted to yell. He would have killed any man who'd touched his wife, but the knowledge that it was the dead Englishman who had proved his better was the most unendurable insult of all. Each week he'd allowed her to visit her dying friend, and each week he'd been cuckolded, Terence was sickened with revulsion and anger. 'Did you like fucking a corpse, Henrietta,' he snarled, 'was that it?'

'Stop it, Terence! Stop it!' She could feel the locket digging into the palm of her hand, and the knuckles of her fingers felt they might break any minute as he crushed her fist. She backed away, trying to wrench her hand from his vice-like grip. For one second she succeeded, but then he seized both her wrists, and dragged her to him so that her face was only inches from his.

'Is that what you liked, Henrietta?' His voice was harsh now, demented, his face twisted and ugly. 'Is that what you liked? Fucking a corpse? A man with one foot in the grave? Is that what you liked?'

'I only slept with him once!' she desperately begged. His rage was frightening. 'Only once! I swear it!'

Did she expect him to believe that? And even if he did, what difference did it make? She'd given herself to another man, she'd had another man's child, and she'd lied to him all these years. All these years he'd been raising another man's son! And for the rest of his life he would be forced to recognise this whore's bastard as his own blood. *Whore! Whore!*

'You're a whore, Henrietta! You're a whore! Say it!' She could feel his spittle on her face. 'Say it, Henrietta!' he yelled. 'Say it! I'm a whore! Say it!'

'I'm a whore,' the words came out in a breathless sob, she was terrified now.

'Say it again!'

'I'm a whore.'

'Again! Again!'

'I'm a whore, I'm a whore, I'm a whore,' she sobbed, her body sagging, but he continued to hold her up, suspended by the wrists.

'That's exactly what you are, you filthy bitch,' he hissed, and he finally released her.

She sank to her knees and, as she did so, she involuntarily clutched the locket to her breast.

Her instinctive reaction was the final straw for Terence. His madness was no longer a mere release of rage and hostility. His madness now had a purpose, and the purpose was murder, it was quite obvious that Henrietta must die.

He pulled her to her feet and supported her as he took the several steps to the edge of the precipice. 'Stay here with your lover, Henrietta,' he said, 'and I'll keep his bastard son.'

Henrietta's eyes were wide with disbelief, her mouth open in protest, but she had no time to utter a word. The gentlest push sent her backwards, and the last thing she saw was the look in Terence's eyes. Not of anger and recrimination, but the burning glow of sheer insanity. Then, as if in slow motion, the world spun as she felt herself fall.

Terence stood, motionless, watching Henrietta's body bounce from a rock ledge and continue to fall, buffeted about like a rag doll amongst the vegetation of the cliff face, until she was finally out of sight.

His anger had left him, and he felt free of any form of emotion. He wondered vaguely whether he had planned to kill her by bringing her to this deserted place. If so, he hadn't been aware of his intention. His intention had been to frighten her into admitting the truth. But it was better the way things had turned out. She deserved to die, and this way his secret would always be safe.

He heard the distant roll of thunder, and behind him Blocker whinnied nervously—Blocker didn't like storms—but Terence made no move, still staring down into the gorge. Her body would never be found, no-one ever came up here. Perhaps a crocodile would get her; in a heavy wet season the odd rogue croc found its way up to the pools of the gorges. In any event he was perfectly safe. But he would miss her, he suddenly realised. He didn't regret her death, it had been necessary, but he would miss Henrietta. He started to feel sad.

A far-off streak of lightning, another crash of thunder, and Blocker tossed his head and pawed the ground, the storm was getting closer. Terence forced himself to think practically, he must make plans.

He untethered the horses and started to lead them down the slopes. He would camp out overnight at one of the sheds near the mustering yards not far from the base of the escarpment. It was the customary thing to do during a heavy storm, no-one would raise the alarm at their failure to return tonight. Then, in the morning, he would go home with the news of the 'accident'.

CHAPTER TWENTY-SIX

Jackie and Nellie were not unduly concerned when the boss and the missus failed to return. The storm was ferocious and it was natural to presume they would stay overnight in one of the many sheds or barns about the property.

But mid-morning the following day, when the storm had cleared and Florian cantered home riderless, they knew there was cause for worry. Jackie raced through the back door and into the kitchen with the news.

'Florian come back to the stables Nellie,' he said. 'No missus.'

'Where's the boss?' Nellie asked, instantly alarmed.

'No boss.'

'You go find her, Jackie.' Nellie, as always, took control of the situation. 'I'll get Boss Nelson.' She headed for the telephone in the lounge room.

From the rise a good half mile away, Terence had watched as Florian headed for home. Early in the morning, he'd circled the homestead with the horses to make his approach from a different direction and, a mile or so from the station, still well out of sight, he'd released Florian and urged Blocker into a gallop. To Florian the race was on.

The horses ran neck and neck until they reached the clearing which led to the homestead, then Terence reined Blocker in and watched as Florian headed for the stables, the horse slowing to a canter when he realised it was no longer a race.

In the distance, Terence saw Jackie run to the horse. The black man calmed the animal, patting him gently as he led him into the saddling yard, then he eased the girth strap. The horse was snorting nervously, unaccustomed to galloping fully saddled and riderless. Terence watched as Jackie sprinted to the back door of the homestead to alert Nellie. It would have been quicker if he'd gone through the front door, but then even in a crisis Jackie avoided that. It was interesting to note that the black man still moved with the speed and agility of a thirty-year-old, and yet Jackie had to be at least fifty-five, fifty-six, maybe more, who could tell. His hair and his beard were greying, his body had thickened, but he was as fit as a mallee bull. Good old, reliable Jackie, Terence thought. He smiled, everything was going according to plan.

Only minutes later, Jackie reappeared. Terence watched as he returned to the saddling yard.

'Where you bin, Florian?' Jackie murmured, stroking the animal's neck. Florian nuzzled his nose into the crook of Jackie's arm. 'Where you bin?' He knelt and checked the horse's knees for signs of a fall, then he tapped each fetlock in turn, the animal obediently lifting each hoof for inspection. The horse was perfectly calm now, he was uninjured, his breathing was not laboured and there was little sweat on him, he'd not been overexerted. The missus must have taken a fall not far from the homestead, Jackie thought.

'You gonna take me to the missus, Florian?' Jackie whispered as he tightened the girth strap. 'We go find the missus, eh?'

From his observation post, Terence saw that Jackie was about to mount the horse and go in search of Henrietta.

It was what he'd expected, but it must be prevented. He dug his heels into Blocker's sides and galloped for the homestead.

Jackie saw Blocker and the boss emerge from the bush on the rise. He waved. The boss was safe, that was good, maybe he knew what had happened to the missus.

Terence dismounted at the saddling yard.

'She's back then,' he said breathlessly, indicating Florian, 'good, I was starting to get worried.'

'Missus not back, boss. Florian back, no missus.'

Terence stared at the horse, as if momentarily not comprehending.

'Don' worry boss, me and Florian gonna find her.' Jackie flung the reins over Florian's neck, but Terence stopped him.

'No, Jackie,' he said with some urgency, 'we need to mount a proper search, she could be anywhere, we stayed overnight in the shed at the graveyard.' He started to stride up to the homestead. 'When you've watered the horses come up to the house, I'm going to ring Buff Nelson.'

'Nellie already ring 'im, boss,' Jackie called after him. The boss was worried, he could tell. Jackie wanted to assure him that the missus couldn't be too far away. The stretch of flats known as 'the graveyard', where a vast field of termite mounds resembled huge tombstones, was a major mustering area with yards and sheds, and it was miles away to the east. Florian couldn't have travelled all the way from the graveyard that morning. The horse would have had more of a sweat up if he had.

Jackie quickly loosened the girth straps and watered both horses. Blocker was not sweating heavily either, he too couldn't have travelled that distance this morning. The boss must be confused, Jackie thought, he sure was worried.

When Jackie returned to the house, he heard the boss on the telephone, and he joined Nellie who was standing listening at the door to the lounge room.

'I thought she'd just gone for a ride,' Terence was saying, 'you know how Henrietta likes to ride at dawn,' his voice sounded desperate, 'I waited at the graveyard for over an hour, Buff, and when she didn't come back . . .'

There was an obvious interruption on the other end of the line whilst Buff Nelson calmed Terence.

Again Jackie was bewildered. 'Blocker and Florian don' come from the graveyard, Nellie,' he whispered, 'there no sweat on 'em.'

'You say nothin', Jackie,' she muttered. 'You keep quiet now.'

'But the boss . . .'

'Sssh,' she nudged him sharply as Terence put down the receiver.

'Boss Nelson's rounding up some men and bringing fresh horses in from the home paddock,' he announced, 'I'm going to meet him at the graveyard, we'll start the search from there.'

'I come 'long you, boss,' Jackie said.

'No you stay here,' Terence ordered. 'You boss man now Jackie. Stay by the telephone, Nellie, Christ knows how long it might take to find the missus, she could be anywhere.'

Jackie looked at Nellie, but she didn't return his glance, simply nodding dutifully. 'Yes, boss,' she said.

They watched from the back door as Terence returned to the saddling yard and remounted Blocker.

'Something bad happen, Jackie,' Nellie said, deeply troubled. 'He don' want you with 'im, and you the best tracker around these parts, the boss knows that.'

'No good trackin' after the storm.' It wasn't that aspect which worried Jackie. 'But them horses don' come from the graveyard this mornin'.'

'I know. The boss and the missus din' go to the grave-yard.'

Jackie looked at her, surprised, how did Nellie know that?

'I was cleanin' the windows in the front room,' Nellie said, 'and I heard the boss talkin' to the missus on the verandah, they was goin' to the waterfall, he said.' Nellie looked at her husband, her face full of the direst misgivings. 'He don' know that I hear 'im, then he tells me they just goin' to the home paddock.' She shook her head. 'Something real bad happen, Jackie. Ain' no waterfall round here for miles.'

They both knew exactly where the waterfall was. Warai country, the escarpment well to the south, Jackie had often travelled the area on walkabout when he'd visited Nellie's clanspeople. Why then was the boss searching the graveyard territory to the east?

'Something real, real bad happen,' Nellie said, 'he done something to her, I tell you. You gotta find the missus, Jackie.'

Twenty minutes later, Jackie saddled up Chloe, his whistle at the horse paddock having brought her trotting up to him instantly; each of his favourite mounts had a special whistle. Chloe was a stocky little brumby and she could negotiate slopes like a mountain goat. If Jackie was to explore the escarpment Chloe's skills would come in handy.

They did. Chloe had no problem at all with the climb, Jackie dismounting only once, where a mudslide from the heavy rain had rendered the slope dangerously slippery. They reached the top of the escarpment in half the time it would have taken a less sure-footed animal.

Jackie dismounted and searched amongst the vegetation for the tell-tale signs of horses. He was not looking for animal or human tracks, they would have been obliterated by the rain; it took him only minutes to find the fresh horse dung and the close-cropped tufts of grass where the animals had grazed. It gave him a starting point. He squatted to examine, minutely, every freshly broken twig, every recently disturbed stone on the rocky ledge over-looking the waterfall. People had stood here, he could tell, very close to the precipice too. Dangerous.

Jackie squatted at the edge of the cliff. He looked down, examining the cliff face and, with a sickening sense of horror, he knew what had happened. A bush on a rock ledge ten feet below had been almost pulled out by its roots, it hung dangling into space. A little further down, several branches of one of the many scrawny trees which grew out of the cliff face were broken. Something, or someone, had fallen, their body cutting a swathe through the vegetation which Jackie's trained eye could discern with ease.

He knew a way down to the pool, but he would have to leave Chloe at the top. Tethering the horse, he walked a hundred yards or so away from the ledge, and started the steep descent to the bottom of the cliff.

A good half hour later, when he had reached the pool, he doubled back to where he presumed he would find the body of the missus.

The bushes were flattened and there was a thick trail of mud, as if someone had dragged themselves towards shelter. An easy trail to follow, he found her in an instant.

Lying on her back, head and shoulders propped up against the protective shelter of the cliff, was the body of the missus. She clutched a fist to her breast and her face was caked with blood. One leg was bent at a horrifying angle, and her whole body was covered in mud.

Jackie knelt beside her, shocked and terrified. Nellie had been right, the boss had killed the missus. What was he to do? Take the body home? The boss would kill him if he did. But he couldn't leave the missus here for the croco-diles. Jackie was distraught with grief, he had loved the missus. He touched the body, stroking her face and her tangled hair, jabbering in his own tongue all the while.

In the merciful oblivion which had overtaken her pain and clouded her world, the oblivion she had presumed was her imminent death, Henrietta heard him. Or at least she heard sounds. Strange, primitive sounds, and she opened her eyes.

'Jackie,' she whispered, her voice barely audible. For just one moment, she was pleased to see him, the kind black man who had been her friend all these years. For just one moment she was glad that she was not going to die alone. But the return of consciousness brought the return of pain, and Henrietta prayed for death to overtake her.

'Missus,' Jackie couldn't believe it, the missus was alive. He was galvanised into action. 'Don' you worry, missus, Jackie goin' to get you out.' He took hold of her wrist, and every atom in Henrietta's body shrieked in agony.

'No, Jackie, no,' she whispered urgently. 'You mustn't move me, please don't move me.'

Jackie recognised her pain and gingerly he rested her hand back on the ground. 'We gotta get you home, missus,' he said. 'We gotta get you better.'

'No.' She tried to sound firm. She was the missus, he must obey her orders. 'My body is broken, you cannot get me better, you understand?'

Jackie nodded. The missus was dying, and he understood death. He would stay with her whilst she died. But what was he to do after that? He couldn't leave her.

Henrietta understood his confusion. She closed her eyes as a wave of pain engulfed her. But she must concentrate, she had orders to give. 'You will not take me home,' she said, 'you will leave me here,' and she slowly opened the fist which she clutched to her breast. In the palm of her hand was the locket. 'But you will take this with you, and you will tell Nellie to give it to Kit when he is grown.' She couldn't stretch out her hand, even opening her fist had been agony. 'When he is of age, Jackie, when he is twenty-one, you understand?'

Jackie understood and, very gently, he took the locket from the palm of her hand. 'Yes, missus,' he said.

As he slid the locket into the pocket of his shorts, Henrietta noticed the knife which he always carried in its sheath on his belt. She was grateful that he'd found her, and thankful that when Kit came of age he would know the truth as she'd always intended he should. The locket would tell her son the whole story. But now, as the pain overwhelmed her, she longed to die.

'Take my breath, Jackie,' she said, staring at the knife. For a moment Jackie didn't understand. 'My body is broken, it cannot be mended. Too much pain, Jackie. Take my breath. Please!'

He knew what she meant and he was shocked. 'I can' do that, missus.'

She closed her eyes, feeling the tears well beneath her eyelids. It was a terrible thing to ask of him, she could see it from the incredulity in his face. She tried to take a breath, to control herself, but breathing was agony. 'Oh dear God, Jackie, help me.' She opened her eyes and the tears spilled down the caked mud and the blood on her cheeks. 'Be kind to me. I've seen you do it to the steers. Take the hurt away, I beg you, take my breath.'

Jackie knew that the missus was in great pain. Her body was broken and she was dying. He must comfort her. He took his knife from its sheath, but still he sat beside her, tormented and undecided.

'You can do it, Jackie,' she gently urged, 'you can do it.' And she closed her eyes, arching her neck sideways against the cliff face.

'I can do it, missus,' he whispered, and he started to sing. A rhythmic chant which seemed to Henrietta like a didgeridoo. A haunting, primeval sound which she found most comforting. He touched his hand to the side of her face, stroking her cheek with his finger. 'You sleep now, missus, you don' feel pain no more.' And he continued to chant his strange song.

Henrietta drifted away, lulled by the ageless sound, the sound of the Territory, she thought, and she knew no fear, aware that she would feel no pain.

BOOK FOUR

Book Four

CHAPTER TWENTY-SEVEN

1938

*T*he somewhat shabby seaport of Darwin housed a surprising heart. One of kaleidoscopic colour and activity, exotic and exciting. Chinatown. In direct contrast to the apathy of the rest of the town where failing businesses sat beneath shaggy palms in half-finished streets, Chinatown was a hive of bustling enterprise.

In the shacks and shops of Chinatown, hard-working tailors could cut and immaculately stitch six suits in one day, if a prospective buyer's ship was docked for only twenty-four hours before its return to Singapore. Jovial laundrymen, undaunted by the heat, joked and chattered away as they spat on their burning-hot irons beside their burning-hot fires. In the open-shuttered doorways of the patriarchal shops, the daughters of Chinatown, beautiful in their shining satin tunics and trousers, sold figurines carved in ivory and silken scarves, jars of sugary sweets and delicacies from the East. Brightly pantalooned children darted amongst the many laneways, happy and playful in the freedom of their world. And everywhere the

*air tantalised the senses. The delicate fragrance of incense
conjured up the mystique of the East, and the lusty aroma
of roasting pork and ginger awakened the appetitie.*

Tom Sullivan walked purposefully through the productive
chaos of Cavenagh Street. It was market day, but he did
not stop to browse in the verandahed shops or the stalls as
most Europeans did. He crossed Peel Street, paused for a
moment, then strode through an open shopfront.

In the welcome shade of the shop he saw two Chinese,
one behind the counter, the other opening a display case,
each tending to a customer. To Tom all Chinese looked the
same, only their age set them apart, and he'd been told to
seek out the younger one. The man at the display case was
wizened and minus several teeth. He looked ancient,
although of course he might not have been, you could
never tell with the Chinese, but he was definitely the older
of the two.

Tom approached the man behind the counter, but then
realised that the younger of the Chinese, although well
dressed and dapper, looked like a boy. Small in stature,
fresh-skinned, he might have been fifteen. Damn, was
there another bloke somewhere, Tom wondered, and he
peered through the open doors at the rear of the shop.

The young Chinese looked up from the wares he'd been
showing his customer. 'Hang on a second,' he said to Tom in
a pronounced Australian accent, 'I won't be long.' He gave a
friendly grin and returned his attention to his customer.

Tom recognised the voice of authority. This was no boy,
he realised, this was the man he'd been told to see. He
waited patiently, browsing about the shop, which was fascinating. Samples of silks and brocades, satins and linens,
hung from pegs, the rolls of fabric neatly stacked beneath
them. A tailor's and dressmaker's business was run in the
back rooms of the shop. Shelves were lined with carved
ivory figurines, jade statuettes and jars filled with things
colourful and mysterious. The valuable merchandise was

displayed in glass cases. Jewellery, some gold and gaudy, some dainty and delicate. An impressive collection. Yes, Tom thought, he'd come to the right place.

Five minutes later the customer, a sailor, left the shop with his purchase and the young Chinese turned to Tom. 'What can I do for you, mate?' he asked in the outback vernacular. He'd recognised the young man as either a drover or a gold miner, bearded, bush-hatted, in khaki shorts and boots, and the Chinese always varied his greeting according to the appearance of the prospective buyer.

Tom walked over to the counter. 'Are you Foong Lee?' he asked.

'I am.' It was young Tom Sullivan, Foong Lee realised. He'd seen him around town often. Foong Lee knew everyone in Darwin, if not personally then by sight. Not all of them knew him of course; to Europeans all Chinamen looked the same it seemed, a fact which Foong Lee found amusing. This young man's grandmother knew Foong Lee, however, he had sold several items to the Sullivan matriarch over the years. Old Emily Sullivan had a penchant for fine jewellery.

Foong Lee did not admit to his recognition of Tom, nor to his contact with the family, but he eased up on his outback Aussie accent. The Sullivans, one of Darwin's 'first families', belonged to the upper echelons of society. They owned the longest established surveying company in town, handed down from father to son, and Tom was well educated, although it was rumoured he was the black sheep of the family. Foong Lee himself had heard that the lad was a bit of a ne'er-do-well.

'What can I do for you?' he asked helpfully.

Tom didn't notice that the Chinese suddenly appeared to be well spoken. 'I have something to sell,' he said.

Foong Lee watched as the young man produced an article wrapped in beige kid cloth from his pocket, placed it on the counter and lifted aside the soft fabric.

Despite all of his experience in the assessment and evaluation of fine jewellery, which Foong Lee considered his specialty, he had never before seen such a beautiful piece. He picked up the locket and held it to the light. It was heavy for an item so small. A mountain carved in solid silver and, above it, a sun of perfectly cut diamonds. He recognised the work of a master craftsman.

'A fine piece,' he said, taking up his magnifying glass. His tone was non-committal, but he never lied to his customers, believing honesty to be the best policy; his superior knowledge always gave him the advantage in any event. The craftsman's insignia was engraved on the back, two tiny 'g's. 'A very fine piece,' he said as he opened the locket and studied the initials engraved inside. Antique, he thought, but the light in the shop was inadequate for a proper examination. 'How did you come by it?'

'My grandmother gave it to me.'

Emily Sullivan had parted with a piece of such magnificence? Foong Lee found it hard to believe. Had young Tom stolen it from his grandmother? Foong Lee never accepted stolen goods. But he was eager to examine the locket closer and he needed to do so in natural light.

Two more customers wandered into the shop, a middle-aged European couple, it was always busy on market day.

'Good morning,' Foong Lee greeted them, but they took little notice of him as they browsed around. Realising there was not much likelihood of a sale, Foong Lee turned to his father, who was closing the display cabinet, his customer having left without buying. 'Baba,' he said, and he indicated the couple, 'ngoh yiu hui chut gai.' He would examine the locket in the open courtyard behind the shop, he had decided.

Foong Shek Mei nodded. 'Ho la,' he said, happy to look after the customers.

'Come with me,' Foong Lee said to Tom and they walked through the rear doors of the shop to a large open

*living area where two tailors' dummies stood in the corner
and a cutting table was strewn with patterns and fabric;
the tailor Foong Lee employed arrived at midday and
worked until midnight. They proceeded through to the
courtyard beyond.*

*'Take a seat,' Foong Lee said as he sat by the rickety old
wooden table in the centre of the courtyard. Tom joined
him, leaning his elbows on the table, studying Foong Lee
as the Chinese studied the locket through the magnifying
glass he'd brought with him.*

*So this was Foong Lee, Tom thought, the man whose
knowledge of jewellery his grandmother so respected.
'Find Foong Lee,' she had said, 'the younger of the two
Chinese who own the shop on the right in Cavenagh
Street, near the corner of Peel. He is an honest man and
he'll give you a good price.'*

*In the daylight, Tom could see that Foong Lee was not
a youth as he'd first supposed. He may even have been
near thirty. Still very young to be such an expert (Foong
Lee was in actual fact thirty-seven), but then, Tom
thought, the Chinese were a mysterious lot.*

*'You say your grandmother gave it to you?' It was a
simple question, there was no accusation in Foong Lee's
tone, but Tom knew that he needed proof of the gift,
his grandmother herself had told him so.*

*'I will write you a letter, Tom,' she'd said, 'you will need
proof of ownership or others will think you have stolen the
locket.' Grandmother Emily was always very direct, even
with her favourite, wayward grandson.*

*'I have a letter,' Tom said, producing a piece of paper
from his pocket, 'from my grandmother stating that it is
a gift to me.'*

*'Excellent,' Foong Lee nodded, as if he'd expected as
much, although in truth he was rather surprised. 'Excellent.' He gave the letter a cursory glance, he could easily
authenticate it later, he had Emily Sullivan's signature on*

several documents which he held in safe keeping, he always kept documents of valuable transactions.

'My grandmother said that you would be able to authenticate the letter without much problem.'

Foong Lee darted a glance at Tom Sullivan, was Sullivan reading his mind? It was certainly a bit of a change, Foong Lee was accustomed to holding the upper hand. But Tom grinned back at him disarmingly, and Foong Lee decided that he liked the young man. He returned his attention to the locket.

'Why do you wish to sell it? Such a magnificent piece.'

Tom suddenly realised that, although he'd not mentioned his name, the Chinese knew who he was and was aware of his family's wealth and position. It further occurred to him that Grandmother Emily must have had dealings with the Chinese, how else would she have had such knowledge of Foong Lee?

Tom sat back in his chair, shaking his head admiringly. Frail and elderly as she was, Grandmother Emily continued to surprise, but then she'd always been a force to be reckoned with. He decided to tell the truth.

'My father has two other sons who have embraced the family business,' he said rather formally. He felt it was right to address the Chinese in a formal manner, he seemed such a polite gentleman.

Foong Lee nodded as if such facts were new to him, although he was fully aware of Matthew Sullivan, and the two sons who helped run the business inherited from their grandfather. Old Benjamin had been one of the first surveyors to settle in Darwin, everyone in town knew of the Sullivan history.

'I don't wish to join the family company, and I don't feel I'm needed when all's said and done, so I want to go my own way.'

Foong Lee nodded again but made no enquiry. The young man was certainly unburdening himself, he'd not expected the full story, but it was most interesting.

'*I need cash to stake my claim,*' Tom boldly announced, '*I'm going to the goldfields.*'

Such an announcement would certainly not have impressed his father, Foong Lee thought. Matthew Sullivan was rumoured to be a stickler for tradition.

'*My father has said he'll disown me,*' Tom continued, '*but my grandmother is sympathetic to my cause. She has no cash of her own, but she gave me this locket, which was a gift to her from my grandfather.*'

'*It is all I have of any great value, Tom,*' *Grandmother Emily had said,* '*all that personally belongs to me, that is. The other pieces I've bought over the years have been courtesy of your father and they're expected to remain in the family.*' *She'd said it without bitterness. When her husband Benjamin had died, it was only natural that his wealth had been left to his son. Just as it was only natural that his son was expected to provide for his own mother until the end of her days. And Matthew had done just that. Even indulging her occasionally in her purchases of objets d'art and fine jewellery but, when complimenting her on her taste, he'd always remarked upon their 'investment value', making her fully aware that her purchases belonged to the family. How Emily had longed for her independence.*

It had been young Emily Soper's independent streak which had led her, against the express wishes of her family, to marry Benjamin Sullivan, forsaking her comfortable middle-class existence in Adelaide to carve out a life in the northern wilderness. She had loved her husband. 'Big Ben' she'd called him, recognising him for the gentle giant he was, covering for his weaknesses and his inadequacies. Little Emily Soper had become the matriarch and the strength of the Sullivan family.

Now, twenty years after Benjamin's death, at the age of

*seventy-five, frail and close to the grave herself, Emily had
recognised the independent spirit in her youngest grandson
and she had been only too happy to help him break free of
the family which was stifling him. She had given him her
greatest possession. The locket, which her own gentle Big
Ben had given her upon their engagement.*

*In the days of their courting, Benjamin had shown it to
her and told her that it had once belonged to a Larrakia
king. She hadn't believed him. Even way back then she'd
recognised his stories as a sign of his insecurity, his need to
impress. But she'd pretended to believe him, which had
spurred him on to tales of a Larrakia princess. On the
night that she'd agreed to marry him, he'd given her
the locket and she'd boldly announced that they were now
officially engaged, knowing that she loved him and that
she had the strength to face her family's fierce resistance.*

*When their son had been born, they had taken the baby
back to Adelaide to show him to his grandparents in an
attempt to heal the rift between Emily and her family. It
had worked. Emily's father had even commissioned a
portrait of Emily holding baby Matthew. And during her
sittings with the portraitist Emily had insisted upon
wearing the locket.*

*Now, all these years later, upon giving the locket to her
grandson, Emily had told him that she had no regrets.*

*'I can't accept such a gift, Grandma Em,' Tom had said,
as he unfolded the kid cloth and stared at the locket which
she'd placed in his hand.*

*'You must, Tom,' she insisted. 'It will give me great
pleasure.' Then she'd taken him into her small sitting room
and showed him the portrait. Tom had seen it often before.
When he was a small child it had even sat over the lounge
room mantelpiece until his father had replaced it with
a McCubbin landscape which had cost him a fortune.
But Tom had never noticed before that, in the painting of
the pretty young woman holding her new baby son, his*

grandmother was wearing the locket.

'You see, Tom,' Emily had said, 'I can always look at the portrait. And when I do, I will pray that the locket has helped you to find a new life. Just as it helped me find mine.'

'She said that she prayed the locket would help me find a new life.' Tom repeated his grandmother's words to the Chinese. He didn't know why but, despite Foong Lee's inscrutable expression, Tom felt that the Chinese was sympathetic.

Foong Lee did believe the young man. He would have Emily Sullivan's signature authenticated certainly, just to be safe, but for all of the rumours which abounded about Matthew Sullivan's youngest son, Foong Lee had come to the conclusion that Tom was an honest man.

'I will need several days to evaluate the true worth of the locket,' he said, 'its antiquity will be difficult to assess, but it will only add to its value.' He rose. 'Come into the shop and I'll give you a receipt of possession.'

'That won't be necessary,' Tom said, also rising from his chair. 'I'll come back next Wednesday, shall I?' He offered his hand to the Chinese.

Foong Lee knew that he should have insisted upon the receipt of possession, it was a matter of protocol, after all. But he didn't. It pleased him to think they were both men of honour. A gwailo and a Chinaman having faith in each other, it should happen more often, he thought. There should be more trust between Europeans and Chinese. 'Wednesday will be fine, Mr Sullivan,' he said as they shook hands.

It was the first time his name had been mentioned, and Tom smiled as he left the shop. There was something very reassuring about Foong Lee. Following the dreadful rows with his father, it now seemed that he had two allies. He had the blessing of his grandmother, and apparently that *of Foong Lee too. Tom felt very confident as he stepped out into the glare of Cavenagh Street.*

Foong Lee stood in the courtyard looking at the locket. He would buy it most certainly, and he would pay a good price. But he doubted whether he would ever sell it. He turned it over and over in his fingers, there was something very special about this beautiful thing.

CHAPTER TWENTY-EIGHT

Aggie Marshall strolled down the Esplanade. She liked to 'stroll'. The days when she had 'clomped' were long gone, certainly, but if she tried to get up any speed her gait was still rather odd, so she 'strolled', and her limp was barely noticeable. Besides, she was getting on now, she told herself, it was not dignified for a woman of fifty-six to charge at things like a bull at a gate. But no matter how many times she reminded herself of her age, and no matter how gently she strolled, metaphorically Aggie continued to charge, as her fellow town councillors were fully aware.

Aggie had retired from full-time teaching and although she now devoted her considerable energy to the improvement of Darwin, battling bureaucracy in the process, she continued to give private tuition to select students. Free of charge if the parents were not well off, which was usually the case. The students she agreed to tutor were either those with learning difficulties in need of help, or those with above-average academic skills who, in Aggie's opinion, should be encouraged to go on to university.

Darwin was looking very beautiful, Aggie thought. The poincianas, frangipanis and bougainvilleas were in bloom, and the wealth of their colour seemed to reflect the town's affluence and new-found civic pride. Darwin was no longer the shanty town of no-hopers it had been when she'd first arrived, nor was it the shelled-out war zone, all but razed to the ground by the Japanese bombs. The Darwin of the sixties was both practical and romantic in Aggie's opinion, a marriage of modern business and beautifully restored colonial architecture. And its wealth, employment and harmony owed much to its multicultural origins. Although the colourful pre-war shacks and shops of Chinatown no longer existed, the Darwin Chinese remained a highly successful business community, and only recently the first Chinese mayor, Harry Chan, had been elected to office. The Chinese were closely rivalled by the Greeks whose milk bars were regular meeting places and whose cafés smelled of freshly ground coffee beans. The Paspali brothers Mick and Nick, who had changed their names to Paspalis and Paspaley respectively, were amongst Darwin's wealthy elite. The Paspaleys' pearling business burgeoned, the Manolis's real estate holdings expanded rapidly, successful Greek family businesses were becoming a power to be reckoned with. Darwin was a truly multicultural society, Aggie always boasted, a place to be proud of.

She passed Admiralty House, appreciating, as she always did, its grace and style. Further evidence of Darwin's elegance, she thought. Designed in the thirties by the innovative B.C.G. Burnett, Admiralty House had inspired the design of many homes which had come to typify Darwin architecture. Elevated on stilts, surrounded by wide, shuttered verandahs, with open-plan, wooden-floored interiors, 'Burnett-style' houses were not only practical given the climate of the tropics, but picturesque. They were proud houses, Aggie thought.

She walked down Herbert Street, then turned and headed up Mitchell bound for Galloway Motors. It was mid-afternoon and, as she arrived, Aggie could see Terence's minions scuttling about. On the opposite side of the street was Galloway and Sons Emporium, another hive of activity, and Aggie thought of Henrietta, as she always did when she stood in Mitchell Street surrounded by the Galloway empire.

It had been over five years since Henrietta's disappearance and rarely a day went by when Aggie didn't think of her. The success of the Galloway businesses was a constant reminder of Henrietta's tragic and untimely death. It didn't seem right to Aggie that, after all the hardship and isolation Henrietta had suffered, she should be deprived of a life of ease which she'd so deserved. How proud she would have been of Terence's success, Aggie thought, and of her sons' achievements.

She entered Galloway Motors and, as she wove her way through the shining vehicles on the showroom floor to the stairs at the rear, she wondered again why Terence wanted to see her and what it was that he didn't wish to discuss on the phone. 'I'd much rather see you in person, Aggie,' he'd said. 'That is, if you have the time.' He'd sounded a little upset, she thought.

'Aggie,' Terence met her at the top of the stairs, a glass of whisky in his hand, 'thank you so much for coming.' He ushered her into his impressive office. 'Scotch?' The offer was perfunctory, he knew she'd refuse, but Terence was glad to see Aggie. There was no-one else with whom he felt he could share his strangely unsettling news. He got straight to the point.

'I had a phone call from my solicitors in Adelaide,' he said as they both sat. 'It appears that Henrietta has now been officially declared dead.'

He was trying to sound business-like, Aggie realised, but as he swigged back his Scotch she could sense his pain.

Henrietta's body had never been found. Extensive searches had been mounted, lengthy interviews conducted by police, despite the fact that there were no suspicious circumstances. Every measure possible had been taken to discover the whereabouts of her body, to no avail. The findings of the coronial inquest had been 'presumed dead by unknown causes'. And now, five years after the inquest, the statutory time having elapsed, she had been officially declared dead, or so the solicitors had informed Terence.

'Her estate has reverted to me,' he told Aggie. 'Just a modest bank account and a small property in Ireland,' he said. He took another swig from his glass, and Aggie felt sorry for him. It was quite obvious that the official declaration of his wife's death had reopened the wound of Terence's grief.

During the months following Henrietta's disappearance, a strange relationship had evolved between Terence and Aggie. When the boys had come home to attend the small family memorial service held in honour of their mother, Aggie had not intruded upon their grief, sending flowers and condolences instead. But several days after Malcolm and Kit had returned to boarding school, Aggie had heard that Terence had moved into the Hotel Darwin, and she'd called upon him to offer her sympathies in person.

'I thought, seeing you're staying in town, I'd pay you a visit,' she'd said a little awkwardly as they sat in the hotel lounge.

'Yes, until the new house is ready,' he'd replied, leaning forward in his armchair and staring down at his tightly clasped hands. 'Just whilst they finish the new house, that's all,' he repeated, his fingers restlessly kneading his knuckles.

He was obviously agitated, and Aggie was shocked by his appearance. His face was pale and unshaven, and he'd lost weight. She felt deeply sorry for him.

'If there's anything I can do, Terence,' she said gently,

'anything at all.' He shook his head and continued wringing his hands, his fingers and knuckles turning white. It was pitiful to watch such a strong man fighting to control his emotions. 'Please let me help you,' Aggie said and she placed her hand upon his forearm.

The gesture seemed to push Terence over the edge. He buried his head in his hands. 'I'm staying here because I can't go back,' he said, his voice strained and muffled. 'I can't go back to Bullalalla. I miss her. I see her everywhere. She haunts me.' His voice finally broke as he lost control and sobbed. 'I can't go back there, I can never go back there.'

At first Aggie was horrified at the sight of him sobbing. She was neither concerned nor embarrassed by the curious glances from the several other guests in the lounge, but the spectacle of Terence Galloway crying was shocking. Terence of all people! Then she realised that it was probably good for him, it was probably very healthy.

She rose and, sitting on the broad arm of his lounge chair, she soothed him as she would a distraught child. 'There, there, Terence,' she said, putting her arm around his shoulders, 'it's all right, everything's going to be all right.'

Gradually, his sobs subsided, and he fumbled for his handkerchief. 'I'm sorry,' he said as he blew his nose and self-consciously mopped away his tears. His outburst had shocked him even more than it had Aggie.

Terence had not been lying. He did miss Henrietta. He missed her desperately. And she certainly haunted him. During the fortnight of investigations and searches following her disappearance, he'd been too busy to ponder upon what had taken place, he'd had to keep his wits about him every minute of every day. Then there'd been the inquest, and the boys' return when he'd had to console them in their grief. That had been the ultimate test for Terence, to comfort both equally, to disguise his contempt for Paul Trewinnard's son. The strain had at times been unbearable, there had been moments when he'd wanted to scream at the boy 'get out of this house, you're not my son', but he'd had to embrace him instead, clumsily, awkwardly, as Kit grieved for the loss of his mother.

The nights offered no relief, sleep seemed impossible. When Terence closed his eyes he saw Henrietta. She was not accusing him, there was no damnation in her eyes, she was simply there, lovely and tempting as ever, haunting him with her beauty. But he refused to regret her death. He had only to visualise the locket, to see the images of the two of them encased inside, to remind himself of her infidelity. And then he knew that she'd deserved to die. When a fitful sleep finally overcame him, the image of the locket would become that of Trewinnard making love to Henrietta, and Terence would awake newly anguished and enraged. And then, throughout the day, there was Trewinnard's son, the brazen proof of his wife's dishonour. Terence felt no guilt over Henrietta's death, but he was a creature in torment.

He had expected some relief when the boys returned to school, when he would no longer be in the presence of the son who was not his. But after Malcolm and Kit left, and he found himself alone in the house, Henrietta seemed to be everywhere. There was not even the distraction of Jackie's and Nellie's company.

Following the official enquiries, Jackie had simply gone walkabout, and this time he'd taken Nellie with him. They hadn't even said goodbye. Some thanks for a lifetime of employment, Terence had thought. Oh well, good riddance.

Terence knew Jackie and Nellie had had misgivings about the death of their mistress, he'd known from the very outset, even before he'd left to meet up with the first search party. Of course they'd said nothing of their unease to the police, blacks never interfered in white men's business, but it was probably for the best that they'd gone, he decided.

But when he'd found himself alone in the silence of Bullalalla, he'd missed Jackie and Nellie. The very air of the deserted house seemed to whisper Henrietta's name, or to echo her laughter. Shaken and unnerved, Terence had driven into town and booked into the Hotel Darwin.

When, two days later, Aggie had contacted him, he had found the prospect of confronting Henrietta's closest friend strangely alarming. Was he losing his nerve? Was he losing his very sanity? He'd not flinched throughout the police investigation, why should he find Aggie Marshall of all people a threat? Perhaps because she had known the younger Trewinnard. Perhaps because Aggie Marshall was the one person capable of putting two and two together. Henrietta herself had told him that Aggie didn't know about Trewinnard, and Terence had believed her. But what if Aggie had guessed?

The endless weeks of tension had taken their toll on Terence and, when he'd seen the concern in Aggie's eyes and realised he was safe, it had been the easiest thing in the world to give in to his sense of loss. Suddenly he'd found himself sobbing. He missed Henrietta, he said, she haunted him, he could never go back to Bullalalla. It was all true.

Terence was shocked by his breakdown, and a little embarrassed as he mopped himself up and Aggie patted him on the back, saying 'there, there'. But when he'd pulled himself together and apologised for making such a scene, he decided the embarrassment was well worth it. In Aggie's eyes were the deepest sympathy and compassion.

'I'll always be here to help you, Terence, if you ever need to call on me. Henrietta was my dearest friend, you know that.'

Terence himself wasn't sure whether his outburst had been one of grief or relief, but he felt utterly exhausted, and grateful at the same time.

'Thank you, Aggie,' he said, ignoring the glances of others in the lounge. Who would have thought Aggie Marshall might become his greatest ally? It was really most convenient.

Since then, Aggie had made it a regular habit to call upon Terence at the hotel and he always seemed grateful to see her. Mostly they talked about Henrietta, and Aggie never stayed long, she was just checking to make sure he was all right.

The boys came home for the Christmas holidays and Aggie stopped visiting, convinced that she would be intruding if she did. It would be a sad Christmas for them, she thought.

Several months later, when Terence moved into the new house on the point at Larrakeyah, he rang Aggie.

'You're the first person invited over for the guided tour,' he said. She was very flattered.

'It's beautiful, Terence.' They clinked glasses, he'd opened a bottle of Dom Perignon especially. 'To toast the house,' he said. 'It's truly beautiful,' Aggie said and meant it. It was one of the most beautiful houses she'd ever seen. But then Burnett-style houses were her favourite.

Surrounded by vibrant purple-flowering bougainvillea, it stood two storeys high on its stilts, with broad wooden steps leading up to the first verandah, the shutters of which could be lifted completely to expose the wide balconies. Fine mesh screens could be dropped to keep out the insects and still retain the view. The furnishings were large but not cumbersome, in keeping with the spacious rooms, and the view across the waters of Darwin Harbour was breathtaking.

'The boys'll be home for the May holidays soon,' Terence said, 'I can't wait for them to see it.'

If only Henrietta was alive to see it, Aggie thought, but she didn't say anything.

'Henrietta would have loved it, wouldn't she?' Terence knew exactly what Aggie was thinking.

'Yes,' Aggie said, 'she would.' She didn't stay long, she never did. Despite her profound sympathy for the man, she was never particularly comfortable in Terence's company. But she would never forget the agony of his grief that she had witnessed in the lounge at the Hotel Darwin, and her friendship was always on offer. She owed it to Henrietta.

Terence sometimes wondered why he kept playing the game, Aggie bored him now, but he couldn't afford the risk of alienating her. Keep her on side or she might start thinking, he'd decided, and he remained always charming and sensitive in her presence.

A fortnight after Terence had shown her the house, Aggie was walking down Smith Street when she suddenly stopped dead in her tracks. It was lunchtime and Smith Street was busy but, through the idling window shoppers and those more intent upon going about their business, she had seen a familiar figure. The breath caught in her throat and she stood frozen to the spot. The ambling gait, the lanky frame, the hair falling over the brow which, even as she watched, was raked back in a characteristic gesture. It was Paul Trewinnard.

The shock lasted for only an instant. She quickly realised that the figure was that of a youth. A gangly boy yet to grow into his frame. It was Kit Galloway. He hadn't seen her. He turned to browse in a shop window.

Aggie paused for a moment, taking a breath to recover, then she walked towards him, wondering what exactly she'd say. Wondering indeed whether he might fail to recognise her, it had been over two years since they'd seen each other, after all. He'd been a boy of twelve then, now it seemed overnight he'd become a young man.

She was nearly abreast of him, and about to say something, when he turned from the window.

'Miss Marshall,' he said with a broad grin of delight.

To Aggie his face suddenly became that of the twelve-year-old she had known so well. Of course he was bound to have recognised her, Aggie thought rather foolishly, middle-aged women didn't change over two years.

'Kit,' she replied, moved beyond measure by the warmth of his smile, which immediately reminded her of Henrietta. 'Kit Galloway.' She offered him her hand and they shook firmly, like men. 'And it's Aggie now, I'm not your school teacher anymore.'

'Okay,' Kit said a little self-consciously, it didn't seem quite right to call his old teacher by her first name. 'Aggie it is.' He was genuinely pleased to see her. Miss Marshall had always been his favourite primary school teacher. She, along with Paul Trewinnard, had nurtured his love of literature; he owed her a lot. 'Gee, it's so good to see you.'

'You too. I hardly recognised you, you've grown so tall.'

'Yes I know,' Kit was used to the comment. 'They tell me I'm "at that age".'

Aggie wanted to say something about Henrietta, but she wasn't sure how to begin so, in her customary fashion, she blurted it out. 'I'm sorry about your mother.'

Kit's smile faded. 'Yep,' he said. 'We all miss her.' It had been seven months now and, although he'd accepted the shock of her death, he missed his mother as sorely as if it had been yesterday.

The boy looked so sad. Damn, Aggie thought, why had she blurted it out like that. She tried to change the subject without being tactless.

'Henrietta would have been very proud of you,' she said. 'Your dad tells me you're doing really well at school.'

But Kit didn't seem to need a change of subject. 'He said you've been a real good friend to him, Miss Marshall, since Mum . . .' Kit never quite knew how to say it. He accepted that his mother was dead, but he could never say the words. Perhaps it would have been different if there'd been a proper funeral with a coffin and everything.

'Aggie,' she gently reminded him.

'Yeah, Aggie,' he responded automatically, 'Dad needs friends, he misses Mum a lot.'

Aggie gave a sympathetic nod, then decided that a

complete change of topic was called for. 'Do you and Malcolm like the new house? It's lovely, isn't it?'

'Yeah.' Kit shook off his mood. 'We both reckon it's great. Hey, it's Malcolm's birthday on Friday, I'm trying to buy him a present, I don't know what the heck I'm going to get. Anyway we're having a bit of a party, why don't you come around? I bet Dad'd love to see you.'

'No, no, I'll pop in and say hello over the weekend,' Aggie promised, and she said her goodbyes, leaving him to his gift shopping.

That night the phone rang. It was Terence. 'Kit told me he bumped into you,' he said. 'The boys'd love you to come around for dinner on Friday, it's Malcolm's seventeenth birthday.'

'Oh no, really, Terence.' Aggie was a little embarrassed that Kit had put his father in such a spot. 'I couldn't possibly intrude, teenage boys don't want their old school teacher at a birthday party.'

But he was insistent. 'Oh yes they do. There's only a couple of other boys coming, two old mates from their primary school days. I don't know who the hell they are but you'd be bound to know them.'

'That'd only make it worse,' she laughed.

'Rubbish.' Terence refused to take no for an answer. 'Kit's mad keen for you to come, and so am I. It was remiss of me not to ask you in the first place. Don't leave me with the kids, Aggie,' he begged, 'I need some adult company, please say you'll come.'

'I'd love to,' she replied, flattered.

When Kit had brought up the subject of inviting Aggie Marshall, Terence had sided with his younger son.

'What the hell do you want to ask Miss Marshall for?' Malcolm had scoffed.

'She was Mum's best friend,' Kit retaliated.

'She's still a school teacher, for God's sake, Pete and Frank'll think you're mad.'

'No they won't, Pete always liked her,' Kit retorted, 'he reckoned she was a good sport. And we're supposed to call her Aggie now.'

Malcolm cursed himself for having automatically referred to his old teacher as Miss Marshall, it seemed infantile. 'Well, I don't want Aggie here, she won't fit in.'

'Yes she will,' Terence interrupted. 'She'll fit in very well. It's an excellent idea, Kit, I should have thought of it myself.' In response to Malcolm's scowl, Terence continued, with a warning edge to his voice, 'I told you Aggie's been a very good friend to me since your mother died.'

'Who the hell's birthday *is* it?' Malcolm grumbled, but he made sure his father couldn't hear, and Terence chose to ignore his elder son's rebellious muttering.

'Don't worry, Malcolm,' he said pleasantly but patronisingly, 'after dinner Aggie and I'll leave you kids together and have a coffee upstairs.'

Malcolm glared at Kit. It meant a loss of respect to be called a 'kid' by his father, and it was all Kit's fault.

Terence had an ulterior motive in inviting Aggie. He was intent upon studying her reaction to Kit. So she'd bumped into him this morning in Smith Street. Very interesting. What had she thought? Had she seen a resemblance to Trewinnard?

Each time the boys had returned home, Terence had convinced himself that he could see more and more of the Englishman in his son, despite the fact that commonsense told him he was being paranoid. Kit looked like Henrietta, everyone who had known her told him so.

Terence's memory of the younger Paul Trewinnard was clouded. He'd taken little notice of the man upon their first meetings, finding him of no interest, and the picture in the locket was now a blurred memory. The image of Trewinnard which remained with Terence was that of a skeletal old man. A cadaver making love to his wife, it revolted him. He'd studied the boy for signs of the Englishman, but all he could see was Henrietta. Her smile, her laugh, her commitment to a subject in which she was interested, Kit was so like her. But then the Englishman had been tall and lean, and so was Kit. Did they look alike? Could others see a similarity? Aggie was the one who would know, she'd been Trewinnard's close friend.

It was not the threat of a murder charge which haunted Terence. With the investigations over, and the coroner's findings on record, he felt safe. But he lived in fear that others might discover the son whom he'd raised as his own was that of another man. He could not, and would not, endure such humiliation.

The birthday party was a success. And Aggie was the star of the show, even Malcolm had to admit the fact. Pete Mowbray and Frank Steriakos, the respective friends of Kit and Malcolm, although surprised at the presence of their old school teacher, were obviously pleased to see her and quickly relaxed in her company.

'It's Aggie now,' she insisted and they happily accepted, particularly Frank, who'd always referred to her as 'Aggie One Foot' anyway, the major contributing factor to Aggie's popularity with her pupils having always been their fascination with her prosthetic foot. 'She had it blown off by a bomb,' the older ones were always quick to inform the newcomers and Aggie's hero status had become legendary as the story had been passed from one generation of students to the next.

As the birthday dinner progressed, Aggie was the common link between the boys who, although they'd been close friends, had lost touch with each other over the years. It was Aggie who recalled every episode of their school days. They talked about the day Pete Mowbray had fallen from the tree and broken his elbow. He showed them how it still wouldn't straighten properly. And they relived the triumphs which Malcolm and Frank had shared on the football field. The older boys drank beer, the younger ones were allowed a small glass which became two, and the roast beef and mounds of vegetables prepared by Fran, Terence's middle-aged Filipino housekeeper whom he'd trained well in the Western ways, disappeared down rapacious teenage throats.

Pete was also home on holidays, he attended boarding school in Perth, but seventeen-year-old Frank had left school the previous year to work in his father's fish shop. Terence approved of Pete Mowbray, whose father was a solicitor, but he'd have preferred to have entertained one of Malcolm's school friends rather than Frank.

'There're no Territorians in my class, Dad,' Malcolm had explained, 'let alone anyone from Darwin.'

'Any of your mates'd be welcome to stay, son,' Terence had said, 'there's plenty of room.'

'They've all gone home for the holidays.' Malcolm wished his father would stop talking about his mates, he didn't really have any to speak of. Not ones he could ask to come and stay at any rate. So when his father had insisted upon a birthday party, Malcolm had asked Frank Steriakos.

Terence didn't really disapprove of Frank. His father, Les Steriakos, a Cypriot by birth, was successful and well liked, with a fish shop and a wholesale vegetable supply business. But, as the Galloways were destined to become a power in the community, it would have been preferable, Terence thought, for Malcolm to mingle with the offspring of families on a similar path. Perhaps the Paspaleys or the Manolises. Oh well, he thought, next year when the boy went to Duntroon he would be mixing with the sons of men of distinction.

During this, his last high school year, Malcolm had passed the initial series of selection tests for entry to Duntroon Military College with flying colours. He'd come through the aptitude test and the battery of psychological tests with an OIR rating of eight. Terence, initially annoyed that his son's Officer Intelligence Rating was not the maximum ten, had telephoned a military acquaintance from his war service days who had explained that a rating between six and eight was considered most suitable officer material.

'Ten ratings are seen as boffin material, Terry,' Lieutenant Colonel Desmond Brigstock had told him. 'They might make good rocket scientists, but they're bloody awful officers. Your boy's done well so far.'

'Thanks, Des.' Terence was glad he'd phoned Des Brigstock before castigating Malcolm as he'd initially intended.

The big test was yet to present itself. In two months' time, Malcolm was to attend Keswick Barracks in Adelaide for a series of assessments and examinations, both practical and psychological, from which only a limited number of candidates would emerge successful.

Terence was supremely confident, and Malcolm was terrified of failure.

'Malcolm's off to Duntroon next year, Frank,' Terence said as he refilled Aggie's wine glass, 'did he tell you?'

'Yeah, he said he's taking the tests.' Young Frank Steriakos raised his beer glass. 'Good luck, eh, Malcolm.'

'Piece of cake, boy,' Terence bellowed, 'piece of cake. Speaking of which . . .' He rose to his feet and applauded as Fran entered with a huge birthday cake sporting seventeen candles. Terence laughed heartily at his perfect timing. 'Lights, Kit, lights.'

Kit jumped up and turned off the lights, the candles flickered in the half-darkness, and the others rose to their feet singing 'Happy Birthday'.

Whilst the boys continued to shovel down sponge cake the way only growing boys could, Terence signalled Fran to bring the coffee and suggested to Aggie that they have it on the upstairs balcony.

'Lovely,' she said, although she would have preferred to

stay in the boys' company. She had been uncomfortably aware that Terence had been studying her, and she had the feeling that he wanted to discuss something. What? Surely not the terrible suspicion she entertained.

For the past few days, Aggie had convinced herself that the apparition of Paul Trewinnard she'd seen in the street had been a product of her own imaginings. The boy had merely grown tall since she'd last seen him, and if he'd acquired some of Paul's mannerisms, then why not? He'd idolised the man during two of the most impressionable years of his young life, it was natural to emulate one's hero. And tonight, as they'd sat laughing and reminiscing over the roast dinner, she'd seen nothing but Henrietta in the boy. It was true he bore no resemblance to Terence, but then Malcolm didn't look the least like Henrietta.

Aggie found the difference between the two brothers fascinating. Malcolm had become a replica of his father. His body was now that of a man's, strong and finely toned; like Terence he was an excellent sportsman. A handsome boy, with a strong, chiselled face, Malcolm's eyes bore the defiance of his father's. He too, Aggie guessed, would be prone to fits of anger, he'd been easily angered as a child, she remembered. But when Terence had mentioned Duntroon, she'd seen the sudden flicker of fear in Malcolm's eyes, and the relief when he'd been saved by the arrival of the birthday cake. Poor child, Aggie thought, he still lives in fear of Terence's disapproval.

Early in the evening she'd been vaguely conscious of Terence studying her reactions and, initially presuming that as proud father he was hoping his children met with her approval, she'd flashed him a smile now and then.

But when Fran had cleared away the plates, the huge roast dinner having been entirely demolished, the conversation and the mood in the room had taken a serious turn. Terence, who enjoyed any topic relating to military events, had commented upon the newspaper report that Australia was to send military advisers to South Vietnam.

'A damn good thing too,' he'd said, 'wipe those dirty commos from the face of the earth. We quelled them in Malaya and we'll bloody well put a stop to them in Indo-China.'

'But Australia isn't sending combat troops, Dad,' Kit had said.

'Eh?' Terence had seemed prepared to deliver a tirade, and looked taken aback at Kit's interruption.

'They're only sending instructors to help train the Vietnamese. South Vietnam hasn't asked for troops.'

'Well, they bloody well will, boy, you mark my words.' Terence had been annoyed. 'It'll just be a matter of time before our boys are over there fighting those commo bastards.'

Ignoring the fact that Kit seemed keen to continue the discussion, Terence directed his attention to his elder son. 'You'll probably end up in the thick of it, Malcolm, when you leave Duntroon.' That was when he'd turned to Frank. 'Malcolm's off to Duntroon next year, Frank, did he tell you?'

Aggie had concentrated on the glass of wine which Terence was pouring for her, but she'd found herself once again in a state of shock. As Kit had leaned forward intensely, eager for discussion, there had been an intelligence and enquiry in his unwavering grey eyes which she had seen before, many years ago and on many an occasion. Kit's eyes were the eyes of Paul Trewinnard.

Then the birthday cake had arrived, and the mood had returned to one of levity.

Aggie had tried not to look at Kit as she ate her small portion of cake slowly, not enjoying one mouthful. Her mind was reeling. Was it truly possible that Kit was Paul's son? And if he was, did Terence know? Was it perhaps why he had been studying her throughout the evening? The cake seemed to lodge in her throat, she was having difficulty swallowing, she wished she could go home. But suddenly Terence was signalling the housekeeper and suggesting they have their coffee upstairs, and Aggie heard herself say 'lovely'.

'Help yourself to the beer, boys,' Terence said with largesse as he rose from the table, 'no more for you younger ones.'

'So how do you find my sons?' Terence now leaned back in his armchair on the upper balcony, as affable and as charming as ever.

It was an innocent enough comment, but Aggie felt strangely as if she was being put to the test. She also felt shaken and nervous, but something told her she must not let it show.

'They're fine young men, Terence,' she sipped her coffee. She was aware of the ceiling fan whirring and, beyond the fine mesh of the insect screen, she could see the navigational lights of a small vessel on its way up the harbour. She forced her eyes to meet his as she smiled. 'You must be very proud of them.'

'Oh I am, I am. But you haven't seen them for so long, surely you must have noticed some changes?'

Again the smile of a proud parent. So why did she feel uneasy? She forced a laugh which sounded surprisingly relaxed. 'Of course I do. My God, I can't believe how tall young Kit's grown.'

'Yes he has, hasn't he?' Does she know, has she guessed, Terence wondered. If so, she was giving nothing away. 'He's a bright boy, very intelligent, an enquiring mind.'

'He was always bright,' Aggie agreed. 'As a child, he was my favourite pupil.' She decided that she would be on safer ground if she played the school teacher.

'He's going to go to university. An arts degree, he says. He wants to be a writer.' In his role of fond father, Terence made the announcement with boastful pride. Actually he no longer cared whether Kit went to university or not, as far as he was concerned the boy could do whatever he liked.

'Oh I'm so glad,' Aggie's response was genuine. 'He always had a great love of literature. Just like Henrietta. He's so like her in every way, Terence.' Was she imagining it, or had her instinctive response hit a chord? 'It must be a great comfort to you,' she added. She sincerely meant it.

Terence breathed an inward sigh of relief. She didn't know, she hadn't guessed. 'It is, Aggie. It is a very, very great comfort to me. Would you like another coffee?'

'Please.'

As Terence poured more coffee from the jug which Fran had left them, Aggie felt herself relax, and they spent a further half hour discussing the boys. Particularly Malcolm who, in Terence's opinion, would make a fine officer, and Aggie agreed, praying that the boy would pass his examinations.

When they went downstairs to phone for Aggie's taxi, they discovered that Frank Steriakos was decidedly drunk and the mood of the party had become raucous. Both older boys had obviously been guzzling copious amounts of beer since the adults had left the table, but although Malcolm too was feeling the effects, he knew better than to allow it to show in front of his father.

Terence grinned at his elder son, fully aware that the boy was drunk but successfully disguising the fact. Excellent, he thought. Old Jock had always said, and quite rightly too, Terence maintained, that the way a bloke handled his liquor sorted the men from the boys. Terence was pleased to note that Malcolm had already taken the lesson to heart.

'Have another beer, son,' he said, interested in testing the lad's threshold of control, 'you only turn seventeen once, eh?'

As the taxi pulled away from the kerb, Aggie looked up at them through the car window. Terence stood at the top of the steps with his sons, an arm around each of their shoulders, Malcolm's body swaying a little unsteadily but his feet firmly planted on the verandah. The three of them waved to her and she waved back.

For the next several days Aggie couldn't get the image of Paul Trewinnard's eyes out of her mind. Had she imagined their likeness in Kit's?

She lifted out her messy old cardboard box of photographs, she had a picture of Paul somewhere, she was sure. She found it easily enough, amongst a host of photographs she'd kept of Henrietta. It was a picture of the two of them together, Henrietta and Paul, and she'd taken it the year before he'd died. He hadn't wanted her to, she remembered, but she'd nagged him into it. She studied the face closely, particularly the eyes, for signs of Kit, but she could see none. The face in the photograph was that of an old man, ravaged by illness, and she had no pictures of the younger Paul.

Had it just been her foolish imaginings, Aggie wondered. Her notion that Terence had been putting her to the test had most certainly been a product of her imaginings. He'd simply wanted to talk proudly of his sons, it was obvious, and Aggie felt ridiculous when she recalled her nervousness. She must forget the entire incident, she told herself. She must stop musing upon the subject of Kit Galloway's parentage which, after all, was no business of hers. Even if, by some remote chance, Paul Trewinnard was the boy's natural father, Henrietta had obviously kept the fact a secret from her husband. My God, Aggie thought, if it were true and if Terence ever found out . . .!

But much as she tried to erase the question from her mind, Aggie couldn't. She was plagued by the need to know. It was far more than mere curiosity. Had Henrietta lived such a lie for all those years? If so, what torment she must have experienced. Had Paul known the truth? In the last years of his life, he and Henrietta had been very close, had it been because they shared a son? For no purpose other than her own peace of mind, Aggie determined to find out the answer. There was one person, and one person only, who might know the truth.

Foong Lee chatted amiably as he poured the *heung ping* into Aggie's small china cup. It was five o'clock in the afternoon and they were sitting in his deserted restaurant in Cavenagh Street. It didn't open for diners until 6.30, but Foong Lee was always there in the afternoons, taking deliveries and organising the specials for the evening menu. He enjoyed being a restaurateur, leaving the financial management of the store and his many other business interests in Albert's capable hands these days.

He was pleased when Aggie called in. She used to call in more often, he remarked, as he poured the jasmine tea. He and Aggie saw each other often at their mutual charity concerns, of which there were many, but they'd socialised rarely of late.

'I know, I've been altogether too busy this past month or so,' Aggie said, 'too many students and too many fights with councillors.' She tapped the knuckles of her middle finger and forefinger on the table as he finished pouring her tea, and Foong Lee smiled his approval. He had long ago taught her the Chinese etiquette of table tapping. 'It's our way of saying thank you when someone serves us food or drink,' he'd explained.

'How courteous,' she'd remarked.

'Not really. It's laziness more than anything. It replaces the *kow-tow* you see.' He'd got down on his hands and knees, touched his forehead to the floor, then stood up and laughed. 'We let our fingers do the bowing instead,' he'd tapped his knuckles on the table, 'it's a lot kinder on the knees.'

Today Aggie made the gesture automatically, not reacting to his smile of approval, which she would normally have returned. She was distracted, Foong Lee thought, and he chatted on politely, waiting for her to get to the point of her visit, knowing that there was one. Aggie being Aggie, it didn't take long.

'Have you seen the Galloway boys since they came home for the holidays?' she asked.

'The Galloway boys,' he looked mystified for a second, then, 'Oh, you mean Terence Galloway's sons, what're their names? Kit and who's the other one?'

'Malcolm.'

'Malcolm, that's it. Yes, I saw young Kit a week or so ago. I was with Albert at the store and he came in looking for a present for his brother, I believe it was Malcolm's seventeenth birthday. By golly he's grown tall, young Kit, I hardly recognised him. Mind you I'd have trouble recognising either of them at the best of times, I haven't seen them since they were kiddies here at school.' Foong Lee sipped his tea and smiled reminiscently. 'They used to come into the shop at lunchtime and buy lollies, all the kids did.'

Aggie was at a loss as to how to introduce the subject of her visit, and Foong Lee's garrulous chatter wasn't helping.

'You were Paul Trewinnard's closest friend, Foong Lee.' It was a statement not a question and it came from nowhere, but Foong Lee appeared to notice nothing out of the ordinary in Aggie's abrupt change of topic.

'Oh yes, I most certainly was,' he said. 'A fine man, tragic that he died so young. He didn't even make it to sixty, you know.' Foong Lee himself was sixty-one and, except for the pouches under his eyes, which he'd had since his youth anyway, he looked like a man in his forties. He certainly felt like a man in his forties. 'And sixty isn't old these days,' he continued. 'Not anymore.'

He was going to go on, Aggie could tell. Foong Lee was in one of his talkative moods. He was always convivial company, but sometimes he was talkative, chattering away like a monkey, and sometimes he simply sat smiling benignly. The latter would have been preferable today, she could have found a more subtle way to approach the conversation. She decided to cut to the chase.

'I couldn't help but notice a resemblance between young Kit Galloway and Paul Trewinnard.' There, she'd said it. In the moment's pause she studied the man's reaction. She'd expected an element of shock, but there appeared to be none. He merely burst out laughing.

'Good heavens above, Aggie,' he chortled, his pouched eyes disappearing into slits, 'what a fanciful notion. Are you suggesting that Paul might have been the boy's father?'

Well, she was wasn't she, although she'd not said the words out loud. 'It's possible isn't it?' she replied a little defensively, Foong Lee was looking at her as if she was a fool.

He stopped laughing. 'No, my dear, it is not remotely possible,' he said, dropping the garrulous mood he'd adopted the moment she'd mentioned Kit Galloway's name. He'd known in that instant the reason for her visit.

Foong Lee spoke kindly, but firmly. 'I was Paul's closest friend, and he told me everything, there were no secrets between us. It's quite true that he loved Henrietta in his own way'—he would give Aggie that much, Foong Lee decided, in order to satisfy the romantic in her—'although of course he never declared himself. And I'm quite sure that, had he had a son, Paul would have wished the boy to be like Kit. The two were very good friends.'

'Yes, I know they were.'

'And young Kit idolised Paul,' Foong Lee continued reasonably, 'so it's quite possible he may have modelled himself upon his hero. Who knows?'

'Yes, that occurred to me,' Aggie admitted. She wondered if she should mention Kit's eyes.

Foong Lee could tell that she was not fully convinced. Aggie Marshall was treading upon dangerous ground. 'My dear,' he said with kindly concern, 'you must put any such notion out of your mind.' Foong Lee was not accustomed to lying but when it was a matter of life and death, as he believed it might well be in this case, he was most adept. Chameleon-like as always, his face now bore the wisdom of the ages, and his words sounded irrefutable. 'Rest assured, Aggie, Kit is most certainly Terence Galloway's son.'

Aggie suddenly felt embarrassed. Had she appeared a meddlesome gossip? Or worse, a dangerous rumour-monger? She must have, surely. 'I know it's none of my business, Foong Lee,' she felt herself flush, 'I hope you don't think that I . . .'

Foong Lee interrupted, quick to put her at her ease. 'Your enquiry springs from your love for Henrietta, I know that.' Aggie nodded fervently. 'You were a very good friend to her, Aggie, and you of all people know that her marriage had its turbulent times. But it was a faithful marriage which produced two fine sons.'

Aggie nodded, her embarrassment replaced by self-consciousness. She felt rather like a child, one of her own pupils in fact, with a benevolent school teacher instructing her upon the finer points of life.

'And Henrietta was most fortunate in having the friends she did to support her through the less pleasant times,' Foong Lee concluded. 'She had you. And she had Paul Trewinnard.' He raised the pot. 'More tea?'

They chatted amiably for a further twenty minutes and, when Aggie left, Foong Lee prayed he had convinced her of the foolishness of her suspicions. For her own sake. He knew of her friendship with Terence, and he was convinced that should Aggie Marshall, in her well-meaning but at times interfering way, ever take it upon herself to tell Terence Galloway the truth, her very life could be in danger.

Foong Lee's words had certainly had an effect on Aggie. Whether she believed him, or whether it was the humiliation she'd felt over her impertinent enquiry, she no longer searched for signs of Paul Trewinnard in Kit. And now, five years after Henrietta's death, she saw none. Kit's eyes had become Kit's, and the query that had plagued Aggie no longer existed.

The news that Henrietta had now been officially declared dead was indeed somehow shocking and, as Aggie sat in Terence's splendid office overlooking the huge showroom of Galloway Motors, she found her heart going out yet again to the man. His wealth and his position were obviously of little comfort to him, she thought as he rose from his chair, agitated.

'I'm signing her estate over to the boys,' Terence said as he crossed to the bar in the corner. 'Malcolm's twenty-one now, and Kit's share will be held in trust until he's of age.'

'She would have been so proud of them, Terence,' she said. 'And of you and the success you've achieved. She would have been so very proud.'

'Yes she would, wouldn't she?' Terence was grateful for Aggie's sympathy, he was feeling maudlin. It was a pity Henrietta wasn't here to share his triumphs. He hadn't realised lately just how much he missed her, the contact from the solicitors had brought it all home to him. If she were here now, he thought, she'd be the most beautiful woman in Darwin, married to one of the most successful businessmen, feted and admired by all.

He poured himself another hefty Scotch. It was a pity Aggie wasn't a drinker, he'd have liked someone to get drunk with, but he was grateful she was here. Good old Aggie. And she was quite right, Henrietta would have been proud of him.

Terence sat back at his desk and looked out through the plate-glass windows of his office at the impressive showroom. Behind their own small glassed-in offices lined along one side, smartly suited salesmen sat at their desks busy with their paperwork, and on the main floor the brand new, glossy green British Landrovers sat invitingly on display. Galloway Motors specialised in four wheel drive vehicles, and the previous year Terence had imported a new line of Japanese four wheel drives called Toyota. Local reaction had initially been adverse to Toyota, given Darwin's relationship with the Japanese, but practicality had won out and the vehicles were currently selling like hot cakes.

On the opposite side of the street, he had acquired an adjoining property and extended the Galloway Emporium to include a department dealing exclusively in outback equipment and camping supplies. Everything from drover's wet-weather coats to gas lamps, from tents to inflatable dinghies could be found at Galloway's. He had cornered a thriving market and business had never been better.

'She would have been very proud,' he agreed. 'I miss her so much, Aggie.' He took another healthy swig at his Scotch.

Aggie was concerned. It was three o'clock in the afternoon, far too early for him to be drinking so heavily, particularly straight whisky with neither ice nor water. But she knew better than to admonish him. She changed the subject instead.

'Tell me about the boys,' she said. 'Kit's doing very well at university, he writes to me occasionally.'

'That's nice.' Terence studied his Scotch for a moment before looking up to give her his warmest smile. 'That's very nice.'

'And Malcolm is to go to Queensland next year, Kit says, to a special training camp.' Aggie looked concerned. 'Does that mean . . .?'

'Yes,' Terence interrupted, beaming with pride. 'The Jungle Training Centre at Canungra.' He stood, glass in hand. 'First Lieutenant Malcolm Galloway will undergo training as a Platoon Commander preparatory to active service in Vietnam.'

'Oh dear,' was all Aggie could say. She'd been prepared

to offer words of comfort, but Terence actually seemed delighted that his son would be training to go to war. He'd all but saluted as he'd announced the fact, but he'd downed the remains of his drink instead.

'Malcolm, like his father and his father's father before him, will fight for his country.'

Well, he'd be fighting for somebody else's country, really, wouldn't he, Aggie thought, but naturally she said nothing of her own views on the war in Vietnam. She sometimes felt she was the only person in Darwin who believed the Australians should never have become involved. Darwin, with its military history, seemed very pro-war, and the newspaper reports about the anti-conscription rallies which had been held in several state capitals following the Battle of Long Tan were discussed with vehement disapproval. As was the symbolic burning of draft cards. Conscientious objectors were considered cowards by most, and even traitors to their country by some, so Aggie kept her mouth shut for the most part.

She could discuss her views with Kit, however. They wrote to each other far more than 'occasionally', she simply hadn't wanted Terence to feel that she favoured one of his sons over the other. She and Kit had become very close through their correspondence, sharing their views and their mutual respect; it was a deeply rewarding relationship for them both. And, according to Kit, the feeling amongst his fellow students, indeed amongst the Adelaide populace in general, was very much against Australia's involvement in the Vietnam War.

'I insist you join me in a toast, Aggie.' Terence crossed to the cabinet, refilled his glass and poured her a Scotch. 'Here's to the third generation of Galloway men to fight for this great country.' He handed her the drink and she took it, she could hardly refuse.

'To Malcolm's safe return,' she said quietly as they clinked glasses.

Eighteen months later, Kit was conscripted. He wrote the news to Aggie before he told his father. She immediately presumed he would defer his military training until after he'd completed his university degree. Perhaps by then the whole ghastly business might be over, she thought hopefully. But as she read on, she discovered, to her horror, that Kit did not intend to apply for a deferment. She was further shocked to hear that, following his training, he intended to volunteer for active service.

'You'll probably think I'm a bit of a phony, Aggie,' he wrote. *'As you know, I'm against our involvement in South Vietnam, so on the grounds of principle I shouldn't give in. But I'm going to go because of Dad. Which means you'll probably think me a bit of a wimp as well. But it's not because I'm frightened of him. I can stand up to Dad. Quite honestly I think I can stand up to him better than Malcolm can, but don't ever tell anyone I said that. It's just that I know Dad would feel such shame if I didn't answer the call-up. I couldn't bear the thought of humiliating him in front of his mates.*

'I haven't told him I've been called up so don't say anything yet. My medical's in ten days. I'll pass it of course, skinny I might be but I'm as fit as a mallee bull. Anyway, just in case I find out I've got flat feet or something, I'm leaving it until after then to let Dad know. If I get knocked back I won't say anything, but if it goes the way I'm sure it will, then let Dad tell you himself, and pretend to be surprised. I hope you don't mind the conspiracy, but I wanted you to be the first to know.'

A week after Aggie received the letter, Kit rang his father. He'd been called up, he said. He'd passed the medical and he'd shortly be off to Puckapunyal for his military training.

'You could have deferred, couldn't you?' Terence's reply was abrupt.

'Yep, but I didn't. I'm going to apply for active service.

I'll finish my course when I come home.'

There was a brief pause on the end of the line, then, 'Good on you, son, well done.'

They were the words which each of Terence's sons longed to hear, and Kit was glad he'd earned his father's approval.

'It'll do you the world of good,' Terence said. 'The army'll make a man out of you.'

As he hung up, Terence delighted in the irony of it all. So the boy who had fought him about joining the army was going to war after all. Serve him right.

Safe from the fear of discovery which had haunted him, Terence no longer imagined he saw Paul Trewinnard in the boy. But he was confronted in so many other ways by the fact that Kit was not his son. The boy simply didn't behave like a Galloway. Perhaps the army would change that. Yes, he thought, as he poured himself a Scotch. The army'd do him good, make a man of him.

CHAPTER TWENTY-NINE

1940

O ld Emily Sullivan had died. She'd been feeling quite 'chipper', a term she'd inherited from her English mother and one she used often, and had just enjoyed her seventy-seventh birthday with her family around her. Then, a week later, she'd died. Peacefully, in her sleep, the way she would have chosen to go. She would not, however, have chosen the family drama which ensued.

In evaluating the old lady's jewels, and deciding which of the less valuable items he might magnanimously give to his daughters-in-law, Matthew Sullivan discovered that the locket was missing. Enquiries within the family led nowhere and all fingers pointed to Tom. Tom had left the fold eighteen months previously and was occasionally seen around town when he returned from the goldfields for supplies, but he never visited the family.

When questioned, Tom openly admitted to having sold the locket. His grandmother had given it to him, he said, with the express wish that he sell it in order to embark upon his new life. His father called him a liar and accused him of theft, so Tom took him to the shop of Foong Lee in Cavenagh Street.

In the privacy of his office overlooking the courtyard, Foong Lee produced Emily's letter stating that the locket was a gift to her grandson.

'It's a forgery,' Matthew Sullivan said. 'It's quite obvious, the boy forged her signature.'

'I'm afraid he didn't, Mr Sullivan,' Foong Lee replied. 'The signature is authentic.'

Matthew Sullivan was unaccustomed to being answered back with such authority, particularly by a Chink. A big man, like his father, and a powerful one at that, people were normally subservient in his presence.

'You're in this with him, aren't you?' he said threateningly to the Chinese.

'I most certainly am,' Foong Lee replied with the utmost politeness, 'your son and I had a business transaction. I paid a good price for property which was his to sell.'

Young Tom grinned openly at Foong Lee, whose expression remained inscrutable, whilst Matthew Sullivan's face grew apoplectic with rage.

Foong Lee continued smoothly, 'I have other documents containing Mrs Sullivan's signature, you are quite welcome to examine them if you wish.'

Matthew Sullivan cursed his mother. It was just what the stupid old bitch would have done, he realised. She'd considered herself a bit of an adventuress in her time, and Tom had always been her favourite, she'd given him the locket along with her bloody blessing. Matthew forced himself to keep calm, he needed to get the Chinese on side.

'Tom,' he said, 'wait out in the shop, I'd like to have a chat with Mr Foong.'

Tom did as he was told and when he'd gone Matthew said expansively, 'Mr Foong, I believe you're an honest man.'

'I believe so too,' Foong Lee replied. He knew men like

Matthew Sullivan. Powerful, self-righteous and confident. Bullies accustomed to getting their own way.

'And I believe you've been misled in this transaction.'

'As I've said, the signature is genuine.' Foong Lee refused to be bullied.

'Ah yes, I'm sure you're right there, but you see the old lady would not have been in a sound mental state when she signed it. My mother's mind had been wandering for years before her death.'

'The entire letter was in her hand,' Foong Lee said, still with the utmost of politeness, 'and the text does not read like the product of an unstable mind.'

'Well, of course not,' damn the Chink's hide, Matthew thought, 'Tom would have dictated it to her, wouldn't he.'

'The handwriting itself is very confident,' Foong Lee replied. 'But of course, if you're convinced Mrs Sullivan was not of sound mind, then perhaps there are others who might attest to the fact. Her doctor perhaps?'

Matthew Sullivan realised that the Chinese's courteous façade masked a will of steel. He decided on a different tack. He would be honest with the man.

'Mr Foong,' he said. 'Let us just say that you're right. Perhaps the old lady did give the boy the locket, but don't you see, in the whim of her old age, she has led him astray. Thomas has responsibilities to a family business, to a respectable name. He must be taught a lesson for failing those responsibilities. He must be led back to the fold.' *The Chinese was listening attentively. Good, Matthew thought. 'May I sit?'*

'Please.' *Foong Lee was interested, what was Sullivan leading up to? Both men sat.*

'I have a proposition for you,' Matthew said, 'one which is distinctly to your advantage. I will give you the amount you paid my son and you will return the locket to me.'

'How is that to my advantage?' Foong Lee asked.

'Hah,' Matthew shook his head in begrudging admiration, 'you Chinese are true businessmen, aren't you. All right, I'll add ten percent to the purchase price. But of course the true advantage you'll be gaining is the fact that you won't be involved in a legal suit. Because I'll tell you here and now, if I don't get that locket back, I'll sue my son. I'll publicly denounce and disown him, teach him a lesson once and for all.'

'And if I agree to exchange the locket for your payment, then what lesson will your son have learned?'

'Humiliation,' Matthew said triumphantly. 'The greatest way to teach a man his place. Humiliation! Amongst those closest to him, my son will be perceived as a thief. His friends and his family will know that Tom stole his grandmother's locket and that I repurchased it to keep it in trust for those who were always intended to inherit it.'

And what will I be perceived as, Foong Lee thought. A receiver of stolen goods. His expression was unreadable, but he was angry. 'I believe the locket was the personal property of Mrs Sullivan,' he said, 'and therefore hers to dispose of as she wished.'

Damn it, the Chink was getting on his nerves. 'It belonged to the family, Mr Foong.' Matthew's voice once again had a threatening edge. 'As did all of my grandmother's valuable possessions.'

'It was given to her by her husband upon their engagement, I'd heard.'

'Well of course that's what Tom would have told you,' Matthew scoffed.

'He did.' Foong Lee rose, he'd had enough of the conversation. 'And I believe him. I'm afraid, Mr Sullivan, that the locket is not for sale.'

Matthew was shocked. The man was not only refusing his offer, but dismissing him from his office. He stood, pushing back his chair so roughly it fell on its side. 'You'll pay for this, you dirty little Chink. I'll take you through the courts. You and my son. You're an accessory to theft and I'll make your name mud.'

'As you wish.' Foong Lee led the way out of the office. 'Any such action is your prerogative of course.'

The Sullivans left, Tom following his irate father from the shop, too fearful to do otherwise. At the door, he turned back briefly and Foong Lee gave him a reassuring nod.

When the two of them had gone, however, Foong Lee stood with his elderly father, who had watched the proceedings in a state of utter bewilderment, and he felt his bravado falter. He was in deep trouble and he knew it. Sullivan was not only rich, powerful and respected, he was a gwailo. It would be a gwailo's word against that of a Chinaman in a gwailo court of law. The odds were severely stacked against him, but Foong Lee knew of one man who could possibly save him.

'Of course I'll take on the case,' Paul Trewinnard agreed having listened to Foong Lee's account of the events, 'but it's a while since I practised, you could perhaps find more experienced representation.'

'You have the most important credential of all, Paul,' Foong Lee said, 'you are a gwailo. No other European solicitor will agree to represent me, I'm convinced of it, not against Matthew Sullivan. And, sad to say, I doubt whether even the most expert of Chinese solicitors would fare very well with such a case. Besides,' he added realistically, 'there is a war on. Who will be remotely interested in the honour of a Chinese shopkeeper?'

'Under the circumstances then, I insist upon taking up your offer.'

Paul knew that Foong Lee was a very worried man. And with just reason. His reputation meant more to him than his very life, and the loss of face he would suffer, particularly in the eyes of the Chinese community in which he was held in such high esteem, would be more than he could *bear. Paul determined to do everything within his power to save his friend. After all, Foong Lee had saved his own life, the least he could do was return the favour.*

When Paul Trewinnard had arrived in Darwin in April of the preceding year, his first port of call had been China-town. Where there were Chinese there was opium and, in Singapore, he had discovered that opium relaxed him. It eased the pain of his memories. Just occasionally, he told himself. He didn't intend to make it a habit.

'I'm looking for Foong Shek Mei,' he said to the young Chinese behind the counter of the shop in Cavenagh Street.

'May I enquire as to why?' the young Chinese queried.

'Personal business,' Paul brusquely replied. 'I was told Foong Shek Mei is the proprietor of this shop.'

The young Chinese nodded. 'He is my father and co-owner indeed, but it is I who conduct all business transactions.' Foong Lee had a nasty suspicion that the Englishman was seeking opium, why else would he wish to see Foong Shek Mei?

Foong Lee was angry that his father had been suggested as a contact, and he knew full well who would have made that suggestion. Kwan Man Hop who imported the drug and from whom Foong Lee bought the regular small supply to assuage his father's addiction. Kwan Man Hop would have been too wary to deal with a gwailo. Perhaps he thought that Foong Lee, with his many European associates, might be prepared to act as a middleman. Foong Lee was insulted and angry, he would have words with Danny Kwan. But he must first ascertain that his suspicions were correct. He walked to the open back door of the shop.

'Lin Mei,' he called, and his wife appeared. 'Lei yiu bo woo po tau,' he said. It was Foong Shek Mei's afternoon off and he was playing mah-jong with his friends at a

Chinese café. Lin Mei nodded, quite happy to look after the shop, and Foong Lee beckoned to the Englishman.

'Would you care to come out into the courtyard?' he said.

Paul followed him through the back door. In the glare of the courtyard he could see that the Chinese was not as young as he'd thought. A man in his thirties, Paul guessed, possibly even close to his own age.

'I am Foong Lee,' the Chinese said offering his hand.

'Paul Trewinnard, how do you do.' They shook.

'How may I help you, Mr Trewinnard?'

The Chinese's gaze was so honest and direct that Paul felt self-conscious, he hoped that the contact he'd been given was correct.

'I've just arrived from Singapore,' he said, hedging a little.

'Ah yes,' Foong Lee smiled, 'welcome to Darwin.'

'Thank you.' The man's courtesy made him feel even more self-conscious. 'And I was wondering whether you might perhaps be able to supply me with, um . . .' Paul hesitated.

'Yes?'

Damn it, Paul thought, the helpful look of enquiry on the man's face was most disconcerting. 'Just a small quantity, um . . .'

Foong Lee decided to put the Englishman out of his pain, he looked so distinctly uncomfortable. 'You wish to purchase a commodity which is easily available in Singapore, but difficult to obtain in Darwin?'

'Exactly.'

'Opium is illegal in Darwin, Mr Trewinnard.' Judging by Trewinnard's discomfort Foong Lee was sure he was aware of the fact, but it was only fair he be given the benefit of the doubt.

'Yes, I did know that.'

'I'm sorry to disappoint you, but I'm afraid you've been

directed to the wrong source. You won't find what you seek here.'

Paul's discomfort multiplied tenfold. In the light of the man's dignity he suddenly felt rather grubby. 'I do beg your pardon,' he said, 'I meant no offence.'

Foong Lee was sorry for Trewinnard, he seemed such a respectable gentleman, and yet there was something very lost about him. Was he an addict? If so, how sad. Foong Lee knew only too well the ravages of opium addiction, he watched it daily with his father. Foong Shek Mei was not yet incapacitated by the drug, but he soon would be. All the signs were there, it was only a matter of time.

'Would you care for some tea?' he asked as the Englishman turned to go.

'No, please, I don't wish to impose.'

'It's no imposition, I'd enjoy the company, we're not busy today and my wife will look after the shop.'

'I'd love some tea, Mr Foong. Thank you.'

They chatted quite comfortably as Foong Lee prepared the heung ping. *The Chinese was such pleasant company that Paul found himself talking more openly than he had in a very long time. He was a solicitor, he said, but he no longer worked for his family's business in Singapore. He earned his living as a freelance journalist these days.*

'For the London Times *mainly,' he said. 'Usually travel, but lately I've been covering the situation in the Pacific. Of course with Europe on the threshold of war, I'm hardly front page stuff, but they're interested in what the Japanese might get up to.'*

'How very interesting.'

'Yes, isn't it? Australia doesn't seem to be taking too much notice of the Japs, but they should, I tell you. They should.'

'Do you know anyone in town, Mr Trewinnard?'

'The desk clerk at the Hotel Darwin,' Paul grinned.

'Then you must allow me to introduce you to my friend

Leon at the Northern Standard, I'm quite sure he'd be eager to acquire the services of someone with your wealth of experience.'

'That's very kind of you, Mr Foong, I'd be most obliged.'

'Foong Lee. Please.'

'Foong Lee,' Paul nodded, he found the man charming. 'And I'm Paul.'

An hour later, as they sat in the courtyard with their second pot of tea, Paul found himself talking, for some unknown reason, about the death of his wife and child. He had spoken to no-one about the accident for years. Not because the subject was too painful, he had learned to accept his loss and the inevitable emptiness of his days. But he had admitted no-one into his life on a personal basis. He didn't question now the fact that he was conversing intimately with a man he'd just met, it somehow seemed quite natural.

Paul was unaware that putting people at their ease and extracting their life story was a particular talent, only one of many, which Foong Lee possessed.

'So this is why you seek opium?' Foong Lee finally took the plunge. He had been working towards it for the past half hour, and he felt now was the time to risk it.

Paul was shocked. Shocked at the fact that he had spoken so intimately to a virtual stranger, and shocked that Foong Lee should think him an addict. His guard was up immediately.

'Perhaps,' he said stiffly. 'It's a distraction certainly, but I only "seek it" as you say on the odd occasion.' He was as defensive as Foong Lee had expected him to be. 'I'm moderate in my use, I don't overindulge, and I'm most certainly not an addict as you seem to imply.'

'There is no such thing as the "moderate" use of opium,' Foong Lee replied, the reasonable tone of his voice only adding to the condemnation of his words. 'You are already overindulging and you are most certainly on the road to *addiction. That is, if you have not already arrived there.'*

Paul rose from the table. 'Thank you very much for the tea.'

'I mean no offence, Paul. Sit down, please, I beg you. Just for a moment.'

Not *wishing to be rude, Paul sat. But he had closed off his mind, Foong Lee could tell. For the moment he was unapproachable. It was to be expected.*

'I sound as harsh as I do, because I wish to help you. I wish to be your friend.'

'I'd rather not speak anymore on the subject.' Paul cursed his own stupidity for having revealed himself, for having walked into the trap which the Chinese had obviously set for him. He was certainly not prepared to listen to a lecture on the evils of his occasional dalliance with opium. He wished he could just get up and walk out, but having accepted the man's hospitality it would be unspeakably rude.

'Of course,' Foong Lee said, 'as you wish. I could, however, obtain opium for you.' Paul's reaction was instinctive and just as Foong Lee had anticipated. He could not disguise his immediate interest.

'You could?'

'Yes. I didn't lie earlier, I do not deal in the drug, but I know where I could acquire opium if you really wished for it. However, I have a proposition, will you hear it?'

'Yes.'

Foong Lee's proposition was that Paul visit him several times a week. They would talk and drink tea, just as they had that afternoon, 'And there will be opium here should you need it,' he said.

The offer was genuine, and it was that simple. But Paul was given no time to reply.

'Now do you have a pen and paper?' Foong Lee's query was brisk and efficient.

'Yes.' A little bewildered, Paul obediently fumbled in his

coat pocket for the notebook which he always carried.

'You must take down the telephone number of my friend Leon at the Northern Standard,' Foong Lee said, and he dictated it to Paul, he knew all of his contacts' numbers by heart and rarely referred to address books. 'I shall telephone him as soon as you leave and he'll be expecting your call.' Foong Lee rose and extended his hand. 'Why don't you come around on Friday, about the same time, mid-afternoon, we're not busy mid-afternoons, then you can let me know how you went with Leon.'

'Right.'

They shook hands and Foong Lee led the way through the shop.

'I'll see you Friday then,' Paul said at the front doors.

'I look forward to it.'

Suddenly Paul found himself out in Cavenagh Street a little dazed by the speed of events. There had been no further mention of opium, but he knew the offer was genuine. Each time he called upon his new-found friend, opium would be available for purchase, Foong Lee had been quite clear.

Paul couldn't sleep that night. Over and over, he analysed his reaction to Foong Lee's words. He had most certainly been defensive. Was Foong Lee right? Did he have a problem? No, bloody ridiculous, he told himself, of course he didn't. He vacillated. One minute he was angry at Foong Lee's interference, the next he recalled the concern and the wisdom in the eyes of the Chinese and again he questioned himself.

He kept his appointment on Friday, determined to make the visit short and to purchase a supply of opium.

'Leon tells me you had a most successful meeting,' Foong Lee said as he poured the tea.

'Yes.' Paul had been surprised when the editor had suggested they meet at the Northern Standard offices upon the very afternoon of his phone call. 'He's interested in my

writing a series of articles.'

'Excellent.'

They discussed the situation in Europe, most particularly Italy's recent invasion of Albania.

'Only a month after Hitler's invasion of Czechoslovakia,' Foong Lee remarked. He had the major newspapers sent up to him from Adelaide and he read them from cover to cover, following the state of affairs in Europe with avid interest.

'Yes,' Paul said. 'There are many who believe it's only a matter of time before Britain declares war on Germany.' He shook his head gravely. 'These are bad times, Foong Lee, the world is about to go mad.'

'We are a little complacent in Australia,' Foong Lee said, 'it all seems so far away from us here.'

'It isn't. Australia can ill afford complacency. In the event of war the British fleet will be deployed in Europe and Australia will be at the mercy of the Japanese.'

Foong Lee nodded. 'Your fellow countryman H.G. Wells said as much when he visited this country recently. "The British fleet is no longer your fleet." Those were his exact words, it was in the newspapers. And then when he warned Australia that the Japanese menace was "no bogey", as he put it, they howled him down. The Australian press are short-sighted fools with regard to the Japanese.' There was a touch of uncharacteristic contempt in Foong Lee's voice. Since the slaughter of hundreds of thousands of Chinese during the invasion and occupation of Shanghai and Nanking the previous year, Foong Lee, like most of his countrymen, detested the Japanese. 'They called Wells's remarks "deplorable",' he scoffed.

'Then I agree with you,' Paul said, 'they're short-sighted fools. Wells was right. Without the protection of the British, Australia's a sitting duck.'

The conversation was stimulating and the afternoon

passed quickly. Suddenly Foong Shek Mei was at the door to the courtyard announcing that it was after five o'clock and the shop was getting busy.

It was only as he said goodbye, that Paul realised he had forgotten to purchase the opium.

'Shall we say Monday, mid-afternoon, around three?' Foong Lee asked.

'Yes, Monday would be fine.' He would purchase the opium on Monday, Paul thought.

But he didn't. He didn't forget, but after another session with Foong Lee, which Paul found both stimulating and relaxing, he somehow didn't want to ask for the opium. Was it because he didn't wish to lose face with the Chinese, he wondered.

And so it went on. Each time Paul visited Foong Lee he knew the opium was there if he wished, but he never mentioned the subject. He briefly contemplated finding another source of supply, but he told himself no, that would be reneging on their arrangement.

Sometimes they would talk very little. Foong Lee would burn incense and they would sit in contemplative silence. Meditation was good for mind, body and soul, Foong Lee said. Paul hadn't realised he'd been meditating, he'd simply found the process relaxing. He was sleeping much better these days, he told Foong Lee a week or so later, perhaps it was the meditation. Foong Lee remarked that there was much to be said for the Eastern ways, perhaps Paul would like to learn the art of tai chi?

Paul had always felt very 'foreign' when he'd witnessed the scores of Chinese in Singapore performing the gentle movements in unison. Tai chi seemed to epitomise the difference between East and West, surely there was little a 'gwailo' could learn from practising such an art. But he didn't wish to be hurtful or rude.

'Yes,' he said, 'that would be very interesting.'

The weeks became months and the two men continued to enjoy each other's company. Slowly, and without realising the fact, Paul Trewinnard had found, possibly for the first time in his entire life, a true friend. They practised tai chi, they meditated, and they talked. Endlessly. And always they drank tea, copious amounts of tea.

One day Paul arrived with a bottle of Scotch under his arm. 'I hope you don't mind, Foong Lee,' he said. 'Please don't take offence, but I'm sick to death of jasmine tea.'

Foong Lee laughed long and loud. Paul Trewinnard was still a lost man in many ways, perhaps he would never fully find himself, but at least he was not destined to follow the path of destruction which had so strongly beckoned.

In taking on Foong Lee's case against Matthew Sullivan, Paul was also representing young Tom and, upon their first meeting, he was pleased to discover that not only did he believe in the lad's innocence, he genuinely liked Tom Sullivan. In fact they had much in common. Like Tom, Paul too had been considered a ne'er-do-well, the black sheep of a very respectable family. Well, Paul would take on that family and, come hell or high water, he said, they'd win.

But it was not going to be easy, Matthew Sullivan was pulling out the big guns. He had purchased the locket for his mother, he swore, along with many other valuable items over the years. His son had either forged the letter, or coerced the feeble-minded old lady into writing it, and the Chinese shopkeeper, Foong Lee, in purchasing the piece, had done so with full knowledge of the facts. Matthew was out to get both of them, and the case was to be heard in the Adelaide Supreme Court.

'It'll be our word against theirs,' Paul told Tom and Foong Lee. 'They'll drop the forgery tack I'm sure, handwriting analysts will vouch for the letter's authenticity. But *they'll try to prove that you dictated it to your grand-mother, Tom, and they'll probably pay a doctor to testify she wasn't of sound mind.'*

Tom was obviously concerned. 'Don't worry,' Paul assured him, 'I'm sure we'll be able to discredit the wit-ness, Foong Lee tells me there are many who can attest to the fact that Emily Sullivan was as smart as a whip.'

Paul looked at the two of them, they were hanging on his every word. 'We've a very good chance of saving both your reputations,' he continued, with a greater confidence than he actually felt, 'but not the locket, I'm afraid. Your father's final defence will be that it was never Emily's to give away in the first place. He'll swear under oath that he purchased the locket and that it belonged to the family along with the rest of her jewellery, and it'll be nigh on impossible to prove otherwise.'

Tom grinned. 'I can help you there,' he said.

CHAPTER THIRTY

Malcolm heard the Huey before he saw it. He'd been anticipating its arrival, but he was in the command post with his replacement platoon sergeant, Hugh McKay, a dour Scot who'd lived in Australia for twenty years but still had an accent you could cut with a knife. Malcolm missed Big Stan, the previous platoon sergeant who'd served with him since he'd first come to Vietnam. Hugh 'Mac' McKay had been with the platoon for the past three weeks, since the battalion had occupied Fire Support Base Tango, but Malcolm found that he couldn't really warm to Mac. It was probably his own fault, he realised. He didn't warm to anyone much these days.

The two men were engrossed in the maps spread out before them, Mac's cigarette smoke wafting irritatingly past Malcolm's nose, when the incessant thud of the helicopter's blades announced its presence overhead. A comforting sound, Malcolm thought.

'I'll make some tea,' Mac said affably as Malcolm went out to greet the new arrivals.

'Good idea.' He knew his reply was surly, and once again he chastised himself. Mac was a nice enough bloke.

It wasn't Mac's fault that he wasn't Big Stan. But Malcolm's moods had been getting the better of him lately. 'Thanks,' he added brusquely, stepping outside.

Sullen bastard, Mac thought.

Malcolm walked the fifty metres or so from the platoon HQ pits to the helipad and watched the Huey descend. Hueys were a welcome presence in the field. Be they gunships mounted with twin 7.62mm mini-guns, an upgrade of the Gatling gun that fired 6,000 rounds a minute, or resupply ships dropping essential ammunition and rations, or CASEVACs, with the Red Cross insignia, collecting the wounded, Hueys meant help was at hand. The familiar sight and sound was a reassurance.

Of course they weren't quite such a reassurance if they were dropping you into a combat zone, Malcolm thought, bracing himself against the blast of air and watching the helicopter come to rest like a giant jungle-green dragon fly. When they were dropping you into battle, they hovered above ground and, as you prepared to make the jump and run for cover, the rapid rhythm of the Huey's blades matched the terrified beating of your heart. Not that you ever admitted to it.

This time, however, the Huey was delivering ammunition and, even more importantly, an officer from the supporting field artillery battery. Malcolm had advised his higher HQ that if his beleaguered men were to maintain their sector of Fire Support Base Tango at all costs, as had been his orders, then immediate direct artillery support was required. His platoon had been under intermittent fire for the past three weeks, and Malcolm was convinced that the North Vietnamese Army, aware of the strategic importance of Fire Support Base Tango, were about to launch a full-scale attack through his sector.

It was a crisp wintry morning in January. Ominously still. No sound from the enemy who, in any event, would not wish to give away their position to the Huey and risk a possible air attack. From his vantage point, Malcolm had a clear view of his platoon's position, its gunsites and their fields of fire. The entire hill had been selectively denuded of vegetation for that very purpose. Throughout his position, the foxholes were linked by a series of trenches to gunpits further down the hill where machine-gun crews were ever at the ready, their M-60s each covering a fixed arc. Beyond the gunpits, sentries covered likely enemy approaches, and barbed wire was positioned to channel the enemy into the machine guns' killing area. A dangerous position, there had recently been two casualties in a ferocious burst of enemy gunfire from the north.

Over the past week the NVA appeared to be probing, in the main from the north. But it was sporadic. Diversionary tactics, with sniper fire from other directions. It was impossible to tell how, or where, they were massed, even with aggressive patrolling outside the position. Beyond the killing area, 800 metres away, lay the impenetrable jungle of trees and lush undergrowth which housed the unseen enemy. Malcolm had ordered the arcs of machine-gun fire altered to concentrate on the north but, because of his uncertainty of the enemy's position, the alteration had been minimal.

'G'day. Bill Perseman, I'm your forward observer.' The captain, having alighted from the Huey, introduced himself with the twang of a Queenslander. He was a tough, leathery little man in his mid-thirties. 'Call me Perse,' he said as he offered his hand.

'Hello, Perse, I'm Malcolm Galloway.' The handshake was a knucklebuster, Malcolm registered.

'This is my signaller,' Perse gestured to the artillery man who had unloaded the radio transmitter from the Huey and was walking towards them, 'I reckon you blokes know each other,' he grinned.

'G'day, Malcolm.' The gangly young gunner put down the transmitter and smiled at the incredulous expression on the lieutenant's face. 'Close your mouth or the flies'll get in,' he said. It was an expression their mother had often used when they were children.

'Kit!' The brothers embraced. 'Jesus, I knew you were in artillery, but what the hell are they doing sending you here?' The pleasure of seeing his young brother was strongly overridden by Malcolm's fear for Kit's safety.

'I'm the signaller,' Kit shrugged, 'I'm here to operate the radio.'

'He's probably here to look after me,' Perse said, and in response to Malcolm's querying look he added, 'he's a crack bloody shot your little brother, best in the whole bloody regiment.'

'Come to the HQ pits,' Malcolm said, 'Mac's brewing us a cuppa.'

'Be with you in a tick.' Perse returned to the Huey, which was preparing for takeoff. He didn't really need to chat with the pilot but he thought the brothers might like a few minutes alone together. Bill Perseman was a tough little bloke, but he could be surprisingly sensitive.

'Crack bloody shot, eh?' Malcolm muttered as he and Kit walked to the HQ pits where the command post had been extended to accommodate the additional artillery men. 'You stupid bastard.'

'Why?'

'Being a crack bloody shot gets you into trouble, that's why.'

'Comes with the territory, eh?' Kit grinned.

'Don't be a smartarse. It's because you're a crack bloody shot that you've got yourself moved to a forward command position. You'd have been much safer if you'd kept your mouth shut and stayed at the rear with the rest of the pack.'

'Oh well, in for a penny, in for a pound.' It was another of their mother's sayings, and Malcolm cuffed Kit good naturedly over the back of the head.

Throughout the day Malcolm and Perse examined their maps, checking coordinates and grid references. From the observation post adjoining the CP, with its raised roof and wide view of the terrain on all sides, they studied the area through binoculars. But, even as they discussed tactics, they agreed there was really nothing they could do. It was up to the enemy to make the first move.

'We can't even be sure where the bastards are,' Malcolm said.

In the CP that night, the corporal section commanders welcomed Perse and Kit in their customary ribald fashion.

'Bloody nepotism it is, mate,' Ben the Tasmanian said to Kit. 'Bloody nepotism landing a cushy job like this. You're a lucky young bastard to be right here where it's all about to happen.' He incited the others with a series of none-too-subtle nudges and winks. 'Always who you know, isn't it?' and the others loudly voiced their agreement.

Perse had spread the word that Kit was a crack shot, he was proud of his young signaller. And, always impressed by marksmanship, the men compared notes.

'Bet he's not as good as Beady,' Ben the Tasmanian said.

'I'd put good money on it that he is.' Perse hadn't even met Beady, but he'd back Kit against any man.

The wager was on. The Kid against Beady. Kit was by far the youngest at the base and was already being referred to as 'The Kid'. He didn't really mind, they were good blokes all round.

Two hours later when Beady, a freckle-faced man with a shock of red hair, came off sentry duty he said, 'I hear you're a crack shot, Kid.'

'I heard the same about you.'

Mac, who'd come off radio duty for a quick smoko, said 'Ben tells me there's a wager.' Mac was a betting man. 'The Kid against Beady, count me in.' He dragged heavily on his Winfield.

In the dim overhead light of the CP, the men hadn't

noticed the arrival of their officer, but they were instantly silenced by the voice which cut through their bonhomie.

'We'll hardly be having a shooting contest when we're about to engage with the enemy.'

Each man turned to the figure of Lieutenant Galloway standing in the shadows of the CP entrance.

'Sure Skipper, we know that,' Ben said hastily.

Mac and Beady exchanged a look, which did not go unnoticed by Bill Perseman. 'We're talking about after,' Beady added.

'After what?'

'They mean after we've sorted out Charlie,' Mac said as patiently as he could. Christ the Skipper was a moody bastard, couldn't he just let the men have a good time?

Malcolm had heard the men's good-humoured jibes about nepotism, and the obvious inference to the danger of their situation had unnerved him all the more. What the hell was Kit doing here? And now the men were setting him up against Beady, the crack shot of the battalion. Kit was already expected to perform like a hero. Hell, he shouldn't have been in Vietnam in the first place, let alone in a bloody battle zone.

'Then that's exactly what we'll do, Mac,' Malcolm replied. Christ, why did the Scot's implacability so get on his nerves, he thought, it was an admirable quality in a platoon sergeant. But he couldn't help himself, he disliked Mac. 'We'll sort out Charlie. Then maybe we'll talk about who's the crack shot.'

'Of course, Skipper.' Mac's reply was casual, but he knew he'd just received an order. He took another drag on his cigarette. 'I'll make that quite clear to the men.'

'See that you do.' Malcolm was agitated, nervy, and the tic in his right eye, which for the most part he managed to keep hidden from the others, was starting its involuntary action. He left the CP, closely observed by Bill Perseman.

That night the dreams were more vivid than ever.

Malcolm could see the village in Phuoc Toy, some of the huts still smouldering, the bodies left to rot, humans, pigs and chickens, all treated with the same disregard. He could smell the cordite and the sickly odour of burned and rotting flesh. He could hear the incessant buzzing of the sluggish, fat blowflies and, despite the stench, he breathed through his nose, not daring to open his mouth for fear he might swallow one. As he dragged a woman's body to the makeshift mass grave, he saw the flesh tear apart to expose the maggots feeding on her insides.

It had supposedly been a routine public relations patrol. They were to keep the villagers happy and gain their confidence, they were to hand out medical supplies, and food and sweets to the children.

But Malcolm's platoon sergeant, Big Stan Munday, a tough seasoned soldier of forty, well versed in the ways of jungle warfare, had known that something was wrong.

'That smoke's not from cooking fires,' he'd said.

They'd circled the village and approached with caution. Upon discovery of the carnage, Malcolm had tried to cover his sickened sense of shock by commenting upon the Vietcong's slaughter of pigs and chickens for no purpose.

'They do it all the time,' Big Stan had said, rolling the body of a piglet over with his boot. 'Bloody waste, they'll be maggot ridden by now.'

Malcolm had tried to adopt Stan Munday's detachment. It hadn't been easy, but he'd done it. He and Big Stan had served together since Malcolm's training camp days, well over a year now, and Big Stan, although his inferior in rank, had been Malcolm's true mentor. Everything Malcolm Galloway knew about active service he'd learned from Big Stan Munday.

It was after they'd dug the mass grave and started burying the bodies that one of the men saw the child.

'Hey, I think that kid's alive,' he called.

No-one had noticed the child, a boy of around ten,

seated on the ground in the shade of a tree, leaning comfortably against its trunk, his eyes open, his hand resting on his stomach.

The young private crossed to the child.

'Don't touch him!' Big Stan bellowed at the top of his voice.

But the private wasn't listening. 'It's okay, little fella,' he said quietly to the boy. The child wasn't moving, perhaps he was dead after all. But he appeared unscathed. Perhaps he was catatonic, in a state of shock. The private knelt beside him.

For a big man, Stan Munday could move with lightning speed. 'Don't touch him!' he roared again as he hurled himself towards the tree and the soldier and the boy.

The private lifted the boy's hand from his stomach to see if the child was wounded and, just as he did so, Stan Munday reached him. The big man bent down and grabbed the soldier's arm to wrench him away. Too late. The grenade planted on the dead child's body, pin removed, the little boy's weighted hand keeping the explosive mechanism in check, went off. The tree, the private and the boy were destroyed, and so was Big Stan Munday.

Malcolm hadn't lost his nerve. Not there and then. The men needed leadership, he was in command, it was up to him to maintain control. They'd got on with the job at hand. It was only afterwards that Malcolm had lost his nerve. In his head, where no-one could see, Malcolm became a mess. He'd relied upon Big Stan and now he was on his own. Well that was war, he told himself, you don't have Stan Munday, so get over it and get on with things.

But he couldn't get over it. He couldn't get over the shock of the booby trap and the sight of Big Stan with half his face blown away. And without Big Stan Munday, Malcolm's professional detachment deserted him. Every memory of the village and its desecration remained a personal horror.

During the day he functioned, the constant duty and activity kept the images at bay, but at night his sleep was fitful, fraught with the horrors which presented themselves, over and over, until he'd awake drenched in sweat, despite the chill of the winter air.

And now Kit was with him, and that night the dreams took on a chilling new aspect. The ghastly image of Big Stan's mutilated face became that of young Kit Galloway. His baby brother, drenched in blood, no eyes, no nose, just gore where his face had been.

Malcolm rose before dawn and prowled about the camp, willing the practicality and purpose of the day to begin, to rid him of his imaginings. But an hour or so later when Kit bounded up, youthful, eager, awaiting his orders, the images returned, and Malcolm found himself shaken and unnerved. Damn them! Why had they sent his little brother!

The day progressed like many others. There was no action from the enemy, so the men maintained their customary routine. Around lunchtime, several who were off sentry duty tossed a baseball about. Not ostentatiously, and not far from the trenches. Just whiling away the time, relieving the boredom and frustration, they would have said if questioned. In truth they were distracting themselves from the underlying anxiety which always accompanied the waiting game.

Bill Perseman knocked back Kit's offer to chuck the ball around. He'd noticed Mac over at the helipad, sitting on the ground, soaking up the sun, enjoying a smoke. Good, he thought, glad of the opportunity for a private chat with the sergeant, he'd been wanting to seek him out.

'G'day, Mac.'

'Sir.' Mac seemed quite happy to have his moment of privacy interrupted. 'Do you want a smoke?' He dived his hand into his top pocket for his Winfields but Perse shook his head. He'd given up a year ago and, like many a reformed smoker, he loathed the habit.

Perse squatted comfortably, elbows on his knees. 'Couldn't help but notice a bit of tension last night.' Perse always got straight to the point. 'Everything all right with your Skipper?'

Mac looked sharply at him. The captain had a bit of a hide expecting him to rat on the Skipper. 'Sure,' he said, 'why shouldn't it be?' Hell, Mac thought as he rose to his feet and ground his cigarette butt out with the heel of his boot, he might dislike the Skipper on occasions, but he'd never be disloyal to his officer.

Perse also rose. He was aware of Mac's unspoken outrage and realised he'd been too abrupt. But, as the harm had already been done, he decided the best way out was to be truthful. 'No offence, Mac, I'm not asking you to badmouth him. I just sensed your Skipper was a bit tense and I wondered if anything had happened, that's all. No offence intended, I swear.'

The honest look of concern in the tough little Queenslander's face was enough to convince Mac that he'd over-reacted. 'None taken,' he said, once again producing his packet of Winfields. 'You sure?' he asked, offering the pack.

'Why not.' Perse grinned and accepted the cigarette. Sharing a fag'd clear the air, he thought, it'd taste like shit but he wouldn't inhale.

They lit up and sat once again, side by side on the helipad, smoking in companionable silence.

'Skipper's always had a bit of a temper,' Mac admitted finally. Hell nothing disloyal in that, everyone was aware of the Skipper's quick temper. 'But the men understand that. They know better than to rile the Skipper, it keeps them in line.' Mac sucked heavily on his cigarette. 'It seems I'm the one who rubs him up the wrong way. For no particular reason,' he added as he exhaled.

'Why do you reckon that is?'

'Personality clash, I suppose,' Mac shrugged, 'and the fact that I'm not Stan Munday.'

This seemed to be going somewhere, Perse thought. 'Oh?' he queried taking a second tentative drag on his cigarette, his mouth tasting like dry camel dung.

'Stan Munday was his previous platoon sergeant,' Mac continued, 'an older bloke, quite a hero with the men, I believe. Or at least that's what Beady tells me.'

Perse nodded, it was all making sense. Stan Munday would have been a hero to Malcolm Galloway too, he thought. He'd seen it before. A young officer losing his right-hand man could be pushed to the brink. 'What happened to Stan Munday?' he asked.

'A booby trap.'

'Ah.' So that was it, Perse thought.

Bill Perseman had witnessed something in Malcolm Galloway's behaviour the previous night, something far more than a quick temper. The lieutenant was losing it, he was sure. Poor bastard. It was a big worry under the circumstances, however. Perse stood and stubbed out his cigarette. He'd have to keep a close eye on Lieutenant Galloway.

'Thanks for the smoke, Mac,' he said.

'You're welcome, sir.'

Shit his mouth tasted foul, Perse thought. 'I'm going to get a cuppa,' he said, 'do you want—'

He stopped mid-sentence as an artillery shell commenced its angry squeal. At the same time, the yell 'incoming!' sounded out clearly from the gunpits, and the squeal became a scream as the missile shrieked its way towards them.

Ben the Tasmanian had his arm raised and was about to throw to Kit when he heard the first chilling sound. He dropped the baseball. 'Run Kid,' he yelled, even before the call sounded from the gunpits, and he dived for the nearest trench, the others following close behind.

Perse and Mac turned to race for the control post, their nearest protective cover. Only fifty metres! Their ears were ringing. The sound was like the demented scream of a banshee, the shell was directly overhead. Thirty metres! Twenty-five! Twenty! It took them only seconds, but then it took the missile only seconds too. They didn't make it. The shell landed a little short of its intended mark. It had been intended to take out the three foxholes on the very peak of the hill, but it landed directly in between the CP and the helipad. As if it had been intended for Perse and Mac.

They've got artillery within range, Malcolm thought the moment he heard the scream of the shell. *I didn't know they had any bloody artillery*. He was in No. 3 foxhole with the machine-gun crew. *But there've been no intelligence reports of artillery movement*. His mind was racing. Even in the seconds before the shell hit, he was trying desperately to analyse the situation. Then there was an almighty explosion. Over near the CP. *Jesus!*

'Check the CP.' In the trenches connecting the foxhole, several men were already racing to the CP to see who might have copped it. 'Only one of you, for Christ's sake,' Malcolm barked, and the men halted. 'You, corporal, check the CP,' and Ben the Tasmanian disappeared. 'Where's the FO, where's Captain Perseman?' Of the three remaining men in the vicinity, no-one seemed to know. Malcolm turned to Kit who'd suddenly appeared by his side. 'Where's Perseman?' he snapped.

Oh God! Kit paled. He'd asked Perse if he wanted to chuck the ball around, and Perse had said no, and he'd headed off towards Mac, and Mac had been sitting over on the helipad. Just past the CP . . .

Malcolm registered the look on his younger brother's face. *Shit, don't tell me I've lost my Forward Observer*, he thought, *don't tell me that!* 'Get the radio,' he ordered.

Barely a minute later Kit returned with the radio transmitter, but by then the news had come back about Perse and Mac.

'Both dead, sir. Direct hit, killed outright.'

Oh Christ! 'And the CP?'

'Damaged. Only two blokes there, neither of them badly injured, sir.'

'Good.' Malcolm instructed the three privates to retrieve the bodies of Perse and Mac, then return to their posts. 'Corporal,' he turned to Ben, 'order all troops to maintain full alert and repair all damage.'

'Yes, sir.'

'Come with me, Kit.' The brusque efficiency of Malcolm's voice belied the shattered state of his nerves. *Two in one hit!* a voice was screaming in his head. *Jesus fucking Christ! You've got no forward observer! You've got no platoon sergeant. Jesus fucking Christ!*

Kit shouldered the transmitter in its backpack and followed Malcolm to the observation post.

'Set up the radio,' Malcolm ordered, and he bent over the map spread out on the ground, 'I'm calling in the artillery.' There was a sheet of paper beside the map with notations in Bill Perseman's surprisingly neat hand. Had it been only yesterday they'd studied the map together? *Shit, why isn't Perse here!*

Kit obeyed the order. He set up the transmitter which was tuned to the special artillery frequency, but as he did so he looked at his brother in amazement. 'You're calling in the artillery?'

'What else would you suggest, private?' It was a patronising sneer, but the tic in Malcolm's right eye had started to flicker. 'They have artillery out there, we need support.' He picked up the binoculars, looping them around his neck, and looked out over the base, mainly to avoid Kit noticing the humiliating tic.

Kit realised, with a sense of shock, that his brother's nerves seemed to be getting the better of him. 'I think they've only got one gun, maybe two at the most,' he suggested reasonably. There'd been silence from the enemy for a full five minutes. If the NVA had more artillery they wouldn't have fired just one shell, he thought, they'd have shot the shit out of the place by now.

'Oh they've only got one gun,' Malcolm said sarcastically, 'that's what you think is it?' *You smartarse bastard, they could have a whole fucking battery down there!* Lowering the binoculars, he turned on his brother. 'And how the hell would you know?'

'If they had more artillery, they wouldn't have fired just one shell. It might be a . . .' Kit stopped mid-sentence. The burgeoning scream of another shell interrupted, as if bent upon proving him a liar.

The brothers stood staring at each other for a split second before they dived to the ground, covering their heads. Again, a massive explosion, dirt and debris showering them. But again, the shell fell short of its mark and, when they rose to their feet and looked out over the position, it was obvious that no real damage had been inflicted.

In Malcolm's fragile state, however, the explosion had been enough to push him to the very edge of the emotional precipice upon which he teetered.

Grabbing the radio handpiece, he pressed the transmit button. He couldn't go to pieces, there was a job at hand, he was in command. He forced his voice to remain steady. 'Golf 41 this is 31 Fire Mission Battery, over.'

'31 this is Golf 41, over.'

As he heard the answering response, Malcolm traced, with his finger, the lines on the map before him. The fire had come from the north, but how far away were they? What distance should he call? What was the east-west grid reference? The lines on the map were dancing in front of his eyes. *Shit! Shit! Shit! What are the bloody coordinates?*

Kit watched, dumbfounded. It was madness to call in the artillery. Surely the fact that it had been five minutes between shells *proved* that the NVA had only one gun. Perhaps it was a setup, perhaps the shells had been intended as a decoy. They should be analysing the situation, Kit thought, not calling for help.

'Golf 41 from 31 . . . request immediate artillery fire . . .' The map was mocking him, the lines wouldn't stay still. *What are the fucking coordinates!*

A moment's pause. The voice once again through the handpiece. This time requesting coordinates.

Shit! Shit! Shit! Perse's notes. *Thank Christ!* Malcolm grabbed the sheet of paper, once again steadying his voice. 'Coordinates are grid 453 658, height 215 metres, over.'

The reply came, 'Require confirmation of coordinates grid 453 658, height 215 metres. Do you confirm? Over.'

Nervous beads of sweat were forming on Malcolm's brow. 'Golf 41 from 31, coordinates confirmed. Counter battery fire, one round fire for effect, over.'

'31 from Golf 41, counter battery fire, one round fire for effect, out.'

Malcolm put down the handpiece, overwhelmed with relief. *Thank Christ that's over.* He looked at his brother, who was staring at him. Rather strangely he thought. He straightened his back, glad that he hadn't lost control. In front of Kit of all people! Hell, it'd been close. He'd nearly lost it altogether. What a terrible thing, what on earth had happened to him? Oh well, they were all right now. The day was saved. Help was at hand. For some unknown reason, a string of cliches ran through Malcolm's mind and he wanted to laugh. Minutes later, when the deafening sound of a half a dozen heavy artillery shells screamed overhead, he did. He laughed out loud.

'Help is at hand,' he said, thinking that he sounded rather like his father as he said it.

From their shelter the two men looked down the hill and out over the killing area to the jungle beyond. But the shells didn't land in enemy territory. The perimeter of the base suddenly disappeared as the missiles detonated, throwing a wall of earth high in the air. God almighty, Kit thought, the shells aren't landing in enemy territory. They're not even landing in the killing area! We're firing on ourselves! He grabbed the handpiece of the radio transmitter.

'Check fire!' he yelled. 'Check fire! Check fire! Check fire!' Even as he yelled it, a shell landed higher up the hill and Kit watched in horror as one of their own gunpits disappeared. A direct hit. Somewhere in that shower of dirt, men had been blown to pieces. Then all was silence.

Malcolm stared down at the gutted position. He stared at the gunpit, clouded with smoke, from which there appeared no movement. But he wasn't seeing anything. The coordinates had been wrong, how had that happened? He tried to remember. Yesterday afternoon he and Perse had made notes. *That's right.* And at one stage Perse had written down their own coordinates. The grid references of Fire Support Base Tango's outer perimeter. *Ah yes, Perse's notes. That's what went wrong.*

Someone was slapping his face. It was very annoying.

'Malcolm, it's me, Kit. Are you all right?'

'Kit?' *Good God, I've shelled my own men.* 'Kit?' Malcolm stared stupidly, uncomprehendingly, back at his brother. Then he turned to once more gaze down the hill. *How could I have shelled my own men!* He raised the binoculars which still hung around his neck and peered through the clearing smoke. *That's where Charlie is,* he thought blankly as he swept the binoculars in an arc over the enemy territory. *That's where the shells should have landed.* He stared at the jungle and the thick, heavy grasses on the edge of the killing area. Then, out of the grasses, he saw figures rising, others stepping from behind the trees. *Charlie.* 'They're coming,' he said.

Kit ripped the binoculars from his brother's neck and followed the direction of Malcolm's vacant gaze.

They were coming from the north-west. In full force, it appeared. His initial instincts had been right, Kit thought. The enemy shell fire had been a decoy.

He grabbed Malcolm, thrusting the radio receiver into his brother's hand as he frantically checked the grid references on the map.

'Ring through these coordinates,' he said urgently, 'grid 454 662!'

But Malcolm was staring at the handpiece as if he wasn't sure what it was. *Ring through the coordinates? But I've already done that. And they were wrong.* He stood in a state of utter stupefaction. *What's the point of ringing through the wrong . . .* Suddenly he felt an almighty blow across his left cheek and he staggered back a step. It was Kit. Kit had hit him. With the flat of his hand, admittedly, but with all his might and it stung like hell. Why would Kit do that? And he was yelling too.

'For God's sake, Malcolm, ring through the coordinates! Grid 454 662!'

A glimmer of clarity found its way into Malcolm's brain. *The coordinates. Of course. I have to ring through the coordinates. Grid 454 662.*

'Grid 454 662,' he repeated, pressing the radio's transmit button.

As Malcolm, still dazed but at least functioning, radioed artillery, Kit raced out into the open and down the hill. In the gunpits, the crews would have their arcs of fire set to cover the wrong direction and, through the mayhem which surrounded them, they wouldn't even see the enemy's approach until it was too late to reposition the heavy guns and make the correction.

'Enemy to the left!' he yelled as he threw himself onto the ground beside the pit. 'Swing 'em left! Swing 'em left!' For a split second, the men looked at the young private as if he was mad. 'Skipper's instructions!' Kit yelled. 'Reposition! Correct your arc!' And he stood, pointing in the specific direction of the advance. Behind him, the men lifted the heavy weapon to reposition it.

Seconds later, Kit was racing on to the next gunpit, yelling, 'Skipper's orders, correct your arc!' Once again he exposed himself to enemy fire as he openly stood, drawing the gunners' attention to the advancing NVA infantry, calling target instructions. Then he was off once more, sprinting, dodging, weaving, to the next gunpit.

He didn't stop at the next gunpit, though. He barely slowed down, there was little point, it no longer existed. As he raced past the remains of men, he saw, briefly but clearly, Beady's freckled face staring up at him, mouth open as if in protest, eyes comically wide with astonishment. Ten metres from the pit, he stumbled and fell. Something had tripped him. It was a leg. He picked himself up and ran on, wondering vaguely if it was Beady's.

At the next gunpit. 'Skipper's orders . . .!' But, aware by now, the crew was already in the act of repositioning their machine gun.

The first wave of enemy troops had crossed into the killing area and were in range of their weapons. Bullets were whizzing all about Kit, whistling past his head, kicking up clods of earth. But, miraculously, he was unscathed, and by now the machine guns were finding their mark, defending their position, slowing the enemy's advance.

They were successfully buying time, Kit thought, but for how long? Fresh hordes of NVA troops were pouring out of the jungle, backing-up the first assault. Where the hell was the artillery?

Even as he thought it, he heard the first distant scream of the shells and, seconds later, the world erupted. Thank God! But he had to get back to the radio, he had to call in air support. The attack was massive, they needed all the help they could get.

As he raced up the hill, Kit barely felt the bullet that caught him in the arm. He barely felt anything except the heaving of his lungs as he once again dodged and weaved, legs pumping, hands clawing the air as if to pull himself along faster and faster, any minute expecting a bullet in the back.

Malcolm stared down at the battlefield, transfixed, his mind numb. There was something he must remember. What was it? Something terrible had happened. He tried desperately to remember what it was, but he couldn't. A safety mechanism had been triggered in his brain. He could not recall the hideous knowledge that he had caused the deaths of his own men. Something would not allow him to do so.

Then, out of the smoke and the chaos of battle, he saw Kit running up the hill, staggering, falling, recovering himself and running on.

Malcolm was galvanised into action. He could see nothing but his young brother. Kit was in trouble. He must save Kit. Nothing else mattered. He ran from the observation post. The noise was deafening as shells shrieked overhead to explode in the distance. Amongst the scream of the artillery which had come to their rescue, it was impossible to discern the one missile heading in the opposite direction.

Malcolm was barely ten metres from the observation post when he felt himself lifted off his feet by the impact. For a split second he was aware that he was airborne. But he didn't feel himself land, by then everything was black.

Kit too felt the blast. He felt it before he saw it. He'd been looking down at the ground as he ran, careful of falling again, aware that, in his exhausted state, he must keep up his momentum. He hesitated briefly as he was sprayed with debris. The bloody NVA gun, he thought, and he looked up. The roof of the observation post had been blown away and he prayed that the radio was intact. Then he noticed the body lying face down on the ground. He ran and knelt beside it. He didn't need to roll it over to know who it was, he saw the pips on the shoulder.

Malcolm was alive. Unconscious but breathing, and Kit dragged him into the nearby trench. He couldn't tell the extent of his brother's injuries and there was no time to examine him. The unit needed air support. Gunships. He had to find the radio.

He did. Amongst the ruins, the radio was mercifully intact. Breath still rasping in his throat, lungs feeling they might burst, Kit made the call.

Malcolm was floating, it could have been for a lifetime, as he lay there in the trench, drifting in and out of consciousness. But it wasn't, it was only a minute or so. He tried to move but he couldn't, not a muscle it seemed, and something told him he was dying. Strangely enough he didn't seem to care. He wasn't in any pain and that was the main thing. It was the pain he feared most, they all did. There wasn't a man amongst them who wasn't terrified at the thought of dying in agony.

It was quite pleasant, just floating. But there was something he needed to remember. Concentration was difficult. What the hell was it? He'd been calling in artillery support. And Kit had been with him.

Kit! He suddenly remembered. Kit! He'd seen Kit racing up the hill like a madman. *Kit! Was Kit all right?* He'd gone out to help him, and that was all he could remember.

'Malcolm.'

Thank God! Kit was kneeling beside him, concern in his eyes, anxiety in his voice. 'Are you all right?' Kit was saying. Malcolm nodded.

'Are you in pain?' How badly hurt was he, Kit wondered. He was in one piece, no limbs blown off, but his body was so limp. Internal injuries? Broken back? His face was stark white and, except for his eyes, he seemed utterly lifeless.

Malcolm stared at Kit. The initial relief at his brother's safety was replaced with the shocking memory which the sight of Kit had restored. They'd been in the observation post. He'd been radioing for artillery support. He'd given the wrong coordinates. It all flooded back. The memory which his brain had so successfully blocked out engulfed him. *I killed my own men!*

Kit saw his brother's eyes widen with horror. Was it death? Was he dying? Malcolm's mouth was open as if he was gasping for air. Kit didn't know what to do. Should he get him some water? No, that wasn't the right thing to do if he had internal injuries.

'I'm sorry, Malcolm.' He stroked his brother's forehead and cheeks, wiping away the dirt and the grime. He felt so useless he wanted to cry. 'I'm sorry. I don't know what to do.'

The plea in Malcolm's eyes was desperate. 'Kit . . . Kit . . .' he whispered and Kit leaned close to his brother's mouth to catch the words.

'What is it? What is it? Tell me what to do?'

'Don't tell Dad.' It was the faintest breath upon Kit's cheek, but the words were as clear to him as if Malcolm had yelled them. 'Don't tell Dad,' Malcolm whispered again, for fear his brother might not have heard. *Tell him I died a hero's death*, he wanted to say, but how could he? He'd killed his own men. *Don't tell Dad*, his mind screamed, *please, please, Kit, don't tell Dad*.

Kit nodded. 'Sshh,' he said, 'sshh,' stroking his brother's forehead as Malcolm drifted into a semi-conscious state.

He sat there for a long time, hearing the arrival of the gunships. Two Hueys with their mini-guns. It'd be over soon, he thought. And it was.

Somebody called in the CASEVACs, he wasn't sure who. But he was feeling very weak by then, he'd lost a fair bit of blood and he kept blacking out. He wanted to walk to the Huey, but they put him on a stretcher instead.

'Jesus Christ,' someone said, 'that's The Kid. He saved the whole fucking lot of us.' But Kit didn't hear.

As they put him on the stretcher, he gestured to Malcolm, and he heard the medic say, not unkindly but practically, 'Too late mate, he's gone.'

CHAPTER THIRTY-ONE

When Tom Sullivan told Paul Trewinnard about the portrait of his grandmother in which she was depicted wearing the locket, Paul was initially confused.

'Your grandmother was a young woman posing with her new baby, you say?'

'Yes,' Tom excitedly responded, 'and the baby was my Dad! They'd even dressed him in his christening robes.'

'But how could your father possibly maintain that he bought the locket if your grandmother was pictured wearing it shortly after he was born?'

'I don't think Dad's ever realised she was wearing the locket in the painting, I didn't myself until my grandmother pointed it out to me. My father hasn't even seen the portrait for the past two years, it's been hanging in Grandma Em's sitting room.'

Paul darted a glance at Foong Lee. Did they dare hope, his eyes said. Could they really be this lucky?

'Can we get hold of the portrait without your father knowing?' Paul asked. 'If he gets wind of its significance you can bet your last penny it'll disappear.'

'Miriam,' Tom said with a confident grin. In response to

the mystified looks on both men's faces, he added, 'she's one of my sisters-in-law, the only one sympathetic to my cause.'

Miriam Sullivan was more than sympathetic to Tom's cause. A bitter woman, she detested her father-in-law only fractionally more than she detested her husband. She'd married for money and, supposedly, the position and power that went with it, but she was paying the price. Within the patriarchal family, Miriam was expected to know her place, like all Sullivan women should, and her place was to bear children and keep well in the background. Miriam didn't like it one bit. She'd wished Tom well when he'd left for the goldfields. 'Good luck to you, Tom,' she'd said, 'get as far away as you can.' And now that the contentious issue of the locket had presented itself and the case was to go to court, she'd said, 'Teach the greedy bastards a lesson, Tom. Win if you can,' although she'd not thought it possible for a moment.

'Miriam will help us,' Tom said.

And Miriam did. The portrait had been removed from Emily's sitting room and stored in the basement of the family home, awaiting general sale along with many of her possessions which Matthew had considered of little individual value to the family. A resourceful woman, and one bent on revenge, Miriam had little trouble smuggling it out and delivering it to Tom.

Tom now propped it up against the wall on Foong Lee's desk and the three men stood back to admire it.

'Well, well, well,' Paul said. So this was Emily Sullivan, he thought. A pretty woman with a feisty glint in her eye, and the locket as clear as daylight around her slim young neck. The shape and dimensions were exact and, on close inspection, one could see the shapes of the mountain and the sun. The artist had obviously found the locket intriguing.

'We've got him,' Paul muttered to Foong Lee. 'We've got the bastard. Oh I'm sorry, Tom,' he hastily added.

'No you're not, and neither am I. You're quite right, we've got the bastard.'

Paul insisted that they talk about their options. 'We could show Sullivan the painting,' he said. 'We could settle out of court.' He looked at Foong Lee. 'No, I didn't think you'd want to do that.'

'It's up to Tom,' Foong Lee insisted.

'It's my reputation too,' Tom said. And the die was cast.

'Well if that's what you call being a "little rusty" . . .' Foong Lee muttered to Paul as they sat in court. The doctor's opinion regarding Emily Sullivan's frail mental condition had been severely undermined in the face of evidence supplied by a number of witnesses whom Paul had called forward, all citizens of fine standing who had known Emily well.

After losing the battle as to Emily Sullivan's sanity, the prosecuting attorney concentrated on the legal ownership of the locket. Every evidence was produced attesting that Emily Sullivan had personally owned not one item amongst her many possessions, they had all been purchased for her by her son. The fact that there was no documentation for the purchase of the locket was incidental, there was no documentation for many of the gifts.

When the defence was called upon to present its evidence, Paul did not immediately produce the portrait. He held a minor card up his sleeve to further undermine Matthew Sullivan's credibility before producing his ace.

Jim 'Bully' Bullmore was a colourful witness. A gold miner by trade, Bully, as a small boy, had known old Benjamin Sullivan.

'He showed that locket to my dad,' Bully said. 'I remember it plain as the nose on my face. Said he got it from a Larrakia princess. Dad said it was a load of bullshit.'

Everyone laughed, except the prosecuting attorney who cast an anxious look at Matthew Sullivan. This was *unexpected. Matthew gave him a confident nod which said Bully's story was sheer fabrication and, after a break in proceedings and a conference with his client, the attorney went on to successfully discredit the witness. Jim 'Bully' Bullmore was a layabout and a drunk, well known to many.*

There was to be no argument about fabrication, however, when the portrait was finally presented. The artist's signature and the year he'd painted his subject were clearly marked in the corner, it was noted, and the locket depicted hanging around the neck of young Emily Sullivan was the very same locket which had been tendered to the court.

As Matthew stared at the painting, utterly flabbergasted, he cursed his son and his mother and the dirty little Chink and the smartarse Pommie lawyer, but there was nothing he could do. He had perjured himself in a court of law and he backed down at the rate of knots. He'd obviously been mistaken, he admitted to the judge, he'd bought so many items for his mother over the years that he'd assumed the locket had been one of them.

'A costly assumption, Mr Sullivan,' the judge dryly remarked.

Matthew Sullivan was ordered to pay damages to his son, Tom, and to Mr Foong Lee. He was further ordered to meet all legal expenses for both parties and, to top it all off, he was severely reprimanded for wasting the court's time. Matthew Sullivan had been made a laughing stock.

'I owe you my life, Paul.'

'Hardly,' Paul grinned. They were sitting in the courtyard at the back of the shop and Foong Lee had accepted a glass of Scotch to toast their success.

But Foong Lee did not return Paul's grin. 'My honour is my life,' he said, 'and as you have saved my honour, therefore you have saved my life.'

Paul had not intended to trivialise the situation. 'I am

simply returning the favour, Foong Lee,' he said in all seriousness.

The two men had never once referred to the threat of Paul's opium addiction, but Foong Lee now bowed his head briefly, appreciating the acknowledgement. A life for a life. It was good. For one man to owe such a debt to another could become a terrible burden.

'Nevertheless,' he said, 'I wish you to accept a gift.'

'It's not necessary.'

But Foong Lee wasn't listening. He took a small parcel of beige kid cloth from his pocket and put it on the table.

'I wish you to have it,' he said as he unwrapped the locket. He handed it to Paul, who held it up to the light, the diamonds sparkling in the sun.

'It is the most glorious thing, isn't it?' Paul said.

'It is,' Foong Lee agreed.

Paul pressed the clasp and opened the locket to reveal the initials inside. 'You know of course I can't possibly accept it.'

'You would insult me if you didn't.'

'It's a symbol of love . . .' Paul said. Foong Lee nodded agreement. '. . . and it should be hanging around the neck of a woman.' Foong Lee nodded again, and Paul laughed out loud. 'So who the hell would I give it to?' he said, handing it back.

Foong Lee accepted the locket, but he would not be deterred. 'It is yours nonetheless.' And before Paul could interrupt, he added, 'I shall look after it for you until the time presents itself.'

'As you wish,' Paul said, politely inclining his head and parroting one of Foong Lee's favourite phrases. 'Now for God's sake, man, will you get drunk with me just this once!'

CHAPTER THIRTY-TWO

Kit Galloway was awarded the Military Medal. His father accompanied him to the Queen's Birthday Awards announcement at Admiralty House in Sydney.

'On 16 January 1969, in the province of Phuoc Toy, South Vietnam, Private Christopher Galloway did, whilst under heavy enemy fire, ensure the security of his battalion's position and aid the repulse of a concerted enemy attack. For his actions he is awarded the Military Medal for bravery in the field.'

Terence stood at attention as Kit's citation was read out by the Governor-General, Sir Paul Hasluck.

Upon their return to Darwin, Kit's photograph was featured on the front page of the *Northern Territory News*, and Terence accepted endless congratulations as the father of a hero, nodding when people said 'you must be so proud'.

But Kit's Military Medal rankled Terence, as did the fact that the boy was seen as a hero in the eyes of others. He considered Kit a pretender. A man with no true military calling. A conscript who, by sheer force of circumstance, had been recognised for bravery.

The truth was, Terence hated Kit because he'd returned. The wrong man had come home, and Terence would never forgive Kit for that.

Terence Galloway was heartbroken at the loss of his elder son. His only son, he now decided. For the past several years he'd lulled himself into an acceptance of Kit. He'd spoken of him with genuine pride, particularly to Aggie, for whom he had a begrudging respect. He was pleased that, in Aggie's eyes, Kit was such a fine student.

It angered him now to think that he'd felt any pride in Kit's achievements. It was disloyal. Traitorous. Kit was alive and Malcolm was dead. It was inconceivable that Paul Trewinnard's son should survive when Malcolm Galloway, the one and only true heir to Terence's empire, had ceased to exist. There were times when Terence could barely disguise his loathing for the boy others thought was his son.

Kit knew that his father was grieving. He even knew that, had his father been given a choice as to which of his sons should survive, he would have chosen Malcolm. Malcolm had always been his father's favourite. Kit was prepared to accept that, he'd lived all of his life in his brother's shadow. But he too had loved Malcolm. Couldn't he and his father grieve together? Couldn't they comfort each other? But his father seemed inconsolable, isolated in his grief. Kit did everything he could to soften the blow of his brother's death.

'I was with him, Dad,' he said shortly after his return as they sat on the verandah in the early twilight. His arm was still heavily bandaged, but the prognosis was good. 'You'll have an impressive scar,' the army doctor had said, 'but no permanent damage.'

'I was right beside him . . .'

Terence Galloway gazed silently through the light mesh screen at the harbour.

'. . . and he didn't feel any pain.'

Terence gave a brief nod, appreciative of the knowledge that Malcolm had not suffered, but he couldn't bring himself to look at Kit.

Kit longed to embrace his father. He couldn't remember a time when they'd ever embraced. Not *really* embraced. Perhaps once, after the death of his mother, but it had been so clumsy, he recalled, so awkward.

'He died bravely.'

Of course he did, Terence thought, he was a Galloway. It had been a magnificent sunset, and the final glow of the sun still glinted pink on the ripples of the water.

Malcolm's words returned to Kit. 'Don't tell Dad.' He could see the plea in his brother's eyes. 'Don't tell Dad.' Of course he would never tell their father. Their father would not be able to stand the truth. And so Kit lied. He lied not only for Malcolm, but also for his father. 'He was a hero, Dad.'

So why didn't *he* get a bloody citation, Terence thought. Even a posthumous award might have been of some comfort. Malcolm Galloway was listed as a casualty, a mere statistic, whilst Kit Galloway was cited for bravery. The thought of it galled Terence beyond measure.

His father remained silent, staring out at the water, and Kit longed to break through his pain, to offer him some form of comfort. 'You would have been really proud of him.'

'I am,' Terence said, focussing on a yacht under full sail heading up river for home. He dared not look at the bastard. He might kill him if he did.

'I feel guilty, Aggie.'

Six months later, following their trip to Sydney and the award presentation, there was still no change in his father, and Kit was deeply disturbed. The only person he could turn to was Aggie Marshall. 'I feel guilty because I came home and Malcolm didn't. I know that's what Dad's thinking, he's wishing it had been the other way around.'

'Oh Kit, that's not true.'

'Sometimes I catch him looking at me and I can see it in his eyes.'

He was agitated, she could tell. He'd refused a cup of tea and he didn't want to sit down, he just paced about by the bay windows occasionally peering out over the Esplanade at nothing in particular.

'He hates me.'

Aggie was concerned. 'You're wrong, my dear. He's proud of you, as we all are.' Kit shook his head, but she continued. 'Your father is in pain, Kit. He's grieving, and he's closing you out along with the rest of the world.'

Kit turned to her, and she could see that he was hanging on to her every word, desperate for reassurance of his father's love. Dear God, she thought, he's only twenty-one. Despite all he's been through, he's little more than a boy.

Aggie wanted to sound wise, although, in truth, she had no idea why Terence would alienate his son. Certainly Malcolm had been his favourite, it had been evident for years. They'd been so alike, Terence had always seen himself in his elder son. But Malcolm was dead, and Kit had come home. Terence could have lost both his boys, Aggie thought, he should be thankful that his younger son had returned.

'It's a pity,' she said in her matter-of-fact way, trying to reach the boy through plain commonsense. 'It's a very great pity that your father's not including you in his grief. It'd be easier for you both if you could share your loss.' Kit's grey eyes were focussed on her with such intensity, anxious for answers she didn't have. 'But grief takes many forms, and he's holding his inside, you just have to give him time.' It seemed such a lame reassurance, she thought, and he looked so young and so vulnerable.

'Think of your mother, Kit. Think how proud of you Henrietta would have been.' She didn't know why she'd said it, in her customary blunt fashion the words had just come out. But, surprisingly enough, they hit the right chord.

'Yes she would, wouldn't she?' Kit thought of his mother, and suddenly the tears welled in his eyes. He didn't attempt to fight them back.

Aggie embraced him and, unashamedly, Kit returned the embrace. He clung to her as he wept for his brother. He'd had no-one with whom to share his own grief and, as he wept, the emotion he'd kept in check was released with his tears until, finally, he was left with an overwhelming sense of relief.

'Thanks, Aggie,' he said when he'd recovered and Aggie had returned from the bathroom with a box of tissues. 'Sorry to be such a baby,' he apologised, grabbing a fistful of Kleenex, 'but I must say I feel a hell of a lot better.'

'It's a pity your father can't have a good cry.'

'Yes, isn't it,' Kit agreed. 'Perhaps you should visit him,' he grinned as he blew his nose loudly, 'you're an excellent therapist.'

He was only joking, but it was a damn good idea, Aggie thought. Terence might well tell her to mind her own business. But then Aggie was used to that.

'He told you this, did he?'

Aggie froze at the animosity in Terence's voice and the dangerous glint in his eyes. She thought she'd chosen the right moment. They had the house to themselves, Kit was at the library studying, as he was most afternoons; he was returning to university in the new year. Fran had served them afternoon tea and they were comfortably settled in the lounge room with the ceiling fan whirring, it was far too hot for the verandah, and Terence, although subdued, had seemed pleased to see her.

Aggie had visited him a number of times over the past months. She had been amongst the first to offer her condolences upon the news of Malcolm's death, and when Terence had returned from Kit's award ceremony, he had responded pleasantly to her congratulations. 'Yes of course I'm very proud,' he'd said. He'd seemed a little distracted, which was understandable, but there'd been no animosity in him as there now was.

'What exactly did he say?'

'Well he didn't *say* it, not in so many words.' Aggie started backing off as quickly as she could. 'It was just something I sensed.'

'How exactly could you *sense* that my son thinks I hate him? Don't treat me like a fool, Aggie, what exactly did he say?'

Aggie cursed herself, her interference had caused trouble for Kit. 'He said he felt guilty that he'd come home and Malcolm hadn't.'

'Well, that's his problem, isn't it,' Terence sneered, 'and then he said that I hated him, is that it?' Terence was angry. How dare the boy go running to Aggie Marshall with his problems, the snivelling little coward.

'As I said,' Aggie hedged, 'I just sensed that . . .'

'Don't lie to me, Aggie.' There was something threatening in the way Terence leaned back in his chair and tapped his fingertips methodically on the wide wooden armrests. 'I will not have lies, do you understand?'

Aggie felt a jab of fear. He was trying to intimidate her, and with some success, she realised. Terence Galloway could be formidable. But her protectiveness of Kit quickly overrode her fear. If he was prepared to bully her in this way, just exactly how far would he go with his son?

'Terence, I know that you're grieving,' she said, 'but you must understand . . .'

'Don't bullshit me, woman,' Terence growled angrily, rising from his armchair. 'What did the boy say?'

At fifty-five, Terence Galloway was still an impressive looking man, but his body had thickened over the years.

Now, as he towered over Aggie, his shoulders bull-like, the veins standing out on his powerful neck, he presented a frightening figure.

Perhaps it was his very power, and his awareness of it, which goaded Aggie. Terence was a bully who liked to instill fear, and Aggie refused to be bullied. She also stood, prepared now to give as good as she got.

'Malcolm was always your favourite, Terence,' she said, and it was the voice of accusation. 'God only knows why, but you favoured him for years, and now that he's dead you're forgetting that you have another son.'

The words struck him like a blow. Terence stared at her. He had gone too far, he realised. Since Malcolm's death he had felt recurring bouts of his madness. There had been times when he could have killed Kit for the fact that he had survived when Malcolm had not. Terence suddenly realised that he had been endangering himself. He must be more guarded.

'I was not aware that I had so favoured Malcolm,' he said a little stiffly. Had it been that obvious, he wondered.

'You always did, Terence. Ever since he was a little boy it was quite obvious he was your favourite.' Aggie was astonished at the effect her outburst had had upon him. She hadn't intended to sound so brutal. 'It's understandable, he was so like you. But Kit is your son too,' she added a little more gently.

'Thank you, Aggie,' he said. Annoyed as he was at Aggie Marshall's interference, Terence was nonetheless grateful. Her warning was timely. 'Since he was a little boy' she'd said. So she'd recognised that Malcolm had been his favourite well before Henrietta's death, that was good. Nothing suspect could be read into that.

'I haven't been kind enough to Kit, I agree.' He sat. Leaning forward in his chair, elbows on knees, hands clenched, he stared at the floor. 'Malcolm's death was such a shock. I haven't been able to think about anything else.

It was wrong of me.'

'I'm sorry,' Aggie said. She remembered the day at the Hotel Darwin when Terence had cried over the death of Henrietta. A broken man. He looked much the same now. 'I'm truly sorry, I didn't mean to be hurtful.'

'No, you're right, and I'm grateful. Kit is my son and I love him.'

'Of course you do, Terence, I know that.' She knelt beside his armchair, her face a picture of concern. 'Just as he loves you.'

Terence wanted to give the interfering bitch a swift backhander, but he played the distraught father instead. 'I hadn't realised I'd been so cruel. I'll make it up to him, Aggie.' Damn Kit, he thought. Thank Christ it was only a couple of months until he returned to university, Terence couldn't wait for the boy to be out of his sight.

He suffered a few more of Aggie Marshall's platitudes and when she'd gone he breathed a sigh of relief. But, irritating as she was, Aggie had given him a great deal to think about. Not only must he take care to disguise his antipathy towards Kit, he must accept Malcolm's death or it would destroy his life. For months now he'd avoided the emporium and the showrooms, ignoring all contact from his associates. He knew that his business had suffered.

Terence poured himself a large Scotch and ice. He'd become obsessed with the death of his son, he realised. He needed distraction. A woman would help. The discreet call-girl service he'd employed on a regular basis over the years wasn't enough. He needed a woman living in the house. Not a wife. Not yet anyway. But a woman who could be at his beck and call.

'You need some help, Fran,' he said when his house-keeper arrived half an hour later to clear away the tea things.

Fran looked at him, mystified, as he sat back in his armchair nursing the fresh Scotch he'd just poured for himself. Why would she need help carrying a tea tray?

'You need some help running the household,' he said, 'you're not getting any younger.'

'No, sir, no help necessary.' Why did he think she needed help, Fran wondered. The young Mr Galloway would be going to Adelaide in less than two months and there would be just the two of them left in the house. She'd even been a little worried that Mr Galloway might dispense with her services.

'Yes, I think it's a good idea,' Terence said taking a hefty swig at his drink. 'A strong young woman who can share some of your burden, she can have the small bedroom near the back stairs. If there's anyone who comes to mind I'd be willing to consider your suggestions.'

Fran knew exactly what he meant. When she had taken up her position in the Galloway household eight years previously, she had rather hoped it might lead to a more intimate and binding relationship than that of a house-keeper. She'd soon realised, however, that she was too old for Mr Galloway, despite the fact that they were approximately the same age. The women who occasionally visited the house, and who Fran recognised as professionals at their trade, were young, not even thirty. Ah well, no matter, Mr Galloway paid well, and she was not worked too hard. But now he was seeking a companion. What a perfect opportunity for her niece, Fran thought.

'I know someone, Mr Galloway,' she said.

'Good. Send her along for an interview.'

When Kit came home from the library in the early evening he was surprised to find his father in a most convivial mood.

'Want a beer?' Terence asked.

'Sure. Thanks.'

'I had a visit from Aggie Marshall today,' Terence said as he prised the top off the beer bottle.

Oh no, Kit thought. Aggie's visited and she's said that

I cried on her shoulder and he's as mad as hell and he's playing one of his games. Kit accepted the glass of beer and waited for all hell to break loose.

Terence stared into his freshly poured glass of Scotch and ice. It was the fifth he'd had, and he always poured stiff ones, but he never showed the effects.

'I'm sorry, Kit,' he said, 'I've been very hurtful.' He gently swirled the contents in the glass. The ice clinked and it was interesting to note the change in the colour of the alcohol as it melded. A pleasant distraction.

Kit stared at his father. He was saying he was sorry. Did he mean it? Had Aggie wrought such a miracle?

'I should have shared my grief with you,' Terence said, studying the Scotch with interest as the melting ice slowly turned it into one shade of brown. 'It was wrong of me.'

'That's okay, Dad,' Kit said. Oh, thank you, Aggie, he thought.

The interesting swirls had gone now, and the Scotch was boring, the colour of weak cold tea. Terence looked up at his son, put down the glass and held out his arms. 'Will you forgive me, Kit?'

The two men embraced.

His father was not a physical man, Kit knew that, and their embrace did not last long, but the relief he experienced was extraordinary. The war, the pain, the agony of his brother's death, all seemed to disappear as he felt Terence's arms around him.

Abhorrent as physical contact was to him, Terence had decided it was easier to embrace his son rather than look him in the eyes. As he felt Kit's body beneath the texture of the light cotton shirt, he was surprised at its strength and muscle development. The gangly youth had a strong man's body. And all Terence could think of was Malcolm. This should be Malcolm's body he was holding.

Terence broke free of the embrace as quickly as he could.

'Thanks, Dad,' Kit said.

'Yes, well, enough said. Another beer?'

'I haven't even started this one.' It was enough, Kit thought, it was all he could expect, and he loved his father for the effort he'd made.

Terence couldn't wait for the day when Kit would leave for Adelaide. I hope to hell he stays there, he thought.

BOOK FIVE

CHAPTER THIRTY-THREE

*J*essica Williams didn't look black. Green-eyed and ginger-haired, she could have been Irish. Indeed she herself didn't know she was black until one day in early January. The day after her eighteenth birthday.

Born in 1950, Jessica had been taken from her black mother as a three-year-old and farmed out to a respectable white couple keen to adopt. Despite the protestations of her natural mother, the Western Australian Aboriginal welfare authorities carried out their duty, as was the custom of the day, in finding the half-caste infant a suitable environment in order that she might be easily assimilated into white society. Such standard practice was for the child's own good. It was to the advantage of all half-caste children that they be brought up as whites, the fact was common knowledge.

It was a shock to Jessica when she discovered she was adopted, although her adoptive parents said all the right things. When they'd found they couldn't have children, they'd been eager to adopt and they'd fallen in love with her the moment they first saw her, they said.

So what about her real parents, she asked. Who were they? Where did they come from?

Dr Williams, a medical practitioner and a sensible man, had discussed such confrontational questions often with his wife. Enid Williams was in agreement that they inform their daughter of her adoption, but not of the fact that her mother had been black.

'And what do we say when she asks about her natural parents?'

'We say we don't know anything about them,' Enid said, 'which is true.'

But Grahame Williams disagreed and, when the time came, his wife reluctantly capitulated.

So, following the shock of discovery that she was adopted, Jessica was further confronted with the fact that her natural mother was black. It was a lot to take in all at once.

Grahame Williams told his daughter all that he could. Jessica's father had been a white drover on a cattle station near Onslow, and her mother a Yamatji woman. Her father had left his Aboriginal mistress shortly after their child was born and three years later Jessica had been taken from her mother by the area welfare officer on the instructions of the Western Australian Aboriginal welfare authorities. And that was as much as he knew.

Jessica was confused and bewildered. Her mother hugged her and told her how much they loved her, as she glared accusingly over her daughter's shoulder at her husband. She told Jessica that she mustn't let herself be upset by the facts, they didn't change anything. After all, she was still their darling girl, her life hadn't changed.

But her life had changed, Jessica thought as she lay in bed that night. She didn't doubt the love that she shared with her adoptive parents, but the facts had most certainly changed her life. They had changed who she was, who she had always perceived herself to be.

She became preoccupied. She stared at herself in the mirror, trying to come to terms with the truth. How could she be black? She didn't look black. She didn't feel black. She didn't even know any black people. She and her parents lived in Claremont, one of the more fashionable suburbs of Perth, and no black people lived in Claremont. Occasionally, when she caught the train into the city she saw Aborigines hanging around the railway station. Usually dirty, sometimes drunk. Was that who she was? Her perception of black people, through her own ignorance and through reports she'd read in newspapers, was negative, she needed to know the truth. Jessica then became determined to find out everything she could about her background and her mother's people.

Enid Williams worried about her daughter's preoccupation with her new-found identity, and she blamed her husband. 'We should never have told her,' she said. But Grahame, after his own initial misgivings at perhaps having opened a Pandora's box, was convinced that he had done the right thing. Jessica was a very intelligent young woman and, having obviously pondered her situation, was now asking questions and seemed bent on discovering her origins. Grahame would help his daughter in any way he could.

They came up against a brick wall with the Aboriginal welfare authorities, and no amount of insistence could alter the fact. It appeared the Williamses had no automatic right to trace Jessica's birth parents and, even if they had, it would prove 'an impossibility', they were informed.

Jessica was shortly to attend the University of Western Australia. She'd had excellent results in her Leaving Certificate the previous year and could have enrolled in any number of courses, but she'd decided on an arts degree, majoring in English literature, although she wasn't sure to what end. She really had no idea what she wanted to do with her life.

The discovery of her adoption altered everything. She now had a purpose. After meeting with university faculty advisers and discussing her reasons, she opted for an arts degree majoring in anthropology. The Chair of the newly created Department of Anthropology was Professor Ronald Berndt, a bald, pear-shaped man with milk-bottle lensed spectacles who puffed incessantly on a meerschaum pipe. His wife, Dr Catherine Berndt, was a senior lecturer and, in contrast to her husband, was a colourful woman with a bird's nest of grey hair and a penchant for hippie-style long floral dresses. They were a bizarre couple, but experts in their field, both specialising in Australian Aboriginal anthropology. The Berndts keenly encouraged Jessica on her journey of self-discovery.

From the outset, Dr Catherine Berndt became Jessica's inspiration. Catherine Berndt was, herself, passionate about her work and, during her many field trips over the years, she had so befriended the Aboriginal women that, in certain areas, she had been accepted into the very fabric of their society. Catherine found Jessica's background of great interest and promised that, upon the successful completion of her bachelor degree, Jessica could accompany her in the field as a research assistant.

Jessica's mother didn't at all approve of the turn her daughter's life was taking.

'She's become obsessed,' Enid said. 'It's not healthy.'

'Of course it is, it's the best thing that could have happened to her.' As his wife shook her head in obvious disagreement, Grahame continued before she could interrupt. 'She's found a direction, my dear. She's enjoying university, she's finding it stimulating. Vastly preferable to stumbling through an arts course with no idea where it's taking her. This will lead to a whole new career, I couldn't be happier.'

Enid, who had been quite content 'stumbling' through her own arts course and meeting the young medical student she was to marry, had presumed Jessica would follow suit. University was an excellent introduction agency through which one could meet the right marital prospect, what was wrong with that? Enid hadn't really considered that Jessica would embark upon a 'career' as such.

Enid Williams didn't lack intelligence. To the contrary she was a bridge player of championship standard, the one extra-curricular activity she allowed herself. In the meantime, she was an excellent cook, hostess, bookkeeper and mother. Like many of her ilk, Enid was a professional housewife, and very good at her job, as her husband fully appreciated. But Grahame Williams knew that Jessica's quest of discovery would give her a much broader life.

He was right. Jessica thrived at university. She loved her studies and was an excellent student. And the more she learned of Aboriginal lore and culture, the more she found herself personally responding to her new-found knowledge. It was as if in unearthing the ancient mysteries of her people she was unearthing her true identity.

Through the university 'hippie' set who, in between anti-war protests and ban-the-bomb demonstrations, keenly affiliated themselves to minority groups with a cause, she discovered the newly formed Aboriginal Arts Society. A small self-funded group, the society worked out of a modest hall in West Perth where they exhibited Aboriginal crafts and paintings and performed ceremonial dances accompanied by the clapping sticks and the didgeridoo.

Most importantly for Jessica, the society was a meeting place. It was through the society that she discovered, not only Aborigines with a pride in their culture, but several like herself, deprived of their heritage, keen to discover their origins and their people.

Jessica Williams was a popular, pretty girl with a wicked throaty laugh and a delicious sense of humour. She made friends with ease, which was unusual in a student who so excelled academically. Most of those who topped their courses each year, as she did, were bookish types devoted to their studies. Jessica lived a gregarious existence and yet maintained a passion for her work, a balance which was enviable to many of her fellow students.

She completed her bachelor degree and applied to do an honours year, and in the summer of late 1971, upon the completion of her honours, she accompanied Catherine Berndt as a research assistant in the field.

Catherine's field trip, tracing the myth of the Rainbow Serpent through the valleys and plateaus of the Murchison and Gascoyne Rivers, started out in the coastal region of mid-Western Australia, and it was here that Jessica finally found herself in the area of the Yamatji people. Her mother's people.

After four years' intensive academic study, Jessica felt an instant and personal sense of oneness with the land of her ancestors. Her mentor, Catherine Berndt, was furthermore an inspiration as, in their four wheel drive vehicle, they traced the routes of ancient campsites from one waterhole to another, Catherine pointing out the middens where piles of shells and refuse remained as evidence of meals shared possibly hundreds of years previously.

They spent several days at an Aboriginal mission near Gascoyne Junction and there Catherine, in her customary manner, joined in the women's corroborees, and sat comfortably amongst them by the fireside ashes, playing with their children.

Jessica met with tribal elders who were initially a little wary of the pretty young white woman with the flame-coloured hair. What did she want of them? They quickly discovered that she knew a great deal of their culture and deeply respected it and, upon the further discovery that she was one of their own, they were generous in their recognition and acceptance. They showed her the sacred sites allowed to women, and she listened to their stories of the Dreaming which, coming from the mouths of the elders, took on a different perspective altogether to the essays of anthropologists and university tutorials. They discussed tribal culture with her, as much as was permitted to be discussed with a woman, and they showed her rock paintings which had existed for centuries.

The paintings were stark white and simple in design. Jessica knew from her studies that the inland Murchison people used white kaolin clay for their paintings, and she was familiar with the imprints of hands, and with the circular swirls of the water symbol. But there was one recurring design which puzzled her. Several of the paintings depicted an oval shape, within which was a mountain peak reaching towards a vibrant sun.

But there were no mountains in this region. Why would the Aborigines paint a mountain when there were none? Jessica discussed it with Catherine, who was equally mystified. Was it related to some story of the Rainbow Serpent myth about which they were unaware? But the elders assured them the picture was not related to the Rainbow Serpent. The paintings had been there for a very long time, they said. On their travels, particularly to the north-east desert region, around the campsites of the Oakover River, and even out to the hills and valleys of the Rudall River, the Yamatji had seen other drawings of such a symbol, but they knew nothing of its origins.

In one painting Jessica pointed out to Catherine the oval shape was hanging about the neck of a man. Was it some form of religious token? But then, as the two women agreed, the Aborigines did not wear religious tokens. Fascinated, Jessica took photographs of the oval object which appeared in the paintings. Dependent upon the results of her honours year, she intended to apply for a masters degree, in which event she would investigate the symbol further in the field trips she hoped to make during the following two years.

CHAPTER THIRTY-FOUR

Aggie Marshall inadvertently changed the lives of Terence and Kit Galloway as well as her own when Kit returned home from university in late 1972.

He had come back to Darwin for most of his vacations over the past three years, but this time it wasn't for a holiday. He'd completed his Bachelor of Arts degree, and an honours year to boot, and although he was set on a career as a journalist, he wasn't sure where to start.

'A mate of mine has contacts at the *Adelaide Advertiser*, and there're no openings there,' he complained to Aggie. 'I could apply, but there doesn't seem much point. I think my best bet's to go to Melbourne or Sydney, and try for a job as a proofreader on one of the dailies.'

'A proofreader!' Aggie's shaggy white eyebrows knitted into a scowl. 'But you've majored in English literature! You're an honours graduate! You've devoted four whole years of your life to . . .'

'Oh Aggie,' Kit laughed, she was as ferocious as ever once she got going, 'no-one's terribly impressed with a BA these days.'

'Well they bloody well should be. And what's wrong with Darwin?'

'Eh?'

'Why Sydney or Melbourne? Why not Darwin?'

Kit shrugged. 'I suppose because everybody heads for the big smoke to make their name.'

'What? As a proofreader?' Aggie scoffed.

'Only to begin with.' She was being deliberately provocative, he knew it. Aggie's inspirational tack was often aimed to provoke anger, but Kit refused to take the bait. 'You have to start somewhere.'

'And what's wrong with the *Northern Territory News*?' she demanded belligerently.

'Nothing. But I'd probably have to start from the bottom there too.'

'We'll see about that.'

'The astrology column!' Kit searched the flinty eyes behind Jim Bowditch's spectacles for a sign that the man was joking. 'I don't know anything about astrology.'

'Who does?' Jim shrugged. It was no joke. Jim Bowditch was good for a laugh during a heavy drinking session at the pub, but in working hours he was a busy man with little time for humour. 'Just for a couple of weeks while Mathilda's on holidays. She's left you all her charts and stuff.'

They chatted for a while longer. Or rather Jim did, laying down the rules. Kit listened for the most part, overwhelmed by the tough little man's energy. But then Jim Bowditch was famous throughout the Territory as a hard-nosed journalist of the no-nonsense variety. He worked with a bottle of Scotch on his desk, and wrote feature articles under the nom de plume 'Silent Sam', cutting a swathe through what he referred to as 'bureaucratic stupidity' and fearlessly tilting at windmills in his fight for human rights.

Finally, satisfied that he'd set the boy straight, Jim shook Kit's hand. 'Welcome to *NTN*,' he said. 'You start next week, Lisa'll show you around.

'Thank you, Mr Bowditch.'

The attractive young front counter receptionist introduced Kit to the gang in the newsroom. Busy with their chattering typewriters and ubiquitous telephones, most looked up from their desks, gave him a cheery nod, said 'welcome to *NTN*' and returned to their work.

'This is only half the gang,' Lisa said, 'the others are out, you'll meet them next week, we've got a staff of fifteen in all.' Then she showed him where the tea urn was, pointed out the small desk in the far corner of the newsroom which was to be his work station, and dumped a pile of charts and notebooks in his arms, presumably Mathilda's notes.

'Welcome to *NTN*,' she said with a radiant smile, before disappearing through the doors to the reception counter.

'What's your star sign, Aggie?' Kit asked as she ushered him expectantly into the lounge room. He'd promised he'd come straight around after his interview.

'Aquarius,' she said mystified, watching him open his briefcase and take out a notebook. 'But from what I've heard I'm not at all typical and it's a load of rubbish anyway, why do you ask?'

Kit flicked through the pages of the notebook. 'Your ruler, Uranus, joins with Mercury which is the planet of the mind. Ah hah!' he proclaimed, snapping the notebook closed. 'I predict an interesting week for Aquarians.'

'Stop mucking around, tell me what happened at the newspaper.'

'I just did. You're looking at your friendly new stargazer.'

His expression was endearingly comical, and Aggie knew that she was expected to laugh, but she couldn't. Deep down, she felt angry.

'How dare he!' she expostulated. 'He promised me personally that he'd give you a chance.' It wasn't as if Jim Bowditch didn't owe her a favour. She'd sided with him on many an issue and helped him cut through bureaucratic red tape on many an occasion. She'd thought they were good mates, the least he could do was give Kit a fair go. And it wasn't as if the lad didn't deserve it on his own merits, he had excellent qualifications. He was a war hero, for God's sake, he'd be an asset to the paper. The more she thought about it the more Aggie's anger mushroomed. 'He gave me his word, damn him!'

'Hey, take it easy.' Kit made her sit in her favourite armchair, she was getting herself far too worked up, but he suddenly knew why. She'd obviously put herself on the line for him. Aggie unashamedly called in favours when she was working for her charitable causes, even gentle blackmail was not beyond her, but she never used her persuasive powers on a personal basis. Of course, it explained everything.

'Jim Bowditch at *NTN* is very keen to see you,' she'd said not long after their initial chat about his future.

'What have you done, Aggie?' He'd been suspicious to start with. Why would the famous Jim Bowditch, editor of the *Northern Territory News*, profess an interest in him?

'Nothing, just a quick phone call.' She'd been the picture of innocence. 'He's impressed with your credentials, he wants to give a local a chance, and you're to ring for an appointment next week.' An insouciant shrug. 'Don't go if you don't want to. Entirely up to you.'

Now she was seething.

'Stop blowing a gasket, everything's all right,' Kit said. She was incorrigible, he thought as he sat on the leather pouffe beside the armchair. It was just as well he hadn't known she'd put pressure on Jim Bowditch or he would never have gone for the interview. 'I'm only filling in on the astrology column for a fortnight.'

'Oh?' Aggie looked hopeful.

'Yep. Then I go on to sport . . .'

'But you don't know a thing about sport.'

'. . . and if I'm lucky I'll score the movie review.'

'Oh Kit!'

Aggie's face was such a mask of horror that Kit could contain himself no longer. He burst out laughing. 'It's a fantastic job, Aggie, thank you. Whatever strings you pulled with Jim Bowditch, I'm really grateful.' Her expression was still dubious and he felt the need to explain. 'Every cadet starts off this way, and I'm on a *one*-year cadetship instead of the normal four.' He leaned forward excitedly, his elbows on his knees, a gangly figure, boyish in his excitement. 'And I can submit feature articles for consideration, Jim says, he told me to call him Jim. So long as I write them in my own time, he said.'

'But that's wonderful,' Aggie replied. 'That's exactly what we wanted.' Then she added hopefully, 'Isn't it?'

'Of course it is.'

'So why did you give me such a shock? Astrology columns and all that.'

'I wanted to see the look on your face,' he grinned. 'It was worth it.'

His grey eyes glowed with affection and gratitude. Perhaps even love, Aggie thought. She hoped so. If he only knew how much she loved him. Kit Galloway was the son she'd never had.

'Thanks, Aggie.' Kit enveloped her in an enthusiastic hug.

'My pleasure,' she said.

The large tin shed which formed the offices of the *Northern Territory News* was on the corner of Mitchell and Chapel Streets, not far from Aggie's place, and it was decided that Kit would stay in her spare room whilst he lined up a flat nearby. He couldn't afford a car, and his father's house at Larrakeyah was not within easy walking distance of the offices.

'Okay,' Kit had agreed when Aggie insisted the arrangement was the only sensible solution. 'It'll only be for a few weeks.'

'Take your time, there's no rush.' She would have been perfectly happy if he'd moved in for good.

Terence's reaction to the entire situation had been enigmatic from the outset. 'I thought you were going to apply for a job in one of the big cities,' he'd said. He hadn't anticipated Kit living with him permanently.

'Aggie thinks I can get a much better offer right here.'

'I see.' When would Aggie Marshall stop interfering, Terence thought.

Kit turned down his father's offer to supply a vehicle. 'No thanks, Dad,' he said, 'If I get the job I'll move into a flat where I can walk to work, and save up to buy a car of my own.' Kit hoped his father wasn't hurt by his refusal, but he felt an intense desire to assert his independence.

Relieved that the boy would not be living under his roof, Terence could afford to be magnanimous and he tried to insist upon setting Kit up in a flat. 'It's the least I can do,' he said. But Kit was adamant, he would accept no help. And far from respecting his desire for independence, Terence was irritated. He would have preferred to have been seen as the generous benefactor.

And now it appeared that Aggie Marshall was to be granted the privilege. It irked Terence to think of Kit staying with the woman who had brought about such a change in their lives. He'd cursed Aggie for the fact that the boy had decided to settle in Darwin in the first place, thereby disrupting the comfortable pattern of his own life, and now, perversely jealous, he cursed her further for being a champion to his son. Why couldn't the woman mind her own bloody business!

'For God's sake, boy,' he snarled, 'why do you want to live with old Aggie Marshall when I could set you up in a decent flat?'

Kit hated it when his father was irritable, which seemed to be a lot of the time lately. And since when had he taken such a dislike to Aggie, whom he'd always professed to be a loyal friend? He'd said 'old' in such a disparaging way. Hell, Kit thought, Aggie's only a few years older than you are. But he didn't say it. 'It'll only be for a few weeks,' he said instead, then he got out of his father's way. Best to leave him alone when he was in one of his morose moods.

Kit was also secretly relieved to be moving out of the house at Larrakeyah. The fact that he appeared to be a source of irritation to his father was hurtful, but at least he knew the reason. It was because of Rose.

'This is Rose,' Terence had said when Kit had returned home for vacation a few years previously, 'Fran's niece, she's going to be helping around the house.'

Rose was a pretty girl. Petite, seemingly shy, and her English was very poor, Fran regularly translating for her as she stood, confused, brown eyes downcast. Kit felt sorry for her.

Privately, Terence had told Kit that of course he didn't need extra staff, but the girl had been in dire straits and he'd given her a roof and a wage as a favour to Fran.

'Fran's been such a loyal employee,' Terence had said. 'It's the least I can do.'

It seemed his father's latest catch phrase, Kit now thought, but he'd naively believed him at the time, and he hadn't realised that his father was having an affair with the girl until a full year later when, again home for vacation, he'd seen Terence sneaking into her little bedroom by the back stairs.

Kit had been shocked at the time. Not only shocked by his father's deception but by the fact that Rose was barely twenty-three years old, the same age as he was himself. He'd tried not to sit in judgement, what right did he have to do so? His father was lonely. And he'd soon realised that Rose was not the innocent she had appeared to be. She'd quickly usurped her position in the house when Terence was not around. Kit observed her rudeness to her aunt, even as they spoke in their native tongue. And Fran appeared to accept Rose's superiority. Then, when Terence came home, the game plan changed, Rose was servile and obeisant, and Fran was the efficient housekeeper she'd always been. In their own ways, both of them waited on their lord and master.

It was an unpleasant and duplicitous household. Couldn't his father see that, Kit wondered. Then he realised that, not only could his father see it, he was perfectly happy with the women's pecking order, it served his purpose.

Kit suddenly viewed his father through different eyes. He tried not to. He didn't want to. His father was his hero, just as he'd been Malcolm's hero. Terence Galloway, World War II fighter pilot, past owner of the renowned Bullalalla cattle station, now a powerful Darwin businessman. Throughout Kit's life his father had always been highly respected. A man of morals, a man with a strict code of ethics which he had instilled in his sons.

Kit hated the disenchantment he felt. Perhaps if his father had spoken to him, man to man, admitted to the fact of his young Filipino mistress, stopped living a lie. But he didn't. Not a word was said and the façade continued. Kit fervently hoped that moving away might restore the respect he'd once felt for Terence Galloway.

'Come off it Aggie, I can't let you do that!'

'Too late, it's done, and you need the space.'

In the several days before Kit moved in, Aggie had rushed about at a feverish pace converting the large front bedroom of her home to suit his needs. A new writing desk stood in pride of place by the windows which looked out over the Esplanade, and upon it sat an Olivetti typewriter and a fresh supply of paper.

'For when the inspiration hits you,' she said. She'd even changed the curtains and bedspread and cushions to give the room a more masculine look.

'But this is your bedroom and that's your typewriter.'

'Not anymore, I'm perfectly comfortable in the spare room, and I'm going to treat myself to a new Olivetti, it's high time I did.'

Kit was taken aback by her generosity, but she was glowing with such joy that he knew there was no point in arguing the case.

The ensuing weeks were amongst the happiest in Aggie's life. Had she been lonely before? If so, she hadn't realised it. But now she delighted in their evenings together, when Kit would return home with stories from the workplace which so obviously stimulated him. Sometimes they'd sit up talking until late in the night. Sometimes he'd retire to his room and she'd listen to the chatter of the typewriter as she made him a fresh pot of coffee.

One night, she pulled out her old cardboard box of photographs and they had what she referred to as a 'sob session' reminiscing over pictures of Henrietta. It was very healthy, Aggie thought.

'Here's one of Paul,' Kit said.

'Yes, it's the only one I have. I took it the year before he died, I wanted something to remember him by. He didn't want me to take it but I bullied him into it.'

Kit laughed, he could well believe it. He looked at the face of the man who had been his childhood hero and wondered if he would ever have aspired to become a writer had it not been for Paul Trewinnard. He owed the man a great debt, he thought. Paul had given him a purpose.

For the first time in her life Aggie enjoyed cooking, it was fun to plan evening meals. Once a week she would allow Kit to take her out to dinner, usually to Foong Lee's restaurant in Cavenagh Street, and after some initial argument, she accepted the rent he insisted upon paying, recognising not only his need for independence but her own tendency to smother.

Kit too was happy. He loved his work, everything about

it. He loved the busyness of the tin shed, stifling though it was in February with no air conditioning. So what? The closeness and humidity intensified the smell of the ink which assailed him the moment he stepped in the door. He loved the smell of the ink, just as he loved the clacking of the typewriters and the insistent ring of the numerous telephones. He sat at his desk, right shoulder hunched, handpiece clamped to his ear, as he speedily tapped out the radio station's programmes. He was doing television and radio this week, next week it might be the weather and shipping news. He loved the variety. Every day he seemed to learn something new. And that's what he loved most of all.

Kit also loved Aggie. But not as a mother figure. Aggie was, as she had been for as long as he could remember, an inspiration. She fed his excitement and fired his ambition. She never tired of hearing about his day, and they endlessly discussed current affairs and literature. When they talked of books, Kit was reminded of the conversations he'd had as a boy with Paul Trewinnard. Aggie had the same love of literature.

The weeks became months and Aggie encouraged him to stay. 'You have an excellent work setup here,' she'd say, 'why bother moving?' Kit was aware that he really should be out flat-hunting. 'Besides,' Aggie would add, 'the rent money certainly does come in handy.' And he'd be further lulled into a state of complacency.

Aggie was lying, she didn't need the rent money, she just couldn't bear the thought of him leaving.

Then one night in mid-April Kit was revisited by one of his dreams. They'd recurred less and less over the years, he hadn't had one for a couple of months now, not since he'd been at Aggie's. But when he had them they were as hideous and as frightening as ever.

He was running. He was always running in the dream. But he was never going anywhere. His lungs were bursting, he couldn't seem to get any oxygen into them, and he was gagging with the effort. His legs were a blur of movement, his fists were pounding the air, but he couldn't make any ground, it was as if he was on a treadmill. And all about him was noise. Explosions and fire and belching black smoke. Then, out of the smoke, things would float towards him, circling slowly in the air then passing him by. Severed limbs, an arm or a leg, then a hand or a foot. And then Beady's head. Always Beady's head. But Beady's head would not pass him by. It would hang in front of him as his feet pounded the ground and, try as he might, he could not run past it. Then the mouth would move and Beady would speak to him. 'Hear you're a crack shot, Kid,' he'd say, but the voice was distorted. Evil. The lips were twisted into a sneer and the eyes were malevolent. Beady's head mocked him.

Sometimes Kit would wake up the moment he saw Beady's head. Sometimes he'd wake up before Beady spoke. He preferred it that way, he hated the sound of the voice.

Tonight, Beady's open mouth started to form the words, but Kit heard another voice.

'Kit, wake up. Wake up, Kit.'

A hand was stroking his matted hair back from his face, wiping the sweat from his brow. Kit sat bolt upright, as he always did when he came out of his dream. Aggie was sitting on the side of the bed, concerned and anxious.

'Oh my dear, are you all right?' she said, once more stroking his forehead.

'Yes I'm fine, Aggie.' He pushed her hand away. He didn't want to be hurtful but he desperately wished she would leave him alone. 'Please. I'm fine.'

Aggie was too worried to get the hint. 'You were having the most shocking nightmare, I could hear you from my room.'

'Yes, well I have them sometimes, please go back to

bed.' He knew his tone was abrupt, but his dreams were not something to be shared, they were his own nightmare world, and he handled them his own way. Aggie, taken aback, didn't move. 'Go to bed, Aggie.'

It was a command, and in that instant Aggie realised her mistake. He was not a little boy to be comforted in a mother's arms. He was a man. A haunted man, fighting battles within himself which she could never know of. And he looked so old and so weary.

'Of course,' she said, mortified, 'I'm sorry.'

Kit was his normal, ebullient self in the morning, but they never spoke of the matter, and he kept his bedroom door closed from then on.

'For God's sake, Kit, when are you going to ask me out?'

A gang of them were at the Victoria Hotel. They invariably went to the Vic on a Friday night after work. Even Jim Bowditch was there, drinking at the bar with a couple of his old cronies.

Kit was at a table with a half a dozen other journos, lounging around in leather chairs. Lisa the receptionist was with them and, when he'd gone to the bar to buy his round, she'd joined him and draped an arm over his shoulder.

'You're pissed, Lisa,' he smiled, 'another jug and two white wines, mate,' he said to the barman.

'No I'm not,' she said. Of course she wasn't. Four glasses of wine, or was it five, she wasn't sure, might loosen her up a bit, but it certainly didn't make her legless. 'I'm asking for a date, what's a girl supposed to do?' Gee, she thought, it wasn't as if she hadn't made it quite obvious that she fancied him. She had from the moment she'd shown him around the office, and that was over three months ago! Kit Galloway was the most attractive man at *NTN*.

Lisa took a hefty slurp from one of the glasses of white

wine the barman had just poured as Kit pulled out his wallet. Hell, Kit Galloway was the most attractive man in Darwin, she thought. Tall, good body, those eyes that looked right into yours, and that *gorgeous* smile! And he was a *war hero*! At least somebody had told her he was. And they'd been terribly impressed as they'd said it, so of course she had been too. Kit Galloway was *famous*!

She cuddled up to him as he paid the bill. 'So come on,' she said, 'ask me out.'

'I will when you're sober.' As she gave a befuddled frown, he added 'Well, when I am.' She really was legless. Not that it bothered Kit, everyone got pissed on a Friday night. In fact people drank far more in Darwin than they did in Adelaide, probably something to do with the tropics, he thought.

He could feel the fullness of her breasts as she snuggled beside him. He had to admit he'd noticed Lisa's breasts. Most men did. Lisa Langello had superb breasts. But did she really fancy him? Probably not, she flirted with everyone, even when she was sober. In a good-natured, harmless way, Kit certainly liked Lisa. But he hadn't realised that she fancied him.

They returned to the table and he couldn't take his eyes off her. Why hadn't he recognised before how extraordinarily good looking she was? Dark-haired, sloe-eyed, full-figured and luscious. She glanced at him teasingly and Kit, aware of his growing erection and the fact that he hadn't made love to a woman for over six months, was having trouble following the conversation.

An hour and three glasses of wine later, Lisa was at the falling down stage and Kit walked her home. Or rather half carried her. She lived nearby in Mitchell Street.

'Do you want to come in?' she said after he'd kissed her at the front door of the dilapidated old wooden house on stilts. Kit did, desperately, but she shared the house with three others, she'd said, and besides, she'd pass out soon.

It wasn't the right time and it wasn't the right place.

'See you Monday, Lisa,' he said, opening the door for her.

'Oh you will, you will,' and she staggered inside.

As he walked home, Kit decided that it was time to leave Aggie's. First the dream and now Lisa. He needed a place of his own. But he wasn't sure how to break the news to Aggie, he knew that she'd become dependent upon his company.

The following night, he insisted upon taking her to dinner at Foong Lee's restaurant.

'A Saturday?' she queried. 'I'm honoured, but what about your friends?'

It had become customary for Kit and two of his work mates, Nick Coustas and Maxie Brummer, to have a rowdy boys' night out on a Saturday, Nick's penchant for gambling inevitably leading them to a card game at one of the illegal gambling houses to which the police turned a blind eye. Kit liked a good game of poker and he particularly enjoyed *pai kew*, the Chinese blackjack-style betting game, but he didn't gamble heavily. He simply relaxed in the male company of his friends and the escape from Aggie's flat which had become claustrophobic. He had lately come to realise, with a sense of disloyalty, that it was even an escape from Aggie herself, and the devotion she lavished upon him.

'Nick and Maxie can survive a Saturday night without me,' he said.

Kit and Aggie arrived at the restaurant at eight o'clock, Foong Lee personally greeting them at the door as he always did. The restaurant was actually called the Golden Dragon, but no-one referred to it as such, it was simply known as 'Foong Lee's'.

'Aggie tells me you've had a feature article accepted, Kit,' Foong Lee said as he escorted them to their table.

'Well it's not really a feature,' Kit said self-deprecatingly, 'it's a follow-up story, just a half a page.'

'On the effects of the French nuclear testing in the Pacific last year, Aggie tells me.'

'Yes, that's right.'

'Excellent. My congratulations.'

Foong Lee recommended the specials and left them with the menus.

'You've been showing off again,' Kit said to Aggie after he'd gone.

'Only to Foong Lee,' she replied, 'he's always asking after you, he follows your career with great interest, you know that.'

Kit smiled good naturedly. It was true, and he was fond of old Foong Lee. But Aggie would have boasted about him with equal pride to anyone who had the time to listen, she'd become a real mother hen. Which only made his decision all the more difficult to impart, he thought. His smile faded.

He waited until they'd finished their main course, he didn't want to spoil the evening. Then he simply made the announcement, there was no easy way, he'd decided.

'I'll be moving out next weekend, Aggie,' he said. He'd also decided it would be easier to name a date. If he hadn't found a flat by then he'd stay with Maxie until he did.

'Oh.' For a moment Aggie looked as if she'd received a physical blow, his pronouncement had been the last thing she'd expected. 'Why?' she asked dabbing at her mouth with her serviette to mask her confusion.

'It's time.' He knew she was shocked, as he'd expected her to be. 'In fact it's way past time, I should have moved out months ago. I've been lazy and complacent, and it's my fault and I'm sorry.'

'Why?' she asked again, this time with a light laugh and an attempt at bravado, 'it's hardly as if you've overstayed your welcome. I enjoy your company, you know that.'

'And I enjoy yours, Aggie. But I need my own space.'

Foong Lee had arrived at the table with the bowls of

lychees and ice-cream. Aggie always had lychees and ice-cream. He made no indication that he'd heard Kit's remark, but he cast a brief glance at Aggie before he left. He had known this would happen, in fact he had tried to warn her.

'You're not his mother, Aggie,' he'd said as gently as he could, 'and he's not a child, he's a man . . .'

She'd cut him off tersely. 'Don't be ridiculous, Foong Lee, of course I know that. And I don't mother Kit,' she'd said, 'we're good friends, he tells me himself I inspire his work.'

Aggie stared at her lychees and ice-cream. She'd been a stupid old woman. Foong Lee had been right. She'd stifled Kit, smothered him with her motherly love, of course he wanted to get away from her. That was why he'd been going out most Fridays and Saturdays for the past several weeks, she'd been getting on his nerves. She felt hurt and humiliated. She stirred the melting ice-cream into the lychee juice, not quite able to raise the spoon to her lips.

She looked hurt, Kit thought. But she shouldn't be. He decided it would be best if he told the truth—well, some of it at least. 'I've met a girl,' he said.

Aggie looked up from her lychees.

'A girl from work, I don't really know her that well, and I'm not pretending she's the woman of my dreams . . .' That sounded a little derogatory, he thought. 'Well, she might be,' he hastily added, 'I don't know yet, but . . .' He grinned self-consciously, 'she reckons she fancies me, and she's bloody good looking.'

Relief, mingled with a sense of her own foolishness, flooded through Aggie. He wasn't fed up with her, he didn't despise her. He was a young man with a young man's lusts, and of course he must move out of the nest she'd built for him. Foong Lee had tried to warn her and she hadn't listened. She'd behaved like an over-possessive mother.

'Well, well, well,' she said with a suggestive smile, hoping Kit hadn't noticed her vulnerability. 'I trust when you come up for air you'll visit me from time to time.'

'Of course I will,' he said, 'you're my best friend.' It was the truth and he meant it from the bottom of his heart. 'You're the best friend I have in the world, Aggie.'

She glowed, it was all she needed to hear.

As Aggie started to hoe into her lychees and ice-cream, Foong Lee, watching from several tables away, breathed a sigh of relief. Catastrophe averted, he thought.

Kit was determined to find a place on his own. Most young people in Darwin shared houses and flats, properties for lease being in such heavy demand that rentals were high, but Kit was adamant. Perhaps because of his fear that flatmates might overhear the cries in his sleep, perhaps simply because of his lust for Lisa, or perhaps, as he told himself, because he needed the privacy to write.

Eventually his determination paid off, and he found a small downstairs bed-sitting room affair, tucked neatly between the stilts of an attractive old house in Lindsay Street, near Frogs Hollow. Bob O'Malley, retired builder, had built the little granny flat himself five years previously for his elderly mother, but the old lady had recently died, and Bob and his wife were keen to let it out.

Tess O'Malley was most impressed by the fact that their tenant was none other than Terence Galloway's son and she initially encouraged Kit to 'come upstairs for a cup of tea whenever you feel like it'. He made it clear, as politely as he could, that all of his spare time was given to writing and she soon got the message and left him alone, thankful that at least he was a 'quiet' young man. Kit revelled in his new-found independence.

The Friday after he'd moved in, he invited Lisa back to his place following the customary session at the Vic and she accepted with alacrity.

He let them in through the private side entrance to the flat, hoping that Lisa's loud giggles wouldn't wake Mrs O'Malley upstairs. Lisa was pissed again, but not legless this time.

'What a cute place,' Lisa said, looking around at the open-plan bed-sitting room. It was a bit pokey, she thought.

There was a kitchenette at the far end, a sofa which pulled out to a bed, a wardrobe, a chest of drawers and a rather impressive desk with two chairs by the windows. Only the barest of essentials, but the overall effect was attractive. Aggie had insisted upon donating the desk, which also served as a dining table, just as she had insisted upon Kit having the cushions, bedspread and curtains from his room at her place.

'I bought them especially for you,' she'd said, 'and they'll make the flat feel homey.' She was right, they did.

'Is there a bathroom?' Lisa asked, she was dying for a pee.

'Through there.' Kit indicated the door to the right of the entrance which led into a tiny bathroom. 'The en suite,' Tess O'Malley had proudly announced when she'd showed him the flat.

He opened the bottle of riesling he'd bought the previous day in the hope that Lisa would come home with him and, by the time she'd returned from the bathroom, he'd filled the two wine glasses which he'd also purchased the previous day.

They sat on the sofa, clinked glasses and sipped.

'How did you win your medal?' Lisa asked.

'Eh?' Kit was nonplussed by the question.

'Janice's dad says you're a war hero.' Kit looked blankly at her. 'You've met Janice,' she prompted him. 'My girl-friend who comes into the office sometimes, we have lunch together. You *know*,' she seemed a little frustrated that Janice didn't spring immediately to his mind, 'Janice Rowlands, she works in the post office.'

'Oh. Janice. Yes.'

'Well her dad says you won a medal for bravery. Janice reckons that's fantastic.'

'Oh.' Kit took another sip of his wine, he really didn't like white wine, he thought as he wondered how to change the conversation.

'So what did you win it for?'

There was only one way. He put the glass down on the floor and stared at her intensely for a moment.

'You're terrific looking, Lisa,' he said. It worked. She smiled, gave a gentle scoff and shook her head in that pseudo-self-deprecating way girls sometimes did when they wanted to hear more.

'You really are, you're beautiful.' He studied the lustre of her hair and the darkness of her thick-lashed eyes and the fullness of her mouth. 'Very, very beautiful,' he repeated softly as he ran his finger along the curve of her jawline and down her neck. He meant it, she was glorious, and he desired her immensely.

Kit Galloway had always had success with women. His unassuming air won them from the outset, he appeared completely unaware of the impact he had on the opposite sex. He was easygoing, friendly, non-threatening, and sometimes frustrating to women who expected flirtation. As a result, they were overwhelmed to discover, when he finally did make a move, that he was a skilful lover. He'd not worked hard to perfect the art of seduction, it came naturally to him. He was honest in his admiration. He genuinely loved women. He loved the look of them, the feel of them, the taste and smell of them. He loved making love to women.

Lisa, mesmerised by his intensity, had been watching him study her. Finally she gave a self-conscious giggle, still unable to take her eyes from his as they wandered from her throat to her breasts. 'I know what you're after, Kit Galloway.'

Kit gazed at the slight moistness he could see between the cleavage which pouted from the scooped neck of her T-shirt. It was a hot humid night. 'Yes,' he said, and he took the glass of wine from her, placing it beside his on the floor.

Lisa was accustomed to chatting for a while before she did it. She was good at flirting. That was what a girl was supposed to do. It was part of the game. Then you pretended that you were taken by surprise, and it just happened. She was about to say something but suddenly he was kissing her, his tongue gently exploring her mouth, his hand caressing her breast, soft but insistent fingers finding her responsive nipple, and Lisa's rules of etiquette went out the window.

The white wine tasted different mingled with her saliva, Kit thought, it tasted womanly and desirable, and he could feel her nipple hardening beneath the thin lace of her brassiere. He knew that he'd have to keep himself in check, it had been so long and she felt so good.

They didn't bother to pull the bed out, they undressed each other and made love on the sofa.

At twenty-three Lisa Langello considered herself a modern young woman, it was the age of sexual liberation, after all, and she'd made love on sofas before, and on floors, and once in the backseat of a Holden. She and her friend Janice shared a theory that sofas, floors and car seats constituted 'quickies' and were never as good as when a man wooed you properly, taking you out to dinner and then back to his place for drinks and intimate conversation before the ultimate seduction. 'Well, it's polite for starters,' Janice maintained, 'and it certainly gets you more in the mood.' Lisa had agreed. But tonight, as she felt herself teased beyond endurance, as every fibre in her quivered with a desire she'd never known, as she heard her animal moans of pleasure and felt her muscles contracting in waves of fulfillment, the theory's credibility was forever undermined.

They lay in a heap on the sofa, chests heaving, skin slippery with mingled sweat and then, when he'd recovered himself, Kit rose, pulling her gently to her feet, and kissed her.

'I'll make the bed up,' he said.

'Okay,' for once Lisa was lost for words.

They lay naked on the bed with just a sheet over them and she nuzzled herself into the crook of his shoulder, he loved the feel of her there.

As they lightly dozed off in each other's arms, Kit realised that he'd been lonely. He'd never really been in love. In fact he wasn't sure if he knew what 'being in love' was, but he'd very much missed having a woman in his life. In his state of semi-sleep, he ran his fingers along the silken curve of Lisa's hip. So beautiful.

She raised her head drowsily and looked at him as he gazed at the ceiling. 'What are you thinking about?' she asked.

'You,' he said. And they made love again.

'Not a good idea, Kit,' Nick Coustas warned.

'What?'

'Screwing a bird from work.' Nick was always direct.

Kit tried to ignore him, but Maxie's advice, although more tastefully voiced, was the same.

'Girlfriends and work don't mix, mate, you should know that.'

'We're just going out together,' Kit said, attempting to dodge the issue, but they were right and he knew it. In fact he was already in trouble. He and Lisa had been sleeping together on a weekly basis for four months now, and she was starting to suggest they move in together.

Kit had been taken aback when she'd first proposed the idea, but as usual he'd decided that honesty was the best policy.

'I'm not ready to live with anyone, Lisa.'

'Oh don't be silly,' she said, 'I don't mean *live together* like *that*!'

'Like what?'

'Like a *couple,* you *know.* I'm not asking you to *commit* yourself or anything.'

Surely that's exactly what she was asking, Kit thought. They were sleeping together, after all.

'It's just that I'm sick of sharing with that bunch of yobbos in Mitchell Street, and you're sick of this pokey little flat and we could find a really beaut place if we shared the rent.'

'But I'm not sick of this pokey little flat.' He loved his pokey little flat. And he loved his independence.

'Oh all right,' she said huffily, '*be* like that!' But minutes later she was snuggling up to him again. 'I hate it when we fight.' He didn't know it had been a fight.

They made love and the subject was forgotten. Until a week later. And then the week after that. But Kit refused to give in, he could be very stubborn when he wished.

The fact was, Lisa did want a commitment. She hadn't really realised it until Janice had pointed out what a catch Kit Galloway was.

'Terence Galloway's son! Jeez, Lisa, you're mad if you don't grab him. You said yourself, everyone at work reckons he's going places, and he'll get all of his Dad's money one day.' Janice had even told her she should get pregnant, 'he'd have to marry you then.' But Lisa didn't go off the pill. She didn't want to get pregnant. She wasn't even sure if she wanted to get married, she'd always felt she was destined to be something more than a housewife. But she always listened to Janice, and if Janice said Kit Galloway was such a catch then of course she was mad if she didn't try to snare him.

'This is Lisa, Dad. Lisa Langello.'

'How do you do, Mr Galloway.' Lisa all but dropped a

curtsy. She'd been nagging Kit for ages to introduce her to his father, and he'd finally taken her along to Galloway Motors on a Saturday morning. She'd rather he'd invited her to dinner at the big house in Larrakeyah, but he said he didn't go there much himself.

'Ah, you're the girlfriend,' Terence loudly declared as he took her hand warmly in both of his. 'Hello, Lisa.'

Lisa beamed and nodded. So Kit had been talking about her to his father, that was good.

Terence had actually heard the news from Aggie who'd met the girlfriend a number of times.

'A lass who works at the newspaper,' she'd simply said, 'they've been going out for a good six months now.'

Terence had had the feeling that Aggie didn't altogether approve of the girlfriend. He could see why. She oozed sexuality. Aggie Marshall, dried up old prune that she was, would probably have preferred to see Kit with a scholarly, bespectacled type. Terence himself was surprised that Kit could attract a girl like Lisa Langello. What could she possibly see in him?

'Why don't we come up to my office for a coffee?' he suggested and, without waiting for an answer, he led the way.

'What a lovely office,' Lisa said admiringly. Office, she thought, it was a bloody movie set, no-one she knew had an office like this. Leather armchairs, mahogany desk, a bar in the corner, and what about the view! She wandered over to the plate-glass windows and looked down at the rows of shiny vehicles on the showroom floor. 'Fantastic,' she said.

'Yes, it's rather impressive, isn't it?' Terence agreed, he liked it when people admired the showroom. 'Business is doing very well at the moment. Booming in fact. The market's good. Sit down, Lisa, please, you too, Kit.' He gestured to the armchairs and they sat. 'Coffee's on its way, anyone like anything a little stronger?' He crossed to the bar to pour himself a Scotch.

'Bit early for me, Dad, coffee'll do fine,' Kit said.

'Lisa? How about a champagne?' Lisa gave a breathless giggle, it wasn't even lunchtime. 'Come on,' Terence urged, 'it's not every day a man meets his son's girlfriend.'

'All right, just a little one.'

'That's my girl.'

The secretary arrived with the pot of coffee and three cups as Terence eased the cork out of the vintage Krug. 'Just pour the one, thank you, Dora,' he said, and when she'd gone he tapped his Scotch glass against Lisa's champagne flute. 'Cheers,' he said.

'Am I the only one having champagne? Oh, you shouldn't have opened the bottle for me.'

'If you don't finish it, my dear, then we'll simply throw it out.'

Christ he was laying it on thick, Kit thought.

Lisa sipped at her champagne, it tasted different to the bubbly she normally drank, she was sure it was the real stuff.

'It's all thanks to television,' Terence announced as he sat behind his desk.

Lisa looked at him blankly. What was?

'He means the boom in the market,' Kit explained.

'Exactly.' Terence resisted the urge to scowl, he'd been waiting for the girl's enquiry and Kit had stolen his moment of triumph. But he curbed his irritation. 'Television advertising most certainly changed the face of the marketplace . . .' It was true, since the arrival of television in Darwin two years previously Terence's profits had doubled. '. . . but everyone's on the bandwagon now, you have to be innovative. And that's exactly what we're doing. I haven't told you yet have I, Kit?' He grinned excitedly at his son.

Told him what, Kit wondered. He hadn't seen his father this enthusiastic in years. He was about to enquire, but Terence continued, once again directing his attention to Lisa.

'We'll be launching a whole new campaign next month,' he said. 'A campaign based on personality. You see it's not just the products one needs to sell. It's the face of the person who sells the products.' He was directly quoting the advertising specialists he'd employed. 'Who instills you with trust? Who do you want to do business with? Who do you like and respect the most?'

He was firing the questions directly at her and Lisa wondered whether she was expected to come up with the answers. Fortunately not.

'It's all a matter of image!' he triumphantly pronounced.

Terence's excitement was genuine. He'd flown a top advertising team up from Sydney a month previously and they were already filming the first batch of commercials to go to air in time for the November sales and the Christmas market. Terence Galloway, the face of Galloway Motors and Emporium. The prospect of television fame excited Terence as much as did the advertising expert's guarantee of a massive boost in sales.

'The image of the person you trust!' He rose from his desk and crossed to the bar.

'So will you be on television yourself, Mr Galloway?' Lisa asked. She was terribly impressed.

'Terence, my dear, please.'

Lisa momentarily pictured herself out with Janice. They'd bump into Mr Galloway and she'd introduce him. 'Janice, this is Mr Galloway.' Then she'd say, 'How are you, Terence?' She could just see the look on Janice's face.

'Yes, I shall most certainly be on television,' he said as he topped up her glass. 'What do you think, Kit?' He turned to his son, arms theatrically outstretched, Krug bottle in hand. 'Terence Galloway! The face of Galloway Motors and Emporium.'

Kit laughed, it was good to see his father in such a jovial mood. 'So that's why you've bunged on the new hairdo,' he said. His father's thick grey hair was elegantly styled and Kit was sure it was a touch more silver in hue than when he'd last seen him. 'You look like an elder statesman.'

Terence was aware it wasn't altogether meant as a compliment, but the image of elder statesman pleased him so he took it as one. Lisa obviously agreed.

'Yes, you look very distinguished,' she said. She wanted to add 'Terence', but she couldn't quite muster the courage.

'Thank you, my dear.'

Terence gave a mock bow and Lisa returned him one of her most radiant smiles.

There was something special in her smile and the way she looked at him, Terence thought. He was sure that she found him attractive. God she was a looker. Then it occurred to him. Of course! She'd be perfect!

Greg Sharman, the advertising guru of Ogylvie and Mather, had suggested that they include a young person's face in the campaign in order to appeal to the younger market. 'Not for Galloway Motors,' he'd said, 'but for the Emporium commercials.' Something in Terence's eyes had caused him to hastily add, 'in a very secondary role of course, say as your assistant or something.' Then the perfect solution had occurred to him. 'I've got it! What about your son?'

It had gone down like a lead balloon. 'My son has no interest in the business,' Terence had icily replied. 'It's why I changed the name.' Which wasn't altogether true. 'Galloway and Sons' had become 'Galloway Motors and Emporium' following Malcolm's death.

Terence had eventually seen Greg's point, however, and they'd decided upon a female image. 'A bit of sex appeal never goes astray,' they'd jointly agreed.

And young Lisa Langello certainly had sex appeal, Terence thought as his eyes strayed to her breasts, then her legs.

Lisa's smile froze, she was starting to feel embarrassed. Mr Galloway was looking her up and down. She hoped he didn't fancy her. Not that he wasn't a handsome man in his own way, but he had to be in his fifties, and she wasn't attracted to old men.

'Forgive me for staring, my dear,' Terence said, aware that she'd caught him looking at her breasts, but he wasn't in the least embarrassed, he'd had every legitimate reason. He returned the champagne bottle to the bar refrigerator and sat once again behind his desk. 'You're an extremely attractive young woman,' he said, continuing his study of her.

Oh my God, Lisa thought, he *does* fancy me.

Kit too was aware that his father was ogling Lisa. 'Time to go,' he said as he rose from his chair. Bloody old perve, he thought, he could at least have been a little more subtle.

'Sit down, Kit, I have a proposition for Lisa.' Kit remained standing. 'Would you be interested in testing for our commercials, my dear?'

Lisa stared back dumbly. Had she heard right? Was he joking?

'We're looking for a young woman to incorporate in the campaign, in order to appeal to the younger market. The director is currently holding auditions.'

He wasn't joking. Lisa was breathless.

'I could arrange a test for you, if you're interested.'

'You're joking,' Kit said. 'Lisa isn't an actress.'

'I'd be very interested, Mr Galloway . . .' Shut up Kit, she thought. '. . . Terence.' There, she'd said it.

'Excellent.' Terence took a business card from the top drawer of his desk and scribbled a telephone number on it. 'It's not actresses we're looking for, Kit,' he said as he circled the desk. 'Just the right image. Besides,' he added as he held out the card, 'I'm sure Lisa has a natural talent. That's the director, my dear, Greg Sharman, I'll tell him to expect your call.'

Lisa took the card. 'Thank you.' She gave him another of her radiant smiles. Yes, he thought, she certainly found him attractive. 'How exciting,' she said.

Terence insisted that they drink a toast, and poured champagne all round.

'She hasn't got the job yet,' Kit said, 'doesn't she have to see the director?'

'I've no doubt Greg'll cast her,' Terence said. He'd make sure that Greg did. 'Cheers.'

It was ridiculous, Kit thought as he joined in the toast. The whole situation was bizarre.

He didn't find it so bizarre when, barely a month later, the commercials went to air and Lisa became an overnight star.

Terence had paid a fortune, the ads saturated NTD8's prime-time viewing slots. When the Northern Territory tuned into 'Happy Days' or 'Number 96', or any of the other top-rating programmes, there they were, Terence Galloway and Lisa Langello. The two of them were suddenly household names. Well, Terence was. Terence Galloway was the impressive pillar of society in whom one could place one's trust. The girl who said 'come in and see us some time' remained simply 'the girl from the Emporium', but Lisa was stopped in the street wherever she went.

She'd had to take a couple of 'sickies' to shoot the ads, and she'd sworn Kit to secrecy.

'Don't you dare tell,' she'd said, 'it might get me the sack.'

Of course he wouldn't, he promised. The whole thing was utterly ridiculous, he thought, as he had from the outset. His father was being shockingly irresponsible, jeopardising Lisa's job and encouraging her fantasies. He tried to tell her as much but she refused to listen.

A fortnight after the ads had gone to air, Lisa announced that she was handing in her resignation. She was going to work for the Galloway Emporium, she told Kit.

'Your father's offering me twice what I get at *NTN*,' she said, 'and all I have to do is greet people at the door.' It appeared there had been a huge enquiry. 'Where's the girl from the Emporium?' customers had been asking.

Kit was forced to admit his mistake. Yes, he agreed, his father had opened up a whole new career for her.

'And he's making another series of commercials in the new year,' she said, 'isn't it wonderful, Kit, I'm the Emporium girl.'

'Yes,' Kit said, 'it's wonderful.' Something didn't seem right, he thought.

Terence held a large Christmas party at the house in Larrakeyah and told Kit to invite his friends from *NTN*.

'Make sure you ask Jim Bowditch,' he said. 'He's a good bloke, Jim.' And a very handy man to have on side, Terence thought.

There were approximately twenty people present from both Galloway Motors and the Emporium. Only those at executive level, Terence having already thrown the obligatory staff parties where he'd made a brief appearance and given a stirring speech on team effort and morale. The other forty invited guests were prominent citizens, including the mayor, Harold Brennan, and the elite of Darwin's businessmen and their wives.

Kit and Lisa arrived in his brand new car, or rather his brand new second-hand Kingswood which he parked alongside the Mercedes and Jaguars.

Lisa was in her element. The house was as grand as she'd expected it to be. A string quartet played on the first-floor balcony welcoming guests as they walked through the floodlit garden and up the stairs. Waiters in dinner suits glided about everywhere with trays of real champagne—she'd lately developed a taste for Krug Vintage—and two Filipino housemaids darted here and there clearing ashtrays and providing fresh ones before they were even needed. Lisa was overwhelmed by the fact that the upper echelons of Darwin whom she'd never met appeared to know her. 'Hello, you're the girl from the Emporium,' they said. She mingled with as many distinguished guests as she could and barely saw Kit all night.

Kit stood with Nick Coustas and Maxie Brummer at the huge buffet table which the caterers had set up in the first-floor lounge room, the dining room having been given over to the serving of desserts and coffee. Nick was filling his plate for the third time. The food was superb and, as fast as it disappeared, fresh platters arrived. Kit picked at his plate of seafood and looked out to the balcony where Lisa was in animated discussion with Nick Paspaley's wife. Well, Lisa was in animated discussion, it looked rather as if Mrs Paspaley was seeking an escape. Lisa was already a bit pissed, he thought, he'd better take her home early. Not that he minded, he was already finding the evening a bit wearisome.

An hour or so later, he went in search of her, to find her standing alone in the small, rear sitting room, bleary-eyed and distinctly unsteady on her feet.

Lisa was lost. She'd been after the bathroom. She'd been there earlier in the evening, she was sure it had been in this direction but she'd taken a wrong turn. Suddenly Kit was by her side.

'Time to go, love, what do you reckon?' He put an affectionate arm around her, more to prop her up than anything, but she pushed him away.

'Don't be silly, Kit.' She smiled brightly, her eyes glassy and wide in an effort to prove she wasn't drunk. He thought she was pissed, she could tell. Well, she wasn't. Perhaps a little bit tiddly, but then everyone was.

'The night is young,' she said. It was one of Janice's favourite sayings. She wished Janice was here. She'd thought of asking Terence if she could invite her friend Janice, but she hadn't quite found the nerve. Although she now called him Terence with ease, and even flirted a little as they drank champagne in the boardroom on Fridays, Lisa was still very much in awe of Terence Galloway.

'Come on, love, you've had enough.' Kit put his arm around her again, but once more she pushed him away, roughly this time, nearly losing her balance as she did so.

'Leave me alone,' she said, her voice suddenly shrill.

A couple passing by the open door looked in their direction. Bugger it, Kit thought, she was going to make a scene.

Lisa pulled herself together, aware that she'd been a little too loud. 'I'm looking for the bathroom,' she said with a dignity verging on the comical as her ankle strap shoes threatened to give way under her, 'I seem to have lost it.'

Then she heard a kindly female voice say, 'I'm after the bathroom too, shall we go together?' Aggie Marshall had come into the sitting room to call for a taxi.

'Yes,' Lisa said. She allowed Aggie to take her by the hand and they went off to the bathroom together, arm in arm, the way she and Janice always did. 'I don't like being bossed about,' she said loudly to Aggie for Kit's benefit.

'Of course you don't, dear, nobody does.'

How funny, Lisa thought, she hadn't particularly liked old Aggie Marshall. Mainly because she'd thought Aggie didn't like her. But Aggie was really very nice.

Kit breathed a sigh of relief.

He was waiting for them when they came out of the bathroom a full fifteen minutes later. Lisa seemed in much better condition, he thankfully observed.

Lisa was. Aggie had suggested that they both wash their faces, touch up their makeup and drink two large glasses of water each.

'A little alcohol goes to my head very badly these days,' Aggie had said. 'And I'm feeling so terribly tired.'

'I've said we'll give Aggie a lift home, Kit,' Lisa said, 'is that all right?'

'Fine by me.' Kit grinned, another Aggie Marshall miracle. But Aggie didn't meet his eye. She and Lisa walked arm in arm down the stairs, Lisa still a little unsteady, but Kit didn't offer his assistance, aware that Aggie had the situation under control. He and Lisa were drifting apart, he thought. The sad thing was, he didn't really care all that much.

When they dropped Aggie off, she bade a fond goodnight to Lisa, kissing the girl on the cheek. 'You looked lovely tonight, dear,' she said, 'quite lovely. Goodnight, Kit.'

Both Terence Galloway and Lisa herself had been quite wrong in their assessment of Aggie's attitude. She neither disapproved of, nor disliked the girl. She felt sorry for her. It would be only a matter of time before Kit tired of Lisa, Aggie thought. He would need more than the obvious sexuality their relationship offered. And what would happen to Lisa after that? Another sexual liaison? Another man dumping her? Lisa had 'victim' written all over her in Aggie's estimation.

Aggie's surmise proved correct on one score. Kit and Lisa broke up a month later, but it wasn't Kit who did the dumping, it was Lisa. Her life had taken a different direction, she told him. She'd earned a lot of money from the commercials, she was moving out of the old house in Mitchell Street, she could afford a place of her own. A stylish place too, she said. Classy. And they moved in different circles now, didn't they? They really didn't have much in common anymore.

Kit wasn't offended. There was something so desperate in Lisa's manner as she rattled on. It was as if she was apologising. But she didn't need to, he thought, he quite understood. He said all the right things. He'd miss her, he wished her every success, but in fact he was secretly relieved. Besides, there was the excitement of his promotion. He'd served his one-year cadetship and was now a fully fledged, fully paid journalist for the *Northern Territory News*.

CHAPTER THIRTY-FIVE

*T*he two years of Jessica's masters degree were enlightening to say the least. In the first year she lost her virginity to a law student. On purpose. At twenty-one she was far too old to be a virgin, she'd decided. She also decided that sex was overrated, until the following month when she lost her heart to a final-year medical student who dumped her six months later. She got over it, she was determined to be tough.

Despite her sexual awakening, Jessica did not neglect her studies, she had always been adept at living life to the full. Much of her time was focussed on the mystery of the oval symbol which she had seen painted in kaolin clay by the inland Yamatji people. She could find no historical record of it so, with Catherine Berndt's encouragement, she made a field trip in the summer vacation of 1972 into the desert area of the Oakover region. This time she travelled alone in the second-hand Landrover her father had bought her for Christmas, a gift of which Enid had strongly disapproved.

'It's a good car,' Grahame had insisted, misguidedly thinking his wife disapproved of the fact it was second-hand. Enid had never driven a second-hand vehicle in her life.

'But a Landrover!' No respectable young woman drove about in a Landrover!

'She needs a four wheel drive for her field research.'

They'd ganged up on her and Enid realised that she didn't have any say in the matter. But when she discovered that Jessica was going to travel alone she was horrified.

'Dr Berndt's arranged an Aboriginal guide for me once I get to the Jigalong Mission, Mum,' Jessica assured her, 'and she's given me contacts all along the way. I have maps, I've studied the route I'll be taking, she's marked the few towns and the best campsites and . . .'

Enid wouldn't listen, it was quite unheard of, she said, and it took Grahame a long time to calm her down enough to pay any attention at all.

'She's twenty-two years old and she's a modern young woman, my dear,' he insisted. 'Besides, she's an anthropologist and she's doing what anthropologists do.' Deep down Grahame rather wished Jessica had a travelling companion, and had suggested as much.

'Can't a fellow student go with you, sweetheart?'

'I'm studying this symbol for my thesis, Dad,' she said. 'I can't expect anyone else to have the same interest in it. Heck, I don't want them to,' she gave one of her attractively throaty laughs, 'it's my personal discovery, I might be onto a whole new breakthrough.' She could see that he was concerned. 'Jessica Williams!' she theatrically announced, 'Youngest anthropologist in history to unearth one of the mysteries of ancient Aboriginal culture!' She threw her arms around his neck. 'Wouldn't you be proud?'

He hugged her warmly, she could always get around him. 'Of course I would, Jess,' he said. He was already proud of her beyond measure, but he knew he'd worry nonetheless.

Jessica herself had no misgivings whatsoever. She was excited and, in the brash confidence of youth, eagerly optimistic that she would discover the rock paintings *which the elders had told her of during her field trip with Catherine Berndt. Her starting point was the Jigalong Mission roughly ninety kilometres east of Newman. From there, with the help of her Aboriginal guide, she would initiate her enquiries as to the exact whereabouts of the paintings.*

She travelled inland along the Great Northern Highway, staying overnight at Paynes Find and Meekatharra, but for the most part choosing to make camp. She liked to squat by her campfire, surrounded by the red earth and the hardy scrub. She liked to watch the glow of the sunset fade to night and the ensuing brilliance of the stars emerge like diamonds in the clear black sky, so close she felt she could touch them. And when she was tired, she simply rolled out her swag by the dying embers of the campfire and slept as she had never slept before.

Jessica's field trip with Catherine had opened her eyes to the wonders of her country and she had felt an affiliation with the land, but now, alone, without the companionable fireside chat by way of distraction, her surrounds begged questions of her which she had never before asked. She found herself wondering what her life might have been, had she not been taken from her birth mother. Would she be nomadically wandering the land with her people? Would she be settled in a mission with her extended family? Would she perhaps be one of the lost and hapless city Aborigines she'd seen hanging around the railway station?

She was not in turmoil. Even as she wondered who she might have been had her life followed its natural path, Jessica knew very well who she was. She was Jessica Williams, anthropologist, loved by her white parents and comfortable in the white society in which she had been raised. But deep inside, Jessica could feel the stirring of her Aboriginal blood. She was proud of her ancestry and felt a tremendous sense of peace in the harsh, outback country of her people.

She stayed overnight at Newman and, when she finally reached the Jigalong Mission, she was a little taken aback by the Aboriginal guide whom Catherine had arranged for her to meet up with.

In his mid-thirties, Wallawambalyl Djarranda wore loud floral shirts, boots with footie socks and gabbled in a twangy ocker accent at such a rate it was sometimes difficult to discern what he was saying.

'Call me Wally,' he said with the cheeky grin which was always at the ready, 'most people call me Wally.' Most white people he really meant, they mucked it up when they tried to say his name, so he preferred Wally.

Wally was a larrikin. But a larrikin, as Jessica quickly discovered, who possessed a great knowledge of, and pride in, the culture of his people. After her initial surprise, she quickly warmed to Wally, it was difficult not to.

There were a number of ancient paintings in the region, he assured her, and he was only too happy to show them to her. 'Got some pretty good stuff around here, I can tell you, it'll open your eyes, I'll bet.'

By way of introduction, he took her north-east up the Oakover River and showed her the white sandstone columns of Hanging Rock. Temple-like, they stood pristine and gleaming as they had for centuries, nature's place of worship, mysterious and spiritual. Wally remained silent as she wandered amongst them and, when she returned, he whispered, 'Told you, good stuff eh?'

He took her on a tour of the waterholes and campsites where there were a number of drawings and, as Jessica had anticipated, with the use of ochre, the paintings of the desert people were far more colourful than those of their inland river cousins. In brilliant reds and yellows and oranges, the drawings were also more intricate and more detailed than the simple kaolin clay outlines she had seen on her previous trip.

She and Wally chatted avidly when they set up camp;

Wally liked a good chat. He was surprised and delighted when she told him her story.

'You don't look black,' he said, stating the obvious. 'Where you get that hair, all ginger like that? And them eyes. Green, they are, you got green eyes.' Jessica laughed, he said it as if she wasn't aware of the fact. Wally often made her laugh, mostly when he didn't intend to. 'Black people don't have green eyes.' He pursued his conversation in all seriousness. 'Where you come from, Jess?'

'My father was a drover. ' She smiled as she shrugged, 'Who knows? I sure as hell don't.'

It was in a cave near Nimberra Well that she found the symbol she'd been seeking. The oval shape. And within it was a vivid red mountain peak which met with a bright yellow sun. But, alongside the symbol, there was another painting which took her breath away. A ship with masts and, within its outline, the small figures of men indicating the size of the vessel. She knew of such paintings and rock carvings. Many existed. Some rock carvings on the coast at the Burrup Peninsula depicted men wearing hats which resembled helmets. Anthropologists had concluded that it was quite possible the Aborigines had been recording the arrival of the first European explorers. Spaniards? Dutch? French? William Dampier's men? Who could tell.

Jessica was overwhelmed with the excitement of her find. Here, in the desert region where there were no boats, was a picture of a massive sea-going vessel and alongside it a painting of the symbol she sought. Of course! The two were linked. The symbol had come from a European ship, it was an artifact of some kind. In one of the kaolin clay paintings it had been hanging about a man's neck. Was it some form of pendant? Had it come ashore amongst the flotsam of a shipwreck off the western coast of the continent? Many a Dutch merchant vessel had foundered on its hazardous route to the East Indies. If so, the pendant had become important enough to the Aborigines for them to record it in their paintings. What part had it played in their lives?

Wally, like the elders she'd encountered on her previous field trip, had no idea. 'No-one knows,' he said, 'no-one from round here anyway, just bin there for years, just a picture, you know?'

They returned to the mission and Jessica took her leave, eager to follow up her research in Perth.

Wally was sorry to see her go. 'You bin a good mate, Jess,' he said, 'had fun with you. Some of these do-gooders and people studying their stuff,' he gave a disinterested shrug, 'well you can tell they don't care, you know? But you different, you one of us, all right.'

'Thanks, Wally.' She was touched.

'You can call me Wallawambalyl if you like. That's my real name.'

'Wallawambalyl,' she said.

He grinned. 'You say it good, just like us.'

So she should, she thought, indigenous language had formed a major part of her studies over the past five years, but she didn't tell him that.

'Goodbye, Wallawambalyl.'

'Goodbye, Jess.'

Upon her return to Perth, Jessica researched the early Dutch shipwrecks off the Western Australian coast. The skeletal remains of the Batavia, *wrecked on the Houtman Abrolhos in 1629, had, after lengthy explorations, been discovered only nine years previously in 1963. A great deal had been written about the mutiny aboard the* Batavia *and the grisly fate of her passengers and crew. And, most interestingly, the riches of her cargo had been itemised. Piece by piece, jewel by jewel. She'd been carrying a king's ransom. Little wonder she'd proved such a temptation. But there was no mention of the pendant. Could it have been a personal item belonging to a passenger? Perhaps it had not*

*been washed up amongst the wreckage at all. Perhaps it
had come ashore with a survivor.*

*But further research proved that, according to the
journals of Commandeur Francisco Pelsaert which he'd
recorded after the trials and which were well documented,
only two men had been left behind. Eighteen-year-old Jan
Pelgrom de Bye, a cabin boy, and Wouter Loos, a soldier,
had been spared execution despite their involvement in the
mutiny, and had been marooned on the mainland and
left to their fate. It was unlikely that the pendant would
have belonged to either of them.*

Jessica turned her attention to the Verguide Draeck, *the
'Gilt Dragon' wrecked off Lancelin just north of Perth in
1656. A crew of seven had set sail in a small lifeboat
leaving sixty-eight survivors on the mainland, who were
never to be seen again. Then there was the* Zuytdorp,
*which had foundered against the cliffs near the mouth of
the Murchison River in 1712. As many as fifty survivors
had made it ashore from the* Zuytdorp *to the mainland to
fend for themselves. They too had disappeared. There was
no further record of any of these Europeans, but surely the
pendant had been the property of one of them.*

*The most exciting prospect of all resulted from Jessica's
further research into genetic differences which had been
noted in Aborigines, particularly amongst the coastal
people. Even a hundred years ago, the strange sight of
light-complexioned Aborigines with blue or green eyes and
fair or red hair had been documented, proof that shipwreck survivors had cohabited with the local natives and
a strain of 'European' Aborigines had resulted.*

*Jessica felt a chill run down her spine as she read it.
'Green eyes and red hair'. Five years ago she had
embarked upon her anthropology course as a means to
discover her black ancestry. Had she unintentionally been
tracing a white ancestor too? It was a fanciful notion, she
knew it, but it was thrilling nonetheless.*

*She was satisfied that she had finally pieced together
the story of the pendant drawings though. The pendant
had to have come ashore with a shipwreck survivor who
had been accepted by the black people and had lived
amongst them. They in turn must have acknowledged the
object as a personal talisman belonging to their clan; it was
therefore not a part of Aboriginal mythology.*

*Her history of the symbol was hypothetical, and she had
unearthed no mystery of Aboriginal culture, but Jessica's
eventual thesis received top marks and she graduated from
the University of Western Australia in early 1974 with a
Master of Arts in Anthropology.*

*But Jessica Williams left university with more than an
MA (Anthrop) to add to her name. She left with an obses-
sion to discover everything she could about the pendant.
Perhaps, one day, even its whereabouts.*

CHAPTER THIRTY-SIX

Terence Galloway was planning a new promotional campaign for the following year. But this time it would not be aimed at boosting sales. The advertising ploy had proved so successful that he was now, via the power of television, one of the most recognised faces in the Northern Territory. It was time to set his sights on the mayoral office. Terence determined that the following year of 1975 would see him the new mayor of Darwin.

He decided that he must prepare the ground before openly mounting his campaign, however, and the first step was a series of generous donations to a number of worthy causes. He found Aggie Marshall extremely helpful, knowing full well that, when he told her he expected no recognition, she made it secretly known that the anonymous benefactor was none other than Terence Galloway. Aggie always believed in giving credit where credit was due, and the word slowly spread that not only was Terence Galloway devoted to charitable concerns, but he expected no thanks.

Then of course his mistresses had to go, their discovery was not worth the risk. He gave Rose a month's wages and sacked her, warning Fran that, should her niece ever make any indiscreet remarks, she too would be given her walking orders.

He feared that Lisa Langello would not be so easy. The only reason the girl had kept her mouth shut this long had been because of his generosity. Terence's ego no longer deluded him, as it first had, that Lisa was a woman in love. She made her liking for money and the trappings that went with it all too obvious.

Lisa's position as 'the Emporium girl' and her exposure on NTD8 had been an easy cover for both her elevated circumstances and the truth of their relationship, but Terence now cursed himself. He'd been a fool to set her up in a flat and assume he could maintain the secrecy. At the time, however, he'd lusted after her so strongly that he'd have done anything to have her. And he had to admit that the sweaty Friday night couplings with a girl less than half his age had made him feel like a young buck again.

Now, eight months later, the novelty had worn off. Already she was an unnecessary threat to his reputation and next year, in his bid to become mayor, she could well prove his undoing. He'd warned her from the outset that if she ever told of their relationship he'd kill her. Just to put the fear of God into her. It had worked, he could tell, she was terrified. But who knew when she might babble on at the mouth with a few drinks in her. Lisa was a walking time bomb.

Terence cursed both his stupidity and his vanity for having landed him in such a predicament. He'd have to get Lisa Langello out of Darwin somehow. He pondered the situation and it didn't take long before he came up with the answer. He rang Sydney.

'You remember her, Greg,' he said, Greg hadn't recalled the name. 'We used her in the ad campaigns, the girl from the Emporium.' Terence laughed at Greg Sharman's response. 'Yes, that's right, great tits. Well I'm good mates with her dad and he asked whether I could pull a few strings for her.'

Terence had no idea who Lisa's father was, Kit had told him once that her family lived in Katherine and that she had nothing to do with them, that she hated her father. Probably some interference there, Terence had thought; hell, Lisa was made for interference.

'She's very keen to go to Sydney and break into the business, and her dad wondered whether I could help. Naturally I thought of you.' Greg probably wouldn't believe the father line, but Terence didn't particularly care.

Greg was not forthcoming, but Terence persevered. 'You're casting things, though, surely,' he said. Oh yes, Greg replied, they were always casting. 'Well just whack her in front of a camera. Give her a screen test, that'll keep her happy. She's really looking forward to a trip to Sydney, and her Dad'll pay the air fare and put her up for a while.'

Greg laughed, he'd got the message. 'Sure. Got to keep Dad happy, don't we?' he said.

All solved, Terence thought as he hung up. He had no fears of Lisa returning to Darwin when the job fell through. She'd have a taste for Sydney by then and some man would pick her up. She was that sort of girl.

It was a fresh September day, hot but not too humid, perfect Darwin weather, when Kit bumped into Lisa outside the Don Hotel. Although her flat was a little way out of town, she still worked at the Emporium and he'd often seen her around since they'd separated. She buzzed about Darwin in her little bright red MGB these days, the famous girl from the Galloway TV ads, and she was always bright and breezy, always the same old Lisa, but Kit had sensed somehow that she wasn't really happy. Today was different.

'Kit,' she exclaimed and she hugged him, 'how wonderful to see you, I was going to ring you to say goodbye and tell you the news.'

'Something fantastic obviously,' he said. She looked

radiantly happy. 'Don't tell me, I'll guess. You're engaged, and you're going away to get married.'

'Oh, better than that,' she scoffed, 'you can get married any day. I'm going to Sydney, I've got a test for a commercial. And if the first one takes off, it'll be a whole *series*. It's for a new line of chocolates, I forget the name, Caramel something.'

'That's great, Lisa.'

'It is, isn't it?' She was literally jumping up and down. 'I only found out the day before yesterday and I leave next week. It's that director, you remember? Greg Sharman?'

'I actually never met him, but I remember the name, he did Dad's commercials, didn't he.'

'Well he *wants* me! He's *asked* for me!'

Kit laughed, her enthusiasm was beguiling, she looked so fresh and so young. 'A star is born!' he announced. 'Lisa Langello,' she twirled in front of him, 'from Emporium Girl to Caramel Queen!' She squealed with delight. 'Let's have a drink to celebrate.'

'Only a quick one, I've got mountains of shopping to do. Although why I don't know,' she said as they walked into the Don arm in arm, 'I'm going to Sydney, shoppers' heaven.'

An hour and three white wines later, Kit reminded her that she had shopping to do.

'Oh my *God*, is that the *time*!' She hadn't noticed. She'd forgotten how much she loved being in Kit's company, he always made her feel beautiful, and she hadn't felt beautiful for a long time now.

Outside in the street, Kit hugged her goodbye. 'I'm so happy for you, Lisa,' he said.

'Thanks, Kit.' She knew that he meant it. 'Still love you a bit,' she said, and she kissed him before she whirled off in a flurry of excitement.

A month later, Kit received a phone call from his father asking him to come to the house for a photo session.

'Just a father and son shot,' Terence said, 'it won't take long. It's for a magazine article about me. Bit of a bore and I don't want to do it, but it's good for business.'

Kit obliged and they were photographed sitting together in the study, Terence's war photographs, of which there were many, dominant in the background. He looked every bit the proud father, arm draped over son's shoulder. Terence didn't bother telling Kit, but it was a further stratagem of the ground-laying plan for his mayoral campaign in the new year. The publicist he'd employed felt the creation of his image as a family man was important.

Several weeks later, the magazine article appeared and Kit was infuriated. 'A family of Territorians' it was headed. Well, he supposed that was all right, although he'd expected the article to be a profile on his father. But 'My Son the War Hero' in bold print beneath the picture of the two of them disgusted Kit. Terence was quoted as being deeply proud of his son's heroic deeds on the battlefield. 'My younger son is the greatest pride in my life,' he said. Then he spoke at length of his family's proud war record. His father had fought at Gallipoli, he himself had served as a fighter pilot in the Second World War. 'Just doing my duty,' he was humbly quoted as saying. And of course there was the grief he'd experienced with the death of his elder son in Vietnam. 'We've been a family serving our country,' he said nobly, 'and I know my son Kit joins me when I say that we're proud to be Australians. Even more so, Territorians.'

It was tasteless self-aggrandisement, and Kit barged into his father's office at the showrooms, slammed the magazine down on the table and told him so.

'They won't see it that way,' Terence replied. He'd been delighted with the article.

'Who won't?' Kit demanded.

'The general public. The people who are going to vote me in as mayor.'

Kit stared at his father. He should have known. Terence Galloway always had an ulterior motive.

'They'll see us quite rightfully as a family of war heroes,' Terence continued implacably. Kit's annoyance didn't upset him one bit. It was too late now, the article was out there and there was nothing he could do about it. 'I don't know why you're upset,' he smiled, 'you should be delighted that I'm so proud of you.'

'You're not proud of me,' Kit said, 'you never have been.' He continued to stare at his father, suddenly aware that he detested the man. Why had he never realised it before? 'And from now on, when you want to use people to further your own gain, leave me out.'

Terence shrugged and said, 'Fair enough.' But he said it to the air. Kit had stormed out of the office.

Shortly before Christmas, on a Saturday morning, there was a knock at Kit's door. He opened it to find an Aboriginal woman standing there. Probably early middle-aged, but she could have been sixty. Slovenly, ill-kempt, in a tattered dress, greying hair matted, she presented a lost and forlorn figure.

Kit was currently writing a feature article on the tragic plight of many of Darwin's indigenous population, a subject close to Jim Bowditch's heart, and the two of them were committed to the importance of the story. He wondered briefly if the woman's arrival had something to do with the article. Had she been sent to see him by one of the many contacts he'd used for research? If so, he wondered why they'd not telephoned him.

'Hello,' he said, waiting for her to introduce herself, but she didn't.

'You're Kit Galloway, aren't you?' she asked.

'Yes.'

'You don' remember me I bet, but I met you coupla times when I come to Bullalalla to visit Mum.'

He looked at her blankly, obviously puzzled.

'My Mum, Nellie,' she said. 'I'm Pearl.'

'Pearl! Of course I remember you. Come in.' He didn't really remember her. He had vague memories, as a small child, of an attractive young woman with two babies who used to visit Nellie from time to time. But he most certainly remembered Nellie. And Jackie. This was Nellie's and Jackie's daughter Pearl. Good God, he thought, she looked so old!

He ushered her to the table by the window and she sat gingerly on the edge of one of the chairs, the small string bag she carried clutched in her lap.

'Can I get you a cup of tea, Pearl?'

'Don' wanna be no trouble.' She looked rather sullen, as if she didn't want to be there. So what on earth had prompted her to come, Kit wondered.

'No trouble, I was just about to get one for myself, I'll make a pot, eh?' He chatted away amiably as he filled the electric jug, trying to put her at her ease. 'It's lovely to see you, how are your kids? They must be all grown up now.'

'Nineteen and twenty,' she said, still without the vestige of a smile, but he could sense she was relaxing a little. 'How old are you?'

'Twenty-six.'

'Yeh, you were only little when I used to visit Mum.'

'And how's Nellie?' Kit asked, 'she must be getting on.'

'She's dead.'

'Oh. I'm sorry to hear that.'

'She bin dead for a long time,' Pearl shrugged, 'seven, eight years. Dad's still alive, but.' She scowled momentarily, it was because of her dad she was here when she didn't want to be. Kit Galloway was being very nice, though, it was good that he remembered her kids. 'Dad always liked you,' she said.

'I always liked him too, Pearl.' Memories flooded back. *You get 'im here, Kit.* Jackie's black thumb pressed against the steer's skull. *You get 'im here, 'im feel no pain.* Jackie picking him up from the ground, his shoulder aching like hell, *you kill 'im good, Kit.*

'He's a fine man, your father.' Kit brought the teapot and two cups to the table. 'How is he these days?'

'Don' see him much. He's gone Warai, lives out in the bush most of the time. Won't work for whites anymore, not since Mum died. He comes in to see me sometimes, though.' She said it with pride.

Pearl and her husband lived in a shanty on the outskirts of town, and the fact that her father visited her was a testament to his love. Jackie Yoorunga was highly respected amongst the black community and he didn't approve of Pearl's husband Eddie and his mates, who were drunk more often than not. Jackie would have nothing to do with those he considered had strayed from the path. 'No way for black fellas to live, Pearl,' he'd said time and again. 'They got no pride for themselves.' *Easy for you to say,* Pearl would think. Her Eddie used to be a good drover, but where was the work for drovers now? And when the St Vincent de Paul's in Stuart Park found him odd-job work, labouring or gardening, she'd have to scrounge whatever she could from his pay before it went on grog. Eddie drank 'cos there was nuthin' else for him to do. *Easy for you to say,* Pearl would think, but she never answered back to her dad. Her dad didn't know what it was like.

Kit fetched the milk and sugar and poured the tea.

'You not married,' Pearl said, looking around at the small apartment, it was not a question.

'No, not yet.'

'You got a girlfriend?'

It appeared she wanted to chat and, although he was still curious as to the reason for her visit, Kit was quite happy to oblige. 'I did have,' he said, 'but we broke up and she went to Sydney.'

Pearl asked what he did and he told her he worked for the newspaper. He asked about her husband and her family, but she obviously didn't want to talk about herself.

'Seen your dad's shops when I come into town,' she said, very impressed. 'I seen your dad on TV too.'

She was probably after money, Kit thought. He'd certainly give her some, although he worried that it might be spent on alcohol.

Eventually, when they'd finished their tea, Pearl said 'I gotta go now. Jus' come 'round to give you this.' She lifted a small crumpled parcel of newspaper out of her string bag and pushed it across the table to him.

Kit opened it. Inside was a locket. The heavy silver was tarnished, it needed a good clean, but the diamonds sparkled with a breathtaking brilliance. A mountain basking in the light of a diamond sun, it was a beautiful piece.

'Where did you get it?' he asked. He was worried. Had she stolen it? Was she trying to sell it to him?

Pearl rose from the table. She wanted to leave. 'It belong to the missus.'

'What missus?'

'She give it to my dad. She told him she wanted you to have it.' Pearl didn't want to answer any questions, and she knew no more than her mother had told her. 'You give this to Kit Galloway in two years' time, Pearl,' Nellie had instructed her daughter as she lay on her deathbed. She had known that, when she died, Jackie would return to the bush, but her Pearl was a good girl, she could rely on her Pearl. 'The missus wanted Kit to have it. "When he comes of age", that's what the missus said to your dad,' Nellie had told her daughter.

'*Who* gave it to your dad?' Kit asked, frustrated. '*What* missus?' He needed answers and Pearl was backing towards the door.

'Your mum. It belong to your mum. My dad said I gotta

give it to you.' She had to get out before he asked her why she'd kept it so long. 'I gotta go now.'

She was out the door in a flash and Kit raced after her. 'Pearl!' he called. 'Pearl!'

But Pearl was tearing down the street as fast as her legs could carry her and she wasn't looking back. Apart from running her down and physically stopping her, there was nothing Kit could do. He went back inside to examine the locket. If there was no evidence of his mother's ownership, he'd take it to the police and perhaps they could trace the rightful owner.

Pearl didn't look back until she'd turned the corner and run another two full blocks. Then, panting from her exertion, she glanced behind and slowed down, thankful that he hadn't followed. She was safe now. Not only safe from any questions about why she'd kept the locket, but safe from the warning curse of her father, which had so terrified her.

'You steal from a dead person, Pearl,' he'd said. Jackie had been shocked when he'd discovered her wearing the locket.

Talk about bad luck, Pearl had thought when her father fronted up to the shanty. She hadn't seen him for a year and she never wore the locket. Not when people were around anyway. Eddie had always been on at her to sell it for grog money so she'd told him she'd lost it. He hadn't believed her and he'd bashed her around a bit. He only ever bashed her when he was bad on the grog, and he was always sorry after. So she'd scrounged all the money she could and told him she'd sold it. He'd stopped nagging her after that. Now she only ever wore the locket when she was on her own. It was such a pretty thing and it made her feel happy.

'No honour in what you done,' her father had said, staring at the locket, 'bad things gonna happen to you, Pearl.' Then he'd looked at her and his eyes had seemed to burn into her skull. 'Bad, bad things.' She'd felt a shiver of terror. 'You find Kit Galloway, and you give that to him from his mother's grave,' Jackie had warned her. "Cos if you don't, you dead yourself, Pearl.'

As Pearl trudged through the streets of Darwin on the long walk home she felt a vast sense of relief. She'd miss the locket, it was so pretty, but at least she was rid of the curse.

Kit sat at the table examining the locket. It was heavy for such a small piece, and valuable if the diamonds were real, which they certainly appeared to be. He turned it over, there was a personal insignia engraved on the back. He fetched the magnifying plate from his atlas. Two tiny g's. Would the craftsman be traceable, he wondered. Perhaps not, the locket appeared very old.

He tried to open it, but the catch had seized up a little and he didn't want to force it. He worked some oil into the clasp and hinge and, after several attempts, it opened to reveal two photographs. They were faded with age but undamaged, the locket's perfect seal having protected them from the elements.

Kit recognised his mother in an instant. So Pearl had been right, the locket had been his mother's. But who was the man? He presumed that the locket dated back prior to the marriage of his mother and father. The man was possibly his mother's first love. He found the thought moving. And she looked so young, so young and so very beautiful.

The man's face seemed familiar. In a weird way it reminded Kit a little of himself. Not the face he saw in the mirror, but the way he sometimes appeared in a photograph. Strange how photographs capture an aspect altogether different from the way one sees oneself, he thought. Who the hell could it be?

Through the magnifying plate, he looked closely at the eyes and the mouth, there was an expression there he knew. The glint of humour in the eye, the slight sardonic curve to the lip. Then he realised. It was Paul Trewinnard. He'd known Paul only as an old man, prematurely aged by his illness. But here, in the locket, the face which gazed back at him was undoubtedly that of the younger Paul Trewinnard.

CHAPTER THIRTY-SEVEN

Jessica Williams' introduction to Darwin had been a violent one. She'd been warned of the monsoon season and had felt fully prepared for the onslaught but, as Cyclone Zelma had buffeted Darwin, Jessica, like most newcomers to the Territory, had been overwhelmed by the vehemence of nature's attack.

'Ah that was nothing,' old cynics boasted, 'we've had worse and we will again.' 'It was a pretty bad one,' others assured her, 'they're not always like that.' Yet others told her, in a blasé fashion, that the warnings which were regularly broadcast on radio and television meant nothing more often than not. 'Most of the time the cyclones head out west, we cop a bit of the flak, but no real damage.'

Jessica wasn't sure who to believe. But thanks to Cyclone Zelma, she was prepared these days. A good torch and a ready supply of candles and batteries in the event of power failure, and she tuned in regularly to the ABC's warning broadcasts, of which there were many lately. As Christmas approached warnings abounded and Jessica was astonished that the locals took such little notice.

'It's always the same this time of the year,' she was assured.

Jessica was returning to Perth for Christmas and, if the current warnings were to prove true, she hoped she'd be well clear before the next cyclone hit, she had found Zelma terrifying.

Apart from Zelma, however, Jessica had thoroughly enjoyed her time in Darwin. On a research grant from the Commonwealth Department of Aboriginal Affairs, she had spent the past two months compiling data on Aboriginal art as a means of historical record. The Top End was the home of a wealth of indigenous art and the work had been stimulating. So had Darwin, where she'd stationed herself for this particular leg of her research trip.

Although she'd always made friends with ease, Jessica found the Darwinese particularly hospitable, only too ready to welcome a stranger in their midst. And she'd quickly realised that Darwin itself dictated an easygoing attitude. Was it just the lazy heat of the tropics? But then the weather was hardly lazy, it was a constant drama, certainly during the monsoon season. Perhaps it was the very drama itself, dished out by the elements on a daily basis, which bonded the Darwinese. Whatever it was, Darwin was unique. As she told her father over the telephone, there was 'something about Darwin'.

She'd finished her assignment and was filling in the last day before her return to Perth. Reneging on the offer of a long boozy lunch—her new-found Darwin friends certainly knew how to drink and she was feeling a little seedy from the preceding night—she took herself off to the library.

Browsing was one of Jessica's favourite pastimes, particularly browsing through the history of a place as fascinating as the Northern Territory and, two hours later, she'd lost all track of time as she found herself locked in The Rise and Fall of Darwin's Pioneering Families. *Written by a journalist, Robert Ashworth, in the 1950s, it was a riveting mixture of gossip and history. She turned a page and read, beneath the picture of an extraordinarily*

handsome bearded man, 'The Sullivans, a family in tur-
moil'. Then a picture on the opposite page caught her eye.

She stared down at it unable to believe what she saw.
It was a photograph of an antique locket, and depicted on
the face of the locket was the symbol she'd seen in the
Aboriginal paintings. There was no mistaking it.

Jessica had continued her search for the elusive symbol
wherever she'd gone, showing people her photographs of
the Aboriginal artwork and making endless enquiries, but
she'd always come up against a dead end. She'd almost
given up on her quest, and now here it was staring out at
her from a book in the Darwin library. The crystal clear
picture of a mountain peak and a brilliant sun. And they
were engraved on an antique locket.

So her theory of the symbol being a pendant of some
kind had been correct, she thought. But how had the
locket come to Darwin? How had it changed hands?

Pulse racing with excitement, she read the brief history
of the Sullivan family, curbing her desire to skip through
to the section on the opposite page which pertained to
the locket. The Sullivans had started a highly successful
surveying company in Darwin's early days. The family
patriarch, Benjamin Sullivan, had been an eminent
surveyor, indeed a member of Goyder's team, and had
settled in Darwin to become a prominent citizen.

The early surveyors, of course, Jessica thought. There
had been a great deal of contact between the blacks and
the first white surveyors. So that was how the locket had
changed hands. Perhaps by force, perhaps by barter, Ben-
jamin himself had acquired the locket from the Aborigines.

She read on. In 1939, Matthew Sullivan had sued his
son and a Chinese shopkeeper over the theft of a valuable
locket, professing that he himself had purchased it for his
mother. But the defence had proved that Matthew's father,
Benjamin, had given the locket to his wife upon their
marriage. The case had been thrown out of court and the

Sullivan name made a laughing stock through Matthew's greed and his implied perjury.

So who now had the locket, Jessica wondered. The son? What was his name, she searched the page, Thomas, that was it. No, it would surely be the property of the Chinese shopkeeper who had purchased it. Once again she searched the page. Foong Lee. She wondered if he was still alive. He'd had a shop in Chinatown before the war. She enquired at the front desk of the library.

'There was a Mr Foong who had a shop in Chinatown in the late thirties,' she said. 'Would you know if it's still here?'

The young girl had no idea, she was relatively new to Darwin, but she wanted to be helpful so she fetched old Jack from out the back. Jack was a walking history book, she said.

Jessica introduced herself and once again enquired after Mr Foong's shop in Chinatown.

'Heavens above no,' Jack said, 'Chinatown was obliterated in the bombing, all the shops went and the Government didn't bother building them again. I think they were glad to see them gone,' he added with a touch of disapproval.

'Oh.' She was about to ask after the Sullivan family when Jack continued.

'Of course Foong Lee himself built another shop, without any Government assistance, immediately after the war. I don't know if that's of any help.'

'Is he still alive?'

'Oh yes, very much so.'

'Were you talking about Foong Lee?' the young girl interrupted. Jessica nodded. 'You should have said,' she smiled, 'everyone knows Foong Lee. He owns the Golden Dragon in Cavenagh Street. It's a restaurant, but no-one calls it the Golden Dragon, it's known as Foong Lee's. He's very famous around Darwin.'

'*I think Miss Williams was enquiring about Mr Foong's shop, Alice,*' Jack said, annoyed that she'd stolen his thunder.

'*Thank you, Alice, you've been very helpful,*' Jessica said. Poor Alice looked severely put in her place. '*Would I find Mr Foong at the restaurant?*'

'*Yes, he's always there,*' Alice beamed. '*It's in Cavenagh Street, near the corner of Knuckey, you can't miss it.*'

'*Thank you so much. And thank you too, Jack.*' Jessica hurriedly departed, leaving the two of them to sort out their differences.

CHAPTER THIRTY-EIGHT

It was four o'clock in the afternoon and Foong Lee had just returned to the restaurant having popped out to the post office to collect his overseas newspapers. They were sent to him regularly in batches, and he was very much looking forward to settling down with a pot of *heung ping* and the overseas news, he always enjoyed the afternoon lull between lunch and dinner, and the papers made the prospect doubly pleasurable.

As he was about to pull the door closed behind him, he saw Kit Galloway crossing the street. He didn't bother calling out to gain his attention, it was obvious that Kit was heading directly for the restaurant. How nice, Foong Lee thought, he was coming to visit, the papers could wait.

But Kit wasn't coming to visit. In fact he walked right past Foong Lee without even seeing him. He was probably preoccupied by whatever assignment he'd been on, Foong Lee told himself, Kit was always very passionate about his work. But in his distraction, he'd appeared worried. Foong Lee didn't call after him, not wishing to interfere. Perhaps when he next saw Aggie he might make some discreet enquiries, he thought as he closed the door; if anyone would know what was troubling Kit it would most certainly be Aggie.

Only seconds later, there was a tap at the door. Foong Lee hoped it was Kit. But then he saw, through the glass with the red-painted dragon on it, the form of a young woman. The restaurant hours were clearly marked on the window for all to read, but Foong Lee never put up the 'closed' sign. He left it to his own discretion whether or not to turn people away. If he liked the look of them, or felt in the mood, he might invite them in for *heung ping*, to while away an hour or so before the evening trade. Today, with the overseas newspapers before him, he decided to tell the young woman the restaurant was closed.

He opened the door. 'I'm so sorry,' he said, 'but we're not open until half past six.'

'I realise that, but I wonder if I might have a quick word with you,' she entreated. 'You're Mr Foong, aren't you?'

'Yes I am,' Foong Lee said. What an extraordinary looking young woman, he thought. Hair the colour of copper and eyes of jade, she was not only attractive, but her origins intrigued him. She was not Irish as some might presume, she was a strange mixture. Pale-skinned admittedly, but there was a fullness to her perfectly shaped upper lip, and a curve to the nostrils of her aquiline nose. He'd seen many white blacks before, and he wondered whether perhaps she might have Aboriginal blood in her. White blacks were usually very attractive, he'd found. Like Eurasians. Nature was prone to choose the best features from both races. Most intriguing.

'Come in, my dear, may I interest you in a cup of jasmine tea?' There was always time to read the papers.

Jessica stepped into the restaurant where the overhead fans created a welcome breeze from the sweltering stillness of the day. 'Thank you, Mr Foong,' she said, 'that would be lovely.'

She watched him as he made the tea. He was a small,

neat man, rather like a penguin, she thought, and she wondered at his age. He looked no more than sixty but he had to be much older. And there was a warmth about him, an old-world courtesy.

'My name is Jessica Williams,' she said as he ushered her to a table by the windows. 'I've been in Darwin for two months on a research trip.'

'And what can I do for you, Miss Williams?' he asked, sitting opposite her and pouring the tea.

'I've just come from the library,' she said. 'And I was reading about the Sullivan family in a book called *The Rise and Fall of Darwin's Pioneering Families* . . .'

'Ah yes,' Foong Lee smiled, 'Robert Ashworth. He was rather unpopular with a number of people after that was published, particularly the Sullivans. They wanted to sue him but they couldn't, he'd got all his facts right, you see.' He chortled, his eyes disappearing into mirthful slits as he recalled Matthew Sullivan's outrage. 'However, Miss Williams, if you're researching Darwin's pioneers, I can suggest a number of books with a little more depth and a little less sensationalism than Mr Ashworth's.'

'I'm not actually an historian, Mr Foong,' she corrected him, 'I'm an anthropologist. I specialise in Aboriginal anthropology.'

'Oh? How very interesting.' He was pleased that he'd been correct, Jessica Williams was Aboriginal, he was sure of it. Foong Lee always prided himself on his powers of observation, particularly when it came to a person's origins. But then one saw such a mixed bag in Darwin, it became quite easy after years of practice.

'And it's not the Sullivans I'm interested in,' she continued, 'it's the locket which the family went to court over. The locket which you yourself had purchased at the time.'

'More and more interesting,' Foong Lee said, plainly fascinated. 'What part could a seventeenth-century locket play in Aboriginal anthropology?' he asked.

'Seventeenth-century?' Jessica felt the familiar quickening of her pulse, could this be another step in the right direction? 'Are you sure?'

'Fairly sure, yes. An educated guess, mind you, I never did have it authenticated. But I'd say seventeenth-century, and the work of a Dutch master craftsman.'

'Oh!' Jessica beamed, she wanted to kiss him. Surely it was proof that her theory of the symbol had been correct. An artifact bearing its image had come ashore from one of the early Dutch shipwrecks. 'Mr Foong,' she said a little breathlessly, 'do you still have the locket? Please. Please may I see it?'

'Sadly, no, my dear, I'm afraid the locket is no longer in my possession.' He knew she was about to ask him where it was, how she could find it, but he cut her off even as she mouthed the question. 'Perhaps you could tell me a little of your interest which appears so avid.'

Jessica realised she'd been grilling him. He really was owed an explanation, he'd been so kind and patient. 'Of course,' she said, 'I'm sorry, it's just that I'm excited about getting so close to it after all this time.'

She told him about her discovery of the simple kaolin clay outlines early in her university studies, then her later discovery of the ochre paintings and the theories she'd developed over the years. He watched her as she spoke, she was so passionate.

When she finally came to the end of her story, Jessica felt the need to once again apologise. 'I'm sorry, I've carried on a bit, haven't I? But it's become an obsession with me.'

'Don't apologise, my dear, may I call you Jessica?'

'Of course,' she said, a little taken aback by the non sequitur, but charmed nonetheless.

'And I am Foong Lee,' he said with a gracious bow of his head which she took as a signal that they were friends. 'I'm very much afraid, Jessica, that I cannot tell you the locket's whereabouts.'

She stared at him. Cannot or would not, she wondered. His tone, although kind, was final.

'I cannot tell you, simply because I don't know,' he said. 'I gave it to my very dearest friend, a man by the name of Paul Trewinnard, and he has since died. Many years ago now.'

'Do you have any contact you could give me?' she asked desperately. To have come so close! 'His family, anyone who might know . . .'

'Certainly you would have no trouble getting in touch with his blood relatives. Trewinnard's is a well-known family firm of solicitors operating in both London and Singapore, as they have for the past fifty years or more. But I'm afraid it would do you little good,' he dashed her hopes as soon as he'd raised them. 'Paul had no contact with his family. He was a solitary man.'

Her disappointment was clearly profound and Foong Lee wished he could tell her the truth. He would like to have told her that Paul Trewinnard had given the locket to a beautiful woman called Henrietta Galloway. That the locket had symbolised the great love they had shared. He would have enjoyed telling such a love story to this passionate young woman. But the story was not his to tell, it was a story which endangered too many people.

'I'm sorry that I'm unable to take you to the locket, Jessica,' he said, 'I would if I could, I'd like very much to be present when you saw it.'

Why did he seem to know more than he was saying, Jessica wondered.

'However,' Foong Lee continued, 'I can tell you a great deal about it which I'm sure will enable you to trace its origins. Do you have a pen and paper?'

'Of course.' She took out the notebook she always carried in her oversized shoulder bag.

He gave her an intricate description of the locket. Its size, weight, silver content, and diamond carat value, all of which he'd evaluated before he'd bought it. He also gave her details of the craftsman's insignia, two small g's, and the initials engraved inside, 'L v.d. M and B v.d. M'.

'It should be easy enough to trace,' he said. 'The initials appear Dutch, and I would suggest you start your search in Amsterdam. Amsterdam was the home of the true diamond cutters and master craftsmen of the seventeenth century.'

Jessica looked up from the notes she'd been scribbling at the rate of knots. She didn't know how to thank him. With this detail she knew she'd be able to trace the locket. The fact that she would never see it was a personal disappointment, but she would know its origins. And that was, after all, she told herself, the most important part of her search. To tie up all the links. She was greatly indebted to him.

'Thank you, Foong Lee,' she said. 'You don't know what this means to me.'

'I'm sure I don't, a passion like yours can be hard to fathom for we non-academics.' He seemed to study her for a moment before continuing. 'I would suggest, however, that such a passion goes far deeper than your academic studies.' Foong Lee knew he was being presumptuous, but he liked to prove himself right. 'Could it perhaps have something to do with the discovery of your people?'

Jessica was astonished. In the whole of her life, no-one, either black or white, had ever guessed at her Aboriginal ancestry. 'My mother was a Yamatji woman,' she said. 'How did you know?'

'It's a hobby of mine,' Foong Lee smiled, very pleased with himself. 'We are such a mixed breed here in Darwin, people's origins are a constant source of interest for me and guessing has become a habit. Will you join me in a fresh pot of tea?'

'I'd love to,' she said. She meant it, she could have talked to the old Chinese for hours, 'but I have to get home and do some packing, I leave for Perth first thing tomorrow.'

'Very wise,' he said, 'with the cyclone coming.'

'Do you think it'll hit Darwin? Everyone seems very blasé.'

'Who knows?' Foong Lee shrugged, 'they're such mercurial things, cyclones, but yes, I think it will.'

'Thank you, Foong Lee.' They shook hands. 'You've been a wonderful help.'

'I only wish I could have done more,' he said.

Was there the faintest hint of regret in his voice, she wondered? Once again she had the vague feeling there was something he wasn't telling her. She rummaged in the side pocket of her shoulder bag.

'I'll leave my card with you,' she said, 'just in case anything else comes to mind.' His expression was quizzical and Jessica was certain that he knew what she was thinking. She found herself rattling on a little self-consciously. 'And of course if you ever come to Perth, I do hope you'll ring me, I'd love to see you, I've enjoyed our chat.'

'Perth,' he said as he took the card. He seemed most interested. 'A very pretty place, Perth.'

'You know it well?'

'No. But I've visited a number of times, I have friends who live there.' As he opened the door for her, she couldn't resist impulsively kissing him on the cheek, and it obviously pleased him.

'Goodbye, Foong Lee, and thanks again.'

'Good luck with your search, Jessica.' He stood deep in thought as he watched her walk down the street.

Two days after Jessica's departure, Foong Lee was concerned that his weather prediction may prove ominously correct. On the morning of Christmas Eve, the cyclone was given a name. She was called Tracy. And although most remained heedless of the warnings, convinced that Tracy would alter her path, Foong Lee, always a man of caution, telephoned his son.

'You will bring the family around and stay the night with your mother and me, Albert,' he said.

The large storage cellar beneath Foong Lee's house, which had been built following the Japanese attack on Darwin, was constructed to also serve as a shelter. It was protection against bombs or cyclones or anything else that might threaten his family, and in the case of Tropical Cyclone Tracy, Foong Lee was taking no chances, particularly with the safety of his beloved grandchildren.

Kit Galloway had more on his mind than an impending cyclone. For three days he had agonised over the locket and what it signified. He'd gazed for hours at the photographs of his mother and the man who must surely have been her lover. He recalled the resemblance he'd initially recognised between himself and Paul Trewinnard. Was it possible that this man was his father? If so, the ramifications were immense. Had his mother lived a lie for fourteen years? Or had her husband known from the outset? It would certainly explain Terence Galloway's antipathy towards him. For as long as Kit could remember he'd felt alienated from his father. Had Paul Trewinnard himself known? Kit recalled, with vivid clarity, their last meeting at Mindil Beach when he'd known that Paul was dying. He remembered the fervour with which the non-demonstrative man had returned his hug. Had Paul been saying goodbye to his son?

The more Kit pondered the subject, the more he convinced himself that Paul Trewinnard was his father. And the more he gazed upon the locket, the more tortured he became in his desire for the truth. He must know. It was his right to know.

There was only one person able to put his mind at rest. Terence Galloway. But what if his mother had lived the lie until the end? What if his father had never known the truth? Should Kit confront him with the proof of his wife's infidelity and the knowledge that he'd raised a son not his own?

Then Kit thought of his mother. She had wished him to have the locket, hadn't she? She had wanted her son to know the truth.

Kit spent the days in an agony of indecision until finally he could bear it no longer. He decided to confront his father.

It was Christmas Eve when he drove out to Larrakeyah. Late in the afternoon. A restless day, ominous and threatening. The weather report which had appeared in that day's edition of the *Northern Territory News* had run only three paragraphs. Tropical Cyclone Tracy was currently 150 kilometres north-west of Darwin, with winds of 120 kilometres an hour buffeting Bathurst Island. Little attention had been paid to the report.

Terence, Scotch in hand, was sitting on the first-floor verandah looking out over the harbour and the blackening sky. Certainly cyclone weather, he thought, but it wouldn't reach them, it wouldn't get past Bathurst Island.

He was surprised when the Kingswood pulled up. He hadn't seen much of Kit lately. There'd been a definite cooling between them since the magazine article and the confrontation which had followed its publication. Not that Terence particularly cared, it was simply further proof of the gulf which existed between him and the boy. By God, he'd thought, how proud Malcolm would have been of that article. Malcolm was a Galloway, with true Galloway pride. And how staunchly Malcolm would have supported him in his forthcoming mayoral campaign. Kit's reaction had irked Terence. The ungrateful young bastard didn't know how lucky he was to bear the Galloway name.

'Well, well, well,' he said, rising from his chair as Kit walked up the steps to the verandah, 'the prodigal son returns.' He gave a hearty beam, there was no point in further alienating the boy, the family image remained

important. 'How nice to see you, what are you drinking?'
He slung an arm around Kit and hooked his hand over his
son's shoulder. Although much slighter in build, Kit stood
a good four inches taller than Terence. 'Scotch? Beer?' he
offered as they walked inside to the lounge room.

Kit had intended confronting his father with the locket
the moment he arrived, but given the enthusiasm of his
welcome, it was difficult.

'Beer thanks, Dad,' he found himself saying. Christ, how
the hell was he to go about it?

'Fran!' Terence bellowed, topping up his Scotch from
the bottle on the sideboard, and she instantly appeared.
'Bring a beer for our boy.'

'Hello, Kit,' she said, pleased to see him.

'G'day, Fran.'

'So what are you getting up to tonight?' Terence asked,
'Want to come to a dinner party? Posh affair, I can tell you.
Who's who there, great food, great booze.' It would look
good if Kit was with him, he thought.

'Sounds great,' Kit said, it sounded awful, 'but Maxie's
having a party and I promised I'd go.'

'Oh yes, I know the sort of thing,' Terence kept up the
bonhomie, 'a right bloody pissup.' He gave a laugh which
sounded decidedly mirthless. 'Darwin on a Christmas Eve,
eh?'

'Yes it'll probably be like that,' Kit admitted. The beer
arrived. 'Thanks Fran.'

Terence wondered what Kit's reply would be if he
said, 'Hey son I'd really like you to come with me tonight
as a favour, politics, you know what I mean?' The boy
would simply say 'no thanks, Dad', he knew it. Malcolm
would never have said that. Malcolm would have done
anything he'd asked.

He looked at Kit with disdain, but the smile remained
painted on his lips. 'Well, cheers, happy Christmas and all
that.' He clinked his glass against Kit's and they drank.

'So to what do I owe the honour?' he said, 'Have you got a Christmas present for me?'

Kit recognised the sarcasm, just as he recognised the fact that his father was angry with him. He was supposed to have accepted the invitation to dinner, but he could hardly do so under the circumstances, could he? Not that he would have accepted under normal circumstances. Oh hell, he told himself, just bite the bloody bullet.

'There's something I want to show you, Dad,' he said, depositing his beer on a coffee table and taking the locket, which he'd carefully cleaned and wrapped in a white handkerchief, from the top pocket of his shirt. 'And there's something I need to ask you. Could we turn on that lamp?' The light was dim in the gathering gloom of the afternoon.

Damn the boy's peremptory tone, Terence thought, but he put down his Scotch, crossed to the standard lamp in the corner and turned it on.

Kit unwrapped the locket and held it beneath the light from the lamp. He shoved the handkerchief back into his pocket, then carefully pressed the locket's clasp. It was only when he had opened it to display the photographs inside that he looked at his father.

Terence Galloway was staring in stupefaction at the locket. He appeared to be in a state of complete disbelief.

So his father hadn't known, Kit thought. His father hadn't known that his wife had had a lover. Damn, he should have been a bit more subtle. He wondered whether he should suggest that perhaps the locket dated from a time previous to their marriage. No, he decided, he wasn't here to mollify his father and invent explanations. He needed answers, even if the answers were hurtful to Terence Galloway. And if Terence Galloway himself hadn't known, which it appeared he hadn't, then surely he too deserved the truth after all these years.

'It's Paul Trewinnard, Dad,' he said. There was no need to explain any further the image in the locket, his father was staring at it, mesmerised, obviously aware of its implications.

In the horrifying instant Terence had seen the locket in the palm of Kit's hand, he had remembered the moment when he'd pressed his wife's fingers around that very same locket. It had been the moment before he'd killed her. *How could it be here?* his mind screamed. Then, as he'd watched Kit open the locket, he'd fought back his panic. There had to be a reasonable explanation for its reappearance. His frenzied brain churned with a dozen scenarios. *Someone had found the body! So why hadn't they reported it? They hadn't reported it because they'd stolen the locket, yes, that made sense. So why had the locket come to light now? Why was it being returned to him after all these years?* Then the sickening realisation struck home. *Someone knew the truth! They'd sent the locket as a signal. Was it money they wanted? Was it blackmail?*

Kit had said something but Terence didn't hear what it was. 'Where did you get that?' he demanded in a menacing growl.

Kit hoped that his father wasn't about to have one of his fits of rage, it would serve neither of them any purpose if he did. They needed to talk calmly and reasonably, to unveil the secrets of the past and find the answers which both of them deserved to know.

'It belonged to Mum,' he said. 'She and Paul Trewinnard . . .' Surely he didn't need to spell it out.

'I said where did you get it?' Terence tore his eyes away from the locket and glared at his son.

Did that really matter? Kit wondered. 'Someone gave it to me,' he said.

'Who?'

Kit recognised something else in his father's face besides rage. Was it fear?

'Who, boy? You tell me right now, who gave you that locket?'

'It doesn't matter who, Dad,' Kit didn't want to get Pearl into trouble. She'd been clearly frightened when she'd returned the locket, better to leave her out of the equation, he thought. 'We just need to recognise the truth,' he said. 'Both of us.'

The familiar madness had come upon Terence, and Kit's composure now infuriated him. He lunged at the locket. 'Give me that thing, you sanctimonious little prick!'

But Kit was too quick for him. He snatched the locket away from Terence's grasp. 'For God's sake, be reasonable,' he yelled, although it appeared that Terence Galloway was beyond all reason. 'It doesn't matter who gave it to me! Mum wanted me to have it!'

Terence had been about to hurl himself at Kit and wrestle the locket from him, but he was stopped in his tracks.

She wanted him to have it! She'd lived long enough to give the locket to someone. Again the realisation rocked him. *And whoever she had given it to as she lay dying knew that Henrietta Galloway had been murdered. Who was it? Who knew that Terence Galloway had killed his wife?*

As his mind screamed the question, Terence forced himself to keep calm. He needed answers.

'Who told you that she wanted you to have the locket, Kit?'

But Kit appeared not to have heard the question. 'She wanted me to know the truth, Dad,' he said, relieved that his father had regained his composure.

Terence froze at the words. *What truth?* He stared at his son. *Did Kit himself know? Was Kit attempting to black-mail him?*

'What truth?' he asked, his voice now deadly calm. He'd kill the boy if need be.

Someone had to say it out loud, Kit thought. The locket's implication must have occurred to his father. He'd been quite sure it had, given Terence Galloway's stunned reaction, but the man seemed unable to admit it. Kit took a deep breath. 'The truth that Paul Trewinnard was my father.'

Terence continued to glare at him with eyes glassy and menacing. Was that all the boy needed to know? Surely whoever had given him the locket had said something about his mother's death.

'I'm sorry, Dad.' Kit took his father's silence as shock. 'It came as a shock to me too. I actually thought you might have known yourself all this time, but . . .' His voice trailed off. The expression on his father's face was enigmatic. Was he still angry? Was he hurt? It was impossible to tell. '. . . but I believe it's the truth. I believe that Paul Trewinnard was my natural father.'

Terence wanted to laugh out loud with relief. The boy knew nothing. Whether someone had stolen the locket or whether they'd been given it by the dying Henrietta, they had said nothing. And that same someone had now relinquished the locket. In Terence's fixated mind, the only proof of her murder was the locket itself, and it was right here in front of him for the taking.

'Of course Trewinnard was your father,' he said. Kit was obviously desperate for an answer, might as well tell him. 'But don't blab it around town, boy, it wouldn't do either of us any good.'

'You knew?' Kit was dumbfounded.

'Naturally.' Not wise to admit to discovering the fact just prior to Henrietta's mysterious death, Terence thought. 'I knew from the very start,' he said, congratulating himself on his cunning. 'Very noble of me, don't you think? Bringing up Henrietta's bastard child.' Now that he felt safe Terence wanted to twist the knife just a little, the boyishly wounded look on Kit's face irritated him.

Kit hadn't known what to expect in confronting his father. Perhaps the rage that he'd already encountered, perhaps the vitriol; neither had surprised him. But this calm, cold reaction was the last thing he'd anticipated. He stood at a loss, not sure what to say. It seemed there was nothing he *could* say.

'Thank you for telling me the truth,' he said when he finally found his voice. It was time to go, he thought. He crossed to the verandah door and opened it.

'Give me the locket, Kit.' It was an order.

'Why?' he asked, turning back.

'Because I don't want photographs of my wife and her lover floating around for everyone to see.'

'I won't show anyone.'

'I said give me the locket, Kit.' Terence crossed to the door, his hand outstretched.

'No.' Kit slipped the locket into his shirt pocket. 'She wanted me to have it.'

'You'll do as you're told, you little bastard,' Terence snarled, his anger once more on the rise.

'Not so little,' Kit said, 'but you got the other part right.' Looking at Terence Galloway's face, twisted with rage as he'd so often seen it, Kit felt light-headed and strangely relieved. So many unspoken questions seemed to have suddenly been answered. 'I'm glad Paul Trewinnard was my father,' he said. 'It explains a great deal.'

'It does, doesn't it.' Terence's years of hatred overwhelmed him. 'Do you think I could ever have sired a spineless little bastard like you! You're the product of that slut of a mother of yours and her wimp of a Pom. Big fucking war hero, my arse.' He shoved Kit roughly in the chest and Kit lost his balance, staggering a step or two back through the door. Terence followed him onto the verandah. 'Let's see what you're made of, big fucking war hero.' Terence wanted more than a fight. He wanted to kill Kit with his bare hands.

Kit looked at the man he'd known as his father throughout his life. He was looking at a madman, he realised. Terence's face was red and distorted, his massive shoulders were hunched, his fists clenched, and he pawed the verandah deck like an enraged bull. A complete and utter madman, Kit thought. Didn't he realise that it wasn't an even match? Didn't he realise that he didn't stand a chance? For God's sake, didn't the man realise that he was nearly sixty years old?

Terence swung at Kit with all his might. Kit dodged aside, easily avoiding the blow, and Terence lost his balance, overturning a chair. He kicked it aside and lunged again at Kit.

There was a scream in the background as Fran raced from the kitchen through the lounge, yelling at them to stop. But neither of them took any notice. Kit was too busy concentrating on evading the lethal punches, Terence was still a strong man, and Terence himself was hell-bent on murdering the kid.

'Cut it out!' Kit yelled above Fran's screams. 'I don't want to fight you!'

'Come on, you bastard. Fight!' Kit's evasion tactics were infuriating him. 'Fight!' Terence's chest was heaving as he lunged about the verandah hurling furniture aside, trying to corner Kit. If he could just land one punch, Jesus he'd teach the prick a lesson!

It was madness, Kit thought, as the housemaid screamed and the decking furniture flew in all directions. Terence Galloway would have a heart attack any second.

Then suddenly Terence landed a punch and Kit found himself sprawled on the verandah, his ear singing, the whole left side of his face throbbing. Christ, he thought, as he grabbed at the stair railings to haul himself up, the old man packed a powerful right.

Terence was elated. 'Come on,' he crowed as Kit struggled to his feet, 'come on, mister big fucking war hero.'

And he charged in for the kill.

Kit reacted instinctively. As Terence threw a punch, he dodged it and drove his left fist hard into the man's solar plexus, feeling the expulsion of air from his lungs. Then, as Terence crumpled, he followed through with his knee, giving it all the strength he could muster, feeling the crunch of nose cartilage beneath his kneecap.

Terence staggered and, in falling, he grabbed for the railings. Too late. Before he knew it he was catapulting, head first, down the stairs. He came to rest at the bottom and lay in a motionless heap on the garden path.

'You have killed him!' Fran screamed as she ran down the stairs. 'You have killed him!'

Oh Jesus, Kit thought, is she right?

But Terence wasn't dead. Kit slung the unconscious body over his shoulders in a fireman's lift and carried him upstairs to the lounge room where he dumped him unceremoniously on the sofa.

'He'll be all right, Fran. You can call a doctor if you like, I leave that up to you.' Kit didn't care one way or another.

'I will look after him.' Fran was not a woman normally given to hysterics and now that the situation had been resolved and the men had not killed each other, she knew what she must do. It would be far more than her job, or indeed her personal safety, was worth should she call in any witness to Mr Galloway's humiliating defeat. 'We will keep very quiet about this,' she said to Kit.

'Yes,' Kit agreed. They were his father's words, he thought, Christ he had her well trained. 'We won't tell anyone.'

As Kit drove home, he dismissed the ugly image of Terence Galloway from his mind. He thought of his mother instead. His mother and Paul Trewinnard. Memories flooded back to him from his childhood years, and it seemed astonishing to him now that he'd never guessed at the truth. He was not only thankful that Paul

Trewinnard was his father, he was thankful that his mother had found such a love whilst she'd suffered life with her monster of a husband.

Hell, he thought, the locket! Had he dropped it when Terence had sent him flying with that punch? He clutched his shirt pocket and felt the reassuring shape beneath the cotton. Thank God. The locket was very precious to him now.

At home, Kit checked the damage in the mirror. His left eyelid was already swollen, he'd have a black eye in the morning. But it didn't hurt as much as his knee. He sat for a while, swapping an icepack intermittently from his eye to his bruised kneecap, wondering what to do. Only one thing for it, he decided, go to Maxie's party and get drunk.

The fog in Terence's brain was slowly lifting. Someone was bathing his face with a flannel. What the hell had happened? His nose was busted, he knew that much for sure, and he could taste blood. He ran his tongue around his mouth, two of his front teeth had been loosened, the gums bleeding. What the hell had happened? Had he been in an accident? Then the fog cleared. Kit!

He pushed Fran aside and got to his feet, then quickly sat down again as the room started to spin. She fetched him a glass of water and he drank it as he gradually regained his senses.

Kit had arrived with the locket. Terence recalled his terror upon seeing it. Then he'd lost his temper when Kit wouldn't give it to him. He'd had one of his fits. Not very smart, but then he'd never been able to control them. And they'd had a fight.

Terence didn't dwell on the humiliating fact that his son had beaten him. The kid got lucky, that was all, and then he'd fallen down the stairs. The most important consideration was the locket. He had to get hold of the locket! By whatever means and at whatever cost.

He stood. The room was no longer spinning. He told Fran to piss off, grabbed the bottle of Scotch and lurched, still a little unsteady on his feet, to his study at the rear of the house.

He took his war service revolver from the drawer and placed it on his desk. It was his pride and joy and he always kept it in mint condition. He sat looking at the revolver as he swigged from the Scotch bottle. He'd have to kill Kit to get the locket, and he relished the prospect. He might even tell him the truth before he did it. He might even say 'I killed your whore of a mother, and now I'll kill her bastard son'. And then he'd put a bullet right between Kit's eyes. He savoured the image as he swigged back the Scotch. Then he put down the bottle and started loading the revolver.

Terence didn't contemplate what the outcome of his actions would be. He was a man obsessed. As he methodically revolved the cylindrical magazine and fed each .38 calibre bullet into its chamber, he didn't question his madness. He didn't realise that every vestige of sanity had deserted him from the moment he'd seen the locket in the palm of Kit's hand.

CHAPTER THIRTY-NINE

'Yoo hoo.'

It was nine o'clock at night as Kit left to go to Maxie's party. He closed the front door to his flat and, as he walked down the side path, hefting the slab of beer he was carrying onto his shoulder, he heard a call from the verandah above. He looked up to see Tess O'Malley in the light of the open front door of the house.

'Would you like to come up for a Christmas Eve drink, Kit?' she called down to him.

He wouldn't particularly like to, he thought, but he'd been knocking back Tess O'Malley's invitations for so long now it seemed rude to refuse; it was Christmas, after all.

'Love to,' he called back, and he put the slab of beer into the boot of the Kingswood and went upstairs to join the O'Malleys.

'How about a sherry?' she said as she welcomed him into the lounge room where Bob, in T-shirt and shorts, was lolling back in his favourite armchair watching television.

'Don't be silly, Tess,' Bob said good naturedly, 'he'll have a beer. G'day Kit.'

'G'day, Bob.'

'Pull up a pew. I'll have another one too thanks, love.'

He handed his empty tinny to his wife.

'I think we can have the telly off, dear.' Tess smiled but there was a slight edge to her voice and, to keep the peace, Bob turned the set off.

The room was dominated by a gigantic plastic pine Christmas tree, complete with fairy lights, which reached to the ceiling. As Tess went off to get the beers, Kit commented upon it.

'Yeah, she's a stickler for convention,' Bob said, jerking his head in the direction of the kitchen. 'We put it up for the kids actually,' he explained, 'Tim was coming up for Christmas.' Bob's son lived in Adelaide with his young family. 'But the baby's got an ear infection and they didn't want to fly, so now we're stuck with the bloody thing.'

'And I'm glad that we are.' Tess arrived with the beers in time to hear the last remark. 'It wouldn't be Christmas without a tree.'

She toasted them with her sherry glass as she sat. 'To Christmas,' she said.

'To Christmas,' they dutifully replied.

'What happened to your eye?' Tess asked.

'Walked into a door eh?' Bob had chosen to ignore Kit's eye, the kid'd obviously been in a fight.

'Yeah, sort of,' Kit replied gratefully. 'You're looking very smart, Tess.'

She was glad that he'd noticed. She'd been to the hairdresser's that afternoon for a new blue rinse and set, and she was wearing her good pearls.

'We have people popping over in an hour or so for a quick drink before midnight mass,' she said, darting a look in Bob's direction. She wished he'd got changed before she'd invited Kit up.

The look on Bob's face warned her that she was lucky he'd agreed to go to midnight mass in the first place so Tess didn't push her luck.

'And what are you doing for Christmas, Kit?' she asked,

offering him a bowl of mixed nuts and raisins which he declined. 'I suppose you'll be spending Christmas Day with your father.' She found it strange that Terence Galloway never visited his son, she had rather hoped that he would when Kit had moved into the flat.

'Nope.' Kit offered no explanation, although Tess O'Malley's raised eyebrows invited one. 'A mob of us have booked in to Foong Lee's for lunch.'

How very un-Christmassy, Tess thought, a Chinese restaurant on Christmas Day, but she smiled. 'Oh you young things,' she said.

They chatted for half an hour or so and then Kit made his farewells. 'I'll leave you to get ready for your guests,' he said.

'Yes,' Tess agreed, glancing at Bob who heaved a sigh. Midnight bloody mass. He'd got out of it last year, staying home to babysit the youngest of the grandkids.

As Kit got into the Kingswood, he could sense the impending storm. The night was restless, the air thick and sticky. It's going to be a beauty, he thought, and during the drive to Maxie's he wondered whether perhaps Cyclone Tracy might hit Darwin after all.

The old stilted wooden house which Maxie shared with several others was at the top of the Esplanade near Daly Street, and the party was in full swing when he arrived. Music was blaring from the open windows, the place was lit up like the O'Malleys' Christmas tree, and as Kit got out of his car, Nick Coustas, who was on the front verandah with a number of others, yelled down to him.

'What took you so long?'

Kit waved back and lifted the beer out of the boot of the Kingswood.

Aggie Marshall was at Mavis Campbell's house in Casuarina along with three other women from the CWA. They'd been finalising the last minute arrangements for the

Christmas festivities at the hospital the following day. The entertainment had been lined up weeks ago, a guitarist who sang just like Bing Crosby and a Father Christmas for the children, so now it was really a case of deciding who was going to get there early to blow up balloons, and who had cars and could pick up supplies.

'Albert's delivering the presents for the kiddies,' Aggie said. Although Christmas held no significance for Albert Foong, he had willingly inherited his father's annual tradition, donating gifts for whatever Christmas cause Aggie had taken up. 'I'm sure he won't mind collecting the soft drinks.' Aggie happily delegated another chore to Albert in the knowledge that he never refused her.

The finer details having been sorted out over several pots of tea, the women took their leave. All except Aggie, who stayed on for a bit of a chat with Mavis. The two women had become firm friends since the death of Mavis's husband three years previously. Over the remains of Mavis's fine Christmas cake and yet another pot of tea, the gossip ran rife. In Darwin very little escaped Mavis Campbell and Aggie Marshall.

At Foong Lee's house, not a word was being spoken. There was no exchange between the five of them but the clack of mah-jong tiles. They sat around the kitchen table, deep in concentration, Foong Lee, his wife Lin Mei, who was winning as she invariably did, Albert and his wife, Wai Li, and their eldest son, seventeen-year-old Edward. Twelve-year-old Sally had been sent off to bed, complaining bitterly at the fact, half an hour previously.

It was eleven o'clock and outside the wind was picking up. The shutters were starting to rattle alarmingly and it was Foong Lee who broke the silence.

'I think we'll continue the game in the cellar,' he said.

Albert had thought his father was being a little alarmist in demanding they all come to the house as a safeguard against the imminent cyclone. It was no hardship, however, to spend an evening together, they were a very close family. So Albert had humoured the old man, he and Edward setting up the cellar as a refuge with emergency supplies and even a couple of camp stretchers.

Now, as the howl of the wind drowned the clack of the mah-jong tiles, and the rattle of the shutters became more frenzied, Albert wondered whether perhaps his father might have been right. He went to wake Sally.

The church was crowded for midnight mass. Tess O'Malley sat in one of the front pews, with Bob squirming uncomfortably beside her. Bob always hated wearing a suit and tie. But he was looking very nice, she thought thankfully. She smoothed her hair back into position, there was such a frightful gale blowing as they'd arrived at the church, and she wished she could check her hair in her compact mirror, but that would look vain. She was glad that she'd had a fresh rinse put in that morning, midnight mass was a very social event.

Barely half an hour into the mass, the wind outside seemed to double in strength, becoming a dull roar, eventually drowning out the priest's voice altogether. The gathered congregation became restless. They looked at one another in growing consternation.

By midnight most of the revellers at Maxie's house were drunk. The more frenzied the wind grew, the more exciting they found it. And when the rain pelted down, a number of them stood on the balcony, drenched, admiring the fury. Trees were bent double and, out in the black harbour, white-topped waves whipped the water as though the harbour itself was a giant cauldron. It was most impressive.

Kit Galloway was trying to join in the party mood, wondering why he couldn't seem to get drunk like the others.

Perhaps it was because they'd all started drinking a lot earlier than he had, or perhaps it was the events of that afternoon, but he felt decidedly sober as he opened yet another can of VB.

Nick Coustas sat on the balcony rail, legs dangling over the side, clutching hold of the downpipe in one hand and a tinny in the other. He yah-hooed and rode the wind as if it was a bucking bronco, before one immense gust forced him backwards and he landed in an untidy mess on the balcony, covered in beer. Undeterred, he sprang to his feet, rescued his tinny and leaned over the balcony toasting the storm's magnificence.

Maxie Brummer was also enjoying the weather's violence, but in a different way. Trish Paterson, the new front counter receptionist at *NTN*, had been frightened and he'd taken her into his bedroom to comfort her. She'd soon forgotten her fear. The howl of the wind excited her now. It excited them both. The storm was a real turn-on and Maxie and Trish were lost in its ferocity and their own mounting passion.

In the lounge room, someone turned the stereo over to the ABC for the latest cyclone report. The ABC was playing 'Raindrops Keep Falling on My Head'. Everyone burst out laughing.

They weren't laughing a little while later. Within minutes, the storm changed. It was no longer a game, nor an impressive show of nature's strength to be admired. And in seconds, Darwin was hit by the full lethal force of Cyclone Tracy. With an angry roar, she swooped, tearing relentlessly at everything in her path. Full-grown trees were uprooted as if they were saplings. In the streets, cars were overturned and smashed against buildings. People clung to the floors of their homes as roofs and walls were ripped away and tossed about in the air like playthings. Power poles crashed to the ground and, in the blackness of the night, electrical fires ignited in flashes of brilliance, only to be quelled by the deluge. Sheets of corrugated iron danced crazily along the pavement, driven as effortlessly as autumn leaves by the gale-force winds, and everywhere the air was thick with flying debris.

Out on the harbour, ships were wrecked where they lay, or torn from their moorings to be washed ashore like so much flotsam.

At Darwin Airport the control tower's wind gauge recorded 217 kilometre an hour winds before the gauge itself was ripped apart and blown to oblivion. Millions of dollars worth of light aircraft were reduced to scrap metal, hangars blown away, steel girders twisted like spaghetti, and the new air terminal gutted and flooded.

The onslaught was relentless. And all the while, above the crash of colliding debris and the scrape of corrugated iron on concrete, was the voice of the cyclone itself. Ominous and omnipotent, Tracy roared like a hundred maddened lions, as if she would be satisfied with nothing less than the entire destruction of Darwin.

The roof of Maxie's house had disappeared in the first swift rage of the cyclone. With it went the downpipe, and with the downpipe, Nick Coustas. Before he knew what had happened Nick had been swept from the balcony.

Kit saw it happen and raced down to help him, yelling above the screams of the terrified partygoers as he did so. 'Get downstairs everyone! Get downstairs!'

Kit dragged Nick into the laundry where several of them huddled against the stone walls. Others fled to the relative safety of the garage.

'I've busted my arm,' Nick loudly complained.

'Shit mate you're lucky,' Kit yelled back. 'If you weren't so pissed you'd probably be dead.'

Upstairs, Maxie and Trish had been in a drunken, post-coital slumber when the roof blew away. Suddenly, the world was roaring around them, the bedclothes were whipped off them and the rain beat down on their naked bodies. Trish screamed hysterically, and Maxie dragged her under the heavy bedstead where they lay quaking with terror as debris crashed onto the very bed where they'd just been sleeping.

At Mavis Campbell's house in Casuarina, Aggie had been persuaded to stay the night. She'd been about to leave at eleven-thirty. 'Goodness,' she'd said, noticing the time, 'we've talked half the night away.'

'You'll never get a taxi in this weather,' Mavis had re-marked, and Aggie had agreed it would be sensible to stay.

The women had retired to their respective rooms for the night and both were rudely awakened by the first wrath of Tracy. They met in the hall and, highly practical women, immediately set about looking for candles and torches; bound to be a power failure, they agreed. Mavis's house, small and solidly built, sat in a shallow gully and they felt relatively safe. As the horrendous noise screamed all about them, they sat silently in the lounge room, well back from the windows should they shatter, and imagined the dev-astation being wrought in the blackness of the streets.

Within the safety of the cellar beneath Foong Lee's home, Albert Foong cradled his terrified daughter and blessed his father's wisdom as the family sat listening to Tracy's anger. There was no point in talking, there was nothing to say. Besides, the human voice could barely be heard above the all-pervasive growl of the cyclone.

In a stupor induced by his semi-concussed state and half a bottle of Scotch, Terence Galloway had slept through the first hour and a half of Cyclone Tracy. It was only when the windows of his study shattered, showering him with glass, that he awakened to the chaos which was destroying his house along with the rest of Darwin.

He sat bolt upright in his chair as the wind howled in through the open window. Jesus Christ, what was happening? It was pitch black. Then he heard Tracy's voice. The ghoulish roar. So the cyclone had hit them, after all. He fumbled about in the drawers of his desk and found the torch which he always kept there. He turned it on, papers were swirling about the study like so much confetti. Then he directed the torch's beam at the revolver which lay on the desk before him, fully loaded, ready for action, and he remembered his plan. The madness of the cyclone might well be to his advantage, he thought as he picked up the gun.

He walked from his study towards the front of the house and the lounge room. But there was no lounge room. The roof and the walls had gone, only the floor remained, covered with shattered glass and timber. The wind was shrieking, tearing at the rear section of the roof, determined that nothing should remain standing.

In the torch's beam, Terence saw Fran's body. She lay sprawled on her back, covered in glass and drenched with blood. Such a lot of blood, he thought. Then he saw the wound to her neck. It was cut to the bone, her jugular vein had been sliced right through. Well, that explained it.

Terence headed for the rear of the house, any minute the whole place would go. He raced down the back stairs, bending double against the gale-force winds that met him, and struggled his way to the garage.

As he backed the Jaguar out into the street, he could feel the wind buffeting the car, threatening to overturn it. He drove slowly, avoiding the hazards he could see everywhere in the high beam of the headlights. A fallen tree, an overturned car. Things were sailing through the air overhead, but he couldn't make out what they were. He swerved to avoid a large sheet of galvanised iron swirling down the road. Too late, they collided, and for a moment his vision was lost before the sheet of iron was whipped away, digging ugly holes in the Jaguar's bonnet, but fortunately leaving the windscreen intact. He slowed down still further. No need to hurry, he had all the time in the world. Behind him the cyclone was ripping his house to pieces, but who cared, he could always build another house, bigger and grander. And who cared about the scarred Jaguar, normally his pride and joy, he'd buy another one. Tonight he had business to attend to, things to sort out. And what better cover could he have than Cyclone Tracy. As he crawled along through the destruction and mayhem which surrounded him, Terence felt a sense of elation.

Unable to withstand the relentless attack, the whole upper section of Maxie's house gave way. With the protection of neither roof nor walls, the supporting poles listed to one side before finally crashing to the ground. And they took with them the bedroom floor, the bedstead, Maxie and Trish.

In the laundry and the garage, Kit and the others crouched on the ground covering their heads with their arms, hearing the house crash all about them, expecting that any second their own shelters would cave in.

Then, only moments later, all was still. It was a minute or so before anyone dared believe it could be over. One by one, they stepped outside into the black, eerie stillness. It seemed Cyclone Tracy had retreated as swiftly as she had attacked.

Everywhere, people surveyed the damage. Some naively attempted to start on the clean up. 'It's the eye,' they were warned. 'It'll be back.'

Kit took a head count, Maxie and Trish were missing. Oh Jesus, he thought, they'd been upstairs. Maxie had taken Trish off to the bedroom. But that had been hours ago.

They turned on car headlights and searched amongst the

wreckage with cigarette lighters and matches. It was only minutes before they found them. The naked bodies of Maxie and Trish lay mangled beneath debris. Beneath the very bedstead under which they had sought safety.

One of the girls was crying hysterically, and several of the young men started trying to dig out the bodies.

'Don't,' Kit told them. 'Get back under cover.'

'Christ alive, Kit, we can't just leave them there.' Nick Coustas stood nursing his broken arm and staring down at the lifeless body of his friend.

'Yes we can.' Kit started to sprint down the street. 'Get everyone under cover!' he yelled back at them. 'It's only the eye!'

Kit had just one objective in mind. Aggie. Aggie lived two blocks further down the Esplanade. If the cyclone had made such mincemeat of Maxie's, what the hell would it have done to Aggie's little weatherboard? Oh Christ let her be alive, he prayed.

As the Jaguar pulled into the drive of the O'Malleys' house, the wind suddenly stopped. Terence left the headlights on and stepped out of the car into an unnatural calm which matched his mood. It was uncanny. He and the cyclone seemed to be as one. There was a sense of deliberation in the cyclone, as if during this brief respite Tracy was mustering her forces for her next dire attack. It suited Terence's purpose to perfection. He would kill Kit and dispose of the body during the cyclone's next onslaught.

In the headlight's beam, the house was clearly a wreck, but the granny flat built beneath it was intact. As he walked up the side path, Terence wondered whether the O'Malleys were dead, that too would serve his purpose. But the entire place appeared deserted. Damn, he thought, where the hell was Kit? Then he realised the Kingswood was missing and he remembered. Of course. 'Maxie's having a party,' Kit had said.

Terence walked back to the Jaguar. He got in and turned off the headlights, no point in drawing attention to himself, up and down the street people were tentatively venturing out of their houses. He could hear the mutter of disbelief as they surveyed the destruction. A baby was screaming, a woman crying. He started up the car and backed out into the road. Where the hell did Maxie live? He contemplated driving around the streets of Darwin looking for the Kingswood. Then the obvious solution occurred to him. Aggie would know where Maxie lived.

In the eerie lull of the cyclone's eye, Mavis and Aggie went out into the street to see if they could help some of the stricken people. The town of Casuarina had been shattered and Mavis's house was one of the few left standing. Hundreds were seeking refuge in the nearby high school, the women were told. There were children and wounded. Mavis and Aggie gathered torches and candles, bandages and medical supplies, all they could carry, and rushed to Casuarina High School. They knew they didn't have long.

It was just as Kit had feared, Aggie's house had been demolished, ripped from its very foundations. Panic seized him.

'Aggie!' he yelled. 'Aggie!' And he raced frantically about the wreckage, heaving aside beams and debris, searching for her body, praying that by some miracle she might be alive.

Terence saw him in the beam of the headlights. So it was going to be this easy, he thought. The entire street was deserted. It had been almost twenty minutes since the cyclone's wrath had subsided, and those naive enough to have believed it was over had now been convinced that it was only the eye. Everyone had taken cover. The whole of Darwin was cowering, waiting for Tracy's return. There were just the two of them, Terence thought. Just the two of them out here in the street.

Terence turned off the headlights and took the revolver from his pocket as he got out of the car.

Kit had wondered who was foolish enough to be out in a vehicle during the eye of the cyclone but he'd been grateful for the headlights. He ran to the shadowy figure standing beside the open car door. 'Turn them on again will you, mate,' he said, breathless from his exertion. 'She's got to be trapped here somewhere, help me find her.'

'I'll help you find her, Kit.'

Kit recognised the voice of Terence Galloway.

'I'll help you find her after you've given me the locket.'

Kit instinctively clutched the pocket of his shirt. He'd forgotten that he'd been carrying the locket all this time. He was relieved to feel it still there, to know that he hadn't lost it amongst the chaos of the past several hours.

Terence laughed. It was getting easier by the minute. He'd thought he might have to take Kit back to his flat to kill him. Here and now was much more convenient.

As if the gods were yet further in his favour, there was an almighty roar and Tracy once again attacked with all the vengeful force she could muster. No-one would even hear the gunshot, Terence thought, and he raised the revolver as he gripped onto the open car door to prevent himself being blown from his feet.

Kit staggered back with the force of the wind. 'Take cover!' he yelled.

Terence fired.

As he dived to the ground, Kit saw the flash from the muzzle of the revolver and, amidst the furore of the cyclone, he heard the sharp report of gunfire.

But in the very instant Terence pulled the trigger, his ally turned against him. It seemed the maddened beast that was Tracy no longer favoured Terence Galloway.

As if in slow motion, Terence felt the car door buckle in

his hands like foil wrapping paper. He turned towards the car and, as it reared up onto its side, he felt himself falling backwards with it, unable to move his feet, pinned to the Jaguar as the full weight of it crashed down on him, the metal framework digging deep into his chest. Terence Galloway's scream of mortal agony mingled with Tracy's roar. Then, as his cry was reduced to a death rattle, he felt himself moving. He felt nothing more after that.

The Jaguar travelled a good fifty metres down the Esplanade, grinding Terence's lifeless body to a pulp beneath it, and finally coming to rest against an uprooted tree. Then Tracy, like a spoilt child having destroyed a favourite toy, turned her attention elsewhere.

As he lay on the ground, Kit's eyes followed the dark shape of the Jaguar, watching its clumsy, macabre dance down the street before it was swallowed up in the blackness.

Terence Galloway had tried to kill him. Kit had seen the flash of gunfire, he'd heard the shot. And now Terence Galloway was dead.

Kit rose and, head down, buckled against the wind, he made for cover.

CHAPTER FORTY

Around the country, newspapers carried reports of Tracy's carnage. 'KILLER CYCLONE TRACY BLASTS DARWIN OFF THE MAP'. 'TRACY DEVASTATES DARWIN'. 'DARWIN TERROR STORM: 40 DIE'.

The reports differed. The death toll varied, but was eventually confirmed at forty-nine. And with rescuers frantically combing the wreckage in the hope of finding survivors, it was feared there might be more lying dead beneath rubble. Thousands had been wounded by crashing masonry, glass and iron. Sixteen people were missing at sea, including two crew members of the navy patrol vessel HMAS *Arrow* which had sunk in Darwin Harbour. It was believed there could yet be many more fatalities at sea— the RAAF had mounted a search for thirteen small ships listed as missing.

Winds were reported to have reached 250 kilometres an hour, cutting all power and communication lines to the rest of Australia as well as destroying ninety percent of the city's buildings. Tens of thousands had been rendered homeless. Army reports described Darwin as looking as though it had been hit by an atomic bomb.

Major-General Alan Stretton, Director-General of the National Disasters Organisation, arrived in Darwin with teams of doctors, nurses and medical supplies. The Prime Minister, Gough Whitlam, was expected to cut short his tour of Europe to return to what was reported as being Australia's worst natural disaster.

Evacuation of the city began immediately. Massive airlifts took place. The homeless needed to be relocated and, with the destruction of water and sewerage systems, outbreaks of typhoid and dysentery were feared.

For the second time in her short history, the city of Darwin, gateway to the north, had been reduced to rubble.

Foong Lee ignored Albert's pleas to join the family in their move to Adelaide. He'd stayed after the bombing, he said, and he'd stay after Tracy. He was one of the few who still had a home; it was his duty to help rebuild Darwin, he said. So Albert stayed with him. The two men farewelled their wives and family and set about resurrecting the restaurant. Albert's home and the store had both been destroyed, but the restaurant was salvageable, and Foong Lee decided it would serve as a soup kitchen. Fresh food supplies were scarce but, as relief poured in, they would be able to garner what they could and serve free meals for the needy.

Aggie Marshall was of the same mind. She moved in to Mavis Campbell's, joined the official relief committee, and started work immediately on the distribution of funds and supplies which were arriving from the federal government and from fundraising bodies all over the country.

Kit Galloway didn't even think of moving. *NTN* was Darwin's link with the outside world and he was too busy reporting on every aspect of the disaster. A new mayor was elected in the aftermath of Tracy, and the irony of the choice was not lost on Kit. Dr Ella Stack was a robust little woman who took great pride in the fact that she had delivered some 2,000 Darwin babies over the years. To her, the city was a sick child in need of care. Kit wondered what Terence Galloway's reaction would have been to the fact that the office he'd so eagerly sought had been won by a woman.

It was several weeks after the disaster, when the final statistics and death lists had been published, that a thought occurred to Foong Lee. He was surprised it hadn't occurred to him sooner, but then in the wake of Tracy he had been understandably preoccupied.

Just before dawn on a Sunday morning, he awoke to the sudden realisation that there was no longer any need for secrecy. He lay staring at the ceiling and wondered how best to go about things. Several hours later, he made two telephone calls.

In West Perth, Jessica Williams put down the telephone receiver, grabbed her car keys and raced out of the house she shared with two other young women. Waratah Avenue, Nedlands, she thought as she drove, good God, it was the adjoining suburb to Claremont, her childhood home where her parents still lived.

A pleasant suburban house, probably built in the fifties, it was surrounded by a low stone fence with a neatly cut front lawn and two healthy cumquat trees.

Jessica walked up the path and knocked on the door. It was opened by a handsome woman. Her copper-coloured hair although streaked with grey was thick and attractive and, despite the fact that she leaned on a cane, she was tall and of regal carriage. Jessica guessed her to be in her fifties.

'Hello, are you Miss Southern?' Jessica asked.

'I am.' The woman nodded pleasantly.

'I'm Jessica Williams.'

'I know.' The woman smiled.

Her smile was extraordinarily beautiful, Jessica thought. 'I hope you don't mind my just calling around,' she apologised, 'but he said . . . Foong Lee that is . . .

'He rang me. I've been expecting you.'

Henrietta Galloway extended her hand and the two women shook. 'How do you do, Jessica,' she said, 'Please come in.'

Henrietta led the way into a pleasant parlour where the clear January sun filtered through lace curtains and Jessica could see the cumquat trees in the front garden. What a pretty place, she thought, airy and feminine. One feature was at odds with the rest of the room, but somehow it managed to add to its interest. The far wall, from floor to ceiling, was a massive built-in bookcase. There must have been hundreds of books cluttering the shelves, some carefully ordered, some piled untidily, as if they were referred to often. Henrietta Southern was obviously an avid reader, Jessica thought.

A tea tray was set out on the coffee table by the windows. Fine china cups and saucers sat beside the teapot, and there was a plate of shortbread biscuits.

Henrietta propped her stick against a hard-backed carver by the windows and sat, indicating the armchair opposite. 'I'm not very comfortable in armchairs myself. Tea?'

Jessica nodded, bemused as she watched Henrietta pour the tea. The brew was piping hot, it had just been prepared.

Henrietta was aware of the girl's bemusement. 'Foong Lee guessed that you'd be around within twenty minutes,' she smiled. 'In fact he said he'd lay odds on it, and he's a very successful gambler, so I made tea.'

Jessica felt relaxed in the older woman's company; it was difficult not to, Henrietta Southern was charming.

'Yes, he's an amazing man, isn't he?' she said, recalling Foong Lee's recognition of her origins. 'I only met him the once, but I found him quite extraordinary.'

'The feeling was obviously mutual,' Henrietta said, handing Jessica her tea. 'You made a very strong first impression on Foong Lee too.'

'Really?' Jessica was surprised—why would Foong Lee have found her impressive? But she was pleased, and somehow very flattered.

Henrietta observed the girl over the rim of her teacup. Jessica Williams was free from artifice and every bit as interesting as Foong Lee had said. Not beautiful in the classical sense, but very attractive. How he had ever picked her Aboriginal blood was beyond Henrietta; she herself would have assumed the girl was Irish.

'Very few people impress Foong Lee upon first meeting,' she continued. She wanted to chat to the girl, to get to know her before they touched upon the reason for her visit. 'He makes them feel that they do, but they don't really. He can be very devious.'

Henrietta remembered Paul's description of Foong Lee. 'Don't let him fool you, Henrietta, he's the quintessence of Oriental inscrutability.' She'd laughed at the time, but he'd been quite serious. 'He's a chameleon,' Paul had said. 'He'll be whatever he thinks people wish him to be. But once he's your friend . . . Oh my darling girl, he's your friend for life. You must always remember that.'

'I can't think why on earth he'd be impressed with me,' said Jessica.

'He told me he admired your passion.'

'Did he?' Jessica was once again surprised, but delighted.

'Yes, your passion and your dedication.' Henrietta offered the plate of shortbread biscuits and Jessica took one. 'But mainly your passion. He believes greatly in passion, although he says it's a quality he doesn't possess.'

Henrietta recalled Foong Lee's words. 'You have a passion which is enviable, Henrietta. A passion for life. And it is that passion which will heal you.' He had been right, as usual.

Comfortable as Jessica felt in Henrietta's presence, she was nonetheless a little puzzled. Henrietta Southern obviously knew why she had called upon her, and yet she seemed to be avoiding the topic.

'Have you lived in Perth long, Miss Southern?' She took a bite of the biscuit, dying to ask leading questions but feeling it would be more discreet to continue with the general conversation.

'Call me Henrietta, please.' The girl was sensitive too, Henrietta noted with approval. 'Thirteen years,' she said. 'Is the shortbread good? I haven't tried it myself, I only opened the tin this morning.'

'Terrific.'

Henrietta decided it was time to put Jessica out of her misery. The girl was obviously aching for answers. She set her cup back on the tray.

'Foong Lee tells me that you're searching for an antique locket which was once in my possession.'

'Yes.' The shortbread stuck momentarily in Jessica's throat as she swallowed. *Once in her possession.* So Henrietta didn't have the locket. Not that Foong Lee had said that she did, Jessica now recalled. 'Miss Southern knows of the next stage in the locket's journey,' that was what he'd said, but in her excitement Jessica hadn't really listened.

The girl's bitter disappointment was palpable and Henrietta wished she could tell her the truth. She decided to buy time and, pouring more tea, she asked about Jessica's research.

'Get her to tell you her story,' Foong Lee had said. 'The locket has a connection with her people; you'll find it most fascinating.'

'Do tell me about your interest in the locket, Jessica,' she implored. 'Foong Lee told me your story was fascinating.'

With a definite sense that Henrietta was hedging, Jessica told of her search for the locket. As she did so, she couldn't help but warm to her theme, and Henrietta recognised the girl's passion just as Foong Lee had.

'. . . then when Foong Lee told me it was most likely seventeenth-century and Dutch into the bargain,' she concluded, having barely drawn breath for a full fifteen minutes, 'I thought all my Christmases had come at once! I mean it simply *had* to have come ashore from one of the early shipwrecks!'

The two fresh cups of tea sat cold before them. Jessica's excitement was contagious and Henrietta had been as immersed in the story as Jessica herself had been in the telling of it.

'And then he described the initials inside,' Jessica said. 'L v.d. M. and B v.d. M. It was easy after that, there's been so much written about the *Batavia* since the wreck was discovered in 1963.'

Henrietta nodded. She'd heard the gruesome stories of murder and mayhem associated with the wreck of the *Batavia*.

'Lucretia van den Mylen was her name,' Jessica continued. 'She was an aristocrat, a woman of great beauty, and she was sailing to the East Indies to meet her husband, Boudewijn.'

Lucretia and Boudewijn van den Mylen. Henrietta recalled her thoughts when she'd looked at the initials in the locket on the night that Paul had given it to her. Who were they, she'd wondered? Had their love survived into the autumn of their years as hers and Paul's could not?

'What became of Lucretia?' she asked.

'She survived the shipwreck and the atrocities that followed, miraculously enough, and she finally reached Batavia aboard the rescue vessel the *Zaandam*. Which means,' Jessica said thoughtfully, 'that the locket came ashore with someone else. Either she gave it to someone or it was stolen. I tend to favour the latter. Why would she give it away? It was surely designed as a love token.'

'Oh yes, I'm quite sure of that,' Henrietta agreed with feeling.

The locket had most certainly been a symbol of the love she had shared with Paul, she thought. But it had also been her undoing. The locket had been the catalyst to Terence's discovery of the truth, the initials of Lucretia van den Mylen and her husband having been masked by the photographs of herself and Paul. Even Foong Lee did not know the ongoing story of the locket—Foong Lee knew no more of the locket than the fact that Paul Trewinnard had given it to her before he had died.

'I'll make us a fresh pot, shall I?' Henrietta said, grasping her cane, about to ease herself to her feet.

'No really, I'm fine,' Jessica insisted.

'I think I'd like another cup myself.'

Jessica jumped up. 'Then let me get it. Please.'

'What an excellent idea.' Henrietta rested the cane back against the arm of her chair. 'The kitchen's just through there, it's all set out.'

As Jessica disappeared with the tea tray, Henrietta gazed thoughtfully out the window. She didn't really want any more tea, but she needed a little space. She wanted to direct the girl to the locket; Jessica deserved the right to find it after the years she had dedicated to her search. But how much of her own story could Henrietta tell? In directing Jessica Williams to the locket, she would be directing her to Kit.

When Foong Lee had telephoned that morning, he had urged Henrietta to make her existence known to her son. 'Terence Galloway is dead,' he'd said, baldly stating the fact. 'He was killed in the cyclone. There is no longer any need for secrecy, Henrietta.'

But it wasn't as simple as that. Much as she longed to make herself known to her son, Henrietta was nervous, unsure as to whether she should so disrupt his life. The locket would by now have told Kit that Paul Trewinnard was his father. Jackie Yoorunga would have honoured his promise, Henrietta was sure, and Nellie would have delivered the locket to Kit when he'd come of age. He must have had it for years now, and she'd often wondered what his reaction had been. But Kit believed that she was dead. How was she to explain her existence for all of these years? How was she to tell him that she had feared for his life? Terence Galloway's warning had remained hanging over Henrietta's head like a curse for the past thirteen years.

'No-one is ever to know that Kit is not my son,' he'd said, his words indelibly imprinting themselves on her brain. 'I would not only kill you, Henrietta, I would kill your bastard child.' Then, only minutes later he'd thrown her to what he'd thought was her death. Terence Galloway was most certainly capable of murdering her son—it had been no idle threat.

The news of Terence's death had put Henrietta in a turmoil of indecision. She wanted desperately to make herself known to Kit, but how would he react to her? She would never regret the fact that she had informed him, through the locket, that Paul was his father. She owed it to Paul and she owed it to her son. Kit should know he'd been blessed with blood that was not Terence Galloway's. But how had Kit reacted to the knowledge of his mother's infidelity? Had he been shocked? Did he despise her? Henrietta didn't know whether she could confront her son's scorn.

Foong Lee's simple solution to return and carry on where she'd left off had bewildered Henrietta. What was she to tell her son? Was she to tell him that his stepfather who had raised him for all these years was a murderer? And then, seemingly unaware of the myriad of implications, Foong Lee had added the girl. 'She is obsessed with the locket, Henrietta, she needs to know its history, and now that Terence Galloway is dead, perhaps she could talk to you. She need not know your true identity of course,' he'd added, as if that presented no problem. 'May she call on you?' And Henrietta had found herself saying yes. Foong Lee was a difficult person to refuse and it was quite obvious he wanted her to meet young Jessica Williams. Besides, it had seemed the least of Henrietta's problems at the time. There would be no harm in telling the girl her story of the locket, she'd decided. She would tell her that it had been a symbol of love. That it had been given to her by a man called Paul Trewinnard who had long since died. And she would tell her that it had been lost over thirteen years ago in the horrific accident which had nearly cost her her life.

But Jessica's quest of discovery had moved Henrietta, just as it had Foong Lee. Had that perhaps been his intention? Had he hoped that Jessica Williams would be the deciding factor? That she would inadvertently persuade Henrietta to reveal her identity? Foong Lee was quite capable of such manipulative strategy, Henrietta knew. Just as she knew that she could not reveal the locket's whereabouts without giving away her secret.

Henrietta was deep in thought and still plagued with indecision when Jessica returned from the kitchen.

Jessica too had been thinking. She knew that Henrietta had been buying time to avoid telling her the story of the locket. Now, as she sat, putting the tea tray on the coffee table, it was quite obvious to her that Henrietta Southern was troubled. She was staring out the window, her fine brow furrowed, her eyes troubled. Jessica felt concerned. Had she raised some spectre from the past in her enquiries about the locket?

'Miss Southern,' she said tentatively. 'Henrietta,' she corrected herself. 'You're upset. If I've been presumptuous in coming here, I'm sorry, I didn't mean to cause you any pain . . .'

It was all Henrietta needed. 'My name is not Henrietta

Southern,' she stated. 'It is Henrietta Galloway. And I have a son. His name is Kit.' Henrietta dragged her gaze from the window to look squarely at Jessica. 'Kit has the locket.'

Jessica stared back at the older woman, not daring to answer. Henrietta's tone was grave and her eyes were begging Jessica's trust.

'I will tell you a little of what has happened in my life,' she said. 'And I must swear you to secrecy—do I have your word?'

'Yes.'

CHAPTER FORTY-ONE

'Come with me, Jessica.' Henrietta eased herself up from her chair a little awkwardly. 'I shouldn't really sit for so long,' she said. 'I tend to freeze up.' Jessica followed her into the hall. 'My hip's deteriorated a little over the past year or so,' Henrietta said, leaning heavily on her cane as she walked. 'They say I may need some revision surgery. Oh well, what will be will be.'

Henrietta was still chatting amiably as they entered the small spare bedroom which she'd converted into a form of office, but Jessica could tell that the woman was preoccupied. 'I'm actually better if I keep mobile,' Henrietta said. 'Please take a seat.'

Jessica looked about at the clutter. A large desk, wedged in one corner, took up half the room, and upon it were a typewriter, manuscripts, open reference books, and endless sheets of paper covered with jottings. There were two bookcases. One, beside the desk, housed hardbacks and the other, beside the door, was stacked with messy piles of paperback editions. Stuck haphazardly up on the wall beside the desk were yet further scribbled notes.

Henrietta offered Jessica the one and only office chair. 'I really am happier moving about for a while,' she insisted. With the cane propped at her side, she leaned against the desk and started sifting through a pile of folders on the middle shelf of the bookcase.

Jessica remained standing. She glanced at the titles of the paperbacks, which appeared to be mostly crime fiction. How strange, she thought, she wouldn't have picked Henrietta Galloway as a crime fiction fan. Then she noticed, on one of the covers, the name Henry South. She picked up the book.

Having taken a scrapbook from amongst the folders, Henrietta turned and gave a wry smile as she saw the paperback in Jessica's hand. 'Oh dear, you've caught me out,' she said. 'They're of the penny dreadful variety, I'm afraid.'

'I'm most impressed.' Jessica looked admiringly at the line-up of Henry South books on the shelf. 'How many have you written?'

'Ten in all. They sell quite well, remarkably enough. I tried writing in a more esoteric form but I found I didn't really have the poetic streak. Not like Kit—there was always a bit of the poet in him, even as a little boy.'

At the mention of her son, Henrietta's face once again clouded. She was still undecided as to how much she should tell the girl. She set the scrapbook down on the desk.

'If you're to meet my son, it might be a good idea for you to know what he looks like,' she said, trying to keep her voice light. Once again she gestured to the chair. 'Please sit down, Jessica.'

'I will if you do.' Jessica removed a pile of books from the stool which stood by the door. How could she possibly sit whilst Henrietta remained standing? She placed the stool beside the chair.

Henrietta was touched by the gesture, and together they sat. 'This is Kit,' she said as she opened the scrapbook.

'Local War Hero'. Jessica read the headlines on the front page of the *Northern Territory News*. She studied the picture of the young man with the attractive smile, wondering as she did where the secrecy was leading. It was not unusual for a mother to keep a scrapbook of her son's exploits.

'He won the Military Medal,' Henrietta said. 'Foong Lee sent me the article. He sends me all of Kit's articles— he's a journalist now, and a very good one.' She watched as Jessica slowly turned the pages of the scrapbook, glancing through Kit's feature stories, each with a picture of him beside the byline.

Henrietta was very proud of her son. He'd become a fine writer. Paul had always said he showed talent. She remembered the two of them together, Paul holding forth about the great writers of the twentieth century, the little boy hanging on his every word. Paul, too, would have been proud of his son, she often thought.

Jessica turned the page to another article, this time from a magazine. 'A Family of Territorians' it was headed, but the article had been mutilated. There was a photograph of Kit with a man's arm about his shoulder, but the image of the man had been cut out. And there was a further photograph, of a young, dark-haired man, very handsome, in army uniform.

'Who's this?' she asked.

'That's my elder son, Malcolm,' Henrietta said. 'He was killed in Vietnam.'

'Oh.' Jessica glanced at Henrietta, not sure what to say, but Henrietta's smile assured her no words were necessary.

'He was a fine young man,' she said. 'A hero.' Poor, dear Malcolm, she had thought, dying in battle. His father would have been broken-hearted but proud. 'My son died for his country,' she could hear Terence boast. Henrietta had thought of nothing but the fear and the pain Malcolm might have known. Dear God let it have been quick, she'd prayed.

'Turn the page,' she said, not wanting to invite enquiry

about the mutilated picture, although she was sure Jessica would be too tactful to make any comment, 'there're some photographs on the next one.'

Jessica turned the page without having had time to read the copy which attended the article. She wondered about the man in the mutilated picture. Was it the husband? Surely it must have been.

Three photographs were pasted onto the following page. 'Foong Lee,' she said recognising the Chinese in the first one. 'Gosh Kit's tall.'

'Yes, he is, but then Foong Lee's short.' Henrietta smiled as she looked at the photograph of Kit and Foong Lee in a playful pose outside the front of the restaurant, Kit propping his elbow on Foong Lee's head.

'And that's Kit and his girlfriend,' Henrietta said. 'She used to work with him at the newspaper, but they've split up now.'

'Who's this?' Jessica asked of the final photograph of Kit and a handsome older woman with a shock of white hair.

'She's a very dear friend who's been like a mother to him,' Henrietta said. Darling Aggie, she thought. She blessed Aggie Marshall daily. And she blessed Foong Lee for sending her the photographs and the articles. They were the only contact Henrietta had with her son and his life, and they were of immeasurable comfort to her.

Henrietta closed the scrapbook and turned to Jessica. Now for the moment of truth, she thought. 'I haven't seen my son for over thirteen years,' she said.

Jessica made no reply, she didn't dare breathe a word, aware that this was the secret Henrietta had agonised over whether or not she should reveal.

'Kit doesn't know that I'm alive.' Henrietta's voice was matter-of-fact, clinical. There, she'd said it, now she'd simply have to trust in the girl's oath of silence. 'He's nearly twenty-seven years old, and since the age of thirteen he has believed that I am dead.'

It was a shocking statement and Jessica didn't know what to say. Why on earth would Henrietta Galloway want her son to believe she was dead? Jessica's eyes obviously asked the question.

'If I had returned to Darwin during those years,' Henrietta explained, choosing her words with care, 'lives would have been endangered—my own, and others. The threat no longer exists—if it did, then of course I wouldn't be telling you this—but there are personal reasons why I don't wish to make myself known now.'

Jessica once again wondered why. But this time the query in her eyes went unanswered.

'If I direct you to the locket,' Henrietta continued, 'and therefore to Kit, you must give me your word that you will say nothing to him about me.'

'Why don't you want him to know you're alive?' Jessica couldn't stop herself asking the question. 'If there's no longer any danger, then surely . . .'

But Henrietta continued as if she hadn't heard. 'It would be quite easy. You would simply tell him the story of your search, just as you told me and Foong Lee. Your search would naturally lead you to Kit, Foong Lee having told you that Paul Trewinnard gave me the locket. And you would have presumed that, upon my death, Kit may have inherited it.'

Jessica repeated her question, gently this time. 'Why don't you want your son to know you're alive, Henrietta?'

There were a dozen answers Henrietta could have given, but Jessica didn't know the full story. So she told her as much of the truth as she could. And strangely enough, as she said it, she realised she was voicing her principal concern.

'He has a life of his own,' she said. 'I've been dead to Kit for over thirteen years—it's best he remembers me the way I was.' She recalled how close they'd been, she and her darling younger son. He had been her world as she knew she'd been his—could she bear to see disenchantment in his eyes? 'Heavens above,' she said lightly in an attempt to suppress her innermost fears, 'he doesn't need a middle-aged cripple of a mother he hasn't known since his childhood.'

'Oh yes, he does.'

It was Henrietta's turn to be taken aback, and she was. Jessica herself was taken aback by her own vehemence. There was a moment of silence, but when she continued it was with the same fervour. 'Do you know what I would have given to find my real mother? To meet her, to discover who she was and what she'd done with her life? To know her as a woman, this person who gave birth to me? Do you know what I would have given?' Jessica didn't wait for Henrietta to reply. 'You owe it to Kit,' she said. 'He's your son and he should be allowed to share your life.'

There was nothing Henrietta could have desired more, but there were extenuating circumstances—the girl didn't know the whole story. 'There are things that have happened in my life, Jessica,' she said slowly, 'things that may have altered Kit's view of me, truths that might shatter his world.'

'Surely it's worth the risk.'

'It's not that simple.'

'I believe that it is.'

The girl was pushing her and Henrietta felt confused and uncertain. 'You don't know the full story,' she said.

'I'm aware of that.' Jessica was also aware of her own bullying tactics, but perhaps, somewhere deep inside, Henrietta wanted to be bullied. It was quite evident that she loved her son and that she missed him desperately. 'But whatever the story is, it obviously involves Kit. Don't you think he should be allowed to know the truth?'

How Henrietta longed to tell Kit the truth. The good truths in any event. She longed to tell him about the love she and Paul had shared, and the love Paul had felt for the son he could never acknowledge as his own. She wanted nothing more than to tell him such truths. But her fear remained.

'What if he hates me?' she whispered, more to herself than the girl.

Jessica was moved. She wanted so much to help Henrietta, but she knew that there was little more she could say. She didn't want to bully her further. Henrietta was too frightened. She was haunted by fear; it was in her eyes.

An idea suddenly occurred to Jessica. 'Why don't we go to Darwin together?' she suggested. The words were out of her mouth before she'd given them any thought and, as they hung in the air, she realised that she'd surprised herself more than Henrietta in the saying of them. Why was she so eager to become involved in the reuniting of Henrietta Galloway and her son, she wondered. Was she trying in some way to help heal the wounds of her own loss? The question was unanswerable but, whatever her motives, Jessica was driven by an intense desire to bring mother and son together. 'You could see Kit from a distance,' she urged, 'and then decide what to do.' Yes, that was it, she thought. Surely once the woman laid eyes on her son she would feel compelled to reveal herself. 'You wouldn't have to make yourself known to him if you didn't want to,' she added encouragingly.

'Yes,' Henrietta breathed. Caught up in Jessica's excitement, she felt the agony of her indecision lifting, 'yes, I could do that, couldn't I? He needn't even know I'm there.' Why hadn't she thought of it the moment Foong Lee had rung with the news of Terence's death? At least then she would be able to see her son in the flesh. To actually lay eyes on him instead of poring over a photograph or a press clipping. Her heart raced at the prospect, and she blessed the intervention of Jessica Williams. 'Yes, I'll come to Darwin with you.'

Her decision made, Henrietta was determined to move quickly—any more thought on the subject might invite a return of her indecision. She was going to see her son and that was all that mattered. She had made the momentous decision and it had to happen *now*. 'Foong Lee can arrange a meeting between you and Kit,' she said, reaching for the telephone on her desk. 'You'll see the locket and I'll see my son,' she said as she started to dial.

For the past half hour, the locket had been the last thing on Jessica's mind as she'd become embroiled in the mystery of Henrietta Galloway's past.

Henrietta paused mid-dial. 'Would you be able to go to Darwin if we can get a flight tomorrow?'

Jessica nodded. And now it appeared she was about to become embroiled in Henrietta Galloway's future.

CHAPTER FORTY-TWO

Darwin was unrecognisable from the air. The two women peered through the windows of the aircraft at what looked like a war zone below.

During the flight, Henrietta had felt the strangest yearnings as she'd watched the landscape unfold beneath her. The red earth, the lush wetlands, the plains and the escarpments. She hadn't realised how much she had missed the vastness of the Territory. And when she stepped off the plane and the heat embraced her, she welcomed it like an old friend. She had thought she would never return, but the Territory had claimed her long ago. She belonged here, she thought.

As they walked through the makeshift terminal, Jessica was appalled. 'This was a brand new airport when I left,' she said. Could it really have been only five weeks ago?

Both women were silent during the taxi drive into town. The pleasant Greek-Australian cab driver registered their shock. 'Yeah, bit of a mess, eh?' Then, realising they didn't want to chat, he tactfully kept quiet. He agreed with them anyway, there was nothing much to be said. Tracy had done a thorough job of it, all right. As far as the eye could see, Darwin had been razed to the ground.

It was early afternoon when Kit arrived at the restaurant.

'You're right on time,' Foong Lee said, greeting him at the door. 'Excellent.'

'Well you made it sound like it was more than my life was worth to be late,' Kit replied. 'What's all the mystery? And why have you got the closed sign up? You never put the closed sign up.'

But Foong Lee didn't answer any of his queries. 'Come in, come in.' And he hustled Kit inside, closing the door. He crossed to the bar where the teapot and cups were set out by the urn. 'Don't worry,' he said, 'it's not for you.' Kit hated *heung ping*. Foong Lee handed him a cold beer from the refrigerator.

'Thanks,' said Kit. 'So who's it for then? Who's the mystery person I'm supposed to meet? Why all the secrecy?'

'All in good time, all in good time. Tell me about work, how are things at the paper?'

Kit gave up. He knew better than to try to badger information out of Foong Lee. If Foong Lee had decided he wasn't talking then that was that. But whatever the mysterious business was, Kit hoped it wouldn't take too long. He had a pile of assignments to tackle.

'Busy,' he said. 'Things are busy at the paper.' He said it good naturedly, but he was making a definite point, hoping Foong Lee would take the hint.

'Really? How exciting. Tell me all about it.' Foong Lee led the way to a table beside the windows. Kit heaved a sigh of frustration, the man was infuriating.

Foong Lee sensed Kit's exasperation, but he refused to explain what was going on, just as he'd refused Henrietta's request that he be part of the deception.

'You must tell Kit all about Jessica and her search for the locket,' Henrietta had instructed him over the phone, 'and you must say that you told Jessica that Paul gave the locket to me.'

'But I didn't tell Jessica any such thing.' Foong Lee had

been surprised to hear that the locket was in Kit's possession. Not that it mattered—the locket had lessened in
importance in the current scheme of things. Its discovery
had served the purpose of bringing Henrietta out of
hiding, and that was all that concerned Foong Lee. But,
to his dismay, Henrietta had insisted upon maintaining
her secret.

'I have no intention of returning from the grave, Foong
Lee. I simply want to see Kit, that's all. From a distance.'

'You're wrong, Henrietta,' he said. 'And you may live to
regret such a decision.'

'Then the regret will be mine,' she replied, very firmly.

'As you wish. Of course I shall say nothing.' But he
refused to play her game. He was not going to make things
easier for her, he'd decided, secretly hoping that, on seeing
Kit, Henrietta would be unable to resist making herself
known to her son.

Kit sat at the table and peered out the window. Foong
Lee had probably set up a meeting with someone who
wanted a favour from the newspaper, he thought. Most
likely something to do with one of the many relief com-
mittees with which he was involved. Kit would vastly
have preferred a more straightforward approach, but then
Foong Lee was a devious old bugger, he thought. There
was no option but to play his game. He took a swig from
his can of beer and started talking about his assignments
and the importance of *NTN* in the aftermath of Tracy,
rapidly warming to his theme. Kit's work was a subject
which never ceased to interest him.

Outside the restaurant, a taxi pulled up. From the moment
they'd reached the outskirts of town, Henrietta had begun
to feel terrified. Why? she'd asked herself, there was no
need. She would simply remain in the taxi, see her son
from a distance, then instruct the driver to return to the
airport.

'Don't be ridiculous,' Foong Lee had scoffed over the phone when she'd told him her intention, but she'd been adamant. It was a day trip only and she would be returning on the early evening flight. Henrietta had decided it would be far too dangerous to stay overnight. She was still well known to many in Darwin and she dare not risk an encounter with someone from the past.

'At least let Albert pick you up,' Foong Lee had suggested. 'Then he can take you to the house until it's time for your flight back to Perth. You can't spend the whole afternoon hanging around the airport.'

'Have you told Albert I'm alive?' she'd demanded.

'Of course not.' He'd been outraged by her suggestion that he might have broken his word.

'Then there is no reason for him to know now.' Henrietta wished that she hadn't involved Foong Lee in the exercise, she knew he was trying to force her hand.

Jessica was about to open the door of the taxi. 'Are you sure you won't change your mind and come in with me?' she asked.

'Quite sure,' Henrietta replied with a strength which belied her emotional state. She'd been tense from the moment they'd left Perth, and the sight and the feel and the smell of the Territory hadn't helped, assailing her with images and sensations from the past. Now she was a bundle of nerves, but she was determined not to show it. 'Go on.'

Jessica said nothing but, impulsively, she clasped Henrietta's hand. Henrietta didn't acknowledge the gesture. She was far too uncertain of her emotional control to accept any show of sympathy and she wished the girl would get out of the vehicle. But, suddenly, just as Jessica was about to open the car door, Henrietta clutched the girl's hand in both of her own. And clutched it so tightly that she startled herself as well as Jessica.

Jessica looked at Henrietta in alarm. The colour had

drained from her face and she was staring fixedly out of the car window. Jessica turned. In the restaurant, only metres away, clearly visible through the large plate-glass window, Kit Galloway was seated at a table in avid conversation with Foong Lee.

Henrietta quickly released Jessica's hand. 'I'm sorry, I'm so sorry, it was just the shock.' But her eyes didn't leave Kit for an instant.

'Come in with me, Henrietta,' Jessica urged.

'No, no,' she said. She didn't dare. But there he was, clear as day. She had only to cross the footpath and tap on the window and he would turn and look directly at her. How she longed to see his eyes. 'Go on, Jessica, go on,' she implored.

Jessica reluctantly pushed the door open, hoping that at any minute Henrietta might change her mind. But Henrietta didn't move a muscle, she remained staring at her son.

Foong Lee had seen the taxi pull up. He paid rapt attention to Kit's conversation, but in his peripheral vision he watched the taxi, and he waited. A minute or so went by before the car door opened and Jessica alighted. 'Ah,' he said, 'our visitor.'

Kit looked out into the street. He studied the girl as she closed the door of the taxi behind her. She had creamy skin and chestnut hair and was rather attractive. So this was the mystery person he was supposed to meet—how very intriguing.

Foong Lee rose from the table. 'Would you mind filling the teapot, Kit?' he asked.

'Sure.' Kit raked his hair back with his fingers as he stood.

Henrietta's heart skipped a beat at the familiar gesture. The instant he'd looked in the taxi's direction, she'd seen a flash of the grey eyes which she knew so well. But now he'd turned away and, as she watched, he stepped out of sight. She gave an involuntary gasp, willing him to return to the window. But even if he did she knew it would not be enough. Staring at him through a plate-glass window was just as unfulfilling as poring over photographs and press clippings. She needed to look into his eyes, to touch his face, to hold him close and feel her arms around him. Her breath was coming in short gasps, she realised, as she opened the car door.

'You okay, lady?' the cab driver asked with a touch of concern.

'Please wait,' she said, and got out of the taxi a little clumsily, her stick momentarily wedging itself in the door. The driver was about to get out and help her. 'No, I'm all right, thank you,' she hastily assured him, so he settled back behind the wheel and opened his newspaper.

Jessica had been about to knock on the restaurant door. She paused and watched as Henrietta slowly, but unhesitatingly, crossed the footpath. When the older woman stood beside her, she gently tapped on the door.

While Kit was busy filling the teapot, Foong Lee had remained standing by the window watching the taxi, and he breathed a sigh of relief when he saw Henrietta get out. He waited until he heard the tap at the door and then went to open it.

Henrietta stood there, white-faced and breathless. He gave her a smile of encouragement which she failed to notice as she stared straight ahead.

'Say hello to our visitor, Kit.' Foong Lee pushed the door wide open and stepped aside.

The figure Kit saw silhouetted in the doorway was not that of the girl who'd alighted from the taxi. It was an older woman. Tall, regal of bearing, despite the fact that she was leaning her weight on a cane. She stepped out of the glare and into the cool of the restaurant, and for one brief second Kit wondered if it was the girl's mother. She was very handsome and they shared the same colouring, creamy skin and chestnut hair.

Henrietta stood motionless. The photographs hadn't prepared her at all. Neither had the sight of him through the plate-glass window. She put a hand to her face and tears sprang to her eyes. She was looking at Paul Trewinnard.

'Oh, my darling,' she whispered, she wasn't sure to whom. Perhaps to Paul, perhaps to Kit; she was overwhelmed.

In the same instant, Kit recognised his mother. He, too, stood frozen, unable to move. How could this woman be his mother? His mother was dead.

They stared at each other across the room, both mother and son in a state of shock.

Henrietta was the first to recover. 'Hello, Kit,' she said. She didn't know whether to hold out her arms, or to hobble her poor lame way over to him. What should she do? He was standing there as if he'd seen a ghost. Well of course he had. 'It's me.' She nodded encouragingly, hopefully.

And then suddenly he was with her and his arms were around her and he was holding her so close, bending over her, his head tucked into her shoulder, and she could feel the dampness of his tears against her bare neck.

Henrietta's cane clattered to the floor as she clung to her son.

'Shall we go for a walk?' Foong Lee whispered to Jessica.

She nodded. 'And I think I'd better pay off the cab driver,' she said.

They closed the door behind them as they left. Neither Henrietta nor Kit saw them go.

After several minutes, Henrietta found herself laughing. Whether through sheer relief or emotional exhaustion, she didn't know. 'Oh my darling, this is ridiculous,' she said, 'just look at us.' They finally released each other, both with tears streaming down their cheeks. 'We're a mess.'

'Hardly surprising,' Kit grinned, wiping his face with the back of his hand. 'Jesus Christ . . .'

'Don't blaspheme,' she said automatically, then laughed. 'Come on, help me sit down.'

There were so many questions, all of which Henrietta had expected, but she'd worried about how she would answer them. The worry was gone now; she would simply tell him the truth.

'I'll tell you everything that happened, Kit,' she said. 'Everything.' And for the first time, Henrietta unguardedly told her story. She held nothing back.

CHAPTER FORTY-THREE

'Take my breath, Jackie. Too much pain. I beg you, take my breath.'

When Henrietta had offered her throat to Jackie's knife, she had prayed for oblivion, and she'd felt it descend thankfully upon her as she'd listened to his chanting. She'd felt herself floating into another world. How kind of him, she'd thought as she floated away. How right. How just.

She'd awoken much later, it could have been minutes or hours, and the pain once again screamed through her. She seemed to be lying on some sort of litter, her whole body tied tightly to it. And she was in a cave, surrounded by black people, the storm raging outside. Jackie was there, kneeling by her side.

'Sorry, missus,' he'd whispered. 'Couldn' let you die.'

Why not, her mind had begged. But he'd started chanting again, and other voices joined in. Hands had touched her, voices had lulled her and, mercifully, she'd once again lost consciousness.

It was the last time she'd seen Jackie Yoorunga. But she'd seen the other people, Jackie's friends of the Warai, as she'd floated in and out of consciousness, thankful each time the world clouded over, hoping that she would not reawaken to the pain.

She'd been aware at one stage of being carried on the litter. The agony had been excruciating and again she'd blacked out.

When she'd awoken it had been to a different sound from the harsh tongue of the black people. A strange sing-song language. And the faces surrounding her were different. They were Chinese faces.

There was more movement, more agony, more blissful oblivion. And finally she'd woken to find herself in a bed. Still she couldn't move, and her limbs seemed strapped, but the pain was finally bearable. It was there but she was somehow disassociated from it, as if she had left her body. She didn't know at that stage that they'd given her opium. And this time, when she'd awoken, it had been to a face she knew.

'Foong Lee,' she'd whispered.

'You are going to live, Henrietta.'

His voice was gentle, and seemed to come from somewhere far away, but, in the cloud of her brain, Henrietta felt a sudden fear. 'Terence,' she said. 'Terence mustn't know.'

'Sssh,' the gentle voice had assured her, 'no-one will know. Rest now.'

The fear in Henrietta's eyes had confirmed Foong Lee's suspicions.

The Warai had taken Henrietta to Daly River, and they'd passed word to the Chinese coolies working on the peanut farms there. A white woman was hurt bad. It was no good business, the Warai had said, and they wanted no part of it. But they'd passed the word on all the same, and the word had soon found its way to the Chinese tai pan, Foong Lee.

Foong Lee had wondered why the Warai had become involved. It was white men's business, after all, and bad business at that, as they'd told the coolies. Had it been sheer luck that news of the injured white woman had reached him? Or had someone specifically mentioned his name, with orders passed along the network to seek him out?

Foong Lee didn't know that the Warai had been following the instructions of Jackie Yoorunga, but he'd been grateful that they'd seen fit to intervene. There was something decidedly sinister about the tragic accident which was purported to have happened at Bullalalla cattle station.

Henrietta Galloway had been reported missing, but Foong Lee's discreet enquiries revealed that the search, instigated by her distraught husband, did not include the high escarpment area of the Warai. Foong Lee had found it very suspect. Terence Galloway had been out riding with his wife when the storm had struck—he would most certainly know which areas to search. So Foong Lee had kept his silence as he nursed Henrietta in the safe house to which he'd brought her. Until he knew the full story, he decided that it would be wiser not to alert Terence, but to allow him the belief that he had succeeded in his crime. Foong Lee was even sure of the man's motive. Terence Galloway must have discovered the truth about Kit.

Foong Lee had always known that Kit was Paul Trewinnard's son, Paul himself had told him. 'Henrietta may well need a friend when I'm gone, Foong Lee,' he'd said. 'It's right that you should know.'

To a man like Terence Galloway, the discovery that he'd raised another man's son might well be enough to incite a murderous rage, Foong Lee realised. But how had he found out? Henrietta would most certainly not have told him.

Henrietta's fearful reaction convinced Foong Lee of Terence Galloway's guilt, and he determined that, when she was well enough, he would help her confront the authorities with the truth.

In the meantime, Henrietta was secretly tended by a Chinese doctor whose connections to the opium trade guaranteed his silence. Foong Lee had lied to Paul Trewinnard from the outset. The opium trade did exist in Darwin, a well-kept secret from all but a select number of Chinese. Foong Lee didn't approve of it, but at moments like this, such a trade served its purpose.

However, when Henrietta had regained her strength enough to talk, and to discuss a plan of action, she was adamant, "No, Foong Lee, no-one must know that I'm alive. It is better for all concerned if I remain dead.'

She had not told him what had actually taken place, and he had not asked for details, but an unspoken understanding rested between them. When he had told her that the search had been called off and she had been presumed dead, she'd breathed a sigh of relief. 'Thank God,' she'd said. Now, as he suggested they inform the authorities of her existence, her fear had returned.

'Kit's life would be in danger,' she said.

She was aware that Foong Lee knew the truth about her son—Paul had told her. 'Foong Lee could be a valuable ally when I'm gone, Henrietta,' he had said, 'and you need never fear: he will take the secret to his grave.'

'Help me, please,' she begged. 'As long as Terence is alive no-one must ever know of my existence.'

They agreed that she must leave Darwin.

It was many months before she was fit enough to travel, and, in the spring, Foong Lee accompanied her south. Even still, Henrietta was barely able to walk, and when she attempted to do so the pain was intolerable.

In Perth he introduced her to Chinese friends of his. The two middle-aged Ling brothers and their large extended family were market gardeners with a profitable business on the South Perth foreshore west of Coode Street. In deference to their old friend, Foong Lee, the Lings asked no probing questions about Henrietta Southern's past, they simply welcomed her into their circle, and after several weeks, comfortable in the knowledge that Henrietta Galloway was safe, Foong Lee returned to his family.

Henrietta was determined to make a full recovery. In Darwin, as she'd teetered on the brink of existence, Foong Lee had sat by her bedside for endless days encouraging her will to live. 'It is your passion for life which will heal you, Henrietta,' he had so often said to her. Henrietta had proved him right. She had survived. And she then resolved to live as full and active a life as was humanly possible.

For many painful months she worked hard on her physical fitness until the orthopaedic surgeon to whom she'd been referred considered her healthy and strong enough to undergo the necessary operations. Her right leg would need to be rebroken and reset in two places, and her right hip would require surgery.

Hungry for a normal life, Henrietta agreed to the innovative hip replacement procedure which the surgeon was eager to practise. She'd be in anything that was offering, she vowed.

The healing process was slow, but with the Chinese family's care and support, and through her own sheer determination, Henrietta recovered. The months became years and she set about building a life of her own. She bought a house and busied herself with the business investments which Foong Lee had made on her behalf, thankful for the fact that she had long ago set aside funds in preparation for the day when she would leave Terence Galloway. Little had she known then that that day would come so soon and in such a violent manner, she often thought with a sense of irony.

She determined not to be crushed by her losses, knowing that Terence would provide well for Kit and Malcolm, and that Foong Lee and Aggie would always look out for her precious sons. She had no choice but to believe these things. She must stifle her longing in order to protect Kit.

So she made her new life full. She had a loving adoptive family in the Lings, she met new people and made new friends through the book clubs she joined, and eventually she even became a published author herself under the nom de plume Henry South.

'I'm not sure if you'd approve of Henry South, darling,' Henrietta said a little nervously in the pause which followed the completion of her story. She looked closely at Kit trying to gauge his reaction. He'd been attentive throughout, but he'd shown no emotion and now he was silent. She was suddenly unsure as to whether or not she'd been wise. Did he believe her about Terence? Did he understand the fear which had kept her away all these years? She was on tenterhooks as she waited for him to say something.

Kit not only understood, he had his own story to tell.

'Terence Galloway was a madman,' he said finally. 'A complete and utter madman. He tried to kill me too.'

Kit had told no-one of the gunshot that night in the midst of Tracy's fury; he too had kept his secret. Terence Galloway, one of Darwin's most prominent citizens, attempting to kill his son? What was the point in telling such a story? No-one would have believed him. It was a relief to be able to speak of it now.

He told Henrietta everything, from Pearl's visit, to his confrontation with Terence over the locket and the ensuing madness of the cyclone.

So Pearl had kept the locket for a whole six years, Henrietta thought. She wanted to ask Kit how he'd felt when he'd seen it, when he'd realised that Paul was his father, but she wasn't sure how to voice the question. She didn't need to.

'It explained a lot of things to me,' Kit said thoughtfully.

'What did, darling?'

'Paul being my father. It explained everything.' How could he tell her of all the questions in his life which had been answered. But Henrietta was nodding, she knew. 'I was glad when I found out,' he said. 'I loved Paul.'

'So did I. Oh God, here I go again.' She laughed, but she didn't try to stem the tears. 'And Paul loved you, Kit,' she said. 'He loved you and he was so proud of you.'

They sat holding hands, and they laughed happily and wept unashamedly as they talked about Paul Trewinnard.

Foong Lee and Jessica had spent a good hour walking through the demolished streets of Darwin. He'd taken her to the *yung si*, the ancient banyan tree at the southern end of the town and he'd told her all about the early days.

'The *yung si* used to be part of Chinatown,' he'd said. 'As children we'd play in its branches. The *yung si* is a symbol of Darwin. It has lived through the bombs and it has lived through the cyclone and it will live on, just as Darwin will.'

They'd walked down to the harbour, then up the hill to the Esplanade and eventually he'd said, 'I think we can go back now.'

When they returned to the restaurant, they discovered Henrietta and Kit huddled together at a table talking nineteen to the dozen.

'We're back,' Foong Lee announced.

'Oh.' Henrietta looked up as if she was seeing them for the first time.

'I didn't know you'd gone.' Kit blinked away the remnants of his tears as he rose from the table. He couldn't remember having cried this much since he was a kid, and a very little one at that. 'Ah, Foong Lee's mysterious visitor.' He proffered his hand to the girl he'd seen alighting from the taxi. 'Hello, I'm Kit Galloway.'

'Jessica Williams.' She looked into the same warm smile she'd seen in the photographs and Jessica felt she knew him as she shook his hand.

'So you're part of the whole conspiracy, Jessica,' Kit said. The girl was obviously some form of secretarial companion to his mother. 'I must say I'm very grateful to you and Foong Lee for planning this reunion.'

Jessica was about to correct him, but Henrietta answered for her. 'Jessica is certainly responsible for my being here, Kit,' she said, 'but we met only yesterday.' Kit looked puzzled. How strange, he thought. How could the girl be responsible? Where did she fit in? 'Jessica's actually come to Darwin to see you, my darling.'

Kit turned to the girl. What on earth was she doing here, he wondered.

'It's true, Kit,' Jessica said. 'You have something I've been searching for for years.'

CHAPTER FORTY-FOUR

1975

The bell on the shop door of the Huize Grij tinkled. Behind the counter, Wouter Eikelboom turned to greet the young couple who stepped in from the paved street.

'Goede morgen,' he said.

'Hello,' the young man replied. Then he smiled apologetically, 'I'm sorry, but do you speak English?'

'Of course,' Wouter nodded. He spoke seven languages, most of them fluently, and his English was impeccable.

The young man shared a relieved grin with his companion.

'Welcome to the House of Grij,' Wouter said. His customary formal greeting was reserved and delivered with an unintended edge of superiority.

Kit felt gangly and out of place as he and Jessica crossed to the dapper, balding man in the pinstripe suit and vest who stood behind the counter. The room was tiny, the ceiling low. I'm too big for this room, he thought.

'How do you do,' Jessica said. 'I'm Jessica Williams.'

She smiled warmly at the man, hoping to break through his reserve, 'and this is Kit Galloway.'

Wouter's eyes glanced at the girl's left hand, no wedding ring. 'How do you do, Miss Williams'—he always liked to address people correctly—'Mr Galloway,' he nodded. 'I am Wouter Eikelboom, how may I help you?'

The man seemed incapable of smiling, Jessica thought. His face was a mask of inscrutability. 'We have an antique piece and we need to authenticate its origins,' she said, getting down to business. 'We believe it may have been designed by the House of Grij.'

'I am most willing to be of service if I am able.'

Kit took the case from his pocket, opened it and put it on the counter. From its silk-lined interior, Wouter lifted out the locket. His hands were small and lily-white, Jessica noticed, his fingers delicate, his nails perfectly manicured.

'An exquisite piece,' he said. He looked up at them and, to their astonishment, his face suddenly contorted. He raised his eyebrows in an exaggerated expression of surprise, set a jeweller's magnifying eyepiece into the socket of his eye then frowned ferociously, wedging the eyepiece firmly in position. Then, facial gymnastics over, he bent to examine the locket.

Jessica and Kit exchanged a glance, their eyes dancing with amusement; they both wanted to burst out laughing. Kit gave a bit of a snort, which he turned into a cough as Jessica nudged him.

'Seventeenth-century,' Wouter said.

'That's what we thought,' Jessica quickly answered, not trusting in Kit's ability to reply—she had a feeling he was about to get a fit of the giggles. He'd returned her nudge with a nod at the dome of the little man's head where long, thin strands of grey hair were painstakingly pasted across his bald pate from one ear to the other.

Wouter turned the locket over. 'Ah,' he said as he studied the two tiny g's of the engraver's mark, 'what a find, most exciting,' although his voice betrayed not an element of excitement. He didn't open the locket. He laid it back on the counter and looked up at them, his face an angry scowl. Then he raised his eyebrows in a reversal of his previous facial contortion, took the eyepiece from his socket, and his face shrank back to its impassive mask. Jessica kicked Kit's foot.

'It is most certainly a piece from the House of Grij,' Wouter said. 'A very valuable piece, I might add.' Jessica and Kit forgot their mirth—this was the breakthrough they had sought. 'There is someone you must meet,' Wouter continued, picking up the handpiece of the telephone on the counter, 'or rather I might suggest, someone who must meet you.' He dialled, then said, 'Please excuse me,' with the utmost deference, before talking briefly in Dutch to whoever it was on the other end of the line.

He replaced the receiver, carefully returned the locket to its case, and handed it to Kit. 'Please come with me,' he said, 'Mr Grij is most interested in meeting you.' He stepped out from behind the counter and crossed to the front door. He was wearing spats, Jessica noticed.

Wouter turned the 'open' sign on the door to 'closed' and stood aside for them. 'After you,' he said, and they stepped outside.

'This is the original home of the Grij family.' The bell tinkled as Wouter closed and locked the door behind them. 'It was built shortly after the canal was completed. Of course it has undergone many restorations over the centuries but little of its original design has changed. It remains a magnificent example of early Dutch architecture.'

The spiel was obviously well rehearsed and had been trotted out to many a tourist on numerous occasions, but it was delivered with pride nonetheless.

Jessica looked up at the tall, slender building, at its many narrow windows and its high, sloping roof intricately tiled in terracotta. It was indeed an impressive *house, reminiscent of a bygone era. But then so was the whole street. The line of terraced houses, the paved road, the linden trees, the canal where barges drifted lazily by. It seemed that in this part of Amsterdam time had stood still for centuries.*

Having locked the door, Wouter turned to them. His face remained a mask, but his voice was most agreeable; he obviously enjoyed delivering his lecture to tourists.

'Mr Grij, whom you are about to meet, converted the adjoining building to a museum in the 1950s, some time after the war. It was not only a tribute to his ancestors and their artistry, but a personal statement of his feelings about war. Come with me, please.'

They followed him to the terrace house adjoining the jeweller's. Above the door was a sign which said 'Museum Grij'.

'Mr Grij is very passionate about the futility and the destruction of war. So many great works of art have been lost through man's foolishness and greed, he is determined to preserve whatever he can for the enjoyment of future generations.'

The front door of the museum led directly off the street into a foyer. Narrow steps to the left led upstairs to the first and second floors where the museum exhibits were displayed, and there were two doors at the rear of the foyer, one leading to the office, the other to the work-rooms out the back. In the corner was a reception desk strewn with brochures and leaflets, and the young woman tending it greeted them with a smile.

'Goede morgen, Wouter,' she said.

'Goede morgen, Riemke.'

'Good morning,' she said to Kit and Jessica, 'Mr Grij is expecting you.'

She walked to the rear door on the left and tapped gently. Only seconds later, she stood aside as the door was opened by a man who, although elderly, appeared in excellent health.

'Hello, hello,' he said expansively, his voice a robust baritone with a thick Dutch accent. 'My English visitors, come in, come in.'

'We're Australian actually,' Kit said as they stepped into the office, Wouter accompanying them and Riemke closing the door behind them.

'All the better, all the better.' He was very jovial and appeared to enjoy saying things twice. 'I am Jaerk Grij.'

'How do you do, Mr Grij, I'm Kit Galloway and this is Jessica Williams.'

'Pleased to meet you,' he shook Kit's hand. 'Pleased to meet you,' he shook Jessica's. 'Please, please, sit down.'

As Jessica crossed to one of the chairs he'd indicated, she looked around at the office. It was devoid of daylight, and would have been a gloomy room, but it was so effectively lit by lamps set in wall brackets that the heavy timber beams, the shelves of books and the solid oak furniture looked warm and cosy. Again she had the feeling that time had stood still. It was a quiet and peaceful room, infused with the fragrance of wood.

Kit didn't notice the room, he was studying Jaerk Grij as he sat. Grij was obviously in his seventies, but with the energy of a man twenty years younger. His thick head of hair was snow white, his eyes, set deep in the wrinkles of his face, were the palest of blue. He was neither tall nor short, neither slim nor fat. Age had added a paunch to his belly but the overall impression was that of a nuggety man, still physically strong, and still with a passion for life.

Jaerk sat behind his desk and looked at the young couple as they seated themselves opposite him. They were a most attractive couple, he thought. Australia. How interesting. He'd often thought he'd like to visit Australia. Not to live there of course, there was little art there that would interest him, except perhaps that of the country's indigenous people. But he would have liked to have seen the texture of the landscape. Ayers Rock, he had always *wanted to see Ayers Rock.*

'*You have something of interest for me.*' He cut his own musings short, which was a pity, he always liked meeting new people, and he'd like to have chatted about Australia. But there were more important things to hand. '*You have a work of Gerrit Grij, Wouter tells me.*'

The young couple looked mystified, so he explained. '*You have a piece with the engraver's mark of two small g's, yes?*'

Kit nodded as he took the case from his pocket.

'*Gerrit Grij was one of the finest master craftsmen ever to have lived, in my opinion and in that of many others.*' Jaerk beamed proudly, his eyes instantly disappearing in the wrinkles of his face. '*I am his direct descendant. It was Gerrit Grij himself who founded the House of Grij.*' The smile vanished as quickly as it had appeared and the pale blue eyes focussed keenly on the small case which Kit placed before him. '*We have only four items of Gerrit's in our possession,*' he said as he turned on the desk lamp. '*His work is very difficult to find these days, and when we do discover a piece, the owner is most loath to part with it, which of course is understandable.*' He took his reading glasses from his top pocket, put them on and opened the case.

Jessica watched the old man's hands as he lifted out the locket. Unlike Wouter's, they were workman's hands. Strong brown fingers with square cut nails. But their touch was delicate; it appeared Jaerk Grij's hands were capable of great strength and sensitivity.

The old man exhaled gently, a soft sigh, barely audible, and his mouth remained open in wonderment as he held the piece up to the light. Kit and Jessica watched him, neither daring to breathe a word. Jaerk Grij appeared transported.

Gently, he caressed the mountain and the diamond sun with his thumb, exploring their texture, then he turned the *locket over and reverently touched the two g's with the tip of his forefinger.*

'Het hangertje,' *Jaerk finally whispered. Wouter had said the young couple had a piece with Gerrit's mark, but he had not said what it was. Any work of Gerrit's was a miraculous find, but* het hangertje? *The locket which he now held in his hands? This locket was Gerrit Grij's lost masterpiece.*

He glanced up at Wouter who stood, as if at attention, beside the desk. Wouter's face remained as implacable as ever, but he gave a slight nod and Jaerk smiled in return. Wouter had deliberately neglected to mention the locket on the telephone, it was obvious he had wished to see Jaerk's reaction.

With the most delicate of touch, Jaerk pressed the clasp and the locket opened to reveal the initials.

'Lucretia van den Mylen,' *he said, and once again it was the softest of whispers.*

'You know of her?' *Jessica found herself whispering back.*

Jaerk Grij appeared to come out of a dream.

'Ah yes. I feel that I know Mevrouw van den Mylen personally.' *He replaced the locket gently in its case, took off his reading glasses and returned them to his top pocket, then he leaned back in his chair.*

'I have devoted many years to the discovery of this piece,' *he said,* 'the van den Mylen locket which disappeared from the face of the earth. Never did I believe that it was lost at sea; I knew that somewhere it existed. But I had given up, I thought that the locket would not come to light in my lifetime.' *He looked down at his desk, the reflection of the diamond sun catching the wrinkles of his face in the lamp's beam.* 'And now here it is.' *He stared at it for a moment longer, then shook his head, as if reprimanding himself for the indulgence of his reverie. It was time to get down to business.*

'Wouter tells me you wish to authenticate the piece,' he said, snapping the case closed and picking it up.

Jessica nodded.

'I can do that.' He seemed instantly revitalised as he rose from his chair and strode to the door. Wouter tried to open it for him but Jaerk was there first. 'Come with me,' he said.

In the foyer, he instructed Riemke to field his calls and then led the way up the narrow stairs to the first floor.

The Grij display rooms were enchanting. The house itself was a museum piece, and the first floor was designed to offer an intimate view of family life in times long past. A sitting room with seventeenth-century furnishings and rugs, works of art from the period adorning the walls; a bedroom with a canopied four poster, a large jug and bowl on a wash stand, a dressing table displaying a woman's vanity set of brushes and combs. Alongside the personal items of everyday existence stood life-sized dummies in costume, including two children, a little boy and girl surrounded by their toys, and throughout, the atmosphere was enhanced by indirect lighting from imitation gas-lamps on the walls.

'It's beautiful,' Jessica said.

But Jaerk would allow them no more than a few minutes to wander the rooms. 'What we seek is on the second floor,' he said. 'Follow me,' and once again he trudged up the stairs, Wouter standing aside for Kit and Jessica to follow first.

The second floor proved to be a workroom. Light flooded through the tall narrow windows which looked out over the canal, and two heavy benches displayed the tools of the diamond cutter's and craftsman's trade.

The adjoining room was a showcase of the results. Magnificent pieces gleamed, perfectly lit, in display cases about the walls. Rings and pendants, necklaces, bracelets and brooches, all hand-crafted works of art. An ancient *wooden desk stood in one corner and behind it was another large showcase housing books, dominant amongst which was a giant leather-bound ledger.*

Jaerk put the locket on the desk, opened the display case and took out the ledger and a smaller volume which appeared to be a diary of some sort. He placed them both on the desk beside the locket.

'These books are nearly 350 years old,' he said, 'and in them is a record of Gerrit Grij's work.'

He put on his reading glasses and opened the smaller book. 'His journal,' he said. 'Gerrit considered the van den Mylen locket his finest piece.' Jaerk turned directly to the page; he knew the exact spot.

Kit and Jessica peered over his shoulder as he traced the handwriting, still clear and unfaded by age, with his forefinger.

'I shall translate for you,' he said.

' "Vrouwe van den Mylen has entrusted the design of the locket to me,"' he read the words slowly, but unfalteringly, ' "her wishes being the depiction of the earth and the sun to symbolise the love she shares with her husband Boudewijn. I have suggested a mountain peak embraced by a diamond sun, to which she has agreed, the initials of her and her husband to be engraved in the locket's interior."'

Jaerk did not look at Kit and Jessica, but turned several pages of the journal to a further entry.

' "Vrouwe van den Mylen appears satisfied with the locket,"' he read, once again tracing the words with his finger, ' "a fact which pleases me as I consider it my finest work. The creation of a piece intended as a symbol of love, I believe added to my inspiration. I admire Vrouwe van den Mylen. For a woman in her position to undertake such a perilous journey is a measure of her love. May the Batavia carry her safely, and may the locket see her united with her husband."'

Jaerk closed the journal. 'It is a very unusual entry for Gerrit,' he said. 'In writing of his work, it is the only time he made a personal comment about one of his clients.'

He peered at them over the top of his reading glasses. 'There is no further mention made of Lucretia van den Mylen in his journal. It is obvious he never heard from her again. No doubt he believed she had perished as so many did following the wreck of the Batavia.'

Jaerk turned back to the desk and opened the large leather-bound ledger. 'Here is the official verification you are seeking,' he said, and once again he translated for them as they peered over his shoulder.

The hand was different to that of Gerrit, the writing small, neat and painstakingly correct. ' "Quantity—one. Silver pendant with diamonds inset . . ." ' Jaerk read. The payment was entered and in the receipt column was the signature 'Pieter Grij'.

'Gerrit's son,' Jaerk explained. 'He was clerk to his father during his apprenticeship and became a well-respected craftsman himself in later years.'

He closed the ledger. 'I will photocopy these documents for you,' he said.

Jaerk took off his glasses and peered at them. He withdrew a handkerchief from his pocket and, as he started to methodically clean the lenses, he said, in a tone which was meant to convey indifference but didn't, 'I don't suppose you would contemplate selling the locket? I would offer you an excellent price.'

Kit turned to Jessica standing beside him. He reached for her hand and clasped it. She was surprised by the gesture.

'I think the locket should stay here, don't you, Jess?'

'Yes,' she replied, clasping his hand in return. 'It belongs in the House of Grij. Besides,' she added briskly, 'I have all the material I need for authentication purposes.' She tried to keep her voice business-like, but Jessica was moved. The locket had finally come home. She looked at Kit, their *fingers entwined, and they shared the moment.*

Jaerk's astonishment and delight were plainly evident, he grinned broadly at Wouter and even Wouter could not conceal the glimmer of excitement in his eyes.

Twenty minutes later, when the material had been photocopied and the young couple were preparing to leave his office, Jaerk was further astounded. Kit refused to discuss any form of payment.

'The locket is not mine to sell,' Kit said. 'I believe I've simply been its keeper for a short time.' It was true, he thought. He would feel wrong if he profited from the locket, as if he was accepting payment for stolen goods. Besides, he didn't need the money, he'd inherited the Galloway empire, he was hardly short of cash.

'May I hold it?' Jessica surprised herself as she asked the question, and she felt a little self-conscious when three sets of eyes turned to her. 'Just a last look, that's all.'

Jaerk was only too happy to oblige. It showed great taste on the girl's part that she should wish to pay tribute to a masterpiece. Not many young people today showed such an appreciation for works of art, he thought as he took the locket from its case and handed it to Jessica.

It was so heavy for such a small thing, Jessica marvelled, and she remembered how surprised she'd been by its weight when Kit had first placed it in her hand two months ago. She angled it towards the lamp on Jaerk's desk, the light from the diamonds dazzling her eyes. So powerful. So brilliant. And again she wondered. What would the black man have felt when he balanced the weight of this perfect object in the palm of his hand? What would he have felt when the rays of its miniature sun dazzled his eyes? Little wonder he had been compelled to record the image of such a wondrous thing in his paintings 350 years ago.

Kit watched Jessica as she studied the locket. He knew exactly what she was thinking. He remembered her passion when she'd told him her story.

'*The locket came ashore with a shipwreck survivor, Kit,*' she'd said. '*And he was accepted by the Aborigines—he became one of them. A member of the family.*' Kit recalled her excitement as she'd added, '*Do you know, there were recorded sightings over a hundred years ago of pale-skinned Aborigines with ginger or fair hair and blue or green eyes?*'

Aware Kit was looking at her now, Jessica turned to him. Their eyes met, and she too remembered. '*Did you ever think, Jess,*' he'd said, '*that when you were tracing the history of the locket, you might be tracing your own ancestors?*'

'*Yes,*' she'd answered. She'd never admitted it to anyone before, but she'd admitted it then to Kit Galloway. '*Yes,*' she'd said, '*it had crossed my mind.*'

She and Kit exchanged a smile as she returned the locket to Jaerk. What a small part they had played in the history of the locket, Jessica thought, and conversely, what a huge part it had played in their lives.

'*Thank you,*' Jaerk said, returning the locket to its case, gratified that two young people should pay such homage to the work of his ancestor.

'*The locket will be exhibited in pride of place,*' Jaerk announced as he and Wouter stepped outside to farewell Kit and Jessica, '*I will have a special cabinet made for the lost masterpiece of Gerrit Grij.*'

They shook hands all round, Jaerk pumping Kit's hand vigorously, and as he and Wouter watched the young couple walk down the street, a thought occurred to Jaerk. Het hangertje, *the symbol of love, had not only returned to its home, it had fulfilled its purpose.*

'Dit stel houdt erg veel van elkaar,' *he murmured to Wouter.*

Wouter nodded. Yes, he agreed, the couple loved each other very much. The faintest suggestion of a smile twitched the corners of Wouter Eikelboom's mouth. He wondered how long it would be before they realised it themselves.

THE BATAVIA AND THE LOCKET

In my chapters pertaining to the *Batavia*, the locket and the character of Dirck Liebensz are fictional, and I have taken dramatic licence in my use of dialogue and interaction between the principal players. With these exceptions, all other events are historically accurate. The characters about whom I wrote existed, and the attempted mutiny, the slaughter and torture inflicted upon the survivors by Cornelisz and his henchmen, and the miraculous and timely return of Pelsaert are historical fact.

A postscript on several of the principal characters, for those who may be interested in their fate:

Lucretia van den Mylen finally reached Batavia aboard the rescue vessel the *Zaandam* only to discover that her husband, Boudewijn, had died shortly before her arrival. She married again, and lived for a number of years in the colonies before returning to Holland towards the end of 1635, where she and her husband settled in Leiden. They remained childless.

The success of Commandeur Francisco Pelsaert's rescue operation and the scrupulousness of the trials he conducted on the Abrolhos were sufficient to stifle the criticism of cowardice directed at him from some quarters. However, he became a physically and emotionally broken man through the illness he had contracted during the voyage and the accusations he suffered consequently. He died in 1630.

The mutineers, under torture on the Abrolhos, accused their skipper, Adriaen Jacobsz, of being a principal instigator in the alleged plot to seize the *Batavia*. Jacobsz successfully defended his innocence to the charge of mutiny. He did not, however, escape the serious, and ironically incorrect, accusation levelled at him by his harshest critics. He was accused of 'abandoning his ship and her occupants, thereby provoking the disasters which occurred'. Despite his repeated requests for freedom, he was left to languish, and doubtless to die, in the dungeons of the citadel of Batavia. There is no record of his release, nor is there record of his death.

JUDY NUNN

Pacific

As she worked on the script, she felt her excitement gather until it charged through every fibre of her being. This was the role of a lifetime. She couldn't wait to get into the heart and soul of this woman.

Australian actress Samantha Lindsay is thrilled when she scores her first lead movie role in the Hollywood epic *Torpedo Junction*, playing a character based on World War II heroine 'Mamma Tack'.

But as filming begins in Vanuatu, uncanny parallels between history and fiction emerge. Just who was the real Mamma Tack? And what mysterious forces are at play? The answers reveal not only bygone secrets but Sam's own destiny.

In another era, Jane Thackeray travels from England to the far distant islands of the New Hebrides. Ensnared in the turmoil of war, Jane witnesses the devastating effect human conflict has upon an innocent race of people. There she meets Charles 'Wolf' Baker, a charismatic fighter pilot, and Jean-Francois Marat, a powerful plantation owner – and soon their lives are entwined in a maelstrom of love and hate …

From the dark days of Dunkirk to the vicious fighting that was Guadalcanal, from the sedate beauty of the English Channel ports to a tropical paradise, *Pacific* is Judy Nunn at her enthralling best.

PROLOGUE

The elements were peaceful. A cloudless sky, a gentle breeze, an unruffled sea. It should have been a perfect summer morning. And the beach should have been inviting. Terrace houses, some five storeys high, fronted onto the broad expanse of sand, a pretty setting, echoing past holiday-makers' delight. But it was no holiday haven today.

Today black smoke dimmed the sun, and the sea and sky merged to a murky grey as layer upon layer of German aircraft swooped from high to unleash their 1,000-pound bombs on the English destroyers. The elements were peaceful, but mankind was bent on death and destruction.

Martin Thackeray lay on the deck, clinging to the gunwales of the small wooden fishing boat as the Stukas roared overhead. The boat had pulled out to sea and was in the midst of the havoc being wreaked upon the British warships. He looked back at the shore barely a mile away, at the beach and the houses. He thought of Margate where his family used to holiday annually when he was a child and he tried to blot out the smoke and the exploding shells and the bodies bobbing about in the oil-blackened sea. He concentrated on the beach and the houses. It could have been Margate, he thought. And the long V-formation of soldiers marching down to the shore could have been holiday-makers. He clung to the thought as rigidly as he clung to the gunwales, fearful of losing consciousness, for the loss of consciousness meant the loss of his life. Why did death frighten him so? he wondered. He'd seen many men die. Now it was his time. He must accept it. But somehow he couldn't. Guilt mingled with his pain. Had he lost his faith? Why was he so fearful of meeting his Maker? He chastised himself, urged himself to make his peace with God, accept his fate, but even as he did so he couldn't resist the need to fight back. The pain once again engulfed him and, desperately, he thought of Margate and his childhood. Stay alive, his mind urged, stay alive.

Despite the chaos which reigned, there was little panic amongst the troops. Thousands waited patiently on the beach for their turn to march crocodile-style into the sea. Like well-behaved schoolchildren they waded, some up to their necks, rifles held high above their heads, to the flotilla of craft waiting to take them home. In the skies overhead dogfights raged as RAF fighters engaged the Luftwaffe, but still the soldiers kept their orderly files until, one by one, two by two, they were hauled aboard vessels where they collapsed, exhausted, on the deck.

Martin had been unable to wade beyond waist-deep. He would not have been able to make it that far had it not been for the man who had saved him.

The humiliation of the British Expeditionary Force had been total, and the troops had retreated as far as they could when orders had been received to assemble on the beach. Few believed the rumours of a rescue mission. They'd be stranded if they went to the beach, they thought. Slaughtered or taken prisoner. But orders were orders and thousands upon thousands of soldiers scrambled through the bombed-out villages to head for the open and vulnerable shoreline.

Martin Thackeray and twenty others of his unit had been trapped in a ruined church as the enemy advance troops entered the deserted village. They'd left it too late to make their escape. They opened fire. The enemy took cover and skirmishing had continued throughout the entire day and into the night as the Germans tried to ascertain the Allied numbers remaining in the village. Fresh enemy troops arrived and dug in for the morning when they'd storm the church and surrounding buildings.

It was just before dawn when the men had made their escape bid, but they were lambs to the slaughter, mercilessly mown down by the surrounding forces which awaited them. Only Martin and young Tom Putney had emerged unscathed, eventually making it to the coastline a full day later.

'Christ almighty!' Tom had muttered in his thick Cockney accent as they'd ducked through a narrow street which led to the sea. 'Jus' look at that!'

'Don't blaspheme.' Martin's reply had been automatic. Tom's blaspheming and his own remonstration had been a running joke between them for months, but he too had stood dumbfounded at the sight of the myriad vessels churning through the water. There must be hundreds, he'd thought. Too many to count, and of every description. There were troopships and mine sweepers, cruisers and yachts, pleasure craft and fishing boats, and others, little more than dinghies. And on the beach sat thousands of men, patiently waiting their turn for deliverance. Some had been waiting for days.

'I wasn't blasphemin', Marty,' Tom had said, 'I was givin' thanks.' Even in the direst of circumstances Tom was always good for a joke, but this time he wasn't joking at all. 'It's a bleedin' miracle, it is. A bleedin' —'

He'd stopped mid-sentence as the building beside them erupted. A shell had found its mark. But they were out of the battle zone, Martin had thought vaguely as the force of the blast lifted him bodily into the air.

When he had come to his senses, seconds or hours later, he couldn't tell, he had realised that the shell had not been fired from the battle zone. The Stukas overhead were determined to halt the escape mission.

Yet more troops were pouring down the narrow street making for the shore, climbing over the rubble of the building, tripping over the body of Tom buried waist-deep in debris.

'Tom!' Martin had dragged himself over to his friend, a searing pain in his left leg and chest. There was a ringing in his ears and his vision was blurred, but he knew Tom was dead. Tom Putney had been barely twenty, ten years younger than Martin. Too young to die.

'Our Father,' Martin had begun as he crossed Tom's hands over his chest, 'who art . . .' Then suddenly he was grabbed by the wrist and hauled to his knees, the pain screaming through his body.

'Don't waste your breath, boyo.'

'Our Father who art in heaven . . .' Martin had protested, as much for himself as for Tom.

'Come on!' Emlyn Gruffudd had urged. Jesus Christ! He was as religious as the next man, but what was the point in saying prayers for a bloke who had half his head blown off! And at a time like this! 'Come on,' he'd repeated, hoisting Martin to his feet. 'You can make it.'

Martin had found himself half carried, half dragged to the beach. He had no idea who the man was but, as his sight cleared, he knew that he was not from his unit. He had tried to thank the man but waves of pain had engulfed him and the words wouldn't come out.

'Don't you worry, boyo,' Emlyn had muttered, 'you'll make it.'

The ringing in Martin's ears blocked out any sound. Once again he'd tried to voice his thanks and his lips formed the words, but nothing came out, not even a whisper.

The wounded were the first to be shepherded into the queue making its way to the water and Emlyn Gruffudd thanked his lucky stars that he'd rescued the Englishman. He might have been waiting his turn with the others for days if he hadn't. It had not been his intention to jump the queue, but when the opportunity had offered itself he didn't say no. He hoisted Martin higher up on to his hip, ignoring the groans of agony. Perhaps the poor lad was already dying, he'd thought, as he started to wade.

Only minutes later they were picked up by one of the lighter craft which had negotiated its way into shallower water.

'Ten's the limit, room for two more,' the skipper of the small fishing boat had said and he and his young crewman, a lad barely out of his teens, had helped them aboard. There was no disorderliness from the other troops in the water. The men simply waded out further or waited their turn in the shallows, aiding the wounded.

'That's it, Billy-boy,' the skipper had said to the lad, 'we've got our load of pongos, we're off.'

So Martin clung to the gunwales and, whilst the boat chugged out into the channel, he watched the beach of Dunkirk and thought of Margate as he fought to retain his consciousness. But once they were out in the boisterous sea, the motion of the boat sent such pain through his shattered leg and his chest that unconsciousness seemed a blessing. If this was death, he thought, so be it. The pain had become unendurable and he prayed to God as he slipped into the merciful blackness.

'Portsmouth's chaos. So's Southampton. The big boats are all makin' for the docks there.' The voice was authoritative, an older man with a thick Hampshire accent. 'We're headin' for Fareham.'

The ringing in his ears had lessened and, as he came to, Martin heard the words clearly. So he was still alive. He didn't know whether he was thankful or not. He steeled himself to the pain which once again galloped through him like an angry stallion, every part of his body now screaming in agony.

'Where's Fareham?' he heard a Welsh voice query. 'Never heard of it.'

'Roughly 'alfway 'tween Portsmouth and Southampton,' the skipper said. 'About four mile upriver. Home eh, Billy-boy?' The skipper smiled through his grey beard at his young crewman. 'We're headin' home.'

'Aye, Skip,' the lad grinned back.

Martin once again felt the blackness slide over him. But this time he didn't think of God and he didn't think of death. He no longer cared, he simply wished to escape the pain.

He awoke once again to the sound of voices. Many of them this time. Voices of command. 'Easy does it. Gently now.' Others scrambled from the boat, willing hands helping the wounded, and he heard the Welshman say, 'You can make it, boyo,' as he felt himself lifted onto the jetty. He gritted his teeth to prevent himself crying out. They laid him on a canvas stretcher and carried him to a waiting vehicle, one of many in the quayside dockyard. Army ambulances, private cars, even several horses and drays: the place was a hive of activity.

Martin was delirious, his brain in turmoil. Where was he? The voices were English, all of them. He wanted to ask, 'Am I home?' but he didn't dare try to speak. Then a hand was holding his. A soft hand, but its grip was firm and reassuring.

'Don't worry, you're home now.' A woman's voice. She had read his mind, and she looked like an angel. He fought against the blackness as he felt himself drift away. He didn't want to lose sight of the vision. An angel, with hair so fair it formed a halo around her face. 'You're home,' she said again, 'you're safe. We're taking you to the Royal Victoria Hospital at Netley.' Her voice was gentle and came from very far away. And then she smiled. He held on to the voice and the vision as they lifted him into the ambulance. His fear and uncertainty had left him now. He was saved, the angel had told him so. 'You're safe,' she'd said, and he believed her.

BOOK ONE

CHAPTER ONE

'*Nora – can I never be anything more than a stranger to you?*'

'*Ah, Torvald, the most wonderful thing of all would have to happen.*'

'*Tell me what that would be!*'

'*Both you and I would have to be so changed that . . . Oh, Torvald, I don't believe any longer in wonderful things happening.*'

'*But I will believe in it. Tell me! So changed that . . .?*'

'*That our life together would be a real wedlock. Goodbye.*'

She left, and he sat, burying his head in his hands.

'*Nora! Nora!*' *He looked around.* '*Empty. She is gone.*' *Hope flashed through his mind.* '*The most wonderful thing of all . . .?*' *Then he heard the sound of the door below as it closed.*

The final performance of Henrik Ibsen's *A Doll's House* at the Theatre Royal, Haymarket, received a standing ovation. The award-winning production had played for over a year to capacity houses for each of its 431 performances, and its success was in most part due to the young actress who had taken London's West End by storm. 2003 was certainly Samantha Lindsay's year.

In the centre of the lineup, hands clasped with her fellow cast members, Samantha walked downstage to take the final of the curtain calls. There'd been twelve in all. She'd accepted the bouquet from the theatre manager, taken several solo calls and now, as the cast bowed, she glanced to the wings and gave a barely perceptible nod to the stage manager. He acknowledged her message, the lights dimmed, the cast left the stage and the audience was still loudly applauding as the house lights came up.

Backstage, cast and crew hugged each other affectionately, some with tears in their eyes, and Deidre, who played the maid, openly cried. It had been a long run and a very happy company; they would miss each other. A celebratory supper had been arranged for the entire cast, but for now they continued to mingle in the wings, savouring the moment. Alexander embraced Samantha.

'My darling doll-wife,' he said, 'you've been a glorious Nora, it's been wonderful.' Then, when he'd kissed her on both cheeks, he couldn't help adding, 'But why on earth did you call a halt? We could have taken at least another half dozen calls.'

Sam recognised it for the genuine complaint it was. 'Always leave them wanting more,' she replied innocently, 'isn't that what they say?'

He appeared not to hear her. 'We took fifteen on the last night of *Lady Windemere*, and that only ran for a hundred performances, we could probably have stretched it to twenty tonight and created a record.' Alexander had never approved of the fact that the cast had been directed to take their curtain calls from Samantha. The girl gave a stellar performance in the role of Nora, he agreed, but she was far too inexperienced in theatre etiquette. In West End theatre etiquette, in any event.

'Oh well, too late now,' Sam shrugged. Alexander's litany of complaints had become water off a duck's back to her. He was a fine actor and they'd worked well together, although she'd had to overcome his open anti-pathy in the early days. Alexander Wright had been unaccustomed to working opposite a virtual unknown. However, the reaction of the preview audiences and the opening night reviews had altered his opinion and, like everyone else, he'd eventually succumbed, albeit begrudg-ingly, to Samantha's natural charm and lack of pretension.

'She's a dear,' he'd say to those who asked what Samantha Lindsay was really like – and, to his secret chagrin, there were many who did. 'Quite the little innocent really.' He always managed to make it sound simultaneously affectionate and patronising.

Sam was not innocent. She was unaffected certainly, but she had realised that it made things easier for everyone if she simply pandered to the actor's ego.

'I'm quite sure you're right,' she now added as she noticed the familiar scowl, 'and yes it's been wonderful.' She hugged him genuinely. 'I've loved working with you, Alexander, you've taught me a lot.' She meant it. She'd learned a great deal from him and she was grateful. Besides, Alexander couldn't help being Alexander. What was the saying? *A pride of lions, a gaggle of geese and a whinge of actors.* After thirty dedicated years in the theatre, Alexander Wright was a product of his profession.

Recognising her sincerity, he replied with the dignity befitting such a compliment. 'Thank you, my dear. I feel it's one's responsibility to encourage young actors.'

He was touched by her remark, she could tell, and was about to embark upon one of his many, and interminable, stories of past productions, so she pecked him on the cheek. 'You have, and I'm very grateful.' She smiled. 'And now I have to get the slap off.' She grabbed the bouquet of flowers which the assistant stage manager was patiently holding for her and headed for her dressing room. 'See you at supper,' she called over her shoulder. 'I'm bloody starving!'

Alexander shook his head with exasperated fondness. She was so ridiculously Australian.

Reginald waited ten minutes before tapping on Samantha's dressing-room door. If it had been another of his female clients he would have waited at least half an hour, but it took Sam only ten minutes to 'get her slap off', as she called it. And, as she never ate before a performance, she was always ravenously hungry after the show and impatient to leave. Furthermore, she preferred to eat at one of the small cafes where the food was good, rather than somewhere one went to be seen. Reginald had found Samantha refreshing from the outset, although it had taken him some time to adjust to being called 'Reg'. He accepted it now and they'd become close friends.

'Reg!' Sam was minus her stage makeup but still in a stocking cap and robe at her dressing-room mirror when the dapper little Englishman entered. She jumped up, wig in hand, and hugged him. 'Take a seat,' she said, 'won't be a tick.' She sat, dumped the wig on the wig stand, pulled off the cap and brushed her fair hair, normally curly and framing her face, back into a severe ponytail. Nothing else you can do with wig hair, she always maintained. She refused to start from scratch and coax back the curls, it took too much time and after a show food was far more important. 'We hung around backstage saying goodbyes,' she explained, 'God only knows why. Everyone's coming to supper.' She jumped up once again and started taking off her robe.

'I'll wait outside.' Reg rose.

'Don't be silly, I'm perfectly respectable.' She dropped the robe. 'Look! Thermals!'

Reg smiled but still discreetly averted his gaze. Even in a winter vest and thigh-length, cotton stretch knickers she looked sexy, lean and lithe, with the body of a healthy young animal. He found it a little confronting and he'd much rather have waited outside.

Sam dressed quickly; she hadn't meant to embarrass him. She'd deliberately donned the thermals before he'd arrived in order not to. What was it with the English? she wondered. Australian actors stripped openly in dressing rooms, but even the English acting fraternity seemed prudish, and her immodesty had often been frowned upon.

'Did you check that the beer's arrived?' she asked as she zipped up her cord trousers and grabbed her jumper. She'd arranged the delivery of two cartons of beer for the stage-hands who had to strike the set and 'bump out' in preparation for the next production.

'Yes, they're holding it at the stage door. The doorman was most amused that it was Foster's.'

'Thought I'd make a bit of a statement. All respectable, you can look now.' She grabbed her overcoat from the peg on the door. 'Come on, I'm starving.'

'We'll be the first there.'

'Goody, we'll grab the best table.'

So much for making the grand late entrance, Reginald thought, and so much for dolling herself up. He cast a circumspect glance at the corduroys. They were going to the Ivy after all, the best table had been booked for the past two months, and even on closing night she was still one of the hottest things in town. 'No need to rush,' he said with a touch of irony, 'Nigel's minding the table for us.'

For the first time Sam drew breath. 'I didn't know Nigel was coming.'

'Sam,' he said patiently, 'I told you last week he needs to do this interview before you leave for Sydney.' Nigel was the publicist Reginald employed to promote a number of his top clients and he knew Sam didn't like the man. Which was understandable, most people didn't, but Nigel was very good at his job. 'He says you've been avoiding meeting him for the past five days.'

'I've had to move out of the flat, for God's sake,' she

protested, 'I've been organising the furniture removal, I haven't had time!'

'Then you should have made time.' Sam could be infuriating on occasions. 'You've won the Olivier Award, for God's sake! You have to be fair dinkum about this.' It was a term she'd taught him as a joke, laughing at the way he said it in his pukka English accent, but it usually proved most effective. 'You can't just disappear from London. We need to keep you hot. We need to make the industry aware that you're about to star in a Hollywood movie.'

'I know, I know. But it's the last night!'

It appeared for once that 'fair dinkum' wasn't going to work. 'Fine,' Reg snapped, 'I'll tell him to come to Fareham then, shall I?' She glared back at him, and her hazel eyes held a glint of defiance, but Reginald was fully prepared to stand his ground. 'He'll be happy to make the trip, I'm sure.'

'All right, you bastard, you win.' She gave a resigned shrug and he knew that she wasn't really angry, just as he knew that the language was not intentionally insulting. Sam's voice held no nasal twang and was not particularly Australian, but her behaviour certainly was and Reg had grown to love her for it. She tossed her scarf around her neck. 'Let's go.'

'Lippy,' he reminded her. Then, whilst she slashed the lipstick across her mouth, he added, 'And a touch of eyes.' She glared at him once again in the mirror. 'Well, at least some mascara,' he said. 'It's the Ivy, Sam, and there's bound to be press photographers sniffing around.'

'I don't know why we're not going to Zorba's,' she grizzled, 'the food's much better.'

'Because the others want to go to the Ivy, that's why. Stop being such a prima donna.'

It was a biting night, unusually cold for so early in September, and as they walked up the broad Haymarket towards Piccadilly Circus, Sam turned to look back at the theatre, at the stateliness of the Corinthian columns with their gold embossed motif and the arches and stonework, all perfectly floodlit. A glorious building, its interior was of equal magnificence, with molded ceilings, crystal chandeliers, polished marble, and layer upon layer of English gold leaf. What a privilege it had been to work there.

She remembered the first time she'd been to 'the Haymarket', as the actors fondly referred to the Theatre Royal. It had been December 1994 and she'd caught the train up from Fareham during the two days she'd had free of rehearsals. So many firsts, she remembered. Her first trip to England, her first visit to London, and her first experience of West End Theatre. She'd seen the new Tom Stoppard play, *Arcadia*, and the Theatre Royal had just that year undergone major restoration. She'd been eighteen years old and it had been the most magical experience of her life. And now, nine years later, she'd worked there. She'd played a leading role at 'the Haymarket', the most elegant theatre in London. During the eight performances a week for over a year, she had never once taken the experience for granted. And now it was over.

'It's been a good run, hasn't it?' Reginald had been standing silently beside her for a full minute or so. He knew what she was thinking.

'Ever master of the understatement, Reggie,' she grinned. It was their secret language. He drew the line at 'Reggie' and she only ever used the term in private.

He took her hand and smiled. 'Onward and upward, Sam. Onward and upward.'

'I hope so.' The forthcoming film role was potentially the biggest step yet in her career, but movies were risky business, as they both knew. And she would miss the theatre.

'*Torpedo Junction*. It's a rather old-fashioned title, don't you think?' Nigel sat, pen poised over his notepad, gin and tonic untouched. He'd graciously waited until Sam had finished her supper, a huge steak – God knew where the girl put it, she was built like a whippet – and then he'd insisted the three of them retire from the main arena of the restaurant to one of the more private leather booths.

'Come on, Sam,' Reg had urged, recognising that she was loath to leave the others. 'They'll be partying for ages, you can join them later.' Then, when she'd looked a little rebellious, he'd muttered, 'You promised you'd be fair dinkum.'

'Okay,' she'd said meekly enough.

'Old-fashioned in what way?' she now asked a little archly. She couldn't help herself: she found Nigel such a supercilious bastard.

'It sounds like a war movie from the 1940s.'

'Well, it is in a way, isn't it? Torpedo Junction was the infamous Japanese submarine hunting ground during World War II.'

Nigel adjusted his Gucci glasses and gritted his teeth. He didn't like Sam any more than she liked him. Little upstart. Didn't she realise that, as a journalist with his own PR company and all of the contacts he had to hand, he could destroy her? And if she wasn't on Reginald's books he'd take great delight in doing so. But he couldn't afford to lose the account of Reginald Harcourt Management, so he gave a glacial smile and continued.

'So that's what it is then? A war film?'

'No.' What a waste of time it all was, Sam thought. She hated playing these games. But it was part of the job, she told herself as she took a breath and tried to sound pleasant. 'It's about love really. Human love.'

'Ah,' he pounced like a hungry cat. It was exactly what he was after. 'So it's a similar genre to *Pearl Harbor* then, a war story with a love theme.' Nigel scratched away at his notepad, delighted. At this early stage, before commencement of filming, the production house was releasing no specific details about *Torpedo Junction*, merely the title, the principal cast, and the fact that it was the next big-budget production from Mammoth.

'No, it's not a war story with a love theme,' she said tightly. That wasn't what she'd meant at all, Sam thought, cursing the man. What the hell did it matter anyway? Whatever she said he'd misquote her.

'Who'd like another drink?' Reg asked, giving Sam a warning glance as he rose from the booth. It was the way Nigel often conducted interviews. Offend the subject just enough to make them defensive. That way they gave away more of themselves or, in this case, more of the project. The subject matter of the script was under wraps, and Sam knew that.

'I'm fine, thank you, Reginald,' Nigel said, taking the mildest sip from his gin and tonic.

'Another red for me, thanks,' Sam gave Reg a nod that said she not only knew exactly where she stood, but she was more than a match for Nigel Daly.

'It's not at all like *Pearl Harbor* actually, Nigel,' she said, draining the last of her glass and smiling, she hoped, sweetly.

'What is it like then?'

'Why don't you ask me how I feel about working with Brett Marsdon? It's what everyone will want to know, surely.'

She was right of course, but he'd be able to sell another whole story on the *Torpedo Junction* theme if he could get it out of her. 'So you don't want to discuss the script?' He gave it one last try.

'It's about people, Nigel. One of the best scripts I've ever read. And it's all about people.'

The smug bitch, he thought. She went on to parrot the details which had been generally released. It was an American production, Mammoth's biggest budget movie of the year, they were shooting offshore, interiors at Fox

Studios in Sydney and on location somewhere in the South Pacific or far north Queensland, the specific details hadn't been released yet. It was nothing he didn't know already. Nigel gave up.

'So tell me about Brett Marsdon,' he said. 'How do you feel about working with Hollywood's hottest property?'

Not all of the questions were trite. In true form, Nigel questioned her about the fact that she would be playing an Englishwoman. 'Film critics are very quick to judge accents,' he said.

'I've been working in the English theatre for the past two years,' she replied, a fact of which Nigel was fully aware, she thought. He'd not only seen a number of her performances, but Reg would have sent him her CV. She glanced at Reginald but he sipped his white wine and said nothing. It was not his job to field the questions.

'Of course,' Nigel replied smoothly, 'but this is your first movie role, is it not?'

Is it not, she thought, whoever said *is it not*? But, aware that he was once again needling her, she gave a cheeky smile instead of biting back. 'Oh no, I was a prostitute in a low-budget thriller three years ago.'

'Really?' It was Nigel's turn to glance at Reginald. 'That wasn't on the CV.'

'I ended up on the cutting-room floor, the whole scene did. And the movie bombed anyway.'

'I see.' Well, he could hardly use that, could he? He asked her about her ties to England. After a year as the darling of London's West End, did she anticipate coming back to Britain, or would Hollywood claim her? Surprisingly enough, she warmed to the theme.

'I'll go where the work is, of course,' she said, 'but I'd like to live in Britain when I can.' She grinned at Reg. 'I've bought a house here.'

'Oh?' Nigel feigned interest. 'Where?'

'Fareham.'

'Fareham!' His surprise pleased her. Had he expected her to say Chelsea or South Kensington? 'Why on earth Fareham? It's miles from anywhere.'

'It's where I did my first panto. Well my only panto actually,' she corrected herself. '*Cinderella* at Ferneham Hall, Fareham, 1994.'

Nigel winced. The traditional Christmas family panto-mime was hardly something to boast of, and certainly not a production in a backwater like Fareham. Really, the girl was impossible.

Sam looked at Reg. She had no intention of cloaking her humble beginnings in secrecy and she couldn't give a damn if others wished that she would. But she didn't want to offend Reg. Reg had been responsible for her success and, in the early days, he'd suggested she neglect to mention her lack of formal training to the press. Surprisingly enough, Reginald Harcourt gave an encouraging nod.

'It was the first time I'd ever worked in the theatre,' Sam said, 'although the producers didn't know it. Not that they would have cared, I suppose. I was only hired because of the soapie.'

Nigel looked incredulously at Reginald. He'd known that Samantha Lindsay had started out as a teenager in an Aussie soap, but surely they didn't want to go in that direction?

Reginald made his one and only contribution to the interview. 'I think it's time Sam's background was dis-cussed. It makes her different,' he suggested mildly. 'I think readers would find it interesting.'

Readers maybe, Nigel thought, but hardly prospective producers and casting agents. Oh well, if the girl wanted to hang herself, and if he had the agent's permission, he was only too happy to oblige.

'How fascinating,' he said as he scribbled in his pad.

Tiger Men

The eagerly awaited new novel by Judy Nunn

'This town is full of tiger men,' Dan said. 'Just look around you. The merchants, the builders, the bankers, the company men, they're all out for what they can get. This is a tiger town, Mick, a place at the bottom of the world where God turns a blind eye to pillage and plunder.'

Van Diemen's Land was an island of stark contrasts: a harsh penal colony, an English idyll for its landed gentry, and an island so rich in natural resources it was a profiteer's paradise. Its capital, Hobart Town, had its contrasts too: the wealthy elite in their sandstone mansions, the exploited poor in the notorious slum known as Wapping, and the criminals and villains who haunted the dockside taverns and brothels of Sullivan's Cove. Hobart Town was no place for the meek.

Tiger Men is the story of Silas Stanford, a wealthy Englishman; Mick O'Callaghan, an Irishman on the run; and Jefferson Powell, an idealistic American political prisoner. It is also the story of the strong, proud women who loved them, and of the children they bore who rose to power in the cutthroat world of international trade.

Tiger Men is the sweeping saga of three families who lived through Tasmania's golden era, who witnessed the birth of Federation and who, in 1915, watched with pride as their sons marched off to fight for King and Country in the Great War.

Available from November 2011

Other titles by Judy Nunn

Heritage

In the 1940s refugees from more than seventy nations gathered in Australia to forge a new identity – and to help realise one man's dream: the mighty Snowy Mountains Hydro-Electric Scheme. From the ruins of Berlin to the birth of Israel, from the Italian Alps to the Australian high country, *Heritage* is a passionate tale of rebirth, struggle, sacrifice and redemption.

Floodtide

Floodtide traces the fortunes of four men and four families over four memorable decades in the mighty 'Iron Ore State' of Western Australia. The prosperous 1950s when childhood is idyllic in the small city of Perth . . . The turbulent 60s when youth is caught up in the Vietnam War . . . The avaricious 70s when WA's mineral boom sees a new breed of entrepreneurs . . . The corrupt 80s, when greedy politicians and powerful businessmen bring the state to its knees . . .

Maralinga

Maralinga, 1956. A British airbase in the middle of nowhere, a top-secret atomic testing ground . . . *Maralinga* is the story of Lieutenant Daniel Gardiner, who accepts a posting to the wilds of South Australia on a promise of rapid promotion, and of adventurous young English journalist Elizabeth Hoffmann, who travels halfway around the world in search of the truth.